Thomas Oswald Cockayne, Sextus Placitus, Barbarus Apuleius

**Leechdoms, Wortcunning, and Starcraft of Early England**

Being a collection of documents, for the most part never before printed - Vol. 2

Thomas Oswald Cockayne, Sextus Placitus, Barbarus Apuleius

**Leechdoms, Wortcunning, and Starcraft of Early England**
*Being a collection of documents, for the most part never before printed - Vol. 2*

ISBN/EAN: 9783337382490

Printed in Europe, USA, Canada, Australia, Japan

Cover: Foto ©Andreas Hilbeck / pixelio.de

More available books at **www.hansebooks.com**

# LEECHDOMS, WORTCUNNING,

AND

# STARCRAFT

OF

# EARLY ENGLAND.

BEING

## A COLLECTION OF DOCUMENTS, FOR THE MOST PART NEVER BEFORE PRINTED,

ILLUSTRATING

## THE HISTORY OF SCIENCE IN THIS COUNTRY BEFORE THE NORMAN CONQUEST.

COLLECTED AND EDITED

BY THE

## REV. OSWALD COCKAYNE, M.A. CANTAB.

## VOL. II.

PUBLISHED BY THE AUTHORITY OF THE LORDS COMMISSIONERS OF HER MAJESTY'S
TREASURY, UNDER THE DIRECTION OF THE MASTER OF THE ROLLS.

LONDON:
LONGMAN, GREEN, LONGMAN, ROBERTS, AND GREEN.

1865.

Printed by
EYRE and SPOTTISWOODE, Her Majesty's Printers.
For Her Majesty's Stationery Office.

# CONTENTS.

# PREFACE.

# PREFACE.

No historical records are complete without the usual
chapter on Manners and Customs; and the true scholar
never feels himself well in possession of the requisite
knowledge of the past age, till he has so learnt its
time honoured tale, as to apprehend in a human and
practical sense those feelings which made its super-
stitions plausible, its heathenism social, its public
institutions tend, in the end, to the general welfare.

The Saxons have not been more fortunate than others
in their appreciation by us, self satisfied moderns. They
have been, and still are, I believe, commonly regarded
as mangy dogs, whose success against the Keltic race
in this country was owing chiefly to their starved
condition and ravening hunger. The children protest
that, positively, as they know from their most reliable
handbooks, these roving savages stuffed their bellies
with acorns, and the enlightened *literati* and *dilettanti*
begrudge them any feeling of respect for their queens
and ladies, or any arts such as befit our "Albion's
"glorious isle" under an English king.

The work now published for the first time, and
from a unique manuscript, will, if duly studied, afford
a large store of information to a very different effect,
and show us that the inhabitants of this land in
Saxon times were able to extract a very fair share
of comfortable food, and healing medicines, and savoury
drinks directly or indirectly from it. Many readers

will be glad to see drawn together into one the scattered notices which occur most plentifully here, and
occasionally elsewhere, upon this matter.

At his noon meat or dinner, at the *hora nona*, or
ninth hour of the day,[1] for the word noon has now
changed its sense, the Saxon spread his table duly
and suitably with a table cloth.[2] He could place on
it for the entertainment of his family and household,
the flesh of neat cattle,[3] now Normanized, as Sir Walter
Scott has made familiar to all, into beef, the flesh of
sheep,[4] now called mutton, of pig, of goat,[5] of calf,[5] of
deer, especially the noble hart,[6] of wild boar,[6] the peacock, swan, duck,[7] culver or pigeon,[8] waterfowl, barn-
door fowl,[9] geese,[10] and a great variety of wild fowl,
which the fowler caught with net, noose, birdlime,
birdcalls, hawks, and traps;[11] salmon, eels, hake, pil-
chards, eelpouts,[12] trout, lampreys, herrings, sturgeon,
oysters, crabs, periwinkles, plaice, lobsters, sprats,[13]
and so on.[14]

The cookery of these viands was not wholly contemptible. It was entrusted to professors of that admired
art,[15] who could, though their accomplishments have
been neglected by the annalists, put on the board
oyster patties,[16] and fowls stuffed with bread and such
worts as parsley.[17] Weaker stomachs could have light

---

[1] Hom. II. 256. Also See ꞅunne
aþꞁꞃeꝺoꝺe.ꞃpaɱ mɩꝺꝺæᵹe oꝺ non,
M.II. 158 a, *The sun was darkened
from midday till noon.* Even here
our dictionaries blunder.

[2] Beoꝺelaꝺ, Æ.G. 8, line 31. Myꞃe
hꝺæᵹel, Lye.

[3] Lb. II. vii., etc.

[4] Coll. Monasticon, p. 20.

[5] Lb. II. xvi.

[6] Coll. Mon. p. 22.

[7] Lb. II. xvi.

[8] Lb. II. xxx. 2.

[9] DD. 504 ; Lb. II. xvi. 2.

[10] Lb. II. xvi. 2.

[11] Coll. Mon. p. 25.

[12] Young eels (Kersey).

[13] Spꝛoꞇꞇaꞅ not in the dictionaries.
Besides two passages in which it
occurs, reserved for reasons which
readers of the Shrine will understand, it occurs Coll. Mon. p. 23.
See French Celerin, Selerin ; the
MS. has Salin.

[14] Coll. Mon. pp. 23, 24.

[15] Coll. Mon. p. 29.

[16] Lb. II. xxiii.

[17] Lb. III. xii.

food, chickens,[1] giblets, pigs trotters,[2] eggs, broth, various preparations of milk, some of the nature of junkets.[3]

From some of their drawings, their cookery of meat seems to have been more Homeric[4] than Roman or modern English, for we see portions of meat brought up on small spits, all hot, to the table. All food that required it was sweetened with honey, before men had betaken themselves to sugar. For fruits, we know they had sweet apples,[5] which are not indigenous to England, pears, peaches,[6] medlars, plums, and cherries.

Saxons, thus well provided with eatables, could satisfy thirst with not a few good and savoury drinks; with beer, with strong beer, with ale, with strong ale, with clear ale, with foreign ale, and with what they called twybrowen, that is, double brewed ale, a luxury, now rare, and rare too then probably.[7] These ales and beers were, of course, to deserve the name, and as we learn from many passages of the present publication, made of malt, and some of them, not all probably, were hopped.[8] I have sufficiently, in the Glossary,[9] established that the hop plant and its use were known to the Saxons, and that they called it by a name, after which I have inquired in vain among hop · growers and hop pickers in Worcestershire and Kent, the Hymele.[10] The hop grows wild in our hedges, male and female, and the Saxons in this state called it the hedge hymele; a good valid presumption that they knew it in its fertility. Three of the Saxon legal deeds

---

[1] As before.

[2] Lb. II. i.

[3] Gl. pleʒan.

[4] Καὶ ἀμφ' ὀβέλοισιν ἔθηκαν.

[5] Mylsce æppla, Lb. II. xvi.

[6] Persocas, Lb. p. 176; Laen. 89; Διδαξ. 31.

[7] Lb. I. xlvii. 3.

[8] IIb. lxviii.

[9] See also Preface, Vol. I. p. lv.

[10] I find Ymele, fem., gen –an, for a roll, scroll, volumen. The Hymele is in glossaries frequently Volubilis; and the two suggest a derivation for either from Ymbe = 'Αμφί, so that Hymele means coiler.

extant refer[1] to a hide of land at Hymel-tun in Worcestershire, the land of the garden hop, and as tun
means an enclosure, there can be not much doubt that
this was a hop farm. The bounds of it ran down to
the hymel brook, or hop plant brook, a name which
occurs about the Severn and the Worcestershire Avon
in other deeds. One of the unpublished glossaries
affords the Saxon word Hopu, *Hops*,[2] and Hopwood in
Worcestershire doubtless is thence named. Perhaps,
to explain some testimonies to a more recent importation of hops, it may be suggested that, as land or
sea carriage of pockets of hops from Worcestershire to
London or the southern ports was difficult, the use of
the hop was long confined to that their natural soil,
while the Kentish hops may be a gift from Germany.

A table is well enough furnished where the flagons
are filled with good malt liquor; it is flat heresy, they
say, to discover mischief in University "particular:"
but, notwithstanding, the Saxons drank also mead, an
exhilarating beverage, which from its sweetness must
have been better suited to the palates of the ladies,
and which was of an antiquity far anterior to written
or legendary history. They had also great store of
wines, which they distinguished by their qualities, as
clear, austere, sweet, rather than by their provinces or
birth. They made up also artificial drinks, oxymel,
hydromel, mulled wines, and a Clear drink, or Claret,[3]
of the nature of those beverages which are now called
cup.

Salt, which is an indispensable condiment to civilized
man, they obtained from Cheshire and Worcestershire,
where they had furnaces for the evaporation of the

---

[1] C.D. 209, 680, 1066.

[2] "Lygistra hopu," Gl. Cleop.
f. 57 a. Ligustra, though known to
every ear, by the line Alba ligustra
cadunt, were long doubtful; we believe them to be the blossoms of
privet.

[3] See the Glossary in Dluzrop
Spene.

brine.[1] Salt for salted meats,[2] which also were quite familiar to them, might be got from the saltpans on the sea shore.

The dishes, on which their meats were served, were sometimes of silver,[3] nor was this esteemed a high distinction.[4] The vessels from which they drank were sometimes of glass;[5] and those they had also transparent in quality.[6] The supply upon the tables of a chieftain, who had many retainers, was abundant, and not over studious of luxury and refinement.[7] When not engaged in war or hunting, the princes thought a good deal of their gormandize.[8] Festive assemblies were more frequent than among other races of men; they were duly ordered, and attended by gleemen, from whose lips the honeysweets of song flowed readily and freely, and whose reward came from the munificence of the prince. The feasts not rarely lasted through the night.[9]

In the monastic colloquy, an exercise for students, who were to be "bilingues," capable of conversing in their own language and in that of Rome, which is, therefore, quite destitute of artifice or ambition, a boy is asked what he has to eat. His reply is, worts (that is, kitchen herbs), fish, cheese, butter, beans, and flesh meats. He drinks ale, and, if he cannot get that, water, for he cannot afford wine. This is the daily diet of a boy under education in a monastery.

Altogether, if the comfortable prejudices of modernism do not shut out trustworthy and contemporary testi-

---

[1] C.D. 451.

[2] Lb. p. 234, etc.

[3] Discus argenteus regalibus opulis refertus, Beda, III. vi.

[4] Est videre apud illos argenteæ vasa, legatis et principibus eorum muneri datæ, non in alia vilitate quam quæ humo finguntur. Tacitus, Germ. 5.

[5] Calicem is translated glæppær, Beda, p. 618, line 12.

[6] C.E. 78, ult.

[7] Epulæ et, quanquam incompti, largi tamen adparatus, Tacit. Germ. 14.

[8] Dediti somno ciboque, Tacit. Germ. 15.

[9] Tacit. Germ. 22.

mony the Saxons must be concluded to be very far
removed from that pasturage upon the herb of the
field which was the regale of human innocence, and
that feeding upon grass which was the doom of an
arrogant Oriental king. They seem to dine like Eng-
lishmen.

The Saxon imported purple palls, and silk, precious
gems, gold, rare vestments, drugs, wine, oil, ivory, ori-
chalchum (a very fine mixed metal of gold and silver),
brass, brimstone, glass, and many more such articles.[1]
Tin came by water from Cornwall. Their enterprise by
sea was distinguished ; they pursued the dangerous
whale, and were known for their adventurous hostile
landings upon the Gallic coasts before they had settled
in this country.[2]

When the Saxons got possession of Britain, they
found it, not such as Julius Cæsar describes it, but
cultivated and improved by all that the Romans knew
of agriculture and gardening. Hence rue, hyssop, fennel,
mustard, elecampane, southernwood, celandine, radish,
cummin, onion,[3] lupin, chervil, flower de luce, flax
probably, rosemary, savory, lovage, parsley, coriander,
olusatrum, savine, were found in their gardens and
available for their medicines. Among the foreign drugs,
or the like, which are mentioned in this volume, we find
mastich, pepper, galbanum, scamony, gutta ammoniaca,
cinnamon, vermilion, aloes, pumice, quicksilver, brimstone, myrrh, frankincense, petroleum,[4] ginger.

The Saxons and Engle for the supply of their tables,
thus, as we have seen, abundantly supplied, kept herds
of cattle. The agriculture was in great measure, with
alterations adapted to the moister climate, and with
improvements from lapse of time and from other coun-

---

[1] Col. Mon. p. 27.

[2] Ammianus Marcellinus, xxviii.
5.

[3] Ynneleac has for its first element a Latinism, unionem, *onion*.
[4] Ib. pp. 53, 57, 61, 101, 125
289, 297.

tries, Roman. Among them arable land was excellently
cared for, much on the same method as we observe on
the downs of Kent, the garden of England. By throwing a thousand small allotments into one great field,
they were well rid of the encumbrance, the weeds, the
birds, the boys going a birdnesting, and the repair of
hedges or other fences. But the pasture land was not
so well managed. The Romans, who had an elaborate
machinery of aqueducts and irrigation, grew hay in their
prata, or meadows, which were artificially supplied with
water, and to get two crops a year, or three or four,[1]
gave a large flow of that element to the soil. This,
of course, had its inconveniences, herbs that thrive in
wet came up stronger than the grass, especially horse-
tail, and a "nummulus" with pods. They had an awk-
ward inefficient way of cutting the grass with a hook,
held in the right hand only, and this was followed
by a second operation, called sickling,[2] to cut what the
hooks had left. They tedded the hay, as is done now,
by hand, with forks,[3] took care it should be dry enough
not to ferment, leaving it in cocks,[4] and when ready
carried it off to the farm,[5] and stored it in a loft.[6]

Our forefathers here were able, from the frequent Hay.
rains, to dispense for the most part with irrigation.
They cut the hay with sithes,[7] the pattern of which
was probably borrowed from the continental Kelts,[8] and,
most naturally, by the subdued British before the settle-
ment of the English, since they were relatives, spoke

---

[1] Interamnæ in Umbria quater
anno secantur etiam non rigua,
Plin. xviii. 67 = 28.

[2] Sicilire; Plin. as above, Varro,
R.R. i. 19.

[3] Furcillis.

[4] Metæ.

[5] Villa.

[6] In tabulato. Sub tecto, Columella, II. xix.

[7] Hom. II. p. 162. Also a Saxon
drawing in MS. Cott. Tiber. B. v.,
where the painter has given straight
handles to the sithes; and has certainly committed an error in drawing haymaking for August, and
reaping for June.

[8] Galliarum latifundia maioris
compendii, Plin. as above.

the language, and were in frequent communication with
Gaul. They stored the hay in ricks[1] and mows,[2] where
it was less likely to get mouldy than in the half close
lofts of the Romans.

But according to the Roman system little hay was
prepared thus, there were legal impediments to extending widely the formation of inclosed pasturages, and
we read often enough of feeding the cattle upon leaves,
or rather on foliage.[3] The man employed in procuring
small boughs for his cattle was called Frondator.[4] The
greater part, by far, of Italian pasture land was common,
overspread by bushes and trees, where the employment
of herdsmen and shepherds was indispensable, and im-
provement was almost impossible.

Cattle thieves. In the same way, in early England, a grass field[5] is
rarely heard of, while the law books are full of pre-
cautions against cattle thieves, whose bad business was
made easy by the threading commons and wide moors,
along which a stolen herd could be driven, picking up
subsistence on its way, and evading observation by
keeping off the great roads. So much were the farmers
pestered with cattle thefts, that the legislature required
responsible witnesses to the transfer of such property,
and would have it transacted in open market; it also
invented a team; that is to say, when Z, who has lost
his oxen, found them and identified them in possession
of A, the said A was bound by trustworthy witnesses
to show that he had them lawfully from B; B was
then compelled to go through the same process, and to

---

[1] This word is not in the Saxon
dictionaries. and I will not at present indicate the passage where it is
to be found. S: *passages ...........*
*.......... .. HREAC .. . ...*
[4] *Mugan*, Exodus xxii. 6.

[3] " Quid maiora sequar? Salices
" humilesque genistæ

" Aut illæ pecori frondem aut
" pastoribus umbram
" Sufficiunt." .
        Virgil. Georgic. II. 434.
" Hic ubi densas agricolæ strin-
" gunt frondes."
        Id. Ecl. ix. 60.
[1] Virgil. Ecl. I. 57.
[5] Gæɲɲꞇun.

show that he gave honest money for them to C; thus a team or row of successive owners was unravelled till it ended in P, who had neglected to secure credible witnesses to his bargain; or in Q, who bought them at a risky price from the actual thief. Then Z recovered his cattle or their value.[1] Under this legislation the chief difficulty of a loser was to trace the direction in which his cattle had been driven off, and the skill of the hunter in tracking the slot of the deer, helped to follow the foot prints of horse or sheep or ox.[2] The less fertile parts of England are still patched by strips of common, or ways with grassy wastes skirting them, and the wanderer may often ramble by hedgerow elms mid hillocks green, among the primroses and violets, by ups and downs, through quagmires and over gates, from his furthest point for the day, till he nears the town and his inn. Elwes, the famous miser, could ride seventy miles out of London without paying turnpike. The Saxon herdsman watched the livelong night.[3]

The Saxons also, like the Romans, fed their cattle, sometimes, so as to make the notion familiar, with the foliage of trees. In his life of St. Cuðberht, the venerable Beda gives an account of a worthy Hadwald (Eadwald), a faithful servant of Ælflæd, abbess of Whitby, who was killed by falling from a tree.[4] Ælfric three hundred years afterwards telling the same story, gives us either from some collateral tradition, by writing may be, may be by word, or from his judgment of what was naturally the mans business at tree climbing, an account that this tree was an oak, and that he was feeding the cattle with the foliage, so that he was killed in discharge of his duty as herdsman.[5] In the summer of 1864 this

*(margin note: Cattle fed on leaves.)*

---

[1] DD. in many passages.

[2] Ηοппεε, For┌ρoп.

[3] Coll. Mon. p. 20. Tota nocte sto super eos vigilando propter fures.

[4] Incautius in arborem ascendens deciderat deorsum, Beda, 256, 22.

[5] Hom. II. 150.

poor resource is said to have been used in some counties of England, notwithstanding the "great strides science " has made."

Sheep.

Sheep were driven to pasture by their shepherd with his dogs, and at night were taken back home and folded.[1] With goats, sheep provided most part of the milk and cheese consumed in early times; cow butter is frequently named in this volume by way of distinction; these smaller beasts were robbed of their milk from the teats between the hind legs. A Saxon calendar heads the month of May with a painting representing sheep and goats under the shepherds care.

Swine.

Swine were entrusted to the swineherd, who pastured them in his masters woods, or on a customary percentage of the stock,[2] in the woods of some other proprietor. He had a perquisite, a sty pig out of the farrow, with another for his comrade or deputy, besides the usual dues of servitors.[3]

Boar hunting.

A drawing of a purely Saxon type, in a Saxon manuscript, represents the hunting of the wild boar; a thane, or as we say gentleman, on foot, has some wild pigs, bristly and yellowish brown, in view; he carries a long boar spear, and his left hand rests on the hilt of his sword, which is to save his life, if the boar charges; he is followed by an unarmed attendant, with a pair of dogs in a leash, and a hunting horn. The painter has probably assigned this drawing to the wrong month.[4]

Hawking.

The same artist has drawn a Saxon gentleman out a hawking on horseback, with an attendant on foot, each provided with a hawk; the wild fowl, ducks or teal, are in the picture, these the hawk dispatched

---

[1] Coll. Mon. 20.

[2] One third of very fat ones, one fourth, and one fifth of less fat. DD. p. 58.

[3] DD. p. 187.

[4] September. To say this painting represents herding swine is a strange inaccuracy. No hand is raised to shake down mast.

quickly, splitting their skulls with a stroke of his beak. A large bird, perhaps a heron, is introduced into the scene.

Feather beds, with bolsters and pillows, were in use in Saxon times. [1]

It seemed necessary to pave the way for an examina- England civilized. tion of the work now published by some such remarks as these, which are not all trite or matters of course; in order that the minds of readers not very familiar with these early times might give the rest of our facts a readier acceptance. The entire scope and tenor of all that we possess in the way of home literature, laws, deeds, histories, poems, regarding these Angles and Saxons, implies a tolerable degree of civilization; and many modern writers have persistently misrepresented their customs, and pretended to unloose the very bonds of society among them. I take leave to touch on one or two points, tending still to prepare us for the facts on the face of the present volume.

Tacitus says that the German races were well pleased Coins. with Roman money, and that such coins as were of approved value, the milled edged, and the pair horse chariot stamped,[2] had currency among them. In England the kings, great and small, learned to imitate on their own account the currency of Rome. Writers on the subject dwell upon this, and we are, in our mended age, ourselves guilty of this want of originality. Saxon pennies are common enough, but the numismatists say that they coined no gold, because no gold coins have been turned up. Saxon gold mancuses are mentioned in twenty different passages of manuscripts: they were not money of account, for we read of mancuses by weight; and a will, now in the hands of a zealous editor, settles the question by the following words: " Then let twenty hundred mancuses of gold be taken

---

[1] Gl. Somn. p. 60 b, line 40.    |    [2] Serratos bigatosque.

" and coined into mancuses;"[1] that is, there was a gold coin of a determinate weight called a mancus, and coined in England. Suppose when the document is fairly before us that this will turn out suspect; suppose it be pronounced a forgery; still we have Saxon authority for coining gold mancuses, and at home. All works that touch the subject, know that there were in those times royal mints and royal moneyers.

**Herbalist learning.**

The Glossary appended to this work exhibits, from among a still wider list, a large number of names of herbs; and materials exist for determining most of these to full conviction. The change of residence produced doubtless some confusion, by depriving the Saxons of specimens of the trees and plants answering to their names. The Germanic races had not before their arrival here pushed down upon the Mediterranean shores, but we all know historically that they had not been confined to cold climates, and one very curious proof exists that in some instances the name they fixed on a plant was appropriate only to its aspect in warmer countries.[2] It is true that the oak, beech, birch, hawthorn, sloethorn, bore native names, but elm,[3] walnut, maple, holly,[4] are equally native names; and, except the walnut, native trees. The cherry was brought to Italy by Lucullus, from Κερασοῦς, Cerasus, a city of Cappadocia, where it was plentiful, and it has ever borne the same name. The students of nature learn that many species of its Fauna, and also, though less so, of its Flora, can be traced to a single spot. Thus the peach, pepproc,

---

[1] þanne mupe (read nime) man rpentiȝ hund mancufa golber ꝺ gemynerige ro mancuyan, HID. fol. 21 a. The transcript is not by any means cotemporary.

[2] I regret I cannot here explain this fully.

[3] Not a Latinism.

[4] Holen, which is originally an adjective, Holeȝn, Holeȝen, and even now so applied to Holn Wood on the banks of the Dart, near Ashburton. Holeȝ, Holly, is the original substantive, C.E. 437, line 19. The old Latin name is Aquifolius: the Ilex was glandiferous, the evergreen oak.

Malum Persicum, was from Persia; there is no other name for it but "the Persian apple." For such as these it was impossible to have any other name; they were fruit trees foreign to all but their own countrymen. The plum is a better sloe; can be raised only by grafting, for seedlings are found to degenerate; which is also the case with the pear, having its native equivalent in the *Pirus domestica*, of Bewdley Forest. The sycamore, which has been alleged to prove the Latinism of the Saxons, is merely a maple. Yet the great influence which a Latin education, and scarce any instruction in old English, has upon ourselves, is traceable even among the Saxons: the true signification of some native names was passing away, and the plants supposed once to have borne them began to be known by some Roman denomination. For so common a plant as mint, seen in every running ditch, on every watery marge, there seems to be no name but that which is Hellenic, and Latin. The Germanic races, on the contrary, were the original patrons of hemp [1] and flax,[2] as against wool. It is, however, with their reach over the material world, and their proficiency in the arts which turn it to mans convenience, after, and not before, their arrival in England, that we are now dealing; and we maintain that a great part of what the Roman could teach, the Saxons, their successors, had learnt.

The most cursory examination of the work now before us will show that we are reading of a civilization such as the above details would lead us to expect. Here a leech calmly sits down to compose a not unlearned book, treating of many serious diseases, and assigning for them something he hopes will cure them. In the Preface to the first volume it was ad-

*Book learning.*

---

[1] Vol. I. p. x. note.
[2] Feminæ sæpius lineis amictibus utuntur. Tacitus, Germ. 17.

mitted that Saxon leeches fell short of the daring skill of
Hellas, or the wondrous success of the leading medical
men of either branch in London or Paris.   Notwithstanding that this is a learned book, it sometimes sinks
to mere driveling,   The author almost always rejects
the Greek recipes, and doctors as an herborist.   It
will give any one who has the heart of a man in him
a thrill of horror to compare the Saxon dose of brooklime and pennyroyal twice a day, for a mother whose
child is dead within her,[1] with the chapter in Celsus
devoted to this subject, in which we read, as in his
inmost soul, an anxious courageous care, and a sense
of responsibility mixed with determination to do his
utmost, which is, even to a reader, agitating.[2]

The manu-
script.

The volume consists of two parts; a treatise on
medicine in two books, with its proper colophon at
the end, and a third of a somewhat more monkish
character.   The book itself probably once belonged to
the abbey of Glastonbury, for a catalogue of the books
of that foundation, cited by Wanley,[3] contains the entry
" Medicinale Anglicum," which is rightly interpreted,
" Saxonice scriptum ;" and this book, rebound in 1757,
has preserved on one of the fly leaves an old almost
illegible inscription, " Medicinale Anglicum."   Search
has been made for any record of the books, which, on
the dissolution of the monasteries, might have found
their way from Glastonbury to the Royal Library, but
in vain.

An earlier, the first, owner is pointed out in the
colophon.[4]

Dald habet hunc librum, Cild quem conscribere iussit.

---

[1] Lb. p. 331.
[2] Adhibenda curatio est, quæ
numerari inter difficillimas potest.
Nam et summam prudentiam mo-
derationemque desiderat, et maxi-

mum periculum affert.  Celsus, VII.
xxix.
[3] Hickes, Thesaur. Vol. II. Præf.
ad Catalogum.
[4] P. 298.

In this doggrel, Bald is the owner of the book; we have no right to improve him into Æðelbald; Cild is, probably, the scribe; some will contend, the author. In classical Latin no doubt would exist, conscribere would at once denote the composing of the work: but in these later days, when millions of foreigners learnt the Latin language as a means of interchange of thoughts, occasionally intruding their own Gothic words, all such niceties of the ear went for nothing; Cild might well be the mere penman. But then the marginal tokens, and private memoranda, show that the work so written had passed either through the hands of the author, which from the use of private marks is probable, or through those of another leech, who was able to discover the sources of the authors information. Bald anywise may have been the author himself.

Let us give a few touches to the, as yet, bare outline of the penman Cild. The famous Durham book is a charming work of ancient Saxon art; those who cannot inspect the original may see a copy of a piece of the ornamentation in the Gospel of St. Matthew, edited by the Rev. Joseph Stevenson, and published by the Surtees society. According to an entry of a later age in the book itself, not of doubtful authenticity, this exquisite piece of pattern work, which is a part of the writing, was the performance of Eadfrið, bishop of Lindisfarne, who occupied that see from 698 to 721. It is of Irish tone, and like many other dignitaries this prelate had, very likely, completed his Christian education in the Isle of Saints. Cild was certainly not of the make and metal of a bishop, for the words "conscribere "iussit" forbid it; Dunstan forefend! It would be somewhat speculative to say, that in Northumbria, A.D. 700, the art of writing was at a higher premium than afterwards. I will not venture to say it, but proceed upon surer data. One of the poems in the Exeter book, of uncertain date, but before the end

*Cild.*

of the tenth century, mentions as a valued accomplishment the art of writing in fair characters.[1]

> One can cunningly
> word speech write.

Ælfric also himself in a sermon on Midlent Sunday,— " Oft one seeth fair letters awritten; then extolleth he " the writer and the letters, and wotteth not what they " mean. He who kenneth the difference of the letters, " he extolleth the fairness, and readeth the letters, " and understandeth what they mean." The honour remained to beautiful writing, but the writer did not stalk in so lofty a station. On the top margin of a page [2] of the Oxford copy of the Herd Book, or Liber Pastoralis, of King Ælfred may be read these words,—

> pıllımoꞇ pjıꞇ þuf oððe beꞇ,

that is, *Willimot, write thus or better.* A little further on,[3]

> pjıꞇ þuf oððe beꞇ oððe þıne hyðe ꞅopleꞇ,

*Write thus or better, or bid good bye to thy hide,* that is, get a good hiding. In an Harleian MS.[4] there is a bit of nonsense, but the same idea of a hiding is uppermost;

> pjıꞇ þuf oððe beꞇ jıbe apeg.
> ælꞅnæppaꞇꞇaꞅox þu þılꞇ ꞅpınȝan ælꞅjıc cılb;

*Write thus or better; ride away; Ælfnarpattafox; thou wilt swinge child Ælfric.* From these marginal scribblings it is plain that the penman had descended from his episcopal throne, to be a tipsy drudge, kept in order by the whip. Cild, " quem Bald conscribere " iussit," was nearer the whip than the crooked staff.

The owner of the book, Bald, may be fairly presumed to have been a medical practicioner, for to no other

*Bald.*

---

[1] " Sum mæȝ ꞅeapolıce,
    " ꞅopð cpıðe ppıꞇan."
           C.E. 42, 14.

[2] Fol. 53 a.
[3] Fol. 55 b.
[4] Harl. 55, fol. 4 b.

could such a book as this have had, at that time, much
interest. We see then a Saxon leech here at his studies;
the book, in a literary sense, is learned; in a professional
view not so, for it does not really advance mans knowledge of disease or of cures. It may have seemed by
the solemn elaboration of its diagnoses to do so, but I
dare not assert there is real substance in it. Bald,
however, may have got some good out of it, he may
have learned to think, have begun to discriminate, to
take less for granted. Thus we see him in his study,
among his books becoming, for his day, a more ac-
complished physician; and he speaks with a genuine
philosophs zeal about those his books. "nulla mihi tam
" cara est optima gaza Quam cari libri:" fees and stored
wealth he loved not so well as his precious volumes.
If Bald was at once a physician and a reader of learned
books on therapeutics, his example implies a school of
medicine among the Saxons. And the volume itself
bears out the presumption. We read in two cases [1] that
" Oxa taught this leechdom;" in another [2] that " Dun
" taught it;" in another " some teach us;" [3] in another
an impossible prescription being quoted; [4] the author, or
possibly Cild, the reedsman, indulges in a little facetious
comment, that compliance was not easy. I assume that
Oxa and Dun were natives, either of this country or
of some land inhabited by a kindred people. Any way,
we make out, undoubtedly, a bookish study of medicine;
the Saxon writers, who directly from the Greek, or
through the medium of a Latin translation studied
Trallianus, Paulus of Ægina, and Philagrios, were men
of learning not contemptible, in letters, that is, not to
say in pathology. Some of the simpler treatment is
reasonable enough; the cure of hair lip [5] contains a true

---

[1] Lb. p. 120.
[2] Lb. p. 292.
[3] Lb. p. 114.

[4] Ibid.
[5] Lb. I. xiii.

element; the application of vinegar with prussic acid[1] for head ache is practical; the great fondness for elecampane, *Inula helenium*, is parallel to the frequent employment, at the present day, of Arnica. But it would be vain to defend the prescriptions, some are altogether blunders, and the fashion of medical treatment changes so much that the prescriptions of Meade and Radcliffe are now condemned as absurd. It suffices that Saxon leeches endeavoured by searching the medical records of foreign languages to qualify themselves for their profession.

Age.

The character of the writing fixes, as far as I venture on an opinion, this copy of the work to the former half of the tenth century; some learned in MSS., who have favoured me with an opinion, say the latter half, 960 to 980. My own judgment is chiefly based upon comparison with books we know to have been written about 900.

King Ælfred.

The inquisitiveness of men at that period about the methods in medicine pursued in foreign countries is illustrated by the very curious and interesting citation from Helias, patriarch of Jerusalem.[2] The account given has strong marks of genuineness. We will assume that King Ælfred had sent to Jerusalem requesting from the patriarch some good recipes; for it would be not in the manner of mens ordinary dealings for the head of the church in the Holy Land to obtrude upon a distant king any drugs or advice of the kind. He returns then a recommendation of scamony, which is the juice of a Syrian convolvulus, of gutta ammoniaca, a sort of liquid volatile salts, of spices, of gum dragon, of aloes, of galbanum, of balsam, of petroleum, of the famous Greek compound preparation called θηριακή, and of the magic virtues of alabaster.[3] These drugs are good in themselves, and such as a resident in Syria would naturally recommend to others. The present author

---

[1] Lb. I. i. 10 and 12.
[2] Lb. p. 290.

[3] On the Phœnician origin of this word, see SSpp. p. 285.

drew his information, we may fairly suppose, from that
handbook which the king himself kept, in which were
entered " flowers, culled from what masters soever,"
" without method,"[1] "according as opportunity arose,"
and which at length grew to the size of a psalter; whence
also most likely came in due time the voyage of Oth-
here. It is very much the custom of the present swarm
of critics to drag up every old author to their modern
standard of truth, to peer into dates, to sift, and weigh,
and measure, and in short, to put an old tale teller into
the witness box of a modern court of justice, and there
teaze and browbeat him because they cannot half understand his simple talk, nor apprehend how small matters, in a truthful story, the exact day of the week
and the twentieth part of a mile become. When one
writer of the Middle Ages copies another there commonly arises a want of clearness in marking the transitions from the text of the old author to the words
of him who cites him. But in this case all seems smooth ;
the man named was patriarch of Jerusalem ; he was
contemporaneous with King Ælfred, and the drugs he
recommended were sold in the Syrian drug shops, or
apothekæ. I am, therefore, well pleased to claim for
this volume the publication in type of a new fact
about the inquiring watchfulness of that illustrious
ruler.

Thus, Oxa, Dun, perhaps some others of the same
sort, and Helias, patriarch of Jerusalem, are sources
of some of the teaching in this book. To these we
may add a mixture of the Hibernian,[2] and of the
Scandinavian.[3] Some of the recipes occur again in the
Lacnunga and in Plinius Valerianus, who, from his
mention[4] of the physician Constantinus, was later than

Many sources.

---

[1] Flosculos undecunque collectos
a quibuslibet magitris, et in corpore
unius libelli, mixtim quamvis, sicut
tunc suppetebat redigere, Asser. p. 57.

[2] Lb. p. 10, I. xlv. 5.
[3] Lb. I. xlvi., I. lxx. lxxi., III.
lviii.
[4] Fol. 14 b. 15 a.

this work. Large extracts and selections are made from the Greek writers. It is not to be expected that many will soon travel over the field of research which the present edition required, and it will be but fair to those who are examining the facts, to present them with at least one passage as a specimen.

Περὶ λυγμῶν. Ὁ λυγμὸς γίνεται ἢ διὰ πλήρωσιν, ἢ διὰ κένωσιν, ἢ δριμέων χυμῶν δακνόντων τὸν στόμαχον. ὧν ἐμεθέντων παύεται. πολλοὶ δὲ καὶ τὸ διὰ τῶν τριῶν πεπέρεων μόνον λαβόντες, ἐὰν εὐθέως ἐπιπίωσιν οἶνον λύζουσιν. ὅτι δὲ καὶ διαφθείροντές τινες τροφὴν λύζουσιν τῶν γινωσκομένων ἐστί. καὶ ῥιγώσαντες δὲ πολλοὶ λύζουσιν. ἔμετον μὲν οὖν εἰρήσομεν αὐταρκες ἴαμα τῶν διὰ πλῆθος ἢ δῆξιν λυζόντων. θερμασίαν δὲ τῶν διὰ ψύξιν. ὅταν δὲ ὑπὸ πληρώσεως ὑγρῶν γένηται λυγμός, βιαίας δεῖται κενώσεως. τοῦτο δὲ ὁ πταρμὸς ἐργάζεται. τοὺς δὲ ἐπὶ κενώσει λυγμοὺς οὐκ ἰᾶται πταρμός. Διδόναι δὲ τοῖς λύζουσιν πήγανον μετ' οἴνου ἢ νίτρον ἐν μελικράτῳ, ἢ σέσελι ἢ δαῦκον ἢ κύμινον ἢ ζιγγίβερ ἢ καλαμίνθην ἢ νάρδον κελτικήν. ταῦτα τῶν ἐπὶ διαφθορᾷ σιτίων ἢ ἐπὶ ψύξεσιν ἢ ἐπὶ πληρώσει βοηθήματα. τοῖς δὲ ὑπὸ πλήθους λύζουσιν ἐπὶ ψυχροῖς καὶ γλίσχροις χυμοῖς καστόριον τριωβόλου δίδου πίνειν δ' ὀξυκράτου, κ.τ.λ. Paulus Ægin. lib. ii. cap. 56.

### TRANSLATION.

Of hiccupings. Hiccup comes on either by reason of repletion, or of emptiness, or of austere juices biting upon the stomach, and when these are vomited forth it ceases. Many also by only taking the medicine called " by the three " peppers," if immediately on that they swallow wine, hiccup. It is also a recognized fact, that some turning their food sour, hiccup ; and many also hiccup after shivering. We shall find then that a vomit is a sufficient cure for those who hiccup from repletion or irritation ; and the application of warmth for those that do so from chill. But when the hiccup comes on by fulness of moistures, it needs a violent evacuation ; and this sneezing produces ; but sneezing does not cure the hiccups which depend on emptiness. Give the sufferer from hiccup rue with wine, or nitre in sweetened wine, or seseli, or carrot, or cummin, or ginger, or calamintha, or Keltic valerian. These are proper for the cases in which food turns sour on the stomach, or for chill, or for emptiness. But for those that suffer by repletion with cold and viscid humours, give castoreum, three obols worth, and to drink some oxymel, etc.

This is to be compared with Lb. I. xviii. The correspondence is so close as to leave no doubt but that the work before us drew from Paulus, or from one of the Greek authors, from whom he compiled his work. The number of passages the Saxon thus draws from the Greek is great; they would make perhaps one fourth of the first two books, and the question of course occurs strongly to the mind whether they came direct from the study of Greek manuscripts.

At first sight a passage[1] which says that the ficus Internal in the eyes is called "on læben" chymosis, may seem testimony. to resolve the question as that this author copied Latin works. So it may have been; but the place is not conclusive, those words may come from Oxa, Dun, or other writers of the native school of medicine; or læben, leben, may be used as it often is in a loose sense for *language,*[2] *foreign language.* It is not at this point, that it will repay our trouble to stay for consideration: we shall much more profitably form an opinion whether the Saxon leeches in general had access to the sense of the Greek authors, than whether in particular the author of these books knew anything of them. If the best men among our leeches of the tenth century could avail themselves of what Paulus of Ægina, Alexander of Tralles, and Philagrios wrote, that will suffice to raise our estimate of that day into approbation.

M. Brechillet Jourdain[3] has shewn that in those Greek early days, before the invention of printing, the wise learning. men of the middle ages possessed Latin translations of Aristoteles. There was therefore no reason for their not possessing other authors. Some among them were able to translate, some to speak Greek. The Byzantine authors in our own hands come down to a late date.

---

[1] Lb. p. 38.
[2] Ealle hiȝ ȝppecaȝ an lyben, Genesis xi. 6.

[3] Recherches critiques sur l'âge et origine des traductions Latines. d'Aristote. Paris. 1819.

Now if an Italian or a Frenchman could acquire Greek, and translate into Latin, a Saxon might do the same. Beda[1] tells of Theodorus the archbishop, and abbot Hadrianus, that they collected pupils, taught them versification, astronomy, and the ecclesiastical arithmetic of the computus, and some remained while Beda wrote who were acquainted with the Greek and Latin languages as well as with their own.[2] Further on[3] Beda gives an example of one of these disciples, Albinus, who understood Latin not less than his own language, English, with not a little Greek. Of Tobias, bishop of Rochester, another of these pupils, he says[4] that he knew the Greek and Latin languages as familiarly as his own.

King Ælfred and Ælfric both lament the decay of learning consequent upon the invasions of the Danes. Of the works translated from the Latin, by order of Ælfred and by his confidential servants or by himself, some are, in scattered passages, turned rather literally than correctly; some are executed with great spirit, and even improved in the version. Ælfric himself is a very pleasing translator, he kept his own faculties alive in the execution of his tasks; thus he translates dactyli, *dates*, as finger apples, plainly shewing that Greek words were known to him; it is also striking to find him correcting Bedas error, "lutræ,"[5] *otters*, the quadrupeds out of the sea, which came and warmed St. Cuðberhts feet with their breath, into "seals."[6]

I have shown, by the curious pieces published in the preface to the first volume of the Leechdoms, that in

[1] Beda, Hist. Eccl. IV. ii.

[2] Latinam Græcamque linguam æque ut propriam in qua nati sunt norunt. The Saxon interpreter gives a full emphasis to æque ut ; that will bear softening down in this late Latin.

[3] Beda, V. xx., p. 209, line 11.

[4] Beda V. xxiii. Ita Græcam quoque cum Latina didicit linguam, ut tam notas ac familiares sibi eas, quam nativitatis suæ loquelam haberet.

[5] Beda, p. 237.

[6] Hom. I. 138.

a fair practical sense, for the purpose they had in view, pupils in old England received instruction in Greek, and though learning decayed in times of distress, still there existed some who wished to acquire this knowledge, and some who were willing to give it. Some day the monstrous compounds, and the absurd spellings of our scientific nomenclature, pretending to be Greek, and a dozen other weak points of the day on this subject, will be regarded as proofs of barbarism.

It appears, therefore, that the leeches of the Angles and Saxons had the means, by personal industry or by the aid of others, of arriving at a competent knowledge of the contents of the works of the Greek medical writers. Here, in this volume, the results are visible. They keep, for the most part, to the diagnosis and the theory; they go back in the prescriptions to the easier remedies; for whether in Galenos or others three was a chapter on the εὐπόριστα, the "parabilia," the resources of country practitioners, and of course, even now, expensive medicines are not prescribed for poor patients.

On the margin of the pages are some private marks, *Private marks.* such as may be observed on the facsimile page. The purport of these marks is evident at fol. 56 a., chap. lxxv., which has something near a H with "totum"; again, at lxxvi. with "totum," at fol. 56 b., chap. lxxx., the figure in the middle of the facsimile margin with "totum," fol. 57 a., top line of lxxxiii. an I. nearly, with "totum." These were plainly memoranda secretly indicating the author from whom the passages so marked were taken, and "totum" means that the whole article was taken from that source. The token nearly an I. occurs at fol. 9 b., at the beginning of ii.; again at fol. 31 a., at the end of the folio; again at I. lxxxiii. with "totum" and the Roman numeral xviii. twice; again at fol. 94 b., line 8, eft to milte feocum men; again at fol. 126 b., to chapter lxvii. These references

contain a problem, which, in our imperfect knowledge
of the works of the physicians of the lower empire, is,
it seems, beyond solution. If the prescription of celandine for the eyes, Lb. I. ii. be supposed to have been
derived from Marcellus 272 g., then the other passages
cannot, as far as, after repeated examination I see, be
discovered in that author. A mark which comes near
to F. is set, in the MS., over against the words þið
eaȝna mifte, fol. 10 b., line 3, and it does not occur
again; compare Marcellus 272 b. It adds to the difficulty of the investigation, that recipes became a tradition passing from one author to another. A cypher
rather differing from H., which I will call h., occurs at
fol. 10 b. at the words Eft pið ðon ilcan celeþonian:
nearly the same on the same folio, towards the end, at
Eft pinoley. That this prescription is found in Plinius
Valerianus does not help us. Another like a plummet
line, sometimes as in the facsimile, and at fol. 30 b.
for angnail, with a ring at top, sometimes with a cross
line, as at fol. 30 b., line 4.    ȝiƒ næȝl he, is so much
like that called I., that it may be meant for the same
name. There is another like F. reversed, occurring at
ol. 11 a. Eft pyrlaƥ, also at fol. 32 a., towards the
end of the leaf, þonne þu ƒyp, at fol. 55 b. as in the
facsimile, twice with a slight difference, at fol 56 b. top
line, with another small variation, at fol. 57 b. at last
line but one; at fol. 94 a., eft ȝenim iƥieƥ leaƥ; at fol.
125 b., by the third line of chapter lxiiii., with these
words, "quia omni potu et omni medicinæ maleficia-
" torum et demoniacorum a[d]miscenda est aqua bene-
" dicta, et psalmis et orationibus vacandum est, sicut
" in hoc capitulo plene docetur." At fol 31 b. by the
word eallunȝa is a mark with a blot, meant probably
for I. At fol. 55 b. ȝiƥ þu pille, at 55 b., as in facsimile, at 56 a., chapter lxxv. lxxvi, is a sign like H.,
with legs of varied length, thus running into reversed F. At folio 56 b., chapter lxxxii., is an orna-

mented cross; this occurs but once. At fol. 94 a., chapter
xli., the mark ⅃. is three times repeated III. The
marginal ꝺ미ꞇꞇе, fol. 108 b., means that the scribe was
getting his task done: he was not aware of the additional book III. If these signs refer to native treatises,
unknown to us, and now irrecoverable, they go to illus-
trate the existence of an English school of teaching
medicines; as do the expressions "as leeches ken," not
of rare occurrence.

Besides these marks and signs as given above, we *More cypher.*
find at fol. 30 b. by the end of the sentence, ꝺo ꝼlyꞇан
ꞇo, etc., in chapter xxxiv., some writing in cypher,
thus:—

$$\text{ⱤⱤ}\Gamma\text{//}\text{//}\text{/Ɽ.\///}\Gamma$$

and again at fol. 89 b., chapter xxxiv., thus:—

$$\text{J}\Gamma\text{/Ɽ: ⱤJⱤ/Ɽ/\///:}$$
$$\text{Ɽ/Ɽ.Ɽ.Ɽ:J}\Gamma$$

The key to writing of this sort has never been published, and now for those who are skilled in such
matters an account of it shall be given,

The letters were divided into groups, and these, of *The law of this*
course, were at the discretion of every man severally, *cypher.*
as regarded their number and how many letters they
might contain. The groups, first, second, third, and so
on were commonly denoted by dots; the upstrokes
shewed by their number what place in the group each
letter held. Thus, to spell Oxa, if the first group
began at A, and contained six letters, then the second
would begin at H, and if it contained eight letters,
omitting J as not ancient, then the third group would
begin at Q, and might go on, combining U and V, to
the end; so that Oxa would be thus spelt:—

$$: ///////\ : ////// \cdot /$$

and Dun would be thus:—

· //// ⁖ ///// : //////

Some of the first letters in the specimens before us have no dot, and may perhaps be reckoned from the beginning, A.

Another method employed a line of dots instead of upstrokes, so that Oxa appeared, if the groups of letters remained the same, thus:—

. . . . . . . .   . . . . . .
. .   . . .

and Dun thus:—

. . . .   . . . . .   . . . . . .
.   . . .   . .

In his Thesaurus, Hickes and his associate Wanley give other methods employed by the Saxons, of which a common one was to employ the next following letter to that meant, so that Oxa would be Pyb, and Dun, Ewo. These devices, which have in them something of the quality of riddles and conundrums, were as amusing to the idle mind in old times as they are now. When among the varied accomplishments with which men are gifted, we read in the Codex Exoniensis,

sum biþ list hendig to awritanne word geryno,
*One is cunning handy to awrite word mysteries,*

we have an allusion to this art of secret writing, or to its kindred riddle puzzles.

There is but little encouragement to unravel these marginal marks of the Leechbook, since the two specimens afford us but a very scant basis for inductive reasoning. But, doubtless, when laid before the inquisitive eyes of restless men, they may naturally give rise to some unhappy conjectures.

Norse element. Perhaps in dissecting the curious mosaic work of this Leechbook, we may be as much struck by the Old Dansk, or as people now say, Norse element in the words Torbegete, Rudniolin, Ons worm, and the

herb Fornets palm, as by its Irish admixture, or its
Greek and Latin basis, or its fragments from King
Ælfreds handbook.

The third book of the volume is a separate produc- Third book.
tion from the two former. This is evident by the
colophon at the end of the second, declaring who owned,
and who wrote the book, and by the word "dimitte" in
the margin of the last section, indicating the approach
of a close. This other book, then, is generally of the
same tone as the preceding; a marginal mark, as mentioned above, is the same as stands by the side of some
recipes given earlier, and the monkish habit of saying
some good words over the sick is as ready to show
itself. We may therefore conclude it to be, at least, of
the same age; possibly by the same hand as the other
two.

On the whole, this work brings into a clear strong light,
the plentiful supply of good English food for the brave
appetites of the AngulSeaxe, the large importation of
foreign wine and ale and plenteous brew of potent home
beer and ale and mead, the mulled and honeyed drinks
for weaker palates; the colleges of leechcraft, the Greek
and Latin medical studies of the most eminent teachers,
the wide and far back traceable herboristic traditions,
the far and wide inquiries of King Ælfred and men
of his time like him, and it will prove every way a
most valuable work to the student of English antiquity.

In the preface to Vol. I. a few pages were devoted
to an examination of some points of grammar; these
were, of course, to some extent a precaution against
idle cavils and ignorant criticism of the translation.
The same considerations make it desirable to set forth
a few more simple observations and to support them
by examples.

It seems clear enough that the modern system of Long vowels.
marking long vowels by an accent is not in harmony

with ancient authorities; a long syllable often gets the accent, but a short vowel also is frequently found to take one.[1] The manuscripts have a method unexceptionable, and discriminative, of showing that a vowel is long by writing that vowel twice, and in some words that mode of spelling prevails now. They give us, occasionally, ʒoob, *good*, boom, *doom*, " aam, cautere,"[2] (whence we may conclude that the cognate Oman, will have O long,[3]) aac, *oak*, pus, *wise*,[4] and so forth. The information contained in this device of our forefathers has not yet attracted a due share of notice ; for example, the word Sið, *a path*, deriving itself probably from the same source as Semita, becomes in the Mœsogothic Sinþ–, and has been supposed to exhibit a vowel necessarily, as before two consonants, short by nature ; thus producing a short I in the old English. But Sið we know to have a long vowel by the spelling Siið.[5] It is not true that a Teutonic or Old English vowel before two consonants is necessarily short. Some glossaries throw the alphabet into confusion for the sake of giving short A first, then long A. Mislead by accentual marks, the compilers presume that the prefix A must be long, whereas the tradition of our language, as in Afraid, Abroad, Abased, and the short vowel of the particles which it generally represents, prove that in those instances it is short. Where A represents An, *one*, as in Anæð for Anþæð, *constant*, the case may be different. In the parallel case of Un– the prefix, the Greek Aν–, the Latin In–, the vowel is undoubtedly short, but in pronunciation it has an accent, as in Unknown, and it is frequently found accented in the MSS. Nothing but a notion that the language of

---

[1] Vol. I. pp. xciv., xcv.
[2] Gl. C.
[3] See also the Glossary.
[4] Beda, 547. 16.
[5] Beda, 571. 34. See Layamon, 25836, 25837. In Bir. Moritz, Heyne has marked the vowel long, rightly. We have also Gesuð, but Gesrððas.

Ælfric and Ælfred is dead could encourage a foreigner
to such experiments.

It is said by those who had opportunities of know-
ing, that the painful accentual system devised by the
late J. M. Kemble was abandoned by him before his
death. It was, indeed, opposed to the elementary laws
of vocalization; for it is known to all, who have gone
fully into the subject, that a prefix, if accented itself,
affects the accentuation and the vocalization of any
word with which it is compounded. The subject might
be largely illustrated and its essential laws developed
from the Oriental languages; but I will confine myself to that which is now before us. There can be no
reasonable doubt but that Þilðe, *wild*, and Deoþ, *deer*,
were pronounced with the vowels long, and the ridiculous
theory that a vowel before two consonants is short
by nature, can mislead but few; it amounts to this,
that we never could say Beast, Least, but must pro-
nounce those words, Best, Lest. These two words Þilðe,
Deoþ, being compounded and formed into one, retained
the accent and full sound on the syllable most important to the sense, and may be found in the genitive
singular under the form Þilðeþ.[1] Thus the affix Deoþ
lost its proper accent because a more powerful claim-
ant had become it close neighbour. Another example
is found in Þitan, *to reproach*, which, as appears from
Layamon,[2] had its vowel by nature long. This word
is often compounded with the preposition Æt, which
by defect of grammatical knowledge among the old
penmen commonly appears as eð-; Layamon[3] exhibits
the compound still retaining the long vowel; but the
Paris Psalter[4] spells eðþitt, where, according to the

---

[1] CE, 258, line 10.

[2] Layamon, 21311.

[3] Ofte heo heom on smiten,
Ofte heo heom atwiten.
                    Layamon, 26584.

[4] Psalm cxviii. 39.

German way of talking, the second ꞇ is "inorganic," and serves only to mark the shortness of the vowel. Under this form the word is our Twit.

Enough has been said to show that the length of the vowels in Saxon English is a very wide subject, and to justify the postponement of any decisions in the Glossary.

**Letters.**

In our oldest manuscripts þonn often occurs where it is the custom to print T. Reꞃð, *bed*, *rest*, Luꞃð, *pleasure*, *lust*, and a hundred others are examples: the superlatives end in þonn, as þ æðeleꞃðe mæðen, *the very noble maiden*, the participles also. In the Codex Exoniensis the editor removed these features of antiquity; they offended him; and were not according to Rask.[1] If any such occur in the present volume they are preserved; they are not dialectic, but archaic.

**Genders.**

In genders the glossaries are untrustworthy; thus, the most recent is found, as regards the few words common to both, much wrong, when compared with the citations in that at the end of this volume. It is unsafe to trust compounds with ᵹe-, for the genders of the simples, for Ge– being a form of Con–, and collective, its compounds are found to have a tendency to run into the neuter.[2] Simples cannot always be relied on for the gender of the compound; all moderns take ꞃoþþyꞃð for a feminine, after þyꞃð, but in a wide scope of unpublished materials I have always found it neuter.[3] Occasionally a new principle comes in, and by attraction the article agrees with the former element in the compound, instead of the latter; hence pæꞇeꞃæðþe

---

[1] For example, Gebieᵹað, Giepel-ᵹað, p. 358; þeoð, p. 357. Aþꞃe-oþeð, p. 337; Blæð, p. 310.

[2] Thus Sþþæc is feminine, Ge-rþþæc, neuter.

[3] Tꞃa eneoþholen, Lb. I. xlvii. 3, perhaps makes kneeholly neuter; or else Tꞃa, is *two parts*. This remark should have appeared in the Glossary.

appears as neuter; Siðþæpc,[1] feminine. Hence the Codex Exoniensis prefers to write þ plæʒchopð.[2]

Numerals with a singular.

Numerals admit of a substantive in the singular, so that our traditional expressions, Twelvemonth, a Six foot rule, he weighs Twelve stone, are correct according to ancient usage.[3] Distinction must be drawn between masculines, which had a plural in s, and feminines, as Night in Fortnight, or neuters, as in Five pound note, Twelve horse power, for these had in ancient time no s in the plural. Thus xii. monaþ,[4] þpie eucleþ,[5] did not require remark : similarly ʒpeʒen pætelp pull ealað,[6] nɪʒantyne pɪnteþ ɡ ʒpeʒen monaþ,[7] iv. monaþ,[8] and the MS. reading in Beowulf, 4342,[9] may stand.

Idiomatic apposition.

Examples are not very rare in other works beside this Leechbook, when of a set of words under one regimen, those that come last in order appear in the nominative, that is, in no regimen at all. Thus popðʒepðum Deurðeðɪc þe Apcebɪpccop, *defuncto Deusdedit archiepiscopo.*[10] Fepðe þa pɪðði ꞏ ɡ ʒepette ænne mæʒpeppeopt policappuþ ʒelaten ꞏ halɪʒ peþ ɡ pnotoþ,[11] which would be literally, *Deinde profectus attulit presbyterum, policarpus appellatus, vir sanctus atque prudens.* þa æteopðe pebaptɪanuþ on ppæpne anþe puðepan ꞏ lucɪna ʒecɪʒcð ppɪðe æppæpt man,[12] which would be equivalent to, *Tunc apparuit Sebastianus in somnio viduæ cuidam, Lucina nominata, homo valde religiosa.* This, when it comes to be acknowledged generally, may be called Idiomatic apposition.

Harsh transitions in pronouns from plurals to singulars, and back again, are not peculiar to this work ;

---

[1] Lb. p. 260, line 1.
[2] CE, 373, line 3.
[3] So in German.
[4] Lib. III. xviii.
[5] Lb. I. xvi. 2. Tpyðæl, Lb. I. vi. 3, viii. 2, is a compound.

[6] OT, 256. 5.
[7] Beda, 539. 23.
[8] Beda, 564. 13.
[9] Thorpe, 4355.
[10] Beda, p. 563, line 6.
[11] MH. 32 a.

they are found in others of an earlier date, bearing episcopal names for their authors.

I desire again to acknowledge many courtesies and kindnesses at Cambridge, Oxford, the Corpus Library, and that of the British Museum.

O. C.

December, 1864.

# ADDITIONS AND CORRECTIONS.

Page 60, sect. xviii., line 2. *for* ᴄɪean *read* ᴄɪhan.

Page 130, sect. lx., line 1. *for* ɼealɼe *read* ɼealɼe.

Page 174, line 24. *for* moniʒe *read* moniʒe.

Page 194, line 11. *for* Taeu *read* Taen.

Page 210, line 18. *for* bloðeff *read* bloðeɼ.    *P252 l.31 read Spelcum ; note 4, read pɪ la ɪ.*

Page 224, sect. xxviii., line 1. *for* uʒeppe *read* uɼeppe.

Page 292, note 2. *add* " they are possibly a corrupt representation of
" ἱερὰ βοτάνη."

Page 324, sect. xxx., line 4. puðupeaxán is one word.

Page 349, line 29. ἅγιος.

Page 391, glossary, v. Ðeaɼ. Cf. Ƿelanð ʒeɼoɼc ne ʒeſɼceð monna
ænɪʒum Saɼa Se mɪmmɪnʒ ean heaɼne ʒehealðan. (Fragments printed
by Prof. Stephens.) *The Wieland work will fail no man, who kenneth
to wield biting Mimming*, where the editor reads heaɼne as *hoar*.

# LEECH BOOK.

A

# [LÆCE BOC.]¹

fol. 1 a.

.I. LÆCE DOMAS² ƿIÐ eallum untꞃymnessum heafdes ⁊ hƿanan calles ȝe healꞃes heafdes ece cume · ⁊ clærnunȝa ⁊ fpilinȝ ƿið hƿum ⁊ ȝilliftꞃum to heafdes hælo · ⁊ hu mon rcyle ȝebꞃoceneſ heafdes tilȝean ⁊ ȝif þæt bꞃæȝen ut fie. :·

.II. Læcedomaſ ƿið eallum tledepnessum eaȝena · ƿið eaȝna mifte ȝe ealdeſ ȝe ȝeonȝeſ manneſ ⁊ hƿanan þ cume ⁊ ƿiþ rlic ⁊ ƿið eaȝna teapum ⁊ ƿið pemme on eaȝum · ƿið rcꞃmælum · ⁊ ȝif mon fuꞃeȝe ꞃie · ƿið pocceſ on eaȝum ⁊ ƿið ȝeꞃiȝom ⁊ ƿiþ pyꞃmum on eaȝum ⁊ eaȝꞃealfa ælceſ cynneſ.

.III. Læcedomaſ ƿið eallum eaꞃena ece ⁊ faꞃe · ƿiþ eaꞃena deafe · ⁊ ƿið yꞃelꞃe³ hlyfte · ⁊ ȝif pyꞃmaſ on eaꞃan ꞃyn ⁊ ƿiþ eaꞃꞃicȝan⁴ ⁊ ȝif eaꞃan dymen ⁊ eaꞃ ꞃealfe ælceſ cynneſ.

fol. 1 b.

.IIII. Læcecꞃæftaſ ƿiþ healꞃȝunde ⁊ hu þu meaht ȝecunman hꞃæþeꞃ hit healꞃȝund fie ⁊ þ fio adl iſ tꞃeȝea cynna oþeꞃ on þǽm ȝeaȝle oþeꞃ on þæꞃe ðꞃotan pyꞃtðꞃenc ⁊ ꞃealf ꞃiþ þon · ⁊ ꞃiþ ceacena fpyle ⁊ ƿið fpeoꞃcoþe ⁊ ȝeaȝleſ fpyle.

---

¹ See II. xlii. contents.
² This first page of the MS. has suffered somewhat from time and use.
³ This reading makes hlyꞃt feminine. See the text.

¹ Wanley reads eaꞃꞃicȝaꞃ. The text seems to my eyes to be as I have given it; ꞃicȝȝan occurs I. lxi. 2.

# LEECH BOOK.[1]

---

[1] See II. xlii. contents.
[2] Or megrim (ἡμικρανία).
[3] ἡμικράνιον.

[4] *A disease so called, sties, wisps.*
[5] Probably from scrofula.

A 2

.V. Læcedomaſ ȝiſ manneſ muð ſaſi ſie ȝe tyðſeð
⁊ piþ ȝebleȝnaðſe tunȝan muþ ſealſ piþ þon ilcan.
Þið ſulūm oſoðe · III. læcedomaſ.

.VI. Læcedomaſ pið toþſæſce · ⁊ ȝiſ pyſm toþ ete
⁊ toþſealſa · eſt pið þam uſeſan toþ ece ⁊ pið þam
mþeſſan.

.VII. Læcedom ȝiſ mon blod hſæce.

.VIII. Læcedomaſ pið blæce ón ᵹ́phtan ⁊ bſiſ piþ
þon ilcan ⁊ ſealſ ealſa ſeopeſ.

.VIIII. Læcedomaſ ȝiſ men yſine blod óſ nebbe eſt
blodſetena ȝe ón to bindanne ȝe ón caſe to ðonne ȝe
hoſiſe ȝe men ealſa · X.

.X. Læcedóm piſ ȝeſnote · ⁊ piſ ȝeſoſūm.

.XI. Læcedomaſ piſ ſaſium ſeoloſūm.

.XII. Læcedóm pið ſcam¹ muþe ⁊ pið ceolan ſpyle ·
þſiy læcedomaſ.

.XIII. Læcedóm piſ hæſiſceaſiðe.

[XIV.] Læcedóm piſ ſeaðan.²

[XV.] Læcedomaſ pið hpoſtan hu he miſſenlice ón
man becymð ⁊ hu hiſ man tilian ſcyle ⁊ pyſitðſeicaſ
piſ hpoſtan ⁊ piſ anȝbſeoſte ⁊ ðſiyȝum hpoſtan cnd-
leſan cſiæſtaſ.

[XVI.] .XIIII. Læcedomaſ pið bſeoſt ſæſice · IIII.
cſiæſtaſ.

[XVII.] .XV. Læcedomaſ piſ heoſitſſeſice · V. cſiæſtaſ.

[XVIII.] .XVI. Læcedomaſ piſ þam miclan ȝicþan ⁊ hu
he cymð oſ acolodum maȝan oþþe to ſpiðe hatum óððe
oſ to micelſie ſylle oþþc læſineſſe oþþe óſ yſelſie
ſſetan ſhitendſie ⁊ hu hiſ món tilian ſcyle piſ ælc
þaſia.

---

¹ In text ſonum, for ſohum.   |   ² ſeaðan ; text.

---

[1] The *lomentum* of the Roman women, a paste of pulse, generally of lentils ; women used it to improve their complexions, and it was eatable though unsavoury.

[2] Colds in the head.

[3] See II. xxxix.

[4] Host, *cough*, pronounced with o short.

[5] *Wark* is *pain*.

[6] *Emptiness*.

[7] *Humour*.

[XIX.] .XVII. Læcebomaꞃ piþ placan ⱦpeȝen æþele. :·

.XX. Læceboma ꞃ piþ ꞃculþoꞃ pæꞃce · III. cꞃæꝼⱦaꞃ.

.XXI. Læceboma ꞃ pið þæꞃe fꞃiðꞃan ꞃiban faꞃe ꞇ þæꞃe pineꞃⱦꞃan ꞃyx cꞃæꝼⱦaꞃ. :·

.XXII. Læceboma ꞃ pið lenðenece ꝼeoꞃeꞃ. :·

.XXIII. Læcebomaꞃ piþ þeohece ⱦpeȝen ꞇ an piþ þoꞃ ȝiꝼ þeoh ꞃlapaꞃ.

.XXIIII. Læceboma ꞃ piþ cneoꞃ pꞃoꞃce ꞇ ȝiꝼ cneoꞃ faꞃ ꞃe. :·

.XXV. Læceboma ꞃ piþ fcancena ꞃaꞃe ꞇ ȝiꝼ fcancan ꞃoꞃaðe fynð oꞃꞃe oꞃeꞃ lim ꝼeoꞃeꞃ cꞃæꝼⱦaꞃ ꞇ hu mon ꞃpelcean ꞃcyle. :·

ª Read fino.

.XXVI. Læcebomaꞃ ȝiꝼ ꞃin[ª] ꞃcꞃince ꞇ æꝼⱦeꞃ þam ꞃe ꞃaꞃ oððe fpelle oððc ȝiꝼ monneꞃ ꝼoⱦ ⱦo hoꞃꞃmum ꞃcꞃꞃmme ꞇ fcꞃꞃnce ꞇ ȝiꝼ ꞃino clæppeⱦⱦe ꞇ cꞃaciȝe ealleꞃ ꝼeoꞃeꞃ cꞃæꝼⱦaꞃ. :·

.XXVII. Læcebomaꞃ piþ ꝼoⱦece oꞃþe oꞃꞃeꞃ liꞃeꞃ oꞃþe ꝼoⱦa ȝefpelle ꝼoꞃ miclan ȝanȝe · VI. cꞃæꝼ[ⱦaꞃ]. :·

.XXVIII. Lacꞇeboma ꞃ piþ ban ece ꞇ ꞃcalꝼ ꞇ ðꞃenc þꞃy cꞃæꝼⱦaꞃ þæꞃ ꞃynð. :·

.XXVIIII. Læcebomaꞃ ȝiꝼ manneꞃ ȝeⱦaꞃa heoþ faꞃe oþþe aþunðene þꞃy cꞃæꝼⱦaꞃ. :·

.XXX. Læcebomaꞃ piþ æcelman ꞇ piþ ðon ðe men acale þæⱦ ꝼel oꞃ þam ꝼoⱦum. :·

.XXXI. Læceboma ꞃ piþ ælcum heaꞃðum þinȝe oþþe fpyle oþþe ȝefpelle ꞇ piþ ælcꞃe yꝼelꞃe fpellenðꞃe pæⱦan ꞇ piþinnan ȝepyꞃfmeðum ȝefpelle þam þe pyꞃð oꞃ ꝼylle oððe oꞃ ꞃleȝe oþþe oꞃ hꞃyꞃca[¹] lꞃilcum ꞇ piþ fꞃiðe ꝼꞃeꞃlicum fpylum ꞇ piþ ðeaðum fpylum ꞇ ꞃcalꝼæ ꞇ ðꞃencaꞃ ꞇ fpeꞃmȝe ꞇ bæþ piþ eallum lichoman fpylum ealꞃa læceboma ⱦꞃam læꞃ þꞃⱦꞃȝ. :·

---

¹ Text hꞃꞃcꞃca: read hꞃꞃcꞃa ?

---

[1] Exactly, *incapable of muscular action.*

[2] *Be drawn up.*

.XXXII. Læcedomaſ ƿið þam yflan blæce hu man þa
ſealfa ꞇ baþu ꞇ ð|encaſ ƿiþ ðon pyſceau ꞃcyle ꞇ ƿiþ
hꞃeoꞃum lice ꞇ ƿið adeadedum lice bæþ ꞇ ſealfa ƿiþ
þon · bæþ ꞇ ꞃealfa ꞇ ð|encaſ ƿiþ þam miclan lice ꞇ
ſpile ealleꞃ ꞃiꞃꞇyne læcedomaſ.                          :·

.XXXIII. Læcedomaꞃ ꞇ ð|encaſ ꞇ ꞃealfa ꞇ [on]leꞡna
ƿiþ ſpꞃinꞡe ꞡe adeadedum ꞡe undeadedum · VIII. cꞃæꞃ-
ꞇaſ.
.XXXIV. Læcedom ꞡiꝼ næꞡl ſy oꝼ handa ꞇ ƿiþ anꞡ-
næꞡle ꞇ ƿiþ peaꞃꞡbꞃædan.                                 :·

.XXXV. Læcedomaꞃ micle ꞇ æþele be aſpeaꞃꞇedum ꞇ
adeadedūm lice ꞇ hꞃanan ſio adl cume ꞇ hu hiꞃ¹ mon
ꞇilian ꞃcyle ꞡiꝼ ꝥ lic ꞇo þon ſpiþe adeadiꞡe ꝥ þæꞃ
ꞡeꝼelneꞃ on ne ſy · ꞇ hu mon ꝥ deade blod aꝛeꞡ
penuan ꞃcyle · ꞇ ꞡiꝼ hīm mōn līm ōꞃceoꞃꞃan ſcyle oððe
ꝼyꞃ onꞃeꞇꞇan hu ꝥ mou don scyle · bꞃꞃaꞃ ꞇ ð|enceaꞃ
ꞇ ꞃealfa ƿiþ þæꞃe adle.                                  :·

ſol. 3 b.

.XXXVI. Læcedomaꞃ ƿið þæꞃe adle þe mon hæꞇ ciꞃcul
adl bꞃꞃ ꞇ ð|encaſ ꞇ ꞃealfa þæꞇ iꞃ ſpiþe ꞃꞃeōnu² adl ꞇ
heꞃ ꞃeꞡþ hƿilcne meꞇe oþþe ðꞃꞃcan mōn ſcyle on
þæꞃe adle ꞃoꞃꞡan.                                        :·

.XXXVII. Læcedomaꞃ ƿiþ ðon ꞡiꝼ mon ne mæꞡe luꞃ
micꞡean ꞡehealdan ꞇ þæꞃe ꞡepeald naꞡe ꞇ ꞡiꝼ he ꞡe-
miꞡan ne mæꞡe ꞇ ꞡiꝼ he blode miꞡe · ꞇ ꞡiꝼ: ꝼiꝼ on þon
ꞇeðꞃe ſie · XIIII. læcedomaſ.                            :·

.XXXVIII. Læcecꞃæꝼꞇaꞃ ꞇ dolꞡꞃealfa ꞇ ð|encaſ ƿiþ
eallum pundum ꞇ clænſunꞡūm ou ælce piꞃan ꞡe ƿið
ealdꞃe punde ꞇobꞃocenꞃe ꞇ ꞡiꝼ ban bꞃꞃyce ōn heaꞃode
ſie · ꞇ ƿið hundeꞃ ꞃliꞇe · ꞇ dolꞡſealꝼ ƿið lunꞡen adle ꞇ
ƿiþ mnan punde ꞃealꝼ · ꞇ ꞃealꝼ ꞡiꝼ þu ꞃaðe ƿille lyꞇle
punde lacnian ꞇ ꞡiꝼ mōn mid iꞃene ꞡepundod ſie · oþþe
mid ꞇꞃeope ꞡeꞃleꞡen · oþþe mid ſꞇane ꞇ eꝼꞇ ſealfa ꞡiꝼ

---

¹ hiꞃ refers to he.          |          ² Read ꞃꞃeenu.

---

[1] *The cautery.*  |  [2] See viii.

men sie lim of lime ofāslegen finger oþþe fót oþþe hand · oððe gif mearh[1] ute sie ⁊ gif dolh fulige ealra fram fruman seoƿer ⁊ þritig læcedoma. :·

.XXXVIIII. Læcedomas ƿið ælces cynnes omum ⁊ fol. 4 a. ōnfeallum ⁊ bancoþūm · ƿiþ ut ablegnedum omūm ⁊ ƿiþ omena geberste · ⁊ ƿið omum ofer hatūm ⁊ ƿið seondūm omum ꝥ is fic · drencas ⁊ sealfa ƿiþ eallum omum ealra tƿām læs þritig. :·

.XL. Læcedomas ⁊ drencas ⁊ sealfa ƿiþ pōc adle ealra syxe. :·

.XLI. Læcedomas þry æþele ƿiþ innan onfealle ⁊ omum. :·

.XLII. Læcedomas ƿiþ ðære geolƿan adle ⁊ stanbæþ ⁊ ƿiþ geal adle sio cymð of þære geolƿan adle · sio biþ adla ƿreust abiterað se lichoma eall ⁊ ageolƿaþ sƿa god geolo seoluc. :·

.XLIII. Læcedomas ƿiþ ƿæter bollan. :·

.XLIIII. Læcedomas ƿið cancer adle þæt is bite ⁊ smerenessa ⁊ sealf feoƿer cræftas. :·

.XLV. Læcedomas ⁊ drencas ƿiþ ælcum attre ƿið nædran slege ⁊ bite ⁊ slite · ⁊ ƿiþ þon gif mōn atter geþicge · ⁊ þæs halgan cristes þegnes Iohannes gebed ⁊ gealdor ⁊ eác oþer scyttisc gecost gealdor gelƿæfer ƿiþ ælcum attre · ƿiþ fleogendum attre ⁊ sƿyle ⁊ deopūm dolgum · gif hƿa gedrince ƿyrm ōn ƿætere fol. 4 b. ƿiþ þon læcedomas · ⁊ gif mōn forboren sie ealles · XX. cræfta ƿið attre. :·

.XLVI. Læcedomas gif ana ƿyrm on men ƿeaxe sealf drenc ⁊ clam ƿiþ þon · V. læcedomas þæs sint. :·

---

[1] meah, MS.

stone; and further salves if for a man a limb be struck off from a limb, finger or foot or hand, or if the marrow be out, and if a wound get foul. Of all from the beginning four and thirty leechdoms.

xxxix. Leechdoms against erysipelas of every kind and fellons, and bone diseases, for erysipelatous affections accompanied by external blains, and for the bursting of erysipelatous cysts, and for excessively hot erysipelatous attacks, and for running erysipelas, that is *the disease called* "fig." Drinks and salves for all sorts of erysipelatous affections. Thirty less by two.

xl. Leechdoms and drinks and salves for pock disease. In all six.

xli. Three excellent leechdoms for inward tubercles and erysipelas.

xlii. Leechdoms for the yellow disease,ª and a stone ª Jaundice. bath,[1] and for the gall disease which cometh of the yellow disease. This is of diseases the most powerful, the body becometh quite bitter and turneth yellow, as good yellow silk.

xliii. Leechdoms for dropsy.

xliv. Leechdoms for the disease cancer, that is, "bite," and smearings and a salve. Four receipts.

xlv. Leechdoms and drinks against every poison, against stroke and bite and rend of snake; and in case a man swallow poison, and a prayer of the holy thane of Christ, Iohannes, and an incantation and also another Scottish approved incantation, *in Gaelic or Erse*, either of them against every poison, against flying poison and swelling and deep gashes. If any one drink a worm[2] in water, leechdoms against that; and if a man be tied with a magic knot. In all twenty receipts against poison.

xlvi. Leechdoms if King Ons worm wax on a man, a salve, a drink, and a plaster for that. There are five leechdoms of it.

---

[1] A stone bath was a vapour bath, water being thrown on heated stones.
[2] Reptile.

.XLVII. Læcedomas ⁊ drencas ⁊ sealfa ƿiþ þeoradlum moniges cynnes þa betstan ƿiþ þeorƿyrme ōn fet · XII. ealra ƿiþ þeor adlūm. :·

.XLVIII. Læcedomas ƿiþ þam ƿyrmum þe innan eglað mōnnūm · ⁊ ƿiþ ƿyrmum þe on cilda innoþe beoþ ⁊ ƿið cilda innoð sare ealra cræfta · XII. ƿiþ þam. :·

.XLVIIII. Læcedom on sundron anlipig ƿiþ þam smalan ƿyrme. :·
.L. Læcedomas ƿiþ hand ƿyrmum ⁊ deaf ƿyrmum ⁊ gif ƿyrm hand ete · ƿeaxsealf ƿiþ hand ƿyrme syx cræftas ealra · IIII. ƿisan. :·
.LI. Læcedomas ƿiþ ƿyrmum þe monnes flæsc etaþ. :·
.LII. Læcedomas tƿegen ƿiþ lusūm. :·
.LIII. Læcedomas tƿeten ƿiþ smoega ƿyrmum. :·
.LIIII. Læcedomas ƿið ƿyrmætum lice ⁊ cƿeldehtum. :·

.LV. Læcedōm ƿiþ aslegenūm lice. :·
.LVI. Læcedomas ƿiþ aslapenūm[1] lice ⁊ bæþ sealf. :·

.LVII. Læcedomas ⁊ drencas ⁊ sealfa ƿiþ fice. :·

.LVIII. Læcedomas to ƿen sealfe · ⁊ to ƿen bylūm. :·
fol. 5 a. .LVIIII. Læcedomas ƿið ƿaralisin ꝥ is on englisc lyft adl ⁊ ƿiþ neurisne þry. :·
.LX. Læcedomas ƿið bryne ⁊ sealfa · VIII. ealra. :·
.LXI. Læcedomas ƿiþ lið ƿærce ⁊ ƿið liþseaƿe ⁊ gif liþseaƿ sio[2] ⁊ hoþole ūtryrne ealra cræfta feoƿer-tyne. :·

.LXII. Læcedomas ƿiþ feferadle to hælanne drencas ƿið þan · ƿiþ þriddan dæges fære ⁊ feorþan dæges fære ⁊ ƿið ælces dæges fere ⁊ ƿiþ lencten adle ꝥ is fefer · ⁊ hu man sceal ƿiþ þære adle on husl dysce þone halgan

[1] The passage of the text has aslegenum.

[2] For siohe, subjunctive.

---

[1] A sort of dry rot : see the glossary. Μαρασμός.

[2] Possibly νευρῶν πάρεσις ; a kind of παράλυσις.

Ᵹ þone miclan ᵹoðeꞃ naman pꞃitan Ᵹ on þone ðꞃenc
mið haliᵹꝥætꞃe ðꝥean Ᵹ haliᵹ ᵹebeð on uꝼan ſinᵹan Ᵹ
cꞃeðo Ᵹ ꝑateꞃ noꞃteꞃ · x. læceðomaꞃ.                      :·

.LXIII. Læceðomaꞃ pið ꝼeonð ꞃeocum men ðꞃencaſ to
þon Ᵹ hu mon ſcyle mꝟ̈an Ᵹ ᵹebeðu Ᵹ ꞃealmaſ oꝼeꞃ
þone ðꞃenc ꞃinᵹan Ᵹ oꝼ cꞃꝟcbellum ðꞃincan · Ᵹ pið
bꞃæcſeocum men · Ᵹ pið ꞃeðen heoꞃte Ᵹ pið þon eallum ſex cꞃæꝼtaꞃ.                                           :·

.LXIIII. Læceðomaꞃ pið ælcꞃe leoðꞃunan Ᵹ ælꝼſiðenne
ol. 5 b. ꝥ iſ ꝼeꞃeꞃcynneꞃ ᵹealðoꞃ Ᵹ ðuſt Ᵹ ðꞃencaꞃ Ᵹ ꞃealꝼ Ᵹ
ᵹiꝼ ſio aðl netnum ſie · Ᵹ ᵹiꝼ ſio aðl pyꞃðe mannan
oððe maꞃe ꞃiðe Ᵹ pyꞃðe ſeoꝼon ealleꞃ cꞃæꝼta.             :·

.LXV. Læceðomaꞃ eꝼt pið lencten aðle Ᵹ þaꞃa ꝼeoꞃeꞃ
ᵹoðſpelleꞃa naman · Ᵹ ᵹeꝑꞃitu Ᵹ ᵹebeðu Ᵹ ſpꞃᵹenðe
ſceal mon ſum ᵹeꝑꞃit ꝑꞃitan · v. cꞃæꝼtaſ.               :·

.LXVI. Læceðomaꞃ unᵹemynðe Ᵹ pið ðyſiᵹum.              :·

.LXVII. Læceðomaꞃ Ᵹ ðꞃencaꞃ pið ᵹenumenum mete
Ᵹ ᵹiꝼ eala ꞃie aꝑeꞃð oþþe meolcen mete þꞃy cꞃæꝼtas.    :·

.LXVIII. Læceðomaꞃ pið þon ᵹiꝼ hunta ᵹebite mannan ꝥ ſꞃiðꞃe oþꞃe[1] naman ᵹanᵹelpeꞃꝑa ꞃex ðuᵹenðe
cꞃæꝼtas.

.LXVIIII. Læceðomaꞃ pið ꞃeðe hunðeꞃ ſliten Ᵹ pið
hunðeꞃ ðolᵹe · vii. læceðomaꞃ.                          :·

.LXX. Læceðomaꞃ ᵹiꝼ mon ſie to ꝑꞃæne oþþe to
unꝑꞃæne.                                                :·

.LXXI. Læceðomaꞃ pið ꝑæᵹe ꞃeoſan ſaꞃe Ᵹ ᵹiꝼ hoh
ſino ꝼoꞃoð ꞃie.                                         :·

.LXXI. Læceðomaꞃ on hꝑilce tið bloð ꞃie to ꝼoꞃᵹanne
fol. 6 a. on hꝑilce to ꝼoꞃlætenne Ᵹ hu ſie attꞃeꞃ ꝼul ſio
lyꝼt on hlaꝼmæꞃꞃe tið · Ᵹ be ðꞃencum Ᵹ utꝼoꞃum
on þam monþe Ᵹ ꝥte pyꞃta on þam monðe ſinð to
pyꞃcanne.                                               :·

---

[1] Compare the chapter, and read ꝥ iſ ſꞃiðꞃe Ᵹ oðeꞃ.

shall write upon the eucharistic paten the holy and the great name of God, and wash it with holy water in to the drink, and sing a holy prayer over it and the Credo and the Paternoster. Ten leechdoms.

lxiii. Leechdoms for a fiendsick man (*or demoniac*), drinks for that, and how a man shall sing masses and prayers and psalms over the drink, and drink out of church bells, and for a lunatic man, and for the wood heart *or frenzy,* and for them all ; six receipts.

lxiv. Leechdoms against every pagan charm and for a man with elvish tricks ; that is to say, an enchantment for a sort of fever, and powder and drinks and salve, and if the disease be on neat cattle ; and if the disease harm a man, or if a mare ride him and hurt him. In all seven crafts.

lxv. Leechdoms again for typhus, and the names of the four gospellers and writings and prayers ; and in silence shall one write some writing. Five receipts.

lxvi. Leechdoms for the idiot and the silly.

lxvii. Leechdoms and drinks for meat taken, and if ale be spoilt or milken food. Three receipts.

lxviii. Leechdoms in case a hunting spider[1] bite a man, that is, the stronger *sort,* and if another by name gangweaver,[2] *bite him.* Six capital receipts.

lxix. Leechdoms for a rent of a mad dog and for wound of hound. Seven leechdoms.

lxx. Leechdoms if a man be too lustful or too unlustful.

lxxi. Leechdoms for sore of the dorsal muscles, and if the heel sinew be broken.

lxxii. Leechdoms *declaring* at what time blood is to be foregone, and at what to be let ; and how the air is full of venom at Lammas[3] time, and of drinks and evacuations on that month, and that worts on that month are to be worked.

---

[1] Now *Salticus scenicus.* Aranea venatoria is American. But here the tarantula was meant.

[2] *Aranea viatica.*

[3] August 1.

Romane ɼ eall ſuð ɼolc poɼhton hīm eoɼþ huſ ƿið
þæɼe unlyɼte · ɼ hu mōn ɼcyle blodlæſe on þæɼa ɼex
ɼiɼa ƿlcon on þæſ monan eldo ɼonȝan on þɼitiȝūm¹
nihta ɼ hponne betſt to lætanne · ɼ ȝiɼ blod dolȝ
yɼeliȝe · ɼ ȝiɼ þu ƿille ōn ſniðe blod ɼoɼlætan oþþe ōn
æðɼe · oððe ȝiɼ þu ne mæȝe blod dolȝ āppiɼþan · oþþe
ȝiɼ þu ne mæȝe ȝeotend æðɼe appɼiðan oððe ȝiɼ mon
on ſinɼe beɼlea æt blodlætan.      :·

.LXXIII. Læcedom ȝiɼ men hɼile him eine.      :·
.LXXIIII. Læcedōm ƿið peaɼtum ɼ peaɼɼum on lime. :·

.LXXV. Læcedom ƿiþ ɼcuɼɼedum næȝle.      :·
.LXXVI. Læcedōm ƿið ȝicþan.      :·
.LXXVII. Læcedōm ȝiɼ þu ƿille þ yɼel ſpyle ɼ æteɼno
ɼiote ut beɼſte.      :·
.LXXVIII. Læcedom ȝiɼ men unluſt ſie ȝetenȝe.      :·
.LXXVIIII. Læcedom ȝiɼ mōn on lanȝūm ɼeȝe teoɼiȝe. :·
fol. 6 b.
.LXXX. Læcedōm ƿið þon þe mon hine ɼoɼðɼince. :·
.LXXXI. Læcedōm ƿið miclūm cyle.      :·
.LXXXII. Læcedōm ȝiɼ men ſie ɼæɼiɼȝa to micel pæcæ
ȝetenȝe.      :·
.LXXXIII. Læcedōm to manneſ ſtemne.      :·
.LXXXIIII. Læcedom ƿið þon ȝiɼ mon þunȝ ete.      :·

.LXXXV. Læcedōm ƿið þon þe mon ɼundiȝe ƿið huſ
ɼeond to ȝeɼeohtanne.      :·
.XXXVI. Læcedōm ƿiþ miclum ȝanȝe oɼeɼ land þy
læſ he teoɼiȝe.      :·
.LXXXVII. Læcedōm ȝiɼ manneſ ɼeax ɼealle ſcalɼ ƿiþ
þon ɼ ȝiɼ man calu ſie.      ·
.LXXXVIII. Læcedōmaſ ƿiþ hoɼɼeſ hɼeoɼle ɼ ȝiɼ hoɼſ
ȝeallede ſie · ɼ ȝiɼ hoɼſ ſie ōɼſcoten oþþe oþeɼ neat.

---

¹ þɼitiȝúm was written ; now partly erased.

The Romans and all the people of the south wrought for themselves houses of earth against the ill air ; and how a man shall forego bloodletting on each of the six fives[1] of the moons age in the thirty nights, and when best to let *blood,* and if the incision for bloodletting take an ill turn, and if thou will let blood on an incision or on a vein, or if thou may not staunch the bleeding incision, or if thou may not bind up the flowing vein, or if one, in bloodletting, cut down on a sinew.

---

[1] Though a sidereal revolution of the moon be but 27·321 days, yet the moon often attains the thirtieth day of her age.

Alex. Trall.
lib. i.
Oɴ þyrrum æpieſtan læcecpæptum ȝeppitene ſint læcebomaſ piꝺ eallum heaꝼꝺer untpymneppum.

ᛗuppa hatte pypt ȝeȝniꝺ on mopiþepe þ̄te peninȝ
ȝepeȝe • ꝺo ſteap ꝼulne piney to poſe ſmype þonne þ̄
fol. 7 a.
heaꝼoꝺ miꝺ 7 ꝺpince on niht neptiȝ. Piꝺ heaꝼoꝺ pæþce
Cf. Galen.
vol. xiv. p. 500,
ed. 1827.
Κεφαλαλγία.
ȝenim puꝺan 7 pepmoꝺ ȝecnupa 7 menȝ piþ eceꝺ 7 ele
aſeoh þuph claꝺ ſmipe miꝺ þ̄ heaꝼoꝺ • oꝺꝺe clam oꝼ
þám ilcan pypc leȝe on þ̄ heaꝼoꝺ 7 beſpeþe pel þonne þu
to peſte pille.

Lacn. 1.
Piꝺ þon ilcan ȝením betonican 7 pipop ȝeȝniꝺ ſpiꝺe
toȝæꝺepe læt ane niht hanȝian on claꝺe ſmipe miꝺ.
ᵃ Plinius Vale-
rianus, de re
Medica,fol.14 b,
for clearing
the head.
ᵇ Seap is neuter.
Piꝺ heaꝼoꝺ pæþceᵃ betan pypttpuman ȝecnupa piꝺ
huniȝ appinȝ ꝺo þ̄ yeap on neb 7 onȝean ſunnan up-
peapꝺ liȝe • 7 þæt heaꝼoꝺ ho oꝼ ꝺune þ̄ yeᵇ yeap mæȝe
þ̄ heaꝼoꝺ ȝeonꝺ ypinan • hæbbe hím æp on muþe ele
oþþe butepan 7 þonne uplanȝ aſitte hniȝie ꝼoþꝺ læte
ꝼlopan oꝼ þam nebbe þa ȝilliſtpan ꝺo ſpa ȝelome oþþæt
hit clæne ſie.                               :•

Piꝺ heaꝼoꝺ pæþce ȝenim hámpypt niþepeapꝺe ȝecnupa leȝe on cealꝺ pætep ȝniꝺ ſpiꝺe oþþ eall ȝeleþpeꝺ
ſie beþe miꝺ þ̄ heaꝼoꝺ.                       :•
Lacn. 1.
Piþ heaꝼoꝺ pæþce ȝením beah heoloþan 7 ȝpunꝺe
ſpelȝean 7 ꝼencepſan 7 ȝitpipan pel on pætepe læt
fol. 7 b.
peocan on þa eaȝan þonne hit hat ſie 7 ymb þa eaȝan
ȝniꝺ miꝺ þæm pyptum ſpa hatúm.              :•

Piꝺ heaꝼoꝺ ece ȝením ꝼealh 7 ele ꝺo ahſan ȝepype
þonne to ꝛlypan ꝺo to hymlican 7 eoꝼop þpotan 7
ꝺa peaꝺan netlan ȝecnupa ꝺo þonne on þone ꝛlipan

i.

1. In these first leechcrafts are written leechdoms for all infirmities of the head.

2. A wort has been named murra,[a] rub it in a mortar *[a] Scandix odorata.* as much as may make a pennyweight, add to the ooze a stoup full of wine, then smear the head with that and let *the patient* drink *this* at night fasting. For head wark, take rue and wormwood, pound them and mingle with vinegar and oil, strain through a cloth, smear the head with it; or work a paste of the same, lay it on the head and swathe it up well, when thou will to bed.

3. For the same, take betony and pepper, rub *them* thoroughly together, let *them* hang one night in a cloth, smear with *them.* For head wark, pound some roots of beet with honey, wring them, apply the juice to the face, and let *the patient* lie supine against the sun, and hang the head adown that the juice may run all over the head. Let him hold before that in his mouth oil or butter, and then sit up *and* lean forward *and* let the matter flow off the face. Let him so do often till it be clean.

4. For head wark, take the lower part of homewort,[b] *[b] Sempervivum tectorum.* pound it, lay it in cold water, rub it hard till it be all in a lather, bathe the head with it.

5. For head wark, take elecampane[c] and groundsel[d] *[c] Inula hele-* and fen cress[1] and gitrife,[2] boil them in water, make *nium.* them steam upon the eyes, when it is hot, and rub *[d] Senecio vul-garis.* about the eyes with the worts, so hot.

6. For head ache, take willow[3] and oil, reduce to ashes, work to a viscid substance, add to this hemlock[4] and carline[5] and the red nettle,[6] pound them,

---

[1] *Nasturtium officinale.*
[2] *Agrostemma githago.*
[3] *Salix.*

[4] *Conium maculatum.*
[5] *Carlina acaulis.*
[6] *Lamium purpureum.*

beþe mið. Wiþ heafod ece hunder heafod ȝebæcin to
ahran ⁊ suið þ heafod leȝe on.  :·

Wið heafod wræcce ȝenim efelastan ȝecnua on cealð
wæter ȝnið betweoh handum ⁊ ȝecnupa cluþþunȝ ðo
þræncto beþe mið. Wiþ heafod ece ȝenim hoþan ⁊ wín
⁊ eced ȝesþet mið huniȝe ⁊ smiþe mið.  :·

¹Wiþ heafod ece ȝenim ðiler blostman seoð on ele
smiþe þa þunwanȝan mið. ²Wiþ þon ilcan ȝenim heoþoter
hoþnes ahran menȝ wið eced ⁊ þosan seaþ binð on þ
wænȝe. Wiþ þon ilcan ȝenim fæt ful ȝþenþe þuðan
leaþa ⁊ reneþes rícdes cuclep fulne ȝeȝnið toȝædeþe
ðo æȝes þ hwite to cuclep fulne · þ sio realþ sie
þicce smiþe mið feþeþe on þa healþe þe ran ne sie.  :·

• 'Ημικρανία.

Wiþ healþes heafdes ᵃ ece ȝenim þa neaðan netlan
ansteleðe ȝetþiþula menȝ wið eced ⁊ æȝes þ hwite ðo
eall toȝædeþe smiþe mið.  :·

fol. 8 a.

Wiþ healþes heafdes ece lauþes croppan ȝetþiþula ón
eceð mið ele smyþe mið þy þæt renȝe.  :·

Wið þon ilcan ȝenim þuðan seaþ þinȝ on þ næs-
þyrel þe on þa rahan³ healþe bið.  :·

Wiþ healþes heafdes ece · ȝenim lauþes croppan ðust
⁊ seneþ menȝ toȝædeþe ȝeót eceð ón smiþe mið þa
rahan healþe mið þy · oþþe menȝe wið wín þær lauþes
croppan · oþþe þuðan sæð ȝnið on eceð ðo beȝa emþela
ȝnið ðon⁴ hneccan mið þy.  :·

⁵Tácnu þære aðle · sio aðl cymð óf yfelþe þætan uþan
floþenðre oþþe æþme oþþe of bám · þonne rceal mon æþest

¹ Plinius, xx. 73.
² Galenus, vol. xiv. p. 398, ed. 1827.
³ maþan, MS.
⁴ Read ðone.
⁵ Alex. Trall. lib. i. cap. 12, partly word for word.

put them then on the viscid stuff, bathe therewith. Against head ache; burn a dogs head [1] to ashes, snip the head; lay on.

7. For a head wark, take everlasting,[2] pound it in cold water, rub it between the hands, and pound cloffing,[3] apply it thereto, bathe therewith. For head ache, take hove [4] and wine and vinegar; sweeten with honey, and smear therewith.

8. For head ache, take blossoms of dill,[5] seethe in oil, smear the temples therewith. For the same, take ashes of harts horn, mingle with vinegar and juice of rose, bind on the cheek. For the same, take a vessel full of leaves of green rue, and a spoon full of mustard seed, rub together, add the white of an egg, a spoon full, that the salve may be thick; smear with a feather on the side which is not sore.

9. For ache of half the head,[6] take the red nettle of one stalk, bruise it, mingle with vinegar and the white of an egg, put all together, anoint therewith.

10. For a half heads ache, bruise in vinegar with oil the clusters of the laurus, smear the cheek with that.

11. For the same, take juice of rue, wring on the nostril which is on the sore side.

12. For a half heads ache, take dust of the clusters of laurel, and mustard, mingle *them* together, pour vinegar upon them, smear with that the sore side. Or mix with wine the clusters of laurel. Or rub *fine* in vinegar the seed of rue,[7] put equal quantities of both, rub the back of the neck with that.

13. Tokens of the disease. The disease cometh of evil humour flowing[8] or *evil* vapour, or of both. Then

---

[1] That the plant called " hounds-head " in Herb. lxxxviii. is meant, I do not think.

[2] *Gnaphalium.*

[3] *Ranunculus sceleratus.*

[4] *Glechoma hederacea.*

[5] *Anethum graveolens.*

[6] *Megrim.*

[7] *Ruta graveolens.*

[8] I hesitate to believe that upan, can mean *from below upwards*; yet Alexandros says κατὰ συμπαθείαν τοῦ στομάχου. Ufan means *from above.*

on ða nöle ꝼoꝛeꝼeaꝛöꝛe bloö lætan oꝼ æöꝛe · æꝼteꝛ
þon ꝛceal man pyꝛt öꝛenc ꝼellan Ᵹ lacnian ꝛiþþan þa
ꝛaꝛan ſtopa · ȝiꝼ ſeo aöl ſie cumen oꝼ micelꝛe hæto
þonne ꝛceal man miö cealöūm læceöomum lacnian ·
ȝiꝼ hio oꝼ cealöum Intinȝan cymö · þonne ꝛceal mōn
miö hatum læceöomum lácnian ȝeliꝛæþeꝛeꝼ ꝛceal mon
nyttian Ᵹ miſcian þ þone líchoman hæle Ᵹ æꝼeꝛ mæȝen
hæbbe · hīm öeah þ him mōn on eaꝛe öꝛype ȝeplæc-
cöne ele miö oþꝛūm ȝoöūm pyꝛtūm.                              ꞉·

fol. 8 b.            ȝenīm ꝛiþ tobꝛocenum heaꝼöe betonican ȝetꝛiꝼula
Ᵹ leȝe on þ heaꝼoö uꝼan þonne ꝛamnaö hio þa punöe
Ᵹ hælö.  Eꝼt ꝛiþ þon ilcān ȝenīm tunceꝛſan ſio þe ꝛelꝼ
ꝛeaxeö Ᵹ mōn ne ꝛæpö öo In þa noſu þ ꝛe ſtenc mæȝe
on þ heaꝼoö Ᵹ þæt ꝛeap.                                        ꞉·

Þiþ þon ilcan eꝼt ȝenim banꝛyꝛt Ᵹ attoꝛlaþan Ᵹ
öolhꝛunan · Ᵹ ꝛuöumeꝛce Ᵹ bꝛunꝛyꝛt Ᵹ betonican · öo
ealle þa pyꝛta to pyꝛt öꝛence Ᵹ menȝe þꝛꝛ ꝛiö þa
ſmalan cliꝛan Ᵹ centauꝛian Ᵹ ꝛeȝbꝛæöan · ealꝛa ſꝛiꝼuſt
betonican Ᵹ ȝiꝼ þ bꝛæȝen ūtꝛiȝe ȝenīm æȝeꝼ þ ȝeo-
luꝛe Ᵹ menȝ lythꝛon[1] ꝛiö huniȝ Ᵹ aꝼyl öa punöe · Ᵹ
miö acumban beſꝛcöc Ᵹ ꝼoꝛlæt ſpa þonne · Ᵹ ēꝼt ymb
þꝛy öaȝaꝛ ȝeſꝛæt þa punöe · Ᵹ ȝiꝼ ꝛe hala ꝼeꝛþe ꝛille
habban ꝛeaöne hꝛiniȝ ymb þa punöe ꝛite þu þonne
þ þu hie ne mealt ȝehælan.  Þiö þon ilcan ȝenīm
ꝛuöuꝛoꝛan Ᵹ ꝛuöu meꝛce Ᵹ hoꝼan Ᵹ pel on buteꝛan Ᵹ

---

¹ Lyhꝛon, MS.

shall one first in the early disease let blood from a
vein ; after that shall be administered a wort drink,
and the sore places shall be cured. If the disease be
caused by mickle heat, then shall one cure it with
cold leechdoms ; if it cometh of cold causes, then shall
one cure it with hot leechdoms, of either shall advan-
tage be taken, and they shall be mixed, *into a mixture*
that may heal the body and have an austere efficacy
in it. It is well for him that one should drip for him
in his ear oil made lukewarm with "other" good
worts.

14. For broken head, take betony,[1] bruise it and lay
it on the head above, then it unites the wound and
healeth *it*. Again for the same, take garden cress,[2]
that which waxeth of itself and is not sown,[3] introduce it into the nose[4] that the smell and the juice
may get to the head.

15. For the same again, take wallflower[5] and
attorlothe[6] and pellitory and wood marche[7] and
brownwort[8] and betony, form all the worts into a
wort drink, and mix therewith the small cleaver[9] and
centaury[10] and waybroad,[11] of all most especially
betony, and if the brain be exposed, take the yolk
of an egg and mix a little with honey and fill the
wound and swathe up with tow, and so let it alone ;
and again *after* about three days syringe the wound,
and if the hale sound part[12] will have a red ring
about the wound, know thou then that thou mayest
not heal it. For the same, take woodroffe and wood-

---

[1] *Betonica officinalis.*

[2] *Lepidium sativum.*

[3] Self sown ; but a garden cress
still.

[4] Ἔρρινον, therefore ; but these
were used like cephalic snuff; and
never for broken head. See Nicolaos
Myreps. xv.

[5] *Cheiranthus cheiri.*

[6] See Herbarium, xlv., to which
assent is not easily given.

[7] *Apium graveolens.*

[8] *Scrophularia aquatica:* see Herb.
lvii.

[9] *Galium aparine.*

[10] *Erythræa centaureum.*

[11] *Plantago maior.*

[12] The sense of ꝛepþe is doubtful ;
but see glossary.

reoh þurh hæþenne[1] claðð do on ꝥ heafod þonne gangaþ
þa ban ut.                                        ⁖

fol. 9 a.

ᵃ þa, MS., but
erase it.

Ƿiþ langsum sare þæs heafdes oþþe ðara eagena oððe
þara toþa þaᵃ þurh hoph oððe þurh snofl ut æteo ꝥ
þær egleþ · ȝeseoþ cerfillan on wætere sele drincan
þonne aþihð ꝥ þa yfelan wætan ut oþþe þurh muð
oððe þurh nosu. Eft þus þu scealt þa yfelan orfe-
tenan wætan utadon þurh spatl ⁊ hwæccean menȝ pipor
ƿiþ hrit crudu sele to ceopanne · ⁊ pyye him to spillanne þone geagl.[2] ȝenim eced ⁊ wæter ⁊ senep ⁊ huniȝ
ƿyl togædere liftum · ⁊ areoh ðonne læt cohan sele
þonne gelome ꝥ geagl to spillanne ꝥ he þy sel mæȝe
ꝥ yfel utahyæccean.

Ƿyrc þus spilinȝe to heafdes clænsunȝe ȝenim eft
seneþes rædes dæl ⁊ næpsædes ⁊ cersan rædes · sume men
hatað lambes cersan ⁊ meyces sæd ⁊ .xx. piporcorna ·
ȝesamna eall mid ecede ⁊ mid huniȝe · ȝehæt on wætere
⁊ habbe on muþe lanȝe þonne yrnð ꝥ ȝillistey ut.
[3]Eft oþþu spilinȝ on sumere cæyeney ȝodne bollan fulne ·
⁊ ecedes medmicelne ⁊ yropum hatte pyrt hiye leaf ⁊
bloscman menȝ togædeye ⁊ læt standan neahteyne ⁊
on morȝen on cyoccan ofeyþylle ⁊ suþe plæc ⁊ ꝥ geagl
spile ⁊ þpea hiy muð. [4]To þon ilean on pintya seneyes
duftes cuclev fulne ⁊ huniȝes healyne cuclev ȝedo on
calic menȝe þonne æftey þon ƿið wætey ⁊ hæte ⁊ reoh
þurh linenne claðð ⁊ spile mið ꝥ geagl · æftey þam
lvcedome ȝelome mid ele spille þa hyacan. [5]Eft ƿiþ þon
ilean ȝenim mealpan ȝeȝnid on plæc þin sele to spillanne ꝥ geagl.    Ƿið toþpocenum heafde ⁊ saysim juþe

fol. 9 b.

¹ hæþenne suggests itself.
² geagl below is neuter.
³ Plinius Valerianus, de re Med.,
fol. 14 a.

⁴ Ibid.
⁵ Plin. Val., fol. 13 b.

marche and hove, and boil in butter and strain through a coloured cloth, apply it to the head, then the bones come out.

16. **For** chronic disorder of the head or of the ears or of the teeth through foulness or through mucus, extract that which aileth there, seethe chervil in water, give it to drink, then that draweth out the evil humours either through mouth or through nose. Again, thus thou shalt remove the evil misplaced humours by spittle and hreaking; mingle pepper with mastic, give it *the patient* to chew, and work him *a garyle* to swill his jowl; take vinegar and water and mustard and honey, boil together cleverly, and strain, then let cool, then give it him frequently to swill his jowl, that he by that may comfortably hreak out the ill *flegm.*

17. Work thus a swilling *or lotion* for cleansing of the head, take again a portion of mustard seed and of navew seed and of cress seed, some men call it lambs cress, and of marche seed, and twenty pepper corns, gather them all with vinegar and with honey, heat them in water and have them long in the mouth, then the flegm runneth out. Again, another swilling in summer; mingle together a good bowl full of wine boiled down with herbs and a moderate one of vinegar, and hyssop, so the wort hight, its leaves and blossoms, and let *the mixture* stand for a night, and in the morning boil it over *again* in a crock (*or earthen pot*), and let him sup it lukewarm and swill his jowl and wash his mouth. For the same in winter, put in a chalice a spoon full of the dust of mustard and half a spoon full of honey, then after that mingle *this* with water, and heat it and strain it through a linen cloth and swill the jowl with it; after that leechdom frequently swill the throat with oil. Again for the same; take mallows, rub them into lukewarm wine, give it *the patient* to swill the jowl. For a broken

ʒeþiʒeladu mið ſealte ꝺ mið huniʒe ſmiꞃe þ heaꝼod
ꝼoꞃeþeaꞃð mid þy ſe cuþeꞃta læcedóm biþ þam þe heaꝼod
þylm ꝺ ſaꞃ þꞃoꞃiað.   Þiþ þon ilcan eꝼt ʒeʒnid ꞃudan
on þin ſele ꝺꞃincan ꝺ ʒemenʒ eced þiþ ꞃudan ꝺ ele
ꝺꞃype on þ heaꝼod ꝺ ſmiꞃe mid.

. ı. (read .ii.)

Alex. Trall.
lib. ii.

fol. 10 a.

Cf. Marcell.
268 h.

Læcebomaſ þiþ eaʒna miſte ʒením celeþenian ſeaþ
oþþe bloſtman ʒemenʒ þið doꞃena huniʒ ʒebo ón æꞃen
ꝼæt þlece liſtúm ón þeaꞃmum ʒledum oþþ hit ʒeſoden
ſie · þiſ bið ʒod læcedóm þiþ eaʒna dimneꞃꞃe.  Þiþ
þon ilcan eꝼt þilðꞃe ꞃudan ʒebeaꞃþe ꝺ ʒetꞃiꝼuladꞃe
ſeaþ · ʒemenʒ þið aſeoꞃneſ huniʒeſ em micel ſmyꞃe
mid þa eaʒan.   Þiþ eaʒna miſte moniʒe men þy læſ
hioꞃa eaʒan þa adle þꞃoꞃian lociað on ceald pæteꞃ ·
ꝺ þonne maʒon ꝼyꞃ ʒeſeon ne þyꞃt þ þa ꞃeón · ac
micel þin ʒedꞃinc ꝺ oþꞃe ʒeſþette dꞃincan ꝺ mettaſ ·
ꝺ þa ſþiþoꞃt þa ðe on ðꝛoꞃe uꞃeꞃan þambe ʒeþuniað ꝺ
ne maʒon meltan · ác þæꞃ yꝼele þꝛætan þyꞃccað ꝺ
þicce.  Poꞃ ꝺ cꝛpel ꝺ eal þa þe ſyn ſþa aꞃeꞃ ſind to
ꞃleoʒanne ꝺ þ þe mon on bedde dꝛeʒeſ úꞃꞃeaꞃð ne
licʒe ꝺ cyle ꝺ þind ꝺ þec ꝺ duꞃt · þaſ þinʒ ꝺ þiſum
ʒelic ælce dꝛeʒe ſceþþað þám eaʒúm.  [1]Þiþ eaʒna miſte
ʒenim ʒꞃenne ꝼinul ʒebo on pæteꞃ .xxx. nihta ón
ꝇnne cꞃoccan þone þe ſie ʒeꞃicod utan ʒeꝼylle þonne
mid ꞃen þꝛeteꞃe · æꝼteꞃ þon úꞃeoꞃꞃe óꝼ þone ꝼinul ꝺ
mid þy þꝛeteꞃe ælce dꝛeʒe þþeali þa eaʒan ꝺ ontyne.
fol. 10 b.   [2]Eꝼt óꝼ homena ꝛeþine ꝺ ſtꝛeme ꝺ óꝼ plꝛtan cymð

---

[1] Cf. Galen. vol. xiv. p. 499, ed.    [2] Plinius Valerianus, fol. 20 b, for
1827.                                       fourteen lines.

and sore head; bruised rue[1] with salt and honey; smear the forehead with it, the most approved leechdom is *this* for *him* whose head hath burning and painful throes. For the same again; rub rue in wine, give *it* to drink *to the sufferer*, and mingle vinegar with rue and oil; drip it on the head and smear therewith.

ii.

1. Leechdoms for mistiness of the eyes; take juice or blossoms of celandine, mingle with honey of dumbledores,[a] introduce it into a brazen vessel, half warm it neatly on warm gledes, till it be sodden. This is a good leechdom for dimness of eyes. For the same, mingle the juice of wild rue,[2] dewy and bruised, mingle with equally much of filtered honey, smear the eyes with *that*. For mistiness of eyes many men, lest their eyes should suffer the disease, look into cold water and then are able to see far; that harmeth not the vision, but much wine drinking and other sweetened drinks and meats, and those especially which remain in the upper region of the wamb and cannot digest, but there form evil humours and thick ones; leek and colewort and all that are so austere are to be avoided, and *care must be had* that a man lie not in bed in day time supine; and cold and wind and reek and dust, these things and the like to these every day are injurious to the eyes. For mistiness of eyes, take green fennel, put it into water for thirty days in a crock (*or earthen vessel*), one that is pitched on the outside, fill it then with rain water; after that throw off the fennel and with the water every day wash the eyes and open them. Again, from the vapour and

[a] Melle Attico, doubtless.

---

[1] The verbs are often suppressed.

[2] Wild rue is a Hellenism, πήγανον ἄγριον, Dioskor. iii. 59, ἁρμόζει πρὸς ἀμβλυωπίας, or ruta silvestris; Plinius, xx. 51. These are *peguuum harmala*.

eaʒna mijt ⁊ jio jceajpnej ⁊ joʒoþa þ ðeþ pjþ þon ij
þij to ðonne. Þið eaʒna mijte ʒenim cileþonian jeapej
enclep julne oþeþne jinolej · þjiððan apjotanan jeapej ·
⁊ hunɩʒej teapej tu enclep mæl menʒ to ʒædeje · ⁊
þonne mið jeþeþe ʒeðo In þa eaʒan on mojʒenne ⁊
þonne mɩððæʒ jie · ⁊ ejt on æjen æjtej þon þonne þ
aðjuʒoð jie ⁊ toʒoten joþ þæje jealje jceajpnejje ·
ʒenɩm pɩjej meoluc þæj þe cɩlð hæbbe ðo on þa
eaʒan.                                                              :·

Ejt æþele cjæjt ʒenɩm baljam ⁊ hunɩʒej teapej
em mɩcel ʒemenʒ toʒædeje ⁊ jmije mɩð þy.

Ejt pɩð þon ɩlcan celeþonian jeap ⁊ jæpjætej jmije
mɩð þa eaʒan ⁊ beðe. Iɩþ þonne jelejt þ þu mɩne
þæpe celeþonian jeap ⁊ mucʒpyjte ⁊ jmðan caljia em
jela ðo hunɩʒ to ⁊ balðjamum ʒɩj þu hæbbe · ʒeðo on
þ jæt þe þu hɩt mæʒe on mɩð ʒejoʒe ʒejeoþan ⁊ nytta
pel þæt bet.                                                        :·

<sup></sup>¹Pɩþ eaʒna mɩjte ʒebæpneð jealt ⁊ ʒeʒnɩðen ⁊ pɩþ
ðojiena hunɩʒ ʒemenʒeð jmije mɩð.                                   :·

fol. 11 a. ²Ejt jinolej ⁊ jojan ⁊ juðan jeap ⁊ ðojian hunɩʒ ⁊
tɩccenej ʒeallan toʒædeje ʒemenʒeð jmije mɩð þa
eaʒan. ³Ejt ʒjiene cellenðje ʒeʒnɩðen ⁊ pɩþ pɩjej
meoluc ʒemenʒeð aleʒe ojeþ þa eaʒan.                               :·

ᵃ Med. de Quad.
iv. 7.
ᵇ Marcellus,
272, e.

ᵃ⁴Ejt hajian ʒeallan ʒenɩme ⁊ jmije mɩð.                          :·
ᵇ Ejt epɩce⁵ pɩne pɩnclan ʒebæpnðe to ahjan ⁊ þa
ahjan ʒemenʒe pɩð ðojiena hunɩʒ.                                   :

¹ Plin. Val. fol. 20 b.          ⁵ For veras our author read
² Plin. Val. fol. 21 b.             vivas. Or Plinius Valerianus, fol.
³ Plin. Valerianus, fol. 19 b.      21 b, where we read "Cochleæ
⁴ Also Plinius Valerianus, fol.    vivæ."
20 b., 21 b.

steam of ill juices and from nausea cometh mist of
eyes, and the sharpness and corrupt humour causes that,
against which this is to be done. For mist of eyes,
take of celandines juice a spoon full, another of fennels,
a third of southernwoods juice, and two spoon measures
of the tear of honey (*virgin honey that drops without
pressure*), mingle *them* together, and then with a
feather put *some* into the eyes in the morning and
when it be midday, and again at evening after that,
when it is dried up and spent; for sharpness of the
salve, take milk of a woman who hath a child, apply
it to the eyes.

2. Again, a noble craft. Take equal quantities of
balsam and of virgin honey, mix together and smear
with that.

3. Again for the same, juice of celandine and sea
water; smear and bathe the eyes therewith. It is then
most advisable that thou take juice of the celandine
and of mugwort[1] and of rue, of all equal quantities, add
honey to it, and balsam, if thou have it, put it then
into such a vessel that thou may seethe it with glue[2]
and make use of it. It does much good.

Cf. Nicol.
Myreps.
xxxviii. 152,
from an older
author, perhaps.

4. For mist of eyes, salt burnt and rubbed *fine* and
mixed with dumbledores honey;[3] smear therewith.

5. Again, juice of fennel and of rose and of rue, and
dumbledores honey,[3] and kids gall, mixed together;
smear the eyes with *this*. Again, lay upon the eyes
green coriander rubbed *fine* and mixed with womans
milk.

6. Again, let him take a hares gall and smear with it.

7. Again, live perriwinkles burnt to ashes; and let
him mix the ashes with dumbledores[3] honey.

---

[1] *Artemisia vulgaris.*

[2] Or some cement; the original
author perhaps meant a covered
vessel sealed up with cement.

[3] Doubtless from "melle Attico,"
read as melle attaci; the dumble-
dore is *apis bombinatrix.*

ᵃ Plinius,
xxxii. 24.
Marcellus,
272, g.

ᵃ Eft ƿyrlaſ ealƿa ea ƿiſca ón ſunnan ȝemylte ⁊ ƿið huniȝ ȝemenȝðe ſmiƿe mið. :·

Ƿið eaȝna miſte eft betonican ſeap ȝebeatenƿe mið liƿe pyƿttƿumán ⁊ apƿunȝenƿe ⁊ ȝeaƿƿan ſeap ⁊ celeþonian em micel ealƿa menȝ toȝædeƿe ðo ón eaȝe.

ᵇ Marcellus,
272, b.

ᵇ Eft ſinoleſ pyƿttƿumán ȝecnuaðne ȝemenȝ ƿið huniȝeſ ſeap¹ ſeoð þonne æt leohtum fyƿe liſtelice oþ huniȝeſ þicneſſe · ȝeðo þonne ón æƿene ámpullan ⁊ þonne þeaƿſ ſie ſmiƿe mið þiſ toðƿiſþ þa eahmiſtaſ þeah þe hie þicce ſynð. :·

Ƿiþ eaȝna miſte eft celeþonian ſeap oþþe þaƿa bloſtmena ȝeƿƿinȝ ⁊ ȝemenȝ ƿið doƿena huniȝ ȝeðo ón æƿen ſæt plece þonne liſtum ón peaƿinum ȝleðum oþþe ón aƿƿan oþ þ̃ hit ȝeðon ſie · þ̃ bið anſƿilðe lyb ƿiþ eaȝena

fol. 11 b.

dimneſſe. :·

Sume þæſ ſeapeſ anliƿiȝeſ nyttiað ⁊ þa eaȝan mið þy ſmiƿað. Ƿiþ eaȝena miſte eft conðiƿies ſeap ⁊ ſinoleſ ſeap ȝeðo beȝea em ſela ón ampullan dƿiȝe þonne on hatƿe ſunnan ⁊ þa eaȝan inneþeaƿð mið þy ſmiƿe.

ᶜ Marcellus,
272, a.

ᶜ Ƿiþ eaȝena miſte eft conðȝeallan² ſeap þ̃ iſ hyrðepyrt ſmiƿe on þa eaȝan ſio ſyn biþ þy ſceaƿƿe ·

ᵈ Marcellus,
272, c.

ȝiſ þu huniȝ to deſt þ̃ ðeah · ȝenimᵈ þonne þæƿe ilcan pyƿte ȝoðne ȝelm ȝeðo ón ceac ſulne ƿineſ ⁊ ȝeſeoþ oƿnete æƿ þƿy ðaȝaſ · ⁊ þonne hio ȝeroðen ſie apƿinȝ þa pyƿt ōſ ⁊ þæſ poſeſ ȝeſƿetteſ mið huniȝe ȝeðƿinc ælce dæȝe neaht neſtiȝ bollan ſulne. :·

ᵉ Cf. Celsus,
VI. vi. 34 and
29.

ᵉ Ealðeſ manneſ eaȝan beoþ unſceaƿpſyno þonne ſceal he þa eaȝan peccan mið ȝniðinȝum mið ȝonȝum · mið ƿaðum oþþe mið þy þe hine mon beƿe oþþe on pæne ſeƿiȝe · ⁊ hy ſeulan nyttian lytlúm ⁊ ſoƿhtlicūm metum ⁊ liuƿa heaſod cemban ⁊ ſeƿinoð dƿincan æƿ þon þe

---

¹ " Tantundem mellis optimi deſpumati " is turned " juice of honey."

² Cf. Alex. Trall. p. 46, line 31, ed. 1548.

8. Again, the fatty parts of all river fishes melted in the sun and mingled with honey ; smear with that.

9. For mist of eyes again, juice of betony beaten with its roots and wrung, and juice of yarrow[1] and of celandine, equally much of all, mingle together, apply to the eye. Again, mingle pounded root of fennel with the purest honey, then seethe at a light fire cleverly to the thickness of honey. Then put it into a brazen ampulla, and when need be, smear with it, this driveth away the eye mists, though they be thick.

10. For mist of eyes again, wring *out* juice of celandine or of the blossoms *of it*, and mingle with dumbledores honey, put it into a brazen vessel, then make it lukewarm cleverly on warm gledes, or on ashes, till it be done. That is a unique medicine for dimness of eyes.

11. Some avail themselves of the juice singly, and anoint the eyes with that. For mist of eyes again ; juice of ground ivy and juice of fennel ; set equal quantities of both in an ampulla, then dry in the hot sun, and smear the inward part of the eyes with that. For mist of eyes again, smear earthgalls[2] juice, that is herdwort,[2] on the eyes, the vision will be by it sharper. If thou addest honey thereto, that is of good effect. Further take a good bundle of the same wort, introduce it into a jug full of wine, and seethe three days in a close vessel ; and when it is sodden, wring out the wort, and drink of the ooze sweetened with honey every day, after a nights fasting, a bowl full.

12. The eyes of an old man are not sharp of sight ; than shall he wake up his eyes with rubbings, with walkings, with ridings, either so that a man bear him[3] or convey him in a wain. And they shall use little and careful meats, and comb their heads and

---

[1] *Achillea millefolium.*
*Erythræa centaureum.*

[3] In a litter.

fol. 12 a.
a Rather
realter.

hne mete þicȝean.　Þiƿ món ſceal unſceaƿſynūm ſealƿe
pyƿcean to eaȝum · ȝenim þiþoþ ꞇ ȝebeat ꞇ ſpeȝleſ
æþþel ꞇ hpon ſealtᵃ ꞇ ſín þ̄ biþ ȝoð ſealſ.　　　　　:·

Þiþ miclum eaȝece manig man hæþþ miccelne ece
on hiſ eaȝum.　Þyſe hīm þonne ȝrunde ſpelȝean ꞇ
biſceop pyſc ꞇ ſinol pyl þa pyſca calle on þætþe ·
meoluc bið ſelþe læc þ̄ ſeocan on þa eaȝan.　Eſt
celeþonian ꞇ puðulmðelſ[1] leaſ ȝeaceſ ſuſe pið pin
ȝemenȝe.　　　　　:·

Eſt to miclum eaȝece cſoþleac moþoþeaþð ꞇ pic-
mæþeſ pyſc moþoþeaþð cnua ón pine læc ſtanðan tpa

b Gr. ἄργεμα;
Lat. Albugo.
c anfan, MS.

niht.　Þið ſheᵇ eaȝſealſ ȝenim bſomeſ ahſanᶜ ꞇ bollan
ſulne haceſ pineſ ȝeot þþiþa lytlum on hace þa ahſan
ꞇ ðo þonne ón æþen ſæc oððe cypeþen ðo huniȝeſ
hpon to ꞇ meng toȝæðeſe ðo on þæſ untſuman manneſ eaȝan · ꞇ aþþeah eſc þa eaȝan on chenſim pylle.
Þiþ ſhe haþan ȝeallan ðo þeaþmne ón ymb tpa niht

d Slah, MS. not
ſlau.

ſhhð óſ þam eaȝum.　Þiþ ſhe ȝenīm onþæþe ſlahᵈ
þ̄ ſeaþ ꞇ þþung þuþh claſ on þ̄ eaȝe ſona ȝæð on
þþim ðaȝum óſ ȝiſ ſio ſlah biþ ȝþene.　Þiþ ſhe eceð
ꞇ ȝebæþneð ſealt ꞇ beþen mela ȝemeng toȝæðeſe ðo
ón þ̄ eaȝe haſa lanȝe hpile þine hanð on.　　　　　:·

e Read oþþe
þone.
fol. 12 b.

Þiþ ſhe eahſealſ celeþonian ſæð ȝenīm on þamᵉ
pyſctſuman ȝmð ón ealð ſín ꞇ on huniȝ ðo þiþoþ to
læc ſtanðan neahteþne be ſyþe nytta þonne þu ſlapan
pille.　Þiþ ſhe oxan ſlyþþan niþeþeaþðe ꞇ aloþ ſunðe
pylle on buteþan.　　　　　:·

Χύμωσις,
Lippitudo.

Þiþ þon ðe eaȝan tyþen ſuðan ſeaþ ꞇ ȝate ȝeallan ꞇ

---

1 Read -binðeſ.

drink wormwood before they take food. Then shall a salve be wrought for unsharpsighted eyes; take pepper and beat it, and beetle nut[1] and a somewhat of salt, and wine; that will be a good salve.

13. For much eye ache. Many a man hath mickle ache in his eyes. Work him then groundsel and bishopwort[2] and fennel, boil all the worts in water, milk is better, make that throw up a reek on the eyes. Again, let him mingle with wine celandine and woodbines leaves and *the herb* cuckoosour.[3]

14. Again, for much eye ache, pound in wine the nether part of cropleek[4] and the nether part of Wihtmars wort,[5] let it stand two days. For pearl, an eye salve; take ashes of broom and a bowl full of hot wine, pour *this* by a little at a time thrice on the hot ashes, and put *that* then into a brass or a copper vessel, add somewhat of honey and mix together, apply to the infirm mans eyes, and again wash the eyes in a clean wyll *spring*. For pearl on the eye, apply the gall of a hare, warm, for about two days, *it* flieth from the eyes. Against white spot, take an unripe sloe, and wring the juice of it through a cloth on the eye, soon, in three days *the spot* will disappear, if the sloe be green. Against white spot, mingle together vinegar and burnt salt[a] and barley meal, apply it to the eye, hold thine hand a long while on it.

[a] A substitute for "sal ammoniacum."

15. For pearl, an eye salve; take seed of celandine or the root of it, rub it into old wine and into honey, add pepper, let it stand for a night by the fire, use it when thou wilt sleep. Against white spot, boil in butter the nether part of ox-slip[6] and alder[7] rind.

16. In case the eyes be tearful, juice of rue, and

---

[1] The evidence, such as it is, for this rendering will be given in the glossary.
[2] Herbar. i. *Betonica officinalis.*
[3] *Oxalis Acetosella.*

[4] *Allium sativum*, probably.
[5] *Cochlearia anglica*, perhaps.
[6] *Primula veris elatior.*
[7] *Alnus glutinosa.*

ðoþan humȝ ealþa em fela. ȝif eaȝan[1] tyþen heoþotej
hoþnej ahjan ðo on ȝefpet þin. Ƿyþc eaȝfealfe þiþ
þænne ȝenim cþopleac ⁊ ȝaþleac beȝea em fela ȝecnupa
þel tofomne ȝenim þin ⁊ feajþef ȝeallan beȝea em
fela ȝemenȝ þiþ þy leace ðo þonne on apfæt læt ftanðan mȝon niht on þam apfate apþinȝ þuþh claþ ⁊
ȝehlyttþe þel ðo on hoþn · ⁊ ymb niht ðo mið feþeþe
on þ eaȝe fe betfta læceðom.                                           :·

Ƿiþ þenne[2] ón eaȝon ȝenim þa holan ceþfan ȝebþæð
ðo on þ eaȝe fpa he hatoft mæȝe.                                     :·

Ƿiþ eaȝece ȝepyþce hím ȝþunðfpelȝean ⁊ bifceoþ þyþt
⁊ beoþyþt ⁊ fmul þyl þa þyþta ealle on þæteþe meoluc
biþ beteþe.                                                           :·

fol. 13 a.     Ƿiþ eaȝna ece ȝenim þa þeaban hoþan apyl on fuþum
fþatum oþþe on fuþûm ealað ⁊ beþe þa eaȝan on þam
baþe beteþe fpa óftoþ.                                                :·

Ƿiþ eaȝece ȝenim þiþoþinðan tþiȝu ȝecnupa apylle
on buteþan[3] ðo on þa eaȝan.                                        :·

Ƿyþc eaȝfealfe ȝenim hnutcyþnla ⁊ hþæte coþn ȝnið
toȝæðeþe ðo þin to afeoh þuþh claþ ðo þonne on þa
eaȝan. Ƿiþ eaȝna þæþce ⁊ ece hþitef hlafef cþuman
⁊ þiþoþ ⁊ eceð menȝ þel leȝe on claþ binð on þa eaȝan
nihteþne. Þuf món fceal eaȝfealfe þyþicean · ȝenim
ftþeapbeþian þifan moþoþcaþðe ⁊ þiþoþ ȝecnupa þel ðo
on claþ bebinð fæfte leȝe on ȝefpet þin læt ȝeðþeoþan
on þa eaȝan ænne ðþoþan. Ƿyþc eaȝfealfe þuðubinðef
leaf þuðumeþce ftþeapbeþian þifan fuþeþne þeþmoð
oxna lyb celeþoman ȝecnupa þa þyþte fþið menȝ þiþ

---

[1] Galen, vol. xii. p. 335, ed. 1826.   [2] Túλos.
Sextus, cap. i. 1, Lat.                 [3] The MS. has biteþan.

goats gall and dumbledores honey, of all equal quantities.  If eyes be tearful, add to sweetened wine ashes of harts horn.  Work an eye salve for a wen, take cropleek and garlic,[1] of both equal quantities, pound them well together, take wine and bullocks gall, of both equal quantities, mix with the leek, put *this* then into a brazen vessel, let it stand nine days in the brass vessel, wring out through a cloth and clear it well, put it into a horn, and about night time apply it with a feather to the eye ; the best leechdom.

17.  For a wen[2] on the eye, take hollow cress,[3] roast it, apply it to the eye, as hot as possible.

18.  For eye ache, let him work for himself groundsel and bishopwort[4] and beewort[5] and fennel, boil all the worts in water ; milk is better.

19.  For ache of eyes, take the red hove,[6] boil it in sour beer or in sour ale, and bathe the eyes in the bath, the oftener the better.

20.  For eye ache, take twigs of withewind,[7] pound them, boil them in butter, apply them to the eyes.

21.  Work an eye salve *thus ;* take nut kernels and wheat grains, rub them together, add wine, strain through a cloth, then apply to the eyes.  For acute pain and ache of eyes, mingle well crumbs of white bread and pepper and vinegar, lay *this* on a cloth, bind it on the eyes for a night.  Thus shall a man work an eye salve, take the nether part of strawberry plants and pepper, pound them well, put them on a cloth, bind them fast, lay them in sweetened wine, make somebody drop one drop into the eyes.  Work an eye salve *thus ;* leaves of woodbind,[8] woodmarche,[9] strawberry plants, southern wormwood,[10] green hellebore,

---

[1] *Allium oleraceum ?*
[2] Wisps or sties are called wuns in Devon.
[3] *Gentiana campestris.*
[4] In Herb. i. *Betonica officinalis.*
[5] *Acorus calamus.*

[6] *Glechoma hederacea.*
[7] *Convolvulus sepium.*
[8] *Convolvulus.*
[9] *Apium graveolens.*
[10] *Artemisia abrotanon.*

ƿín ðo on cyþeþen fæt oþþe ón æþenum fate hafa
læt ftanðan feofon niht oþþe ma apþinȝe þa pyrta
fƿíðe clæne ȝeðo pipoþ ón ȝ ȝefpet fþiþe leohtlice mið
fol. 13 b. huniȝe ðo riþþan on hoþn ȝ mið fefeþe ðo on þa eaȝan
ænne ðropan. Þype eaȝfealfe ðþiȝe · ȝenim fpeȝlef
æppel ȝ fpefl cþecife attþium ȝ ȝebæþneð fealt ȝ pipoþef
maþt ȝeȝrinð eall to ðufte aþíft þuþli cla ðo on
næþe hæbbe hím ón þy læf hit þine · ðo meðmicel
on þa eaȝan mið toþ ȝaþe ȝeþefte hím æfteþ ȝ flaþe
ȝ þonne aþþeah hiþ eaȝan mið clæne þœtþe ȝ on þ̄
þœteþ lociȝe. Þype eaȝfealfe cymen ȝ ftþeaþbeþȝean
pife ȝecnuþa fþiðe pel ȝ óf ȝeot mið ȝefpette pine ðo
In cyþeþen fæt oððe ón æþen læt ftanðan fela nihta
ón apþinȝ þa pyrte þuþli cla ȝ ahluttþa fþiþe pel ðo
þonne on þa eaȝan þonne þu þille þeftan · ȝíf fío
Imminutiones. fealf fíe to heaþi[1] ȝefpet mið huniȝe. Þið æþmælum
ȝením attþium ȝemenȝ þið fpatl þa[2] eaȝan uteþeaþð
nalæþ innan.


Þið æþmælum niþeþeaþð[3] æþcþþotu ȝecopen ón muþe
ȝ apþinȝen þuþli cla ðon eaȝe ȝeðon punðoþlice hælþ.
Þiþ þon þe mon fuþeȝe fíe ȝenim aȝþimonian pelle
fþiþe oþ þþiððan ðæl þþeah ȝelome þa eaȝan mið þy.
Pustula. Þiþ pocce on eaȝum · ȝením pað ȝ þibban ȝ hleomocan
fol. 14 a. þyl on meolce on buteþan iþ beteþe ȝ þype beþinȝe ·
þyl hleomóc ȝ ȝeaþþan ȝ puðu ceaþfillan on meolcum.

---

[1] Heaþ MS. If any word closely
answering to Germ. Herbe, Lat.
Acerbus, occurs in Saxon, it has
not met my eyes; the context is our
guide here. *See* Gl.

[2] fmþþe must be supplied.
[3] inþeþeaþð, MS.

celandine, pound the worts much, mingle with wine,
put into a copper vessel or keep in a brazen vat, let
it stand seven days or more, wring the worts very
clean, add pepper, and sweeten very lightly with honey,
put subsequently into a horn, and with a feather put
one drop into the eyes. Work a dry eye salve *thus;*
take beetle nut (?) and sulfur, Greek olusatrum[1] and
burnt salt, and of pepper most, grind all to dust, sift
through a cloth, put it on a fawns skin, let him keep
it about himself, lest it get moist. Introduce a small
quantity into the eyes with a tooth pick; afterwards
let him rest himself and sleep, and then wash his eyes
with clean water, and let him look in the water,
*that is, keep his eyes open under water.* Work eye
salve *thus;* pound thoroughly cummin and a strawberry plant, and souse with sweetened wine, put into
a copper vessel or into a brazen one, let it stand
many nights, wring the wort through a cloth and clear
*the liquid* thoroughly, then apply to the eyes when
thou may wish to rest; if the salve be too biting,
sweeten it with honey. For imminution of the eyes,
take olusatrum, mingle with spittle, *anoint* the eyes
outwardly not inwardly.

22. For imminutions, the nether part of *the herb*
ashthroat[2] chewed in the mouth and wrung through a
cloth, *and* applied to the eye, wonderfully healeth. In
case a man be blear eyed, take agrimony, boil it
thoroughly *down* to the third part, wash the eyes
frequently with that. For a pock *or pustule* in the
eyes, take woad[3] and ribwort[4] and brooklime,[5] boil in
milk, in butter is better, and work a fomentation.
Boil brooklime[5] and yarrow[6] and wood chervil[7] in
milk.

---

[1] *Smyrnium olusatrum.*

[2] In Herb. iv. *Verbena officinalis,*
but in the gll. *Ferula.*

[3] *Isatis tinctoria.*

[1] *Plantago lanceolata.*

[5] *Veronica beccabunga.*

[6] *Achillea millefolium.*

[7] *Anthriscus silvestris.*

Ƿiþ ƿyrmum ón eaȝum ȝením beolonan sæð rceað ón ȝleda · do þra bleda fulle pæteþes to fet ón þra healfe ꝧ site þær ofer bræð þonne ꝥ heafod hiden ꝧ ȝeond ofer ꝥ fyr ꝧ þa bleda cñc þonne rceabaþ þa ƿyrmas on þæt þretep.

Ƿiþ þeoraðle ón eaȝũm þe món ȝefiȝo hæt on læden hatte cimosis · hænne æȝes ȝeolocan ꝧ meþces ræb ꝧ attrum ꝧ tunmintan. Eft ƿið ȝefiȝon sceaþes holhscancan unfodenne tobþec ȝebo

þæt meaþh on þa eaȝan. Ƿiþ þiccum bþæþfimᵃ ȝením þþeo hand fulla mucþyrte þþeo realtes · þþeo papan² ƿylle þonne oþ ꝥ sic tþæde beþylleð þær rofes heald þonne on cyþeþenum fate. þam men³ þe habbað þicce bþæþas ȝením cyþeþen fæt do þæþón lybcorn ꝧ realt ȝemenȝ · ȝením celeþonian ꝧ bifceoþþyrt ꝧ ȝeacer rujan ꝧ at-

toþlaþan ꝧ spþunȝpyrt ꝧ enȝlifce moþan · ꝧ hþon þæðices ꝧ hþefnes fot aþæþc þonne calle ȝeot þonne þfin ón · læt standan aþeoh eft on ꝥ cyþeþene fæt · læt þonne standan fiftyne niht ꝧ þa deþftan beoþ ȝode · haþa þe clæne fletan do on ꝥ fæt þe þa deþftan on ryn sþa fela sþa þaþa fletna þæþi ón cliþian mæȝe · sceþer þonne of þam fæte ꝥ biþ spiðe ȝod realf þam men þe hæfð þicce bþæþas.

.III.

Læcedomas ƿið eallum eaþena fáþe ꝧ ccc ꝧ ƿið eaþena adeafunȝe · ꝧ ȝif ƿyrmas ón caþan fynd oþþe

---

¹ See the glossary on ⸀Fic. ȝe. ; it is σύκη, σύκωσις, not χύμωσις ; this is a misinterpretation of an Hellenic word.

² Read rapan.

³ þām, MS. Read þā m̄.

23. For worms[1] in eyes, take seed of henbane,[2] shed    
it on gledes, add two saucers full of water, set them
on two sides of the man, and let him sit there over
them, jerk the head hither and thither over the fire
and the saucers also, then the worms shed *themselves*
into the water. For " dry" disease in the eyes, which
is called *the disease* fig, and in Latin is called χύμωσις[a]    [a] No. Σύκωσις.
the yolk of a hens egg and seed of marche[3] and
olusatrum and garden mint.[4] Again for *the disease*
fig, break to pieces a hock shank unsodden of a sheep,
apply the marrow to the eyes. For thick eyelids, take
three handfuls of mugwort,[5] three of salt, three of
soap, boil them till two parts out of three of the
ooze be boiled away, then preserve in a copper vessel.
For him who hath thick eyelids, take a copper vessel,
put therein cathartic seeds and salt there among,
take celandine and bishopwort and cuckoosour and
attorlothe[6] and springwort[7] and English carrot, and a
somewhat of radish, and ravens foot,[8] then wash them
all, then pour wine on; let *it* stand, strain again into
the copper vessel; then let it stand fifteen nights and
the dregs will be good. Have with thee clean curds and
introduce into the vessel on which the dregs are, as
much of the curd as may cleave thereon. Then scrape
*the scrapings* off the vessel, that will be a very good
salve for the man who hath thick eyelids.

### iii.

1. Leechdoms for all sore of ears and ache, and for
deafness of ears, and if insects are in the ears or an

---

[1] Worms are all creeping things, here insects, acari : Celsus has a chapter " de pediculis palpebrarum," Lib. VI. vi. 15,—" sive etiam vermi-" culos (*oculi*) habeant aut brigan-" tes qui cilia arare et exulcerare " solent." Marcellus, 275, c. Cf. ibid. f. The disease in Hellenic was φθειρίασις, and by keen eyes the insects could be seen to move, Actuarios.

[2] *Hyoscyamus niger.*

[3] *Apium.*

[4] *Mentha sativa.*

[5] *Artemisia vulgaris.*

[6] Uncertain. See Herb. xlv. vol. I. Pref. lvi.

[7] *Euforbia lathyris.*

[8] *Ranunculus ficaria.*

40　　　　　　　LÆCE BOC.

caɲpıeᵹa · ꞇ ᵹıꝼ eaꞃan ꝺynıen · ꞇ eaꞃꞃealꝼa ꝼıꝼꞇyne
cꞃoꝼꞇaꞅ.

Marcellus,
285, f.

Ƿıþ eaꞃena ꞅaꞃe ꞇ ece beꞇonıcan nıꞃan ᵹeꞃoꞃhꞇe þa
leaꝼ ꞃelꝼ[1] ᵹecnupa ón ƿeaꞃmum ƿæꞇeꞃe ꝺo hꞃon ᵹeꞃo-
ꞅoꝺeꞅ eleꞃ ꞇo · ᵹenım þ ꞅƿa placu mıꝺ þıcꞃe pulle ꝺꞃype
on þ eaꞃe. Eꝼꞇ ƿıþ þon ılcan ᵹenım cıeꞃan ᵹeꞅeoþ ón
ele ꝺꞃype on þ eaꞃe þone ele. Ƿıþ eaꞃꞃæꞃce ꞇ ƿıꝺ
ꝺeaꝼe hunꝺeꞃ ꞇunᵹe ꞇ ꞃenmınꞇe ꞇ cellenꝺꞃe ᵹecnupa ón
ƿın oþþe ón eala aꞅeoh ꝺo on eaꞃe. Ƿıþ þon ılcan

fol. 15 a.

Marcellus,
286, d.

Sextus, cap.
xi. 1. Lat.

ᵹenım hænne ꞃyꞃele ᵹemylꞇe ꞇ þonne ᵹeꝺo placo ón
eaꞃe ᵹeꝺꞃype ón. Ƿıþ þon ılcan ᵹenım ele · ᵹenım eac
ᵹoꞃe ꞃyꞃele ᵹeóꞇ on þonne ᵹeꞃıꞇ þ ꞃaꞃ apeᵹ.

Ƿıþ þon ılcan ᵹenım beolonan ꞃeap ᵹeplece ꞇ þonne
ón eaꞃe ᵹeꝺꞃyp · þonne þ ꞃaꞃ ᵹeꞅꞇılꝺ.

Cf. Marcell.
284, c.

Ƿıþ þon ılcan ᵹenım ᵹaꞃleac ꞇ cıꞃan ꞇ ᵹoꞃe ꞃyꞃele
ᵹemylꞇe ꞇoᵹæꝺeꞃe ꞃꞃınᵹ on eaꞃe.

Marcellus,
287, d.

Marcellus,
285, b.

Cf. Alex. Trall.,
lib. iii. 1.
= p. 56, line 21,
ed. 1548.

Ƿıꝺ þon ılcan ᵹenım æmeꞇan æᵹꞃu ᵹeꞇꞃꞃula ꞃꞃınᵹ
ón eaꞃe. Ƿıꝺ eaꞃena ꞃaꞃe ᵹenım ᵹaꞇe ᵹeallan ꝺꞃype
on þ eaꞃe · menᵹ ƿıꝺ cu meolúc ᵹıꝼ þu ꞃılle. Ƿıꝺ
eaꞃena ꝺeaꝼe · ᵹenım hꞃyþeꞃeꞅ ᵹeallan ƿıþ ᵹæꞇen hlanꝺ
ᵹemenᵹeꝺ ᵹeꝺꞃype ᵹepleceꝺ on þ eaꞃe.

Ƿıþ þon ılcan ᵹıꝼ eaꞃan ꞃıllen aꝺeaꞃıan oþþe yꝼel
hlyꞅꞇ ꞅıe · ᵹenım coꞃoꞃeꞅ ᵹeallan ꞃeaꞃꞃeꞅ ᵹeallan ·
buccan ᵹeallan ᵹemenᵹ ƿıþ hunıᵹ ealꞃa em ꞃela ꝺꞃype
on þ eaꞃe.

Ƿıþ þon ılcan ᵹıꝼ[2] yꝼelne hlyꞅꞇ hæbbe ıꞃıeꞅ ꞃeap
þæꞃ þe be coꞃþan ꞃlıhð þ clænoꞅꞇe ꞅeaꞃ ᵹemenᵹ ƿıþ
ƿın ꝺꞃype on eaꞃe.

fol. 15 b.

Eꝼꞇ ꞃıbban ꞃeap ꞇ ᵹepleceꝺne ele ꞇoᵹæꝺeꞃe ᵹemenᵹeꝺ
ꝺꞃype ón ꞃunꝺoꞃlıce hælð. Ƿıþ þon ılcan ᵹenım ꞃam-

---

[1] Read ꞃelꞃe ?　　　　|　　　　[2] Add hꞃa, or mon.

earwig, and if the ears din, and ear salves. Fifteen receipts.

2. For sore and ache of ears, pound new wrought betony, the leaves themselves, in warm water, add a somewhat of rose oil, take that lukewarm with thick wool, drip it into the ear. Again for the same, take an onion, seethe it in oil, drip the oil on the ear. For ear wark and for deafness, pound *the herb* hounds tongue[1] and fenmint[2] and coriander in wine or in ale, strain it, apply to the ear. For the same, take hen grease, melt it, and then apply it lukewarm to the ear, drip it on it. For the same, take oil, take also goose grease, pour into *the ear*, then the sore departs.

3. For the same, take juice of henbane, make it lukewarm, and then drip it on the ear; then the sore stilleth.

4. For the same, take garlic and onion and goose fat, melt *them* together, squeeze *them* on the ear.

5. For the same, take emmets eggs, crush *them*, squeeze *them* on the ear. For sore of ears, take goats gall, drip it on the ear; mingle, if thou will, cows milk with *it*. For deafness of ears, take neats gall mixed with goats stale, drip it, when made lukewarm, on the ear.

6. For the same, if the ears have a tendency to grow deaf, or if the hearing be ill, take boars gall, bulls gall, bucks gall, mix equal quantities of all with honey, drip *this* on the ear.

7. For the same, if one have ill hearing, mingle juice of ivy, that which runneth by the earth, the cleanest juice, with wine; drip it into the ear.

8. Again, drip into *the ear* juice of ribwort and oil made lukewarm, mingled together, it wonderfully healeth. For the same, take rams gall, with urine *of*

---

[1] *Cynoglossum officinale.*    |    [2] *M. silvestris.*

mey ȝeallan mið hiy yelfef nihtnertiȝey iniȝoþan ȝemenȝe wið butepan ȝeót on eape. Eft wiþ þon ilcan
hnutbeamey pinðe feap ȝepleceð ðpype ón eape.        :·

Cf. Marcell.
284, g.

Þiþ ðon ilcan ȝenim celenðpan feap ȝpenpe menȝ
wiþ wiyef meoluc ꝛ huniȝey ðpiopan ꝛ piney ȝeplehc
tofamne. Viþ eapena aðeafunȝe eft ellencpoppan ȝe-
Cf. Marcell.
285, a.
cꝛiyulað þ feap ppinȝ on þ eape. Eft wiþ þon ilcan
ȝenim eoyoper ȝeallan · ꝛ feaꝛꝛef ꝛ buccan menȝ wiþ
huniȝ oþþe ón ele ppinȝ on eape.        :·

Marcellus,
282, d.

Eft wið þon ilcan ȝenim ȝpenne æyeenne ftæf leȝe
on fyp ȝenim þonne þ yeap þe líím oy ȝæþ ðo on þa
ilcan pulle ppinȝ ón eape ꝛ mið þæpe ilcan pulle foꝛ-
ftoppa þæt eape.        :·

Þiþ þ ilce eft ȝenim æmetan hopf ꝛ cpopleác ꝛ
neoþopeaꝛðe ellenpinðe oþþe beolonan ꝛ ele ȝecnupa to
Somne pypme on feille ðo þonne on eape þaꝛa ꝛeaðena
fol. 16 a.
æmetena hopf · ȝenim þonne ꝛæðic ꝛ eceð cnupa to
Somne ppinȝ on þ eape. ȝif pypmaf on eapan fyn
ȝenim coꝛð ȝeallan ȝpeney feap · oþþe hunan yeap ·
oþþe yeꝛmoðey yeap fpile þaꝛa an fpa þu pille ȝeot þ
feap on þ eape þ cihð þone pyꝛm út. Þyꝛe fealfe
ȝecnupa finyullan ꝛ leoþopypt[1] ꝛ poꝛ ȝeðo þonne on
ȝley fæt mið eceðe ꝛ þuꝛh clað apꝛinȝ ðꝛype on þ
eape. Þiþ þon ȝif eapan ðynien · ȝenim ele ðo ón mið
eopocizpe pulle ꝛ foꝛðytte þ eape mið þæpe pulle þonne
þu ꝛlapan pille ꝛ ðo eft óf þonne þu onpæene.        :·

---

[1] Read leaþoꝛꝛypt.

*the patient* himself after a nights fasting, mix with butter and pour into the ear. Again for the same, drip into the ear juice of the rind of a nut tree made lukewarm.

9. For the same, mix with womans milk juice of green coriander, and a drop of honey and of wine, warmed together. For deafening of the ears again, *try* alder[1] bunches triturated, wring *out* the juice into the ear. Again for the same, take boars gall and bullocks and bucks, mingle with honey or in oil, wring into the ear.

10. Again for the same, take a green ashen staff, lay it on the fire, then take the juice that issues from it, put it on the same wool, wring into the ear, and stop up the ear with the same wool.

11. For the same, take emmets horses[2] and cropleek[3] and the lower part of alder rind or henbane and oil, pound *them* together, warm in a shell, then introduce into the ear the red emmets horses; than take radish and vinegar, pound them together, *and* wring into the ear. If there be insects in ears, take juice of green earthgall,[4] or juice of *hor*ehound, or juice of wormwood, whatsoever of these thou mayest wish, pour the juice into the ear, that draweth the worm out. Work a salve *thus;* pound sinfull[5] and latherwort[6] and leek, then place *them* in a glass vessel with vinegar, and wring through a cloth, drip *the moisture* on the ear. In case that there is a dinning in the ears; take oil, apply it with ewes wool, and close up the ear with the wool, when thou wilt sleep, and remove it again when thou awakest.

---

[1] *Sambucus nigra.*

[2] This talk of "emmets horses" is merely a misunderstanding of the Ἱππομύρμηκες of Aristoteles. Hist. Anim. viii. 27. The translation by Plinius, "formicæ pennatæ," that is, *male ants*, is commonly accepted as true, of course, but it is both philologically and physically unsatisfactory.

[3] *Allium sativum.*

[4] *Erythræa centaureum.*

[5] One of the *sedum* tribe, or all.

[6] *Saponaria officinalis.*

Eſt piþ þon ilcan peꞃmoð ᵹeſoðenne on piœteꞃe on
nipſim cytele ðo oꝼ heopðe læt ꞃeccan þone ſtéam on
þ eaꞃe ꞃ ꞃoꞃðytte mið þꞃoꞃe ꞃyꞃte ſiþþan hit mᵹeᵹan
ꞃie. Piþ eaꞃꞃieᵹan · ᵹením þ micle ᵹꞃiœte ꞃiiðel ſtꞃeaꞃ
tꞃyœeᵹe þ on poꞃꞃium ꞃixð ceop on þ eaꞃe he bið oꝼ
ꞃona.

.IIII.

Alex. Trall.,
lib. iv.

[1] Læceðomaꞃ pꞃð healꞃᵹunðe ꞃ þœꞃ tacn hꞃœþeꞃ he
hit ſie · ꞃ eác pꞃð ᵹealhſꞃile ꞃ þꞃotan · ꞃ paꞃenðe · piþ
ſpeoꞃcoþe · XIIII. cꞃœꝼtaſ. ⁖

fol. 16 b.

Marcellus,
306, a.

Piþ healꞃᵹunðe þonne œpeſt onᵹinne ꞃe healꞃᵹunð
peſan ſmiꞃe hine ꞃona mið hꞃiþeꞃeſ oþþe ſpiðoſt mið
oxan ᵹeallan þ iꞃ acunnoð ymb ꞃeapa niht bið hal.

Marcellus,
306, b.

ᵹiꝼ þu polðe pitan hꞃœþeꞃ þ healꞃ ᵹunð ſie · ᵹením
anᵹeltꞃœccean ᵹehalne leᵹe on þa ſtope þœꞃ hit aꞃꞃuten
ſie ꞃ beꞃꞃeoh ꝼœſte uꞃan mið leaꞃúm · ᵹiꝼ hit healꞃᵹunð bꞃð ſe pᵹꞃm pyꞃð to eoꞃꞃan · ᵹiꝼ hit ne biþ he
biþ ᵹehal. Eſt piþ healꞃ ᵹunðe ᵹením celenðeꞃ ꞃ beana
toᵹœðeꞃe ᵹeſoðene ꞃ aleᵹe ón Sona toꞃeꞃeþ. Eſt læce-

Marcellus,
306, b.

ðom piþ þon ilcan ᵹením pœteꞃhœꞃeꞃn ᵹebꞃœꞃneðne ꞃ
þonne ᵹeᵹniben ſmale ꞃ piþ huniᵹ ᵹemenᵹeð ꞃ ón ᵹeðon
Sona bið ꞃel. Piþ þon ilcan eꝼt ᵹalbanum hatte

Marcellus,
306, a.

ſuþeꞃne þyꞃt leᵹe þa ón þone ſpeoꞃꞃœꞃc · þonne atihð
hio mið ealle þa yꞃclan pœtan út ꞃ þone ᵹunð.

Piþ þon ilcan eꝼt beꞃeꞃ melo ꞃ hluttoꞃ pic ꞃ peax ·
ꞃ ele menᵹ toſomne ſeoþ ðo emhteſ oþþe eilðeꞃ miᵹe-

fol. 17 a.

þan to to onleᵹene ðo on þone ᵹunð. Pið healꞃ ᵹunðe

---

[1] Cf. Galen, vol. x. p. 881, ed. 1825.

12. Again for the same, *try* wormwood sodden in water in a new kettle, remove it from the hearth, let the steam reek upon the ear, and when *the application*[1] has gone in, close up *the ear* with the wort. Against earwigs, take the mickle great windlestraw[2] with two edges, which waxeth in highways, chew it into the ear, he, *the insect,* will soon be off.

### iv.

Leechdoms against a purulent humour in the neck, and tokens of it, whether it be such, and also for swellings in the jowl and throat and weasand, and against quinsy. Fourteen receipts.

2. Against a purulence[a] in the neck, when first the neck ratten begins to exist, smear it soon with gall of a beeve, or best of an ox ; it is a tried *remedy ;* in a few nights he will be whole. If thou wouldst know whether it be neck purulence,[b] take an earthworm entire, lay it on the place where the annoyance is, and wrap up fast above with leaves ; if it be neck ratten the worm turneth to earth, if it be not, he, *the patient,* will be whole. Again for neck ratten, take coriander and beans sodden together, and lay on, soon it removes *the disease.* Again, a leechdom for the same, take a water crab burnt and then rubbed small and mingled with honey and done on, *or applied,* soon he will be well. For the same again, a southern wort has been called galbanum, lay it on the neck pain, then it draweth altogether out the evil wet *or humour* and the ratten.

a Struma, Marcellus.

b A strumous swelling.

3. For the same again, mingle together bere *or barley* meal and clear pitch[c] and wax and oil, seethe *this,* add a boys or a childs mie, *make* into an external application on the matter. For ratten in the

c Resin.

---

[1] It ; the application, because *ream* is masculine.

[2] *Cynosurus cristatus,* some ; *Agrostis spica venti,* some.

eft þröpe ꞃeaðan netelan pyꞃttꞃuman ᵹeꞃoðenne on
eceðe ꞇ ᵹebeatenne ꞇ on ꞃeaxhlaꝼeꞅ pıꞃan ón aleð · ᵹıꝼ
ꞅe ᵹunð bıþ þonne onᵹınnenðe ꞅıo ꞃealꝼ hıne toðꞃıꝼþ ·
ᵹıꝼ he bıþ ealð hıo hıne ontynð ꞇ ꞅpa aꞅtıhð þ̃ yꝼel
ꞇıꞇ oþ þ̃ he hal bıð.                                        :·

Eꝼꞇ pıþ þon manıᵹꝼealð tacn ꞇ læceðom pıð healꝼ-
ᵹunðe oþþe ᵹeaᵹlꞅpıle [1] oððe þꞃotan oþþe paꞃenðe · Sıo
aðl íꞅ tꞃeᵹea cynna.   Oꝺeꞃ ıꝼ on þam ᵹeaᵹle ꞇ þonne
mon þone muþ ontynð bıþ ᵹehꞃæþeꞃ ᵹeꞅpollen ꞇ bıþ ꞃeað
ymb þa hꞃæctunᵹa ·  ꞇ ne mæᵹ ꞅe man eþelıce eþıan
ac bıþ aꞅmoꞃoð ·  ne mæᵹ eác naht ꝼoꞃꞅpelᵹan ne pel
ꞅpꞃecan ne ꞅtemne næꝼþ ·  ne bıð þeoꞅ aðl hꞃæþeꞃe to
ꝼꞃecne.   Oþeꞃ íꞅ þonne on þꞃöpe þꞃotan bıþ ꞅpyle ꞇ
lyꞃꞅeu ꞅe ne mæᵹ naht ᵹecꞃeþan ꞇ bıð ꞅe ꞅpıle ᵹe on
þam ꞅpeoꞃan ᵹe on þꞃöpe tunᵹan ·  ne mæᵹ ꞅe man pel
eþıan ·  ne þone ꞅpeoꞃan on ceꞃꞃan ·  ne hıꞅ heaꝼoð
ꝼoꞃð ón hylðan þ̃ he hıꝼ naꝼolan ᵹeꝼeon mæᵹe ·  ꞇ
butan hıꞅ man ꞃaþoꞃ tılıᵹe he bıþ ymb þꞃeo nıht
ᵹeꝼaꞃen.   ᵹıꝼ ꞅıe þæꞃe aðle bꞃyne Innan þæꞅ ꞅtꞃanᵹ
þ̃ món ne mæᵹe utan ᵹeꝼeon ꞅıo bıþ ðy ꝼꞃecenꞃe.
ᵹıꝼ þonne ꞅıe [2] on ᵹehꞃæþeꞃe healꝼe þa ceacan aꞅpollen
ꞇ ꞅıo þꞃotu ꞇ þu þa tacn ᵹeꝼeo þonne ꞅona læt þu
hım bloð ón æðꞃe ·  ᵹıꝼ þu þ̃ þuꞃhteon ne mæᵹe
ꞅceaꞃꞃa hím þa ꞃcancan þ̃ hím ðeah.                   :·

Sele hím ꞅceaꞃꞃne pyꞃtðꞃenc pyꞃne hım meteꞅ æꝼteꞃ
þon bepınð þone ꞅpeoꞃan ꞇ leᵹe ón læceðomaꞅ þa þe
utteon þa yꝼelan pætan ꞇ þæt ꞅaꞃ þonne bıþ þæꞃ pyꞃꞃe
pen.   Pyꞃc hım þa ꞃealꝼe ᵹením ꞅpıneꞅ ꞃyꞅle ᵹeꞅınꞃpe
ane bꞃaðe ꞃannan Inneꞃeaꞃðe mıð þam ꞃyꞃcle pyl þonne
ꞃeoꞃꞃ ᵹoꞅe ꞅceapn to on þa ꞃannan ꞇ ᵹeꞃlöce ꞇ þonne
hıt ꞅy ᵹemylt ðo þonne on lınenne clað leᵹe on þ̃ ꞃaꞃ ꞇ
beꞅꞃeþe ðo þ̃ pel óꝼt on on ðæᵹ ·  ꞇ bıþ ꞅpa beteꞃe ꞅpa

---

[1] ᵹeaᵹlꞅꞃꞃþe, MS.        [2] Read ꞅıen.

neck again, *use* a root of the red nettle sodden in
vinegar and beaten, laid on in the manner of a cake
of wax; if the matter be then beginning, the salve
driveth it away; if it be old it openeth it, and so the
evil riseth out till he be hale.

4. Again for that, a manifold token and a leechdom
for the neck ratten or jowl swelling or *swelling of the*
throat or weasand. The disease is of two kinds; the
one is in the jowl, and when one openeth the mouth
it is both swollen and is red about the uvula; and
the man can not easily breathe, but will be smothered;
he can not also swallow aught nor speak well, nor
hath he voice; this disorder, however, is not dangerous.
Another *sort* is when there is a swelling in the throat
and purulence, he, *the patient,* may not speak aught,
and the swelling is both on the neck and on the tongue;
the man can not well breathe, nor turn his neck nor
lean forward his head so that he may see his navel;
and except one attend to him somewhat speedily, in
about three days he will be deceased. If the burning
of the disease within be strong, yet there are no
external signs of it, it is so much the more dangerous.
If then on either side the jaws be swollen and the
throat, and thou see the tokens, then soon let thou
him blood on a vein; if thou may not carry that
through, scarify for him his shanks, that doth him
good.

5. Give him a sharp wort drink, warn him off meat,
after that bandage the neck, and lay on leechdoms
which may draw out the evil humour and the sore,
there will be then hope of recovery. Work him the
salve *thus;* take swines fat, smear the inside of a
broad pan with the fat, boil up, then cast goose sharn
into the pan, and make lukewarm, and when it be
melted then put it on a linen cloth, lay it on the
sore, and swathe up, apply that pretty often in a day,
and it will be the better the oftener thou renewest

þu oftop edmpaft þa fealfe ⁊ oftop onlegeft fio tihð
þ yfel ut.⠆

Ƿiþ healfgunde genim peax ⁊ ele gemeng þiþ noran
bloftman ⁊ gemelt togædene do þæp on.    Ƿiþ fpeop-
fol. 18 a.
coþe pypc on lecgende fealfe · genim feannef gelynðo
⁊ bepan fmepu ⁊ peax ealpa em fela pypc to fealfe
ª Alex. Trall.,
p. 67, ed. 1548.
Paul. Ægin.
iii. 27.
fmipe mið. ªEft þiþ þon ilcan gif þu finde hpitne
hunðep þoft abpige þone ⁊ gegnið ⁊ afyft ⁊ gehealð þ
þiþ þæpe fpeopcoþe ⁊ þonne þeapf pie meng þiþ hunig
fmipe þone fpeopan mið þ biþ ftpang fealf ⁊ god pið
fpelepe ablapunge ⁊ bpunepan ⁊ þiþ þapa ceacna ge-
fpelle oððe afmopunge · fceal þeah fe hunð ban gnagan
tep · þy biþ fe þoft hpit ⁊ micel gif þu hine nimeft ⁊
gadepaft æt fylne¹ þonne ne biþ he to unfpete to
geftmcanne · þonne pceal mon þone geagl eac fpillan
gelome on þæpe able · ⁊ fpolgettan eceð þiþ pealt gemenged. Eft fifleapan feapef þpy bollan fulle lytle
pceal fopcuuolftan.    Ƿiþ fpeopcoðe eft gapleac gegniðen
on eceð þ þe fie þiþ pætep gemenged fpille þone geagl mið
þy.    Ƿiþ fpeopcoþe eft pigef feopoþa feoþ on gefpettum
fol. 18 b.
pætepe fpille þa ceolan mið þy gif pe fpeona pap pie
pyn eac þa fpillinga hpilum hate þonne if eac to þyppe
able gepet þ mon unðep þæpe tungan læte bloð oþþe óf
eapme ⁊ on mopgen ón fppenge · gif hit þonne cniht
fie læt on þam fpeopan · ⁊ on þæpe able if to fop-
pypmanne pinef ⁊ flæpcef fpiþopt þy læp fio ceole fie
afpollen.⠆

.V.

Ƿiþ þon gif mannef muð fap fie genim betonican ⁊
getpifula lege on þa peolope. To muð fealfe ⁊ to

---

¹ Read fylle.  In Lye fillen, *omentum*, is an error for fylmen.

the salve and the oftener thou layest on. It will draw the evil out.

6. For matter in the neck, take wax and oil, mingle with rose blossoms and melt together, put *this* thereon. For swereccothe *or quinsy*, work an onlaying salve. Take suet of bull and grease of bear, and wax, even quantities of all, work to a salve, smear with it. Again for the same, if thou find a white thost[a] of hound, dry it and rub it, and sift it, and hold it against the swerecothe, and when need be mingle with honey, smear the neck with it, that is a strong salve and good for such upblowing *or inflation* and brunella,[1] and for swelling of the jaws, or smothering. The hound must gnaw a bone ere *he droppeth the thost*, then will the thost be white and mickle; if thou takest and gatherest it at the fall, then it is not too unsweet of smell; one shall further often also swill the jowl in this disease, and swallow vinegar mingled with salt. Again, he shall swallow down three bowls of the juice of cinquefoil, little ones. For swerecothe *or quinsy* again, *use* garlic rubbed in vinegar which be mingled with water, swill the jowl with that. For quinsy, again, seethe the siftings of rye on sweetened water, swill the gullet with it, if the swere be sore, let the swillings also be whilom hot. Besides it is also laid down for this disease, that blood be let under the tongue or from an arm, and on the morrow apply a clyster. Further if it be a boy, let (blood) on the neck; and in this disease it is well to warn off (the sick) from wine, and specially from flesh *meat*, lest the gullet be swollen.

[a] Album Graecum.

## V.

In case that a mans mouth be sore, take betony and triturate it, lay it on the lips. For a mouth

---

[1] A disease resembling diphtheria; otherwise, Pruna.

ȝeblegenaðre tunȝan ſiſleaȝe · ꝺ bꞃembel leaf ꝼyl on
ꝧætepe haꝼa lanȝe on muðe ꝺ ȝelome.　ȝiꝼ monneꞃ
oꝼað ſie ꝼul ȝenim beꝥen mela ȝoꝺ · ꝺ clæne huniȝ ꝺ
lꝑꞇ ꞃealꞇ ȝemenȝ eall ꞇoſomne ꝺ ȝniꝺ þa ꞇeþ mid
ſꝑiðe ꝺ ȝelome.　　　　　　　　　　　　　:·

### . VI.

Læcedomaꞃ ꝑiþ ꞇoð ꝧæꞃce ꝺ ꝑiþ ꝼyꞃmſim ȝe ꝑiþ þam
uꝼeꝥan ꞇoðeee ȝe ꝑiþ þam[1] niþeꝥan.　　　　　:·

ᵃ Herbar.
Apul. i. 8.

þiþ ꞇoþ ꝧæꞃce ·ᵃ beꞇonican ſeoð on ꝑine oþ þꞃiꝺꝺan
ꝺæl ſꝑle þonne ȝeonꝺ þone muð lanȝe hꝑile.　　　:·

fol. 19 a.

þið ꞇoþ ꝧæꞃce ȝiꝼ ꝑyꞃm eꞇe · ȝenim calꝺ holen leaꝼ
ꝺ heoꞃoꞇ cꞃoꝑ neoþeꝥeaꞃðne ꝺ ſaluian uꝼeꝥeaꞃðe beꝑyl
ꞇꝑy ꝺæl on ꝧæꞇꝑe ȝeoꞇ on bollan ꝺ ȝeona ymb þonne
ꝼeallað þa ꝑꝼyꞃmaꞃ on þone bollan.　ȝiꝼ ꝑyꞃm eꞇe þa
ꞇeð ȝenim oꝼeꝥ ȝeaꝥe holen ꝥinꝺe ꝺ eoꝼoꝥ þꞃoꞇan
moꝥan ꝼel on ſꝑa haꞇum[2] haꝼa on muþe ſꝑa haꞇ ſꝑa
þu haꞇoſꞇ mæȝe.　þiþ ꞇoð ꝑyꞃmum ȝenim ac mela ꝺ
beolonan ꞃæꝺ ꝺ ꝥeax ealꝥa em ꝼela menȝ ꞇoſomne
ꝑyꝥc ꞇo ꝥeax canꝺelle · ꝺ bæꞃꝥ læꞇ ꝥeocan on þone
muð ꝺo blæc hꝥæȝl unꝺeꝥ þonne ꝼeallaþ þa ꝑyꞃmaꞃ
on.　　　　　　　　　　　　　　　　　　　:·

þið ꞇoþ ꝧæꞃce ȝebꞃæꝥn hꝑiꞇ ꞃealꞇ ꝺ ȝaꝥleſic beꝥce on
ȝleꝺum ȝebꞃæꝺ ꝺ beꝥenꝺ ꝺ ꝑiꝥoꝥ ꝺ ſꞇꝥælꝑyꝥꞇ ȝeȝniꝺ
eal ꞇoſomne leȝe on.　　　　　　　　　　　　:

þiþ ꞇoþ ꝧæꞃce hꝥeꝼneꞃ ꝼoꞇ ꝥel on ꝑine neoþoꝥeaꞃðne
oðða on eeeꝺe ſuꝥ ſꝑa ðu haꞇoſꞇ mæȝe.　þiþ ꞇoðꝧæꞃce

---

ꝥiþā, MS.　　　　　|　　ᵓ haꞇum ꝥæꞇꝥe ?

salve and for a blained tongue, boil in water fiveleaf,
*that is, cinquefoil*, and bramble leaves, have it long in
the mouth and frequently. If a mans breath be foul,
take good barley meal and clean honey and white
salt,[1] mingle all together, and rub the teeth with *it*
much and frequently.

### vi.

1. Leechdoms for sharp pain in the teeth and for
worms, either for the upper tooth ache or for the
nether.

2. For tooth wark, seethe betony in wine to the
third part, then swill the mouth thoroughly for a long
while.

3. For tooth wark, if a worm eat *the tooth*, take an
old holly leaf and one of the lower umbels of hart-
wort,[2] and the upward *part of* sage, boil two doles[3]
in water, pour into a bowl and yawn over it, then the
worms shall fall into the bowl. If a worm eat the
teeth, take holly rind over a year old, and root of
carline thistle, boil in so hot *water?* hold in the mouth
as hot as thou hottest may. For tooth worms, take
acorn meal and henbane seed and wax, of all equally
much, mingle *these* together, work into a wax candle,
and burn it, let it reek into the mouth, put a black
cloth under, then will the worms fall on it.

4. For tooth wark, burn white salt and garlic,
make them smoke on gledes, roast and tear to pieces,
and *add* pepper and clubmoss, rub all together and
lay on.

5. For tooth wark, boil in wine or in vinegar the
netherward part of ravens foot,[4] sup as thou hottest
may. For tooth wark, bray together to dust rind

---

[1] That is, the best, purest salt.

[2] *Seseli*; perhaps, however, Hart-
bramble, *Rhamnus*, may be meant.

[3] That is, two of worts to one of
water.

[4] *Ranunculus ficaria.*

hnutbeames rinde ⁊ þorn rinde gecnua to duste adrig ōn pannan snið utan þa teþ scead on gelome. :·

Wyrc þus toþsealfe ofersæwisc rind ⁊ hunig ⁊ piper meng tosomne lege ōn · wyrc eác sealfe of wenwyrte on þa ilcan wisan. :·

fol. 19 b. Wiþ þām uferan toþece genīm wiþowindan leaf wring on þa nosu. Wiþ þam niþeran toþece slit mid þe foþorne oþ þæt hie bleden. :·

Eft genīm elmes rinde gebærn to ahsan gemeng þa ahsan wiþ wæter ⁊ aseoh hafa þæt wæter lange on Marcellus, 296, h. muþe. Eft genīm gearwan ceow swiþe. :·

.VII.

Herbar. Apul. i. 13. Gif mon blode hræce genim betonican swilce swa .III. penegas gewegen gegnid on gæte meolc sele þry dagas þry bollan fulle to drincanne. :·

.VIII.

Wiþ blæce ōn ⁊wlitan wyl to baþe fencersan ⁊ neoþoweardne secg · æscrinde earfan wyl ōn wætere lange beþe mid. :·

To sealfe wiþ blæce ōn ⁊wlitan · ompran neoþowearde þa þe swimme do sealt to ⁊ fletan ⁊ æg. Briw wiþ blæce ōn ⁊wlitan gemelte eald spic briw on þon · do gegrundenne piper ōn · ⁊ cropleác hwætenes melwes twy dæl swilce þæs piperes āwyl hwæt hwega · genim þæs þreo snæda gewest æfter wearme. fol. 20 a. Wið blæce genīm heorotes horn gebærn to ahsan ⁊ swefl ⁊ gebærned sealt ⁊ píc to ahsan ⁊ swa ostrer scella ⁊ gecnuwa ompran smale ⁊ gemeng eall to briwe ⁊ smire

of nut tree and thorn rind, dry then in a pan, cut[1] the teeth on the outside, shed on frequently.

6. Work a tooth salve thus, mingle together oversea rind[2] and honey and pepper, lay on. Work also a salve of wenwort in the same wise.

7. For the upper tooth ache, take leaves of withewind, wring *them* on the nose. For the nether tooth ache, slit with the tenaculum, till they bleed.

8. Again, take elms rind, burn to ashes, mingle the ashes with water and strain, hold the water long in the mouth. Again, take yarrow, chew it much.

### vii.

1. If a man break up blood, take as much betony as three pennies weigh, rub in goats milk, give for three days three bowls full to drink.

### viii.

1. For a blotch on the face, boil for a bath fencross[3] and the netherward *part of* sedge,[4] ash rind, tares, boil long in water, bathe therewith.

2. For a salve against a blotch in the face, *use* the netherward part of dock, which will swim,[5] add to it salt and curds and egg. A brewit for a blotch on the face, melt old lard, on that a brewit, add ground pepper, and cropleek,[6] two doles of wheaten meal as well as of the pepper, boil a little, take of it three slices, after that go to bed and get warm. For a blotch, take harts horn, burn to ashes, and sulfur, and burnt salt and pitch burnt to ashes, and so oyster shells, and beat sorrel[7] small, and mingle all into a brewit, smear

---

[1] By Sect. 7, it appears by top is meant the gums, toþþeoman.

[2] *Cinnamon.*

[3] *Nasturtium officinale.*

[4] *Carex.*

[5] This seems by Gerarde to be *duckweed, Lemna.*

[6] *Allium sativum.*

[7] *Rumex Acetosa.*

mið.  Eft ꞃealꝼ pel on aþyðūm ſceapeꞃ ſmeꞃupe hæᵹ-
þoꞃneꞃ bloſtman ⁊ þa ſinalan ſinᵹꞃenan ⁊ ꞃuðuꞃoꞃan
menᵹ þonne hꞃꞇꞇepuðu ꞃiþ ⁊ hꞃon buꞇeꞃan.                :·

### .VIIII.

Cf. Marcell.
290, c.

Ᵹiꝼ men yꞃne bloð oꝼ nebbe ꞇo ſꞃiðe ᵹenīm ᵹꞃene
beꞇonican ⁊ ꞃuðan ᵹecnupa ūn eceð ᵹeꞃꞃinᵹ ꞇoſomne
ſꞃilce ꞃie an ꞃlah ꝼꞇmᵹ on þa noſu.  bloð ꞃeꞇen biſceoꝥ
ꝥyꞃꞇ moꞃoꞃeaꞃðe eꞇe oððe on meolce ðꞃince.  Blod
ſeꞇen eft ᵹenīm heᵹecliꞃan ᵹebmðe ūn ſꞃeoꞃan.      :·

bloð ſeꞇen eꝼꞇ ſꞃꞃinᵹ ꝥyꞃꞇ ðo ūn eaꞃe.

Bloð ꞃeꞇen eꝼꞇ ꞃeᵹbꞃaðan ðo ūn eaꞃe.                  :·

bloð ꞃeꞇen eꝼꞇ ᵹehal beꞃen eaꞃ beꝼꞇinᵹe on eaꞃe
ſꞃa he nyꞇe.  Sume þiꞃ ꞃꞃꞇað ✠ æᵹꞃyn · ꞇhon · ꝼꞇꞃuꞇh ·
ꞃ
fol. 20 b.
ꞃola aꞃᵹꞃenn · ꞇaꞃꞇ · ſꞃꞃuꞇh · on · ꞇꞃia · enn · ꞃiaꞇh ·
haꞇhu · moꞃꞃana · on hæl ✠ aꞃa · caꞃm · leou · ᵹꞃoꞇh ·
ꞃeoꞃn · Ꞁ · ꝼꞃil · eꞃonði · ꞃ · |✗| · mꞃo · eꞃon · aꞃeꞃuo ·
eꞃuuo · aeꞬ · leᴎo · ᵹe hoꞃſe ᵹe men bloð ſeꞇen.      :·

### .X.

Þiþ ᵹeſnoꞇe ⁊ ᵹeꞃoſum · ᵹenīm oxna lyb nꞃeꞃeaꞃð
ᵹecnupa ꞃel ꞃið ꞃaꞇꞃe · ᵹiꝼ huo ſie ᵹꞃene ne ðo þu
þæꞃ ꞃaꞇeꞃ ꞇo ꞃꞃuᵹ þonne on ꝥ neb.                  :·

### .XI.

Marcellus,
291, e.

Þiþ ꞃaꞃum peoloꞃūm ᵹeſuuꞃe mið huniᵹe þa peoloꞃaꞃ
ᵹenīm þonne æᵹeꞃꝼclnan beꞃceað mið ꞃiꞃoꞃe leᵹe on. :·

### .XII.

[1]Þiþ ꞃouum muþe ᵹenīm omꞃꞃan ⁊ ealðne ſꞃineſ
ꝥyꞃſle ꝥyꞃꞃ ꞇo ꞃealꝼe ſeꞇe on þone ꞃon[2] ðæl.  Þiþ ceolan

---

[1] Κυνικὸς σπασμός.
[2] ꞃon, here is a contraction of ꞃohan, ꞃoᵹan.

therewith. Again, a salve, boil in pressed sheeps grease, hawthorns blossoms, and the small stonecrop and wood-roffe, then mingle mastic therewith and a little butter.

### ix.

1. If blood run from a mans nose too much, take green betony and rue, pound them in vinegar, twist them together like as it might be a sloe, poke it into the nose. A blood stopper; eat the netherward part of bishopwort or drink it in milk. To stop blood again, take hedge cleavers, bind it on the neck.

2. As a blood stancher again, put springwort[1] into the ear.

3. To stop blood again, put waybroad[2] into the ear.

4. To stop blood again, poke into the ear a whole ear of bere *or barley;* so he be unaware of it. Some write this: . . . . . . . . . either for horse or man, a blood stancher.

### x.

For snot and poses *or catarrhs;* take the netherward part of stinking hellebore,[3] pound it well with water; if it be green do not apply water to it, then wring on the nose.

### xi.

For sore lips, smear the lips with honey, then take film of egg, scatter it with pepper, and lay on.

### xii.

For distorted mouth, take dock and old swines grease, work to a salve, set on the wry part. For swelling of gullet, for that, everfern[4] also shall *come*

---

[1] *Euforbia lathyris.*
[2] *Plantago maior.*
[3] *Helleborus viridis.*
[4] *Polypodium vulgare.*

ſpile ƿiþ þon ſceal eoſoꞃꞅeaꞃꞃ ene ſꞃa ⁊ ȝyþꞃꞃꞃan ƿyl
on meolce ſuꞃ þonne ⁊ ȝebeþe miꝺ.    Þiþ ceolan ſpile
biꞃſceop ꞃyꞃc aceꞃꞃlaꝺe niꝺeꞃeaꞃꝺe ⁊ clacan ƿyl on
ealaꝺ.                                                 :·

### .XIII.

Þiꝺ hæꞃ ꞃeeaꞃꝺe hꞃic eꞃuꝺu ȝeenuꞃa ſꞃiꝺe ſmale
ꝺo æȝeꞃ þ hꞃice co ⁊ menȝ ſꞃa þu ꝺeſc ceaꞃoꞃ ōn-

ꝼniꝺ miꝺ ꞃeaxꝼe ſeoꞃa miꝺ ſeolee ꞃæſce ſmiꞃe miꝺ þonne
miꝺ þæꞃe ꞃealꞃe ucan ⁊ innan ꞃꞃ ꞃe ſeolōe ꞃociȝe ·
ȝiꝼ cofomne ceo ꞃece miꝺ hanꝺa ſmiꞃe eꝼc ꞃona.     :

### .XIIII.

Þiþ ꞃeaꝺan · ꞃeeelꞃ lycel ſꞃeꝼl ſꞃeȝleſ æꞃꞃel ꞃeax
ȝinȝiꝼeꞃ þuꞃh hoꞃn ꝺꞃince · hunan haꝼōeꞃyꞃc on
hluccꞃūm ealoꝺ.                                       :·

### .XV.

[1]Þiþ hꞃoſcan hu he miꞃꞃenhee ōn mon becume ⁊ hu
hiꞃ mon ciliaꞃ ꝼeyle.    Se hꞃoſca hæꝼꝺ maniȝꝼealōne
cocyme ſꞃa þa ſꞃacl beoꝺ miꞃꞃenheu · hꞃilum eynꝺ
ōꝼ unȝemecꞃæꞃcꞃe hꞃco · hꞃilum oꝼ unȝemecꞃæꞃcum
eyle · Dꞃilum oꝼ unȝemeclheꞃe ꝺꞃuȝneꞃꞃe.

Þꞃꞃe ꝺꞃene ƿiþ hꞃoſcan · ȝeniꞃ mueȝꞃyꞃc ſeoþ on
eyꞃeꞃenum ciele ⁊ ƿyl oþ þ hio[2] ſie ſꞃꞃþe ꞃieee · ⁊ hio[2]
ſie ōꝼ hꞃæcenum mealce ȝeꞃoꞃhc ȝeniꞃ þonne eoꞃoꞃ-
ꞃeaꞃneꝼ mæꞃc biſceop ꞃyꞃc · hinꝺ  heoloꝺan · ꝺꞃeoꞃȝe
ꝺꞃoſclan ſinȝꞃenan ꝺo to eall on ꝼæc ſele ꝺꞃinean miꝺ-

ꝺelꝺaȝum ⁊ ꞃoꞃȝa ꞃuꞃ ⁊ ſealceꞃ ȝehꞃæc.    Þiþ hꞃoſcan

---

¹ Bꝺ́ȝ.                    |         ² Read he.

*into use,* and boil cockle in milk, them sup *some* and bathe with it. For swelling of gullet, boil in ale bishopwort, the netherward part of attorlothe, and burdock.

### xiii.

For hair lip, pound mastic very small, add the white of an egg, and mingle as thou dost vermillion, cut with a knife *the false edges of the lip,* sew fast with silk, then smear without and within with the salve, ere the silk rot. If it draw together, arrange it with the hand; anoint again soon.

### xiv.

For watery congestions[1] called κλύδωνες, a little incense, some sulfur, beetle nut, wax, ginger; let *the patient* drink through a horn *hor*ehound and hawkwort[2] in clear ale.

### xv.

For host *or cough,* how variously it comes upon a man, and how a man should treat it. The host hath a manifold access, as the spittles are various. Whilom it cometh of immoderate heat, whilom of immoderate cold, whilom of immoderate dryness.

2. Work *thus* a drink against cough. Take mugwort,[3] seethe it in a copper kettle, and boil till it[4] be very thick, and let it[4] be wrought of wheaten malt; then take of everfern most, bishopwort, water agrimony,[5] pennyroyal,[6] singreen,[7] set all in a vat, give to drink at the middays, and forego *what is* sour and every-

---

[1] Βρογχοκήλη, perhaps.
[2] *Hieracium.*
[3] *Artemisia vulgaris.*
[4] The gender of the pronoun makes it refer to the wort, whereas the process seems to require a masculine, referring to the potion.
[5] *Eupatorium cannabinum.*
[6] *Mentha pulegium.*
[7] *Sempervivum tectorum.*

eft · genīm hunan seoð on wætere sele swa wearme drincan. :·

Eft genim clifwyrt sume men hatað foxes clife sume eawyrt · ⁊ hio sy geworht ofer midne sumor seoþ þa ōn wætere oþ ꝥ driddan[1] dæl þæs woses ōf sie sele drincan þriwa on dæg. :·

Wið hwostan eft genīm fæmnitan wyl on ealaþ sele drincan. Eft genim sprácen berindred wyl ōn ealað sele drincan. :·

Eft gen[i]m hofan geaspan reade netelan wyl ōn meolce. Eft genīm wiþ hwostan ⁊ wiþ angbreoste slarian godne dæl do bollan fulne wines to bewyl þriddan dæl on þa wyrte supe on niht nestig. :·

Eft genim marubian wyl on ealað do piwor on. Eft wiþ angbreoste gif men sie drige hwosta · genīm spices snæde þynne lege on hatne stan sceað cymed ōn sete horn ōn drince þonne smic. :·

Wiþ drigum hwostan eft genīm colonan ⁊ galluc ete on huniges teare. :·

fol. 22 a. .XVI.

Wiþ breost wærce genim þa lytlan culmillan ⁊ cymed wyl on hluttrūm ealaþ supe ⁊ drince. Eft genīm dweorge dwostlan ⁊ gyþrifan kyncean welle on hluttrum ealað drince scene fulne ōn neaht nestig. :·

Wyl ōn ealað wiþ þon ilcan finul marubian betonican ⁊ drince. Wiþ breost wærce genīm rudan · hunan ⁊

[1] Read ðriddan = ðridda.

thing salt. Again for host, take horehound, seethe in water, administer it so warm to drink.

3. Again, take cliffwort,[1] some men call it foxes cliff, some riverwort, and let it be wrought past midsummer, seethe it in water till the third part of the wash be off, give it thrice a day to be drunk.

4. For host again, take sea mint, boil it in ale, give to drink. Again, take black alder rendered *and purified*, boil *it* in ale, give *it* to be drunk.

5. Again, take hove,[2] yarrow, red nettle,[3] boil *them* in milk. Again, take against host and against breast anguish,[4] a good portion of slary,[5] add a bowl full of wine, boil away a third part on the wort; let *the patient* sup it at night fasting.

6. Again, take marrubium, boil it in ale, add pepper. Again, for breast anguish, if a man have a dry host, take a thin slice of lard, lay it on a hot stone, shed cummin on it, set it on a horn,[6] let *the patient* drink in the smoke.

7. For a dry cough again, take elecampane and comfrey; let *the patient* eat them in virgin honey.

### xvi.

1. For acute pain in the breast, take the little centaury and cummin, boil in clear ale, let *the patient* sip and drink. Again, take pennyroyal and cockle, artichoke, let him boil in clear ale, let him drink a cup full at night fasting.

2. Boil in ale for the same, fennel, marrubium, betony, and let *the patient* drink. For pain in the breast, take rue, *ho*rehound and abrotanon,[7] rub to-

---

[1] *Arctium lappa.*

[2] *Glechoma hederacea.*

[3] *Lamium purpureum.*

[4] *Angina pectoris* seems too limited.

[5] *Salvia sclarea.*

[6] Lye understands cymeþ as χαμαιδρύς, germander, going by the syllables.

[7] *Artemisia abrotanon.*

appotanan ᵹeᵹniꝺ toSomne ſmæle on mo�007tepe menᵹ
piꝺ huniᵹ ꞇ þiy ꝺaᵹaſ ælce bæᵹ æp mete þine cucleþ
ꝼulle ᵹeþicᵹe.

## .XVII.

Þiþ heopt pæpcc þuban ᵹelm ſeoþ on ele ꞇ ꝺo alpan
anc yntſan to ſmipe miꝺ þy þ ſtilꝺ þam ſape. Þiþ
heopt ece ᵹiꝼ him ón Innan heapꝺ heopt pæþe ſie
þonne him pyxþ pinꝺ on þæpe heoptan ꞇ hine þeᵹeꝺ
þuþſt ꞇ biþ unmehtiᵹhc.

Þyþc him þonne ſtan bæꝺ ꞇ ón þam ete ſupepne
þaebic miꝺ pealte þy mæᵹ peſan ſio punꝺ ᵹchæleꝺ.

fol. 22 b.

Þiþ heoþot ece eꝼt ᵹením ᵹiþþiꝼan ſeoþ ón meolce pele
ꝺpincan · VI. ꝺaᵹaſ.

Eꝼt moþepeapꝺ eꝼoþꝼeapin ᵹyþþiꝼan · peᵹbpæ[ꝺan]
pyl topomne pele ꝺpincan. Þiꝺ hopot ece eꝼt ᵹenim
pipoþ · ꞇ cymen · ꞇ coſt ᵹeᵹniꝺ on beoᵹ oþþe on
þætpe pele ꝺpincan.

## .XVIII.

Paul. Ægineta,
ii. 56.
Alex. Trall.
vii. 15.
Αυγμός.
°tilian

Ðponan pe micla ᵹeoxa cume oþþe hu hiſ mốn
tican° pcule. Se cymꝺ óꝼ þam ſpiꝺe acoloꝺan maᵹan ·
oþþe oꝼ þam to ſpiꝺe ahatoꝺan · oꝺꝺe óꝼ to micelþe
ꝼylle · oþþe oꝼ to micelþe læþneppe · oꝺꝺe oꝼ yꝼelum
þætan · phtenꝺum ꞇ ſccoþꝼenꝺum þone maᵹan · ᵹiꝼ
þonne ſe peoca man þuþh ſpipeꝺþenc aſpipꝺ þonc yꝼelan
bitenꝺan þætan ón peᵹ · þonne ꝼopſtent pe ᵹeohſa · ſpipe
þa ꝺeah þam monnum þe ꝼoᵹ ꝼylle ᵹihſa phhꝺ oꝺꝺe
ꝼopþon þe hie Innán pcypꝼꝺ ꞇ eác pe ᵹeohſa pe þe oꝼ
þaeſ yꝼelan þætan micelnyppe cymꝺ hæꝼꝺ þeapꝼe ſpip-
ꝺþinceſ · pe pypeꝺ micelne pnoþan eác ꞇ ſe hine bet ·
þonne pe ᵹeohſa oꝼ þæpe iꝺlan pambe cymꝺ ꞇ oꝼ þæþe

gether small in a mortar, mingle with honey, and for three days, every day before meat, let *the patient* take three spoons full.

## xvii.

For pain in the heart, seethe a handful of rue in oil, and add an ounce of aloes, rub *the body* with that, it stilleth the sore. For heart ache, if there be to him within, a hard heart wark, then wind waxeth in the heart for him, and thirst vexes him and he is languid.

2. Work him then a stone bath, and in that let him eat southern radish[1] with salt, by that the wound may be healed. For heart ache again, take githrife, seethe it in milk, give to drink for six days.

3. Again, boil together the netherward part of everfern, githrife, and waybroad ; give to drink. For heart ache again, take pepper and cummin and costmary, rub them into beer, or into water, administer to drink.

## xviii.

*We here explain* whence the mickle hicket[2] cometh, and how a man should treat it. It cometh from the very chilled maw, or from the too much heated *maw*, or from too mickle fulness, or of too mickle leerness, *that is emptiness*, or of evil wet *or humour* rending and scarifying the maw. If then the sick man by a spew drink speweth away the evil biting wet, then the hicket abateth. A spew then is good for the men whom hicket teareth for fulness, or in case it scarifieth them within ; and also the hicket which cometh of the mickleness of the evil wet *or humour*, hath need of a spew drink, which eke worketh mickle sneezing, and amendeth *the sick*. When the hicket cometh of the

---

[1] *Rhafanus sativa.*
[2] Holland and old writers spell Hicket, the moderns " hiccup," " hic-
" cough."

fol. 23 a.

ʒelæpan ne bet þone fe ꝼnoꝑa. ʒiꝼ fe ʒeohfa oꝼ cile
cume þonne fceal mon mið pyꝑmenðum þinʒum lacnian
fpile fpa ꝑiꝑoꝑ iꝼ ꝼ oþꝑa peꝑmenða pyꝑta oþþe ꝑuðan
ʒeʒniðe mon opin[1] ꝼelle ðꝑincan · oþþe meꝑcef ꝼæð
mið pine[2] oþþe eceð[2] ꝼelle ðꝑincan oððe mintan bꝑoð

Correct cymen,
from the Hel-
lenic.

oþþe moꝑan · oððe cymenef oþþe ʒinʒiꝼꝑan hꝑilum an-
lepiʒ fpa ʒeꝑenoðe · hꝑilum þa pyꝑta toʒædeꝑe ʒeðon
on þ pof ꝼelle ðꝑincan · ʒiꝼ oꝼ hatum pætan yꝼelum
on þone maʒon gefamnoðum fe ʒeohfa cume ꝼ he ʒeꝼele
þ fe hine innan fceoꝑꝼe on þone maʒan · ꝼele him þonne
placu pæteꝑ ðꝑincan fpiþe hat · ʒeðo þonne ꝼeþeꝑe on
cle ftinʒe him ʒelome on þa hꝑacan þ he maʒe fꝑꝑan ·
ꝼele him piþ ʒeohfan cealð pæteꝑ ꝼ eceð ðꝑincan ꝼ
apꝑotanan ʒeʒniðene on pine.

Cf. Paul.
Æginet.
lib. iii. 37.
ed. Ald. fol.
43 a. line 35.
Ναυτία,
'Ανορεξία.
fol. 23 b.

.XVIIII.

Þiþ plættan þam men þe hine ne lyft hiꝑ meteꝑ ne
liþeꝑ oððe on maʒan fintꝑum fie · oþþe biteꝑe hꝑæce ·
eoꝑð ʒeallan ꝼ ꝑiꝑoꝑ ðꝑince on peaꝑmum pæteꝑe þꝑy
bollan ꝼulle on niht neꝑtiʒ. Eꝼt piþ platunʒe ꝑuðan
peꝑinoð bifceop pyꝑt maꝑubian pyl on calað fpiþe ʒefpet
mið huniʒe leohtlice · ʒeðꝑinc fpa hateꝑ fpa þin bloð
fie fcenc ꝼulne ðo fpa þonne þe þeaꝑf fie.                    ⁖

.XX.

Þiþ ꝼculðoꝑ ꝑæꝑce calðeꝑ fpineꝑ toþð þæꝑ þe ꝼelð-
ʒanʒenðe fie menʒ pið ealðne ꝑyꝼele ʒeꝑyꝑme leʒe on
þ ðeah piþ ꝼculðoꝑ ꝑæꝑce ʒe pið ꝑið ꝑæꝑce · piþ breoft
pæꝑce · ꝼ piþ lenðenꝑæꝑce. Eꝼt ꝑyl hetonican ꝼ neꝼtan on ealað ꝼele ðꝑincan ʒelome ꝼ fimle æt ꝼyꝑe
ʒefmiꝑe mið penpyꝑte. Eꝼt ʒenim fpineꝑ ꝑceaꝑꝑ þæꝑ þe
on ðun lanðe ꝼ pyꝑtum libbe mænʒ piþ ealðne ꝑyꝼele

---

For on ꝼín.                        |        [2] Not the same case.

foul wamb and of the leer *or empty* one, the sneezing
doth not amend it. If the hicket come of chill, then
shall a man cure it with warming things, such as
pepper is, and other warming worts, or let one rub
rue and give it in wine to drink; or give seed of marche
with wine or vinegar, or broth of mint or carrot,[a]
or cummin, or ginger, at times singly *and* so prepared. At whiles give to drink the worts together
put into the wash. If the hicket come of hot evil
humours collected into the maw, and *the sick man*
feel that it scarifieth him within in the maw, give
him then lukewarm water to drink " very hot," then
put a feather in oil, poke him frequently in the throat
that he may spew; give him against hicket cold water
and vinegar to drink, and abrotanon rubbed in wine.

## xix.

Against loathing *or nausea,* for the man who hath
no lust for his meat nor for his cup, or be infirm in
the maw, or breaketh bitter, *as in heartburn,* let him
drink earthgall and pepper in warm water, three
bowls full at night fasting. Again for loathing, boil
strongly in ale slightly sweetened with honey, rue,
wormwood, bishopwort, marrubium, drink of this as
hot as thy blood be, a cup full, do so when need be
to thee.

## xx.

Against shoulder pain, mingle a tord of an old swine,
which be a fieldgoer, with old lard, warm it, lay it on,
that is good for shoulder pain or for side pain, for
breast wark and for loin wark. Again, boil betony and
nepeta in ale, give to drink frequently, and always
at a fire smear with wenwort. Again, take sharn of
swine, which liveth on the downland and on worts,
mingle with old lard, lay on, and let *the patient* drink

leȝe ón ꝺ ðꞃince¹ betonican on ȝeꞅpettum ꝑine · ȝiꝼ
ꝼeꝼeꞃ habbe ðꞃince on pæteꞃe.          :·

### .XXI.

Þiþ ꞃiban ꞅaꞃe þæꞃe ꞅꝑiþꞃan boȝen ꝺ ꞃebic ꝺ hꝑite
clæꝼꞃan ꝑyꞃc to clame ꝺ to ðꞃence. Þiþ þæꞃe ꝑineꞅ-
tꞃan ꞅiban ꞅaꞃe ꝑuðuꞃꞃan ȝecnupa on eceb ꝺ ꝑyꞃc to
clame ȝebinb on þa ꞅiban. Eꝼt betonican ꞅꝑile ꞅꝑa
þꞃy peneȝaꞅ ȝeꝑeȝen · ꝺ ꝑiꝑoꝑeꞅ ꞅeoꝼon ꝺ xx. coꞃna to
Sómne ȝetꞃiꝼulab · ȝeót ealbeꞃ ꝑineꞅ þꞃy bollan ꝼulle
to · ꝺ ȝeplece ꞃele nihtneꞃtiȝúm ðꞃincan. Eꝼt ꝑib
ꞅiban ꞅaꞃe ꝑubon ꝑib ꞃyꞃele² ȝemenȝeb ꝺ ȝebeaten
lecȝe on þa ꞅiban þ bet. Þiþ ꞃiban ꞅaꞃe eꝼt lauꞃeꞃ
cꞃoppan ȝebeate ðꞃince on pæteꞃe ꝺ on þa ꞅiban
binbe. ³Þiþ ꞅiban ꞅaꞃe eꝼt canleꞅ ꝑyꞃttꞃuman ȝebæꞃn
to ahꞅan ꝺ ꝑiþ ealbne ꞃyꞃele ȝemenȝ ꝺ aleȝe on þa
ꞃiban.

### .XXII.

Þiþ lenben ece ȝenim betonican ꞅpilce tꞃeȝen peneȝaꞅ
ȝeꝑeȝen bo þæꞃto ꞅꝑeteꞅ ꝑineꞅ tꞃeȝen bollan ꝼulle menȝ
ꝑiþ hat pæteꞃ ꞃele nihtneꞃtiȝ ðꞃincan. Eꝼt ȝenim
ȝꞃunbe ꞅpelȝean ȝebeat ꝺ þ ꞅeaꝼ ꞃele ðꞃincan niht-
neꞃtiȝum.

Þiþ lenben ece caliꝼeꞃ hatte ꝑyꞃt ȝnib on ealaþ ꝺ
ðꞃince þa. Þiþ þon ilcan hunbeꞃ tunȝe hatte ꝑyꞃt
ȝenim þa leaꝼ aðꞃiȝ ꝺ ȝeȝnib to meluꝑe ȝenim þonne
beꞃen mela ȝemenȝ ꝑiþ þa ꝑyꞃt ꝺ ȝebꞃinȝ þonne ón
meolce.

### .XXIII.

Þiþ þeoh ece · ꞅmice mib ꞃeaꞃne ꞅꝑiþe þa þeoh. Eꝼt
to ðꞃence · ꝑiꝑoꞃ · ꝑin · pealꝑyꞃt · huniȝ. Eác to þon

---

¹ Read ðꞃince.
² Τῇ πηγανερᾷ, Paul. Æg. and Galen, *a preparation of rue.*
³ Paul. Æginet., lib. iii. cap. 33.

betony in sweetened wine. If he have fever, let him drink it in water.

### xxi.

For sore of the right side, work thyme and radish and white clover to a paste, and to a drink. For sore of the left side, pound woodroffe in vinegar, and work it to a paste, bind it on the side. Again, betony as much as three pennies weigh, and twenty-seven corns of pepper triturated together; pour in three bowls full of old wine, and make lukewarm, give *to the patient* after his nights fasting to drink. Again for sore of side, lay rue mingled with lard and beaten, on the side; that amendeth it. For sore of side again, let him beat bunches of laurel *flower*, let him drink them in water, and bind them on the side. For sore of side again, burn to ashes roots of colewort, and mingle with old lard, and lay on the side.

### xxii.

For loin ache, take betony, as much as two pennies weigh, add thereto two bowls full of sweet wine, mingle with hot water, give it to drink after his nights fasting. Again, take groundsel, beat it, and give the juice to drink after his nights fasting.

2. For loin ache, a wort is called ealiver,[a] rub it in ale, and let *the patient* drink it. For the same, a wort hight hounds tongue, take the leaves, dry them, and rub them to meal, then mingle with the wort barley meal, and then apply it in milk.

### xxiii.

For thigh ache, smoke the thighs thoroughly with fern. Again, for a drink, pepper, wine, wallwort, honey;

apulðop · þopn · æpc · cpicbeam · copopþpote æpcþpote · clone · bipceop pypt · ipiᵹ · betonica · pibbe · pædic · fppacen · pipop · hpit cpuðu · coft · ᵹinᵹifep · moniaca · netle · blinðe netle pipe þip to ðpence. ᵹif þeoh plapan aðelf moþopeapðne pēcᵹ pyl on pætepe læt peocan ōn þæt lim þte plape smipe miö pealfe þe mōn þup pypce. Of fpinef fmeppe · pceapef fmepu · butepe · fcipteapo · pipop · hpit cpuðu · fpeᵹlef æppel · fpeᵹl · coft · eceð · ele · hpeppette · pædic · eolene · bifceop pypt · pealt · æpc · apulðpe · āc · þopn.

<br>

### .XXIIII.

Þiþ cneop pæpce · pnðu peaxe · ᵹ heᵹepipe ᵹecnupa þa toᵹæðepe ᵹ ðo ōn ealu læt heᵹean neahtepne pele him þ þonne ðpincan beþe miö ᵹ leᵹe ōn. Þiþ þon ᵹif cneop pap fie · ᵹenīm pealpypt ᵹ cluppunᵹ · peaðe netlan apyl ōn pætepe beþe miö.

fol. 25 a.

<br>

### .XXV.

ᵹif feancan pape fynð ᵹenīm ᵹipþipfan ᵹ ðolᵹpunan · ᵹ hamop pypt · ᵹ betonican ᵹ ban pypt · ᵹ linpypt ᵹ pnðu mejpce · ᵹ copðᵹeallan · ᵹ bpunpypt peoþ on butepan fmipe miö:-

Gif[1] fcancan fynð fopoðe nīm banpypt ᵹecnupa ᵹeot æᵹep þ hpite menᵹ tofomne fcancfopeðum men. Þið fopeðum lime leᵹe þaf pealfe on þ fopoðe lim ᵹ fopleᵹe miö elmpinðe ðo fpile to · eft fimle nipa oþþ ᵹehaloð fie ᵹepenðpa elm pinðe ᵹ apyl fpiðe ðo þonne of þa pinðe ᵹenīm linpæð ᵹeᵹpinð bpipe pið þam elmef ðpænce þ bið ᵹoð pealf fopeðum lime.

<hr>

¹ Gif, MS.

also in addition, apple tree, thorn, ash, quickbeam, everthroat, ashthroat, helenium, bishopwort, ivy, betony, ribwort, radish, spraken,[a] pepper, mastic, costmary,[a *Rhamnus frangula.*] ginger, sal ammoniac, nettle, blind nettle, work this to a drink. If thighs be paralyzed, delve up the netherward *part of* sedge, boil it in water, make it reek on the limb that is helpless, smear with a salve, which a man may thus work; from swines grease, sheeps grease, butter, ship tar,[1] pepper, mastic, beetle nut, sulfur, costmary, vinegar, oil, cucumber, radish, helenium, bishopwort, salt, ash, apple tree, oak, thorn.

### xxiv.

For knee pain; pound together woodwax[2] and hedgerife, and put into ale; let it lie for a night, give him then that to drink, bathe with it, and lay it on. In case that a knee be sore, take wallwort and cloffing, and red nettle, boil in water, bathe therewith.

### xxv.

1. If the shanks be sore, take githrife and pellitory and hammerwort and betony and bonewort and flaxwort and wild marche and earth gall and brownwort, seethe in butter, smear therewith.

2. If shanks be broken, take bonewort, pound it, pour the white of an egg *out*, mingle these together for the shank broken man. For a broken limb, lay this salve on the broken limb, and overlay with elm rind,[3] apply a splint, again, always renew *these* till the limb be healed; clean some elm rind, and boil it thoroughly, then remove the rind, *and* take linseed, grind it for a brewit *or paste* with the elms drink; that shall be a good salve for a broken limb.

---

[1] Pix navalis is frequent in Latin medicine of the time.

[2] *Genista tinctoria.*

[3] Cf. Aetius. J. i. v. πτελέα.

## .XXVI.

Ἀγκύλωσις. Marcellus, 403, d.

Gif sino gescrince ⁊ eft · æfter þon sƿelle genīm gate tord gemeng ƿið eced smit ōn sona halað. Monegum men gescrinceað his fet to his homme ƿyrc baþo do earban to ⁊ cersan ⁊ smale netelan ⁊ beoƿyrt do on troh hate stanas ƿel gehætte gebeþe þa hamma mid þam stan baðe þonne hie sien gesƿate þonne ƿecce he þa ban sƿa he sƿiþost mæge do sƿelc to ⁊ betere sƿa mon oftor mid þy beþige. gif sino clæppette mucgƿyrt gebeatenu ⁊ ƿiþ ele gemenged ⁊ ōn aled. Mycgƿyrte seaƿ ƿiþ geƿosodne ele gemenged smire mid þy sona biþ ætstilleð sio cƿacung.

fol. 25 b.

## .XXVII.

Ποδάγρα.

Ƿiþ fôt ece betonican · geormenleaf · finul · rubban · ealra emfela gemenge meoluc ƿiþ ƿæter ⁊ ꝥ tosƿollene līm fram ƿære ufeƿran healfe beþe þy læs se sƿile Ingeƿite · genime þonne galluc gesodenne lege ōn. Ƿið fota sare oþþe gesƿelle fram miclum gange ƿegbræde getrifulad ⁊ ƿið eced gemenged. Ƿiþ þon deah grunde sƿelge gebeatenu ⁊ ƿið ƿysele gemenged. :·

Apul. Herb. ii. 17.

Cf. Marcellus, 405, f. g.

Ƿiþ fôtece gif se fôt ace ingesƿice genīm mucgƿyrte ƿyrtruman meng ƿiþ ele sele etan. Ƿið fôt ece eft hunān seaƿ ƿiþ ele gemenged smire þa sƿaþan fet mid. :·

fol. 26 a.

Ƿiþ fotece genīm elleneſ leaf · ⁊ ƿegbrædan ⁊ mucgƿyrt geenuƿa lege on ⁊ gebind ōn.

## .XXVIII.

Ƿiþ ban ece tuningƿyrt ·[1] beolone · ƿealƿyrt ealde grut ⁊ eced · heoroteſ sinera oþþe gate · oþþe gose

---

[1] Tunsing ƿyrt, Herbarium, cxxxviii. So read.

### xxvi.

Book I.
Ch. xxvi.
a That is, when
a leg is broken.

If a sinew shrink,[a] and again after that swell, take a she goats tord, mingle with vinegar, smudge *it* on, soon *the sinew* healeth. In the case of many a man, his feet shrink up to his hams, work baths, add tares and cress and small nettle and beewort,[1] put hot stones well heated in a trough, warm the hams with the stone bath, when they are in a sweat, then let him, *the patient*, duly arrange the bones as well as he can, apply a splint, and it is so much the better the oftener a man bathes with the *preparation*. If a sinew have pulsation, mugwort beaten and mingled with oil, and laid on *is good*. Juice of mugwort mingled with rose oil, smear with that, soon will the quaking be stilled.

### xxvii.

1. For foot ache, betony, germen leaves, *that is* Ποδάγρα. *mallow*, fennel, ribwort, of all equal quantities; mingle milk with water, and bathe the swollen limb, from the upper part of it, with that, lest the swelling go inwards; then take sodden comfrey, lay it on. For sore of feet or swelling from much walking, waybread triturated and mingled with vinegar. For that *disorder*, groundsel beaten and mingled with lard is good.

2. For foot ache; if the foot ache go inwards, take mugworts roots, mingle with oil, give to eat. For foot ache again, juice of *hore*hound mingled with oil, smear the sore feet with it.

3. For foot ache, take leaves of elder and waybroad and mugwort, pound, lay on, and bind on.

### xxviii.

For leg ache, white hellebore, henbane, wallwort, old groats and vinegar, harts or she goats or goose

---

[1] *Acorus calamus.*

menᵹ toſomne leᵹe þonne on.  Ƿiþ banece eft to ðpence
elene · cneopholen · pealpypt · hune · cluꝼþunᵹ ᵹecnupa
ðo on pætep þ oꝼep yɪne beþe to ꝼype ſpiðe þone
ece þpea mið þy pæcepe ðo þ þpɪpa on dæᵹ · pypc
þonne ſealꝼe oꝼ tun[ɪ]nᵹ pyptc oꝼ eolonan · oꝼ þunᵹe ·
oꝼ pepmoðe ðo ealþa emꝼela pylle ſpiðe.

## . XXVIIII .

ᵹɪꝼ manneſ ᵹetapa beoþ ſaɪe oððe aþunðene betonican ᵹetpiꝼula on pɪne beþe þa ſaþan ſtopa ɥ þa
aþunðenan mið þy.  Eꝼt ᵹɪꝼ hɪe ðylꝼtihte ſien oððe
ᵹeboꝛſtene ᵹenɪm ſaluian feoð on pætepe beþe mɪð þa
ᵹetapa.

Eꝼt ðile ᵹebæpneð ᵹemenᵹ pɪð ahpan hunɪᵹ[1] pype to
ſealꝼe aþpeah þonne ɥ ᵹebeþe þa punða aþept mɪð
hate pætepe æꝼtep þon mɪð pcaþɪne elc ᵹe ſmɪpe on
þam þe pæþe pɪp ᵹeſoðen leᵹe þonne þa ſealꝼe on.

## . XXX .

Ƿɪſ ſceal pɪþ æcelman ɥ pɪð þon þe men acale þ ꝼel
oꝼ þam ꝼotum · ᵹenɪme neoþopeapðe meðopypt ɥ luſt-
mocan · ɥ acpɪnðe ᵹecnua eall to ðuſte ᵹemenᵹ pɪð
hunɪᵹ lacna mɪð þy.

## . XXXI .

Vɪþ æleum heapðum ſpɪle oððe ᵹeſpelle aðpɪᵹe beana
ɥ ᵹeſeoþ butan ſealte menᵹ þonne pɪþ hunɪᵹ leᵹe on.
Ƿɪþ þon ilcan ᵹenɪm beþen melo ſeoþ on ecede ðo on

---

[1] Read ᵹemenᵹ þa ahpan pɪð hunɪᵹ.

grease, mingle together, then lay on. For leg ache
again, for a draught, helenium, kneeholly, *or butchers
broom*, wallwort, *or dwarf elder*, horehound, clofling,[1]
pound these, put them in water, so that it run over,
warm at the fire thoroughly, wash the ache *or aching
part* with the water, do that three times a day; then
work up a salve of white hellebore, of helenium, of
thung *or wolfs bane*, of wormwood, put equal quantities
of them all, boil thoroughly.

### xxix.

1. If a mans instrumenta genitalia be sore or puffed
out, triturate betony in wine, bathe with that the sore
and puffed up places. Again, if they be mucous, or
in eruption, take sage,[1] seethe in water, bathe with
that the instrumenta.

2. Again, *take* dill burnt, mingle the ashes with
honey, work up to a salve, then wash and bathe the
wounds first with hot water, after that with warm
oil or grease, on which myrtle has been sodden, then
lay the salve on.

### xxx.

This shall *be good* for chilblain and in case that the Pernio.
skin of a mans feet come off by cold,[2] let him take
the netherward part of meadowwort and lustmock and
oak rind, pound all to dust, mingle with honey, effect
a cure with that.

### xxxi.

1. For every hard tumour or swelling, dry beans
and seethe them without salt, than mingle with honey,
lay on. For the same, take barley meal, seethe in

---

[1] *Ranunculus sceleratus.*
[2] Cf. **Myreps. xlvii. 10.**

[3] Or þam fotum, *off the feet.*
not *of.*

Eft ƿiþ þon belenan menȝ ƿið ƿyrele leȝe ón. Þið ſƿile eft ȝebeat hunan menȝ ƿiþ ƿyrele leȝe ón oððe ȝate hoƿn ȝebræƿneð ⁊ ƿiþ ƿœteƿ ȝemenȝeð. Eft ƿyrele oþþe ȝelynðo ƿiþ ȝaƿleác ȝemenȝeð ⁊ ón aleð þone ſƿile þþænþ.

Þiþ ſƿile eft ceƿƿille ȝecnuƿað mi̋ð ƿyrele ⁊ on ȝemelt ƿeax ȝeðon ⁊ ón aleð bet.

Við ſƿile eft ȝate ſlæȝc ȝebræƿneð to ahſan mið ƿœteƿe ón ȝeſmiten calne þone ſƿile toƿeƿeþ. Eft iuniƿeƿu þ iſ ȝoƿſt þ ƿæð ȝecnuƿa ⁊ ſeoþ on ƿœteƿe. Eft ſinſulle ƿiþ ƿyrele ȝemenȝeð ⁊ ƿiþ hlaſ ⁊ ƿiþ celenðƿan æt · ſomne ȝemenȝeð. Þiþ yſlum ƿœtan ⁊ ſƿile ȝeƿím heoƿoteſ ſceaƿoþan óſ þám hoƿne oþþe þæſ hoƿneſ melo menȝ ƿiþ ƿœteƿ ſmit ón eal þ ſoƿuiſ ⁊ þone yſelan ƿœtan aƿeȝ ðeþ ⁊ aðƿiſþ.

Þiþ ſƿile ȝeƿím ȝate tyƿðlu on ſceaƿƿum eceðe ȝeſoðen ⁊ ón ſelſe ƿiſan ón ȝeðon.

Þiþ ælcum yſlum ƿœtan mucȝƿyƿte þa ȝƿenan leaſ ȝetƿiſulað ⁊ ƿiþ ƿyrele ȝeȝniðen toȝœðeƿe ſmiƿe an ȝe þeoh þæƿ ðylſtan on ſynð þ ðeah ƿiþ þan · ȝe þ ðeah eác ƿiþ ſota ȝeſƿelle. Þiþ innan ȝeƿyƿſmeðum ȝeſƿelle þam þe ƿyƿð oſ ſylle oþþe óſ ſleȝe oððe óſ hƿicƿea hƿilcſim · þa ƿyƿt þe hatte ſíſleaſe · ȝeniƿ ⁊ ȝebeat ⁊ leȝe on ȝelome oþ þte open ſie ſe ſƿile lacna þonne þa ƿunða ſƿa oþƿe ƿunða. Þið ſƿile eft hluttoƿ ƿíc ȝeƿím ðo ahſan to ſeoð œtȝœðeƿe ȝeleȝe þonne þone ſƿile mið þy ȝelome. Þiþ ſƿile eft ȝate tyƿðlu ðƿuȝe ȝeȝmið ⁊ aſiſte þuƿh ſmæl ſiſe ðo þonne ƿyƿle

vinegar, put on. Again for that, mingle henbane with lard, lay on. For a swelling again, beat *horehound*, mingle with lard, lay on, or goats horn burnt and mingled with water. Again, lard or suet mingled with garlic, and onlaid, dwindleth the swelling.

2. For swelling again, chervil pounded with lard and added to melted wax, and laid on, is to boot *or amend*.

3. For a swelling again, goats flesh burnt to ashes, smudged on with water, removes all the swelling. Again, pound the seed of juniper, that is gorse,[1] and seethe in water. Again, houseleek mingled with lard and with bread and with coriander, mingled together. Against ill humours and swelling, take shavings off the horn of a hart, or meal of the horn, mingle with water, smudge it on, it doth away and driveth off all that ratten and the evil wet.

4. Against swelling, take goats treadles sodden in sharp vinegar, and applied in the same manner.

5. For every evil humour,[2] mugwort, the green leaves *of it*, triturated, and rubbed together with lard, both smear on the thighs on which the mucus is, that is good for them ; and that is good also for swelling of the feet. For a swelling purulent within, such as cometh of a fall or of a blow or of any crick, take the wort that hight fiveleaf *or cinquefoil*, and beat it and lay it on frequently till that the swelling be open, then tend the wounds as other wounds. For a swelling again, take "clear pitch,"[3] add ashes, seethe together, then overlay the swelling with that frequently. For swelling again, dry goats treadles, grate and sift them through a small sieve, then add lard, as much as

Φλέγμα and χυμός.

---

[1] Some verb must be supplied to form a sentence, as frequently happens. And of course iuniperus is not gorse.

[2] Pituita molesta, of Horatius.

[3] Probably resin, as solid.   See Blæcrepu, *pale tar*, in Lye.

to ſpa ſpa ꝼyn tꝛa þunð ⁊ ealdeſ pincer ſpa micel ſpa
þe þince pyꝛc to ſealꝼe.

Eꝼt ᵹebæꝛneð ꝛealt ᵹeᵹnið pel on ᵹepleceð pꝛæteꝛ
oþ þ̄ hit ſie ſpa þicce ſpa huniᵹeſ teaꝛ leᵹe ōn þone
ſpile oꝼeꝛ leᵹe mið claðe ⁊ mið eoꝛciᵹꝛe pulle bmð
ōn. Þiþ ꝼæphcum ſaꝛe ⁊ ᵹeſpelle nīm peax ⁊ hemhc
ᵹetꝛuꝼula pyꝛc ſpa peaꝛm to ꝛealꝼe bmð on þ̄ ꝛaꝛ. :·

Þiþ ꝼæꝛ ſpile · nīm hunan ᵹebeat ⁊ ᵹemenᵹ piþ
pyꝛele leᵹe ōn. Eꝼt maꝛe tꝛynihte ᵹꝛut mealteꝛ
ſmeðma · cepſan · aᵹeꝛ þ̄ hpite biſceop pyꝛc · clene ·
ontꝛe · elehtꝛe · ſiᵹſonte · ᵹalluc menᵹ toſomne leᵹe
ōn. Þiþ ðeaðum ſpile · ꝣim ᵹꝛunðeſpelᵹean leᵹe on
ᵹleða ⁊ ᵹepyꝛme ⁊ leᵹe þonne ſpa peaꝛme on þone ſpile
⁊ bebmð mið claðe læt beon mhteꝛne ōn ᵹiꝼ hiꝛ þeaꝛꝼ
ſie. Uið ðeaðum ſpile āᵹꝛimonian ᵹebeat menᵹ pið pm
⁊ piþ ꝛealt ðo on þone ſpile ꝛona ᵹepit apeᵹ. Þiþ ſpile
attoꝛlaðan ᵹecnupa leᵹe on þone ſpile leᵹe læſt ōn þ̄
ðolh ꝛelꝼ. Ðꝛenc piþ ðeaðum ſpile þ̄ he utꝛlea eoꝛoꝛ-
þꝛote · eolone · ᵹotꝛoðe · tꝛa penpyꝛta ðo ōn ealu
ðꝛmce. Þiþ ðeaðum ſpile ᵹenīm ſpane pyꝛc ᵹecnupa
pel ᵹemenᵹ pið ꝼeꝛſcꝛe buteꝛan leᵹe on þone ſpile oꝼ
þ̄ ᵹelacnoð ſie. Þiþ ſpile cunille · ſpꝛinᵹ pyꝛc clate
pyl ōn buteꝛan ⁊ on huniᵹe leᵹe on þa pyꝛta ᵹemenᵹ
pið aᵹeꝛ þ̄ hpite. Speþinᵹ piþ ſpile · ban pyꝛc uꝛe-
ꝛeaꝛðe ᵹecnupa ſmæle þa pyꝛte ᵹemenᵹ pið aᵹeꝛ þ̄
hpite beclæm þ̄ hm mið þe ꝛe ſpile on ſie.

Þyꝛc þ̄ bæþ ōꝼ þam ilcum pyꝛtum on cealðum pylle
ꝛætꝛe ᵹecnupa þa pꝼꝛta ſꝛiþe pel leᵹe ōn þ̄ ꝛætꝛꝛ
laꝼa on þone ſpile. :·

Við ſpile cnupa miðeꝛeaꝛðe hamoꝛ pyꝛc ⁊ ꝛecᵹ bmð
on.

two pounds, and as much of old wine as to thee may seem good, work to a salve.

6. Again, rub burnt salt well in water made luke-warm, till that it be as thick as a tear of honey, lay on the swelling, overlay with a cloth, and with wool of ewe, bind on.  For sudden sore and swelling, take wax and hemlock, triturate, work this so warm into a salve, bind on the sore.

7. Against a sudden swelling, take *horehound*, beat and mingle it with lard, lay on.  Again, mingle together the cottony potentilla, *commonly called silver-weed*, groats of malt, smede *or fine flour*, cress, the white of an egg, bishopwort, helenium, ontre, lupins, " sigsonte," comfrey, lay on.  For a dead[a] swelling, take groundsel, lay it on gledes and warm it, and lay it so warm on the swelling, and bind on with a cloth, let it be on for a night, if need be for that.  For a dead swelling, beat agrimony, mix with wine and with salt, apply it to the swelling, *which* soon will depart away. For swelling, pound attorlothe, lay on the swelling, lay least on " the wound" itself.  A draught for a dead swelling, that it may break out, put carlina, helenium, goutweed, the two wenworts into an ale drink.  For a dead swelling, take " swanwort," pound it well, mingle with fresh butter, lay on the swelling till that it be healed.  For a swelling, boil cunila, springwort,[1] clote, in butter and in honey, lay the worts on, mingle with them the white of an egg.  A swathing for a swelling, pound small the upper part of bonewort, mingle with the wort the white of an egg, plaster the limb on which the swelling may be, with that.

8. Work the bath of the same worts in cold well water, pound the worts very well, lay on, leave the water on the swelling.

9. For a swelling, pound the netherward part of hammerwort and sedge ; bind on.

[a] Without feeling.

---

[1] *Euforbia lathyris.*

.XXXII.

Ἀλφός. Λεύκη. Læcedomas wiþ blæce ⁊ bæþ fiftyne ealra.

Wel eolenan niþewearde ⁊ mintan ón[1] sealtes rynian
fol. 28 b. þ hit sie þicce swa briw gemeng togædere smire mid. Wiþ blæce ním eolonan niþewearde ⁊ ompran eác swa sio þe swimme ⁊ ontran ⁊ biscop wyrt ⁊ æscrinde seoþ on buteran aseoh þurh clað meng þonne wið pipor ⁊ wiþ teoran gegrind smire mid. Wiþ blæce wyl eolonan on buteran meng wiþ sote sealt · teoro · hunig · eald sape smire mid. Wið blæce gením gose smero ⁊ niþewearde elenan ⁊ haran sprecel biscop wyrt ⁊ hegrifan þa feower wyrta cnuwa tosomne wel awring do þæron ealdre sapan cucler fulne gif þu hæbbe lytel eles meng wiþ swiþe ⁊ ón niht alyþre. Sceawa þone sweoran ofer sunnan setlgange geot swigende þ blod ón yrnende wæter spiw þriwa æfter · cweþ þonne hafa þu þas unhæle · ⁊ gewit aweg mid gange eft ón clænne weg to huse ⁊ gehwæþerne gáng swigende. Bæþ wið blæce awyl tyn ribum þa wyrte on hwere ⁊ syndrigea betonican · neftan marubian[2] agrimonian · gearwe ·
fol. 29 a. minte elhheoloþe hindheoloþe · curmealle · eorð gealla · dile · merce · finul ealra emfela gewyrc þonne stol of þrim treowum niþan ðyrele site ón bydene ⁊ þe oferhref ufan mid hwitle þy læs se æþm ut · geót under þone stol on þa bydene læt reocan ón · swa þu meaht on þam wyrtum þriwa don · ⁊ under niþan styre mid sticcan gif þu hattre wille · ⁊ ær þam bæþe smire þone lichoman ⁊ þone wlitan mid geswette wætre ⁊ gehwer twa ægru on hatum wætere gesmire ealne þone lichoman mid.

---

[1] ón ón, MS.

[2] maribian, MS.

### xxxii.

1. Leechdoms for blotch and baths. Fifteen in all.

2. Boil the netherward part of helenium and mint in the runnings of salt, that it be as thick as brewit, mingle together, smear therewith. Against blotch, take the netherward part of helenium, and so also of dock (that which will swim), and ontre, and bishopwort, and ash rind, seethe in butter, strain through a cloth, then mingle with pepper and with tar, grind *these*, smear therewith. For blotch, boil helenium in butter, mingle with soot, salt, tar, honey, old soap, smear therewith. For blotch, take goose grease and the netherward part of helenium and vipers bugloss, bishopwort and hayrife, pound the four worts together well, wring them, add thereto of old soap a spoon full, if thou have it, mingle a little oil with them thoroughly, and at night lather on. Scarify the neck after the setting of the sun, pour in silence the blood into running water, after that spit three times, then say, " Have thou this unheal, and depart away with it ;" go again on a clean way to the house, and go either way in silence. A bath[1] for blotch, boil ten times the worts in a basin and separately betony, nepeta, marrubium, agrimony, yarrow, mint, horseheal,[a] hindheal,[b] churmel,[c] earthgall,[d] dill, marche, fennel, of all equally much, work then a stool of three pieces of wood, with a hole below, sit on a bucket,[2] and robe thee over from above with a garment lest the vapour escape ; pour *the prepared hot liquor* under the stool into the bucket, let it reek on thee. So thou mayst do thrice with the worts, and underneath stir with a stick if thou wilt *have it* hotter ; and before the bath smear the body and the forehead with sweetened water, and shake up two eggs in hot water, smear the whole body therewith.

a *Inula helenium.*
b *Eupatorium cannabinum.*
c *Chlora perfoliata.*
d *Erythræa centaureum.*

---

[1] Πυρίη. Hippokr.    |    [2] Byden, now Bidet.

Læcedom þiþ hþeoｆūm lice · aðelｆe omþþan Ᵹ ȝeloð-
pyｆ ȝecnuþa · pyl þonne on buteþan ðo hpon ｆealteｆ
to. Þiþ ðeaðum lice ｆtæþþyｆ meþce ȝnið ōn ealoð
ｆele ðｆincan. Þið hþeoｆle pell ōn hlonðe cｆicｆinðe [1] ·
ellenｆinðe niþepeaｆinðe · æｆc ｆinðe · Ᵹ pað · elm ｆinðe ·
heinlic ðo þonne buteþan on Ᵹ huniȝ. Þiþ hþeoｆle
peȝbｆæðe læcepyｆ · leac · minte · maȝþa · eolone ·
ｆpeｆl ȝecnuþa þiþ ｆyſle ðo þæｆ ｆ[þ]eｆleｆ ｆpilcan þaｆa
pyｆ tｆæðe.

fol. 29 b.

Þiþ hþeoｆle eｆ ȝenīm hoｆｆeｆ ｆyｆele ȝemen[ȝ] ſpiþe
þiþ ｆealte ſmiｆe mið. bæþ þiþ hþeoｆle · pyl ōn pæteｆe
æｆcｆinðe · cｆicbeam ｆinðe · liolen ｆinðe · ｆulanbeameｆ ·
ananbeameｆ · ｆēcȝ · þeoｆpyｆ · heȝeｆiｆe · maｆubian ·
beþe mið · Ᵹ þ̄ lic ȝnið mið þæｆe heȝeｆiｆan. Þyｆc
ｆealｆe ōｆ maｆubian on buteþan · ōｆ pyｆm meluþe · ōｆ
haｆan ｆþｆecele · heȝeｆiｆan · ȝenīm healｆe þa ｆealｆe
ȝemenȝ þiþ ȝecnuþaðe elenan ſmiｆe oþ þ̄ batiȝe · ｆiþþan
mið þæｆe oþeｆｆe. bæþ þiþ þam miclan lice eolone
bｆūm · iｆiȝ · mucþyｆ ælｆþonc · beolone · cottuc · eｆe-
laｆan pyl ōn þｆoteｆe ſpiþe ȝeōt on byðene Ᵹ ｆitte ōn.
ðｆince þｆｆne ðｆenc þiþ þon · betomcan · cuｆmille hoｆe ·
aȝｆimonia · ｆpｆinȝȝpyｆ · ｆeaðe netle · elehtｆe · Saluie ·
ſinȝｆene · alexanðｆia · ſie ȝepoｆht ōｆ þiliｆcūm ealað
ðｆince on þam laþe Ᵹ ne læte ōn þone cþm. Sealｆ þiþ
þam miclan lice · elene · þūnȝ omｆｆe · ȝｆunðeｆpelȝe ·
hole ceｆſan · peȝbｆæðe · eｆelaｆe · ōntｆe · hoｆe · ȝallūc ·

fol. 30 a.

celeþonian · cottūc pel on buteｆan eal toȝæðeｆe healｆ

---

[1] Read cｆicbeamｆinðe.

3. A leechdom for a leprous body, delve up dock and silverweed, pound them, then boil them in butter, add a trifle of salt. For deadness of the body, rub in ale staithwort, marche, give *to the patient* to drink. For a leper, boil in urine[1] rind of quickbeam, the netherward part of elder rind, ash rind, and woad, elm rind, hemlock, then add butter and honey. For a leper, pound with lard waybroad, leechwort, leek, mint, maythe, helenium, sulfur, put of the sulfur two parts to one of the worts.

4. For a leper again, take fat of a horse, mingle thoroughly with salt, smear with that. A bath for a leper, boil in water ash rind, quickbeam rind, holly rind, the foultree *or black alder rind*, rind of spindle tree, sedge, ploughmans spikenard, hayrife, marrubium, bathe therewith, and rub the body with the hayrife. Work a salve of marrubium in butter, of worm[2] meal, of vipers bugloss, hayrife, take half the salve, mingle with pounded helenium, smear till it get better, then *smear* with the other half. A bath for the mickle body *or elphantiasis,* boil in water thoroughly helenium, broom, ivy, mugwort, enchanters nightshade (?), henbane, mallow, everlasting, pour into a byden, and let *the patient* sit upon it. Let a man drink against that *disorder* this drink; betony, churmel, hove, agrimony, springwort, red nettle, lupin, sage, singreen, alexanders, let it be wrought out of foreign ale, let *the sick* man drink it in the bath, and let him not allow the vapour to reach it. A salve for the mickle *leprous* body, helenium, wolfsbane, dock, groundsel, field gentian, waybroad, everlasting, ontre, hove, comfrey, celandine, mallow, boil all in butter together, let half *the salve*

---

[1] Cf. Aetius. I. ii. 108.

[2] Thus in later times : " Fair large Earthworms gathered in May when they couple ; put them into a Pail of Water at night till the next morning, so will they have cleansed themselves, then dry them before the fire, or in an Oven, which when through dry, beat into Pouder." Salmon's English Physician. p. 697, ed. 1693. He adds the cures.

ħe ſpineſ nyrele oððe hoꝑreſ ſmeꝑu · ſmiꝑe þonne miŏ.
Þiŏ ſpile ᵹenîm peᵹbꝛæŏan moþoꝛeaꝛŏe ᵹecnupa ꝑiþ
nyſele leᵹe ꝼ ᵹebinŏ ûn þone ſpile.

Φλύκτ<i>aιναι.</i>   Dꝛencaſ ꝼ ꝛealꝼa ꝑiþ ſꝑꝛinᵹe · ſꝛꝛinᵹꝛyꝑꞇ ꝛeaŏe hoꝛe ·
peᵹbꝛæŏe · ꝼeꝛeꝛ ꝼuᵹe · apꝛoꞇane · maᵹeþe · piꝛoꝛ ·
ꝛîn · ᵹiꝼ he ôn eaꝛan ħe ᵹebeaꞇe peᵹbꝛæŏan · ꝼ ꝼeꝛeꝛ
ꝼuᵹean ꝼ piꝛoꝛ · ꝑꝛinᵹ ôn ꝥ eaꝛe. To ꝛealꝼe piŏ
ſꝛꝛinᵹe · nîm ŏolhꝛunan · peᵹbꝛæŏan maᵹeþan · þone
bꝛaŏan caꝑel moþoꝛeaꝛŏne · ᵹeoꝛmenleaꝼ niþeꝛeaꝛŏ ·
ŏocce niþeꝛeꝛŏ · ꝛeaŏe hoꝛe · buꞇeꝛe ꝼ huniᵹ.   Sealꝼ
eꝼꞇ meŏoꝛyꝛꞇ · acumban · hinŏ hioloŏe · ᵹeaꝛꝛe · cneoꝑ-
holen · æþelꝼeꝛŏinᵹ ꝛyꝛꞇ · aᵹꝛimonia.

Þiþ ŏeaŏum ſꝛꝛinᵹe.  Þyl on buꞇeꝛan ſelꝼæꞇan
æꝼꞇeꝛ þam[1] · ꝼ ſꝛꝛinᵹꝛyꝛꞇ.   Þiþ ſꝛꝛinᵹe maᵹeþa · ꝛuŏu
meꝛce · ꝛyꝛc ꞇo ꝛealꝼe ŏꝛince ᵹoŏe ꝛyꝛꞇa.   Uiþ ſꝛꝛinᵹe ·
nim elehꞇꝛan ᵹecnupa ôn huniᵹ menᵹ ꞇo ſomne leᵹe
on þone ſpile oþþæꞇ hal ꝛie.   Þiŏ ſꝛꝛinᵹe ſꝛꝛinᵹꝛyꝛꞇ
ceꝛꝼillan ꝼ huniᵹ ꝼ ᵹoꝛe ſmeꝛa ᵹecnupa ꝑyl ꞇo ꝛomne
leᵹe on ŏone ſꝛꝛinᵹ.

ᵹiꝼ næᵹl ħe oꝼ hanŏa ꝼ ꝑiþ ꝛeaꝛhbꝛæŏan nîm liꝛæꞇe
coꝛn menᵹ piŏ huniᵹ leᵹe on þone ꝼinᵹeꝛ.   Þiŏ anᵹnæᵹle
aꝛᵹeſꝛeoꝛꝛ · ꝼ ealŏe ꝛaꝛan ꝼ ele ᵹiꝼ þu hæbbe ᵹiꝼ þu
næbbe ŏo ꝼlyꞇan ꞇo menᵹ ꞇoſomne leᵹe ôn.[2]                    :·

Þiþ ꝛeaꝛhbꝛæŏan · maᵹoþan cꝛoppan ꝑyl on buꞇeꝛan
ꝼ ſealꞇ ſmiꝛe miŏ.

---

[1] Read æꝛeꝛþan.        |        [2] In the margin is some cypher.

be swines fat or horse grease ; then smear therewith.
Against swelling, take the netherward part of waybroad, pound with grease, lay and bind on the swelling.

### xxxiii.

1. Drinks and salves against pustule; springwort, red
hove, waybroad, feverfuge, abrotanon, maythe, pepper,
wine. If it, *the pustule*, be on an ear, beat waybroad
and feverfuge and pepper, wring *them* into the ear.
For a salve against a pustule, take pellitory, waybroad,
maythe, the netherward part of the broad colewort,
the netherward part of mallow, the netherward part of
dock, red hove, butter, and honey. A salve again,
meadow wort, tow,[1] water agrimony, yarrow, butchers
broom, stichwort, agrimony.

2. For a dead pustule; boil in butter the herb wild
oat, æferth, and springwort. For a pustule, maythe,
wood marche, work *these* into a salve, let him drink
good worts. For a pustule, take lupin, pound in honey,
mingle together, lay on the swelling till it be hole.
For a pustule, pound springwort, chervil, and honey
and goose grease, heat them together, lay this on the
pustule.

### xxxiv.

1. If a nail be off the hand, and against a warty
eruption,[a] take wheat corn, mingle with honey, lay on <sup>a</sup> Πτερύγιον,<br>probably.
the finger. For an angnail,[b] brass filings and old soap, <sup>b</sup> Παρωνυχία.
and oil if thou have it, if thou have it not, add cream,
mingle together, lay on.

2. For warty eruption, heat in butter bunches of
maythe and salt, smear therewith.

---

[1] Understand, in ashes. "Lin-
teorum lanugo e velis navium ma-
ritimarum maxime, in magno usu
medicinæ est ; et cinis spodii (*ivory
filings*) vim habet." Plinius, xix. 4.

## .XXXV.

Μελανία.
Μελασμός.
Cf. Galenum de
Simpl. Med.
lib. viii. 43,
ed. 1826.

Be aſpeaᵽtedum ⁊ abeadedum lice ſio aþl cymð oᵽtoſt
óᵽ omum æȝteᵽ aðle þelme ón peȝ ȝeᵽitenᵽe þeoᵽþeð
liᵽilum lic aſpeaᵽtoð · þonne oᵽ þam ᵽᵽum þelme ſio
aðl mið cealðum þinȝum biþ to celanne ⁊ to lacnianne ·
⁊ þonne ſio aðl cymð utan butan ſpeotolúm tacne ·
þonne ᵽcealt þu æþeᵽt þa hæto celan mið cellenðᵽe
ȝetᵽᵽulaðᵽc mið hlaᵽeſ cᵽuman oᵽþenðum mið cealð
pᵽctᵽe oþþe mið þy ᵽelᵽan ſeape ᵽæᵽ cellenðᵽe · oþþe

ſbl. 31 a.

mið æȝeᵽ þy hᵽᵽte oþþe mið ᵽine oþþe mið oþᵽum
þinȝum þam þe þ̃ ilce mæȝen hæbbe · þonne ᵽe þelma
⁊ ſio hæto ſie apeȝ ȝepᵽten ⁊ ᵽe ðæl þæᵽ lichoman
ſie ȝepenðeð hᵽon oððe blæc oþþe pón oþþe ſᵽlceᵽ
hᵽæt ᵽccaᵽᵽa þonne þa ſtoᵽe þonne betſt þu ða · ⁊
ðᵽᵽȝe mið ónleȝene ſᵽa ſᵽa món on peax hlaᵽe ⁊ oᵽ
peaᵽmum beþe · ⁊ oᵽ ſþelcum þinȝum pyᵽcð.¹ Niſ him
bloð to lætanne ón æðᵽe ac ma hiᵽa man ᵽceal tihan
mið pyᵽtðᵽencúm utyᵽnenðum oþþe ſᵽᵽlum oþþe miȝo-
lúm mið þy þu meaht clænſian þ̃ ómcyn ⁊ þæᵽ ȝeallan-
coðe þa ᵽeaðan · ȝe þeah þ̃ yᵽel cumen ne ſie oᵽ þaᵽa
omena þelme ſᵽa þeah ðeah ſᵽlcum mannum ᵽe ᵽceaᵽᵽa
pyᵽtðᵽenc. ȝiᵽ þa omihtan ᵽannan þinȝ oþþe þa ᵽeaðan
ſyn utan cumen oᵽ punðum oþþe óᵽ ſniþinȝum oððe
oᵽ ᵽleȝúm ſona þu þa þinȝ læcna mið ᵽceaᵽᵽinȝe ⁊
ónleȝena beþeſ æᵽteᵽ þæᵽe ᵽiſan þe læcaſ cunnan þel
þu hit betſt. ȝiᵽ þ̃ aſpeaᵽtoðe lic to þon ſᵽᵽe abeaðiȝe

fol. 31 b.

þ̃ þæᵽ nan ȝeᵽelneᵽ ón ne ſic þonne ᵽcealt þu ᵽona
eal þ̃ ðeaðe ⁊ þ̃ unȝeᵽelðe óᵽ aſniþan oþ þ̃ cᵽice lic ·
þ̃ þæᵽ na miht þæᵽ ðeaðan liceſ to laᵽe ne ſie þæſ þe
ᵽeᵽ ne ᵽᵽen ne ᵽyᵽ ȝeᵽelðe. Æᵽteᵽ þon lacniȝe món
þa ðolh ſᵽa þu þone ðæl þe þonne ȝít hᵽilce hᵽeȝa

---

¹ pyᵽc, MS.

### XXXV.

Of swarthened and deadened body. The disease
cometh oftenest of corrupt humours after the inflammation of the disease which has passed away, the body
whilom becometh swarthy. Then, from the original
inflammation, the disease is to be cooled and to be
tended with cold appliances. And when the disease
cometh from without, without a manifest token *of its
cause*, then shalt thou first cool the heat with triturated
coriander, with crumbs of bread moistened with cold
water or with the juice itself of the coriander, or with the
white of egg, or with wine, or with other things which
have the same virtue. When the inflammation and the
heat are gone away and the part of the body is turned
somewhat *to be* either pale or livid or somewhat such,
then scarify the place, thou wilt then better it; and
dry it with an application such as a man works of
wax cake and warm beer and of such things. He is
not to be let blood on a vein, but rather *the symptoms*
shall be tended with wort drinks, of a perfluent
nature, either emetic or diuretic, with which thou
mayest cleanse the corrupt humour and its red gall-
sickness. Yea, though the evil be not come of the
inflammation of the corrupt humours, yet for such men
the sharp wort drink is beneficial. If the pituitous
livid or red symptoms be come from without, from
wounds or from cuttings or from blows, soon do thou
heal those matters with scarifying and onlayings[a] of ᵃ 'Επιθέματα.
barley, after the manner which leeches well know;
thou shalt amend it. If the swarthened body be to
that high degree deadened that no feeling be thereon,
than must thou soon cut away all the dead and the
unfeeling *flesh*, as far as the quick, so that there be
nought remaining of the dead flesh, which ere felt
neither iron nor fire. After that one shall heal the
wounds, as thou wouldst the part which as yet may

ȝeþelneȝȝe hæbbe • ⁊ eallunȝa ðeaðe ne fynð.[1] Þu rcealt
mið ȝelomheþe fceappunȝe hþilūm mið mielum • hþilum
mið reapūm pene ⁊ teoh[2] þ bloð fram þæþe aðeaðeðan
ftope lácna ða rceaþþan þur • ȝennn bean mela oþþe
ætena • oððe beþef • oþþe fþilcer meluþer fpa þe þnnce
þ hit ōnnnman þille ðo eceð to ⁊ huniȝ reoþ ætȝæðeþe
⁊ leȝe ōn ⁊ binð on þa raþan ftopa. Ȝif þu polðe þ
fio realf fþiðþe fie ðo lytel realter to ōn binð hþilum ⁊
þþeah mið eceðe oþþe mið þine. Ȝif þeaþf fie rele
hþilūm pyþtðþene • ⁊ ȝerceapa finle þonne þu þa ftþanȝan læceðomar ðo hþile þ mæȝen fie ⁊ fio ȝecynð þær
lichoman • hþæþeþ hio fie ftþanȝ þe heaþð ⁊ eaþehce
mæȝe þa ftþanȝan læceðomar abeþan þe hio fie hneþce
⁊ meaþþe ⁊ þynne ⁊ ne mæȝe abeþan þa læceðomar.
ðo þu ða læceðomar fþilce þu þa lichoman ȝefie • roþ
þon ðe micel ȝeðal īr on ræþneðef ⁊ þiſer ⁊ eilðeʃ
lichoman • ⁊ on þam mæȝene þæf ðæȝhþamlican
pyþhtan ⁊ þær iðlan þær ealðan ⁊ þær ȝeonȝan ⁊
þær þe fie ȝeþin[3] þþoþunȝum • ⁊ þær þe fie unȝe-
þuna fpelcum þinȝum • ȝe þa hþitan lichoman beoð
meaþuþþan ⁊ teðþan þonne þa blacan • ⁊ þa þeaðan.
Ȝif þu þille līm aceoþfan oððe afniðan of lichoman
þonne ȝefceapa þu hþilc fio ftop fie • ⁊ þæþe ftope
mæȝen • roþ þon ðe þaþa ftopa fum þaþe þotaþ ȝif
hiþe mōn ȝimeleaflice tilað • fume latoþ felað þaþa
læceðoma fume þaþoþ • ȝif þu rcyle aceoþfan oððe
afniþan unhal lim of halum lice þonne[4] ceoþf þu þ on
þam ȝemæþe þær halan licef • ac micle fþiþoþ fnið oððe
ceoþf on þ hale ⁊ þ eþice he fpa þu hit rel ⁊ þaþoþ
ȝelacnoft. Þonne þu ryþ fette ōn mannan þonne nim
þu meþþer þoþþer leaf ⁊ ȝeȝniben realt oþeþ leȝe þa

[1] Read ſy.
[2] Read þenian ⁊ teohan.
[3] Read ȝeþuna.
[4] Insert ue.

have some feeling, and be not altogether dead. Thou shalt with frequent scarifying, whilom with mickle, whilom with slight, wean and draw the blood from the deadened place. Cure the scarifyings thus; take bean or oat or barley meal, or some of such meal as to thee seemeth good, so that it will serve, add vinegar and honey, seethe together and lay on, and bind upon the sore places. If thou shouldst wish that the salve be stronger, add a little salt, bind on at whiles and wash with vinegar or with wine. If need be, give at whiles a wort drink, and observe always when thou art applying the strong leechdoms, what the power be, and what the nature of the body *of the patient;* whether it be strong and hardy, and easily may bear the strong leechdoms, or whether it be nice and tender and thin, and may not bear the leechdoms. Apply the leechdoms according as thou seest *the state of* the body. For a mickle difference is there, in the bodies of a man, a woman, and a child; and in the main *or constitution* of a daily wright *or labourer* and of the idle, of the old and of the young, of him who is accustomed to endurances, and him who is unaccustomed to such things. Yea, the white bodies be tenderer and weaker than the black and the red. If thou wilt carve off or cut off a limb from a body, then view thou of what sort the place be, and the strength of the place, since some *or one* of the places readily rotteth if one carelessly tendeth it: some feel the leechdoms later, some earlier. If thou must carve off or cut off an unhealthy limb off from a healthy body, then carve thou not it on the limit of the healthy body; but much more cut or carve in on the hole and quick body; so thou shalt better and readier cure it. When thou settest fire on a man, then take thou leaves of tender leek and grated salt, overlay the places, then shall be by that the more readily the heat of the fire drawn

ſtope þonne bið þy þe naþon þær ꝼyneꞃ hæto apeᵹ
atoᵹen · ꝥ ilce biþ nyttol iceꞃ ꞃlite oþþe hundeſ ᵹiꝼ
hit man ꞃona to deð · ⁊ eꝼt ymb þꞃeo niht ſmiꞃe
mið huniᵹe ꝥ þy þe naþon ſio hꞃyꝼinᵹ oꝼ ꝼealle.


. XXXVI.

[1] Ƿiþ þæne adle þe mon hæt cineul adl ᵹením cꞃicbeam
ꞃinde · ⁊ æꞃ ſan · ⁊ apuldoꞃ · mapuldoꞃ · ellen · ꝥiþiᵹ ·
ꞃealh · ꝥiꞃ · ꝥicc · ac · ꞃlahþoꞃn · biꞃcean · elebeam ·
ᵹatetꞃeop · æꞃceꞃ ꞃceal mæꞃt · ⁊ ælceꞃ tꞃeoꝡeꞃ dæl
þe man beᵹitan mæᵹ · butan hæᵹþoꞃne ⁊ aloꞃe þaꞃa
tꞃeoꝡa mæꞃt þe heꞃ aꝥꞃiten ꞃynd ⁊ eac ᵹaᵹel ⁊ cneoꞃ
holen · ſinᵹꞃenan eolonan · ꞃedic pealpyꞃt · þa ᵹꞃeatan
netlan · peꞃꞃnoð coꞃþ ᵹeallan. ᵹením þonne tynam-
beꞃnc cetel do þꞃibban bæl þaꞃa ꞃinda ⁊ þa pyꞃta
pylle ſꝥiþe on maxpyꞃte ᵹiꝼ þu hæbbe · ᵹiꝼ þu næbbe
pyl on ꞃætꞃe ſꝥiþe · do þonne oꝼ þa ꞃinda ⁊ do niꝥe on
innan ꝥ ilce poſ do ſpa þꞃiꞃa aſeoh þonne clæne ſpa
hatne þone dꞃenc ⁊ do þonne mele ꝼulne buteꞃan on
ſpa hatne ⁊ ᵹehꞃeꞃe toᵹædeꞃe læt ſtandan tꝥa niht
oþþe þꞃeo · ado þonne oꝼ þa buteꞃan ⁊ ᵹením þonne
ᵹaᵹel cꞃoppan · ⁊ iꝼiᵹ cꞃoppan · helban · ⁊ betonican
eolonan · ꞃedic · banpyꞃt · eoꞃð miſtel ᵹebeat toᵹædeꞃe pylle on þæꞃe buteꞃan ado þonne þa buteꞃan
clæne oꝼ þam pyꞃtum þæꞃ þe mon mæᵹe · ᵹením þonne
ſmæl beꞃen mela ⁊ ᵹebꞃæꞃneð ꞃealt bꞃiꝥe þonne on

fol. 33 a.

---

[1] Ζώνη, or Ζωστήρ.

away. The same *process* is advantageous for frogs[1] or
hounds bite, if one soon applieth it. And again, for
about three nights, smear with honey, that thereby the
more readily the scab or crust may fall off.


## xxxvi.

Against the disease which is hight circle addle[2] *or
shingles*, take quickbeam rind, and aspen and apple
tree, maple tree, elder, withy, sallow, myrtle, wich
elm, oak, sloe thorn, birch, olive tree, the lotus tree,[3]
of ash there shall be most, and a part of each tree
which a man can get at (except hawthorn and alder),
the largest quantity of the trees which are here written,
and also gale and knee holly, *that is, butchers broom*,
singreen, *that is, house leek*, helenium, radish, wallwort,
the great nettle, wormwood, earthgall.[4] Take then
a kettle holding ten ambers, put *therein* a third part
of the rinds and the worts, boil strongly in mashwort,
*that is, the unfermented wort of beer*, if thou have it, if
thou have it not, boil strong in water, then remoth
rinds, and put new *rinds* into that same decoction, do
so three times, then strain out clean the drink so hot,
and then add a basin full of butter so hot, and shake
*them up* together : let *this* stand two nights or three,
then remove the butter, and then take catkins of gale,
berry branches of ivy, tansy, and betony, helenium,
radish, bonewort, basil, beat together, boil in the butter,
then remove the butter clean off the worts, as far as a
man may : then take fine barley meal and burnt salt,

---

[1] No doubt *frog*, Cod. Ex. p. 426-9.
Dioskorides Alexifarm. 31. has a
chapter on the Φρύνη, or *toad*, and
the Βάτραχος ἕλειος, or " marsh
frog," as poisonous.

[2] In Plinius Valerianus, Circinus.

" Vesicæ si hominem cinxerint oc-
cidunt."

[3] Are we to suppose Carpinus
was read as Caprinus, and say horn-
beam for lotus ?

[4] *Erythræa centaureum.*

þæpe butepan Ᵹ hpepe þonne ſpiþe butan fype Ᵹ do
pipop to ete þonne æpeſt þone bpip ón nealht neſtiȝ.
ðpince þonne æftep þone dpenc Ᵹ nanne oþepne pætan
tyn nihtum þuptiȝ ȝif he mæȝe • ȝenim þonne acmiſtel
ȝebeat ſmæle Ᵹ aðpiȝe Ᵹ ȝeȝnid to melupe ápelh þonne
piþ ænne peninȝ do þ on þ betſte pín. ðpinc ſpa
miȝon daȝaſ Ᵹ ne ete nipne ciſe ne feppce ȝoſ • ne
feppene æl • ne fe[p]pc ſpin • ne naht þæſ þe of
mopode cume • ne fixaſ • únpcellehte • ne flohtenfote
fuȝelaſ • ȝif he hpilc þipſa ete ſie þ pealt Ᵹ nane
þinȝa beop ne ðpince Ᵹ ȝemethce pín Ᵹ eala • ȝif mon
þiſûm læcedome befyliȝð þonne biþ ſe man hal; Þiþ
cipcul able ȝením doccan þa þe ſpimman pille ȝebeat
ſpiþe ſmale apylle on caldum mopode ȝode hand fulle
do þonne þa pypta óf do eft oþpe hand fulle þæpe
ilcan pypte pylle eft ſpíðe ȝedo þonne þa pypta óf
ȝenim þonne ſpefl ȝebeat ſpiþe ſmale ȝedo þonne on
þa pealfe þ hio ſie ſpa þicce ſpa bpip ſmipe þonne þa
ſpeccan mid þæpe ſealfe oþ þ hun pel ſie.

.XXXVII.

Marcellus,
362, d.

Þiþ þon þe mon ne mæȝe hiſ micȝean ȝehealdan Ᵹ
þæpe ȝepeald naȝe cofopeſ clapa oþþe oþpeſ ſpineſ ȝebæpn to ahſan pceað þonne þa ahſan on þæſ peocan

Marcellus,
362, d. c.

manneſ dpincan. Eft ſpineſ blædpan untydpendeſ þ iſ
ȝylte ȝebæpn to ahpan do on pín ſele dpincan. Þiþ
þon ilean eft ȝate blædpe ahypſte pele etan • ſume ſpa
ȝehypſte ȝeȝnidaþ to duſte ſceað on pín pellað dpincan

fol. 34 a.

ȝif hie beoð butan feppe. ȝif mon ne mæȝe ȝeniȝan
eft cymeneſ ȝenim ſpa micel ſpa ðu mid þpim finȝpum

next make a brewit of them in the butter, and shake it well up without fire, and add pepper, then let *the patient* eat first the brewit at night fasting.   Further after that let him drink the draught and none other liquid for ten nights, for thirty if he can *endure it ;* then take mistletoe of the oak, beat it small and dry it, and rub down to meal, then weigh it against one penny, put that into the best wine ; let *the sufferer* drink *this* accordingly for nine days, and let him eat neither new cheese, nor fresh goose, nor fresh eel, nor fresh pig, nor aught of that which cometh of a decoction, nor fishes without shells, nor web footed fowls ; if he eat any of these, let it be salted, and by no means let him drink beer, and wine and ale moderately.   If this leechdom be followed then shall the man be hole. Against circle addle *or shingles,* take dock that will swim, beat it very small, boil in old inspissated wine a good handful, then remove the worts, afterwards add another handful of the same wort, boil again thoroughly, then remove the worts ; then take brimstone, beat it very small, then apply the salve, so that it may be as thick as brewit, then smear the specks with the salve till it be well with him, *the patient.*

### xxxvii.

In case that a man may not retain his urine and have not control over it, burn to ashes claws of a boar or of another swine, then shed the ashes on the sick mans drink.   Again, burn to ashes the bladder of an unprolific, that is a gelt, swine, put it into wine, administer it to drink.   For the same, fry a goats bladder, give it *to the man* to eat ; some, when so fried, reduce it to dust, and *when shed* into wine, give it *to the men* to drink, if they be without fever.   Again, if a man may not pass water, take of cummin as much as thou mayst lift with three fingers, triturate it, and add

úp ahebban mæȝe ȝetpifula ꝼ ȝeðo to pineꝼ tpeȝen
bollan fulle • ꝼ oþꝛe tpeȝen pætepeſ ꞃele ðꞃincan niht-
neꞃtiȝum. Eꝼt ȝiꝼ mon ne mæȝe ȝemiȝan ðꞃincc ȝyþꞃiꝼan on pætꞃe ȝeȝniðene. Eꝼt ȝenime eac ȝeappan ꝼ
ꞃeȝbꞃæðan pyl on pine ꞃele ðꞃincan. Eꝼt ꝼammeꞃ
Marcellus,
358, g.
blæðꞃe ȝeſoðene þicȝe he. ȝenim ꝼinoleſ pyꞃttꞃuman
eꝼt • ꝼ þa pyꞃt ꞃelꝼe ȝebeat ꝼ ȝeȝnið ðn pin oꝼþæne
Marcellus,
362, d.
pel ꝼ aꞃeoh ꞃele ðꞃincan. Eꝼt ȝoſa tunȝan ȝebꞃæððe
ꝼ ȝeþicȝe. Eꝼt ȝiꝼ þu ꝼinðe ꝼiſc on oþꞃum ꝼiſce
innan ȝenim þone ꝼ ȝebꞃæð ſpiþe ꝼ ȝebꞃyte on ðꞃincan ꝼ ꞃele þam ꞃeocan men ðꞃincan ſpa he nyte ſpa
þu ꞃcealt þa oþꞃe ætaſ ꝼ ðꞃincan ꞃellan. ȝiꝼ mðn ne
mæȝe ȝemiȝan ðꞃincc he lihan pyꞃttꞃuman apylleðne
on pine oððe on ealað. ȝiꝼ he þonne to ſpiðe miȝe
fol. 34 b.
ðꞃincc ȝyþꞃiꝼan on pætepe ȝeȝniðene. ȝiꝼ mðn bloðe
miȝe ȝenim puðu ꞃoꞃan ſeoþ on pætꞃe oððe on ealað
ꞃele ðꞃincan.

Giꝼ ꝼiꝼ ne mæȝe ȝemiȝan nim tuncepꞃan ſæð ſeoð
on pætꞃe ꞃele ðꞃincan. ȝiꝼ mðn ne mæȝe ȝemiȝan
ȝecnupa luꝼeſtice ꝼ ellenꞃinðe ꝼ oleaſtꞃum þ íꞃ pilðe
elebeám ȝemenȝ pið ſuꞃum hluttꞃum ealað ꞃele
ðꞃincan.

### .XXXVIII.

Ðeꞃ ſinðon ðolh ꞃealꝼa to eallum punðum ꝼ ðꞃencaſ
ꝼ clænꞃunȝa[1] on ȝehpilce piſan ȝe utan ȝe on þam
innoþúm. Þeȝbꞃæðe ȝebeaten pið ealðne pyꞃele ȝemenȝeð ꞃepꞃe ne nyt biþ.

[2]Eꝼt ðolhꞃealꝼ ȝenim peȝbꞃæðan ſæð ȝetꞃiꝼula ſmale
ꞃceað on þa punðe ꞃona bið ꞃelpe.

---

[1] clæꞃnunȝa, MS.     |     [2] Herbar. Apul. ii. 6.

thereto two bowls full of wine and two others of water, give it *to the sick* to drink after his nights fasting. Again, if a man cannot mie, let him drink githrife, rubbed *fine* in water. Again, take also yarrow and waybroad, boil *them* in wine, give *them* to be drunk. Again, let him eat a rams bladder sodden. Again, take roots of fennel and the wort itself, beat it and rub it *fine* into wine, moisten well and strain *it, and* administer *it* to drink. Again, let him roast[1] and partake of the tongues of geese. Again, if thou find a fish within another fish, take and roast it thoroughly, and break it to bits into a draught, and give it to the sick man to drink in such a manner that he know it not. So shalt thou give the other meats and drinks. If a man may not pass water, let him drink a root of a lily boiled in wine or in ale. If he then mie too strongly, let him drink githrife in water, rubbed to *dust*. If a man mie blood, take dog roses, seethe them in water or in ale, administer them to drink.

If a woman may not pass water, take seed of garden cress, seethe it in water and give it her to drink. If one may not pass water, pound lovage and elder rind and oleaster, that is wild olive tree, mix *this* with sour clear ale, *and* give to drink.

### xxxviii.

1. Here are wound salves for all wounds and drinks and cleansings of every sort, whether without or in the inwards. Waybroad beaten, mixed with old lard; *the* fresh is not of use.

2. Again, a wound salve; take seed of waybroad, bray it small, shed it on the wound, soon it will be better.

---

[1] Our Saxon has not been careful in the selection of his recipes ; this is set down in Marcellus as restraining " profluvium urinæ."

Ƿiþ ealdre ƿunde toþrocenre ȝrundeſƿelȝe ƿiþ ealdne
nyrele ȝemenȝeð ⁊ on aleð lacna ſpilce ƿunda. To
ƿunde clænrunȝe ·[1] ȝenim clæne huniȝ ȝeƿyrme to
fyre ȝeðo þonne on clæne fæt ðo realt to ⁊ hrere oþ
þ hit hæbbe þriƿer þicnerre ſmire þa ƿunde miþ þonne
fullað hio. ȝif banbrice on hearðe ſie maȝeþan ⁊
ȝotroþan ȝecnuƿa ƿel on huniȝe ðo þonne buteƿan on
þ bið ȝoð ðolhrealf. Eft prið þon eac biþ ȝoð luſt-
mocan croƿ to lecȝanne ón ȝeþrocen hearoð ⁊ ȝif
hunð rlice. Ƿiþ hunðer rlice ȝenim þa readan netlan
⁊ attorlaþan ⁊ ſpicer ælcer emrela ſeoð on buteƿan
ƿyre to realfe rona beoð þa unnyttan ban ute.

ðolh realf ƿið lunȝen able · hleomoce hatte ƿyrt ſio
reaxeð on broce ȝeƿyrc þa ón morȝenne þonne hio
ȝebear ſie ſume beoð unðeare ⁊ ȝoſe ſceapr þonne
hio ne ete · ȝecnuƿa þa hleomocan menȝ ƿiþ þam ȝoſe
rceaƿre · ðo lær þær ſceaƿrer ƿyl on buteƿan apƿinȝ
þ biþ ȝoð realf. Sealf haƿan ſpƿecel nim on ealdum
lande ⁊ lunȝenƿyrt ſeo biþ ȝeolu urereaƿð ⁊ æȝer
ðyðrin miþ þy rceal mon lacrian þone man þe biþ
lunȝenne ƿunð. Ƿiþ innan ƿunde realf · ſin ele ·
ȝalluc · huniȝ. ðolhrealf ȝyþþife ⁊ ȝeloð ƿyrt ⁊ þa
brunan ƿyrt brraðleaƿan ſio reaxeþ on ƿuða ⁊ luſtmoce croppan · ȝecnuƿa þa ealle ⁊ ƿyl æreſt on buteƿan healfe ⁊ apƿinȝ.

ðolh realf eft ȝrunde ſpelȝe þa ðe reaxað ón ƿorþi-
ȝun ſio biþ ȝoð to ðolhrealfe ⁊ ribbe ⁊ ȝearre ⁊ ȝiþ-
rife ȝecnuƿa þa ƿyrta ealle ƿyl on buteƿan ⁊ apƿinȝ.
Eft ðolhrealf ȝoð acrinð aðriȝe þa rinde ⁊ ſpiðe ſmale
ȝecnuƿa ⁊ aðelf niþereaƿðne rlah ðorn ærcar þa yte-

3. For an old bruised wound, groundsel mingled with old lard, and laid on : tend such wounds *thus.* For cleansing of a wound ; take clean honey, warm it at the fire, put it then into a clean vessel, add salt, and shake it till it have the thickness of brewit, smear the wound therewith, when it turneth foul. If there be a bone breach in the head, pound maythe and goutweed well in honey, then add butter, that is a good wound salve. Again for that, a bunch of " lustmock" is good to lay on a broken head, and *also* if a hound tear *a man.* For tearing by a hound, take the red nettle and attorlothe and some lard, of each an equal quantity, seethe in butter, work to a salve, soon the useless bones will be out.

4. A wound salve for lung disease. A wort is called hlemock, which waxeth in brooks, *and is now brook-lime,* work it, *that is, deal with it* in a morning when it is dewy, (some *plants of it* are undewy), and sharn of goose *dropped* when the goose eats not ; pound the brookline, mingle with the dung of goose, put in less of the sharn *than of the wort,* boil in butter, wring *through a cloth,* that will be a good salve. A salve : take vipers bugloss, *grown* on an old tilth, and golden lungwort,[a] and a yolk of egg, with this shall one tend a man who is wounded in the lung. For an inward wound, a salve : wine, oil, comfrey, honey. A wound salve : githrife and silver weed, and the broadleaved brownwort which waxeth in woods, and a bunch of the flowers of " lustmock"; pound all these and boil first in a half proportion of butter, and wring *through a cloth.*

[a] *Hieracium murorum* and *pulmonarium.*

5. Again, a wound salve : the groundsel which waxeth in highways, that is good for a wound salve, and ribwort, and yarrow, and githrife ;[b] pound all the worts, boil in butter, and squeeze *through a cloth.* Again, a good wound salve : oak rind ; dry the rind and pound it very small, and delve up the nethermost *part of a*

[b] *Agrostemma githago.*

meſtan punde ⁊ ſpiðe ſmale ȝecnupa ariƿt ſmale þurh
ſmæl ſiƿe bo beȝea emƿela þ mela bið ȝob on to
ſceadenne. ȝiƿ þu paðe pille lytle punde ȝelacnian
eneeƿiſan ȝetƿiƿula oððe ȝeſeoð on buteƿan pyƿe to
realƿe ſmiƿe mið. ðolh realƿ · ȝeaƿƿan · ȝyþƿiƿan ·
ſinȝƿenan · ȝotþoþan kæſt ȝecnupa pið buteƿan ſpiðe
pel leȝe neahteƿne ſpa ȝeeneben · bo þonne ôn pannan
ƿyl ſpiðe bo þ ƿam ôƿ clæne aƿeoh þurh clað bo on hƿit
realt hƿeƿ ſpiðe oþ þ ȝeſtanden ſie. ðolhrealƿ meƿſe
hoƿe æþelƿeƿðinȝpyƿt ⁊ ȝyþƿiƿan ⁊ ſinȝƿenan on þa

fol. 36 a.

ilean piſan ƿƿiee. ðolhrealƿ ȝenim paðeſ eƿoppan ⁊
netelan eñe ȝecnupa pel · ƿyl on buteƿan aƿeoh þurh
clað bo hƿit ſealt ôn hƿeƿe ſpiðe.


ðolhrealƿ ãeƿinð · æƿeƿðe · meoðopyƿt aðƿiȝe ealle
⁊ ȝecnupa ſmale ariƿt þurh ƿiƿe menȝ pið huniȝe ⁊
æȝeƿ þ hƿite. ðolhrealƿ ȝiƿ mon ſie mið iƿene ȝe-
pundoð · puðmiƿoƿe · ſinȝƿene · ȝeloðpyƿt ſpƿinȝ pyƿt ·
ȝyþƿiƿe · ȝƿundeſpelȝe · maȝoðe pyƿm pyƿt moþoƿeaƿð
ȝeenna pel toſomne ealle menȝ pið buteƿan pyl þa
ƿƿƿta on þæƿe buteƿan ſpiðe aƿleot þ ƿam oƿ clæne
aƿeoh þurh clað bo on bleðe hƿeƿ pið oþ þ ȝeſtanden
ſie.

ȝíƿ mon mið tƿeoƿe ȝeƿleȝen ſie oððe mið ſtane
oþþe byl on men ȝebeƿſteð · to þon ðolhrealƿ · ȝyþƿiƿe · ontƿe · ȝeloðpyƿt · ƿiȝellhƿeoƿƿa · ȝecnupa þa
pyƿta ſpiþe ȝemenȝ pel pið buteƿan ⁊ on þa ilean
piſan ȝeƿena þe ie æƿ eƿæþ.

ȝiƿ men ſie lim ôƿ aƿleȝen · ƿinȝeƿ oððe ƿôt oþþe
hand ȝiƿ þ meaƿh ute ſie · ȝenim ƿeeaƿeƿ meaƿh ȝe-

blackthorn, shave off the outermost *part of the* rind
and pound it very small, sift it small through a small
sieve, put *together* equal quantities of both, the meal is
good to shed on *a wound.* If thou wilt quickly cure
a little wound, bruise or seethe in butter water cress,
work it into a salve, smear therewith. A salve for
wounds : pound very well with butter, yarrow, cockle,
singreen, *or houseleek,* of goutweed the least, lay them
by for a night so bruised, then put them into a pan, boil
thoroughly, remove the foam clean off, strain through
a cloth, add white salt,[1] shake it well up till it
be got firm. A wound salve ; work *up* in the same
wise marsh hove, stichwort, and cockle, and singreen.
A wound salve ; take heads of woad and of nettle,
also pound them well, boil in butter, strain through a
cloth, add white salt, shake thoroughly.

6. A wound salve : oak rind, "æferthe," meadowwort ;
dry all *these* and pound them small, sift *the dust*
through a sieve, mingle with honey and the white of
an egg. A wound salve, if a man be wounded with
iron : woodroffe, singreen, silverweed, springwort,[a] githrife, groundsel, maythe, the lower part of wormwort,
pound them all well together, mingle with butter, boil
the worts in the butter thoroughly, skim the foam
off clean, strain through a cloth, put *it* on a saucer,
shake *it* till it be concrete.

7. If a man be smitten with wood or with stone,
or if a boil bursteth on a man, for this a wound salve :
cockle, "ontre," silverweed, turnsole, pound the worts
thoroughly, mingle well with butter, and prepare in
the same wise which before I quoth.

8. If a limb be smitten off a man, a finger, or a foot,
or a hand, if the marrow be out, take sodden sheeps

[a] *Euforbia lathyris.*

---

[1] Salt not quite pure is not white ; much comes red from the pits ; much dirty from the saltpans. Sal ammoniacum is often prescribed in the Latin and Greek authors ; perhaps this is an evasion of that drug.

roðen leȝe on þ oþeŋ meaŋh · apŋiþ fpiðe pel neahteŋie.

ðolh ŋealf · hæŋlef ŋaȝu ꝼ holen ŋiŋðe ŋþepeaŋðe · ꝼ ȝyþŋiꝼan ȝecŋua fŋiðe pel þa pꝼŋta ȝemenȝ ŋið buteŋan feoð fŋiðe ꝼleot oꝼ þ ꝼam afeoh þuŋh cla∂ fŋiþe clæne ȝiꝼ þæŋ ðolȝef oꝼŋaŋ ꝼynð to hea ymb ftŋic mið hate iŋene fŋiðe leohtlice þ þ ꝼel hŋitiȝe.

ðolhŋealf ȝōtpoþan ȝecnuŋa fŋiðe pel meȝ pŋð buteŋan feoð fŋiðe ꝼ ŋyll ꝼ apŋinȝ þuŋh cla∂ ꝼleot þ ꝼam ōꝼ ȝeŋelt fŋiðe pel · ȝiꝼ ðolh ꝼuhȝe ceop ftŋæl pyŋt ōŋ ꝼ ȝeaŋŋan. ðolhŋealf ȝenim ŋibban · ꝼ ȝeaŋŋan · ꝼ ðolhŋunan ŋoþopeaŋðe · ꝼ ðoccan ꝼ ȝoŋe ŋceaŋŋ ꝼ ŋicef lytel · ꝼ huŋiȝ ŋylle on buteŋan ðo on þ ðolh þonne clænfa∂ hit ꝼ hala∂. ðolhŋealf ȝenīm ȝeaŋŋan ꝼ lŋcce pyŋt pyl on buteŋan.

Sealf piþ þon þ ðolh ne ꝼuhȝe ȝenim bŋcŋ þe lŋopan on ŋeaxaþ ceop þa ŋiŋðe on þ ðolh ne ꝼulaþ hit. ðolhŋealf meðopyŋt ŋoþepeaŋð · luftmoce · hoꝼe · coꝼoŋ ꝼeaŋŋ · pyl on huŋiȝe ðo þicce maxŋyŋt on ȝemanȝ.

ðolhðŋenc · coꝼoŋþŋote ŋoþopeaŋð ꝼ meðopyŋt cāc fpa aȝŋŋŋonia ŋoþopeaŋð ꝼ uꝼepeaŋð pyl ōŋ calaþ þa pyŋta ȝebŋŋŋ mið ȝifte ŋele ðŋŋncan.

ðolhðŋenc ȝeaceŋ fuŋan puðu cuŋille ȝiþŋŋꝼe · coꝼoŋþŋote ŋþepeaŋðe ŋeŋcþŋote cnuŋa fmale ðo ōŋ cealð ŋæteŋ ȝŋ∂ betŋeoh hanðuŋ afeoh þuŋh cla∂ ŋele

marrow, lay it on the other marrow, bind it well up for a night. A wound salve : the lichen of hazel, and the netherward part of holly rind and githrife, pound the worts very well, mingle with butter, seethe thoroughly, skim off the foam, strain through a cloth very clean ; if the edges of the wound are too high,[1] run them round with a hot iron very lightly, so that the skin may whiten.

9. A wound salve: pound very thoroughly, gout-weed, mingle with butter, seethe thoroughly, and boil, and wring through a cloth, skim off the foam, salt it very well; if the wound get foul, chew strailwort upon it and yarrow. A wound salve: take ribwort and yarrow, and the netherward part of pellitory, and dock, and goose dung, and a little pitch, and honey, boil in butter, apply it to the wound, then it cleanseth and healeth. A wound salve : take yarrow and leechwort, boil in butter.

10. A salve to the end that a wound may not foul : take briar, on which hips wax, *that is, dog rose,* chew the rind *and let it drop* on the wound, *then* it will not foul. A wound salve: the netherward part of meadow wort, lustmock, hove, everfern, boil in honey, add thick mashwort among *them.* A drink for wounds : the netherward part of everthroat, *that is, carline thistle,* and meadow sweet, so also the nether and upward part of agrimony, boil the worts in ale, barm them with yeast, *that is, introduce fermentation with yeast,* administer to drink.

11. A wound drink : pound small, cuckoo sour, wild cunila,[2] cockle, the netherward part of carline thistle, ashthroat, put them into cold water, rub between the hands, strain through a cloth, administer to

---

[1] Probably, if the edges are likely to coalesce, before the parts that lie deeper.

[2] Plinius, xx. 63.

ðrincan scenc fulne neahtnestig. dolhdrenc ribbe nioþeƿeard ⁊ ufeƿeard. eoforþrotan. ⁊ æsc þrotan nioþoƿearde cnupa smale do on ƿeallende ƿæter gnid betƿeoh handum ⁊ aseoh þurh clað sele drincan. To ælcum dolge sealf. gesomna cue mesa cu migoþa geƿyrce to flynan þa sƿa mon sapan ƿyrceð micelne citel fulne. nim þonne apuldor rinde ⁊ æsc rinde slahþorn rinde. ⁊ ƿir rinde. ⁊ elm rinde. ⁊ holen rinde. ⁊ ƿiþig rinde ⁊ geongre ace. sealh rinde. do þa ealle on micelne citel geot þa flynan ōn ƿyl sƿiþe lange. do þonne of þa rinda ƿyl þa flenan ꝥ hio sie þicce do simle ōn læssan citel sƿa hio læsse sie. geōt on fæt þonne hio genoh þicce sie. geæl þonne cealcstan sƿiðe ⁊ gesamna sōt ⁊ asift þurh clað ⁊ þone cealcstan eāc on þa flynan smire mid ꝥ dolh. Eft ƿiþ þon ilcan genim hofan ⁊ gelodƿyrt ⁊ brune ƿyrt ⁊ lustmocan crop ⁊ haran sprecel ƿyl on buteran ⁊ ƿring þonne of þa ƿyrta do oþre ōn. ribban. biſceopƿyrt gearƿan attorlaþan do þa on þa ilcan buteran ƿyl eft sƿiðe aƿring þa ōf ꝥ biþ god dolhsealf.

## .XXXVIIII.

Her sint læcedomas ƿiþ ælces cynnes ōmum ⁊ ōnfeallum ⁊ bancoþum eahta ⁊ tƿentig.

Nim grenes merces leaf gegnid oþþe getrifula ƿið ecedes dærstan smire mid þy þa saran stoƿa. Ƿiþ omum utablegnedum nim sur molcen ƿyrc to cealre ⁊ beþ mid þy cealre. Ƿið omum eft genim beorðræsta ⁊

drink a full draught *to the sick* after his nights fasting.[1]
A wound drink : pound small the netherward and upward part of ribwort, carline thistle, and the netherward
part of ashthroat, put them into boiling water, rub
between the hands, and strain through a cloth, administer to drink. A salve for every wound : collect
cow dung, cow stale, work up a large kettle full into
a batter as a man worketh soap, then take appletree
rind, and ash rind, sloethorn rind, and myrtle rind,
and elm rind, and holly rind, and withy rind, and the
rind of a young oak, sallow rind, put them all in a
mickle kettle, pour the batter upon *them*, boil very
long, then remove the rinds, boil the batter so that it
be thick, put it ever into a less kettle as it groweth
less, pour it, when it is thick enough, into a vessel,
heat then a calcareous stone thoroughly, and collect
some soot, and sift it through a cloth with the quick-
lime also into the batter, smear the wound therewith.
Again for the same, take hove and silverweed and brownwort, and a bunch of the flowers of "lustmock," and
vipers bugloss, boil in butter and wring the worts off,
and put others in, ribwort, bishopwort, yarrow, atterlothe, put them into the same butter, boil again strongly,
wring these off ; that will be a good wound salve.

### xxxix.

1. Here are leechdoms for erysipelatous inflammations
of every sort, and fellons, and leg diseases of every
sort ; eight and twenty *in number*.

2. Take leaves of green marche, rub or bruise them
with the lees of vinegar, smear with that the sore
places. For erysipelas which hath broken into blains,
take sour curds, work them to a chalder, and foment with
the chalder. For erysipelatous inflammations again, take

---

[1] Neɲcɪʒ must be understood as neɲcɪʒum.

rapan ꞇ æƷef þ lipiꞇe ꞇ ealde Ʒꞃuꞇ leƷe on þiþ omena
Ʒerpelle. Þiþ omena Ʒebeꞃrꞇe Sιꞇꞇe on cealdum pꞃeꞇeꞃe
oþ þ hιꞇ adeadod rιe ꞇeoh þonne úp ꞃleah þonne ꞃeopeꞃ
rceappan ymb þa poccar uꞇan ꞇ læꞇ yꞃnan þ rꞇιcce þe
hιꞇ pιlle; pyꞃc þe ꞃealꞃe þuꞃ · ᴋim bꞃune pyꞃꞇ ꞇ meꞃrc
meaꞃ Ʒeallan ꞇ ꞃeade neꞇlan pyl on buꞇeꞃan ꞇ rmιꞃe
mιð ꞇ beþe mιð þam ιlcum pyꞃꞇum.

[^1] Þιþ þon ιlean Ʒemm anƷolꞇpꞃæccean ƷeƷnιd rpιꞃe ðo
eced ꞇo ꞇ on bιnd ꞇ rmιꞃe mιð. Þιþ þon ιlean Ʒenīm
raꞃman Ʒnιd ꞇo durꞇe ꞇ menƷ þιþ hunιƷ ꞇ rmιꞃe mιð.
Uιð þon ιlean Ʒenιm Ʒebꞃædde æꞃꞃu menƷ pιð ele
leƷe ōn ꞇ beþe rpιꞃðe mιð beꞇan leaꞃum. Eꞃꞇ Ʒenīm
cealꞃer rceaꞃιn oꞃþe caldery hꞃyþeꞃer peaꞃm ꞇ leƷe ōn.
Eꞃꞇ þιþ þon Ʒenīm heoꞃoꞇer rceaꞃoþan oꞃ ꞃelle arcaꞃen
mιð pumιce ꞇ peꞃe mιð ecede ꞇ rmιꞃe mιð. Eꞃꞇ Ʒenim
eoꞃoꞃer Ʒeallan Ʒιꞃ þu næbbe nιm oþꞃer rpιner ƷeƷnιd
ꞇ rmιꞃe mιð þy þæꞃ hιꞇ raꞃ rιe. Þιþ þon ιlean Ʒenīm
rpealþan nerꞇ bꞃιec mιð calle apeƷ ꞇ Ʒebæꞃιn mιð rceaꞃne
mιð calle ꞇ Ʒnιd ꞇo durꞇe menƷ þιþ eced ꞇ rmιꞃe mιð.
Pιð þon ιlean Ʒehæꞇ ceald pꞃeꞇeꞃ mιð haꞇan ιꞃene ꞇ beþe
Ʒelome mιð þy. Þιþ haꞇum omum · nιm beꞇonιcan ꞇ
peꞃιnoð ꞇ ꞃιnul Ʒnιd ōn eala ꞇ ꞃedιe ꞃele hīm dꞃιncan.
Þιþ haꞇum omum nιm ꞃen omþþan ꞇ þa rmalan claꞇan
pyl on Ʒaꞇe meolce ꞇ rúpe. Þιþ haꞇum omum nīm

[^1]: Plinius Valerianus, fol. 76, d, for eight lines.

dregs of beer, and soap, and the white of an egg, and old groats, lay *this* on against erysipelatous swellings. Against bursting of erysipelatous inflammations, let the man sit in cold water till the sore becometh numbed, then get him up, then strike four scarifying slashes about the pocks on the outside, and let the lymph run as it will. Work thyself a salve thus: take brownwort, and marsh gall, *or marsh gentian,* and red nettle, boil in butter, and smear and bathe with the same worts.

3. For the same, take an earthworm,[1] rub it thoroughly *fine,* add vinegar to it, bind it on and smear therewith. For the same, take savine, rub to dust, and mingle with honey and smear therewith. For the same, take roasted eggs, mingle with oil, lay on, and foment freely with leaves of beet. Again, take a calfs sharn, *that is dung,* or an old bullocks, *still* warm, and lay it on. Again for this *same,* take harts shavings, shaven off the fell or skin with pumice, and wash, *that is macerate,* with vinegar and smear therewith. Again, take a boars gall, if thou have not *that,* take *gall* of another swine, rub and smear with that where it is sore. For that ilk, take a swallows nest, break it away altogether, and burn it with *its* dung and all, and rub it to dust, mingle with vinegar and smear therewith. For the same, heat cold water with a hot iron, and bathe frequently with that. For hot erysipelatous humours, take betony, and wormwood, and fennel, rub them into ale, and radish *with them,* give *the mixture to the sick man* to drink. For hot erysipelatous humours, take fen ompre, *that is water dock,* and the small clote, *that is, cleavers,* boil in goats milk and sup. Against hot erysipelatous humours,

---

[1] Bjorn Haldorson mentions this treatment: the earthworm is called A'mumadkr (read ma'ðkr), because erysipelas is usually cured by it; " his lumbricis probari et curari " solent, cum applicati marcescant " et moriantur." (On A'mumadkr.) A'ma is the Ome of the text.

hunan ⁊ cɼelaſtan ⁊ alexanꝺɲian ⁊ beⱦonican ⁊ celeþonian ⁊ cepliceɲ ɼæꝺ ꝺɲince on pine. Scalɼ nïm
elleneſ bloſtman ⁊ þone cɲop pyl on buⱦeɲan ⁊ ſmiɲe
miꝺ · ᵹiɼ hiⱦ ɲille pynſman ſmiɲe miꝺ æᵹeſ ᵹeolcan oɼeɲ
ſmiɲe miꝺ þy ⁊ ꝺɲiᵹe ⱦo ᵹleꝺum oþ þ hiⱦ heaɲꝺ ſie
ɲpeah þonne apeᵹ ⁊ ſmiɲe cɼⱦ miꝺ þæɲe ɲealɼe. Þiþ
haⱦum omum nïm pineſ ꝺɲæſtan menᵹ piþ hɲeap æᵹɲu
⁊ miꝺ ɼeþeɲe ſmiⱦ ön ⁊ ne ɲpeah æɲ hiⱦ hal ſie.
Þiþ ſeonꝺüm omum nïm cneopholen micle æɲ oðɲum
meⱦe ꝺæᵹhpam ⱦo þam ꝺolᵹe · ⁊ hɲyþeɲeſ ᵹeallan
humᵹ ſoⱦ · ꝺo ⱦoſomne lacna miꝺ. Þiþ þon ilcan þ iſ
ɼïc · luſtmoce þa cɲoppihⱦan nïm ⱦo baþe ⁊ ᵹebæɲne
ⱦo ɲealɼe pulɼeſ ceacan þa pineſⱦɲan ⁊ þa ⱦeþ ſunꝺoɲ
menᵹ piꝺ huniᵹe ⁊ ſmiɲe miꝺ ⁊ ɼeɲɲene cyɲe ön leᵹe
menᵹ þ oþeɲ piꝺ meoluce ſupe þɲy moᵹᵹenaſ niᵹon
ſupan. Þiþ bancoþe þ iſ oman nïm niᵹonⱦyne ſnæꝺa
colonan ⁊ nyᵹon onⱦɲan ⁊ enꝺleɼan ɲeaꝺeɲ ſecᵹeſ ꝺo
on eala ⁊ ꝺɲinc micle æɲ þonne þu eⱦe · ⁊ þa colonān
ane ſeoð oþ þ luo meɲpe ſie cnupa ⱦoſomne ſmiɲe miꝺ
þæɲ uⱦ ɼlea. Ðɲenc piþ onɼeallum cymeꝺ · pipoɲ · coſⱦ ·
meɲceɲ ɼæꝺ · ceaſⱦeɲ pyɲⱦe ſæꝺ cnua pel ꝺo on eala.
Ðɲenc piþ onɼeallum · cnua ön eala oþþe ᵹeſeoð celeþonian ⁊ heah luoloþan biſceop pyɲⱦ ᵹyþɲiɼan. Ðɲenc
piþ onɼeallum · ſiᵹɲouⱦe · cipe · leac · peᵹbɲæꝺe moþo-
peaɲꝺ · pyl calle on pæⱦɲe ⁊ ᵹeſpeⱦ miꝺ huniᵹe. Ðɲenc
piþ þon nïm þa ſmalan clæɼen pyɲⱦ moþopeaɲꝺe pyl on
ealoþ oððe ön beoɲe. Ðɲenc piþ onɼealle pyl ön ealoð

fol. 39 a.

take horehound, and everlasting, and alexanders, and betony, and celandine, and charlock seed, drink them in wine. A salve : take blooms of elder, and the crop, *or bunch or umbel*, boil them in butter, and smear therewith ; if it will, *that is, if it shew a tendency* to form ratten *or purulent matter*, smear with yolk of egg; smear over with that, and dry it by gledes, *or hot coals*, till that it be hard, then wash away and smear again with the salve. For hot erysipelatous eruptions, take dregs of wine, mingle with raw eggs, and with a feather smudge it on, and wash not till *the place* be hole. For oozing erysipelatous blains, take knee holly, *that is, butchers broom*, much ere other meat, daily for the wound, and put together bullocks gall, honey, soot; cure therewith. For the same, that is, for *the disease called* fig, take for a bath *that sort of* "lust-mock" which beareth crops *or flower bunches*, and for a salve, burn a wolfs jaw, the left one, and the teeth apart, mingle with honey and smear therewith, and lay on fresh cheese, mingle the other *ingredient*[1] with milk, sup for three mornings nine sips. For leg disease, that is hot red blains, take nineteen snips of helenium, and nine of "ontre," and eleven of red sedge, put them in ale and drink much ere than thou eat; and seethe the helenium alone till that it be tender, pound together, smear therewith where *the disease* may be striking out. A drink for fellons ; cummin, pepper, costmary, seed of marche, seed of black hellebore, pound well, put into ale. A drink *or potion* for fellons ; pound in ale or seethe celandine, and elecampane, bishop wort, githrife. A drink for fellons ; sigsonte, onion, leek, the netherward part of waybroad, boil all in water and sweeten with honey. A drink for that ; take the netherward part of the small cloverwort, boil in ale or in beer. A drink for fellons ; boil in ale

---

[1] What other ingredient is not clear by the grammatical construction.

ꝼınızlan bıꞃceoppıꞃt heah hıoloþe. ꝺꞃenc ꝥıþ ōnꝼealle
pyl on ealaꝺ ſpꞃınᵹ pyꞃt oþþe on beoꞃe. ꝺꞃenc eꝼt ꝥıꝺ
onꝼealle pyl on ealaþ cꞃoꞃleac ꝺꞃeoꞃᵹe ꝺꝛoſtlan pyꞃm
pyꞃt. ꝺꞃenc ꝥıþ onꝼealle meꞃce aꞇꞇoꞃlaþe · beꞇoce ·[1]
ꞃuꝺe · ſecᵹ · onꞇꞃe · claꞇe · bıꞃceop pyꞃt ᵹepyꞃc on
ealaꝺ. Eꝼꞇ ꝥıþ onꝼealle ᵹenım æꞇ ꝼꞃuman hæꞃlenne
ſꞇıccan oþþe ellenne pꞃıꞇ þınne naman ōn aꞃleah þꞃy
ꞃſceaꞃꞃan ōn ᵹeꝼylle mıꝺ þy bloꝺe þone naman peoꞃꞃ
oꝼeꞃ eaxle oþþe beꞇꞃeoh þeoh on yꞃꞃnenꝺe pæꞇeꞃ ⁊
ſꞇanꝺ oꝼeꞃ þone man þa ꞃſceaꞃꞃan aꞃlea ⁊ ꝥ eall ſpı-
ᵹınꝺe ᵹeꝺo.

Þıꝺ ōnꝼealle ᵹeꝼoh ꝼox aꞃleah ōꝼ cucum þone ꞇuxl
læꞇ hleapan apeᵹ bınꝺ on næꞃce haꝼa þe ōn.

Þıþ pōc aꝺle · onꞃeꝺ hampyꞃꞇ · moþoꞃeꞃıꝺ · ꝼelꝺmoꞃe
mꞃeꞃeaꞃꝺ onꞃeꝺeꞃ emꝼela ⁊ þaꞃa oþeꞃꞃa ꞇꞃeᵹea ꝼelꝺmoꞃan heal꙼e keꞃꞃe þonne hampyꞃꞇe cnupa ſpıꝺe ꞇo
ſomne ꝺo hluꞇꞇoꞃ ealu ꝥ þa pyꞃꞇa oꝼeꞃſꞇıᵹe · læꞇ ſꞇanꝺan þꞃeo mıhꞇ ꞃele ꞃcene ꝼulne ōn moꞃᵹen. ꝺꞃenc ꝥıꝺ
ꝥoc aꝺle pyl pæꞇeꞃ ōn cꞃoccan ꝺo hunıᵹ ōn ꝼleoꞇ ſımle
ꝥ ꝼām ōꝼ oþ ꝥ hıꞇ nelle ma ꝼꞃeman · ſuꞃ þonne ⁊ ꝺꞃınc
ōꝼꞇ ⁊ ᵹelome ſꞃa ꝼu haꞇoſꞇ mæᵹe ⁊ mıꝺ þꝼ hunıᵹe
ſmıꞃe þæꞃ hıꞇ uꞇꞃꞃlea on þoné pōc ne bıþ ꞃona nān
ꞇeona. Sealꝼ ꝥıþ pōc aꝺle pyl on buꞇeꞃan ſınᵹꞃenan ·
ᵹeaꞃꞃe · ᵹyþꞃıꝼe ꞃeaꝺꞃe neꞇelan cꞃoꞃ. ꝺꞃenc ꝥıþ poccum

---

[1] Read beꞇonıce.

fennel, bishop wort, elecampane.  A drink for a fellon;
boil in ale or in beer springwort.  A drink again for
a fellon ; boil in ale cropleek, penny royal, wormwort.
A drink for fellons ; marche, attorlothe, betony, rue,
sedge, "ontre," clote, bishop wort, work *them up* in
ale.  Again for fellons, take, to begin, a hazel or an
elder stick or spoon, write thy name thereon, cut three
scores on *the place*, fill the name with the blood, throw
it over thy shoulder or between thy thighs into running water and stand over the man.  Strike the scores,
and do all that in silence.

For fellon, catch a fox, strike off from him *while
quick, that is alive*, the tusk, *or canine tooth*, let *the
fox* run away, bind it in a fawns skin, have it upon
thee.

### xl.

For pock disease,[1] *use* "onred," houseleck, the nether
*part of it*, fieldmore, the nether *part of it;* of "onred"
an equal quantity, and of the two others by half less
of the fieldmore *or carrot* than of the houseleck,
pound them thoroughly together, add so much clear
ale as may mount above the worts ; let them stand
three nights, administer in the morning a cup full.
A drink for pock disease; boil water in a crock, add
honey, skim continually the foam away till it will
foam no more ; then sip and drink oft and whilom
as thou hottest may, and smear with the honey where
it may be breaking out into the pock, soon there will
be no mischief.  A salve for pock disease ; boil in
butter singreen, yarrow, githrife, the crop, *or flower
head,* of red nettle.  A drink against pocks ; bishop

---

[1] *Small pox.* The disease was unknown in classical medicine ; it
appeared in France in 565, A.D.,
and in Arabia in 572, A.D.  The
Arabic physician Razi treats of it
in a separate monograf about 923,
A.D., not long before this copy of
the Leech Book was written out.

biſceop pyṛt · aττoplaþan · ſpṛinᵹpyṛt · claτan moþe-
peaṛde ōn ealað ᵹepoṛhτ. Þiþ poccum ſpiðe ſceal mōn
blod læτan ⁊ ðṛincan amylτe buτeṛan bollan ꝼulne ·
ᵹiꝼ hie uτꞏlean ælene man ṛceall apeᵹ adelꝼan nið
þoṛne · ⁊ þonne pin oððe aloþ¹ ðṛenc ðṛype on innan
þonne ne beoð hy ᵹeſyne.

Þiþ poccum ᵹenim ᵹloꝼpyṛt apyl on buτeṛan ⁊ ſmiṛe
mið.

<h2 style="text-align:center">.XLI.</h2>

Þiþ innan onꝼealle næᵹlæṛ² haττe pyṛt ſuþeṛno ſio
bið ᵹob τo eτanne þiþ innan ōnꝼelle on nihτ neṛτiᵹ.
Þiþ innan onꝼealle pyl clonan eluhτpan ōn ealað ðṛinc
haτeſ bollan ꝼulne. Eꝼτ pyṛtðṛenc ōꝼ ꝼeṛmode betonican · oꝼ þæṛe ṛuṛan peᵹbṛædan ðṛince ꝼela nihτa.
Þiþ þæṛe ᵹeolþan able · hune · biſceop pyṛt · helbe ·
hoꝼe menᵹe þa τoᵹædeṛe do ælene ᵹoðe hanð ꝼulle
maxpyṛτe do τo poꝼe ambeṛ ꝼulne ⁊ τo ſτanbæꞏþe
ðyþhomaṛ · hune peṛinoð. Sτanbæþ³ ðṛince ðṛenc ōꝼ
omþṛan ōꝼ pine ⁊ oꝼ pæτṛe · ᵹeſpeτe ſpiðe.

<h2 style="text-align:center">.XLII.</h2>

⁴Oꝼ ᵹeal able ſio biþ oꝼ þæṛe ᵹeolþan · cymeþ ᵹṛeaτ
yꝼel ſio biþ ealṛa abla ṛicuſτ · þonne ᵹepeaxeð on innan
unᵹemeτ þæτan þiṛ ſinτ τacn · ꝥ him ſe lichoma eall
abiτepað ⁊ aᵹeolþað ſpa ᵹob ſeoluc · ⁊ him beoð undeṛ
τunᵹan τulᵹe ſpeaṛτe æðṛa ⁊ yꝼele ⁊ lim bið mieᵹe
ᵹeolu · læτ lim oꝼ lunᵹen æðṛe blob ꝼele him ōꝼτ
ſτyṛᵹenðne ðṛenc ſτanbaðu ᵹelome. ⁵Þyṛe lim ðonne

---

¹ Alop, *alnus glutinosa*, has no
medical properties. Probably the
Alnus nigra, now *Rhamnus frangula*,
Sppacen, was meant by the Latin
author copied.

² Read cunæᵹlæṛre, *cynoglossum*.

³ By Sτanbæþ understand Sτan-
bæþðṛenc, or amend thus.

⁴ Ἴκτερος.

⁵ Cf. Plinius Valerianus, fol. 61 d.

fol. 40 b.

wort, attorlothe, springwort, the netherward part of clote, *or burdock*, worked up in ale. Against pocks, a man shall freely employ bloodletting and drink melted butter, a bowl full *of it :* if they break out one must delve away each one *of them* with a thorn ; and then let him drip wine or alder drink within them, then they will not be seen, *or no traces will remain.*

Against pocks : take glovewort, boil in butter, and smear therewith.

### xli.

For inward fellon, there is a southern wort hight cynoglosson, which is good to eat against inward fellon, at night fasting. Against inward fellon, boil helenium *and* lupins in ale, drink a bowl full of the hot *infusion.* Again, a wort drink from wormwood *and* betony, *and* from the rough waybroad *or plaintain*, let him drink it many nights. For the yellow disorder, *or jaundice*, horehound, bishop wort, tansy, earth ivy, mingle them together, of each employ a good handful, add of mash-wort, for an infusion an amber full, and for a stone bath *use* dithhomar, *or papyrus*, horehound, *and* worm-wood. A stone bath; *that must be, to use with a stone bath ;* let *the man* drink a drink from ompre *or sorrel*, from wine and from water ; sweeten thoroughly.

### xlii.

From gall disease, that is from the yellow *jaundice*, cometh great evil; it is of all diseases most powerful, when there wax within *a man*, unmeasured humours; these are the tokens : that *the patients* body all be-cometh bitter and as yellow as good silk ; and under the root of his tongue there be swart veins and perni-cious, and his urine is yellow. Let him blood from the lung vein, give him often a stirring drink, stone baths

ſtilne drenc oᵹ omppan on pine ꝺ on pæꞇꞃe ꝺ ōn þam
baðe ᵹehpilce moꞃᵹene drince mylſce drincan ſio ᵹebeꞇ
þa biꞇeꞃneꞃꞃe þæꞃ ᵹeallan.

.XLIII.

fol. 41 a.

¹Þiþ pæꞇeꞃ bollan beꞇomean ſpilce aneſ peninᵹeꞅ ᵹe-
poᵹe on peaꞃmum pæꞇeꞃe ᵹꝺde drince þꞃy daᵹaꞅ ꞇulce
dæᵹ ᵹodne bollan ꝼulne.  Eꝼꞇ ᵹenꝼm ꞇeꞃꞇꞃoꞇan oþþe
pealpꝑnꞇe pꝑꞇꞃuman þæꞃ ꞅeaꝑeꞅ ꞅeopeꞃ euclepaꞅ ꝼulle
ᵹedo on bollan ꝼulne pineꞅ ſele drincan.

.XLIIII.

Þiþ canceꞃ adle þ̄ iꞅ biꞇe · ꞃuꞃe · ꞅealꞇ · ꞃibbe ·
æᵹ · ꞃōꞇ · ᵹebæꞃned lam · hpæꞇeꞅ ſmeðma menᵹ pið
æᵹꞃu medoꝑꞃꞇ ꞃoꝝeꞃþe acꝑꝺd · apuldoꞃ piꞃd · ꞃlah
þoꞃn piꞃde · ᵹiꝼ ꞅe biꞇe peaxe on men ᵹeꝑꞃe nꝑne
eealꝑe ꝺ leᵹe ōn clænꞃa² þa puꞃde mid.

Þiþ canceꞃe ōn eꝑꞃeꞃeꞃum ꝼæꞇe ᵹebæꞃn ſpeꝼl ᵹe-
ᵹꞃid ꞇo duſꞇe ſpa þu ſmaloſꞇ mæᵹe ꝺ aꞃiꝼꞇ þuꞃh clað
menᵹ pið ealde ſaꞃan ꝺ ꞃe ſpeꝼl jueꞃa do huniᵹeꞅ
ꞇeaꞃeꞅ medmieel ꞇo³ ſeeaꞃe · ᵹiꝼ ꞇo ſꞇið ſie þæm mid þꝼ
huniᵹe leᵹe on ᵹeoꝑnen leaꝼ þonne hiꞇ haliᵹe pyl on
buꞇeꞃan ᵹeaeeꝑ ſaꞃan ꝺ ſinᵹꞃenan ꝺ pudupoꞃan ſmiꞃe
mid þa oꞃꞃaꞅ þæꞃ hiꞇ ꞃeadiᵹe læꞇ þa oðꞃe ꞃealꝼe clænſian þ̄ dolh ne do nan pæꞇeꞃ ꞇo.  Sealꝼ piþ canceꞃe ·
ᵹenꝼm eu meolue buꞇan pæꞇeꞃe læꞇ peoꞃꞃan ꞇo ꝼleꞇum
ᵹeꞃꞃeꞃ ꞇo buꞇeꞃan ne pæꞃe on pæꞇꞃe. Nꝼm ſiᵹel-
hpeoꞃꝼan þa ſmalan unpæꞃeene do clæne enua ſpiðe
ᵹemenᵹ pel pið þæꞃe buꞇeꞃan do on pannan oꝑeꞃ ꝼꝑꞃ
aꝑyl ſpiðe aꞅeoh pel þuꞃh claðlaena mid þy. Þiþ canceꞃ
adle · ꞅe piꞃd ōn noꞃþan ꞇꞃeoꞃe be coꞃþan · ꝺ medo-

fol. 41 b.

---

¹ "Τοδρωψ.
² clæꞃna, MS.

³ Supply a point after ꞇo, not in
MS. Read þæn.

often. Work him then a composing drink of sorrel in
wine and in water, and in the bath, every morning,
let him drink a mulled draught; it will amend the
bitterness of the gall.

### xliii.

For dropsy, rub betony, as much as a penny weight,
in warm water, let *the patient* drink for three days,
each day, a good bowl full. Again, take of the juice
of the roots of ashthroat or of dwarf elder four spoons
full, put them into a bowl full. of wine, give them to
drink *to the patient.*

### xliv.

1. Against the disease cancer, that is, bite: sorrel,
salt, ribwort, egg, soot, burnt loam, smede *or fine flour*
of wheat; mingle with eggs, meadow sweet, "æferth,"
oak rind, appletree rind, sloethorn rind: if the cancer
wax on a man, work up some new chalder and lay
on; cleanse the wound therewith.

2. Against cancer; burn sulfur in a copper vessel,
rub it to dust, as small as thou may, and sift through
a cloth, mingle with old soap, and let the sulfur pre-
dominate, add a moderate quantity of virgin honey;
see if it be too stiff, moisten it with the honey; lay on
a mallow leaf; when it healeth, boil in butter cuckoo
sour and singreen and woodroffe, smear therewith the
borders, where it is red; make the other salve cleanse
the wound, put no water. A salve for cancer; take
cows milk, without water, make it become cream, turn
it to butter, wash it not in water. Take the small
turnsole unwashen, make it clean, pound it thoroughly,
mix it well with the butter, put it into a pan over
the fire, boil it thoroughly, strain well through a cloth,
cure therewith. Against disease of cancer: oak rind
on the north side of the tree by the earth, and the

pyꞃt nioþepeaꞃð · æꝼeꞃðe niþepeaꞃð · cunezlæꞃꞃe nio-
þopeaꞃð · ðo ealꞃa emꝼela ȝecnua to ðuſte · ðo henne
ꞇeȝeꞃ ꝥ hꞃiꞇe ꞇo · ⁊ huniȝ ðo beȝea emꝼela ȝemenȝ
ꞃið þam ðuſꞇūm clæm on ðone canceꞃ ne ðo nan
ꝑꞇeꞃ ꞇo.

. XLV.

Þiþ attꞃe ðꞃencaſ ⁊ læcedomaſ · betonican meꞃce ·
peꞃꞃnoð · ꝼinul · ꞃedic · cnua on ealað ꞃele ðꞃincan.
Þꞃð attꞃe betonican ⁊ þa ſmalan attoꝑlaþan ðo on
haliȝ ꝑꞇeꞃ ðꞃinc ꝥ ꝑꞇeꞃ ⁊ eꞇ þa pyꞃꞇa. Uið ælcum
attꞃe · ꞃedic ⁊ claꞇe eꞇe æꞃ ne mæȝ þe nan man attꞃe

fol. 42 a.

apyꞃðan. Þꞃð ælcum attꞃe biꞃceoppyꞃt niþepeaꞃð ⁊
elehtꞃe · ⁊ ſpꞃꞃnȝ pyꞃt nioþepeaꞃð eoꞃoꞃþꞃotan · ⁊
claꞇan · apyl on ealað ꞃele ðꞃincan ȝelome. Ȝiꝼ næð-
ꞃe ꞃlea man þone blacan ſneȝl apæꞃc on haliȝ ꝑꞇꞃe
ꞃele ðꞃincan oþþe hpæt hpeȝa ꞃæꞃ þe ꞃꞃam ſcottum
come. Eꝼt peȝbꞃæban ȝeȝꞃð ſꞃꞃþe ðꞃīnc on ꞃine.
Þiþ næðꞃan biꞇe betonican ꝥꞇe þꞃy peneȝaſ ȝeꞃeȝe ðo
on þꞃy bollan ꝼulle ꞃineſ ꞃele ðꞃincan.

Þiþ næðꞃan biꞇe eꝼt ꞃīꞃleaꞃe apꞃunȝenu ⁊ þiþ ꝼīn
ȝemenȝeð ȝoð biþ ꞇo ðꞃincanne. Uiþ næðꞃan biꞇe eꝼt
celeþonie ȝeꞇꞃiꝼulaðe ðꞃince ūn neahꞇ neꞃꞇiȝ · III.
bollan ꝼulle. Þiþ næðꞃan ꞃleȝe ſpꞃꞃnȝpyꞃt · atoꝑlaþan ·
eoꞃoꞃþꞃotan · biꞃceoppyꞃt pyꞃe ꞇo ðꞃence.

Þiþ þon þe mōn þꞃeȝe atoꞃ · ȝenim þa haꞃan hunan
ȝepyꞃc micelne bꞃæl ⁊ næðeꞃꞃpyꞃce cnua ꞇoȝæðeꞃe ⁊
ꞃꞃinȝ ꝥ ꞃeap ðo ꞃineſ þꞃie mel ūn ⁊ ꞃele ðꞃincan.
Þiþ næðꞃan ꞃliꞇe nīm peȝbꞃæban · ⁊ aȝꞃimonian · ⁊

fol. 42 b.

næðëeꞃ pyꞃt ꞃele ȝeȝnidene ūn ꞃine ðꞃincan · ⁊ þyꞃe
ꞃealꝼe oꝼ þām ilcum pyꞃtum · ⁊ nīm þa aȝꞃimonian

netherward part of meadow sweet, the netherward part
of "æferthe," the netherward part of cynoglosson, employ of all equal quantities, pound to dust, add thereto
the white of a hens egg, and honey, employ equal
quantities of the two, mingle with the dusts, clam *or
make it cling* on the cancer, put no water to it.

### xlv.

1. Drinks *or potions* and leechdoms against poison.
Pound in ale betony, marche, wormwood, fennel, radish;
administer *this* to drink. Against poison; put in holy
water betony and the small atterlothe, drink the water
and eat the worts. Against any poison; eat ere *the
danger cometh* radish and clote; no man may *then* do
thee a mischief with poison. Against any poison; boil
the netherward part of bishopwort and lupin, and the
netherward part of springwort, everthroat, and clote
in ale; give to drink frequently. If an adder strike
a man, or *for* whatever of that which cometh of shots,
wash the black snail in holy water, give *to the sick*
to drink. Again, rub waybroad thoroughly *fine*, drink
it in wine. For bite of snake, put so much of betony
as may weigh three peanies into three bowls full of
wine, give it *the man* to drink.

2. For bite of snake again; cinqfoil wrung and mingled with wine is good to drink. For bite of snake
again; celandine bruised, at night fasting, let *the man*
drink three bowls full. For adders wound, work euforbia, attorlothe, stemless carline, ammi, into a drink.

3. In case a man swallow poison, take then horehound, work up a mickle deal of it, and adderwort,
pound them together and wring the juice, pour thereon
three measures of wine and give this *to the poisoned
man* to drink. For hurt from snake; take waybroad,
and agrimony, and adderwort, administer them rubbed
*up* in wine to be drunk; and work *up* a salve of the

ȝepyꞃe anne hꞃinȝ ymb þone ꞃlite utan ne oꝼeꞃꞅtihð hit ꝼuꞃþoꞃ • ꞅ binð þa pyꞃte eꝼt oꝼeꞃ ꝥ dolh. Þiꞃ næðꞃan ꞃleȝe do oꝼ þinū eaꞃan ꝥ teoꞃo ꞽ ꞅmiꞃe mid ymb ꞽ ꞅinȝ þꞃiꞃa þæꞃ halȝan Scē Iohanneꞃ ȝebeð ꞽ ȝealdoꞃi.

From the legendary Assumptio scī Iohannis apostoli.

ðeuꞃ meuꞃ et pateꞃ et ꝼiliuꞃ et ꞅpiꞃituꞃ Sanctuꞃ. Cui ōmnia ꞃubiecta ꞅunt. Cui omniꞃ cꞃeatuꞃa be-Sꞃuit et omniꞃ poteꞃtaꞃ ꞃubiecta eSt et metuit et expaueꞃcit et dꞃaco ꝼuȝit et ꞅilit uꞃeꞃa et ꞃubeta illa que diciuꞃ ꞃana quieta toꞃꞃeꞃcit et ꞃcoꞃꞃiuS ex-

a phalangius Al.

tinȝuituꞃ et ꞃeȝuluꞃ uncituꞃ et ꞅpelauꞃ[a] nihil noxium oꞃeꞃatuꞃ et omnia uenenata et aðhuc ꞃeꞃocioꞃa ꞃeꞃen-tia[1] et animalia noxia te ueꞃentuꞃ[2] et omneꞃ aðueꞃꞃe Saluti[3] humane ꞃadiceꞃ aꞃeꞃcunt. Tu domine extinȝue hōc uenenatum uꞃuꞃ extinȝue oꞃeꞃatjoneꞃ eiuꞃ moꞃti-ꝼeꞃaꞃ et uꞃeꞃ quaꞃ In ꞃe habet euacua et da In con-

fol. 43 a.

ꞅꞃectu tuo ōmnibuꞃ quoꞃ tu cꞃeaꞃtj • oculoꞃ ut uiðeant auꞃeꞃ ut auðiant coꞃ ut maȝnituðinem tuãm Intelle-ȝant •[4] et cum hōc dixiꞃꞃet totum ꞅemet jꞃꞅum ꞅiȝno cꞃuciꞃ aꞃmauit et bibit totum quod eꞃat In calice•peꞃ ꞃiȝnum Sancte cꞃuciꞃ • et peꞃ te xꞃe ihū et[5]ðeo ꞅūmmo patꞃe uuiS ꞅaluatoꞃ mundi In unitate ꞅpiꞃituꞃ Sancti peꞃ omnia Sæcula Sæculoꞃum amen ;

Þiꞃ ꝼleoȝendum atꞃe ꞽ ælcum æteꞃinum ꞅpile • on ꝼꞃuȝedæȝe aꞃꞃeꞃ Luteꞃan þe ꞅie ȝemolcen oꝼ aneꞃ bleoꞃ nytne oððe hinde • ꞽ ne ꞅie ꞃiþ pætꞃe ȝemenȝed • aꞃinȝ oꝼeꞃ niȝon ꞅiþūm letania • ꞽ niȝon ꞃiþum pateꞃ noꞃteꞃ • ꞽ niȝon ꞅiþum þiꞃ ȝealdoꞃ • Acꞃæ • æꞃcꞃæ • æꞃnem • naðꞃe • æꞃcuna hel • æꞃnem • niþæꞃn • æꞃi • aꞃan • buiꞃꞃie • aðcꞃiice • æꞃnem • meoðꞃe • æꞃnem • ꞃcþeꞃn • æꞃnem • allū • honoꞃ • ucuꞃ • iðaꞃ • aðceꞃt • cunolaꞃi • paticamo • helæ • icaꞃ xꞃita • hæle • tobæꞃt teꞃa • ꝼueh • cui • ꞃobateꞃ • plana • uih • ꝥ deah to

---

[1] ꞃeꞃentꞃe, MS.
[2] teuebantuꞃ, MS.
[3] aðueꞃꞃe Salutiꞃ, MSS.

[1] -ȝunt, MS.
[5] Supply cum. This doxology is an addition, not in the legend.

same worts, and then take agrimony, form a ring around the incision on the outside, *the mischief* will proceed no further, and bind the wort also over the sore. For stroke of viper, remove from thine ears the wax and smear around therewith, and say thrice the prayer of Saint John.

4. Dominus meus et pater et filius et spiritus sanctus; cui omnia subiecta sunt; cui omnis creatura deservit et omnis potestas subiecta est et metuit et expavescit; et draco fugit, et silet vipera, et rubeta illa quæ dicitur rana quieta torpescit, et scorpius extinguitur et regulus *the basilisc* vincitur et σπήλαιος[a] nihil noxium operatur, et omnia venenata et adhuc ferociora, repentia et animalia noxia, te verentur; et omnes adversæ saluti humanæ radices arescunt; tu, domine, extingue hoc venenatum virus, extingue operationes eius mortiferas, et vires, quas in se habet, evacua, et da in conspectu tuo omnibus quos tu creasti, oculos ut videant, aures ut audiant, cor ut magnitudinem tuam intelligant. Et cum hoc dixisset, totum semet ipsum signo crucis armavit, et bibit totum quod erat in calice : per signum sanctæ crucis, et per te Christe Iesu, *qui cum* domino summo patre vivis, salvator mundi, in unitate Spiritus Sancti, per omnia secula seculorum. Amen.

[a] The tarantula lies hid in a hole watching for prey.

5. For flying venom and every venomous swelling, on a Friday churn butter, which has been milked from a neat or hind *all* of one colour ; and let it not be mingled with water, sing over it nine times a litany, and nine times the Pater noster, and nine times this incantation. *The charm is said in the table of contents to be Scottish, that is Gaelic,*[1] *but the words themselves seem to belong to no known language.* That is valid

---

[1] Or Gadhelic, or Irish. An early instance of the mention of Ireland, | as not Scotland, occurs in Ælfrics Homilies, vol. ii. p. 346.

ꞃeleꞅm ⁊ hupu co ꝺeopum ꝺolᵹum. Sume an ꞃoꝝꝺ ꝝiꝺ
nꝏꝺꞃan luce kꝏpaꝺ co eꝥeꝥenne ꝥ iꞅ ꞃaul ne mꝏᵹ hīm
ꝺeꞃian. Ꝥiꝺ nꝏꝺꞃan ꝝlice ᵹiꝼ he beᵹec ⁊ yc ꝡiꝺe ꞅio
ꝥe eymꝺ oꝼ neoꞃxna ꞃonᵹe ne ꝺeꞃeꝺ him nan acceꞃ·

fol. 43 b.
ꝥonne eꝥaꝥ ꞃe ꝝe ꝥaꞃ boc ꝝꞃac ꝥ luo ꝝꝏꝥe coꞃ
beᵹece.

Ᵹiꝼ hꝝa ꝺꞃince ꝝyꞃm on ꝝꝏceꞃe ōꝼ ꞅmꝺe ꞅceap ꞃaꝺe
ꝺꞃince hac ꝥ ꞃeeaꝥeꞅ bloꝺ.    ᵹiꝼ mon ꞅie ꝝyꞃcum ꞃoꞃ-
boꞃen ꞃele ꞅꝥꞃinᵹꝝyꞃc ꝥ he ece ⁊ haliᵹ ꝝꝏceꞃ ꞃupe.
Ꝥꝝ ꝥon ꝥe mon ꞅie ꞃoꞃboꞃen· ᵹiꝼ he hꝏꝥ on lim
ꞅeyccꝑꝼe peax· ꝥa ꞅmalan accoꞃlaꝺan oꝺꝺe ōn apylꝺum
ꝏlaꝺ ꝺꞃince ne mꝏᵹ hine ꝝyꞃcum ꞃoꞃbeꞃan.


## .XLVI.

Ᵹiꝼ ana ꝝyꞃm on men peaxe· ꞅmꝑꞃe mꝺ ꝥꝏꞃe blacan
ꞃealꝼe ᵹiꝼ he uc ꝥuꝥh ece ⁊ ꝥyꝥel ᵹeꝥyꞃee· ᵹenīm
hunꝑᵹeꞅ ꝺꞃopan ꝺꞃype on ꝥꝏc ꝥyꝥel· haꝼa ꝥonne ᵹe-
bꞃocen ᵹlꝏꞃ ᵹeapa ᵹeᵹꞃunꝺen ꞅeeaꝺ on ꝥ ꝥyꝥel ꝥonne
ꞃona ꞅꝝa he ꝥꝏꞃ onbꝑꞃᵹꝺ ꝥonne ꞅꝥilc he. Sealꝼ ꝝiꝺ
anaꝝyꞃme· ꝥuꞅ mōn ꞃeeal ꝝyꞃeean.    ᵹenīm quinque-
ꞃolian ꝥ iꞅ ꝼiꝼleaꝼe· ꞃuꝺan ꝝyl on buceꞃan ᵹeꞅꝥec mꝺ
hunꝑᵹe.

Ꝺꞃene quinqueꞃoliam ꝥ iꞅ ꝼiꝼleaꝼe ꞃele ōn ealaꝺ ꝺꞃinean ꝥꞃicꝑᵹ nihca.    Ꝺꞃene ꝝiꝺ ꝝon ꝥꝏꝺieeꞅ ꞅꝏꝺ ⁊ eauleꞅ
ᵹmꝺ ōn eala oꝥꝼe on ꝼīn ꝺꞃinee ꝝꝥ anaꝝyꞃme lanᵹe ⁊
ᵹelome oꝥ ꝥ ꞃel ꞅie.    Clam ꝝꝥ ꝥon ꝥa ꞃeaꝺan ciᵹelan
ᵹeenupa co ꝺuꞅce ᵹemenᵹ ꝝiꝺ ᵹꞃuc alꝥꝏꝺ eieel leᵹe on
fol. 44 a.
ꝥ ꝺolh ꝝyꞃe oꝥeꞃne ᵹiꝼ ꝥeaꞃꝼ ꞅie.

for every, even for deep wounds. Some teach us against bite of adder to speak one word, that is, Faul;[1] it may not hurt him. Against bite of snake, if *the man* procures and eateth rind, which cometh out of paradise, no venom will damage him. Then said he that wrote this book, that *the rind* was hard gotten.

6. If one drink a creeping thing in water, let him cut into a sheep instantly, let him drink the sheeps blood hot. If a man be "restrained" with worts,[2] give him springwort for him to eat, and let him sup up holy water. In case that a man be "withheld;" if he hath on him Scottish wax, *and* the small atterlothe; or let him drink it in boiled ale, he may not be "restrained" by worts.

### xlvi.

1. If Ons worm[a] grow in a man, smear with the black salve. If *the worm* eat through to the outside and make a hole, take a drop of honey, drop it on the hole, then have broken glass ready ground, shed it on the hole, then as soon as *the worm* tastes of this he will die. A salve against an Ons worm, thus shall a man work it: take cinquefoil, that is five leaved grass, and rue, boil *them* in butter, sweeten with honey.

2. A drink; administer in ale cinquefoil, that is five leaved grass, or *potentilla*, to drink for thirty nights. A drink for that; rub down into ale or into wine seed of radish and of colewort, let *the man* drink that long and frequently against Ons worm, till that *his case* be bettered. A plaster for the same: pound to dust a red tile *or brick*, mingle with groats, bake a cake, lay it on the wound; work another *plaster* if need be.

---

[1] Cf. "Duo," to drive away scorpions, Plinius, lib. xxviii. 5.

[2] From hæmebliñg. See ropbepian in Glossary.

## . XLVII.

Læcedomaſ pið þeopaðlum · æpepınð · æſpan þınð ·
elm þınð · epıcþınð · ſıo mıcle poþþıg netle moþopeaþð ·
peþmoð · hınðhıoloðe · beſopeaða þa þınða ealle utan ⁊
ᵹecnua ſpıȝe pyl toſomne · ðo ealþa empela oſ ᵹeot
mıð hluttpe ealoþ læt ſtanðan þone ðpenc nıhtepne
on ſate æþ mon hıne ðpıncan pılle · ðpınce on mop-
ᵹenne ſcene ſulne þıȝeſ ðpenceſ · to mıððeſ meþᵹeneſ
ſtanðe eaſt peaþð ⁊ bebeoðe hıne ᵹoðe ᵹeoþınlıce ⁊ hıne
ᵹepemᵹe cyþþe hıne ſunᵹonᵹeſ ymb æſteþ þam ðpence
ᵹanᵹe ſıþþan ⁊ ſtanðe ſume hpıle æþ he hıne þeſte
ᵹeote ſpa mıcel on ſpa he þæþ oſ ðo · ðpınce þyſne
ðpenc mᵹon nıht ⁊ þıeᵹe ſpılene mete ſpa he pılle.
ðpenc pıþ þeopaðle · ſunð[1] omþþan ymb ðelſ ſınᵹ þþıþa
pateþ nþı · bþeð up þonne þu cpeþe ſet[2] lıbeþa noſ a
malo · ᵹenım þreþe ſıſ ſnæða ⁊ ſeoſon pıþoþı coþn
ᵹecnua toᵹæðeþe ⁊ þonne þu þ̄ pyþce ſınᵹ .XII. ſıþum
þone ſealm · mıſeþeþe meı ðeuſ · ⁊ ᵹloþıa In excelſıſ
ðeo · ⁊ pateþ noſteþ · oſᵹeot þonne mıð pıne þonne ðæᵹ
⁊ nıht ſeaðe[3] ðpınce þonne þone ðpenc ⁊ beþþeoð ðe
peaþıne.    ᵹenım þonne hınð hıoloþan ane[4] oſᵹeot mıð
pæteþe ðpınce oþþe möþᵹne ſcene ſulne þonne oþþe
ſıþe ſeoſon ſnæða ⁊ nᵹon pıþoþcoþn · þþıððan ſıþe
nᵹon ſnæða ⁊ XI. pıþoþcoþn. ðþíne ſıþþan ſpıðne ðpenc
ſeþe pılle up yþnan ⁊ oſ ðune · læt þonne bloð unðeþ
ancleoþ.

---

[1] Read ſupe ?
[2] That is, feð ; the MSS. usually
ſet.

[3] At morning twilight.
[4] Some words are here, it seems,
omitted.

### xlvii.

1. Leechdoms for "dry" diseases; a ash rind, aspen rind, elm rind, quickbeam rind, the netherward part of the mickle highway nettle, wormwood, bindheal, *that is, water agrimony,* empurple all the rinds on the outside, and pound them thoroughly, boil them together, apply equal quantities of all, souse them with clear ale, then let the drink stand for the space of a night in a vessel, before a man shall choose to drink it. Let him in the morning drink a cup full of this drink; in the middle of the morning hours,[1] let him stand towards the east, let him address himself to God earnestly, and let him sign himself with the sign of the cross, let him *also* turn himself about as the sun goeth *from east to south and west;* after the drink let him next go and stand some while ere he repose himself; let him pour as much *liquid into the vessel* as he removes from it: let him drink this potion for nine nights and eat what meat he will. A drink for the "dry" disease; delve about sour ompre, *that is, sorrel dock,* sing thrice the Pater noster, jerk it up, then while thou sayest sed libera nos a malo, take five slices of it and seven pepper corns, bray them together, and while thou be working it, sing twelve times the psalm Miserere mei, deus, and Gloria in excelsis deo, and the Pater noster, then pour *the stuff* all over with wine, when day and night divide, then drink the dose and wrap thyself up warm. Then take hindheal alone, souse it with water, drink the next morning a cup full, then the next time seven slices and nine pepper corns, the third time nine slices and eleven pepper corns; afterwards drink a strong potion which will run up and adown;[2] then let blood below *the* ancle.

---

[1] This should be read as beginning the morning at dawn, and ending it at undern, our nine o'clock. The middle will be about seven on the average.

[2] Purgative and emetic.

ðrenc ƿiþ þeoþable mme healf puðu ꝼ bulentꝼan þa
ſmalan · þunoꝛ ꝛyꝛt · puðuꝛeaxan moþoꝛeaꝛið · ƿealꝼyꝛt
moþoꝛeaꝛiðe ᵹecnua þonne ealle toꝛomne ꝛyꝛee hīm to
ðꝛence ðo on ꝛylſe ealo · oþþe on beoꝛ læt ſtanðan
mhteꝛne · ðꝛince þonne ſꝛilene nᵹon moꝛᵹenaſ · nme
þy ceoþan moꝛᵹne þæꝛ ðꝛinceſ tꝛa bleða ꝼulle · beꝛylle
ōn ane ꝼ þa ꝛyꝛta ſien mið aꝛeoh þuꝛh claþ aꝛete
ū̄ꝛ þꝛoꝛ hæ eoꝛþan hꝛman ne mæᵹe oþ þ hæ mōn
ðꝛincan mæᵹe ; [1] þonne þu hæ [2] ᵹeðꝛuncen hæbbe be-
ꝛꝛeoh þe ꝛeaꝛme liᵹe on þa ſiðan þe he þonne ᵹecenᵹe
ſie · ᵹiꝼ he [3] on þam innoþe biꝛð þonne aðꝛiꝛð hine þeſ
ðꝛinc ū̄t. Sealꝼ ƿiþ þeoꝛe nīm ᵹaꝛleāc ꝼ ᵹꝛeate ꝛyꝛt ·
ꝛeꝛmoð leaðe [4] netlan eið ᵹecnua ſmale ꝼ hioꝛōt ſmeꝛu
ᵹemanᵹ þ hæ ſie ſꝛilc ſꝛa ðah ðo þonne ōn lncenne
cla ð ꝛyꝛime þonne ᵹehꝛæþeꝛi ᵹe þ he ᵹe þa ꝛealꝼe to
ꝼyꝛe þonne þu hæ ſmyꝛian ƿille þꝛoꝛ ſio aðl ſie ꝼylᵹe
hīm mið þyꝛꝛe ſealꝼe ꝼ mið þyꝛ [5] ðꝛence. ðꝛenc ƿiþ
þeoþable ðꝛiᵹe ꝛeꝛmoð · ꝛeðic ƿealꝛyꝛt ealꝛa þꝛeoꝛa
em ꝛela ðo on ealu ᵹnið ƿel læce æt æꝛeꝼtan ſtanðan
þꝛeo niht æꝛi þon he hine ðꝛince · ꝼ ꝛiþþan he hine
ðꝛince ymb ſeoꝼon niht ꝛoꝛlæce bloð unðeꝛ þam ancleoꝛe ðꝛince ꝼoꝛþ þone ðꝛenc ꝼeoꝛeꝛtyne niht · læte
þonne eꝼt bloð unðeꝛ þam oþꝛan ancleoꝛe. ðꝛince
ealleſ þone ðꝛenc þꝛitiᵹ nihta ōn unðeꝛn ᵹoðe bleðe
ꝼulle oþꝛe þonne þu ꝛeſtan ƿille. Þiþ þeoꝛꝛyꝛme ōn
ꝼet nim þa ꝛeaðan netlan ᵹecnua ðo ꝛꝛeteꝛ to leᵹe ōn
hatne ſtan læt æꝼꝛeoꝛan binð on þone ꝛōt nealhteꝛne.
Eꝼt ꝛealꝼ ætan ᵹecnua leᵹe ōn. Þiþ þeoꝛe on ꝼet
ᵹeᵹnið ƿealꝛyꝛt ōn ᵹeſꝛet ƿin · ꝼ hꝛiteruðu ꝼ ꝛiꝛoꝛi
ðꝛince þ.

---

[1] mæᵹe, MS.
[2] hæ, MS.
[3] The only antecedent aðl ought
to be followed by feminine pronouns.

[1] This word seems corrupt ; perhaps ꝛeaðe ; red nettle, a plant
of it. ꝛee Line 26
[3] þyꝛ, MS., understand as þyꝛum.

2. A drink against the "dry" disease; take field balm[a] and the small bulentse, thunderwort,[b] the nether part of woodwax, the netherward part of wallwort, then pound all together, work it for him (*the patient*) for a drink, put it into foreign ale or beer, let it stand for the space of a night, then let him drink such *drink* for nine mornings, take on the tenth morning two cups full of the drink, boil them both in one, and let the worts be therewith, strain through a cloth, set it up where it may not touch the earth, till that a man may drink it; when thou have drunken it, wrap thee up warm; lie on the side to which the *pain* is incident, if it be in the inwards, then this drink will drive it out. A salve against the "dry" disease; take garlic and great wort, wormwood, a plant of nettle, pound small, and along with it harts grease, that it may be such as dough is, place it then on a linen cloth, then warm both the body and the salve at the fire; when thou wilt smear *the body or the spot* where the disease may be, follow up *the patient* with this salve and with this drink. A drink for the "dry" disease; dry wormwood, radish, wallwort,[c] of all these equal quantities, put into ale, rub *the herbs down* well, *the man* should have *the liquid* stand at first for three nights before he drink it, and subsequently let him drink it for about seven nights, let him let blood under the ancle, let him drink the drink straight on for fourteen nights; let him next let blood under the other ancle. Drink the dose for thirty nights in all, a good cup full at nine A.M. or when thou wilt go to bed. For a "dry" worm in the foot; take the red nettle, pound it, add water to it, lay it on a hot stone, make it froth, bind it on the foot for the space of a night. Again, a salve; pound oats, lay on. For the "dry" rot in the foot, triturate wallwort into sweetened wine, and mastic and pepper; let him drink that.

Book I.
Ch. xlvii.
[a] *Calamintha nepeta.*
[b] *Sempervivum tectorum.*

[c] *Sambucus ebulus.*

Oxa hæþe þýne lacedom · ᵹenime pealpýpt ꝫ cluf-
þunᵹ ꝫ eneopholen ꝫ eƿelaptan ꝫ camecon ꝫ tunᵹilpm-
pýpt · VIIII. bpune bipceop pýpt · ꝫ attoplaþan ꝫ peade
netlan · ꝫ peade hopan ·ꝫ pepmoð ꝫ ᵹeappan · ꝫ hunan
ꝫ dolᵹpunan · ꝫ dpeopᵹe dpoftlan do calle þap pýpta
on pylipe ealo ꝫ dpince þonne niᵹon daᵹaf ꝫ blod læte.
Þiþ þeop pæpce pýpe to dpence alexandpe · finfulle
pepmoð · tpa eneopholen · paluian · fapne · pealmope ·
lupeftice · pepep puᵹe · mepce · coft · ᵹapleñc · æpc-
þpotu · betonice · bifceop pýpt · on tpybpopnũm ealað
ᵹepýpce þet mid huniᵹe dpine niᵹon mopᵹenaf nanne
oþepne pætan dpine æptep fpiþne dpene ꝫ læt blod
oxa læþde þifne lacedom. Þiþ þeope eneopholen mþe-
peapð · acumba · epið · ꝫ bpune pýpt ealpa empela do
on pilife ealu · bepyl oþ þpiddan dæl ꝫ dpince þa hpile
þa he þupfe · ꝫ þæp fio adl ᵹefitte pylᵹe him fimle
mid tiᵹe hopne oþ þ hal fie.

[1] Þiþ þam pýp mumþe innan eᵹlað þam men · ᵹenim
peᵹbpædan ᵹetpipula ꝫ þ feap pele on euclepe fupan
ꝫ þa pýpt pelfe fpa ᵹeenupade leᵹe on þone napolan.
Þið cilba innoþep pýpmium · ᵹenim ᵹpene mintan ænne
ᵹelm ᵹedo on ppiy pepepaf pætepef peoð oþ þpiddan dæl
apeoh þonne pele dpincan. Þið cilba innoþ fape dpeopᵹe
dpoftle · ꝫ cymen ᵹenim ᵹebeat ᵹemenᵹe þiþ pætep
leᵹe opep ðone napolan fona bið hal. Við pýpmum þe
innan eᵹlað · ᵹeealdep heoptep hopnep ahfan oððe duft

3. Oxa taught *us* this leechdom: take wallwort, and
clofing, and kneeholn, and everlasting, and cammock,[1]
and white hellebore, in the proportion of nine to one,
brownwort, bishopwort, and atterlothe, and red nettle,
and red hove, and wormwood, and yarrow, and *hore-*
hound, and pellitory, and pennyroyal, put all these worts
into foreign ale, and then let *the man* drink for nine
days and let blood. For the "dry" pain; make into a
drink, alexanders, sedum, wormwood, *the* two kneeholns,[2]
sage, savine, carrot, lovage, feverfue, marche, costmary,
garlic, ashthroat, betony, bishopwort, work them up
into double brewed ale, sweeten with honey, drink
for nine mornings no other liquid; drink afterwards a
strong potion, and let blood. Oxa taught this leechdom. Against "dry" rot; put into foreign ale, the
netherward *part of* kneeholn, tow,[3] matricaria (?), and
brownwort, of all equal quantities; boil down to one
third part, and let *the patient* drink while he may
require it; and where the disease has settled, follow
him up ever with the drawing horn[4] till the place
be hole.

### xlviii.

Against the worms which ail men within; take
waybroad, triturate it, and give the juice in a spoon
to sup, and lay the wort itself, so pounded, on the
navel. Against worms of the inwards of children;
take green mint, a handful of it, put it into three
sextariuses of water, seethe it down to one third part,
strain, then give to drink. For inward sore of children take pennyroyal and cummin, beat them up,
mingle them with water, lay them over the navel, soon
it will be whole. Against worms which ail *a man*

---

[1] *Peucedanum officinale.*

[2] Only *Ruscus aculeatus* grows
wild in England. There are three
others.

[3] Understand as reduced to ashes.
See note on I. xxxiii. 1.

[4] Cupping glass.

ᵹemenᵹ ƿið huniᵹ ᵹeſmiꞃe inið þone bæcþeaꞃm ⁊ þone naꞃolan inið þy þonne ꝼeallað hie. ¹ Ƿið ƿyꞃmum þe innan eᵹlað ᵹetꞃiꞃolað² coſt to duſte · ᵹedo ᵹodne dæl in hat pæteꞃ ſele dꞃincan.

fol. 46 b.

Marcellus, 374, c.

Marcellus, 374, a.

³Ƿiþ ƿyꞃmum eꝼt ᵹate toꞃð heaꞃð ⁊ ſpiðe dꞃuᵹe ᵹemenᵹ ⁊ ᵹeᵹniið ƿiþ huniᵹ ſele dꞃincan þæt adꞃiꝼþ hie apeᵹ. Ƿið ƿyꞃmum þe innan eᵹlað eꝼt ꞃedic ſeoð on pætꞃe oþ ſone þꞃiððan dæl menᵹe ƿiþ ƿin ſele dꞃincan. Eꝼt ƿiþ þon ᵹate ᵹeallan ᵹedo on pulle leᵹe ⁊ bind on þone naꞃolan. Ƿiþ þon ilean · mintan ꞃel ᵹetꞃiꞃulaðe menᵹ ƿiþ huniᵹ ƿyꞃc to lytlum clipene læt ꞃoꞃſpelᵹan. Eꝼt ele ⁊ eceðeꞃ em micel ᵹemenᵹeð ſele þꞃy daᵹaꞃ dꞃincan. Eꝼt coꞃoꞃþꞃote · meꞃce · betonice · neꝼte · ᵹiðcoꞃn pyl on pine. Ƿiþ ƿyꞃmum þe innan eᵹlað ƿyꞃtðꞃene oꝼ oꞃtꞃan · oꝼ ꝼelðmoꞃan ſele dꞃincan · Sealꝼ · ete celeþonian · bꞃunepyꞃt apylle on moꞃoðe · do þonne ſeꞃp teaꞃo ⁊ ſpeꝼl to ſmiꞃe mið.

### .XLVIIII.

Aukapis,

Ƿiþ þam ſmalan pyꞃme. Ƿiþepinðan tꞃiᵹ ꞃoꞃꞃeaꞃð · ⁊ þa ꝼealꞃan doccan næꞃ ſa ꞃeaðan · ⁊ þiꞃ ᵹꞃeate ꞃcalt ᵹebeaten toᵹæðeꞃe ſpiðe ſmale ⁊ lytel buteꞃan.

### .L.

fol. 47 a.

Ƿiþ hoꞃð ƿyꞃmum ⁊ deaꞃ ƿyꞃmum · ᵹenim doccan oððe clatan ſa þe ſpꞃiman polðe ſa ƿyꞃttꞃuman menᵹ ƿið ꝼletan ⁊ ƿið ꞃealt læt ſtanðan þꞃeo niht ⁊ þy ꝼeoꞃþan daᵹe ſmiꞃe inið þa ꞃaꞃan ſtoꞃa.

---

¹ Plinius Valerianus, ut infra.
² Read ᵹetꞃiꞃola.
³ Plinius Valerianus, fol. 41, c.

within; mingle with honey, ashes or dust of burnt harts horn, smear therewith the fundament and the navel, then they fall *away.* For worms which ail within; triturate costmary to dust, put a good deal into hot water, give to drink.

2. For worms again; mingle and rub up with honey a hard and very dry goats tord, administer it to be drunk, that will drive them away. Against worms which ail *a man* within, again; seethe in water radish to the third part, mingle with wine, give to drink. Again for that; put goats gall on wool, lay and bind it on the navel. For that ilk; mingle with honey, mint well triturated, work it into a little bolus, make him swallow it. Again, give for three days to drink oil and of vinegar an equal quantity. Again, everthroat.[1] marche, betony, nepeta, githcorn; boil *them* in wine: For worms which are troublesome within; give to drink a wort drink of "ontre" and of parsnip. A salve; let him eat celandine; let him boil brownwort in inspissated wine, then add thereto ship tar and sulfur; smear therewith.

### xlix.

For the small worm; the forepart of a twig of withewind, and the fallow dock,[a] not the red one, and this coarse salt beaten together very small and a little butter.

### l.

1. For hand worms[2] and dew worms; take dock or clote, such as would swim, mingle the roots with cream and with salt, let it stand for three nights, and on the fourth day smear therewith the sore places.

---

[1] *Carlinā acaulis.*

[2] Some Gl. make gad flies the hand worms; are they rather here Κειρία = tœniœ ? *þe pe worms,* worms like ribands or tapes; read as χειρίας.

ȝɪꝼ ƿyꞃm hanð ete · ȝenɪm meꞃſe mꞏeaꞃ ȝeallan ꞇ
ꞃeaðe neꞇlan ꞇ ꞃeaðe ðoccan ꞇ ſmæle cliꝼan ꝥyl on cu
buꞇeꞃan þonne ſio ꞃealꝼ ȝeſoðen ſie ꞃuꞃꝥum nim þonne
ꞃealꞇeꞃ þꞃy men ſceað ón hꞃeꞃ ꞇoſomne · ꞇ ſmiꞃe mið·
lyþꞃe mið ſapan ymb nihꞇ ſmiꞃe mið. Ƿiþ ðeappyꞃme
ſꞇæppe on haꞇ col cele mið ꞃꞅꞇꞃe ſꞇæppe ón ſꞃa haꞇ
ſꞃa he haꞇoſꞇ mæȝe. Ƿɪð ðeappyꞃme · ſume nnnað
ꞃeaꞃm cꞃeað monneſ þynne bınðað neahꞇeꞃne ón·
ſume ſpıneſ lunȝenne ꞃeaꞃme. Ƿɪþ honð ƿyꞃme ɴim
ſcꞃꞇeaꞃo · ꞇ ſpeꝼl ꞇ pıpoꞃ · ꞇ hꞃɪꞇ ꞃealꞇ menȝ ꞇoSomne
ſmıꞃe mið. Ƿeax ꞃealꝼ ƿɪþ ƿyꞃme · ƿeax ꞃealꝼ · buꞇeꞃe
pıpoꞃ hꝼɪꞇ ꞃealꞇ menȝ ꞇoſomne ſmıꞃe mið.

## .LI.

Ƿɪþ ƿyꞃmum¹ þe manneſ ꝼlæꞃe eꞇað ꝥꝼm ȝeallan
þone ꝼaȝan cnua on nꞃe ealo æꞃ þon hɪꞇ aꞃꞃen ꞃe
ꞃele ꝥ oꝼeꞃ ꝼyllo ðꞃıncan þꞃeo nihꞇ. Eꝼꞇ ȝenɪm ȝꞃunðe
ſꞃelȝean þe ón eoꞃþan ꞃeaxeþ ꞇ ſceaꞃeꞃ ſmeꞃu menȝ
ꞇoſomne ȝehce ꞃela leȝe ón. Eꝼꞇ ȝenɪm bꞃen eaꞃ
beꝼenȝ leȝe ón ſꞃa haꞇ ꞇ haꞇ pæꞇeꞃ laꝼa ón. Ƿɪþ
ꝼlæꞃe ƿyꞃmum ȝenɪm monneſ ſuꞃan Ꞹa leaꝼ ȝeꞃel
ꞇoȝæðꞃe ȝebꞃæð on ȝꞃeꞃſe ȝeenua þonne leȝe on ſꞃa
þu haꞇoſꞇ mæȝe aꞃꞃeꝼnan.

## .LII.

Ƿɪþ luſum aeꞃmð ꞇ hꞃon ꞃeꞃmoð ȝeenua ón ealu
ꞃele ðꞃıncan. Uɪð luſum eꝼɪc ꞃeolꝼoꞃ ꞇ ealð buꞇeꞃe
an penıȝ ꞃeolꝼꞃeſ · ꞇ cu penıȝ ꝼæȝe buꞇeꞃan menȝ
on aꞃꞃæꞇ eal ꞇoSomne.

fol. 47 b.

¹ Φθειρίασις ?

2. If a worm eat the hand; take marsh maregall[a] and red nettle, and red dock, and *the* small bur, boil in cows butter; when the salve is sodden, then further take of salt three parts, shed thereupon, shake together, and smear therewith; lather with soap, about night *time* smear therewith. Against a dew worm; let *the man* step upon a hot coal, let him cool *the foot* with water; let him step upon it as hot as he hottest may. For a dew worm, some take warm thin ordure of man, they bind it on for the space of a night; some *take* a swines lung warm. Against a hand worm; take ship tar, and sulfur, and pepper, and white salt, mingle them together, smear therewith. A wax salve against a worm; a wax salve; butter, pepper, white salt, mingle *them* together, smear therewith.

Book I.
Ch. 1.
[a] *Gentiana pneumonanthe*.

## li.

Against worms which eat a mans flesh; pound into new ale, before it be strained, the party coloured ram gall,[1] give the running over to drink for three nights. Again, take groundsel which waxeth on the earth, and sheeps grease, mingle *them* together, alike much *in quantity*, lay on. Again, take an ear of beer *or barley*, singe it, lay it on so hot, and hot water, leave it on. Against flesh worms; take mans sorrel, boil the leaves together, spread them out on the grass, then pound them, lay them on, as thou hottest may endure *them*.

## lii.

Against lice; pound in ale oak rind and a little wormwood, give *to the lousy one* to drink. Against lice; quicksilver and old butter; one pennyweight of *quick*silver and two of butter; mingle all together in a brazen vessel.

---

[1] *Menyanthes trifoliata.*

### .LIII.

Við smeʒa pyrme nipe cyre ⁊ beobread ⁊ hrætenne hlaf ete. Eft monney heafod ban bærn to ahran do mid pipan on.

### .LIIII.

Wið pyrmæðum lice ⁊ epelbehtum ꞅepinde duꞅt · æꞅepinde duꞅt · ellen pinde duꞅt on norþan neoþan þam treope · colonan moran duꞅt · doccan moran duꞅt · pyrm ꞅemeluper duꞅt pipores duꞅt ꞅiʒlan duꞅt · spexley duꞅt · ele · ⁊ hopres smeru to pore ⁊ rcipteapoꞅ læꞅt · þyrra ealra emxela ⁊ þara duꞅta ealra emxela ʒemenʒ eal ceald toromne þ hit xram þam poꞅum eal pel ꞅmitende ꞅmire mid on niht ⁊ on morʒen alethe.

### .LV.

Wið arleʒenum lice · bpom · xeltere · ʒearre · hore · pyl on burepan ⁊ on hun[1] ꞅmire mid.

### .LVI.

Wyrc bæþ pið arleʒenum lice · ʒeniim þ micle xearn morþopeard · ⁊ elm pinde ʒrene ʒecnua toromne ⁊ medðroꞅua do to þætan ʒnid ꞅpiðe toromne leʒe ūn lanʒe hpile oþ þ he pearm ꞅie oþþe onꞅtæppe.

Wið arleʒenum lice realx colone ꞅpiðe ʒeꞅoden ⁊ niðepeard homorreʒ ⁊ cald ꞅpic cnua eal toromne pyrm þyph clað to xyre ꞅmire mid · rceappa þonne ꞅmle ymb · VII. niht rete horn on þa openan rceappan

---

### liii.

Against a boring worm ; let *the man* eat new cheese and beebread and wheaten loaf. Again, burn to ashes a mans head bone *or skull*, put it on with a pipe.

### liv.

For a wormeaten and mortified body ; dust of oak rind, dust of ash rind, dust of elder rind, taken on the north of the tree, and the nether part, warm, dust of the root of helenium, dust of root of dock, dust of acorn meal, peppers dust, dust of rye, sulfurs dust, oil, and horses grease for a liquid, and the least proportion of ship tar, of all these equal quantities, and of all the dusts equally much ; mingle all cold together, so that by means of the liquids may be all well smudging, *or thoroughly uncluous*, smear therewith at night, and in the morning lather.

### lv.

For slain, *that is, stricken*, body, broom, fel terræ,[a] yarrow, hove, boil *these* in butter and in honey, smear therewith.

[a] *Erythræa centaureum.*

### lvi.

1. Work a fomentation for a stricken body ; take the mickle fern,[b] the netherward part, and elm rind green, pound them together, and for a liquor add mead dregs, rub them up thoroughly together, lay on for a long while, till that *the sufferer* be warm or walk about.

[b] *Aspidium filix.*

2. For a stricken body, a salve ; helenium thoroughly sodden, and the netherward part of hammersedge, and old lard, pound all together, warm through a cloth at the fire, smear therewith ; then scarify continually about the bruise for seven nights, set a horn [1] upon

---

[1] A cupping horn.

fol. 48 b.

fmɪɾe mɪð þæɾe blacan ɾealɾe ɾƿa nɪht ɾƿa tɾa ɾƿa þeaɾɾ ɾɪe ⁊ hy opene ɾynð.

## .LVII.

Συκῆ.

Þɪþ ɾɪce ðɾene ⁊ ɾealɾ· pyɾm ɾyɾt ɾylle on meolce ⁊ ðɾɪnce. Sealɾ cnua ȝlæɾ to ðuɾte ðo hunɪȝeɾ teaɾɪ ōn lacnu þ ðolȝ mɪð.

## .LVIII.

To penɾealɾe ⁊ ɾen bylūm· pyɾɪc hɪe ōɾ moþopeaɾɪðɾe netlan ⁊ ōɾ hemlɪce ⁊ oɾ þæɾe cluɾɪhtan penpyɾte ⁊ oɾ þæɾe fmalan moɾɾyɾte pyl ealle ɾeoɾeɾ ōn buteɾan ⁊ ōn ɾceaɾeɾ fmeɾɾe oþþ ȝenoh ɾɪe ȝecnua eɾt þa ɪlcan pyɾta on þæɾe ɾealɾe ⁊ ɾcɪp teaɾɪo ⁊ ȝaɾɪleāc ⁊ cɾoɾleāc ⁊ ɾecȝleāc ⁊ ɾealt menȝ pel ðo on cla̋ pyɾm to ɾyɾe fɾɪðe¹ fmɪɾe mɪð.

Þenɾealɾ ōntɾe ceɾɾan ɾeaðc netlan peɾɪnoð· tɾa penpyɾta· ellen ɾɪnðe· peȝbɾæðe· fuɾɪan· bɪɾceop pyɾt· bulot mðeɾeaɾð· fmeɾe pyɾt· ɾealt· ɾcɪpteaɾɪo· ⁊ ɾceaɾen fmeɾa. Þɪþ pen byle xɪm cɾoɾleāc· ontɾe· colone· cluɾehte penpyɾt· ȝecnua ealle þa pɾɾɪta fɾɪþe pel leȝe ōn.

Þenɾealɾ hɪoɾoteɾ meaɾɪh· ɪɾɪȝ teaɾɪo ⁊ ȝebeaten pɪɾoɾ ⁊ fcɪp teaɾɪo.

²[Þɪþ þa blacan bleȝene fýle þam men etan tɾeȝen cɾoɾɾaɾ oððe þɪý oɾ þæɾe pýɾte þe man on þɾeo pɪɾan hateð mýxenɾlante.]

fol. 49 a.

---

¹ fɾɪð, MS.

In the margin, in a different and later hand.

the open scarifications, smear with the black salve, be it for a night, be it for two, as need be, and as they be open.

### lvii.

For the disease called fig, a drink and a salve; let him boil wormwort in milk and drink it. A salve; pound glass to dust, add a drop of honey, leech the wound therewith.

### lviii.

1. For a wen salve and for wen boils; work *the salve* of the netherward part of nettle and of hemlock, and of the wenwort which has cloves *or bulbed roots,*[a] and of the small moorwort, boil all four in butter and in sheeps grease till there be enough, pound again the same worts in the salve, and ship tar, and garlic, and cropleek, and sedgeleek,[b] and salt, mingle well, put on a cloth, warm thoroughly at the fire, smear therewith.

[a] Probably *Ranunculus ficaria.*

[b] *Allium schœnoprasum.*

2. A salve for wens; ontre, cress, red nettle, wormwood, *the* two wenworts, elder rind, waybroad, sorrel, bishopwort, the nether part of lulot, smearwort, salt, ship tar,[1] and sheeps grease. For a wen boil; take cropleek, ontre, helenium, the clove rooted wenwort, pound all the worts thoroughly well, lay *the stuff* on.

3. A wen salve; harts marrow, ivy tar, and beaten pepper, and ship tar.

4. [Against the black blain, give to the man to eat two bunches or three off the wort, which is called in three ways, *the* mixen plant.[2]]

---

[1] Pix navalis is occasionally prescribed by the medical authors, as Nic. Myreps, 481, c., in the Medicæ Artis Principes.

[2] *Atropa belladonna.*

### LVIIII.

[1] Þiþ lyft adle · nim ƿcene fulne feallendef þæteƿef
oþeƿne eleƿ · ꝺ hƿiteƿ ƿealtef ſpile ſpa mæȝe mid feo-
ƿeƿ finȝƿum ȝeniman · hƿeƿ toȝædeƿe oþ þ hit eall
on an ſie.  ꝺƿinc eall be dƿopan ƿeſt hƿile ſtinȝ finȝeƿ
on ciolan aſpiƿ[2] eft eall ꝺ ma ȝif þu mæȝe · þonne on
moƿȝen foƿlæt blod of eaƿme · oððe of ſpeoƿan ſpa
mæyt aƿæfnan mæȝe · ꝺ ƿceaƿpiȝe · ꝺ hƿon onfette
oƿeƿ eall ſmiƿe þonne mid hatan ele ꝺ hìm æȝhƿæt
ƿealtef beoƿȝe · bƿuce ȝlædenan ꝺ eoƿoþƿeaƿnef uppe on
tƿeoƿe ꝺ mid hneƿce ƿulle oƿeƿ þƿide ealle þa ſceaƿpan
þonne hie ſien ȝeſmyƿede.  Þiþ neuƿiƿne bauƿyƿt do
on ſuƿe fletan ꝺ on huniȝ æȝef ȝeola menȝ toſomne
ſmiƿe mid.  Eft þenpyƿmaf cnua do on.

.LX.

Þid bƿyne pyƿc ƿealfe · ȝenim ȝate toƿd ꝺ hƿæte
healm ȝebaƿn to dufte ȝemenȝ butu þiþ buteƿan do
on pannan oƿeƿ fyƿ apyl ſpide þel aƿeoh þuƿh clad
ſmiƿe mid.

Þiþ bƿyne ȝenim finulef iþþeƿeaƿdef ȝebeat þid
ealdne þyƿele ꝺ leȝe on.  Eft ȝenim liliaƿ ꝺ ȝeaƿpan
þyl on buteƿan ſmiƿe mid.  Þiþ. þon ilcan þylle ƿibban
on buteƿan ꝺ ſmiƿe mid.

Þiþ þon ilcan þylle ȝeaƿpan on buteƿan ſmiƿe mid.

Þiþ þon ilcan þylle cottuc on ƿceapef ſmeƿƿe ꝺ
attoƿlaþan ꝺ coƿoþƿeaƿn do on huniȝ oððe on þeax.
Þiþ þon do æȝef þ hƿite on ȝelome.

---

### lix.

Against palsy; take a cup full of boiling water, another of oil, and of white salt so much as one may pick up with four fingers; shake together till that it be all one: drink all this by drops, rest awhile, poke thy finger into the gullet, spew up again all and more if thou [1] may; then in the morning let blood from the arm or from the neck, as much as he [1] may bear; and scarify and let him put something on, then after all smear with hot oil and let him taste a trifle of salt; employ gladden and everfern *picked high* up on the tree, and cover over with nesh wool all the scarifications when they have been smeared. Against "neurisn" put bonewort into sour cream, and into honey, mingle together *with this* the yolk of an egg, smear therewith. Again, pound up earthworms, apply them.

### lx.

1. Against a burn work a salve; take goats tord and halm of wheat, burn them to dust, mingle both with butter, put into a pan over the fire, boil thoroughly well, strain through a cloth, smear therewith.

2. For a burn, take some of the netherward part of fennel, beat it up with old grease, and lay on. Again, take lilly and yarrow, boil *them* in butter, smear therewith. For the same, boil ribwort in butter and smear therewith.

3. For that ilk, boil yarrow in butter, smear therewith.

4. For that ilk, boil mallow in sheeps grease, and attorlothe, and everfern, put them into honey or into wax. For that *same*, put the white of an egg on frequently.

---

[1] The careless use of pronouns belongs to the text.

Þiþ bliyne það ȝecnua þyl on buteþan fmiþe mið.

. LXI.

[1]Þiþ hð þæþce cnua hð þyþt þð humȝe oþþe ceop ꝺ
leȝe ón. Eft þulꝼeꝛ heaꝛoð ban bæþn fþiðe ꝺ ȝecnua
fmale aꝛyꝼt þuꝺh cla ꝺ ꝺo on þ̊ ðolȝ. Þð liþ þæþce
cnua þeꝺmoð þiþ teoꝺþe ꝺ ꝼenceþfan aþꝺinȝ þ̊ fcaþ óꝼ
menȝ tofomne clæm on þ̊ hð ꝺe þaꝺ faꝛ ꝛie ȝebinð
ꝼaeꝛte ón. Þiþ hð ꝛeaþe ȝeloð þyþt · bꝺune þyþt ·
ꝺ haꝺe þyþt lyteln óꝼtoꝼt þeaxeþ ón tune hæꝼð
hþite bloftmau ȝecnua ða þꝛeo þyꝛta ȝemenȝe þ̊ biþ
ȝoð ꝛealꝼ. Œaneȝum men hð ꝛeau ꝛyhð[2] ȝeꝛþunȝ
æþleꝛ fcaþ ón · ꝺ hoþneꝛ fceaꝛoþan fþiðe fmale ȝeꝛceaꝼ
cꝺim on þ̊ ðolli mnán ðo þ̊ óꝼ ꝺ fmle nꝛe ón. Þiþ
hð fcaþe liþþyþt hunðeꝛ heaꝛoð ȝebæꝺne ꝺ ȝecnuꝛȝe
ꝺ ȝebꝛaðeðne æþþel · menȝ þ̊ eall tofomne ðo þ̊ ón.
Eft ȝením fuꝺme æþþel ȝebꝛæð ꝺ leȝe ón · ðo ȝꝺiut
ón uꝼan þone æþþel                          :·

Þiþ hð ꝛeaþe · ȝenim maȝeþan menȝ þð humȝ ðo on
þ̊ ðolȝ ꝺ binð ꝼæfte. Þiþ ꝛeaþe ȝenim ñcꝛinðe ꝺ ðꝺiȝe
ꝺ þꝺe to fmeðman ꝺ ꝛlahþoꝛn ꝛinðe nioþoþeaꝛðe fyꝛt

---

[1] 'Αρθρῖτις.
[2] Subluvium. We find the out-
flowing of the synovia an object
of legal enactment. See Ælfreds

Dooms, p. 42. art. 53. "Si quis in
" humero plagietur ut glutinum
" compagum effluat:" Laws, Henry
I, p. 265.

fol. 50 a.

5. For a burn, pound up woad, boil it in butter, smear therewith.

### lxi.

1. Against racking pain in the joints, pound lithwort with honey, or chew it and lay it on. Again, burn thoroughly the head bone *or skull* of a wolf and pound it small, sift it through a cloth, put it on the wound. Against pain in the joints, pound wormwood with tar and fen cress, wring out the juice, mingle together, stick *the residue* upon the joint where the sore is, bind it on fast. For the synovia of the joints, silverweed, brownwort, and the little harewort,[1] it oftenest waxeth in a garden, it hath white blossoms, pound the three worts, mingle them, that is a good salve. With many men the synovia of the joints oozeth out,[2] wring on *the spot* the juice of an apple, and shave very small some shavings of horn, crumble them on the wound within it, remove that and ever apply *the same* anew. For the synovia of the joints, burn lithwort,[a] houndshead, and pound them up with roasted apple; mingle all that together, apply it. Again, take a sour apple, roast and lay it on; apply groats over above the apple.

2. For the synovia of the joints, take maythe, mingle *it* with honey, apply it to the wound and bind it fast. For *the secretion of the joints*, take oak rind and dry it and work it to a fine *flour or smede*, and *further* sloethorn rind, the netherward part of it, sift them

[a] *Sambucus ebulus.*

---

[1] *Lepidium?*

[2] " Tune articuli tumentes inflantur, ac deinde durescunt et solidati saxeam faciunt qualitatem ; tum etiam nigriores efficiuntur, atque contorti, ut in obliquas partes digiti vertantur, aut reflexi supinentur, aut vicinis adfixi incumbant, et aliquando humore purulento vel mucilento collecto, aut viscoso, generent poros, quos nos transitus dicere poterimus."— Cælius Aurelianus, about A.D. 230, Chron. lib. v. cap. 2.

þa þuph claðᵹ fceað on þ dolȝ. Þið hð feape · ȝením cetelhpúm ᵹ beþenhealm ȝebæþu ᵹ ȝuið toȝiedepe ᵹ fcað ón. ȝif liþule útypne ȝením meþce moþopeaþóne ᵹ hunȝ ᵹ hpætencf meluþef fmeðman ᵹ picȝȝan Innel [1] beȝmð tofómne leȝe ón. Eft ȝením meðopypte moþo- peaþóe ȝecnua fmale menȝ piþ hunȝe leȝe ón þæt ȝebatoð fie.

fol. 50 b.

ȝif liþule útypne ȝením eceð ᵹ fuþe cþuman beþe- nef hlafeᵹ ᵹ þeupyþmaþ menȝ [2] toSomne binð ón þæt þ hþ mið ecebe oþþe mið fuþan ealað. ȝif liþule útypne · ȝením pepmoð ᵹ ȝecnua ðo ón teoþo clæm ón ᵹ binð ón fæfte.

## .LXII.

[3] Þiþ fefen aðle · elehtþan · ȝyþþufe · peȝbpæde ȝecnua ón ealu læt ftandan tpa niht fele ðpincan. Þiþ fefne eft betonican ðpince fpiðe · ᵹ ete þpeo fnæða. Eft ðpinc on hluttpúm ealað pepmoð · ȝyþþufan · betonican · bifceoppypt · fen minte · boȝen · fio clufihte · pen- pypt · maþþubie · ðpince þpitiȝ ðaȝa. Þpenc piþ þon · betonican · fpþinȝpypt attoplaðe · beþbine · eofoþþþote · hunðeptunȝe · ðpeoþȝe ðpoftle · pepmoð. Þið þþiððan ðæȝef fefþe ón peaþinum þætþe ðpince betonican tyn fopan þonne to pille. Þið feoȝþan ðæȝef fefþe ðpince peȝbpædan feap on fpetum þætþe tpam tiðum æþ him fe fefeþ to pille. Þiþ ælcef ðæȝef fefeþe ðpince ón cealdúm þætepe betonican ðuftef þ ænne þeninȝ ȝepeȝe · oþeþ fpile peȝbpædan.

fol. 51 a.

Þiþ fefþe eft hylpð fynðpiȝo maþubie to ðpincanne. Þiþ lencten aðle pepmoð eofoþ þþote · elehtþe · peȝ- bpæde · þibbe · ceþfille · attoplaðe · fefepfuȝe · alex- anðþe · bifceoppypt · lufeftice · Salue · eaffíe pype to through a cloth, and shed that on the wound. For synovia of the joints, take kettle soot and barley halm, burn and rub them together, and shed on. If the synovia run out, take the netherward part of marche and honey, and the smede of wheaten meal, and the bowels of an *ear* wig, rub them together, and lay on. Again, take the netherward part of meadowwort, pound it small, mingle with honey, lay on till it be mended.

3. If the synovia run out, take vinegar and sour crumbs of a barley loaf, and earthworms, mingle together, and bind on ; wet the joint with vinegar or with sour ale. If the synovia run out, take wormwood and pound it, put it on tar, plaster it on, and bind it on fast.

## lxii.

1. For fever disease ; pound in ale lupins, githrife, waybroad, let it stand for two nights, administer to drink. For fever again ; let him drink betony much, and eat three bits *of it.* Again, drink in clear ale wormwood, githrife, betony, bishopwort, fen mint, rosemary, the clove rooted wenwort, marrubium, drink for thirty days. A drink for that, betony, springwort, attorlothe, vervain, everthroat, houndstongue, dwarf dwosle, wormwood. For a tertian fever, let *the sick* drink in warm water ten sups of betony, when *the fever* is approaching. For a quartan fever, let him drink juice of waybroad in sweetened water two hours before the fever will to him. For a quotidian fever, let him drink in cold water so much of the dust of betony as may weigh a penny ; as much more of waybroad.

2. For fever again it helpeth, to drink marrubium alone. For lent addle, *or typhus fever,* work to a drink wormwood, everthroat, lupin, waybroad, ribwort, chervil, attorlothe, feverfue, alexanders, bishopwort, lovage,

ꝺꞃence on pelſcum ealað ꝺo haliȝ pæꞇeꞃ ꞇo · ⁊ ſpꞃinȝ
ꞃyꞃꞇ.

Þiꞃ mon ꞃceal pꞃiꞇan on huꞃlꞃice ⁊ on þone ꝺꞃene
mið haliȝ pæꞇeꞃe þꞃean ⁊ ꞃinȝan on ·

+ + + Λ + + + + + C D + + + + + + + + +

In pꞃincipio epaꞇ ueꞃbum eꞇ ueꞃbum epaꞇ apuꞇ
ꝺeum eꞇ ꝺeuꞃ epaꞇ ueꞃbum. Ðoc epaꞇ In pꞃincipio
apuꞇ ꝺeum omnia peꞃ ipſum ꞃacꞇa Sunꞇ. Þꞃeah þonne
þ ȝeꞃꞃiꞇ mið haliȝ pæꞇꞃe oꞃ þam ꝺiꞃce on þone ꝺꞃene·
ſinȝ · þonne epeꝺo ⁊ paꞇeꞃ noꞃꞇeꞃ ⁊ þiꞃ leoþ. beaꞇi
Immaculaꞇi þone ꞃealm mið aꝺ ꝺominum þam .xii.
ȝeheꝺ ꞃealmum. Aꝺiuꞃo uoS ꞃꞃiȝoꞃeſ[1] eꞇ ꞃebꞃeS · peꞃ
ꝺeum paꞇꞃem omnipoꞇenꞇem eꞇ peꞃ eiuꞃ ꞃilium ieꞃum
epiꞃꞇum peꞃ aꞃcenſum eꞇ ꝺiꞃcenſum[2] Saluaꞇoꞃiꞃ noꞃꞇꞃi
uꞇ ꞃeceꝺaꞇiS ꝺe hoc ꞃamulo ꝺei · eꞇ ꝺe coꞃꞃuSculo
eiuꞃ quam[3] ꝺominuꞃ noꞃꞇeꞃ Inluminaꞃe Inꞇiꞇuꞇ. Uinciꞇ uoſ leo ꝺe ꞇꞃibu iuꝺa ꞃaꝺix ꝺauiꝺ. Uinciꞇ uoſ qui
uinci non poꞇeSꞇ · + xꝑſ naꞇuſ· + xꝑſ paꞃꞃuꞃ· +
xꝑſ uenꞇuꞃuꞃ · + amꞃ ·[4] + amꞃ · + amꞃ · + Seꞃ ·
+ Seꞃ · + Seꞃ · Jn ꝺieᵃ Saluꞇiꞃeꞃiꞃ mceꝺenꞃ ȝꞃeꞃſibuꞃ
uꞃbeꞃ · oꞃꞃiꝺa ꞃuꞃa uicoꞃ caꞃꞇꞃa caſꞇella peꞃaȝꞃanꞇ.
Omnia ꝺepulꞃꞃ ꞃanabaꞇ coꞃꞃoꞃa moꞃbiꞃ·[5] ⁊ þiuꞃa þonne
onꞃuꞃe þæꞃ pæꞇeꞃeſ ſpelceſ ȝehꞃæꞃeꞃ þaꞃa manna.

.LXIII.

Þiþ ꞃeonð ꞃeocum men · þonne ꝺeoꞃol þone monnan
ꞃeꝺe oððe hine innan ȝepealꝺe mið aꝺle. Spiꞃeꝺꞃene
eluhꞇꞃe · biꞃceoꞃꞃyꞃꞇ · beolone eꞃoꞃleac ȝeenua ꞇoSomne
ꝺo eala ꞇo pæꞇan læꞇ ꞃꞇanꝺan ueahꞇeꞃne ꝺo ꞃiꞃꞇiȝ
lybcoꞃꞃa on ⁊ haliȝ pæꞇeꞃ. ꝺꞃene piþ ꞃeonꝺꞃeocum
men oꞃ eiꞃebellan ꞇo ꝺꞃincanne · ȝyþꞃiꞃe · ȝlæꞃ ·[6] ȝeaꞃꞃe ·
elehꞇꞃe · beꞇonice · aꞇꞇoꞃlaþe · eaꞃꞃuc · ꞃane · ꞃinul ·

---

[1] Frigora.
[2] Descensum.
[3] Quem.
[4] amꞃ=ἅγιος.
[5] Read Oppida, rura, casas, vicos,

castella  peragrans ;  Sedulius,
Carm. Pasch., Lib. III., 23.  Inter-
woven in the text of Beda, III.
xxviii.

[6] For neȝleꞃ, eynæȝlæꞃꞃan ?

sage, cassock, in foreign ale; add holy water and springwort.

3. A man shall write this upon the sacramental paten, and wash it off into the drink with holy water, and sing over it . . . . In the beginning, etc. (John i. 1.) Then wash the writing with holy water off the dish into the drink, then sing the Credo, and the Paternoster, and this lay, Beati immaculati, the psalm;[1] with the twelve prayer psalms, I adjure you, etc. And let each of the two[2] men then sip thrice of the water so prepared.

Inde salutiferis incedens gressibus urbes,
Oppida, rura, casas, vicos, castella peragrans
Omnia depulsis sanabat corpora morbis.
                              SEDVLIVS.

### lxiii.

For a fiend sick man, *or demoniac*, when a devil possesses the man or controls him from within with disease; a spew drink, *or emetic*, lupin, bishopwort, henbane, cropleek; pound *these* together, add ale for a liquid, let *it* stand for a night, add fifty libcorns, *or cathartic grains*, and holy water. A drink for a fiend sick man, to be drunk out of a church bell; githrife, cynoglossum, yarrow, lupin, betony, attorlothe, cassock, flower de luce, fennel, church lichen, lichen, of

---

[1] Psalm, cxix.
[2] Two, the leech and the sick; two is in ᵹeһрæþep.

cincpaʒu · cnifter mæler paʒu · lufeſtice · ʒepype þone
dnenc ōf hluttnum calað ʒefinʒe feofon mæʒʒan ofen
þām pyntum do ʒapleñc Ᵹ haliʒ pæten to Ᵹ dnype ōn ælcne
dnincan þone dnenc þe he dnincan pille ēft · Ᵹ finʒe
þone ſcalm · beati Inmaculati Ᵹ exunʒāt · Ᵹ Saluum
me fāc deuſ · Ᵹ þonne dnince þone dnenc ōf cincbellan Ᵹ
ſe mæʒſe pneoſt hīm finʒe æften þam dnence þiſ ofen.
domine Sancte paten omnipotenſ. Þiþ bnæcſeocum
men · coſt · ʒotpoþe · cluhtne · betonice · attoplaðe ·
cnopleñc · holecepſan · hofe · finul · afinʒe mōn mæſſan ofen pynce ōf pyliſcum cāloð Ᵹ of haliʒ pætepe.
dnince þiyne dnenc æt æʒhpilcum nipe niʒon monʒenaſ
Ᵹ nane oþne pætan ꝥ þicce Ᵹ ſtille fie · Ᵹ ælmeſſan
ſelle Ᵹ hīm anena ʒoð ʒeopnlice bidde. Þið peden
heopte biſceoppynt · clehtne · banpynt · eoponfeapn ·
ʒiþfne · heahhiolope þonne dæʒ ſcade [1] Ᵹ niht þonne
finʒ þu ōn cincean letaniaſ ꝥ iſ þapa haliʒpa naman ·
Ᵹ paten nonten mid þy ſanʒe þu ʒa ꝥ þu ſie æt þam
pyntum Ᵹ þnipa ymbʒa Ᵹ þonne þu lic nime ʒanʒ eft
to cincean mid þy ilcan ſanʒe · Ᵹ ʒerinʒ .XII. mæſſan ofen Ᵹ ofen ealle þa dnencan þe to þnepe aðle
belimpaþ ōn peopðmynde þapa tpelfa apoſtola.

. LXIIII.

Περίαπτον.

Þiþ ælcne yfelne leodnunan Ᵹ pið ælfſiðenne þiſ
ʒepnit pnit hīm þiſ ʒneciſcum ſtafum · + + Λ + +
O + y° + ı ᵱ ᴜ ʏ ᴍ ⧓ : ᴮ e ᴾ ᴾ ɴ NIKNETTANI.
Eft · ofen duſt Ᵹ dnenc pið leodnunan · ʒenīm bnembel
æppel Ᵹ clehtpan Ᵹ polleʒian ʒecnua. fift þonne do on
pohhan leʒe undeſ peofod finʒ niʒon mæſſan ofen do
ōn meolōc ꝥ duſt dnyp þnipa on haliʒ pætepeſ [2] ſele

---

[1] At morning twilight.

[2] A partitive genitive ; haliʒ in haliʒ pætep is commonly undeclined, or regarded as part of a compound.

Christs mark *or cross*, lovage ; work up the drink off
clear ale, sing seven masses over the worts, add garlic and
holy water, and drip the drink into every drink which
he will subsequently drink, and let him sing the psalm,
Beati immaculati, and Exurgat, and Salvum me fac, deus,
and then let him drink the drink out of a church bell,
and let the mass priest after the drink sing this over
him, Domine, sancte pater omnipotens.[1]   For a lunatic;
costmary, goutweed, lupin, betony, attorlothe, cropleek,
field gentian, hove, fennel; let masses be sung over,
let it be wrought of foreign ale and of holy water ;
let him drink this drink for nine mornings, at every
one fresh, and no other liquid that is thick and still,
and let him give alms, and earnestly pray God for his
mercies.   For the phrenzied; bishopwort, lupin, bonewort,
everfern,[2] githrife, elecampane, when day and night divide, then sing thou in the church litanies, that is,
the names of the hallows *or saints*, and the Paternoster ; with the song go thou, that thou mayest be
near the worts, and go thrice about them, and when
thou takest them go again to church with the same
song, and sing twelve masses over them, and over all
the drinks which belong to the disease, in honour of
the twelve apostles.

### lxiv.

Against every evil rune lay,[3] and one full of elvish      A holy amulet.
tricks, write *for the bewitched man* this writing in
Greek letters: alfa, omega, IESVM (?) BERONIKII.[4]   Again,   ΙΧΘΥΣ ?
another dust *or powder* and drink against a rune lay ;
take a bramble apple,[a] and lupins, and pulegium, pound     [a] *A blackberry.*
them, then sift them, put them in a pouch, lay them
under the altar, sing nine masses over them, put the

---

[1] A formula of Benediction ;
several such are found in the
Missals.

[2] *Polypodium vulgare.*

[3] Heathen charm.

[4] Invoking the miraculous portrait of Christ on the kerchief of
St. Veronica.

ðrincan on þrio tida · on undern · on middeȝ · on
nón · ȝif sio adl netrum sie ȝeot mid haliȝ wætre ón
muð þ ilce duft.  Sealf elehtre heȝeruce · birceoppyrt ·
þa peadan maȝoþan · apmelu · cropleac · realt pyl on
buteran to sealfe smire ón þ heafod ꝺ þa breost.
ðrenc hapan spiccel · alexandre · rude · elehtre
heȝeruce · birceoppyrt · maȝoþe · cropleac · apmelu ·
sio eucoehte · penpyrt do on haliȝ wætere.    ȝif món
mare rude · ȝenim elehtran ꝺ ȝapleac · ꝺ betonican ·
ꝺ recelf bind on nægce hæbbe him món ón ꝺ he
ȝanȝe in on þær pyrte.

fol. 53 a.

.LXV.

Eft ðrenc pið lencten adle refenfuȝe · hram ȝealla ·
finul · reȝbræde · ȝefinȝe mon fela mærran oþen þære
pyrte ·¹ ofȝeót mid ealað do haliȝ wætere ón pyl spiþe
pel ðrince þonne spa he hatoft mæȝe micelne scence
fulne ær þon sio adl to pille :·  feoren ȝodspellara
naman ꝺ ȝealdor ꝺ ȝebeð · ▦ .    Matheus · + + + + +
MarcuS + + + + · lucaS · ▦ · Iohannes ⁺⁺ Interᵖᵖ
cedite ppo me · Tiecon · leleloth · patron · adiuro uoS.
Eft ȝodcund ȝebeð · In nomine domini sit benedic
tum · beromce · beromcen · et habet In uestimento et
In femore suo · scriptum rex reȝum et dominus domi
nantium * · Eft ȝodcund ȝebeð ·  In nomine sit bene
dictum · ⋈ M M R M þ · ᴺꝺ · þ T X ⋈ M R F p N ꝺ · þ T X .²
Eſt reeal mon spiȝende þiſ ppitan ꝺ ꝺon þaſ poɼð
spiȝende on þa pinſtran bɼeoſt ꝺ ne ȝa he in ón
þ ȝeppit ne in on bep · ꝺ eac spiȝende þis on ꝺon ·
HAMMANYᵒEL · BPONice · NOYᵒᵉPTAYᵒEPᴦ.

Runes.

Rev. xix.<br/>16.

---

¹ This use of the singular is mere    ⋈MRMþ · Nꝺ · þTX, and under-
carelessness.    stand the T as an I.
² Read ⋈ MMRMþ · Nꝺ · þTX ·

dust into milk, drip thrice some holy water upon them, administer *this* to drink at three hours, at undern, *or nine in the morning*, at midday, at noon, *hora nona, or three in the afternoon*. If the disease be on cattle, pour that ilk dust into the mouth with holy water. A salve; boil lupin, hedgerife, bishopwort, the red maythe, harmala,ᵃ cropleek, salt, in butter to a salve, smear it on the head and the breast. A drink; put into holy water, vipers bugloss, alexanders, rue, lupins, hedgerife, bishopwort, maythe, cropleek, harmala, the wenwort which hath knees.ᵇ If a mare[1] or *hag* ride a man, take lupins, and garlic, and betony, and frankincense, bind them on a fawns skin, let a man have the worts on him, and let him go in *to his home.*

ᵃ *Peganum harmala, Bot.*

ᵇ *Lolium temulentum?*

## lxv.

1. Again, a drink against lent addle *or typhus;* feverfue, the herb rams gall,[2] fennel, waybroad; let a man sing many masses over the worts, souse them with ale, add holy water, boil very thoroughly, let *the man* drink a great cup full, as hot as he may, before the disorder will be on him; *say* the names of the four gospellers, and a charm, and a prayer, etc.[3] Again, a divine prayer, etc., DEEREÞ· HAND· ÞIN· DEREÞ· HAND· ÞIN· thine hand vexeth, thine hand vexeth.

Again, a man shall in silence write this, and silently put these words on the left breast, and let him not go in *doors* with that writing, nor bear it in *doors.* And also in silence put this on, EMMANUEL, VERONICA.[4]

---

[1] As in night mare.
[2] *Menyanthes trifoliata.*
[3] Leliloth is an Arabic idol.

(Freytag.) Cf. Alilat Herod. iii. 8.
[4] The image on the kerchief.

### .LXVI.

fol 53 b.

Ƿiþ unȝemynde ꞇ ƿið ðyſȝunȝe ꝺo ōn ealo biſceoꝓ
ꝓyꝓꞇ · elehꞇꝛan · beꞇonican þa ſuþeꞃꞃan ſmuȝlan ·
neꝼꞇan luꞃðhioloðan · ȝyþꞃiꝼan · meꝛce · ꝺꞃince þonne.
Ƿiþ unȝemynde ꞇ ꝺiſȝunȝe ꝺo ōn eala caꝛſiām · ꞇ elehꞇꝛan · biſceoꝓꝓyꞃꞇ · alexanꝺꞃan · ȝiþꞃiꝼe · ꝼelꝺmoꞃan
ꞇ haliȝ ꝓæꞇeꝓ ꝺꞃince þonne.

### .LXVII.

Ƿið ȝenumenum meꞇe · ȝenīm elehꞇꝛan leȝe unꝺeꝛ
ꝓeoꝼoꝺ ſinȝ niȝon mæꞃꞃan oꝼeꝓ þ ꝛceal ƿiþ ȝenumenum meꞇe leȝe unꝺeꝓ þ ꝼæꞇ · þe þu ꝓille ōn melcan.[1]
ȝiꝼ ealo aꝓeꝛð ſie · ȝenim þa elehꞇꝛan leȝe on þa
ꝼeoꝓeꝓ ꝛceaꞇꞇaſ þæſ æꝓꞃeſ ꞇ oꝼeꝓ þa ꝺuꝛu ꞇ unꝺeꝓ
þone þeꝛxꝛolꝺ ꞇ unꝺeꝓ þ caloꝼæꞇ ꝺo mið haliȝ ꝓæꞇꝛe
þa ꝓyꞃꞇ on þ eala ;

ȝiꝼ meꞇe ſy aꝓyꝛð ꞇ unȝehꝓæꝺe mylcen oððe ꝛilꝺ
oþþe bꞃyþen · halȝa þa ꝓyꞃꞇe ꝺo ōn ꞇ unꝺeꝓ þ ꝼæꞇ ·
ꞇ unꝺeꝓ þa ꝺuꝛu · ꝺo elehꞇꝛan ꞇ cliꝼan · ꞇ beꞇonican
ꞇ biſceoꝓꝓyꞃꞇ.

### .LXVIII.

fol. 54 a.

Ƿiþ þon ȝiꝼ hunꞇa ȝebiꞇe mannan þ iſ ſpiꞃꞃa ꝛleah
þꞃy ꝛceaꝓꝓan neah ꝼꞃomꝓeaꝓꝺeſ læꞇ yꞃnan þ bloꝺ ōn
ȝꝛeꞃꞃꞃe ſꞇiccan hæꝓꝛenne ꝓeoꝓꝓ þonne oꝼeꝓ ꝓeȝ aꝓeȝ
þonne ne biþ nan yꝼel. Eꝼꞇ aꝛꝛleah ane ꝛceaꝓꝓan oꝺ ꞃ
þam ꝺolȝe ȝeeꞃꞃa læcepyꞃꞇ leȝe ōn ne biþ hīm nan
yꝼel. Ƿiþ ȝonȝelꝓæꝼꝓan biꞇe · nim æꝼeꝓꝓan moþo-

---

[1] The Saxons used milk and preparations of milk for the food of the
churls family. Hence the churls    cow is called his Meat cow, DD.
187, 188,

### lxvi.

Against mental vacancy and against folly; put into
ale bishopwort, lupins, betony, the southern *or Italian*
fennel, nepte, water agrimony, cockle, marche, then let
*the man* drink. For idiotcy and folly, put into ale,
cassia, and lupins, bishopwort, alexanders, githrife, fieldmore, and holy water; then let him drink.

### lxvii.

1. For *the better digestion of* meat taken; take lupins, lay them under the altar, sing over them nine
masses, that shall avail for meat taken; lay it under
the vessel into which thou hast in mind to milk. If
ale be spoilt, then take lupins, lay them on the four
quarters of the dwelling, and over the door, and under
the threshhold, and under the ale vat, put the wort
into the ale with holy water.

2. If meat be spoilt,[1] and a good quantity of milken
food, or a milking,[a] or brewing, hallow the worts,[2] put
them into and under the vat, and under the door; use
lupins, and clifwort, and betony, and bishopwort.     [a] See III. liii.

### lxviii.

In case that a hunting spider[3] bite a man, that is
the stronger *spider*, strike three scarifications near, in
a direction from the bite, let the blood run into a
green spoon of hazel wood, then throw it over the road
away; then no harm will come of it. Again, strike a
scarification on the wound; pound leechwort; lay it
on, no harm will happen to the man. Against bite of
a weaving spider,[4] take the netherward part of æferthe,

---

[1] Cf. Luke xiv. 34. Marshall.
[2] By one of the benisons in the
ecclesiastical Manuale.
[3] *Salticus scenicus* is now described by this name; but it is very

appropriate for the *Aranea tarantula*, the habits of which our
author had, doubtless, learnt.
[4] *Aranea viatica*.

ƿeaɲðe ⁊ ſlahþoɲn · þaȝe aðɲiȝ co ðuſce ȝeþæn mið
hunıȝe lacna þ̃ ðolh mið. Þıþ huncan bıce blace ſneȝlaſ
ōn haccɲe pannan ȝehyɲſce¹ ⁊ co ðuſce ȝeȝnıðene · ⁊
pıɲoɲ · ⁊ becomean ece þ̃ ðuſc ⁊ ðɲınce ⁊ ōn lecȝe.
Þıð huncan bıce ꝼ́ım nıþeɲeaɲðne² coccuc leȝe on
þ̃ ðolh. Eꝼc aɲleah · v. ſceaɲɲan ane on þam bıce
⁊ ſeopeɲ ymbucan þeoɲþ mıð ſcıccan ſpıȝenðe oꝼeɲ
pænɲeȝ.

### . LXVIIII.

Þıþ þeðe hunðeſ ſlıce aȝɲımonıan ⁊ peȝbɲæðan ȝemenȝe mıð hunıȝe ⁊ æȝeſ þ̃ hpıce lacna þa punðe mıð
þ.y. Þıþ hunðeſ ðolȝe ꝼoxeſ clace · ȝɲunðeſpelȝe þyl
on bacepan ſmıɲe mıð. Eꝼc becomean ȝecɲıɲula leȝe
ōn þone bıce. Eꝼc peȝbɲæðan ȝebeac leȝe ōn. Eꝼc
cɲa eıɲan oððe þɲeo ſeoþ ȝebɲac ōn ahſan menȝ pıð
ɲyſle ⁊ hunıȝe leȝe ōn. Eꝼc ȝebæɲne ſpıneſ ceacan
co ahſan ſceað ōn. Eꝼc ȝenꝼ́m peȝbɲæðan moɲan
ȝecnua³ pıþ ɲyſle ðo on þ̃ ðolh þonne aſeɲyɲð lno þ̃
aceɲ aɲeȝ.

### . LXX.

Ȝıſ mon ſıe co þɲæne þyl hınðheoloþan on ɲıhſeꝼ́m
ealað ðɲınce on neahc neſ́cıȝ. Gıſ mon ſıe co un-
þɲæne ſyl on meolce þa ılean þyɲc þonne apɲænſc þu.
Þyl ōn eope meolce eꝼc hınðhıoloþan alexanðɲıan ꝼoɲ-
neceſ ꝼolm hacce þyɲc þonne bıþ hıc ſɲa hꝼ́m leoꝼoſc
bıð.

---

¹ For ȝehyɲɲcebe.
² nıþeɲeaɲðe corrected to the masculine, MS.
³ ȝecna, MS.

and lichen from the blackthorn, dry it to dust, moisten with honey, tend the wound therewith. Against bite of hunting spider, black snails fried in a hot pan and rubbed to dust, and pepper, and betony, let *the man* eat the dust, and drink *it,* and lay it on. For bite of hunting spider, take the netherward part of mallow, lay it on the wound. Again, strike five scarifications, one on the bite, and four round about it, throw *the blood* with a spoon silently over a wagon way.

### lxix.

For bite of mad dog; mingle with honey agrimony and waybroad, and the white of an egg, dress the wound with that. For wound by a hound; foxes clote,[a] groundsel, boil *these* in butter, smear therewith. Again, triturate betony, lay it on the bite. Again, beat waybroad, lay *it* on. Again, seethe two or three onions, roast them on ashes, mingle with fat and honey, lay on. Again, burn a swines cheek *or jaw* to ashes, shed *this* on. Again, take more *or root* of waybroad, pound it, put it on the wound with lard, then it will scrape the venom away.

[a] *Burdock.*

### lxx.

If a man be too salacious, boil water agrimony in foreign ale, let *him* drink *thereof* at night fasting. If a man be too slow ad venerem, boil that ilk wort in milk, then thou givest him corage. Boil in ewes milk, again, hindheal, alexanders, *the* wort *which* hight Fornets[1] palm,[a] then it will be with him as he would liefest have it be.

[a] Unknown.

---

[1] For Fornet or Fornjot, see the index of names.

peapðe ꞏ ſlahþoꝝn ꞏ ꝑaȝe aðꝝiȝ ꞇo ðuſꞇe ȝeþæn mið
humȝe læna þ ðolh mið. Þiþ hunꞇan biꞇe blace ſneȝlaſ
ōn haꞇꞇꝛe ꝑannan ȝehyꝛſꞇe[1] ꞏ ꞇo ðuſꞇe ȝeȝꞏnſdene ꞏ ꞏ
ꝑiꝑoꝝ ꞏ ꞏ beꞇonican eꞇe þ ðuſꞇ ꞏ ꝺꝛince ꞏ ōn lecȝe.
Þið hunꞇan biꞇe ᛉ́im niþepeaꝝðne[2] coꞇꞇuc leȝe on
þ ðolh. Eſꞇ aꝛleah ꞏ v. ꝛecaꝝꝛan ane on þam biꞇe
ꞏ ꝛeoꝑeꝛ ymbuꞇan ꝑeoꝝꝛ mið ſꞇiccan ſꝛȝenðe oꝝeꝝ
pænꝑeȝ.


## .LXVIIII.

Þiþ ꝑeðe hunꝺeſ ſliꞇe aȝꝝꞏnꞏomian ꞏ ꝑeȝhꝝæðan ȝemenȝe mið humȝe ꞏ æȝeſ þ hꝛiꞇe læna þa ꝑunðe mið
þy. Þiþ hunðeſ ðolȝe ꝛoxeſ claꞇe ꞏ ȝꝛunðeſꝑelȝe ꝑyl
on buꞇeꝛan ſmꞏꝛe mið. Eſꞇ beꞇonican ȝeꞇꝝꞏꝛula leȝe
ōn þone biꞇe. Eſꞇ ꝑeȝhꝝæðan ȝebeaꞇ leȝe ōn. Eſꞇ
ꞇꝛa ciꝛan oððe þꝛeo ſeoꝝ ȝehꝝaꝝ ōn ahſan menȝ ꝝið
ꝑyſle ꞏ humȝe leȝe ōn. Eſꞇ ȝebæꝝꞏne ſꝑꞏneſ ceacan
ꞇo ahſan ꝛceað ōn. Eſꞇ ȝenꞏꞏm ꝑeȝhꝝæðan moꝝan
ȝecnua[3] ꝑiþ ꝝyſle ðo on þ ðolh þonne aſcꝛyꝝð luo þ
aꞇeꝝ aꝛeȝ.


## .LXX.

Ȝiſ mon ſie ꞇo ꝑꝝæne ꝑyl lunðheoloþan on ꝑiliſeſꞏm
calað ꝺꝛince on neahꞇ néꝛꞇꞏȝ. Ȝiſ mon ſie ꞇo un-
ꝑꝝæne ꝑyl on meolce þa ꞏlean ꝑyꝝꞇ þonne aꝝꝝænſꞇ þu.
Þyl ōn cope meolce eſꞇ lunðꞏꝝoloþan alexanꝺꝝꞏan ꝛoꝝ-
neꞇeſ ꝛolm haꞇꞇe ꝑyꝝꞇ þonne biþ luꞇ ſꝛa hím leoꝝoſꞇ
bið.

---

fol. 54 b.

and lichen from the blackthorn, dry it to dust, moisten
with honey, tend the wound therewith. Against bite
of hunting spider, black snails fried in a hot pan and
rubbed to dust, and pepper, and betony, let *the man*
eat the dust, and drink *it*, and lay it on. For bite of
hunting spider, take the netherward part of mallow,
lay it on the wound. Again, strike five scarifications,
one on the bite, and four round about it, throw *the*
*blood* with a spoon silently over a wagon way.

## lxix.

For bite of mad dog; mingle with honey agrimony
and waybroad, and the white of an egg, dress the
wound with that. For wound by a hound; foxes
clote,[a] groundsel, boil *these* in butter, smear therewith.
Again, triturate betony, lay it on the bite. Again.
beat waybroad, lay *it* on. Again, seethe two or three
onions, roast them on ashes, mingle with fat and
honey, lay on. Again, burn a swines cheek *or jaw* to
ashes, shed *this* on. Again, take more *or root* of waybroad, pound it, put it on the wound with lard, then
it will scrape the venom away.

[a] *Burdock.*

## lxx.

If a man be too salacious, boil water agrimony in
foreign ale, let *him* drink *thereof* at night fasting. If
a man be too slow ad venerem, boil that ilk wort in
milk, then thou givest him corage. Boil in ewes
milk, again, hindheal, alexanders, *the* wort *which* hight
Fornets[1] palm,[a] then it will be with him as he would
liefest have it be.

[a] Unknown.

---

[1] For Fornet or Fornjot, see the index of names.

## .LXXI.

Ƿiþ þæȝe neofan nuðan ſpa ȝnene ſeoþ on ele ⁊ on
peaxe ſmɲe mið þone pæȝeneofan. Eſt nɪm ȝate hæɲi
ſmec unðeɲi þa bɲec ƿiþ þæɲ næȝe neofan. ȝɪſ holi
ſino ſoɲað ſie · nɪm ſoɲneteſ ſolm ſeoð on pætɲe
beþe mið þ lɪm ⁊ þpeah mð þ lɪm ⁊ pyɲice ɲealſe
óſ buteɲan ſmɲe æſteɲi baþe.

## .LXXII.

fol. 55 a.

On hpɪlce tɪð bloð ſie to ſoɲȝanne on hpɪlce to
lætenne. bloblæſ iſ to ſoɲȝanne ſiſtyne nɪhtum æɲ
hlaſmæɲſe ⁊ æſteɲi ſɪſ ⁊ þɲitiȝ nɪhtum ſoɲ þon þonne
calle æteɲino þɪnȝ ſleoȝaþ ⁊ mannum ſpɪðe ðeɲɪað ·
læcaſ læɲdon þa þe pɪɲoſte pæɲon þ nan man on þam
monþe ne ðɲenc ne ðɲunce ne ahɪɲæɲi hɪſ lichoman panɪȝe
butan hɪſ nyðþeaɲſ pæɲie · ⁊ þonne on mɪððelðaȝūm
ɪnne ȝepunoðe ſoɲ þon þe ſio lyſt bɪþ þonne ſpɪþoſt ȝemenȝeð. Romane hɪm ſoɲþon ⁊ calle ſuð ſolc poɲihton
eoɲþ huſ ſoɲ þæɲe lyſte pylme ⁊ æteɲineſſe. Eác
ſecȝeað læcaſ þte ȝeblopene pyɲta þonne ſien betɪte
to pyɲceenne ȝe to ðɲencum ȝe to ſealſum ȝe to ðuſte.
Þu món ſcule blob/læſe ón þaɲa ſix ſiɲa ælcūm on
monðe ſoɲȝan ⁊ hponne hɪt[1] betɪt ſie · læcaſ læɲað
eūc þ nan mán on þon ſiſ nɪhta calðne monan ⁊ eſt
x. nɪhta ⁊ ſiſtyne ⁊ tpentɪȝeſ ⁊ ſɪſ ⁊ tpentɪȝeſ ⁊

---

[1] The idea is blóð ſoɲlætan, for bloblæſe is feminine.

### lxxi.

For the dorsal muscle, seethe in oil and in wax, rue so green, smear the dorsal muscle therewith. Again, take goats hair, make it smoke under the breech up against the dorsal muscle. If a heel sinew be broken, take Fornets palm, seethe it in water, foment the limb therewith, and wash the limb therewith ; and work a salve of butter, smear after the fomentation.

### lxxii.

On what season bloodletting is to be foregone, on what to be practised. Bloodletting is to be foregone fifteen nights ere Lammas,[1] and after it for five and thirty nights, since then all venomous things fly and much injure men.[2] Leeches who were wisest, have taught, that in that month no man should either drink a *potion* drink, nor anywhere weaken his body, except there were a necessity for it ; and that in that case, he during the middle of the day should remain within, since the lyft *or air* is then most mingled *and impure.* The Romans for this reason, and all south folk, wrought to themselves earth houses, for the boiling heat and venomousness of the lyft.[3] Also leeches say that blossomed worts are then best to work, either for drinks, or for salves, or for dust. *Here is set forth* how a man shall forego bloodletting on each of the six fives in the month, and when it is best. Leeches teach that no man on the five nights old moon, and again on the ten nights *old,* and fifteen *nights old,* and twenty, and five and twenty, and on the thirty

---

[1] August 1.
[2] This refers to Italy and to its plumbeus auster, Autumnusque gravis, Libitinæ quæstus acerbæ.

[3] The Italian sirocco, per autumnos nocentem corporibus.

þurtiȝes nihta ealdne monan ne læte blod ac betþeox
þapa þex fifa ælcũm · Ᵹ nif nan blodlæytið fþa ȝod
fþa on þoþeþeaþdne lencten þonne þa yfelan þætan
beoþ ȝeȝaðeþode þe on þmtþa ȝeðþuncene beoð Ᵹ on
kalendaſ apꞃilif ealþa þeleſt þonne tþeop Ᵹ þyꞃta
æþeſt úp fþꞃyttað þonne þeaxeð fio yfele ȝilleftꞃe Ᵹ
ꝥ yfele blod on þam holcum þæꞃ lichoman.  ȝif monneꞃ blod ðolh yfeliȝe ȝenĩm þonne ȝeoꞃmen leaf apylle
on þætꞃe Ᵹ beþe mið · Ᵹ ȝecnua moþoþeaþde leȝe ón.
ȝif þu pille on fnͬiðe blod foplͬætan · nͬim ecteleſ hꞃum
ȝeȝnͬið to ðuſte þcead ón þa þunðe.  ȝenĩm ꞃuȝen healm
eft Ᵹ beꞃen ȝebꞃꞃ to ðuſte · ȝif þu ne maȝe blod
ðolh apꞃꞃan ȝenĩm hoꞃfef toꞃð nꞃpe aðꞃuȝe ón funnan
oððe be fyꞃe ȝeȝnͬið to ðuſte fpꞃþe þel leȝe ꝥ ðuſt
fpꞃþe þꞃece on lnenne clað þꞃꞃ mið þy ꝥ bloððolh
neahtepne.  ȝif þu ȝeotenð æðꞃe ne maȝe apꞃꞃan
ȝenͬm ꝥ þelfe blod ſe oꞃyꞃͬð ȝebæꞃn ón hatum ſtane
Ᵹ ȝeȝnͬið to ðuſte leȝe on þa æðꞃe ꝥ ðuſt Ᵹ¹ apꞃͬð
fpͬðe.  ȝif mon æt blodlͬætan ón fnͬpe beꞃlea menȝ
toꞃomne þeax Ᵹ pͬic Ᵹ feeapen fneꞃa leȝe on clað Ᵹ
on ꝥ ðolh. .

### .LXXIII.

Ȝif men cine hpile lm ȝenĩm ꞃuȝen mela ðo on ꝥ
lim Ᵹ nane þͬætan · ȝif þu þͬætan ðeſt to oꝥþe fmeꞃa
ꞃealꝼe ne meaht þu lͬit ȝelacnian Ᵹ ſe man ꞃeeal fpꞃþe
ſtille beon þy þu ꞃeealt lᵐne halne ȝeðon.

### .LXXIIII.

Þꞃþ þeaꞃtum Ᵹ þeaꞃꞃum¹ ón lᵐne · ȝenĩm fuȝþenan
Ᵹ huniȝef ꞃeap menȝ toȝæðeꞃe ðo on þa þeaꞃtan Ᵹ

---

¹ So in Latin Verrucæ are distinguished from Vari.

nights old moon should let blood, but betwixt each of the six fives: and there is no time for bloodletting so good as in early lent, when the evil humours are gathered which be drunken in during winter, and on the kalends of April best of all, when trees and worts first up sprout, when the evil ratten waxeth, and the evil blood, in the hulks *or hollow frame-works* of the body. If a lancet wound grow corrupt in a man, then take mallow leaves, boil them in water, and bathe therewith, and pound the netherward part *of the wort;* lay on. If thou wilt stop blood running in an incision, take kettle soot, rub it to dust, shed it on the wound. Again, take rye and barley halm, burn it to dust; if thou may not stanch a blood*letting* wound, take a new horses tord, dry it in the sun, or by the fire, rub it to dust thoroughly well, lay the dust very thick on a linen cloth, tie up for a night the blood-*letting* wound with that. If thou may not stanch a gushing vein, take that same blood which runneth out, dry it on a hot stone and rub it to dust, lay the dust on the vein, and tie up strong. If in bloodletting a man cut upon a sinew, mingle together wax, and pitch, and sheeps grease, lay on a cloth, and on the cut.

## lxxiii.

If for a man any limb *of his* become chinked *or chopped,* take rye meal, apply it to the limb and no wet ; if thou puttest wet to it, or a grease salve, thou mayest not cure it, and the man shall be very still, in that way thou shalt make him hole.

## lxxiv.

Against warts and callosities on a limb ; take sin-green, and juice of honey, mingle together, apply to the

ƿeaꞃꞃaꝼ. Eꝼꞇ cealꝼeꞃ ſccaꞃn ⁊ ahſan ᵹemenᵹ ƿið eceð
⁊ leᵹe ón. Eꝼꞇ ꞃiþieꞃ ꞃinðe ᵹebæꞃn ꞇo ahſan ðo eceð
ꞇo ꞇꞃiꝼula ſꞃiðe ⁊ leᵹe ón.

### .LXXV.

Ƿiþ ſcuꞃꝼeðum næᵹle · ním ᵹecyꞃnaðne ſꞇiccan ꞃeꞇe
ón þone næᵹl ƿið þa ꞃeaꞃꞇa ꞃleah þonne þ þ bloð
ſꞃꞃinᵹe úꞇ · ꞃyꞃc þonne þymel ꞇo ⁊ leᵹe ealð ſꞃic ón
uꞃan þone næᵹl healð þꞃiꞇiᵹ nihꞇa ƿiþ ꞃæꞇan · Nim
þonne hꞃæꞇen coꞃn ⁊ huniᵹ menᵹ ꞇoſomne leᵹe on ðo
þ ꞇo oþ þ hal ꞃie.

### .LXXVI.

Ƿiþ ᵹicþan ðoccan ⁊ ꞃyꞃm melu ⁊ ꞃcalꞇ[1] ealꞃa emꝼela
menᵹ ƿið ſuꞃe ꝼleꞇan ⁊ ſmiꞃe mið þy. Ƿiþ ᵹicþan
ním ſcꞃꞃꞇeaꞃo ⁊ iꝼiᵹꞇeaꞃo ⁊ ele ᵹnið ꞇoᵹæðeꞃe ðo
þꞃiððan ðæl ſealꞇeꞃ[2] ſmiꞃe mið þy.

fol. 56 b.

### .LXXVII.

Ᵹiꝼ þu ꞃille þ yꝼel ſꞃic ꞃaðe uꞇbeꞃ ſꞇe nim ꞃeax ⁊
heꞃnlic haꞇꞇe ꞃyꞃꞇ ᵹeheaꞇ ᵹeꞃyꞃmeð ꞇoſomne ꞃyꞃc ꞇo
ꞃcalꝼe binð on þa ſꞇoꞃa.

### .LXXVIII.

Giꝼ men unluſꞇ ſie ᵹeꞇenᵹe · nꞃne beꞇonican þ ꞃille
þꞃy ꞃeneᵹaꞃ ᵹeꞃeᵹan ðꞃꞏnc ón ſꞃeꞇꞃm ꞃꞇeꞃe.

### [LXXVIIII.]

Ᵹiꝼ món ꝼꞃaꞃn lonᵹum ꞃeᵹe ᵹeꞇeoꞃoð ſie ðꞃꞃnce be-

---

warts and the callosities. Again, mingle with vinegar
calfs sharn and ashes, and lay on. Again, burn to
ashes withys rind, add vinegar, triturate thoroughly,
and lay on.

### lxxv.

For a scurfy nail;[1] take a granulated bit of wood,
set *it* on the nail against the warts, then strike, so that
the blood may spring out, then work a thumbstall for
it, and lay old lard above upon the nail, hold it for
thirty nights against wet, then take wheaten corn and
honey, mingle *these* together, lay on, apply that till
all be well.

### lxxvi.

For itch, *take* dock and worms *reduced to* meal, and
salt, of all equally much, mingle with sour cream, and
smear with that. Against itch, take ship tar, and ivy
tar, and oil, rub together, add a third part of salt,
smear with that.

### lxxvii.

If thou shouldst desire that an evil swelling should
rathely burst, take wax and a wort hight hemlock,
beat them together when warmed, work to a salve,
bind on the places.

### lxxviii.

If to a man loss of appetite happen, let him take
betony, so much as will weigh three *silver* pennies,
and drink it in sweetened water.

### [lxxix.]

If a man is tired by a long journey, let him drink

---

[1] Thus. " Unguium scabritiem " : Plin. xxx. 37.

tonican on þam suðpeuan oxumelle · þ¹ eeeð ðpenc
þe þe æp befopan ppiton þiþ þiope healf ðeaðan
aðle.


### . LXXX.

Þiþ þon þe mon hine fopðpince. ðpince betonican
on pætpe æp oþepne ðpincan. Eft pyl betonican ⁊
copð ȝeallan on hluttpum calað oþþe on spilepe pætan
spa he ðpincan feyle ðpince simle æp mete. Eft
ȝenim spinej lunȝenne ȝebpæð ⁊ on neaht neptiȝ ȝenim
fif snæða simle.


### . LXXXI.

Þiþ miclan cele nim netelan feoþ on ele smipe ⁊
ȝnið ealne þinne lichoman mið se cyle ȝepit apeȝ.


### . LXXXII.

Ȝif men sie micel piece ȝetenȝe popiȝ ȝeȝnið on ele
smipe þinne þphtan mið ⁊ þone lichoman ealne pun-
ðopliee þaþe him biþ sio piecce ȝemettȝoð.


### . LXXXIII.

To monnej stemne nim ceppillan ⁊ puðuceppillan
hisceoppypt ontpan · ȝpunðefpelȝean pype to ðpence on
hluttpūm calað · xim þpco snæða butepan ȝemenȝe
pið hpæten mela ⁊ ȝepylte þiȝe mið ʌy ðpence ðo spa
niȝon mopȝenaf ma ȝif hiy þeapf sie.

---

betony in the southern drink, oxymel; the acid drink of which we before wrote in *treating* of the half dead disease.[1]

### lxxx.

In case a man should overdrink himself; let him drink betony in water before his other drink. Again, boil betony and earthgall in clear ale, or in such drink as he, *the drunkard*, may have to drink, let him drink this always before meat. Again, take a swines lung,[a] roast it, and at night fasting take five slices always.

### lxxxi.

Against mickle cold; take nettles,[b] seethe them in oil, smear and rub all thine body therewith: the cold will depart away.

### lxxxii.

If to a man there betide much wakefulness, rub down a poppy in oil, smear thy forehead therewith, and all thy body, wonderfully soon the wakefulness will be moderated for him.[2]

### lxxxiii.

For a mans voice; take chervil, and wood chervil, bishopwort, "ontre," groundsel, work *these* to a drink in clear ale. Take three slices of butter, mingle with wheaten meal, and salt it, swallow this with the *above* drink; do so for nine mornings, more if there be need of it.

---

[1] No such disease had been mentioned in this book; it is found, II. lix, with the receipt for oxymel.

[2] The change of pronouns is an error of the text.

### .LXXXIIII.

Ȝif mon þung ete aþeȝe buteþan ꞇ drince · se þung
ȝepiꞇ on þa buteþan. Eft ƿiþ þon stande on heafde
aflea him mon fela sceaþþena on þam scancan þonne
ȝepiꞇ uꞇ þ atter þuꞃh þa sceaþþan.

### .LXXXV.

Gif mon fundiȝe ƿiþ his feond to ȝefeohtanne stæþ
sƿealpan hꞃiððas ȝeseoþe on ƿine ete þonne æꞃ · oþþe
ƿylle ƿætꞃe seoðe.

### .LXXXVI.

Ƿiþ miclum ȝonȝe ofeꞃ land þy læs he teoꞃiȝe
mucȝƿyꞃt nime him on hand oþþe do on his sco þy
læs he meþiȝe ꞇ þonne he niman ƿille æꞃ sunnan
upȝanȝe cƿeþe þas poꞃð æꞃest. Tellam[1] ꞇe antemeꞃia
ne lasfus sum[2] In uia · ȝesena hie þonne þu up teo :·

fol. 57 b.

### .LXXXVII.

Ȝif manneſ feax fealle ƿyꞃc him sealfe nim þone
miclan þung ꞇ haꞃan sꞃꞃecel ꞇ eaꞃwiꞇe moþoþeaꞃðe ·
ꞇ feꞃðƿyꞃt · ƿyꞃc of þæꞃe ƿyꞃte ꞇ of þisum eallum
þa sealfe ꞇ of þæꞃe buteꞃan þe nan ƿæteꞃ on ne
come. Ȝif feax fealle apylle eoforfeaꞃn ꞇ beþe þ heafod
mid þy ipa ƿeaꞃme. Ƿiþ þon ȝif man calu sie · plimuſ

Nowhere.

se micla lęce seȝþ þiꞃne læcedom · ȝenim deade beon
ȝebꞃæꞃne to ahsan ꞇ linsæð eac do ele to on þ feoꞃe
sƿiþe lanȝe ofeꞃ ȝledum ascoh þonne ꞇ aꞃꞃinȝe ꞇ nime
ƿeliʒ leaf ȝecnuþiȝe ȝeote on þone ele · ƿylle eft
hƿile ón ȝledum ascoh þonne smiꞃe mid æfteꞃ baþe.

---

¹ Read Tollam.　　　　|　　² Read sim.

### lxxxiv.

If a man eat wolfs bane, let him eat and drink butter, the poison will go off in the butter. Again for
that, let him stand upon his head, let some one strike
him many scarifications on the shanks, then the venom
departs out through the incisions.

### lxxxv.

If a man try to fight with his foe, let him seethe
staith swallow nestlings[1] in wine, then let him eat
them ere *the fight,* or seethe them in spring water.

### lxxxvi.

For mickle travelling over land, lest he tire, let him
take mugwort[a] to him in hand, or put it into his shoe, Vol. I. xi. 1.
lest he should weary, and when he will pluck it, be-
fore the upgoing of the sun, let him say first these
words, " I will take thee, artemisia, lest I be weary on
the way," etc. Sign it with the sign of the cross,
when thou pullest it up.

### lxxxvii.

1. If a mans hair fall off, work him a salve, take
the mickle wolfs bane, and vipers bugloss, and the
netherward part of burdock, and ferdwort, work the
salve out of that wort, and out of all these, and out
of that butter on which no water hath come. If hair
fall off, boil the polypody fern, and foment the head with
that, so warm. In case that a man be bald, Plinius,
the mickle leech, saith this leechdom : take dead bees,
burn them to ashes, and linseed also, add oil upon that,
seethe very long over gledes, then strain, wring out,
and take leaves of willow, pound them, pour *the juice*
into the oil, boil again for a while on gledes, strain
them, smear therewith after the bath.

---

[1] *Sand martins, hirundines ripariæ.*

Þeaꝼoð bæþ ƿið þon · pehȝeꝼ leaꝼ ꝼylle on ƿæteꝛe
þƿeah mid þꝼ æꝛ þu hit ſmeꝛuꝛe ꝼ þa leaꝼ cnua ſpa
ȝeſoden ƿꝛið on niht ōn oþ þ hio ſie[1] dꝛiȝe þ þu mæȝe
ſmeꝛꝛan æꝼteꝛ mid þeꝛe ſcalꝼe do ſpa .xxx. mihta
leng ȝiꝼ hiꝛ þeaꝛꝼ ſie. Ƿiþ þon þe[2] hæꝛ ne ꝛeaxe
æmettan æȝꝛu ȝenim ȝnid ſmit on þa ſtope ne cymð
þæꝛ næꝼꝛe æniȝ ꝼeax ūp;

ȝiꝼ hæꝛ to þicce ſie ȝenīm ſpealpan ȝebæꝛn undeꝛ
tiȝelan to ahſan ꝼ læt ſceaðan þa abꝛan ōn.

. LXXXVIII.

Ƿiþ hoꝛꝛeꝛ hꝛeoꝼle · nim þa[3] haꝛanƿyꝛt cnua ƿel
ȝemenȝ þonne ƿið ꝼepꝼeꝛe buteꝛan ƿyl ſƿiðe ōn butꝛan ðo on þ hoꝛꝛ ſpa hit hatoſt mæȝe ſmiꝛe ælce
dæȝe ðo ſimle þa ꝛealꝼe ōn · ȝiꝼ ſio hꝛeoꝼol ſie micel
ȝenīm blond ȝehæt mid ſtanum þƿeah mid þy hlonde
ſpa hatum þ hoꝛꝼ · þonue hit dꝛiȝe ſie ſmiꝛe mid
þeꝛe ꝛealꝼe lacna mne. Eꝼt ȝenīm ƿyman ſcalt[2]
ȝehæt þƿeah mid þy · ꝼ ðonne dꝛiȝe ſie ſmiꝛe mid
ꝼꝛcceꝛ ſmeꝛꝛe. ȝiꝼ hoꝛꝼ ȝeallede ſie · nim æ·elꝼeꝛðinȝ
ƿyꝛt ꝼ ȝotꝛoþan · ꝼ maȝeþan ȝeenua ƿel ðo buteꝛan
to ꝛꝛinȝ pætende þuꝛh clað ðo hꝛit ſcalt ōn hꝛeꝛ
ſꝛiþe lācna þone ȝeallan mid. Ƿiþ hoꝛꝛeꝛ ȝeallan nīm
æꝛcþꝛotan ꝼ ȝōtꝛoþan uꝼeꝛeaꝛðe ꝼ boȝen eāc ſpa cnua
toſomne ƿyl on ƿyꝛle ꝼ ōn buteꝛan aſeoh þuꝛh clað
ſmiꝛe mid.

ȝiꝼ hoꝛꝼ ſie ōꝼꝼcoten oþþe oꝛeꝛ neat nīm omꝛꝛan
ꝛæð ꝼ ſcꝛtiſc ꝛeax ȝeꝛꝛinȝe mōn .XII. mæꝛꝛan oꝼeꝛ ꝼ
ðo hahȝ ꝛæteꝛ ōn þ hoꝛꝛ oððe on ſpa hꝛꝛlc nēat ſpa
hit ſie haꝼa ðe þa ƿyꝛte ſimle mid.

Ƿiþ ꝼon ilcan nīm tobꝛꝛeccenꝛe næðle eaȝe ſtꝛꝛȝe
hꝛndan on þone byꝛꝛlan ne lꝛþ nan tcona.

fol. 58 a.

fol. 58 b.

---

[1] For ſien.
[2] Read ƿiþ þon þ.
[3] After þa a word appears wanting.

[1] Read ƿyman ſcalteꝛ, as before,
xxxii. 2. ?

2. A head bath for that; boil willow leaves in water, wash with that, ere thou smear it, and pound the leaves so sodden, bind on at night, till they be dry, that thou may after smear with the salve; do so for thirty nights, longer if need for it be. In order that the hair may not wax; take emmets eggs, rub *them up*, smudge on the place; never will any hair come up there.

3. If hair be too thick, take a swallow, burn it to ashes under a tile, and have the ashes shed on.

### lxxxviii.

1. For a horses leprosy,[1] take the . . . . . harewort, pound it well, then mingle with fresh butter, boil thoroughly in butter, put it on the horse as hot as possible, smear every day, always apply the salve. If the leprosy be mickle, take piss, heat it with stones, wash the horse with the piss so hot; when it is dry, smear with the salve, apply *also* leechdoms inwardly. Again, take runnings of salt, heat them, wash with that, and when it is dry, smear with fishes grease. If a horse be galled, take stichwort, and goutweed, and maythe, pound well, add butter, wring it wetting it through a cloth, add white salt, shake thoroughly, leech the gall therewith. For a horses gall, take ashthroat, and the upward part of goutweed, and rosemary also, pound together, boil in fat and in butter, strain through a cloth, smear therewith.

2. If a horse or other neat be elf shot,[2] take sorrel seed and Scottish wax, let a man sing twelve masses over it, and put holy water on the horse, or on whatsoever neat it be, have the worts always with thee.

3. For the same; take an eye of a broken needle, give *the horse* a prick *with it* behind in the barrel, no harm shall come.

---

[1] Grease in the legs?
[2] The Scottish phrase for this disease; see the Glossary.

## Book II.

.I. Þas læcedomas belimpað to eallum innoþa met-trymnessum.

.II. Læcedomas wiþ magan sare ealra · X. ⁊ ᵹif se maᵹa aþeneð sie ⁊ hwæt he þicᵹean scyle on þære adle.

.III. Læcedomas be ᵹespelle ⁊ sare þær magan hu him mon scyle blod lætan.

.IIII. Læcedomas wiþ heardum spyle þær magan ⁊ smeresses ⁊ hwæt he þicᵹean scyle.

.V. Læcedomas wiþ magan awundenesse ⁊ hwæt he on þære adle þicᵹe.

.VI. Læcedomas wiþ unluste ⁊ plætan þe of magan cymð ⁊ hwæt he þicᵹean scyle · IIII. cræftas.

.VII. Læcedomas wið abeadodum magan ⁊ ᵹif he for-soᵹen sie ⁊ tacn abeadodes magan hu þ ne ᵹemylt þ he þicᵹeþ · VI. læcedomas.

.VIII. Læcedomas wiþ sare ⁊ unluste þær magan se þe ne mæᵹ ne mid mete ne mid drincan beon ᵹelacnod ⁊ bitere hwæcetunge þropað · IIII. cræftas.

.VIIII. Læcedomas wiþ iwunde magan.

.X. Læcedóm wið plættan ⁊ to hætenne untrumne magan ;

.XI. Læcedóm wiþ awundenesse magan windiᵹre ⁊ eþunge.

.XII. Læcedóm wiþ spiwþan ⁊ wiþ þon ðe him mete under ᵹewunian nelle.

.XIII. Læcedóm wiþ magan springe.

.XIIII. Læcedóm wið eallum magan untrumnessum.

.XV. Læcedóm wiþ þær magan springe þonne þurh inuþ bitere hræð oþþe healcet oþþe him on þam

# BOOK II.

i. These leechdoms belong to all disorders of the inwards.

ii. Leechdoms for sore of the maw, in all ten, and if the maw be distended, and what the patient shall eat in that disorder.

iii. Leechdoms for swelling and sore of the maw, how one must let him, *the patient*, blood.

iv. Leechdoms for hard swelling of the maw, and smearings, *or unguents*, and what *the patients* diet shall be.

v. Leechdoms for puffing up of the maw, and what *the patient* shall partake of in this disorder.

vi. Leechdoms for want of appetite and for nausea, which cometh of the maw, and what *the patient* shall eat; four crafts, *or skilful recipes*.

vii. Leechdoms for deadened maw, and if it have bad lymph, and tokens of deadened maw, how that digests not, which it eateth; six leechdoms.

viii. Leechdoms for sore and want of appetite of the maw, which may be cured neither with meat nor drink, and suffereth bitter risings in the throat; four receipts.

ix. Leechdoms for an inward wound of the maw

x. A leechdom for nausea, and to heat an infirm maw.

xi. A leechdom for windy inflation of the maw, and for puffing up.

xii. A leechdom for spewing, and in case that *a mans* meat will not keep down.

xiii. A leechdom for flux of the maw.

xiv. A leechdom for all infirmities of the maw.

xv. A leechdom for irritation of the maw when there is a bitter heart burn in the mouth, or there is belching,

maʒan þe mete abþceþað ꞇ þyʒeþ[1] ꞇ hu ſio ablaþunʒ
þæþ maʒan cymð oꝼ þam blacum omum.

.XVI. Lærcedomaſ ꞇ ꞇaen þæþ haꞇan omihꞇan maʒan
unʒemeꞇ ꝼæþꞇa ꞇ þæþ unʒeſceaðlice cealdan maʒan
ꞇaen hu þe haꞇa omihꞇa maʒa unʒemeꞇ þuþſꞇ ꞇ ſþol
þþoþað ꞇ neaþoneþþe ꞇ ʒeſþoʒunʒa ꞇ ʒemodeſ ꞇþeonunʒe
unluſꞇ ʒe plæꞇꞇa · ꞇ hu ðone cealdan maʒan unʒelic-
lice meꞇꞇaſ lyſꞇe · lærcedomaſ ꞇo bþem micle ꞇ eþele ·
ꞇ be laꞇꞇþe melꞇunʒe ſumþa meꞇꞇa.

fol. 59 b.

.XVII. Lærceeþaeſꞇaſ be liþþe miþðenlice ʒeeyndo ꞇ
adlūm ꞇ hu hio on þa ſþiðþan ſidan aþeneð biþ oþ
þone nuſeoþan · ꞇ hu hio biþ ꝼꞇþkeþþeðn · ꞇ hu hio iſ
blodeþ ꞇimbeþ ꞇ huþ ꞇ þꞇe þex þinʒ þyþceaþ hþeþ-
þæþice ꞇ lærcnunʒ þaþa ealþa ꞇ ſpeoꞇol ꞇaen þaþa ealþa
ʒe be miezean ʒe be unluſꞇe · ʒe be hiþ hiþe · ꞇ
oþþūm maneʒum ꞇaenum.

.XVIII. Lærcaſ heþað þyþne lærcedōm þið liþþe ſþyle ꞇ
aþundeneþþe.

.XVIIII. Lærceaſ ſeezeaþ þaſ ꞇaen be aſpollenþe ꞇ
ʒeþundaðþe liþþe · ꞇ lærcedomaſ þið þon · ꞇ be þæþe
liþþe heaþðunʒe.

.XX. Lærcaſ læþað þiſ þið þaeþe liþþe þunde þonne
þe ſþyle ʒe þyþmſ ꞇobyþſꞇ.

.XXI. Lærcedomaſ ꞇ ꞇaen aheaþðoðþe liþþe · ꞇ āblaþ-
enþe ōn maniʒꝼealde þiſan ʒe on þām heþþum ʒe on
þām uꝛeþmm ʒe on þam ꝼilmenum ʒe on þam holcum
þaeþe liþþe.

.XXII. Lærcedomaſ þið þaeþe ʒeꝼelan[2] heaþðneſſe þaeþe
liþþe ꞇ þealꝛa ꞇ þyþꞇðþeneaſ oþþe ʒiꝛ hio ꞇobyþſꞇ ꞇ
uꝛeþm ʒeꝛíꞇ oðða ūþaſꞇihð oþþe ꞇo lanʒſum þyþð ſio
unʒeꝼele aheaþðunʒ þaeþe liþþe;

fol. 60 a.

---

[1] The text has þuʒeð.
[2] As the same reading occurs in | the full text we cannot alter to
| unʒeþelan.

or if the meat turns bitter in the maw and he hickets, and how the upblowing of the maw cometh of black bile.

xvi. Leechdoms and tokens of the hot inflamed maw, inmeasurably fast, *and not to be moved*, and of the unreasonably cold maw ; tokens how the hot inflamed maw suffers infinite thirst, and swealing heat, and oppression, and swoonings, and vacillation of the mind, loss of appetite or nausea ; and how variety of meats pleases the cold maw ; leechdoms for both, mickle and noble ; and of the late digestion of some meats.

xvii. Leechcrafts of the various nature and disorders of the liver, and how it is extended on the right side as far as the pit of the belly, and how it is five lobed, and how it is the material and home of blood ; and that six things work acute pain in the liver, and the cure of all these, and a plain token of them all, either by the urine, or by loss of appetite, or by *the mans* complexion, and by many other tokens.

xviii. Leeches teach this leechdom for swelling and puffing up of the liver.

xix. Leeches speak of these tokens of a swollen and wounded liver; and leechdoms for that; and of hardening of the liver.

xx. Leeches teach this for wound of the liver, when the swelling or matter bursteth forth.

xxi. Leechdoms and tokens of a hardened and puffed up liver in manifold wise, either in the lobes, or in the margins, or in the membranes, or in the hollows, of the liver.

xxii. Leechdoms for the sense of hardness of the liver, and salves, and wort drinks, or if it burst and descend downwards or mounteth up upwards,[1] or if the insensibility and hardness of the liver become too prolonged.

---

[1] All the viscera were supposed to get out of place.

.XXIII. Læcedomas hƿæt him sie to forganne on lifer adle hƿæt him sie to healdanne ge on læcedomum ge ōn mete · ⁊ tacn ꝥ se sƿile ƿyrman ne mæg ne utyrnan ōn þære lifre. :·

.XXIIII. Læcedomas ⁊ ƿyrtdrencas ƿiþ eallum lifer ƿærcum ealra þreotyne ⁊ gīf lifer ƿeaxe. :·

.XXV. Læcas eac be eallum ƿambe coþum ⁊ adlūm sceotol tacn fundon ⁊ læcedomas ⁊ hu mōn þa yfelan ƿætan þære ƿambe lācnian scyle ⁊ þonne adl to þære ƿambe ƿile for þære yfelan ōmihtan ƿætan cneoƿ hatiað[1] lendenu hefegiað sƿriað þara lendena hrian · togeoteþ[2] betƿeox sculdrūm utgong gemenged.

.XXVI. Læcedomas gif sio ƿamb ƿund bið hu ꝥ mōn ōngitan mæge ⁊ gelācnian · V. cræftas. :·

.XXVII. Læcedomas be ƿambe misSenlicre gecyndo oþþe misbyrdo hu ꝥ mōn mæge ongitan ⁊ gelacnian ⁊ be ƿambe hatre gecyndo · ⁊ be cealdre ⁊ ƿætre
fol. 60 b. gecyndo ⁊ be hatre ⁊ drigre gecyndo ⁊ ꝥ hæmed þing ne duge · þynnum lichoman ⁊ ne sceþeþ hatum ne ƿætum · feoƿer cræftas ⁊ ꝥte hæmed þing sƿiðost eglað þam ðe horn adle habbað. :·

.XXVIII. Læcedomas ƿiþ þon þe monnes ꝥ ufeƿƿre hrif sie gefylled ƿið yfelre ƿætan ⁊ be ƿindigre ƿambe. :·

.XXVIIII. Læcedomas ƿiþ þon þe mete untela myltte ⁊ cirre ōn fule ⁊ yfle ƿætan oþþe scittan. :·

---

[1] Read healtiað? but hatiað is in the full text.

[2] Read togetteþ from the full text.

---

[1] The maw is the organ of digestion, the stomach; the wamb is the venter, whatever that may mean.

[2] The "hot and cold, wet and "dry" theory was an attempt of the "rationalis disciplina" of the Hellenes to arrive at scientific generalizations; it is traceable among the works attributed to Hippokrates and in Aristoteles.

.xxx. Læcedomaſ ᵹiſ þu ƿille þ þin ƿamb ſie
ſimle ᵹeſund ⁊ be coðe ⁊ ſaƿe be ƿambe coðe ⁊ inne
ƿaƿan ſaƿe ⁊ to ƿambe ᵹemetlicunᵹe ſyxtyne cƿæſ-
taS.

.xxxi. Læcedomaſ ⁊ tacnunᵹ on þam ƿoppe ⁊ ſmæl
þeaƿme ⁊ ōn utᵹonᵹe hu hie þroƿiað oƿmætne þurſt ·
⁊ unluſt · ⁊ be hnopa hipe ⁊ þām naſolan ⁊ ſæᵹſeoſan
⁊ bæc þeaƿme ⁊ niƿeſeoþan ⁊ milte[1] ſcaƿe ⁊ hu un-
hæcaſ ƿenað þ þ ſie lendenaðl oþþe milt ſæƿe ⁊ hƿæſi
þa ƿamb ſeocan þa aðle þroƿien ⁊ hu hun ſie · ⁊ hu
fol. 61 a. hnopa mon tilian ſcyle ſeoƿeſ ƿiſa.[2]

.xxxii. Læcedomaſ hu mon ſƿa ᵹeƿaðne mān lacnian
ſcule · ᵹe mid blodlæſe ⁊ ſealſe ⁊ baðo ⁊ lācnūnᵹ on
þ hƿiſ to Senðanne · ⁊ þaſ læcedomaſ maᵹon ƿið
lendenece · ⁊ ᵹiſ mōn ſonðe miᵹe · ƿiþ ut ƿæƿce · ƿið
maᵹan aðlum ⁊ claſunᵹa ⁊ ƿiſa dedteƿneſſum · ⁊ be
þæƿe coðe hu man lyſte utᵹan ⁊ ne mæᵹ · ⁊ ᵹiſ ſe
utᵹanᵹ ſie ƿinðiᵹ ⁊ ſæteƿiᵹ ⁊ blodiᵹ · XII. ƿiſan.

.xxxiii. Læcedomaſ ƿið þæƿe ſƿecnan coðe þe ſe
mōn hiſ utᵹanᵹ þuƿh ðone muð him ſƿām ƿyſƿð ⁊
aſƿiƿan ſceal · ⁊ ƿið Innoðrunðum ⁊ ſmæl þeaƿma
ſaƿe · ⁊ ƿið tohƿocenum mnoþīim ⁊ ƿiþ ſoƿtoᵹeneſſe
innan · ⁊ ƿið þæƿe ƿambe þe late mylt ⁊ ſe þaƿa læcedoma ne ᵹiinð þonne becymð him ōn ſæteƿ bolla hƿeſi
þæƿe milteſ ſaƿ mieᵹean ſoƿhæſðneſ ƿambe ablaƿunᵹ
lendenƿæƿe ſonð ⁊ ſtanaſ ōn blæðƿan ƿeaxað þƿeotyne
cƿæſtaſ.

[1] Read milte ⁊.         [2] Before erasure, ƿiƿan.

xxx. Leechdoms if thou will that thy wamb be al-ways sound, and of disease and sore; and of disease of the wamb and sore of the intestines, and for the moderation[1] of the wamb; sixteen receipts.

xxxi. Leechdoms and symptoms marking of the rope gut and small gut, and of the fæcal discharge; how they suffer unbounded thirst and loss of appetite; and of their *complexion or* hue, and of the navel, and the dorsal muscles, and rectum, and pit of the belly, and milt, and share *or pubes,* and how bad leeches ween that that is loin disease or milt wark, and where the wambsick suffer the disorder, and how it is with them, and how a man shall treat them: four methods.

xxxii. Leechdoms how a man shall cure one so afflicted, whether with bloodletting, and salve, and baths, and *how* to send curatives into the belly. And these leechdoms are efficacious against loin ache, if a man mie sand, for dysentery, for diseases of the maw, and gripings, and womens tendernesses, and of the disease where a man would evacuate and is not able (*tenesmus*), and if the discharge be windy, and watery, and bloody. Twelve methods.

xxxiii. Leechdoms for the perilous disease in which a man casteth from him and speweth, as they say, his excrement through the mouth; and for wounds of the inwards, and sore of the small guts, and for laceration of the inwards, and for inward spasm; and for the wamb which digests late, and the man who is not affected by the leechdoms; there cometh on him dropsy, pain in liver, sore of spleen, retention of urine, inflation of belly, pain in loins, sand and stones wax in the bladder. Thirteen receipts.

---

[1] The "temperies" and "commoderatio ventris," that it be neither too hot nor too cold.

.XXXIIII. Læceðomaɼ ꞃ be þæɼ manneɼ mılꞇum ꞅceal
mōn þa læceðomaꞅ ꞃellan þe þonne ᵹeꞃoᵹe ꞅynð · ᵹe
heaꞃðe · ᵹe heoꞃꞇan · ꞃ þambe · ꞃ blæðꞃan ꞃ ꞃoᵹeþan ·
ꞃ hu ᵹeaꞃ̈eꞃ hıꞇ ꞅie be hæꞇo ꞃ cele ꞃ ƿıþ laꞇꞇꞃe ınel-
ꞇınᵹe · oððe ᵹıꞃ þamb ꞃoꞃꞃeaxen ꞃ ꞃoꞃꞃunðoð ꞅie ·
ꞃ ᵹıꞃ mon ꞅie ınnan ꞃoꞃblaƿen · ꞃ ƿıð þambe ƿꞃınum[1]
ꞃ ᵹıeþūm · nyᵹan ƿıꞃan.

.XXXV. Læceðomaɼ be cılða oꞃeꞃꞃyllo ꞃ þambe ꞃ ᵹıꞃ
lı̄m meꞇe ꞇela ne mylꞇe ꞃ lı̄m ꞅꞃaꞇ ōꞃᵹa ꞃ ꞅꞇınce
ꞃule.

.XXXVI. Læceðomaꞅ be mılꞇe ꞃꞃꞃce ꞃ þ̈ he bıð on
þa ƿınꞃꞇꞃan[2] ꞅıðan ꞃ ꞇacn ðæꞃe aðle hu huᵹeleaꞅe hı
beoð ꞃ hu lanᵹ ꞅe mılꞇe ꞅıe ꞃ be þæꞃ mılꞇeꞃ ꞃılmene
on þa ƿınꞅꞇꞃan healꞃe be hleahꞇꞃe þe ōꞃ mılꞇe cymð ·
hu ꞃe mılꞇe æᵹhꞃæꞇ þꞃoꞃað þæꞃ þe oþeꞃ lımo ᵹe hāꞇ
ᵹe cealð · ꞃ be bæðe ꞃ hæmeð þınᵹe ꞃ hꞃanan ꞅıo
hæꞇo cume ꞃ cele þæꞃ mılꞇeꞃ eahꞇa cꞃæꞃꞇaꞅ.

.XXXVII. Læceðomaꞅ hu mōn ꞅcyle þone mōnnān
lnnan ꞃ uꞇan mıð cealðum ꞃ haꞇum læceðomum lácnıan ꞃ hƿılc meꞇe hım ꞅie ꞇo þıcᵹenne ꞃ hƿılc hım ꞅie
ꞇo ꞃoꞃᵹanne.
.XXXVIII. Læceðomaꞅ hu mon ꞃceal þa ꞃæꞇan ꞃ þon-
ꞃceaꞃꞇa uꞇan lácnıan ꞃ be þam ꞃæꞇum yꞃlum þæꞃ
mılꞇeꞃ ꞃ ƿıð ꞅlıꞃunᵹe ꞃæꞇan þæꞃ mılꞇeꞃ.

.XXXVIIII. Læceðom ƿıþ ƿınðıᵹꞃe aþunðeneꞃꞃe þæꞃ
mılꞇeꞅ ꞅıo cymð oꞃ æpla æꞇe ꞃ hnuꞇa · ꞃ ꞃyꞅena · ꞃ
hunıᵹeꞅ æꞇe ꞃ þone ꞃoꞃ ꞃ ınneꞃoꞃan ꞃ þambe ꞃ

---

xxxiv. Leechdoms; and the leechdoms which are suitable to the case shall be administered according to the mans powers, whether in head, or heart, and of wamb, and bladder, and lymph; [1] and according as the time of year may be, in regard to heat and cold; and for late digestion, or if the wamb be overgrown and wounded; and if a man be blown out inwardly; and for prurience, and itchings of the wamb; nine methods.

xxxv. Leechdoms for the overfilling *or surfeit* of children, and for their wamb, and if their meat digest not well, and if sweat pass from them and stink foully.

xxxvi. Leechdoms of pain in the milt, and that *the milt* is on the left side, and tokens of the disease, how reckless *the sick* are, and how long the milt is, and of the film *or membrane* of the milt on the left side, and of *splenetic* laughter, which cometh of the milt, how the milt suffereth everything of that which other limbs *suffer* either hot or cold; and of the bath, and of sexual commerce, and whence the heat cometh and the cold of the milt: eight receipts.

xxxvii. Leechdoms how a man shall tend the man within and without with cold and hot leechdoms, and what meat he is to take, and what he is to forego.

xxxviii. Leechdoms how a man shall cure the humours and the livid complexion by external applications, and of the evil humours of the milt, and of the lubricity of the humours of the milt.

xxxix. A leechdom for a windy swollen state of the milt, which cometh of eating of apples, and of nuts, and of peas, and of honey, and which puffeth up throughout the rope gut, and the intestines, and the

---

[1] Gastric juice.

maȝan þa ȝeond blapað · ⁊ pið roȝeþan ⁊ feadan þe öf nilte cymð · ⁊ hu fio aðl ȝepent ön pæteþ bollan ealleþ tyn cþæftaþ.           :·

.XL. Læcedomaf be ablapunȝe ⁊ aheaþðunȝe þæf bloðef on þam nilte.                          :·

.XLI. Læcedomaf pið þæpe heaþðneƴþe ⁊ fape nilteƴ ⁊ hu mon mæȝ fpineƴ blæðpan mið ecebe ȝeƴlðþe ȝehneƴcan þa heaþðneƴþe ⁊ pið callum maðlum þƴy cþæftaS.                               :·

.XLII. Læcedomaf ȝiƴ omihtpe bloð ⁊ yƴele pætan on þam nilte ƴyn þinbenbe þonne ƴceal him mön bloð lætan on þaƴ pyƴan þe þeoƴ læceboc feȝþ · ⁊ be þæƴ bloðeƴ lupe.                      :·

.XLIII. Læcedomaƴ hpæt lim on þæpe able to þiȝenne fie hpæt to ƴoƴȝanne.        :·

.XLIIII. Læcedom eƴt ƴe þe þ yƴel uttihð oƴ þam nilte fpiðe æþele · ⁊ ƴe eac beah pið maȝan ablapunȝe ⁊ Innoþa hneƴceþ þa pambe þynnaþ þa oman · bitepe hpæcetunȝe apeȝ beþ ⁊ hþeoft coþe · ⁊ ƴið þæþe · ⁊ hƴeþ able ⁊ nilte pæþe · ⁊ pambe pinð eal þa hliht.   :·

.XLV. Læcedomaƴ ⁊ fpiððþene pið afpollenum.        :·

.XLVI. Læcedomaf pið ȝehpæþeþþe fiðan ƴaþe ⁊ tacn punðopheu hpanan fio cume ⁊ hu fio aðl topeaþð fie · ⁊ hu mon þaþa tilian ƴcyle.            :·

.XLVII. Læcedomaƴ þa ðe þynnunȝe hæbben ⁊ fmal unȝe mæȝen · þam lichoman þe þa lueto meðmicle oþþe ftþanȝe þþopien ⁊ hu mön fcyle fpineƴ blæðpan ön ðon.                                :·

.XLVIII. Læcedomaf ƴelþan ȝiƴ þaƴ oþþe helpe ne fyn hu him mön eac bloð ƴcyle lætan.     :·

.XLVIIII. Læcedomaf ⁊ peax ƴealƴa ⁊ ƴccaþþunȝa pið fiðan ƴaþe ⁊ hpæt he þiȝean ƴcyle.         :·

wamb *or venter*, and the maw *or stomach*, sobbing and watery congestions which come from the milt, and how the disease turneth into dropsy: in all ten crafts.

xl. Leechdoms for inflation and for hardening of the blood in the milt.

xli. Leechdoms for the hardness and sore of the milt, and how a man may with a swines bladder filled with vinegar, make nesh the hardness; and for all *its* inward diseases; three recipes.

xlii. Leechdoms in case inflammatory blood and ill humours in the milt are enlarging it: then shall *the sick* be let blood in these ways which this Leech book saith; and of the hue of the blood.

xliii. Leechdoms *telling* what during that disorder is to be the diet, and what *food* is to be foregone.

xliv. A leechdom, again, a very noble one, which draweth out the evil out of the milt; and this *leechdom* is also efficacious for puffing up of the maw and of the inwards; it maketh nesh the wamb, it thinneth the hot secretions, it doth away bitter throat risings, and breast disease, and side pains, *pleurisy*, and liver disease, and milt pains, and wamb wind; all them it lighteneth.

xlv. Leechdoms and a powerful potion for the swollen.

xlvi. Leechdoms for sore of either side, and wondrous tokens whence the disease cometh, and how it is imminent, and how it should be dealt with.

xlvii. Leechdoms which have the main *or virtue* of thinning and smalling *or small making;* for the bodies which suffer a moderate or strong heat, and how a swines bladder should be applied.

xlviii. Better leechdoms if these others are not for a help, how, also, *the patient* shall be let blood.

xlix. Leechdoms, and wax salves, and scarifications for sides sore, and *a declaration* what he, *the sick*, shall take *for diet.*

fol 63 a.

.L. Læcedomaſ eft ƿið ſiðan ſare. :·

.LI. Læcedomaſ ƿið lunȝen adle ⁊ laþhƿen tacn hƿanan ſio adl cume ⁊ hu mon lacnian ſcyle · ðrencaſ ⁊ ſealfa ⁊ briƿaſ ȝe ƿið lunȝe punde ⁊ ȝif lunȝen breoþe · ⁊ ȝif lunȝen ðruȝiȝe an ⁊ tƿentiȝ craſta. :·

.LII. Læcedomaſ ⁊ ſriƿeðrencaſ mannum to hæle ⁊ ȝif man hine ofeſi ȝemet bþcce to ſriþanne ⁊ eſt þece ðrenc oþþe ȝif ðrenc oſ men nelle callcſ tƿentiȝ ðrencea. :·

.LIII. Læcedomaſ ⁊ leohte ðrencaſ mannum to hælo ⁊ ũnſpiule ðrenceaſ þiþ untþumum innoþum eahta craſtaſ. :·

.LIIII. Læcedomaſ ⁊ ðrencaſ ƿið miſtice ⁊ ȝif ſtice butan innoþe ſie. :·

.LV. Læcedomaſ ⁊ ðrencaſ ȝif mõn innan ſoþhæſð ſie ⁊ þiþ incoþe ⁊ ſæp coþe. :·

.LVI. Læcedomaſ ȝif mon ſie õn utræþce ⁊ tacn be utþihte ȝe õn þam uſerþan hriſe ȝe õn þam niþerþan ⁊ hƿanan ſio adl cume ⁊ hu mõn hie ſcyle lacnian ⁊ hƿæt mon þicȝean ſcyle ⁊ eſt þiþ þon ȝif mon blode ane utȝrne ⁊ þiþ miclum ſare ⁊ ablanneſſe þæſ in-

fol. 63 b.

noþeſ oþþe ȝif mon ſoſi ſoþþeſ untþumneſſe utȝrne oþþe ȝif hƿa blodryne þrorȝe on þam niþerþan dælum hiſ lichoman oþþe ȝif hƿam ſie micȝe on blod ȝif hƿo ȝehryſþ · oððe ȝif mõn ũtȝanȝ næbbe ⁊ eſt ũt-yrnende hriſ ſiſ ⁊ hund ſeoſontiȝ læcedoma. :·

.LVII. Læcedomaſ þiþ þeaſmeſ ũtȝanȝe ⁊ ȝif men hilyhte ſie ymb þone þeaſm ⁊ ƿið blæc¹ þeaſmeſ ũtȝanȝe niȝon ſiſan. :·

---

¹ Read bæc.

*Prolapsus.*

---

[1] Cloudy.

uꞇꞃæꞵce · ⁊ ȝiꝼ mon bloðe ſꝑiꝑe · ⁊ ꝑiþ blóðꝛyne · ⁊
ȝiꝼ him ꝼæꝛunȝa ace · ⁊ ꝑiþ blæce on ꝑlican.     :·

   .LXIIII. Læceðóm ꝛe moꝿan[1] ꝑiþ innoþeꝛ ꝼoꝛhæꝼð-
neꞃꞅe ⁊ ȝuꞇomon.[2] ꝑið milꞇe ꝛæꝑce ⁊ ſꞇice ⁊ ſꝑican
ꝑiþ uꞇꞃihꞇan ⁊ ðꞃaconꞇjan ꝑiþ ꝼule hoꝛaꞅ on men · ⁊
alꝑan ꝑiþ unꞇꞃymneꞃꞅum · ⁊ ȝalbaneꞅ ꝑiþ neaꞃꝑúm
bꞃeoſꞇum · ⁊ balʒaman ſmiꞃinȝ ꝑiþ eallúm unꞇꞃúm-
neꞃꞅúm ⁊ ꝑeꞇꞃaoleum ꞇo ðꞃincanne anꝛealð ꝑiþ innan
ꞇyðeꞃneꞃꞅe ⁊ uꞇan ꞇo ſmeꞃꝑanne · ⁊ ꞇyꝛiaca iꞅ ȝoð
ðꞃenc ꝑiþ innoþ ꞇyðeꞃneꞃꞅum · ⁊ ꞅe hꝛiꞇa ſꞇan ꝑið
eallúm uncuþum bꞃocum.

   .LXV. Læceðóm ȝiꝼ hoꝛꞅ ꞅie óꝼꞅcoꞇen ⁊ ꝑiþ úꞇꞃæꞵce ·
⁊ ȝiꝼ uꞇȝanȝ ꝼoꞃꞅeꞇen ꞅie · ⁊ ꝑiþ lencꞇen aðle · eꝼꞇ
ꝑiþ uꞇꞃæꞵce ⁊ ꝑiþ unlybbum ⁊ ꝑiþ þæꝛe ȝeolꝑan aðle
⁊ ȝiꝼ men ſie ꝼæꝛlice yꝼele ⁊ ꞇo ȝehealðanne lichoman
hælo ⁊ ꝑiþ ȝicþan ⁊ ꞅlue ⁊ ꝑiþ lonð aðle ⁊ ȝonȝel-
ꝑæꞃꝑan biꞇe · ⁊ ꝑið uꞇꞃihꞇe ⁊ heaꝼoð ꞅealꝼa.

   .LXVI. Þe þam ſꞇane þe ȝaȝaꞇeꞅ haꞇꞇe.
   .LXVII. Þe ꝛæȝe eleꞅ ⁊ oþeꝛꝛa miꞅſenlicꝛa þinȝa.    :·

## [I.]

Alexander
Trallianus, lib.
vii. cap. *i*, ed.
R. Stephani,
1548.

Þiꞅ ſinꞇ ꞇacn aðleꞅ maȝan · æꝛeſꞇ ȝelome ſꝛæꞇunȝa
oððe hꝛæcunȝa · cⅰꞃneꞅ ⁊ ꞅe man hine ȝelome ꞇo ſꝛi-
ꝑanne · ⁊ he ónꝼinðeþ ſꝛile ⁊ þ́ þa oman beoð inne
beꞇynðe þuꝛh þa ablaꝑunȝe · ⁊ him bið uneþe þuꝛſꞇ
ȝeꞇenȝe. Éac oꝼ þæꞅ maȝan aðle cumað moꝿȝe ⁊
miꞅſenlica aðla ȝeboꝛſꞇena punða ⁊ hꝛamma ⁊ ꝼylle
ꝛæꝛe ⁊ ꝼienða aðl · ⁊ micla muꝛnunȝa ⁊ unꝛoꞇneꞃꞅa
buꞇan þeaꝛꝼe ⁊ oman ⁊ unȝemeꞇlica meꞇe ꞅócna ⁊
unȝemeꞇlice unluſꞇaꞅ ⁊ cⅰꝛneꞃꞅa · ⁊ ſaꝛa inaðle ón ꝑiꝼeꞅ

---

¹ Read ꝛeamoꝿan, which is mentioned elsewhere in this book II, iii, 3.,
and is a strong purgative.
² Read ȝuꞇ ammon.

blood, and for blood running ; and if a limb suddenly ache, and for a blotch on the face.

lxiv. A leechdom; scamony for constipation of the inwards, and ammoniac drops for pain in the milt, and stitch, and spices [1] for diarrhœa, and gum dragon for foul disordered secretions on a man, and aloes for infirmities, and galbanum for oppression in the chest and balsam dressing for all infirmities, and petroleum to drink simple for inward tenderness, and to smear outwardly, and a tryacle, that is a good drink, for inwards tendernesses, and the white stone, *lapis Alabastrites,* for all strange griefs.

lxv. A leechdom if a horse be elf shot, and for pain in evacuation of the fæces, and if the evacuation be stopped, and for the "lent disease," *or typhus;* again for pain in evacuation, and for poisons, and for the yellow disease *or jaundice,* and if sudden evils come on a man; and to preserve the bodys health, and against itch and elf, and for "land disease" *or nostalgia,* and for bite of the gangway weaver, *spider,* and for diarrhœa and head salves.

lxvi. Of the stone which agate hight.

lxvii. Of the weight of oil, and of other various things.

### i.

These are tokens of diseased maw ; first, frequent spittings or breakings, choiceness *or a daintiness about food,* and for the man to spew frequently ; and he will have a sense of swelling, and that the hot inflamed humours are shut up within him by the inflation ; and an uneasy thirst is contingent upon him. Also from disease of the maw come many and various diseases of bursten wounds, and cramps, and epilepsy, and fiends disease, and mickle murmurings and uneasiness without

---

[1] Cinnamon is much administered.

gecyndon ⁊ on fotum ⁊ blædran · ⁊ on unmode · ⁊
on ungemet ƿæccūm[1] ⁊ ungeƿitlico ƿord · se maga biþ
neah þære heortan ⁊ þære gelodr ·[2] ⁊ geadortenge þam
bræg[en]e · of þam cumað þa adla swiþost of þas magan
intingan ⁊ on[3] yflūm seawum ƿætan ætterberendum ·
þonne ða ƿætan[4] þa yfelan weorþaþ gegaderode on
þone magan · ⁊ þær rixiað mid scearfunga innan ·
fol. 65 b. swiþost on þam monnum þe habbað swiþe gefelne ⁊
sarerenne magan swa þ hie sume somnunga sweltaþ ·
ne magon aberan þa strangan scearfunga þæra
ætterna ƿætena · hƿilum ƿyrmas of þām inþerran[5]
dælūm geseceað þa uferran dælas to þam magan · ⁊ eāc
heortcoþe ƿyrceað · ⁊ angnessa ⁊ geswogunga swa þte
hƿilum sume men fram þara ƿyrma slitunge sweltað
⁊ forƿeorþað · for þon þæm mannūm deah þ him mon
on fruman þa mettas gife þe celunge ⁊ strangunge
mægen hæbben swa swa[6] beoþ æppla nales to swete
ealles āc surmelsce ⁊ peran ⁊ persucas ⁊ hlaf gedon
ōn ceald ƿæter oþþe ōn hat be þære gelicunge þæs
magan þe þa yfelan ƿætan sceorfendan ⁊ scearƿan
hæfð. þis deah eāc ōn fruman þam ðe þa heortcoðe
⁊ þ gesceorf ðrowiað ælcra gewist þ him mon lytlum
þa mettas selle þa þe late melten · leax[7] ⁊ þa fixas
þa ðe late meltan gose innefle[8] ⁊ swines fet þa ðe
mægen ƿiþ habban[9] þam yfelan ƿætan · ⁊ þonne him
sel sie þonne þicge he swetran mettas · ne biþ hīm
fol. 66 a. nanƿuht selre þonne he þa þicge þa þe late melten[10] ⁊

[1] The construction is faulty; it should be ⁊ unmod ⁊ ungemetƿæcce.

[2] Read gelodre? See Lye in geloda. Also bræge, MS

[3] Read of.

[4] At this point our author skips over seven folio pages and goes on at lib. vii. cap. ιά, p. 114, ed. 1548.

[5] The interpreter omits *οἱ τῆς ῥοᾶς κόκκοι, the seeds of the pomegranate,* and *ῥοδάκινα, nectarines,* and *ἡ αὐστηρὸν καὶ ψυχρὸν ἔχουσα σταφυλή, grapes of a dry and cold flavour.*

[6] Read inþerran.

[7] The interpreter takes *ἰσικοί* for *salmon, esoces*, as was and is usual; and he neatly escapes *βοῦλβα, στέρνιον, ἀστακοί, cray fish, κτένια, scallops, κηρύκια, conch shell fish.*

[8] Read innelfe.

[9] Read habban ƿiþ.

[10] Our interpreter here varies from the printed text, which recommends frequent snacks of food; very wisely.

occasion, and erysipelatous eruptions, and immoderate
desires for meat, and immense want of appetite, and
daintinesses, and sore internal diseases in fœminæ natu-
ralibus, *that is, the uterus,* and in the feet, and in the
bladder, and despondency, and immoderately *long* wak-
ings, and witless words. The maw is near the heart and
the spine, and in communication with the brain, from
which the diseases come most violently, from the cir-
cumstances of the maw, and from evil juices, humours
venombearing. Then the evil humours get gathered
into the maw, and there they rule with excoriations
within ; especially in the men who have a very
sensitive and soon sore maw, so that some of them
suddenly die ; they are not able to bear the strong
excoriating effects of the venomous humours. At whiles
worms from the nether parts seek the upper parts, up
as far as the maw ; and they also work heart disease,[1]
and oppressive sensations, and swoonings ; so that sometimes some men by the gnawing of the worms die and
go to the dogs. Wherefore it is well for those men, that
at the first the meats be given them which have the
virtue of cooling and strengthening, such as be apples,
by no means too sweet, but by all means sourish, and
pears, and peaches, and loaf bread put into cold water or
into hot, according to the liking of the man which hath
the evil humours scarifying and sharp. This also is of
importance in the first place to them who suffer the
heart disease[2] and the abrasion ; it is fitting that one
should give them by little *at a time* the meats which
tardily digest, as lax *or salmon,* and the fishes which
slowly digest, goose giblets, and swines feet, and such
as have a virtue against the evil humours ; and when
he[3] is better, then let him partake of sweeter meats.

- - - -

[1] The Saxon version misses the
meaning of καρδιακὰς διαθέσεις.

[2] Καρδιαλγίαν, *disease of the
digestive organ,* as the Hellenic

author had himself many times
said.

[3] The previous clauses were plural
unless Ŏnopaŏ stand for Ŏnopaŏ.

ſpa þeah ne ſynð ſcɪtole · þɪcɟe to unðeꞃneſ hlaꝼ ɟe-
bꞃocenne on hat pæteꞃ¹ oþþe æppla beꞃɪnðeðe.² Eac
bɪþ ɟoð ꝼultum on ɟoðum pyꞃtðꞃencum ſpa læcaſ
pyꞃcað · oꝼ eceðe ꞩ oꝼ ꝼɪnoleſ pyꞃttꞃuman ꞩ oꝼ ꞃɪnðe ·
ꞩ oꝼ alpan ꞩ oꝼ ðoꞃan hunɪɟe ·³ ɟemenɟ þ ꞩ ꞃele þæſ
cucleꞃ ꝼulne oþþe tꞃeɟen þonne hꞃeꞃcað þ þa ꞃamðe ꞩ
tꞃymeþ · ꞩ þ ðeah pɪþ bꞃeoſt þæꞃce ꞩ pɪþ heoꞃtcoþe ꞩ
pɪð ꝼellepæꞃce · ꞩ pɪþ þon þe mon ſie on þam maɟan
omɪɟꞃe pætan ɟeꝼylleð · ꞩ pɪð maneɟum aðlum þ ðeah ·
ða þe cumað oꝼ oꝼeꞃꝼyllo · ꞩ oꝼ mɪſꞃenhcum yꝼlum
pætum.    ɟɪꝼ hie cumen oꝼ oꝼeꞃꝼyllo mɪð ſpɪþe þan⁴
hy mon ꞃceal lythan.    ɟɪꝼ hie þonne cumað oꝼ oþꞃum
bɪteꞃūm ꞩ yꝼelum pætūm þa þe pyꞃceað oman þonne
beoþ þa elcꞃan to ſtıllanne oþþ þe hie unſtꞃanɟꞃan
peoꞃþan · ſpɪþoſt ɟɪꝼ þa pætan beoð þɪcce ꞩ ꞃlɪꞃeɟꞃan.

Alex. Trall.,
cap. ẏ., ed.
1548.

be ꞃamðe coþe oþþe ɟɪꝼ oꝼ þæꞃe ꞃamðe anꞃe þa
yꝼelan pætan cumen ꞩ ne oꝼeꞃyꞃnen ealne þone lɪchoman þ mon ꞃceall mıð halꝼenðūm mettum anum lac-
fol. 66 b.
nıan ·⁵ ɟɪꝼ þonne ſio yꝼele pæte oꝼ þæꞃe ꞃamðe oꝼeꞃ-
yꞃneþ ealne þone lɪchoman þæꞃ mon ꞃceal mıð maꞃan
lácnunɟe tɪhan · hpɪlum bīm mon ꞃceal oꝼ æðꞃan bloð
lætan ɟɪꝼ þæꞃ bloðeſ to ꝼela þınce ꞩ þæꞃe yꝼlan pætan
ꞩ eac pyꞃtðꞃenc ꞃellan.    Ac æꞃeſt mon ꞃceal bloð
lætan æꝼteꞃ þon pyꞃtðꞃenc ꞃellan.

.II.

Pıþ ꞃaꞃūm ꞩ aꝼunðenum maɟan ɟenɪm ele ꞩ ɟeðo
lɪꞃɪt cꞃuða ꞩ ðıle ꞩ ſuþeꞃne peꞃmoð ón þone ele

---

¹ ὕδωρ ψυχρόν.  Al. Trall.
² ἢ μῆλον ἢ κίτρον ἐκτὸς τοῦ λέπους
αὐτοῦ, Α. Τ.
³ μέλιτος ἀττικοῦ, Α. Τ.
⁴ Not very literally.
⁵ Alex. Trall. has more words.

Naught is better for him than that he take those which digest late, and are notwithstanding not purgative; let him eat at undern, or nine o'clock, loaf bread broken into hot water, or apples peeled. There is also good support in good wort drinks, as leeches work them, of vinegar, and of fennels roots, and of its rind, and of aloes, and of dumbledores[1] honey; mix that up and administer a spoonful of it or two, then that maketh the wamb nesh and firm; and it is efficacious against breast wark, and heart disease, and epilepsy, and in case that a man be filled with inflammatory humour in the maw, and that is valid against many disorders which come of surfeit and of various evil humours. If they are come of surfeit with spewing, by that *remedy* shall they be lessened. If however they come of other bitter and evil humours, which work inflammations, then are the latter to be stilled till that they become less strong; chiefly if the humours be thick and rather slippery.[2]

2. Of wamb disease, or if the evil humours come from the wamb alone and do not overrun the whole body, that *case* shall be treated with healing meats alone. If moreover the evil humour from the wamb overrunneth the whole body, this shall be dealt with by means of the stronger remedies: at whiles one shall let him blood from a vein, if there seems to be too much of the blood and of the evil humour, and also give a wort drink; but he shall first be let blood and after that have the wort drink given him.

## ii.

1. For a sore and swollen maw; take oil, and put mastic, and dill, and southern wormwood into the oil,

---

[1] Attic.                    |            [2] γλίσχροι.

M 2

læt ſtandan þreo niht ⁊ ᵹedo þ þa pyrta ꞃyn ᵹe-
ꞃodene on þam ele · ᵹedo ðonne on hneꞃce pulle
ſmiꞃe þone maᵹan mid. Eꞃt piþ þon ilean ᵹenim
ealdne ꞃyꞃle ᵹetꞃiꞃula on tꞃeopenum moꞃteꞃe menᵹ
pið æᵹeſ þ hpite do on cla ð leᵹe ón. Piþ ꞃaꞃum
maᵹan eꞃt ᵹedo ón ꞃeaꞃinne ele þa pyꞃt · þe hatte
ꞃenoᵹꞃecum ⁊ lauꞃeꞃ cꞃoppan ⁊ ðile ſmiꞃe þone
maᵹan mid þy.                                             :·

Piþ ꞃaꞃum maᵹan ꞃeᵹhꞃædan ꞃeaꞃ ⁊ eceð do on
cla ð leᵹe ón. Eꞃt ᵹiꞃ ꞃe maᵹa apunden ſie oþþe apened ·
ᵹenim þæꞃ ꞃeleſtan pineſ ⁊ ᵹꞃeneſ eleꞃ ſpilc healꞃ ſeoþ
ꞃeꞃmoðeꞃ cꞃoppan do on hneꞃce pulle ſmiꞃe mid. Selle
him þonne ꞃlæꞃc etan lytelꞃa puhta ſmælꞃa ꞃuᵹla ᵹeꞃo-
ðenꞃa ⁊ ᵹebꞃædꞃa ⁊ maniᵹꞃeald æppelcyn peꞃan æpenin-
ᵹaꞃ · piSan oꞃꞃænda ⁊ ᵹeſoðena ón eceðe ⁊ on pætꞃe ⁊ on
pine pel ſceaꞃꞃum. Piþ ꞃaꞃum maᵹan · poſan leaꞃa .v.
oþþe .vii. oððe miᵹon ⁊ pipoꞃeſ coꞃna emꞃela ᵹeᵹnid
ſmale ⁊ on hatúm pæteꞃe ꞃele dꞃincan. Eꞃt piþ þon
ilean ᵹenim oꞃ pulhnyte .xx. ᵹeclænſoðꞃa cyꞃnela ⁊
cymeneꞃ ſpa micel ſpa þu maᵹe mid þꞃim ꞃinᵹꞃum
ꞃoꞃeꞃeaꞃiðum ᵹemman ᵹetꞃiꞃula þonne bollan ꞃulne
pyl on moꞃteꞃe ᵹedo cealdeſ pæteꞃeꞃ to .ii. ᵹode
bollan ꞃulle ꞃele ðonne æꞃeſt þ healꞃ to dꞃincanne.

Eꞃt iꞃ onleᵹen[1] to tꞃymmanne þone maᵹan ⁊ to
bindanne æꞃteꞃ utꞃihtan oþþe æꞃteꞃ pyꞃtdꞃence ᵹe-
baꞃꞃnedne hlaꞃ clæmne ſeoþ on ealdum pine ᵹiꞃ þu
hæbbe · ᵹiꞃ hit ſie ſumoꞃ do peꞃmoðeſ ſædeſ duꞃt to
ſeoþ ætᵹædeꞃe do on cla ð oꞃeꞃſiꞃt mid ele leᵹe ón
þone maᵹan · ᵹiꞃ hit ſie pinteꞃ ne þeaꞃꞃt þu þone
peꞃmoð to ðon.

### .III.

Be ᵹeſpelle ⁊ ꞃaꞃe þæꞃ maᵹan · ᵹiꞃ ſe man þ mæᵹen
hæbbe læt him blod æꞃteꞃ þon mid þy ele ſmiꞃe þe

---

[1] Enleþeua.

let it stand three nights, and arrange that the worts
be sodden in the oil, then put *that* upon nesh wool,
smear the maw therewith. Again, for that ilk; take
old lard, triturate it in a treen mortar, mingle therewith the white of an egg, put on a cloth and lay on.
For a sore maw, again; put the wort into warm oil,
which hight fenugreek, and bunches of laurel flowers,
and dill; smear the maw with that.

2. For a sore maw; put on a cloth juice of waybroad and vinegar; lay on. Again, if the maw be
swollen or distended; take some of the best wine, and
of green oil half so much, seethe the heads of wormwood *therein*, put *this* on nesh wool, smear therewith.
Then give him the flesh to eat of little creatures, as
of small fowls, sodden and roasted, and manifold kinds of
apples, pears, medlars, peas moistened and sodden in
vinegar and in water, and in pretty sharp wine. For a
sore maw; leaves of rose, five, or seven, or nine, and of
pepper corns as many, rub them small, and administer
in hot water to be drunk. Again, for that ilk; take
twenty cleansed kernels of the nuts of the stone pine,
and of cummin so much as thou mayest take up with
the tips of three fingers, then triturate a bowl full, boil
in a mortar, add of cold water two good bowls full,
then give the half *thereof* in the first instance to be
drunk.

3. Again, here is an onlay" *or application* to com-* initial.
fort the maw, and to bind it after the diarrhœa, or
after a wort drink; seethe clean toasted bread in old
wine, if thou have it; if it be summer, add dust of
the seed of wormwood, seethe together, put on a cloth,
smudge over with oil, lay on the maw; if it be winter,
thou needst not apply the wormwood.

### iii.

Of swelling and sore of the maw; if the man have
the strength *to bear it*, let him blood; after that,

þa pypta ſyn on ȝeroðene þe pe ær nemdon · æſteɲ
þon mið hate huniȝe ſmiɲe Ᵹ oſeɲſceaðe þonne mið
hpiteɲ cpiðueſ Ᵹ alpan ðuſte Ᵹ pipoɲeſ hpæt hpeȝa ·
oſeɲleȝe · þonne mið linene claðe oððe mið eopo-
ciȝɲe pulle Ᵹ ſele peɲmoð ōn peaɲmum ɲæteɲe tpam
nihtum æɲ oſȝotenne Ᵹ ſe þam omūm ſtille · Ᵹ ſele
þonne ȝepipoɲoðne pyɲtðɲenc · Ᵹ ðonne ſceal mōn þam
men mið ðɲium handum on moɲȝenne Ᵹ on æſenne
þa handa Ᵹ þa ſet ȝniðan ſpɪðe Ᵹ þyn · Ᵹ ȝiſ hit ſie
ȝoð peðeɲ he hīm on unðeɲne ȝiſe · ȝanȝe him ut
hpɪðeɲ hpeȝa ſume hpile · ȝiſ hit ne ſie peðeɲ ȝanȝe
hīm in ȝeonð hiſ huſ.

### .IIII.

Þɪþ heaɲðum ſpile þæſ maȝan ſele þu him ſealte
mettaſ Ᵹ haɲan ſlæſc Ᵹ eoſoɲeſ · ɲuðan pypttɲuman ·
Ᵹ ceɲſan · Ᵹ ſcɪɲ þīn · Ᵹ eaðmelte mettaſ Ᵹ onleȝena
utteonðe þone heaɲðan ſpile · Ᵹ bæð þenða ſineɲpunȝa
pyɲce oſ ele Ᵹ oſ peɲmoðe · Ᵹ oſ hpitum cpiðue Ᵹ pine ·
beþe ðonne ſmiɲe mið þy · oſleȝe þonne mið eopeciȝɲe
pulle Ᵹ beſpeþe · ȝenim eāc milſce æppla ȝeðo neah-
teɲne ōn pin Ᵹ þonne ȝeſeoð · ȝeſpete þonne ꝥ pōſ
mið huniȝeſ tcaɲe Ᵹ ȝepipeɲa mið .xx. coɲna ſele
hīm þonne on moɲȝenne lytelne bollan ſullne oððe
cucleɲ ſulne þuſ ȝepoɲhteſ ðɲincan.

### .V.

Læcedom pɪþ þæſ maȝan aþunðenneſſe · þæſ manneſ
ſet Ᵹ handa man ſceal ſpiþe on moɲȝentiðum þȳn ·
Ᵹ hine mon ſceal ſpiðe hluðe hatan ȝɲæðan oððe

smear with the oil on which the worts, which we ere
named, have been sodden ; after that smear with hot
honey, and sprinkle over with dust of mastic and aloes.
and somewhat of pepper; then overlay *this* with a
linen cloth or with ewes wool, and give *him* wormwood in warm water, poured off *the wormwood* two
nights (*days*) previously, that it may still the inflammation,[1] and then administer a peppered wort drink ;
and then one shall at morning and evening rub
smartly and squeeze the mans hands and feet with dry
hands, and if it be good weather let him at undern,
*that is at nine in the morning,* by Gods grace, go out
somewhither for a while ; if it be not *fair* weather,
let him walk about within his house.

iv.

For a hard swelling of the maw ; give *the sick* salt
meats, and hares and boars flesh, roots of rue, and
cresses, and sheer (*clear*) wine, and easily digested
meats, and applications drawing out the hard swelling,
and baths ; work moist smearings, *that is, lotions,* of oil
and wormwood, and of mastic and wine ; bathe *him*,
then smear with that, then overlay with ewes wool,
and swathe up ; take also mild apples, put them for
the space of a night into wine and then seethe *them ;*
then sweeten the wash *or infusion* with virgin honey,
and pepper it with twenty peppercorns ; then give him
in the morning a little bowl full or a spoon full of
the thus wrought *potion* to drink.

v.

A leechdom for swelling of the maw ; one shall in
the morning hours squeeze hard the mans feet and
hands, and one shall bid him cry or sing very loud,

[1] φλεγμονή, I suppose.

ſingan ⁊ hine món ꝼeel neahtneꞃtigne[1] ꞃyhtan ⁊ ꞃpe-
man to ſpipanne • ⁊ on mopʒen ſmipepan mið cle on
þam ðe ſie ʒeꞃoðen ꝼiuðe ⁊ peꞃmoð ⁊ þa ꞃeꞃ ʒenemneðan mettaꞃ þieʒe.

## .VI.

[1] Ƿiþ unluſte ⁊ plættan þe óꝼ maʒan cymð ⁊ be hiꞃ
mete • ꞃele him neahtneꞃtiʒúm peꞃmoð oððe þꞃeo-
lꞃeað[2] ʒeðon ón ꞃceaꞃp ꝼín ꞃele neahtneꞃtiʒum • ⁊
ꞃeꝼteꞃ þon ꞃealte mettaꞃ mið eceðe ʒeꞃpete • ⁊ ʒeꞃenoðne
ꞃeneꞃ ⁊ þꞃæðie þieʒen ⁊ ealle þa mettaꞃ ʒe ðꞃincan
þa þe habban hat mæʒen ⁊ ꞃceaꞃp ꞃele þieʒean • ⁊
ʒebeoꞃh þ̵ hie unʒemeltneꞃꞃe ne þꞃopian • ⁊ ʒoð ꝼín
ʒehæt ⁊ hluttoꞃ þieʒen ón nealt neꞃtiʒ • ⁊ neaht.
neꞃtiʒe lapien on huniʒ • ⁊ ꞃecen him bꞃóc ón onꞃaðe •
⁊ on pæne oððe ón þon þe hie a þꞃopian mæʒen.
Eꝼt piþ meteꞃ unluſte • ʒenim ꞃuþeꞃne cymen oꝼꞃæne
mið eceðe aðꞃiʒe ðonne • ⁊ ʒeʒnið ón moꞃteꞃe • ⁊
ꝼinoleꞃ ꞃæðeꞃ • ⁊ ðileꞃ þꞃeo cucleꞃ mæl ʒeʒnið eall
toʒæðeꞃe ʒeece piꞃoꞃeꞃ þꞃeo cucleꞃ mæl ⁊ ꞃuðan

leaꝼa .VII. cucleꞃ mæl ⁊ þæꞃ ꞃeleꞃtan hunigeꞃ aꞃꞃeneꞃ
an punð • ʒeꞃꞃꝼula eal toʒæðeꞃe • ꞃce þonne mið
eceðe ꞃpa þe þince þ̵ hit ſie ón þa onlieneꞃꞃe ʒeꞃoꞃht
þe ꞃenoꞃ bið ʒetempꞃioð to ipiꞃan • ʒeðo þonne on
ʒlæꞃ ꝼæt • ⁊ þonne mið hlaꝼe oððe mið ꞃpa hꞃileum
mete ꞃpa þu pille lapa ón ⁊ nytta ʒe þeah þu mið
cucleꞃe þ̵ ꞃupe þæt hylpþ • þiꞃeꞃ þu nytta ʒe ón
aꝼꞃenne • ʒe ón undeꞃne • niꞃ þ̵ piþ þam unluſte anum
ʒoð þeꞃ maʒan • ꞃic eallum þam lichoman þ̵ ðeah.

Ƿiþ meteꞃ unluſte ðꞃeoꞃʒe ðꞃoꞃtlan on pætꞃe oꝼ-
þꞃenðe • ʒeʒnið mið eceðe ꞃele ðꞃincan pið plættan • Þiþ

---

[1] neahteꞃtiʒne, MS.

[2] Ἀνορεξία. In the first sentence
are some traces of Alexander Tral-

lianus, lib. vii., cap. 7, pp. 108. 109
ed. 1548.

[3] beahꞃeað? πρόπολις is one of the
ingredients in A. I.

and one shall exhort him after his nights fast, and pro-
voke him to spew; and in the morning smear him
with oil on which has been sodden rue and wormwood, and let him diet on the before named meats.

## vi.

Against want of appetite and nausea which cometh
from the maw, and from the mans meat; give him after
his nights fast wormwood or beebread, put into sharp
wine; give it him at night fasting, and after that salt
meats with sweetened vinegar, and prepared mustard,
and radish to eat, and make him eat all the meats
and drinks which have a hot and sharp quality; and
beware that "they" suffer not indigestion, and let
them take at night fasting good wine heated and clear;
and let them after the nights fast lap up honey; and let
them seek for themselves fatigue in riding on horseback, or in a wain, or such *conveyance* as they may
ever endure. Again, for want of appetite for meat;
take southern *or Italian* cummin, moisten it with
vinegar, then dry it and rub it to pieces in a mortar,
and of fennel seed, and of dill, three spoon measures,
rub all together, add of pepper three spoon measures,
and of leaves of rue seven spoon measures, and of the
best strained honey one pint; triturate all together;
eke it out then with vinegar as may seem fit to
thee, so that it may be wrought into the form in
which mustard is tempered for flavouring; put it then
into a glass vessel, and then with bread or with whatever meat thou choose, lap it up, and make use of it;
even though thou shouldst sup it up with a spoon, that
will help. This use thou either at even or at nine
o'clock. The *remedy* is not good for want of appetite
of the maw only, but it is valid for all the body.

For want of appetite for meat; rub up with vinegar
pennyroyal moistened in water, give it to be drunk
against nausea. For want of appetite again; give to

˅ unluſte eꝼt mínꞇan ꝺ pipoꝛeſ mꝺan coꝛn ᵹeᵹniðen ón
pine ꝛele ðꝛincan.

.VII.

Þiſ ſceal pið aðeaðoðum maᵹan · ᵹením hunıᵹeſ ꝺ
eceð toᵹæðeꝛe ᵹemenᵹeð ꝺ ᵹeðeaꞇenne pipoꝛ ꝛele ón
moꝛᵹenne cucleꝛ ꝼulne neahꞇneꝛꞇıᵹum nyꞇꞇıᵹe ſceaꝛ-
peꝛa ðꝛıncena · ꝺ meꞇꞇa · ꝺ ıeꞇ baþe mıð ſinope ᵹnıðe ꝺ
ſıneppe. Sele hím eac neahꞇneꝛꞇıᵹum þiſ · ᵹením eceð
ꝛıþ ᵹlæðenan ᵹemenᵹeð hꝛæꝛlıpeᵹa ꝺ lanᵹeſ pıpoꝛeſ .x.
coꝛn oþþe cꝛoppan ꝺ ſeneꝛ menᵹe eall toᵹæðeꝛe · ꝺ
ꞇꝛıꝛoliᵹe ſele nihꞇneſꞇıᵹúm an cucleꝛ mæl · ᵹeþenc ðu
þonne hꝛæþþe þꞇe calle þa ıeꝛ ᵹenemneðan læceðomaſ
ꝺ þa æꝼꞇeꝛ ꝛꝛıꞇenan ne ſculon ón ane þꝛaᵹe ꞇo lanᵹe
beón ꞇo ᵹeðone ác ſculon ꝼæc habban beꞇꝛeonum ꝺ
ꝛeſꞇe · hꝛılum ꞇꝛeᵹen ðaᵹaſ hꝛılum þꝛy · ꝺ þonne hım
món bloð læꞇe ón æðꝛe ón þam ðaᵹúm ne ðo hím mon
nanne oþeꝛne læceðóm ꞇo · nymþe ymb .v. nihꞇ oþþe
ma. Þiſ ꝼoꝛſoᵹenum maᵹan oþþe aþunðenum · ᵹením
hꝛyþeꝛen ꝼlæſc ᵹeꝛoðen ón eceðe ꝺ mıð ele ᵹeꝛenoð
mıð ꝛealꞇe · ꝺ ðıle · ꝺ poꝛ þıcᵹe þ ꝼeoꝛon nihꞇ þonne
lıhꞇ þ þone ᵹeſpenceðan maᵹan · þıſ ſynð ꞇacn aðea-
ðoðeſ maᵹan þ he þıᵹð ne ᵹemylꞇ þ · ác ſe ᵹeþıᵹeða
meꞇe heꝛeᵹaþ þone maᵹan ꝺ he þone ꝛammelꞇan þuꝛh
ða paınbe uꞇꝛenꞇ.

.VIII.

Þıþ ſaꝛe ꝺ unluſte þæſ maᵹan ſe þe ne mæᵹ ne
mıð meꞇe ne mıð ðꝛıncan beon ᵹelacnoð ꝺ bıꞇeꝛe
hꝛæcceꞇunᵹe · Ním cenꞇauꝛıan þ iſ ꝼelꞇeꝛꝛe ſume ·
haꞇað hyꝛðc ꝛyꝛꞇ · ſume eoꝛð ᵹeallan ᵹeᵹnıð án punð

drink mint and nine corns of pepper rubbed *small* in wine.

### vii.

This shall apply for a deadened maw;[1] take some honey and vinegar mingled together, and pepper beaten up, give in the morning a spoon full *of it* to the man after his nights fast, let him employ sharp drinks and meats; and at the bath let him rub and smear himself with mustard. Give him also, after his nights fast, this : take vinegar mingled with somewhat of gladden, and of long pepper ten corns or clusters, and mustard ; mingle all together, and triturate; give him after a nights fasting, one spoon measure. Then consider thou, notwithstanding, that all the aforenamed leechdoms and the after written ones, shall not be to be done at one too long season, but must have space and rest between them, whilom two days, whilom three ; and when one lets him blood on a vein, on those days let none other leechdom be done to him, except about five days *later* or more. For a stomach troubled with hicket or puffed up, take beeves flesh sodden in vinegar and with oil, prepared with salt, and dill, and porrum, let *the sick* diet on that for seven days, then that relieves the labouring maw. These are tokens of a deadened maw ; what he taketh, that melteth *or digests* not, but the meat swallowed oppresseth the maw, and it sendeth out the half digested food through the wamb.

### viii.

For soreness and loss of appetite in that maw, which may not be cured neither with meat nor with drink, and for the bitter breaking *or retching* ; take centaury,[2] that is fel terræ, some call it herdsmans

---

[1] Now called a torpid liver.  |  [2] *Erythræa centaureum.*

ꞏꝺ ȝeðo þæꞃon hateꞃ pæꞇeꞃeꝼ .IIII. bollan ꝼulle ꞃele
hīm neaht neꞃꞇiȝūm ꝺꞃincan þꞃy ꝺaȝaꝼ.

Eꝼꞇ ȝeꞅīm þa ꞃeaꝺe neꞇlan uꝼeꞃeaꞃꝺe hæbbenꝺe
ꞃaꞃꝺ aþþeah clæne ꞉ꝺ ꝼyꞃce ꞇo ꞅuꝼanne. Eꝼꞇ ȝꞃeneꞅ
meꞃceꞅꞏ ȝeꞇꞃiꝼulaꝺeꞅ ꞃeap ꞉ꝺ apꞃunȝeneꞅ ꞃele ꝺꞃincanꞏ
꞉ꝺ on þa ilean piꞃan ꞃele hīm ꝺꞃincan hunan ꞃeap.
Eꝼꞇ piꝺ maȝan ꞃaꞃe þiꝺan ꞉ꝺ mīnꞇanꞏ ꝺileꞏ ꝺꞃeoꞃȝe
ꝺꞃoꞅꞇlan ꞏ aȝꞃimonian ꞅume haꞇaꝺ ȝaꞃcliȝcꞏ ꞉ꝺ ceꞃꞅan
ȝecnua calle ōn pine oþþe on calaꝺ ꞃele ælce ꝺæȝe ꞇo
ꝺꞃincanne.

## .VIIII.

Þiþ Inꞃunꝺe maȝanꞏ nīm ȝaꞇe meoluc þonne hio
ꞃuꞃþūm amolcen ꞅie ꞃele ꝺꞃincanꞏ ꞅume peaꞃme copo
meoluc ꝺꞃincaꝺ piþ maȝan ꞅaꞃeꞏ ꞅume þone ꞃeleꞅꞇan
ele ȝeꞃyꞃmeꝺneꞏ ꞅume piþ þa ȝaꞇe meoluc menȝaꝺ oþ
þ̄ hie ꞅpipaꝺ þ̄ hi ꝺe yþ ꞅpipan maȝon.

## .X.

Viꝺ plæꞇꞇan ꞉ꝺ ꞇo hæꞇanne maȝanꞏ pæꞇeꞃ beꞃoðen
ōn peꞃmoꝺeꞏ ꞉ꝺ ōn ꝺile oþ þone þꞃoꝺꝺan ꝺæl ꞃele þ̄
ꝺꞃincan þ̄ pyꞃmꝺ ꞉ꝺ heaꞃꝺaþ þone maȝan.

fol. 70 b.

## .XI.

[a] Þiþ aþunꝺeneꞃꞃe ꞉ꝺ eþinȝe maȝanꞏ ꝼinoleꞅ pyꞃꞇꞇꞃu-
man ꞉ꝺ meꞃceꞅ ōꝼ ȝeoꞇ imꝺ ꞅeꞃꞃe pine ealꝺe ꞉ꝺ oꝼ þon
ꞃele ꝺꞃincan nehꞇneꞃꞇiȝūm .II. bollan ꝼulle lyꞇle. Þiþ
ꝼinꝺiȝꞃie aþunꝺeneꞃꞃe maȝan ꞇo pyꞃmanne þone ceal-
ꝺan maȝanꞏ þiꝺanꞏ ꞉ꝺ ꝺileꞏ minꞇanꞏ ꞉ꝺ meꞃce ꝼynꝺ-
ꞃiȝe ꞃecaꞃaꝼ ȝeꝼeoꝺ on þꞃim ceac[b] ꞃuꞃlum pæꞇeꞃeꞅ þ̄
þæꞃ ne ꞅie buꞇan an ꝼul ꞅele þonne þ̄ pæꞇeꞃ ꝺꞃincan.

[a] Πρὸς ἐμπνευ-
μάτωσιν. Alex.
Trall., lib. vii.
cap. 10; p. 112,
ed, 1548 ; but
the remedies
differ.

ᴠ

---

[1] The method of Alex. Trallianus is, it seems, kept in view;
Ηερὶ τῶν δι᾽ ἄμετρον ψύξιν ὑπερεκ-
τούντων, lib. vii., cap. 7 ; p. 109, ed.
1548.

[2] ceacum ?

wort, some earth gall, rub *small* a pound of it, and
apply thereto four bowls full of hot water; give it *to
the sick* to drink for three days after his nights fasting.   Again, take the upper part of the red nettle,
while having seed, wash it clean, and work it up to
sup.   Again, administer to drink juice of green marche
triturated and wrung out, and in the same wise, give
him to drink juice of *hor*ehound.   Again, for sore of
maw; rue and mint, dill, dwarf dwosle, agrimony,
some call it garcliff, and cress, pound them all in wine
or in ale, give *of this* each day to drink.

## ix.

For an inward wound of the maw; take goats milk
just when it is milked, administer to be drunk.   Some
drink for sore of maw warm ewe milk, some the
best oil warmed, some mingle *that* with the goats
milk till they spew, that they may spew the more
easily.

## x.

For nausea and to heat the maw; water sodden on
wormwood and on dill, down to the third part, give
*the man* that to drink; it warmeth and hardeneth the
maw.

## xi.

For puffing up and blowing of the maw; overpour
roots of fennel and marche with clear old wine, and
of that give *the sick* to drink after his nights fast two
little bowls full.   For a windy puffing up of the maw,
to warm the maw, rue and dill, mint and marche;
seethe bundles of them separate in three jugs full of
water, and *continue seething* so that there be only one
cup; then administer the water to be drunk.

### .XII.

* Πρὸς ἔμετον.    ᵃǷið fpiþþan ɥ ƿið þon þe ħim mete undeɲ ne ȝe-
puniȝe · ȝenim finɲullan ȝeȝnið ón fceaɲp ƿin ɲele
bollan ɲulne to ȝeðɲincanne æɲteɲ æɲen ȝeɲeoɲce ·
ȝeńim ƿiþ þon ilcan ɲinoleɲ ɲeapeɲ tɲeȝen dælaf huni-
ȝeɲ ænne fcoþ oþ þ ꝥ hæbbe huniȝef þicneɲɲe ɲele
þonne nealit neɲtiȝum cuclen mæl ɲull · ꝥ plættan
ȝeftineð ꝥ lunȝenne bet ꝥ liɲɲe hælð.    Þið miclan
fpiɲeþan ɥ he ne mæȝe nanne mete ȝehabban · ȝeńim
fol. 71 a.    ðileɲ ɲæðeɲ ane yntɲan · piɲoɲeɲ ɲeopeɲ · cymeneɲ
þɲeo ȝeȝnið fpiþe fmale · ðo þonne on pæteɲ þe pæɲɲe
minte ón ȝeɲoden ɥ fupe æppla oððe ƿinȝeaɲðeɲ tɲiȝu
uɲeɲeaɲð meɲpe ȝiɲ ɲe món ne fie on ɲeɲɲe yce mið
pine ɥ ɲele ðɲincan þonne ne to ɲefte ȝan ɲille · ɥ le²
utan ón þone maȝan ȝefoðene ɲuðu æpla ɥ hlaɲeɲ
cɲumán ɥ fpilce ónleȝena.

### .XIII.

ᶜ Ρευματισμύς.    Þonne ɲceal þiɲ ƿiþ þæɲ maȝan fɲiинȝe Súm pyɲf
cyn hatte lenticulaf ete þaɲa hunð teontiȝ liɲeaɲɲa.
Eɲt ɲceaɲɲeɲ eceðeɲ ȝefupe þɲeo cuclen mæl þonne he
ɲlapan ɲille on æɲen.

### .XIIII.

Þiþ callum maȝan untɲumneɲɲum · ȝeńim ɲinoleɲ
pyɲttɲuman utepeaɲðɲa ꝥ þæɲ mæɲɲoft fie aðo oɲ
þam ɲinole fpa micel fpa oþeɲ healɲ punð fie · ȝeot

---

¹ The method of Alex. Trallianus    μαχον ἀπεμοῦντα τὴν τροφήν, p. 112,
is still preserved; he has a short    ed. 1548.
chapter, lib. vii. cap. 9, Πρὸς στό-    ² For leȝe.

### xii.

For spewing, and in case that *a mans* meat will
not keep down; take sinfulle, rub it *fine* into sharp
wine, give *the man* a bowl full to drink after evening
work. Take, for that ilk, two parts of juice of fennel,
one of honey, seethe *or boil down* till *the mixture*
have the thickness of honey, then give after a nights
fast a spoon measure full; that restraineth nausea,
that bettereth the lungs, that healeth the liver. For
mickle spewing, and *in case a man* may keep *in his*
*stomach* no meat; take one ounce of seed of dill, four of
pepper, three of cummin, rub very small; then put
into water in which mint has been sodden and sour
apples, or the tender upper part of the twigs of a vine;
if the man be not in a fever, eke it with wine, and
give *it him* to drink when he willeth to go to bed;
and lay outside on the maw sodden wood apples
(*crabs*), and crumbs of bread, and such applications.

### xiii.

Besides, this shall be good for flux[1] of the maw;
one sort of peas hight lentils, let *the man* eat of them
raw one hundred. Again, let him sip three spoon
measures of sharp vinegar, when he willeth to sleep
at evening.

### xiv.

For all infirmities of the maw; take of the out-
ward parts of the roots of fennel, what is there most
tender, remove from the fennel as much as may make

---

[1] For this translation I partly rely
on the guidance of Alexander
Trallianus, who has remedies πρὸς
στόμαχον ῥευματιζόμενον; lib. vii.,
cap. 8; p. 111, ed. 1548; p. 337, ed.
1556. Properly ῥευματισμὸς is of
the wamb, or venter, not of the
maw; and Aretæos says as much,
Chron. lib. ii., cap. 6. But other
authors have the same expression
as Alex. Trall; for instance Cœlius
Aurelianus, Chron. lib. iii., cap. 2.

f.d. 71 b.

þonne eceðes ón ſpa oþeſi healf ſyſteſi ſie hæt þonne
þſieo mihz ſtandan ſpa æzzædeſie · æfzeſi þon oſeſiſeoð
þa pyſizzſiuman hſiæt hſieza ón þam eceðe ꞃ apſiinꞬ óſi
þam eceðe clæne · Ɡeðo þonne on ꝥ eceð huniꞬeſ mi◌̃
þ̵ſ eceðe · Ɡeðo þonne alþan Ɡoðne ðæl þæſi on ꝥte
yntſian ꞬeſieꞬe oððe ma ꞃ oþeſi ſpile hſiizeſ eſieoðoſieſ
ꞃ ameoſ hatte ſuþeſine pyſiz oþeſi aſiaſiu ðo þaſia hſieſ
ꞬemenꞬe hſiæþeſie ealle zoꞬædeſie ·ꞃ þonne ſelle him
þſieo eucleſi mæl · ðo þiſ þið maꞬan bſiyne ꞃ þuſiſte
þlaceo ſaſieſi menꞬe þið þone ſeleſtan ele ſele ðſiincan
ꝥ ſzyſið[1] þam þuſiſte.

<h3 style="text-align:center">.XV.</h3>

ᵃ Οἰυρεγαία.

Þiſ þæſ maꞬan ſpſiinꞬe þonne þuſih mið biceſie
hſiæcð[a] oþþe healcet oððe him on þam maꞬan ſuꞬeð ·
Ɡenim piþoſieſ ſpile an mynet ꞬeſieꞬe · ðileſ ſæðeſ
ſpile .IIII. mynet ꞬeſieꞬen · oþeſi ſpile cymeneſ ꞬeꞬnið
eall ꞃ ſele ón þine eucleſi mæl þonne he ſlaþan Ɡan
þille. Siõ aþenunꞬ þæſ maꞬan ꞃ ſio ablaſiunꞬe hæto
cymeð oſ þam blacum omum · ac Ɡenim þonne ſpſiun-
Ɡean[2] Ɡeðo ón ſceaſiſi eceð Ɡeſiæte ſþiðe leꞬe oſ̜eſi
þone maꞬan þonne hiz ſpile ſie. Æſzeſi þon Ɡiſ þæſ
ne ſele leꞬe oþſia onleꞬena ón ſzſienꞬþan ꞃ aſeſiſian
ſpa ſpa ïſ ſaſi[a] óm þið humiꞬ ꞬemenꞬeð ꞃ þon Ɡehe
ſpa læcaſ cunnon.

fcl. 72 a.

<h3 style="text-align:center">.XVI.</h3>

Þiſ ſint zacn þæſ hatan maꞬan omihtan unꞬemet
ſaſzhcan · ꞃ þæſ oſeſicealdan · þæſ hatan maꞬan un-

---

[1] From ſzeoþan.

[2] Understand as ſpouꞬean from

the Hellenie. Alex. Trall., lib. vii.,
cap. 8; p. 110, foot, ed. 1548.

[a] Read aþ. See the Glossary.

a pound and a half, then pour on of vinegar as
much as be a sextarius and a half, then let these
stand thus together for three nights; after that seethe
the roots somewhat in the vinegar, and wring them
clean from the vinegar. Then put into the vinegar
some honey with the vinegar; then put a good deal
of aloes therein, so much as may weigh an ounce or
more, and as much more of mastic and of ammi, as
a foreign wort hight; or asarabacca; put in less of
them, mingle, however, all together, and then give him
three spoon measures. Do this against burning of the
maw and thirst; mingle lukewarm water with the best
oil, give to drink, that checketh the thirst.

### XV.

For irritation of the maw when *the man* through the
mouth has bitter breaking or belching, or there is an
ill lymph in his stomach; take of pepper as much as one
coin may weigh, of seed of dill as much as may weigh
four coin, as much besides of cummin, rub all fine and
administer in wine a spoon full when *the man* willeth
to go to sleep. The swelling of the maw and the heat
of the puffing up cometh from the black flegms; but
then take sponges, put them into sharp vinegar, wet
it thoroughly, lay it over the maw, when it is such.
After that, if it feel not this, *or be insensible to these
remedies*, lay on some other applications, stronger and
more austere, such as is copperas mingled with honey,
and the like of that as leeches know.

### xvi.

1. These are tokens of the hot flegmatic[1] maw, irretentive,[2] and of the overcold. Of the hot or irretentive

---

[1] Full of φλεγμονή.

[2] The diet is drawn from a passage thus headed; Θεραπεία τῆς διὰ
θέρμην ἀσθενούσης δυνάμεως. Unge-
μετγαιτ, ungemetγæγche are therefore the opposites of Καθεκτικός;
and not what Somner supposed.

ȝemetƥæƿtan tacn sindon þonne he bið mid omum
ȝeſƿenced þam men bið þuƿſt ȝetenȝe ⁊ neaƿoneſ ⁊
ȝeſƿoȝunȝa ⁊ modeƿ tƿeonunȝ ⁊ unluſt ⁊ plætta · him
iſ nyt[1] þ he hlaƿ þicȝen[2] on cealdum ƿætƿe oððe on
ecede[3] ⁊ ſƿiðe ƿæſte ȝeƿoden æȝƿia oþþe ȝebƿædde to
unðeƿneſ ⁊ pyƿta · ⁊ lactucaſ þ iſ leahtƿic ⁊ mealpan
⁊ hænne ſlæƿc næƿ ſƿiþe ȝeƿoden · ⁊ ȝoſe þa ytmeƿ-
tan limo · ⁊ ſixaſ þa þe heaƿd ſlæƿc habban ·[4] ⁊
pine pinclan · ⁊ oſtƿan ⁊ oþƿu pyƿena cyn ⁊ mylſce
æppla ⁊ bæþ oſ ſƿetum ƿenſcum ƿæteƿum ſceal beon
ȝeƿoƿht hat bæþ him ne ðeah.     Tæn[5] þæſ oƿcƿiceal-
dan maȝan þ þa men ne þyƿſt ne hi ſpol ȝeſelaþ on
maȝan ⁊ ne bið him æniȝ peaƿm þƿopunȝ ȝetenȝe.
Ac hy ȝiƿnað metta ſƿiþoƿ þonne hit ȝeſiclic ſie ⁊ ȝiſ
him oſſtondeþ on Innan æniȝu cealð þæte þonne
ſƿipað hie þ hoƿh ⁊ þa mettaſ ȝehabban ne maȝon
þe hie ȝeſƿicȝeað · ⁊ æſteƿ þam ſƿipað[6] ƿona him to
ȝiſanne biððað · þa men þu ſcealt ſmeƿƿan mið þy
ele þe mon peƿmoð on ſeoðe · ⁊ þa þiccan ȝeuƿnen
on ⁊ þa ſliƿinȝa[a] ƿætan on þam maȝan ⁊ þa acolodan ·
⁊ þ oſſtandene þicce ſliƿiȝe hoƿh þu ſcealt mið þam
æƿ ȝenemnedan læcedomum pyƿman ⁊ þynnian. Ƿyƿc
him þonne pyƿtðƿenc oſ ſinoleſ pyƿttƿuman ſinde ⁊
meƿƿoſt ſie þte ſix yntſan ȝepeȝe ⁊ ecedeſ anne ſeſ-
teƿ · ⁊ alpan þƿeo yntſan · ſeoþ þonne on þam ecede
þone ſinol oþ þ hit ſie pel ȝeƿoden apƿinȝ þonne þa
pyƿta oſ þam ecede ȝedo þonne to þam ecede clæneſ
huniȝeſ pund ſeoþ þonne ætȝædeƿe oþ þ hit ſie ſpa
þicce ſpa huniȝ ſceað þonne þa alpan on pel ȝeȝnidene
⁊ ſele þƿeo cucleƿ mæl mið ƿæteƿe þ ðeah piþ heoƿt
ece ⁊ piþ ſelle pæƿice.

---

[a] ſliƿiȝa?

[1] Alexander Trall., lib. vii., cap. 5 ;
p. 106, ed. 1548 ; cap. 3, p. 323, ed.
1556.

[2] Read þicȝe.

[3] Gr. εἰς ἄκρατον, *dipped in wine
unmixed with water*, (as if brandy).

[4] ὀστρακοδέρμων, *shell fish*.

[5] From Alexander Trall., lib. vii.,
cap. 5; p. 105, ed. 1548 ; p. 319, ed.
1556, for a few lines only.

[6] Read ſƿiþþan ?

maw are tokens, when it is vexed with inflammations,
thirst is incident to the man, and oppression, and
swoonings, and vacillation of mind, and loss of appetite,
and nausea. It is beneficial for him that he should
eat bread in cold water or in vinegar, and eggs very
hard boiled or roasted, (at nine o'clock in the morning,)
and worts, and lactucas, that is lettuces, and mallow,
and hens flesh not much sodden, and the extremest
parts of the limbs of goose, *that is giblets*, and fishes
which have hard flesh, and periwinkles, and oysters,
and others; various sorts of peas, and mild apples, and
a bath of sweet fresh waters shall be wrought; a hot
bath will not suit him. Tokens of the overcold maw,
that the men feel no thirst nor burning heat in the
maw, nor is there any warm symptom incident upon
them. But they yearn for meats more strongly than
is proper, and if in their inwards there lodges any
cold humour, then they spew up the filth and are not
able to retain the meats which they swallow; and after
the spewing soon they pray that *somewhat* be given
*them to eat*. Those men thou shalt smear with the oil
on which wormwood has been sodden. And the thick
coagulated and the viscid humours in the maw, and
the chilled *humours*, and the intractable thick viscid
foulness, thou shalt warm and thin with the afore
named leechdoms. Work then *for the sick man* a
wort drink of the rind of the root of fennel, and let
it be very tender, *and such* that it may weigh six
ounces, and one sextarius of vinegar, and three ounces
of aloes; then seethe the fennel in the vinegar till it
be well sodden, then wring the worts off the vinegar,
then add to the vinegar a pound of clean honey, then
seethe *these* together, till it be as thick as honey, then
shed the aloes into it, well rubbed up, and give three
spoon measures with water; that is good for heart
ache and for epilepsy.

Alexander Trallianus, ibid.
Κυνώδης ὄρεξις.
Βούλιμος.

be þære oferinnelan friclo þonne of þære selfan cealdan adle þæs magan cymð ꝥ sio oferinnelo friclo ⁊ gifernes ærest of þæs hores wætan þe of þam magan cymð ⁊ hie beoþ spirende ⁊ swa swa hund ett sona secað þa mettas · þam þu scealt sellan clæne ⁊ hluttor win[1] ⁊ read swiðe gehæt ne sie to scearp · ne se mete ne sie to scearp ne to swiþ þe þu him selle · ac smeþe ⁊ fæt · gif[2] ormæte hungor cymð of ungemetlicre hæto þæs magan ⁊ tyddernesse ꝥ hie swa sona geswogene gif hie þone mete næbben. Wiþ ormætum hungre þonne scealt þu sona þæs mannes tilian bind his ytmestan limo mid byndellum teoh him þa loccas ⁊ wringe þa earan ⁊ þone wangbeard twiccige þonne him sel sie sele him sona hlaf on wine gebrocenne ær he oþre mettas þicge · sele him þa mettas þa þe ne sien to raðe gemelte · late mylt hryþeres flæsc gæten · ⁊ hrorota · buccena is wyrrest ⁊ ramma · ⁊ fearra ⁊ þa þe swiðe ealde beoð on feoþorfotum netenum ⁊ fuglas þa þe heard flæsc habbað · pawa · swan · æned þam ðe cealde wambe habbað þu scealt sellan wel meltende mettas scellihte fiscas · ⁊ culfrena briddas · hænne flæsc ⁊ gose fiþru swa betere swa fættran sien ⁊ fersceran þa ytmestan leomo · swina beoð eaðmelte ⁊ geong hryþer ⁊ ticcenu · ⁊ swete win sel mylt þonne ꝥ arre.

fol. 73 b.

## .XVII.

Wiþ eallum lifer adlum ⁊ gecyndum ⁊ wæstmum ⁊ be þam sex þingum þe ðone lifer wærc wyrceað ⁊ lacnung þara earna ⁊ sweotol tacn ge be miegean ge be unluste ge hira hiwe. Sio biþ on þa swiþran sidan aþened oþ þone

[1] τῷ ἀκράτῳ οἴνῳ καὶ τοῖς λιπαροῖς τῶν ἐδεσμάτων. Alex. Trall., who goes on to order legs of pheasants, φασιανῶν μὲν τοὺς μηρούς.

[2] Alex. Trall., lib. vii, cap. 6; p. 106, ult. ed. 1548; p. 323, ed. 1556.

2. Of the overmickle appetite, when from the same cold disease of the maw it cometh that the overmickle appetite and greediness ariseth from the foul humour, which cometh from the maw, and *the sick* are spewing, and, as it were a hound, again soon seek the meats: to them thou shalt give clean and clear wine, and red, much heated; let it not be too sharp; nor let the meat be too sharp, nor too sour, which thou mayst give them, but smooth and fat. If extreme hunger cometh from immoderate heat and tenderness of the maw, so that they are soon in a swoon, if they have not the meat; then, for extreme hunger[1] thou shalt soon treat the man; bind the extremities of his limbs with ligatures, pull his locks for him, and wring his ears, and twitch his whisker, when he is better, give him soon some bread broken in wine, before he take other meats. Give him the meats which are not too soon digested. Beeves flesh, and goats, and harts digests late: bucks is worst, and rams, and bulls, and those of four footed neat which are very old, and fowls which have hard flesh; peacock, swan, duck. To those that have a cold wamb thou shalt give well digesting meats, shell fishes, and young of culvers, hens flesh, and gooses wings; they are the better as they are fatter and fresher. The extremities of the limbs of swine [a] are easy of digestion, and young beeves, and [a] Pigs trotters. kids; and sweet wine digests better than the rough.

### xvii.

For all liver diseases, and of its nature, and increment, and of the six things which work the liver pain, and curing of all these, and plain tokens, either by the mie, or by the loss of appetite, or by the hue of *the*

---

[1] In Trallianus these appliances are meant for the fainting just mentioned, Λειποθυμία.

7 nepeſeoþan ſio hæfð ſíf læppan helt þa lendenbrædan ·
ſio iſ bloðeſ timber · ⁊ bloðeſ huſ · ⁊ ſoſtop · þonne
þaſa metta meltunᵹ biþ ⁊ þynneſ þa becumaþ on þa
liſeſ þonne ſendaþ hie hſoſa hiſ ⁊ ceſſað on bloð ·

fol. 74 a.

⁊ þa unſeſeſneſſa þe þæſ beoþ hio apyſþþ ut ⁊ þ
clæne bloð ᵹeſomnaþ ⁊ þuſli ſeoſeſ æðſa ſſiþoſt ón-
ſenc to þæſe heoſtan ⁊ eac ᵹeonð ealne þone lichoman oþ þa ytmeſtan hino. þe ſex þinᵹúm þe þone
liſeſſæſe þynceað æſeſt ᵹeſſel þ iſ aþunðeneſ þæſe
liſeſ.¹ Oþeſ iſ þæſ ᵹeſſelleſ tobeſſtunᵹ. þſiððe íſ punð
þæſe liſſe · ſeoſþe iſ ſelmeſ hæto mið ᵹeſelneſſe ⁊ mið
ſaſe ᵹeſſelle · ſiſte iſ aheaſðunᵹ þæſ maᵹan mið ᵹeſelneſſe ⁊ mið ſaſe. Sexte iſ heaſðunᵹ þæſe liſſe butan
ᵹeſelneſſe ⁊ butan ſaſe. þæſe liſſe ᵹeſſel oþþe aþun-
ðeneſſe þu meaht þuſ onᵹitan · on þa ſſiðſan healſe
unðeſ þám hneſcan² ſibbe biþ æſeſt ſe ſſile ón þæſe
liſſe ⁊ ᵹeſelð ſe món æſeſt þæſ heſiᵹneſſe ⁊ ſaſ ⁊
oſ þæſe ſtoſe oſeſ ealle þa ſiðan afſihð oþ þ ſſþoþan
⁊ oþ ðone ſſiſſan ſculðoſ þ ſaſ · ⁊ hiſ micᵹᵹe bið
bloðſeað ſſilce hio bloðiᵹ ſie · biþ hím unluſt ᵹetenᵹe
⁊ híſ hiſ blac ⁊ he biþ hſæt hſeᵹa hſiþenðe · ⁊ ſin-
ᵹalne cyle þſoſaþ ⁊ cſacaþ ſſa món on lencten aðle

fol. 74 b.

deþ · ne mæᵹ hım mete unðeſ ᵹeſuſian þinc ſio liſeſ
⁊ ne mæᵹ þam ſaſe mið hanða ónhſunan bið to þon
ſtſanᵹ ⁊ næſþ nanne ſleſ þonne hit ſtſanᵹoſt biþ ·
þonne ſe ſſile tobyſſt þonne bið ſeo micᵹe lyſſen
ſſilce poſinſ · ᵹiſ he utyſnð þonne biþ þ ſaſ læſſe.

---

¹ Read liſſe.     |     ² Read nextan, last?

*patients.* The *liver* is extended on the right side as far as the pit of the belly, it hath five *lobes or* lappets, it has a hold on the false ribs, it is the material of the blood, and the house and the nourishment of the blood ; when there is digestion and attenuation of the meats, they arrive at the liver, and then they change their hue, and turn into blood ; and it casteth out the uncleannesses which be there, and collects the clean blood, and through four veins principally sendeth it to the heart, and also throughout all the body as far as the extremities of the limbs. Of the six things which work liver pain : first swelling, that is, puffing up of the liver; the second is the bursting of the swelling ; the third is wound of the liver ; the fourth is a burning heat with sensitiveness and with a sore swelling; the fifth is a hardening of the maw with sensitiveness and with soreness; the sixth is a hardening of the liver without sensitiveness and without soreness. Thou mayest thus understand swelling or puffing up of the liver ; on the right side is under the nesh [a] rib first the swelling of the [b] liver *observed,* and the *disordered* man there first feeleth heaviness and sore, and from that place the sore riseth over all the side as far as the collar bone, and as far as the right shoulder, and *the mans* mie is bloodred as if it were bloody ; loss of appetite is incident unto him, and his hue is pale, and he is somewhat feverish, and he suffereth remarkable chill, and quaketh as a man doth in lent addle *or typhus fever ;* his meat will not keep down, the liver enlarges, and he may not touch the sore with his hand, to that degree is it strong, and he hath no sleep when it is strongest. When the swelling bursteth then is the mie purulent, as ratten ; if it runneth off then is the sore less.

[b] Read *last.*

.XVIII.

Ƿiþ þære hype sfile oððe aþundenesse ȝif fe utȝanȝ
foɲfitte him iſ on fɲuman blod to foɲlætenne ōn
æðɲe on þa pineſtɲan healfe ƿyɲc him þonne beþinȝe
þuɲ ꝺ ɲealfe of ele ꝺ ɲuðan · ꝺ ðile ꝺ ōf mepcey
ſiede ſƿa micel ſƿa þe þince ɲeoð eall mid þy ele ꝺ
þonne mid hnefcpe pulle beþe mid þy poɲe lanȝe þa
ſpiðþan ſiðan ꝺ þonne ofepleȝe mid pulle ꝺ befpeþe
ꝼæſte ymb .III. niht ƿyɲc him eft ōnleȝende fealfe
ꝺ beþen ȝɲytte ȝeond ȝotene mid pine ꝺ þonne
ȝeɲodene ꝺ mid ecede ꝺ mid hunȝe eall ȝetpiꝼulad
ꝺ eft ȝeɲoden leȝe ōn þone þɲeceɲtan cla mid oþðe
on ꝼel ſpiðe[1] mid ſƿa peapine ꝺ on þ ꝼaɲ bind ꝺ
hpilum teoh mid ȝlæſe oþþe mid hoɲne.     ȝif ſe utȝanȝ
foɲſitte mid ƿyɲtðɲeneum atceoh hine ut.    Ƿyɲc ōf
pepinoðe · ꝺ of hiɲðe ƿyɲce · ꝺ of ɲuðan ɲæðe · ða
afceoponeſ hunȝeſ ȝenoh to ɲele neahtneɲtiȝūm eueleɲ
mæl.

.XVIIII.

Tacn be afpollenɲe ꝺ ȝepundaðɲe hype læcedomaɲ
ɲiþ þon · ꝺ be þære hype aheapðunȝe.  Se þe bið ȝe-
runðoð þonne on þa hyɲɲe · ꝺ ȝif he ne biþ þon ɲaþoɲ
ȝelacnoð þonne becymð he ōn þa aðle þe mōn poɲinſe
ſpiɲeþ.  ȝif ſe ȝefɲollena mon ōn þære hype oððe ſe
aþundena ſƿa afpollen ȝebit oþ þone ꝼiɲ ꝺ tpentiȝeþan
dæȝ ſƿa ſe ſpile ne beɲiſteþ þonne ōnȝind ſio hyɲp
heapðian ȝif hio ȝebyɲiſt þonne bið þæɲ pinð[2] ōn
þære hype.  þære punðe tacn ɲinðon þonne ſio punð

[1] Rather ſpeðe.
[2] Read punð, because þæɲe punðe follows.

### xviii.

For swelling or puffing up of the liver; if the out-going [1] lodge, *the man* must first be let blood on a vein, on the left side, then work him a bathing thus, and a salve of oil, and rue, and of dill, and of marche seed, as much as may seem good to thee, seethe all with the oil, and then bathe with nesh wool with the wash for a long time the right side, and then overlay with wool, and swathe up fast for about three nights; work him again an onlying salve, and lay barley groats soused with wine, and then sodden, and *this* all triturated with vinegar and with honey, and sodden again, lay on the thickest cloth or on a skin, swathe up therewith so warm, and bind upon the sore, and at whiles draw with glass or horn, *as with cupping glass.* If the secretion lodge, draw it out with wort drinks; work *such* of wormwood and of herdwort, and of seed of rue, add enough of strained honey; give *the man* a spoon measure after his nightly fast.

### xix.

Tokens of a swollen and wounded liver; leechdoms for that; and of the hardening of the liver. He who is wounded in the liver, if he be not sooner cured, then arriveth at the disorder in which a man speweth purulent matter. If the man swollen in the liver, or the bloated one, abideth so swollen until the five and twentieth day, so as that the swelling bursteth not, then beginneth the liver to harden; if it bursteth, then is there a wound in the liver. Tokens of the

---

[1] se uɪꭗauꭗ would be presumed to be fæces, the outgoing of the intestines; but, since this chapter must be based on Alexander Tral-

lianus, πρὸς ἔμφραξιν ἥπατος, the writer ought to mean, the outgoing of bile from the liver.

ʒeboꝛſten biþ þonne bið þuꞃh þa ꝛambe ſe utꞃyne
ſpilce bloðiʒ ꝼæʈeꞃ ⁊ biþ hiꞅ neb ꞃeað ⁊ aſƿollen · ⁊
þonne þu him þine hanꝺ ꞃeʈeſʈ on þa liꝼꞃe þonne ʒeꝼelþ
he ſƿiþe micel [1] ſaꞃ ⁊ biþ ſe man ſƿiðe meaꞃo · ⁊ oꝼ
þæꞃe aðle cymð ꝼul oꝼʈ ꝼæʈeꞃ bolla. Þiþ ʒeſƿollenum
ſaꞃe. On ꝼꞃuman miꝺ onleʒenum ⁊ ꞃealꝼum ſceal
mon lacnian · ſio ꞃceal beon oꝼ beꞃenum ʒꞃytʈum
on leaʒe ʒeſoðenum ⁊ oꝼ culꝼꞃena ꞃceaꞃne ʒeꝛoꞃht miꝺ
huniʒe ⁊ þonne alecʒe mon þa ſealꝼe on hatne claꝺ
oþþe ꝼel oþþe caꞃʈan beſꝛeþe miꝺ þonne hnercaꝺ ꞃe
ſpile ſona ⁊ ʒebeꞃſʈeþ innan. Dꞃince mulſa þ iꞅ ʒe-
milſceðe Dꞃincan ælce dæʒe · ⁊ ʒaʈe meoluc ʒeſoðene
⁊ ƿæʈeꞃ on þam ſien ʒeſoðene ʒoðe ƿyꞃʈa.

### .XX.

Lꞇcedomaꞅ ꝛiþ þæꞃe liꝼꞃe punde þonne ſe ſpile ʒe-
ꝛyꝛſmeð ʈobyꞃſʈ · Nim ʒaʈe meoluc ſƿa ƿeaꞃme niꞃan
amolcene ꞃele Dꞃincan. Do eac ʈo Dꞃence nꞇðꞃan
ʒeꝛoꞃhʈe ſƿa lꞇcaꞅ cunnon ⁊ þonne hie æleꞃa Dꞃincan
ƿillen Dꞃincan hie nemne ꝼæʈeꞃ · æꞃ ʒeſoðen oꝼ ƿyꞃ-
ʈum · on ꝛeꞃmoðe ⁊ on oþꞃum ſꝼelcum ⁊ ſƿica onle-
ʒena ſƿa ƿe æꞃ ꞃꞃʈon. Ac mon ꞃceal æꞃ miꝺ ƿeaꞃmum ſꝛꞃinʒum ⁊ hate ꝼæʈꞃe beþian ⁊ þƿean þa ſʈoꝛe
⁊ on þam ꝼæʈꞃe ſien ʒeſoðene lauꞃeſ cꞃoꝛꝛan ⁊ hꞃꝺe-
ꝛyꞃʈ þ iꞅ eoꝛðʒealla ⁊ ꝛeꞃmoð miꝺ þy þu þa ſaꞃan
ſʈoꝛa lanʒe æꞃeſʈ beþe ⁊ læʈ ꞃeocan on · ʒiꝼ þonne
ꞃio puny ſƿiðe ꞃoʈiʒe þæꞃe liꝼꞃe oþ þ he þ ꝛuꞃſm oꝼ
muðe hꞃꞇce · ʒeꝛyꞃce him ʒemilſcaðe Dꞃincan · þ iꞅ
micel ðꞇl beꝛylleðeꞅ ꝼæʈeꞃeꞅ on huniʒeꞅ ʒoðum ðꞇle ·

---

fol. 75 b.

fol. 76 a.

wound are *these ;* when the wound is bursten out then the outrunning through the wamb is as it were bloody water, and *the mans* face is red and swollen ; and when thou settest thine hand upon the liver then *the man* feeleth very much soreness, and the man is very tender, and from this disorder there cometh full oft a dropsy. For a swollen sore: at starting one shall cure with onlayings, *that is, external applications,* and salves ; the *salve* shall be of barley groats sodden in ley, and of culvers sharn wrought with honey, and then let one lay the salve on a hot cloth, or on a skin, or on paper, beswathe with that, the swelling soon becometh nesh and bursteth within. Let *the man* drink "mulsum," that is, dulcet drinks, every day, and goats milk sodden, and water on which good worts have been sodden.

### XX.

Leechdoms for the abscess of the liver, when the purulent swelling bursteth ; take goats milk so warm, newly milked, give *the man that* to drink. Form also into a potion an adder, wrought so as leeches ken *how to work it,* and when *the sick* will to drink anything, let them drink nothing but water previously sodden with worts, on wormwood and on other such, and such onlayings as we before wrote of. But one shall previously bathe and wash the places with warm squirtings and with hot water, and on the water let there be sodden bunches of laurel *berries or flowers,* and herdwort, that is, earth gall, and wormwood ; with these do thou long previously foment the sore places, and make *the reek* smoke them. If further the wound of the liver be very ratteny, so much as that *the man* breaketh the ratten from his mouth, let him work himself a mulled drink, that is, a mickle deal of boiled water in a good deal of honey ; from it shall the scum

oꝛ þam ꞃceal beón þ̵ ꞃoꞇ ᵹelome aðon þenðen hꞇ món
ꝛelð oꝛ¹ þ̵ þꞇp nan ne ꞅie · lꝫꞇ þonne cohan ⁊ ꞅele
þonne ðꞃincan.²

### .XXI.

Σκίῤῥωσις.

Đꝛꞇꞃ ꞅinꞇ ꞇacn aheaꞃðoðꞃe hꝛꝛe ᵹe ón þam læppum
⁊ healocum ⁊ ꝛilmenum. Sío aheaꞃðunᵹ ꞇꞅ on ꞇꞃa
pꞅꞅan ᵹeꝛað. Oþeꞃ bꞇþ ón ꝛꞃuman æꝛ þon þe ænᵹ
oþeꞃ eaꞃꝛeþe ón hꝛꝛe becume · oþeꞃꞇ æꝛꞇeꞃ oþꞃum eaꞃ-
ꝛeþum þæꞃe hꝛꝛe cymð · ꞅio bꞇþ buꞇan ꞅaꞃe · ⁊ þonne
ꞅe man meꞇe þꞇᵹð þonne apyꞃꞇþð he eꝛꞇ ⁊ ónꞃenðeþ
hꞇꞅ lꞇþ ⁊ hæꝛð unᵹeꝛealðene paꞇmbe ⁊ þa micᵹean · ⁊
þonne þu ðꞇne hanða ꝛeꞇꞅꞇ uꝛan on þa hꝛꝛe þonne
beoð ꞅpa heꝛꞇᵹe ꞅpa ꞅꞇan ⁊ ne bꞇþ ꞅaꞃ · ᵹꞇꝛ þ̵ lanᵹe
ꞅpa bꞇþ þonne ᵹehæꝛþ hꞇꞇ ón uncþehene³ pꞃæꞇeꞃbollan.

fol. 76 b.

Calle⁴ þa blaþunᵹe ⁊ þa pelnaꞅ þa þe beoþ ᵹehꝛꝛæꞃ
ᵹeonð þone lichoman · þa cumað óꝛ haꞇum bloðe ⁊
þeallenðum · ꞅpa bꞇð eac ꞅpꞇlce on ðæꞃe hꝛꝛe ꞇo ónᵹꞇ-
ꞇanne hꝛꝛæþeꞃ ꞅio hæꞇo ⁊ ꞅꞇo ablaþunᵹ ꞅie on þæꞃe
hꝛꝛe ꞃelꝛꝛe on þam ꝛilmenum · ⁊ on þam þꞇnᵹum þe
ymbuꞇan þa hꝛꝛe beoþ · ⁊ hꝛꝛæþeꞃ hꞇo ꞅie on ðam
hꝛꝛeꞃbylum ⁊ læppum þe on þam hꝛꝛeꞃholum ⁊ healcum þe on þam ðælum bæm. þonne ꝛe læce þ̵ onᵹꞇꞇ
þonne mæᵹ he þone kꞇceðóm þe ꞃaðoꞃ ꝛinðan · Đꞇꞅ
ꞅynð þa ꞇacn · ᵹꞇꝛ ꞅio ablaþunᵹ ꞅio haꞇe bꞇþ on
þæꞃe hꝛꝛe oꝛꞃum oðꞇe byhꞇm þonne bꞇþ þæꞃ micel
aþunðeneꞃ ⁊ ꞃeꝛeꞃ mꞇð ꞅꝛeopunᵹa⁵ omena ⁊ ꞅꞇꞇ-
ᵹenðe ꞅaꞃ oþ þa ꞃꞇþoban oð ða eaxle ⁊ hꞃoꞅꞇa ⁊
neaꞃoneꞃ bꞃeoꞅꞇa · ⁊ maꞃe heꝛꞇᵹneꞃ þonne ꞅaꞃ · ⁊

---

¹ MS. has on.

² This passage may be from Philagrios on the preparation of ἀπόμελι,
as preserved in Nikolaos Mycreps-
ios, v. 3.

³ For uncþelcacne.

⁴ These words are found in Alexander Trallianus, vii. 19 ; p. 126,
ed. 1548.

⁵ Read ꝛꞃeolunᵹa, from the words
καὶ πυρετὸν ἐπιφέρει καυσώδη.

be frequently removed, while it is a boiling, till that there be none there; then let it cool, and then give it to be drunk.

## xxi.

Here are tokens of a hardened liver, whether on the lobes or the hulks, *that is, the hollows of it*, or the films *and membranes*. The hardening occurs in two ways; the one is in the outset before any other mischief cometh upon the liver; the second cometh after other mischiefs of the liver; it is without sore, and when the man taketh meat, then he casteth *it* up again, and changeth his hue, and hath not under control his wamb and his mic; and when thou settest thine hand from above upon the liver, then it is as heavy as a stone and is not sore: if that continues long so, then it involves a not easily cured dropsy. All the *up*blowings and the burnings which be anywhere throughout the body, come of hot and boiling blood. So also in like manner it is to be understood of the liver, whether the heat and the upblowing be on the liver itself, on the films, *that is, membranes*,[1] and on the things[2] which be about the liver; and whether they be on the liver prominences and lobes, or in the liver holes and hulks,[3] or in both those parts. When the leech understandeth that, then he may the more easily find the leechdom. These are the tokens; if the hot upblowing is on the margins or prominences of the liver, then is there much distention and fever with burning heats and a piercing soreness as far as the collar bones, and as far as the shoulder, and there is host, *or cough*, and oppression of the breast,

---

[1] χιτῶσιν, *tunics, coats*, Alex. Trall.

[2] μυσί, *muscles*, id.

[3] Ζητεῖν ἄρά γε τὰ κυρτά πεπόνθασι μᾶλλον, ἢ τὰ σιμά ἢ καὶ τὸ συναμφότερον; *the convexities or concavities, or both at once.*

þonne ſio ablaþunᵹ biŏ ón þam ſilmenum ⁊ on þam
æðrum þe ón ⁊ ymb þa liᵹne beoð þonne biþ þ ſaſ
ſceaſiþe þonne þaſ ſelmeſ ſaſi þe on þæſe liᵹne
ſelſſe beoð · ⁊ þu meaht he þon onᵹitan þ ſio abl
biþ þæſe liᵹne læppum ⁊ oſſium. ᵹiſ þonne ſio liᵹne

aheaſðunᵹ ⁊ ſio abl ⁊ ſio ablaþunᵹ biþ on þæſe liᵹne
healcum ⁊ holocum ᵹecenneð þonne þincþ him ſona ón
ſſuman þ ſio þæte ſpiþoſ niþoſ ᵹepite þonne hio
ūpſtiᵹe · ⁊ ſe món ᵹeſpoᵹunᵹa þſoþað ⁊ modeſ ᵹeſþæ-
þſunᵹa · ne mæᵹ him ſe lichoma batian āc he biŏ
blāc ⁊ þynne ⁊ acoloð ⁊ ſoſþon iſtſiŏ him þæteſ-
bolla.

.XXII.

Þiþ þæſe ᵹeſelan heaſðneſſe þæſe liᵹne ŏonne iſ
ſio to beŏianne mið hatan þætſe ón þam ſien ᵹeſoðene þyſta. Þeſſmoð · ⁊ pilðſe maᵹþan þyſtſſuman ·
ſenoᵹſecum hatte þyſt · ⁊ coſŏ ᵹealla · þonne þa
ſſen ealle ᵹeſoðene beþe þonne mið mielum ſpſſynᵹum þa
ſaſan ſtoþe lanᵹe · ſoſſiæſ ſpa .III. ðaᵹaſ. Þyſc þonne
ſealſe ōſ hpætenum ᵹſſyttum ᵹepoſhc oŏŏe ōſ bſiſe
ōſ peſſmoðe · ⁊ ōſ pine · ⁊ ōſ apſſotaneaſ ⁊ cymene · ·
⁊ oſ lauſeſ cſſoppan ðo huniᵹeſ ſo þ þu þyſſe ſele
him þ þſiy ðaᵹaſ · oþſe þſine ſete him hoſſ ón oþþe
ᵹlæſ ſeoh uſ. Sel þu lācnaſc ᵹiſ þu ſeoþeſc ſuban
ón ele ⁊ ᵹſſenne peſſmoð oŏŏe ðſiᵹſe · ⁊ hpiſ cpuðu

þy ealle beþe leᵹe on uſan · læt beón ealne ðæᵹ ⁊ eſſc
ſela ðaᵹa þaſ þinᵹ ſinc ſo ðonne ⁊ þám monnum ſynð
ſo ſellanne miᵹole ðſincan · þa þyſſc peſeſſſihan · ⁊

and more heaviness than sore. And when the upblowing is on the films, and on the veins which be in and about the liver, then is the sore sharper than the sore of the inflammation which is on the liver itself, and thou mayest by that understand that the disorder is on the lobes and margins of the liver. If moreover the liver hardening, and the disease, and the upblowing is kindled on the hulks and hollows of the liver, then it soon seems to *the doctor* that the humour descends downwards rather than ascends; and the man suffers swoonings and failings of the mind;[1] his body cannot amend, but it is pale, and thin, and chilled, and hence there falleth upon him dropsy.

## xxii

For the sensitive hardness of the liver; it is to be bathed with hot water, on which worts have been sodden, wormwood and roots of wild maythe, a wort that hight fenugreek, and earth gall; when they are all sodden, then bathe the sore places for a long time with copious water fomentations ;[2] leave it so for three days ; then work a salve wrought of wheaten groats or of a brewit of wormwood, and of wine, and of abrotanum, and of cummin, and of bunches of laurel berries; add thereto as much honey as thou needest ; give *the man* that for three days; on other three set on him *a cupping* horn or glass, draw out *by that, what comes out.* Thou shalt treat *the sick* better if thou settest rue in oil, and green or dry wormwood, and gum mastic, with all that bathe *him, also* lay it upon *him;* let it be for a whole day, and also for many days these things are to be done, and to the men must be given diuretic drinks; give thou him

---

[1] λειποθυμίας for the two.
[2] Medicated baths were well known, as to Oribasios.

dile · ⁊ merces sæd oððe ƿyrttruman mid hunige sele þu him ælce dæge drincan · gif him fefer ne sie ne þæt mid ƿine æfter þon oþþe ƿyrtdrencas sculon siþþan þæt geswel biþ gehƿeled ⁊ tobyrst ⁊ ƿyrð ūnsarre ⁊ niþer gewit þurh ða ƿambe ⁊ se mān mihð ƿormse · talaþ þæt he þonne hal sie · þonne beoþ him to sellanne

Aretæus, Chron. i. 13.

spiþost þa migolan drincan þætte eall þæt yfel þurh ða ƿambe ⁊ þurh þa micgean ƿeorðen[1] aƿeg adon · þy læs se mon ƿeorþe þurh þone muþ ƿorms spiƿende ⁊ hine huru ƿiþ bæð healde ⁊ ƿiþ grene æpla gif þonne se spile ⁊ þæt ƿorms upstihð to þon þæt þe þince þæt hit mon sniþan mæge ⁊ ūt forlætan · ƿyrc him þonne sealfe ærest of culfran scearne ⁊ of þam gelica · ⁊ ær mid spryngum beþe þa stoƿe mid þy ƿætre ⁊ ƿyrtum þe ƿe ær ƿriton þonne þu ongite þæt þæt geswel hnescige ⁊

fol. 78 a.

spiþrige · þonne hrin ðu him mid þy snid irene ⁊ snið

Celsus, iv. 8.

lyt hƿon ⁊ listum þæt þæt blod mæge ūt furþum þylæs þider in yfel ƿolha gesige · Ne forlæt þu þæs blodes

Aret. Acut. vi.

to fela ōn ænne siþ · þyles se seoca mān to ƿerig ƿeorðe oððe sƿylte · āc þonne þu hit tostinge oþþe sniþe þonne hafa þe hnesne ƿætlan gearone þæt þu þæt dolh sona mid forƿride · ⁊ þonne þu hit eft ma lætan ƿille teoh þone ƿætlan of læt lytlum sƿa oþþæt hit adrugie · ⁊ þonne sio ƿund sie clæne · gerynme þonne þæt þæt þyrel to nearo ne sie · āc þu hie ælce dæge mid ƿipan geond sƿæt · ⁊ aþƿeah mid þam ƿin-

[1] Read ƿeorðe.

every day to drink the wort parsley, and dill, and seed
of marche or its roots with honey: if he hath no fever
eke that with wine. After that other wort drinks
are proper, when the swelling is become an abscess and
bursteth,[1] and is becoming more free from soreness, and
is passing off downwards through the wamb, and the
man pisseth ratten, reckoneth that he then may be
hole;[2] then must be given him principally the diuretic drinks, in order that all the mischief through the
wamb and through the mic may be done away, lest
the man should take to spewing ratten through the
mouth; and let him withhold himself somewhat from
the bath and from green apples. If however the
swelling and the ratten mounteth up to that degree
that it seem to thee that a man may cut *into* it and
let it out, then work him a salve first of culvers sharn
and the like of that, and previously bathe the places
with sousings, with the water, and with the worts
which are wrote of before. When thou understandeth
that the swelling is growing nesh and mild, then touch
thou it with the cutting iron,[3] and cut *in* a little,
and cleverly, even that the blood may come out, lest
an evil *sinus* or pouch descend in thither. Do not
let too much blood at one time, lest the sick man become too languid or die; but when thou dost prick or
cut it, then have for thyself a linen cloth ready that
therewith thou mayst soon bind up the cut; and
when thou wilt again let more *blood* draw the cloth
off, let it *run* by a little at a time till it gets dry;
and when the wound is clean, then enlarge it that the
thirl *or aperture* may not be too narrow; but do
thou every day syringe through it with a tube, and

---

[1] The words are not from Trallianus, but he speaks in the same
order of ἀρχομένης πέττεσθαι τῆς
φλεγμονῆς καὶ γὰρ δί' οὔρων ὑποκλέπ-
τεται καὶ σμικρύνεται ὁ ὄγκος.

[2] τὰ τῆς πέψεως σημεῖα ἀσφα-
λέστερα. Trallianus, p. 128, ed.
1548.

[3] Cf. Aretæos: chron. I. xiii.

ʒum ɲþþan ðɲleʒe þe þa ƿunde clænɲien.[1] ʒiɟ hio
ſƿiþoɲ unſyɟɟe þeoɲɲa clænɲa[2] miþ huniʒe ɟ ʒelæt eɟt
toʒædeɲe. Eɟt þonne ſeo unʒeɟelde aheaɲdunʒ þæɲe
hɲþe to lanʒſum ƿyɲð. þonne ƿyɲcþ hio ɲæteɲ bollan
þone þe mon ʒelacnian ne mæʒ. Ac mon ſceal ſona
ðn ɟɲuman þa æɲ ʒenemnedan beþunʒa. ne dɲince he
ɲiþeɲ naht. ɟ ʒiɟ ɲe hɲeɲſioca mon blodeſ to ɟela
hæbbe þonne ſceal him mon æɲ eallum oþɲum læcedomum blod lætan oɟ þam ſɲiðɲan eaɲme on þæɲe
ɲiþeɲɲan æðɲe. ʒiɟ ſɲa mon ne mæʒe eaþe ʒeɲeðɲan
þonne ſceal mon on þæɲe middel æðɲe blod lætan.
þa þe þ ne doþ on micel eaɲɟeþum becumað.

fol. 78 b.

### .XXIII.[3]

Ƿɲæt him ſie to ɟoɲʒanne ðn hɲeɲ adle hƿæt him
ſie to healdanne ʒe on læcedomum ʒe on mete. ɟoɲþon iſ þeaɲɟ micel þ mon nauþeɲ ne ɲcalɟa ne baþu.
ne ðnleʒena æɲ to nyde. æɲ him mon blod læte þam
þe ɟela blodeſſ hæþ.[4] æɟteɲ þon þe ɲe lichoma ſie
þuɲh þa blodlæɲe ʒeclænɲað.[5] þæſ manneſ bileoɟa[6]
iſ to beɲceapianne. æþeſt him iſ to ɲellanne þ
þone innoð ſtille ɟ ſmeþe. ne ſie ɲceaɲp ne to aɟoɲ.
ne ɲlitende. ne ſpiʒene. æle bɲoþ iſ to ɟoɲʒanne
ɟoɲ þon þe hit biþ þindende ɟ yɟele ɲætan ƿyɲeþ.
æʒɲu ſint to ɟoɲʒanne ɟoɲþonþe hiɲa ɲæte bið ɟæt ɟ
maɲan hæto ƿyɲeð. hlaɟeſ eɲuman ʒiɟ hie beoþ oɟ-
þænde oþþe ʒeɲodene ſint to þiʒanne ac na to ſƿiðe.

fol. 79 a.

oþɲe ɲætan[7] mete ʒeaɲɲa ɟ eðcnunʒa ealle ſint to
ɟoɲbeodanne. ɟ eal þa ɲætan þinʒ ɟ þa ſmeɲeɲiʒan ɟ
oɟæþhlaɟaſ[8] ɟ eall ſƿete þinʒ þe ƿyɲeað aþundeneɲɲe.
ʒe þa ɲceaɲɲan aɟɲan þinʒ ſint to ɟleonne. ɟoɲþon þe

---

[1] claɲmen, MS.
[2] claɲna, MS.
[3] Alexander Trallianus, p. 127,
line 9, ed. 1548, by the general
sense.
[4] Εἰ αἷμα πλεονάζει.

[5] ʒeclæɲnað, MS.
[6] Alex. ut supra, line 17.
[7] Read hƿætene ; τὰ δὲ ἄλλα πάντα
σιτώδη.
[8] The Saxon leech skips four
lines of Alexandros of Tralles.

wash it out by those means; after that, lay thereon what may cleanse the wound. If it turn off very impure, cleanse it with honey and draw it again come together. Again, when the insensible hardening of the liver is of too long duration, then it forms a dropsy which cannot be cured. But one must soon at the outset employ the before named fomentations; let him drink nothing new, and if the liversick man have too much blood, then one must, before all other leechdoms, let him blood from the right arm on the nether vein. If that may not easily be got at, then shall a man let blood upon the middle vein; they who do it not, come into mickle difficulties.

## xxiii.

*Here we treat of* what *a man* must forego in liver disease, what he must hold by, whether in leechdoms or in diet. For as much as there is much need that for a man who has much blood one should employ neither salves, nor baths, nor external applications, ere he be let blood; after the body is cleansed through the bloodletting, the mans diet is to be examined: first must be given him what may still and soothe the inwards, *what* is neither sharp nor too austere, nor rending, nor caustic; all broth [1] must be foregone because it is inflating and worketh evil humours; eggs must be foregone because their liquor is fat and worketh more heat; crumbs of bread, if they be moistened or sodden, may be eaten, but not in excess; other wet [wheaten] meat-preparations, and cookings up must be forbidden, and all the moist things and greasy, and oyster patties,[2] and all sweet things which work inflation. Yea the sharp austere things [3] must be

---

[1] Ζέμα.

[2] ὀστρακόδερμα, *shell fish.*

[3] τὰ στύφοντα; but just above ἀγορ translated δριμύ.

þa ſinꞇ ꝼoꞃꞇᵹnenᵭe þa innoþaꞃ · ⁊ ᵹeꝼamnaᵭ þone ſpile
⁊ unᵹþelice melꞇaᵭ · ꝼoꞃ ᵭonne æppla ·[1] ne þin niꞃ ꞇo
ꞃellanne · ꝼoꞃ ᵭon þe hie habbaᵭ haꞇne bꞃæþ · þam iꞃ
ꞇo þiᵹᵹanne ſuꞃceaꞃp þin · eac ꞃocal mon oxunelliꞃ[2]
ꞃellan þ biᵭ uꝼ eceᵭe ⁊ oꝼ huniᵹe ᵹeꝺoꝛhꞇ ᵭꞃenc
ſuþeꞃne · ⁊ þonne onᵹinᵭ þæꞃe hæꞇo þelm paniaɴ
ſꝑþolꞇ þuꞃh ᵭa micᵹean · ⁊ him iꞃ ꞇo ꞃellanne læ-
ꞇucaꞃ ·[3] ⁊ ſuþeꞃne popiᵹ[4] unꞃeꞃeaꝑᵭ.   Taen[5] þ ſe ſpile
þꞃman ne mæᵹ · ne uꞇyꞃnan on þæꞃe hꞃꝑe · þ ſe
moɴ hæꝼᵭ heꝼiᵹ ꞃaꝑ oɴ mꝑeꞃeaꝑᵭꞃe hꞃꝑe ᵭælum ·
emne ſꝑa he ꞃie miᵭ hꝑilcꝑe hꞃeᵹa byꝓþenne ᵹeheꞃeᵹoᵭ
oɴ þæꞃe ſꝑꝑꝑan healꝼe · ⁊ næꝼᵭ he ꝼeꝼꞃeꞃ hæꞇo oɴ
þam ᵭælum · þam men ſinꞇ ꞇo ꞃellanne þa ᵭꞃncan ⁊
þa lececᵭomaꞃ þa ᵭe þe læꝺon þ mon ᵭyᵭe ꞇo þæꞃe
unᵹeꝼelan heaꝑᵭneꞃꞃe onᵹunnenꝑe on þæꞃe hꞃꝑe ᵹeh-
neꞃeiᵹe miᵭ þy þ ꝼoꝑſeꞇene yꝼel · ᵹiꝼ hꝑa þone leee-
ᵭoɱ ᵭeþ ꞇo þe þa ꝼoꝑſeꞇꞇan þinᵹ oɴꞇyne ⁊ uꞇꞇeo aꞃp
þon ᵭe he þone ꝼoꝑheaꝑᵭoᵭan ſpile ᵹehneꞃce · þeneþ þ
he hiꞇ beꞇe · ᵹiꝼ þaꞃp ahꞇ biᵭ læꞃeᵭ þaꞃ heaꝑᵭan · ne
beꞇ he hiꞇ ac ꝑyꝑꞇ · ⁊ aᵭꝑꞃᵹþ miᵭ þy læceᵭome þa
ꝑaꞇan ⁊ ꝑiꞃᵭ ꞃe ſpile ſꝑa heaꝑᵭ ſꝑa ſꞇan · ⁊ ne mæᵹ
hine moɴ ᵹemelꞇan ne ᵹehneꞃcian.[6]


## .XXIIII.

Pyꞃꞇᵭꞃeneaꞃ piᵭ eallum hꞃeꝓ aᵭlum · pyꝓce moɴ
ꞇo ᵭꞃeneum hꞃeꝓ feocum mannum · meꞃ̃ceꝼ[7] ꞃaᵭ ·
ᵭileꞃ · peꞃꞃmoᵭeꞃ · þy ᵹemeꞇe þe læeaꞃ eunnon ᵹniᵭ oɴ
pæꞇeꞃ ꞃele ᵭꞃncan.   Eꝼꞇ[8] coꞃꞇeꞃ ⁊ ꝓpoꝓeꞃ ᵭuꞃꞇ ⁊
oþꞃa ꝑyꞃꞇa þiſum ᵹeliea ᵭꞃnce .III. ᵭaᵹaꞃ · ⁊ lieᵹe on

---

[1] For ροιαί, pomegranates.
[2] As before, foot of page ; miss-ing four lines.
[3] For τὸ ἄσαρ, asarum Europæum, and mœum, meum.
[4] For nardus keltica. Valeriana c. The Saxon perhaps means Glaucium luteum. Cf. Dioskorid. I. vii.
[5] The editions of Alex. Trall. make a new chapter here, p. 127, line 6, ed. 1548. The Saxon ver-sion is free.
[6] This passage ends at Alex. Trall., p. 127, line 16, ed. 1548.
[7] From Alex. Trallianus, p. 129, line 24, ed 1548, with omission of asarabacca and almonds.
[8] Alex. Trall., p. 129, line 32.

avoided, inasmuch as they have a bad effect in closing
the inwards, and they collect the swelling, and it doth
not easily disperse,[1] hence neither apples nor wine
must be given, since they have a hot breath or *aroma*.
The man must take a not sharp wine; one must also
give him some oxymel, which is a southern or *Italian*
drink, wrought of vinegar and of honey: and when
the burning of the heat beginneth to wane away,
chiefly through the mie, he must have lettuces and
the inward part of southern poppy. Tokens that the
swelling in the liver may not abate, nor run off; that
that man hath a heavy sore in the parts of the nether
liver, even as if he were weighted with something of
a burden in the right side, and he hath not a heat of
fever in these parts. To such a man must be given
the drinks and the leechdoms, which we taught one
should use for the insensible hardness begun in the
liver; with them let him make the obstructive mischief
nesh. If any one applieth the leechdom which unlocketh
and draweth out the obstinately lodged matters, before
he hath made nesh the badly hardened swelling, he
weeneth that he is amending it; *but* if there be aught
left of the hard *matter*, he amendeth it not, but
harmeth, and with the leechdom he drieth the humours, and the swelling becometh as hard as a stone,
and it cannot be dissipated nor be made nesh.


### xxiv.

Wort drinks for all liver diseases: let one work for
drinks for a liversick man, seed of marche, of dill,
of wormwood, rub *these fine* into water in the manner
in which leeches ken *how, and* give to drink. Again,
let *the patient* drink for three days dust of costmary,
and of pepper, and of other worts like these, and let
him lie on the right side for half an hour, and drink

---

[1] Τοὺς ὄγκους δυσφορήτους ἐργάζεται.

þa fpiðran fiðan healpe tið Ꝙ dꝛince eft ón æꝛenne.
healðe hine þonne piþ eceð. Þiþ bæþ[1] piþ pifan Ꝙ
beana • Ꝙ næpal'. Ꝙ piþ þa þinȝ þe pindiȝne æþm'ón men
pypeen.   Eft[2] coft • ꝛenum ȝpecum pipoꝛ haꝛan typðlu
ealꝛa emꝛela • ȝebeat oþþe ȝeȝniᵭ Ꝙ aꝛiꝼte • ȝeðo cuclep
fulne þær ón pin ꝛele dꝛincan þam þe butan ꝼeꝼꝛe
fie • þæm ðe ꝼeꝼeꝛ hæbbe þ iꝼ micel hæto Ꝙ hꝛuð[3]
ꝛele þám ón peaꝛmum pꝛeteꝛe • ȝelieȝe þonne on þa
fpiþꝛan fiðan Ꝙ aleeȝe hiꝼ fpiþꝛan hanð lím unðeꝛ
heaꝼoð aꝛeahte healꝛe tið.[4]   Eft pyꝛtðꝛencaf piþ liꝼeꝛ
aðle • clæꝛꝛan ꝛeapeꝛ .II. lytle bollan fulle mið lytle
huniȝe ȝemenȝðe • ðo peaꝛ fulne ȝehætteꝼ pineꝼ' to
ꝛele dꝛincan þꝛy ðaȝaf ȝiꝼ hꝛæt yꝼleꝛ on þeꝛe[5] bið
fie dꝛenc læcnað.   Eft pilðꝛe mealpan feapeꝛ þꝛy lytle
bollan fullan[ᵃ] ȝemenȝðe piþ fpile tu pꝛeteꝼ ꝛele dꝛincan .IIII. ðaȝaf • Ꝙ ȝiꝼ lím hꝛuð aðl ȝetenȝe bið þa
toðꝛiꝼþ ꝼe pyꝛt dꝛenc.   Eft ꝼin cymen Ꝙ huniȝ
ȝeȝniᵭ toSomne ꝛele dꝛincan.   Eft iꝼiȝ cꝛoꝛꝛenu on
þam monðe ȝeȝaðeꝛoð þe pe hatað iuiuaꝛuiꝼ ón læðen •
Ꝙ on enȝlifc ꝛe æꝼteꝛꝛa ȝeola • ꝼiꝼ Ꝙ XX. Ꝙ pipoꝛeꝼ eác
fpa • ȝeȝniᵭ þonne mið þy felextan pine • Ꝙ ȝehæte ꝛele
þam fcocan men neahtneftiȝum dꝛincan.   Læcedóm piþ
liꝼeꝛ aðle eft cauleꝼ tpiȝu oþþe ftelan mið þam cꝛoꝛ-
ꝛum aðꝛiȝe clænlice bæꝛne to ahfan ȝehealð þa ahꝛan •
Ꝙ þonne þeaꝛꝼ fie ȝeðo þeꝛe ahfan cuclep fulne mið
.XI. ȝeȝniᵭenꝛa pipoꝛ coꝛna ón cald fpiꝼe hluttoꝛ . .
. ." ȝehæt þonne ꝛele dꝛincan oþꝛe ꝛiꝼe niȝon coꝛn •
þꝛiððan fiðe feoꝛon. Læcedom piþ liꝼꝛe aðle eft lauꝛeꝛ
cꝛoꝛꝛan Ꝙ pipoꝛeꝼ coꝛna .XX. ȝeȝniᵭ fmale • ȝeðo ón
bollan fulne ealdeꝼ pineꝼ • Ꝙ ȝemenȝ toȝæðeꝛe mið

_fol. 80 a._

_ᵃ Read ꝛulle._

_fol. 80 b._

---

[1] The text of Alex. Tra. 1528, has βαλάνων, but Albanus Torinus " balneum."

[2] Alex. Trall., p. 130, line 3, ed. 1548.

[3] Otherwise found hꝛuᵭ.

[1] This last clause, not in the text of Alex. Tr., is in the Latin of Albanus Torinus.

[3] Add liꝼe, omitted in MS.

[a] Some word, perhaps ꝛin, is here omitted by MS.

again in the evening. Let him withhold himself also from vinegar, from the bath, from peas, and beans, and navews, and from the things which work in a man a windy vapour. Again, beat or rub up and sift costmary, fenugreek, pepper, hares treadles, equal quantities of all; put a spoon full of this into wine, and give it to him who is without fever, to drink. To him who hath fever, that is mickle heat and fire,[1] give it in warm water; then let him lie on the right side and lay his right hand stretched out under his head, for half an hour. Again, wortdrinks for liver disease: to two little bowls full of juice of clover mingled with a little honey, add a bowl full of heated wine; give this to be drunk for three days, if anything of evil be on the liver, the drink will cure it. Again, give to drink for four days, three little bowls full of the juice of wild mallow, mingled with two such of water. and if fever disease be on him, the wort drink driveth it away. Again, rub together wine, cummin, and honey, give him *this* to drink. Again, five and twenty bunches of ivy berries, gathered in the month which we hight in Latin Januarius, and in English the second Yule, and of pepper as much, rub *these up* with the best wine, and heat it; give it to the sick man, after his nights fasting, to drink. A leechdom again for liver disease: dry clean some twigs or stalks of colewort with the flower heads, burn *them* to ashes, store the ashes, and when occasion is, put a spoon full of the ashes with eleven ground pepper corns into old very clear *wine*, then heat it, give to be drunk the next time nine corns, the third time seven. A leechdom again for liver disease: rub small a bunch of bay berries and twenty pepper corns, put them into a bowl full of old wine, and mingle them together with a glowing

---

[1] Properly *fever*; the Saxon seems to interpret Fever, as a Latinism, by pure English words.

ȝlopenðe irene sele ðrincan ⁊ ȝeleȝe stille. Wiþ lifre
aðlum puðan sceafas þry ȝeðo on pine cnoccan ⁊ þry
micle bollan fulle pæteres oferpylle oþ þone þriddan
ðæl ⁊ spete spiðe mið huniȝe ⁊ þonne eft oferpylle
sele ðrincan. Eft pintreopes þa ȝrenan trigu ufe-
peard ȝeȝnið on þ selefte þin sele ðrincan. Eft heorotes lungena mið þære þrotan aspyinðlað ⁊ apeneð ⁊
aðriȝeð on fece · ⁊ þonne hie ful pel aðriȝoðe synð
ȝebryte ⁊ ȝeȝnið ⁊ þonne ȝeromna mið huniȝe sele
to etanne lifer seocum men þ is halpende lecedom.
ȝif lifer peaxe ðrince se man spirolne ðrenc. ðrince
eft pucan æfter þon beon broð ⁊ mæniȝe oþre pætan ·
oþre pucan ðrince perinoð on maxpyrte apyllede · ⁊
nane oþre pætan ⁊ califer hatte pyrt apylle þa eac on
maxpyrte ðrince þriddan pucan ⁊ nanne oþerne[1] pætan.
ðrince æfter speoropolne ðrenc ane ripe.


.XXV.

ÐER sint tacen speotol be panbe coþum ⁊ aðlum ⁊
hu mon þa yfelan pætan þreþe panbe lacnian scyle.
þonne panb aðl toreapð sie þonne beoþ þa tacen.
Þent[2] hie sio panb ⁊ hpyt ⁊ ȝefelð sar þonne
se mon mete þiȝeð ⁊ punȝetunȝa ⁊ inluft metes.
Cneop hatiað[3] lenðenu hefeȝiað ⁊ toȝetteþ betreox
seulðrum ⁊ eall lichoma sticce mælum hefeȝað ⁊ latiað
þa fet · ⁊ þa lipan þapia lenðena rapiað · þonne mon
þar tacen onȝite · þonne is se repesta lecedom ðræȝ-
fæsten þ mon mið þy þa panbe clænsiȝe[4] þ hio þy þe

---

[1] The change of gender is according to the MS.

[2] Diokles apud Paullum Æginc-
tam : col. 376, B. in Medicæ Artis
Principes, for five lines only.

[3] *Gravantur*, Lat., healtiað ?

[4] clænriȝe, MS.

iron, give *to the patient* to drink, and let him lie still.
For liver diseases ; put three bundles of rue into wine
in a crock, and three mickle bowls full of water, boil
them down to the third part, and sweeten them thoroughly with honey, and then again boil off; give *this*
to be drunk. Again, rub into the best wine the upper
part of the green twigs of a pine tree ; administer this.
Again, a harts lungs with the throat ripped up, and
spread out, and dried in the reek; and when they are
full well dried, break them and rub *them small* and
then collect them with honey; give *this* to the liversick man to eat ; it is a healing leechdom. If the
liver wax *large,* let the man drink an emetic drink.
Again, for a week after that let him drink bean broth
and no other liquid, next week let him drink wormwood boiled in mashwort, and no other liquid, and
there is a wort called ealiver,[1] boil that also in mashwort, let him drink that for the third week and no
other liquid. Let him drink after *that* an emetic drink
for one turn.

## XXV.

Here are plain tokens of disorders and sicknesses of
the wamb, and how a man shall cure the evil humours
of the wamb. When wamb disease is present then the
tokens are ; the wamb turneth itself, and is fevered,
and feeleth sore when the man eateth meat, and prick-
ings, and loss of appetite for meat. The knees are
slow, the loins are heavy, and there are spasms between the shoulders, and all the body by piece meal[2]
is heavy, and the feet are tardy, and the muscles of the
loins are sore; when a man observes these tokens, then
the first leechdom is a days fasting, that with that he
may cleanse the wamb, that it may be the lighter. Well,

---

[1] *Jack in the hedge ; Erysimum alliaria.*

[2] "*citra occasionem,*" the modern translation of the unprinted Greek.

leohtne ꞃie · ȝiꝼ ꞃio aðl ꞃie þonne ȝit peaxenðe ꝼaerte
.II. daȝar toȝaðeꞃe ȝiꝼ hun maeȝen ȝelaerte · ȝiꝼ he þ
ne maeȝe ꞃelle hun mon leohter hpaet hpeȝa to þic-
ȝanne rpa aeȝꞃu beoð ɔ ðon¹ ȝelic. Sume to þaeꞃe
paInbe claenꞃunȝa² reoþað netelán on paeꞃe ɔ on
pIne · ɔ on ele · rume þaeꞃe ꞃeaðan netlan tpIȝu
ȝꞃene · rume betan oþþe ðoccan³ on ȝerpettum pIne
reoꞃað ɔ ꞃellað to þicȝenne · ɔ ȝiꝼ ꞃio aðl maꞃe pyꞃð
ɔ re ꞃeoca man þ maeȝen haeꝼð þonne reoþan hIe hun
ꞃtꞃenȝꞃan pyꞃta ɔ ðoþ hpaet hpeȝa ꞃIpeꞃ to ; Sceapiȝe
món ȝeoꞃne hpIlc ꞃe utȝanȝ ꞃie þe mIcel þe lytel þe þaeꞃ
nan ne ꞃie · leoꞃnIȝe be þon ꞃe laece hu hun þInce
hpaet món ðon ꞃeule · ȝiꝼ þ ꞃie omihte paete Innan
ónbuꞃnenu tyhte hIe món ut mIð hꞃIm mettum ꞃin-
cenðum ɔ ne laet Inne ȝeꞃIttan on þam lIchoman · ɔ
pyꞃð ȝeȝaðeꞃoðu omIȝ paete ón þaeꞃe paInbe oððe
on þam rmaelþeaꞃme · ɔ naeꝼð þonne utȝanȝ ꞃio ꞃtoꞃ
ac bIð apyꞃðeð ꞃio ꞃtoꞃ ɔ ꞃe maȝa onpent ɔ tóbꞃocen
· ɔ þ heaꝼoð aþꞃuten ɔ ꞃaꞃ · ɔ þa Innoþaꞃ ablapene ɔ
hate ꝼeꞃꞃaꞃ · ɔ mIcel þuꞃꝼt ɔ ealleꝼ lichoman aðla
peoꞃꞃað apealhte. Sceal món laennan ꞃpIlce able ȝiꝼ he
ꞃóꝼeꞃ naeꝼð · mIð cu meolcum oððe ȝate ꞃpa mIȝe mol-
cene ðꞃInce. Eác hylꞃð ȝiꝼ món mIð ea ꞃtanum on-
baeꞃInebdum · oþþe mIð hatene iꞃene þa meolꞃIc ȝeꞃyꞃð
ɔ ꞃelþ ðꞃIncan · ɔ ȝiꝼ þ bIþ ȝeonȝ man ɔ þa tIð haeꝼð
ɔ mIhte hím mon ꞃceal óꝼ eaꞃme blod ꞃpIþe laetan
ɔ ymb .III. niht ðꞃInce eꝼt þa meoluc.

¹ ðon, MS.

² claeꞃnunȝa, MS.

³ Paul. Ægin, as before.

if the disease be still on the increase, let *him* fast for two days together, if his strength will endure it; if he be not able to do that, let him have somewhat light to eat, as eggs be and the like of them. Some, for the cleansing of the wamb, seethe nettle in water, and in wine, and in oil, some seethe in sweetened wine twigs of red nettle green, some beet or dock, and give *this* to be taken; and if the disease groweth stronger, and the sick man hath the strength *for it*, then they seethe stronger worts and add some little pepper. Let it be earnestly observed what the outgang, *or fæcal discharge*, is, whether mickle, or little, or whether there be none; let the leech learn by that how it seems to him a man should act. If there be an inflammatory flagrant humour within, let it be got out by gentle aperient diet, and let it not lodge within in the body, *for then* there will be gathered an inflammatory humour in the wamb, or in the small guts, and then the place has no passage out, but the spot is corrupted, and the maw is disturbed and upbroken, and the head is vexed and sore, and the inwards upblown; and hot fevers, and mickle thirst, and diseases of all the body become awakened. Such a disease must be treated, if *the patient* have no fever, with cows milk, or let him drink goats milk newly milked. Also it helpeth if a man with water stones[1] put in the fire, or with heated iron, turneth the milk and *so* giveth it to be drunk; and if it be a young man and he hath a suitable time *for it* and strength *to bear it*, he must be freely let blood from the arm, and let him drink the milk for about three days.

---

[1] Understand such stones as would bear to be heated and plunged in water.

## .XXVI.

Be ƿambe coþum ⁊ ȝɪſ: hɪo man punð bɪþ hu
þ món onȝɪtan mæȝe ⁊ ȝelācman · æþeſt ȝɪſ hɪpe
bɪð ón man punð þonne bɪþ þæp pap ⁊ beotunȝa ⁊
ȝeſceopſ · ⁊ þonne hɪe mete þɪcȝeað ⁊ ðɪncað þonne
platað hɪe ⁊ bɪð hɪopa muð ſul ⁊ hɪpðɪað ⁊ hɪpa
utȝanȝ blobɪȝ ⁊ ſtɪncð yſcle · þam mannum ſceal man
ſellan æȝpa to ſupanne · beþen bpeað clæne mpe
butepan ⁊ mpe beþen mela oððe ȝpytta toȝædpe
ȝebpɪpeð ſpa cocaſ cunnon · ſelle mon neahtneſtɪȝum.
Eſt pyſena ſeap ⁊ peȝbpædan menȝe mon pɪð aſcopen
hunɪȝ ſelle neahtneſtɪȝum. Eſte pɪþ þon bo man ȝode
ſealſa¹ ónleȝena utan to þa þe þ yſel út teon eað-
mylte mettaſ ⁊ ſcɪp ſɪn ⁊ ſmeþe.

## .XXVII.

þe ƿambe mɪſSenhepe ȝecynðo oððe þæpe mɪſbypðo
hu þ mon mæȝe ónȝɪtan. þonne² hɪo bɪð hatpe
ȝebypðo ⁊ ȝecynðo · þonne mæȝ hɪpe ſona lytel ðpɪnca
helpan· ȝɪſ he mapa bɪþ ſe ðpɪnca ſona bɪþ ſeo pamþ
ȝeheſeȝoð ⁊ cloccet ſpa ſpa hɪt on cylle³ ſleȝete ⁊ ȝepɪhð ðpɪnm mettum þonne ſio pæte pamb ne þpopað ſeo
þupſt ⁊ ſio ſpɪðe pætpe ȝecynðo bɪþ ne þpopað ſeo þupſt ne
heſɪȝneſſe metta · ⁊ ȝepɪhð pætum mettum. þe hatpe
ȝecynðo pambe· Sɪo pamb ſeo þe bɪð hatpe ȝecynðo
ſio melt mete pel ſpɪþoſt þa þe heaþde beoð ⁊ úneað
mylte ⁊ ȝepɪhð peapmum mettum ⁊ ðpɪncum · ⁊ ne
bɪþ hɪpe ȝeſceðeð ſpam cealdum mettum mɪð ȝemete
ȝepɪȝðum. Seo þe bɪð ſætepɪȝpe ȝecynðo ſio hæſð
ȝode ȝɪpneſſe meteſ· hɪo næſð ȝode meltunȝe ſpɪþoſt
ón þam mettúm þe uneaðe melte beoð · ȝepɪhð cealdum

---

¹ Read ſealſa ⁊ ?
² Twelve lines found in Aetius
Tetrabibl. I. Seom. iv. capp. lxxii.,
lxxiii., lxxiv., consecutively; also in
Paulus of Ægina, lib. I. cap. lxiv.

³ By the printed books ſylle
would seem to be the true reading.
" Fluctuationes habeant, si id quod
" redundat, innatet."

### xxvi.

Of sickness of the wamb, and if it be wounded
within, how a man may understand that and cure it.
First if there be a wound upon it within, then is there
sore, and grumblings, and irritation ; and when they
take meat and drink, then they have nausea, and their
mouth is foul, and they are fevered, and their discharge
is bloody and stinketh foully: to those men shall be
given eggs to sup up, barley bread, clean new butter,
and new barley meal or groats made into a brewit
together, as cooks ken *to do*; let it be administered to
them after their nights fast. Again, let one mingle
juice of peas and waybroad with strained honey, and
give it after the nights fast. Again for that, let one
apply good salves, *and* external applications, such as
may draw out that evil, *also* easily digested meats, and
sheer and smooth wine.

### xxvii.

Of the various nature of the wamb or of its caprice,
how a man may understand that. When it is of a
hot temper and nature, then a little drink may soon
help it. If the drink be more powerful soon the wamb
is oppressed and palpitates, as if in cold it were
beating, and it rejoiceth in dry meats. When the
wamb is moist it doth not suffer thirst, and it is of a
very moist nature ; it doth not suffer thirst nor heaviness from meats, and it rejoiceth in moist meats. Of
the hot nature of the wamb. The wamb, that *namely*
which is of a hot nature, digests meats well, especially
those which be hard and of difficult digestion, and
rejoices in warm meats and drinks, and it is not harmed
by cold meats, taken with moderation. That which
is of a watery nature hath a good appetite for meat ;
it hath not a good digestion, chiefly of the meats
which be of difficult digestion, it rejoices in cold meats.

meттum. he cealðpe ȝ pæтpe ȝecynðo pambe. Sio
pamb fio ðe bið cealðpe oððe pæтpe ȝecynðo oððe
miſbyrðo· hím cymð bpaȝeneſ aðl ȝ unȝepiтſæȝтneſ
him bið· ȝ þonne fio ſopðpuȝaðe ȝecynðo on þam
fínum ȝ on þam banum bíþ· þ́ þa ſyn ſonþypſioðe
fol. 83 a.
þonne ne mæȝ món þa ȝelacnian· ȝiſ hio þonne bíþ
mnoſ on þam ſlæſcehтum ſтopum mið ſynðpiȝum
ſтopum ȝ pæтinȝum ȝ meттum þ́ món mæȝ ȝelácnian
þenðen oſ þæpe líſpe fio blodſceapunȝ ȝeonð ȝeт ealne
þone lichoman. Seleſт kecehom iſ тo ſpilcum þinȝum
þ́ món ȝelome nyттiȝe piceſ[1] ȝ þa pambe mið þy
ȝeſlea þonne hio ȝepypmeðu ſie ȝ baþu oſ þen pæтepe
ȝ niȝe molcen meoluc mið hunȝe ȝeſmeþeð hím ðeah·
baþiȝe hine ȝelome ón ðæȝe ȝ hpilum mið ele ſmipe.[1]
Dim hylpð eác þ́ him ſæт cilð[1] æтſlape· ȝ þ́ he þ́
ȝeðo neah hiſ pambe fimle· him hylpð eác oſen bacen
hláſ[1] ȝ ſcellehтe ſipcaſ ón poſe·[1] ȝ þone meтe þe pel
myltan pille. be haтſpe[1] ȝ ðpiȝpe pambe ȝíſ ſio pamb
aðliȝ bið haт hpæт hpeȝa· eac þæpe ðpiȝneſſe· þonne
ne ſceal he hunȝeſ ónbiтan ác ealð píu plæce meттaſ·
ȝiſ ſio yſle pæтe тo micel fie· þonne ðuȝon him
cealð pæтep ȝ ſceappe meттaſ buтan haттu· hpilum
fol. 83 b.
beoþ þa pæтan on þæpe pambe ſihnenum· þonne
ſceal món þ́ piplice ſecean ȝ pæplice clenſian[2] mið
alpan· ȝ mið ſpelcum úттyppenðum ðpencum aтeon uт
þa hophehтan pæтan. Þpæne mið þy æpeſт ȝ þonne
pypce leohтe ſpipole ðpencaſ oſ pæðice ſpa þ́ lҽcaſ
cunnon. be hҽmeðþinȝum[3] eallúm þyppum lichomum
hҽmeðþinȝ ne ðuȝon ác ſpipoſт þyppum ȝ cealðum·
ne ðeþeþ luт haтum ȝ pæтum pyppeſт luð þam ceal-
ðan haтan[4] ſpipoſт þam ðe hopnable habbað. Spelcúm
mannum ðeah þ́ hie hím ȝeſpinc anȝeſecen ȝ hie ſelſe

---

[1] Oribasius Synops., lib. V. liii.;
also Paulus Ægineta, lib. I. lxxii.

[2] clæpnau, MS.

[3] Five or six lines found in

Paulus Ægineta, lib. I. cap. lxxi. in
Med. Art. Priuc.

[4] Read pæтau from the original.

Of the cold and moist natured wamb. The wamb which is of a cold or moist nature or caprice; on *the man* cometh disease of the brain and loss of his senses; and when the desiccated nature is upon the sinews and on the bones, so that they are dried up, then they cannot be cured. Then if *this dryness* be more within on the fleshy parts, one may cure that with change of residence, and wettings, and meats, as long as from the liver the blood gushes through the whole body. The best leechdom for such things is, that a man should frequently make use of pitch, and strike the wamb with it, when it is warmed; and baths of rain water, and newly milked milk, softened with honey, is good for *the patient*. Let him bathe himself frequently in the day, and at whiles smear himself with oil. It is also helpful to him that a fat child should sleep by him, and that he should put it always near his wamb. Oven baked bread also helpeth him, and shell fishes in liquor, and (let him eat) the meat which will readily digest. Of the hot and dry wamb, if the diseased wamb be somewhat hot, besides, for the dryness; then shall *the patient* not taste of honey, but old wine and lukewarm meats. If the evil humour be too mickle, then are good for him cold water, and sharp meats without heat. At whiles the humours be on the membranes of the wamb; then shall a man wisely seek into that, and warily cleanse *them* with aloes, and draw out the turbid humours with such purging drinks: first clear *the wamb* with them, and then work light emetic drinks of radish, as leeches ken how to do it. Of venery: to all dry constitutions venery is not beneficial; but most to dry and cold ones; it harmeth not hot and wet ones; it is worst for the cold moist ones and them which have disorder of the gastric juices. To such men it is of benefit that they should seek to themselves exercise, and should dose themselves, without bath, and with

ðpencen[1] butan baðe ꞇ mið smipenejjum hie smeppan.
be cealðpe ꞡecynðo pambe. Se þe cealðpe ꞡecynðo sie
nyttiꞡe se ꞡemetlicej yfelej spilce je þe ðpꞡne oððe
pætpe sie. Se þe hattpe sie sio ꞡeꞡaðpaþ ōman · þa
mōn jceal ꞡif hie mjꞇen beoð þpih þa pambe utpih-
tan mið pyptðpence ūt aðon · ꞡif hie sipsꞇꞡen þpih
spipfan jceal mōn apeꞡ aðon.

## . XXVIII.

Þiþ þon[2] þe mannej þ uꞡeppe hpif sie ꞡefylleð mið
yfelpe pætan hopihehtpe þ þām mannum ꞡelimþð þe ōn
miclum ꞡeðpince pel jeðenðe mettas þiꞡeað oþþe spipað
ꞌ spipust æfтep mete ꞌ him bið plætta ꞡetenꞡe ·
heoð ꞡeonð blapene ꞌ bið sio pamb apeneð ꞌ hpæcꞇað
ꞡelome. Ðam monnum jceal[3] jellan oxumelle mið
pædice þ ij suþepne læceðōm · ꞌ þonne spipað hie jona
þone þiccan hoph ꞌ him liþ jel. Gepjjne[4] þe læceðōm
þuj ōf ecede ꞌ ōf huniꞡe · ꞡenīm þ jelesꞇe huniꞡ ðo
ofen heoð ajeoþ þ peax ꞌ þ hjōt ōf · ꞡeðo ðonne to
þam huniꞡe emfela ecedes þæj ne sie spiþe afop ne spiðe
sꞑete menꞡ to ꞡæðepe ꞌ ðo to fypne ōn cpoccan ofep
pylle on ꞡoðum ꞡleðum clænum · ꞌ epicum oþ þ hit sie
ꞡemenꞡeð þ hit sie ān ꞌ hæbbe huniꞡej þicnejje ꞌ ne
sie on bejꞡnejje to speotol þæj ecedej afjne jceappnej ·
ꞡif sio pamb liþ pinðej full þonne cymð þ of plācpe
pætan · sio cealðe pæte pypiþ japan. Þiþ þon jceal mōn
seopan cymen ōn ele · ꞌ mejcej jæð · ꞌ mojan sæð ·
ꞌ ðilej · ꞡif je cyle sie mapa ðo þonne puðan ꞌ laupej
bleðe · ꞌ finolej jæð ꞡejoðen ōn ele · ꞡif þonne ꞡiꞇ
sio aðl eꞡle ꞡeðpinꞡe mne þuph pipan oððe hopn spa

---

[1] " Victus attenuans," Lat. version of P. Ægin.

[2] Nine lines found in Paulus
Ægineta, lib. I. cap. xli.

[3] Read jceal mon.

[4] Oribasius Med. Coll., lib. V., cap.
xxiv. ; tom. i., p. 395, ed. Darem-
berg. Also Galenos, vol. VI.
p. 271, ed. Kühn.

smearings smear themselves. Of the cold nature of the wamb; he who is of a cold nature should avail himself of moderate discipline, as he who is of a dry or moist nature. He who is of a hot nature, *with him* the *wamb* gathereth inflammatory humours; these, if they be low down, one must get rid of by wort drinks, through purging of the wamb; if they mount up high one must get rid of them by vomitings.

### xxviii.

In case that the upper part of the belly is filled with evil sordid humour, a thing which happeneth to the men who in much continued drinking take nutritious meats, or who spew, and chiefly after meat, and who are subject to nausea, they are all over blown *as with wind*, and the wamb is extended and they frequently have breakings. To these men one must give oxymel with radish; that is a southern leechdom: and then they soon spew up the thick corruption, and it is well with them. Work up the leechdom thus, from vinegar and from honey; take the best honey, put it over the hearth, seethe away the wax and the scum, then add to the honey as much vinegar, so as that it may not be very austere nor very sweet; mingle together, and set by the fire in a crock, boil upon good gledes, clean and lively, till the *mixture* be mingled, so that it may be one, and have the thickness of honey, and on tasting it the austere sharpness of the vinegar may not be too evident. If the wamb is full of wind, that cometh from lukewarm humour; the cold humour worketh sores. For that shall one seethe cummin in ale, and seed of march, and seed of more *or carot*, and of dill. If the chill be greater, then add rue, and leaf of laurel, and seed of fennel sodden in oil. Then if the disease still annoy, introduce this through a pipe or a horn, as

læcaʃ cunnan þonne ðeþ þ̄ þ̄ ʃaʃ apeʒ. ʒiʃ þonne ʒit
ʃio aðl eʒle ðo ʃpatl to Ᵹ ʒelauʃeðne ele þ̄ iʃ lauʃeʃ
ʃeap oððc bloʃtman ʒemenʒeð Ᵹ eác oþʃiu þinʒ ʒiʃ
þeapʃ ʃie ʃece món.

## .XXVIIII.

Þiþ þon þe men mete untela melte Ᵹ ʒeciʃʃe ón
yʃele pʃotan Ᵹ ʃcittan · þam monnum ðeah þ̄ hie ʃpiʃen.
ʒiʃ him to uneaþe ne ʃie · ʒeʒʃemme mið pyʃtðʃence
þ̄ he ʃpiʃe · þ̄ he mið ʒeʃpette ʃine ʒepyʃice ʒiʃ þæʃ
oʃeʃþeaʃʃ ʃie æʃ mete þ̄ he ʃpiʃan mæʒe · ʃleo þa
mettaʃ þa þe him ðylʃta Ᵹ ʃoʃbæʃnunʒa Ᵹ ʃtiem on
Innan ʃyʃicen Ᵹ to hʃæðlice meltan · þicʒen þa ðe ʒoð
ʃeap ʃyʃicen Ᵹ þambe hneʃcen. Ðʃilum him ðeah þ̄
him món ʃelle leohte ʃyʃtðʃencaʃ ʃpilce ʃpa bið ʃel
ʒeteað alʃe. Seo ʃæte ʃyʃicþ ʒiʃ hic món ne ðeþ apeʒ
uneaʃlacna aðla þ̄ iʃ ʃót ʃæʃic · liþ ʃæʃic · lenðen
ʃæʃic Ᵹ oʃt ʃtʃanʒ ʃeʃeʃ becymð on þa men þe þa
aðle habbað.

## .XXX.

Ʒiʃ[1] þu ʃille þ̄ þin pamb ʃic ʃimle ʒeʃunð þonne
ʃcealt u hiʃe þuʃ tihan ʒiʃ þu ʃilt · ʒeʃceapa ælce
ðæʒe þ̄ þin utʒonʒ Ᵹ micʒe ʃie ʒeʃunðlic æʃteʃ ʃihte ·
ʒiʃ ʃio micʒe ʃie lytelu ʃeoð meʃice Ᵹ ʃinul ʃyʃic ʒoð
bʃoð · oððc ʃeap[2] Ᵹ oþʃa ʃpeta ʃyʃta · ʒiʃ ʃe utʒanʒ ʃie
læʃʃa[3] nim ða ʃyʃt þe hatte on ʃuþeʃne teʃebintina ʃpa
micel ʃpa ele benʒe · ʃele þonne to ʃeʃte ʒan ʃille. þaʃ
ʃyʃta ʃinðon eác betʃte to þon Ᵹ eað beʒeatʃia · bete · Ᵹ

---

[1] The substance is found in Paulus Æg., I. xliii.

[2] ʃeap : the name of some wort is
omitted in MS. ; or strike out Ᵹ.

[3] Four lines occur in Paulus of
Ægina, lib. I., cap. xliii.

leeches ken to do it; then it removes the sore. If
however the disease still vex, add spittle and laurelled
oil, that is to say, juice or blossoms of laurel mingled
*with oil*, and if need be, let also other things be
sought out.

### xxix.

In case a "mans" meat doth not well digest, and
turneth to evil humour and to excrement, it is good
for those "men" that "they" should spew, if it be
not too uneasy to "him," irritate him to spew by a
wort drink. If there be extreme need that he may
be able to spew before meat, let him manage that
with sweetened wine. Let him flee the meats which
work him mucus, and burnings, and heat in his inside,
and which too readily digest: let him take those
which work a good juice, and make the wamb nesh.
At whiles it is good for him that one should give
him light wort drinks, such as are aloes well prepared. The humour, if one doth not get rid of it,
worketh not easily cured diseases, that is to say, foot
pain, joint pain, loins pain; and often a strong fever
cometh on the men who have that disease.

### xxx.

If thou wish that thy wamb be always sound, then
shalt thou thus treat it, if thou wilt. Look to it every
day that thy fæcal discharge, and thy mie, be of sound
aspect as right is. If the mie be little, seethe marche
and fennel, work a good broth, or *seethe* juice of
. . . and of other sweet worts. If the fæcal discharge
be too little, take the wort which in southern lands
hight turpentine tree, as much of it as the size of
an olive; give it *the sick* when he will go to bed.
These worts are also very good for that, and more

mealƿe · ⁊ bɲaʄʄıca ⁊ þıſum ȝelıca ȝeɲobene ɱtȝædɲıc
mıð ȝeonȝe ſpıneſ ꝼlæɲce · þıcȝe þ bɲoð · ⁊ eac bealh[1]
netle ȝeſoben on ꝼætɲıe · ⁊ ȝeɲelt to þıȝȝanne · ⁊ eac
elleneſ leaꝼ ⁊ þ bɲoð on þa ılcan pıſan. Sume alpan
leaꝼ ɲ᷑ellað þonne mon pıle ꝼlapan ȝan · ſpelc ſpa bıð
þɲeo beana[2] ælce ðæȝe to ꝼoɲſpelȝanne ⁊ þıſum ȝelıce
ðɲencaſ ⁊ ſpıðɲan ȝıꝼ þeaɲꝼ ſıe ɲynbon to ꝼellanne ·
ſpıðoſt on ꝼoɲepeaɲbne lencten æɲ þon ſıo yꝼele ƿæte ſe
þe on pıntɲa ȝeSomnað bıð lıe toȝeote ȝeonð oþeɲa
lıma. Woɱȝe[3] men þæɲ ne ȝymbon ne ne ȝymað
þonne becymð oꝼ þam yꝼlum ƿætum · oððe ſıo healꝼ-
beabe aðl oþþe ꝼylle ƿæɲc oððe ſıo hɲıte ɱeɲþo þe
mon on ſuþeɲne leppa hæt oþðe tetɲa oþþe heaꝼoð
hɲıneꝼðo · oþþe oman. Foɲþon ɲccal mon æɲ clænɲıan[4] þa
yꝼlan ƿætan apeȝ æɲ þon þa yꝼelan cuman ⁊ ȝepeaxen
on pıntɲa · ⁊ þa lımo ȝeonð yɲɲnen. Þıþ pambe coþe
⁊ ſaɲıe · lınſæbeɲ ȝeȝnıben oððe ȝebeaten bolla ꝼull ·
⁊ II. ɲceaɲɲeſ cccbeɲ oꝼeɲɲpylle ætȝædeɲe ɲele ðɲıncan
nealhtneɲtıȝum þam ſeocan men. Eꝼt leȝe ðɲeoɲȝe
ðɲoſtlan ȝecopene on þone naꝼolan ſona ȝeſtılleþ; Eꝼt
ðıleɲ ſæbeɲ lytelne[5] ȝeȝnıð on ƿæteɲ ɲele ðɲıncan.
Þıþ pambe coðe ⁊ ƿıþ ınneɲoɲan ſaɲıe. þonne ɲoɲ
mıclum cele pamb ſıe unȝepealben · bo ða þınȝ to þe þe
be uꝼan pɲıton. ȝıꝼ þæɲ þonne ſıe þæɲ hɲıɲeſ penbunȝ
oððe ȝeɲcceoɲꝼ · ȝenım þɲeo cɲoppan lauꝼeſ bleba ȝeȝnıð
⁊ cymeneɲ · ⁊ peteɲɲıhan ɲynðɲıȝe cuclepaɲ ꝼulle · ⁊
pıpoɲeɲ .XX. coɲna · ȝeȝnıð eall toȝæbeɲe ⁊ þɲıe ꝼıl-
menna on bɲıbba pambum aðɲıȝe · æꝼteɲ ðon ȝenım
ƿæteɲ ȝeȝnıð bıle on · ⁊ þaɲ þınȝ ȝehæte ɲele ðɲıncan · oþ þ þ ɲaɲ ȝeſtılleb ſıe. Þıþ þon ılcan ȝenım
hlaꝼ ȝeſeoð on ȝate meolce ɲoppıȝe on ſuþeɲne.[6]

---

[1] Four more lines found in P.
Æg. The Latin version, the original being unpublished, has *mercurialis* for *nettle*.

[2] The Latin gives, *aloes as big as
three retches*.

[3] Paulus Ægineta, lib. I. cap. c.,
cites Diokles to similar purport.

[4] clænɲıan, MS.

[5] Read lytelne ðæl.

[6] Read on ſuþeɲne ðɲenc.

easily procured, beet, and mallow, and brassica *or cab-bage*, and the like to these, sodden together with young flesh of swine; let *the man* swallow the broth: and also nettle sodden in water and salted is good to swallow; and also leaves of elder and the broth in the same wise. Some give leaves of aloe, when a man willeth to go to sleep, as much as three beans, every day to be swallowed; and drinks like these, and more powerful ones, if need be, are to be administered; especially in early spring, before the evil humour, which is collected in winter, spread itself through the other limbs. Many men have not attended to this, no, nor do yet; then there cometh of the evil humours, either hemiplegia, or epilepsy, or the white roughness, which in the south hight leprosy, or tetter, or headroughness, or erysipelas. Hence one must cleanse away the evil humours before the mischiefs come and wax in the winter, and run through the limbs. For wamb sickness and sore; a bowl full of linseed, rubbed or beaten, and two bowls of sharp vinegar; boil together, give to the sick man to drink after his nights fast. Again, lay chewed pennyroyal on the navel, soon the pain will be still. Again, rub a small quantity of the seed of dill into water, give it to be drunk. For wamb sickness and sore of the bowels; when from much cold the wamb is not under control, do to it the things which we wrote above; then if there be a subversion or irritation of the stomach, take three bunches of laurel flowers, and separate spoons full of cummin and of parsley *seed* (?), and twenty pepper-corns, rub all together, and dry three membranes *which are* in the wambs of young birds; after that take water, rub dill into it, and heat these things; give *the man this* to drink till the sore is stilled. For the same, take bread and seethe it in goats milk, sop it in a southern *drink, such as hydromel, perhaps, or oxymel.*

Þiþ þambe coþe feoð þuðan ón ele ꝼ þicȝe on ele.
Eꝼt ƿilde culꝼre ón eceðe ꝼ ón þætþe ȝeſoðen ꝛele to
þicȝenne. Þið þambe coðe eꝼt lauꝛeſ leaꝼ ceoƿe ꝼ þ
feaƿ ſpelȝe ꝼ þa leaꝼ lecȝe on hiſ naꝼolan. Eꝼt heo-
ꝛoteꝛ meaꝛh ȝemylt ꝛele ón hatum ƿætꝛe ðꝛincan.
To þambe ȝemetlicunȝe · ȝenim betan aðelꝼ ꝼ ahꝛiꝛe
ne þꝛeah þu hie ác ſƿa lanȝe feoð ón cetele ꝼ ꝼylle
oþ þ hio ſie eal toꝛoðen ꝼ þicȝe[1] ȝeuꝛnen · ðo þonne
lytel ꝛealteꝛ to ꝼ huniȝeꝛ · v. cucleꝛ mæl · eleꝛ cucleꝛ
mæl ꝛele bollan ꝼulne. Eꝼt heaꝛðehteꝛ poꝛꝛeꝛ ȝeꝛo-
ðeneꝛ[2] ꝛynðꝛiȝne ꝛele þicȝean. Eꝼt þꝛeꝛe ꝛeaðan netlan ſæð ón hlaꝼ ꝛele þicȝean. Eꝼt byꝛiȝbeꝛȝena feaꝛ
ꝛelle ðꝛincan. Eꝼt plum bleða ete neahtneſtiȝ. Eꝼt
elneꝛ ꝛinðe ȝebeatene þte þeninȝȝe ƿeȝe ón cealðeꝛ
ƿætꝛeꝛ bollan ꝼullum ꝛele ðꝛincan.

## [3].XXXI.

Be þambe coþum ꝼ tacnum on þoppe ꝼ ón ſmæl
þeaꝛmum. Sum cyn bið eác þꝛeꝛe ilcan aðle on þꝛeꝛe
þambe · ꝼ on þam þoppe ꝼ ſmæl þeaꝛmuꝛ þe þiꝛ bið
to tacne · þ hie þꝛoꝛiað oꝛꝛætne þuꝛſt · ꝼ meteꝛ unluſt ꝼ óꝼt ut yꝛꝛað ȝemenȝðe utȝanȝe hꝛilum heaꝛð ·
hꝛilum hꝛit · hꝛilúm óꝼt on ðæȝe ſitȝað ꝼ þonne lytlum · hꝛilum æne · ꝼ þonne micel · hꝛilum hie[4] ƿel
ȝelyꝼt utȝanȝan · ꝼ him þa byꝛþenne ꝼꝛam aꝛeoꝛꝛan ·
ꝼ ȝeoꝛne tilian ac ne maȝon nabbað þ mæȝen þꝛeꝛe
meltunȝe ꝼ ðꝛoꝛeteð blod · ſƿa þon ȝelicoſt þe tobꝛo-
cen ꝼæt. be hioꝛa liꝛe ꝼ þam naꝼolan · ꝼ þam ꝛæȝe-

---

[1] þicȝe, that is þicce.
[2] Add eþoppan or the like.

[3] Plainly a chapter περὶ κωλικῆς διαθέσεως.
[4] Read hine.

2. For wamb sickness seethe rue in oil, and let *the sick* swallow it in oil. Again, give him to eat a wild pigeon sodden in vinegar and in water. For wamb sickness, again, let him chew leaves of laurel, and swallow the juice, and let him lay the leaves on his navel. Again, give melted harts marrow in hot water to drink. For moderating[a] *the action of* the wamb; take beet, delve it up and shake *the mould off*, do not wash it, but seethe and boil it in a kettle so long, that it be all sodden to pieces, and run thick, then add a little salt, and of honey five spoon measures, of oil one spoon measure, give *the* man a bowl full. Again, give *to the sick* to eat, separate, the *top* of a sodden leek, having a head to it. Again, give him to eat some seed of the red nettle on bread. Again, give him to drink juice of mulberries. Again, let him eat after his nights fasting plum fruits. Again, give him to drink elder rind beaten, as much as may weigh a penny, in a bowl full of cold water.

[a] Note, p. 165.

## xxxi.

Of wamb sicknesses, and of tokens in the colon and in the small guts. There is a kind of that ilk disease in the wamb, and in the colon, and small guts, of which this will be for a token; that *the sick* suffer immoderate thirst and loss of appetite for meat, and often they have a flux with a mingled fæcal discharge, at whiles hard, at whiles white, at whiles they discharge often in the day and then little at a time, at whiles once and then much; at whiles a desire is upon them to go to stool and to cast the burthen from them, and gladly would they attend to it, but they are not able,[1] they have not the power of digestion, and they drop blood, very much like a broken vessel. Of their hue, *or*

---

[1] Tenesmus.

ɲeoſan · ⁊ bæcþeaɲme ⁊ neɲeſcoþan · ⁊ mɪlꞇe¹ ſcaɲe ·
beoð ᴚblæcc ⁊ eal ſe lichoma áſcimoð · ⁊ yꝼel ſꞇenc
nah hiꞃ ꞅelꝼeꞃ ᵹeɲealð ⁊ biþ ꝥ ꞃaɲ on ða ſɲiðɲan
ſiðan · healꝼe² on þa ꞃcaɲe · ⁊ þa ꞃambe ſɲɪþe ᵹeneaɲ-
ɲoð · ⁊ eꝼꞇ ꝼɲam þam naꝼolan oþ þone mɪlꞇe · ⁊ on þa
ɲɪneſꞇɲan ɲæᵹɲeoſan ⁊ ᵹecymð æꞇ þam bæcþeaɲme ⁊
ꞇꞇ þam neɲeſeoþan · ⁊ þa lenðenu beoð mɪð micle ꞃaɲe

fol. 87 a.

beᵹyꞃðebu. Þenað unɲiꞃe læcaꞅ ꝥ ꝥ ſie lenðen aðl
oððe mɪlꞇe ꝥæɲc · ac hɪꞇ ne bɪð ſpa · lenðen ſeocc
men ɪnɪᵹað bloðe ⁊ ſanðe þonne þam þe mɪlꞇe ꝥæɲc
bɪð · þinðeþ him ſe milꞇ ⁊ biþ aheaɲðoð ón þam ɲɪneſꞇɲan ðælc þæɲe ſiðan. þa ꞃambſeocan men þɲoɲað
ón þam bæcþeaɲme ⁊ ón þám niþeɲɲan hɲiꝼe ⁊ loſað
him ſona ſio ſꞇeꝼn ⁊ cele þɲoɲað ⁊ ꞅlæp oꝺꞇoᵹen ⁊
mɪhꞇ ⁊ ꞇɪhð ɪnnan þone ɲoɲ ⁊ on ꝥ ſmæl þeaɲme.


## .XXXII.

Þiꞃꞅe aðle ꝼɲuman mon mæᵹ yþelice ᵹelacnian · on
þa ɪlcan ꞇiꞃan þe þa uꞇyɲmenðan ⁊ æꝼꞇeɲ uneð · ᵹiꝼ
hio bɪð unɲiꞅlice ꞇo lanᵹe ꝼoɲlæꞇen. On ꝼɲuman món
ſceal ðæᵹ oððe .II. ꞇoᵹæðeɲc ᵹeꝼæꞅꞇan ⁊ beþan þa
bɲeoſꞇ mɪð ɲɪne · ⁊ mɪð ele ⁊ ɲyɲcean ónleᵹena oꝼ
ɲoſan ⁊ beɲenum melþe pɪð ɲin ᵹemenᵹeð ⁊ on huniᵹe
ᵹeſoðen ⁊ mɪð ele on moɲꞇeɲe ᵹeſamnoð leᵹe oꝼeɲ þa
ſcaɲe oþ þone naꝼolan ⁊ oꝼeɲ þa lenðeno oþ þone bæc-
þeaɲm ⁊ þæɲ hɪꞇ ꞃaɲ ſie · læꞇ him bloð þuꞅ ⁊³ ꞅeꞇe
ᵹlæꞅ ón oððe hoɲn ⁊ ꞇeo ꝥ bloð uꞇ ⁊ ſmeɲe mɪð ele

fol. 87 b.

⁊ beꝝɲeoh hinc ɲeaɲme ꝼoɲ þon þe cile biþ þæɲe aðle

---

¹ Add ⁊.
² The former of these synonyms should be erased.
³ Omit ⁊.

*complexion*, and of the navel, and of the dorsal muscles, and of the back gut *or rectum*, and of the lower belly, and the milt, *and* the share; they are horribly pale, and all the body is glazed, and an evil stench hath not control over itself,ª and the sore is on the right side on the share, and on the wamb, much troubled[1] *by it*, and again from the navel to the spleen, and on the left dorsal muscle, and it reacheth to the anus, and to the lower belly, and the loins are girt about with much soreness. Unwise leeches ween, that it is loin disease, or milt wark: but it is not so; loinsick men mie blood and sand; on the other hand those, who have milt wark, the milt distendeth in them, and is hardened on the left part of the side. The wambsick men suffer in the back gut, and in the lower belly, and their voice soon is lost, and they suffer chill, and sleep is taken from them, and strength, and it draweth the colon from within and upon the small gut.

## xxxii.

One may easily cure the first stage of this disease in the same wise as the outrunning disease, *or relaxation of the bowels*, and afterwards less easily, if unwisely it be too long neglected. In the first instance a man must fast for a day or two, and foment the breast with wine, and with oil, and work poultices of roses and barley meal, mingled with wine, and sodden in honey, and gathered up with oil in a mortar, lay *these* over the share, as far as the navel, and over the loins as far as the back gut, and where it is sore. Let him blood thus; set on him a *cupping* glass or horn, and draw the blood out, and smear with oil, and wrap him up warm, in as much as cold is an enemy in the

---

[1] It seems best to consider ȝeneaȝȝpoð as for ȝeneaȝȝpoðe, with termination dropped.

ƿeonð. Þyne him ſealƒe þuſ ƿiþ þambe coþum oƀ epicum
ſpeƿle ꝺ oƀ blacum pipoʃe · ꝺ oƀ ele ȝnibe mon ſmæle
ꝺ menȝe toȝæbeʃe ꝺ ƿeax calƿa emƿela. Þeaxeſ þeah
læſt · ȝiƀ ſio aðl ſie to þon ſtʃanȝ þ þaʃ læcebomaſ ne
onnime ȝiƀ ſe mon ſie ȝeonȝ ꝺ ſtʃanȝ læt him blob oƀ
innan eaʃme oƀ þæʃe miclan æðʃe þæʃe middel æðʃe.

╬ This seems
a mark of dis-
content with
the text : pro-
bably oʃ þæʃe
miclan æðʃe
should be
erased.

╬ Þyne þuſ ſealƒe ꝺ ſmiʃe þa ſaƿan ſtoƿa ſeoþ ʃubau
on ele bo ƿeteʃʃilian to ȝiƀ þu hæbbe ꝺ ƿeſn ƿyʃt-
cʃiuman · ꝺ ƿoʃiȝ ſiþþan cal ȝeʃoben ſie bo þonne ƿeax
on þ ele ·[1] þte þ eall peoʃðe to hneʃcum ƿeaxhlaƿe þ
hit ſie hʃæþþe ſƿiþuſt ȝeþuht ſealƒ ſmiʃe þa ſtoƿa þ
hit ſie ʃaʃ mib þy · ſƿiþoſt þone bæcþeaʃim baþo ƿiþ
þambe coþum · him oƀ ſealtum pætʃum ſine to ƿyƿe-
anne · ȝiƀ he þa næbbe ſelte mon hioʃa mettaſ. Þiþ
þambe coþum eƀt ſpineſ claƿe ȝebæƿnbe ꝺ to buſte
ȝeȝnibene bo on ſceaƿʃ ƿin ʃele bʃincan. Þið þambe
coþe ȝate hʃeʃ ȝebæƿnebu ꝺ hʃæt hʃeȝa ȝeȝniben ꝺ
on þa þambe aleb him biþ þe bet. Þiþ þambe coþum
eƀt lacnunȝ on þ hʃiſ to Senbanne · ȝením ȝaƿleaceʃ
þʃeo heaƀbu ꝺ ȝʃene ʃubau tʃa hanb ƒulle · ꝺ cleʃ
.IIII. punb oððe ſpa þe þince. ȝcbeat þ leac ꝺ þa
ʃubau ȝeȝnib toȝæbeʃe aþʃinȝ oððe aʃeoh · bo to þam
ele clænʃe buteþan punb hlutʃeſ piceʃ ƒiƀtan healƒe
yntſan · ꝺ clæneʃ ƿeaxeS .III. yntſan ȝemenȝe cal to-
ȝæbʃe bo on ȝlæʃ ƒæt · clænʃa[2] þonne æƿeſt þa þambe
mib bʃenceſ anƒealbbʃe onȝeotunȝe · ȝiƀ þ ʃaʃ þonne
maʃe ſie bo maʃan ele to · ȝemenȝ þonne þa þinȝ þe
ic æʃ nembe ȝeƿlece bo on. þaʃ þinȝ maȝon ȝe ƿiþ
lenben ece · þonne mon ʃonbe mihð ȝe ƿið ʃoppeʃ ȝe
ƿið þambe ꝺ ſmæl þeaʃmeſ ablum ꝺ út ƿaʃpce ȝe ƿiþ

fol. 88 a.

---

[1] ele is usually masculine.        [2] clæʃna, MS.

disease.  Work him a salve thus, against wamb disorders; from live brimstone, and from black pepper,
and from oil; let them be rubbed small and mingled
together; and wax *also;* of all equal quantities, of
wax however least.  If the disease be to that degree
strong that it will not accept these leechdoms, if the
man be young and strong, let him blood from the
inner arm, from (the mickle vein of) the middle vein.
Work a salve thus, and smear the sore places; seethe
rue in oil, add parsley, if thou have it, and roots of
rushes, and poppy; after all is sodden, then add wax
to the oil, in order that the whole may become a
nesh waxen cake,[a] that it may be however a highly   [a] A cerote.
approved salve; smear the places, so that soreness
may come with it, especially the fundament.  Baths
for wamb disorders; they must be wrought for them
of salt waters; if none can be had, let their (*the sick
mens*) meats be salted.  For wamb disorders again;
put into sharp wine a swines claw burnt and rubbed
to dust; give *the man* this to drink.  For wamb disorder; a goats liver burnt, and rubbed somewhat *small,*
and laid on the wamb, it will be the better for him.
For wamb disorders again; to send medicine into the
belly: take three heads of garlic, and green rue, two
handfuls *of it,* and four pints of oil, or as much as
seemeth good to thee; beat the leek and the rue, rub
together, wring out or strain, add to the oil a pound
of clean butter, and four ounces and a half of clear
pitch, *perhaps naphtha,* and three ounces of clean wax;
mingle all together, put into a glass vessel, then first
cleanse the wamb with the simple onpouring of a drink:
then if the sore be greater, add more oil, then mingle
the things which I before named; apply lukewarm.
These things are valid either against loin ache, when
a man pisseth sand, or for diseases and pain of the
long gut, or of the wamb, or of the small gut, and
for dysentery, or for diseases of the maw, and gripings,

maᵹan aðlum ⁊ elapunᵹa · ⁊ ƿiþ ƿiſa teðrum ᵹecyn-
ðum. Sum coþu iſ þeþe painbe þ þone ſeocan mönnan
lyſteð utᵹanᵹeſ ⁊ ne mæᵹ þonne he ute betyned
bið. Þiþ þon ſceal mön nædþan æſmoᵹu ſeoþan on
ele · oððe ön buteþan · oþþe on pine ön tinum[1] ſæte
⁊ ſmiþe þa painbe mið þy · ᵹiſ ſe utᵹanᵹ ſie pindiᵹ ⁊
pætþiᵹ · ⁊ blodiᵹ beþiᵹe mon þone bæcþeaþm on ᵹonᵹ-
ſtole mið ſenuᵹþeco ⁊ meþiſc mealpe · ſume mið pice ⁊
ſmieað ⁊ beþiað. Sume oſ þiᵹenum melpe pyþeeað
hþuþaſ ⁊ cöenunᵹa mið ſealte. Sume ðþeoþᵹe ðþoſtlan
ᵹeeeopað ⁊ leeᵹeað on þone naſolan.

## .XXXIII.

Be[2] þeþe ſþecnan coþe þe ſe mön hiſ utᵹanᵹ þuþh
ðone muð him ſþam þeoþþe ſeeal aſþiþan. De ſeeal
öſt bealeettan ⁊ eal ſe lichoma ſtineð ſule ſelle hïm
mon ðile ᵹeſoðenne ön ele oððe ön þætþe to ðþincanne
⁊ hatne hlaſ ðo on þone ðþincan. Þiþþe aðle eac piþ-
ſtandeþ toſmiðenþe hþeaþemuſe blod ᵹeſmiten on þæþ
ſeocan manneſ þambe. Þið Innoð þundum ⁊ piþ ſmiel
ſeaþma ſaþe · ön ᵹodne ele ᵹeſpetne ðo þone ſuþeþnan
peþmoð þ iſ þþutene · ⁊ oþeþne peþmoð ⁊ ſeoþ þiᵹe
þ ſpa hïm eſoit ſie. Eſt piþ innoþ þundum heoþoteſ
meaþh ᵹemylt on hatum þotþe ſele ðþincan. Þiþ
toþþoeenum Innoþum ⁊ ſaþum þildþie mintan ðiel ᵹe-
elænſa þel ſpa mieel ſpa mön mæᵹe mið þþïm ſinᵹþïm
ᵹenimän ðo ſmoleſ ſædeſ to ⁊ meþeeſ eueleþ mæl ·
ðo eall toᵹæðeþe ᵹeᵹnið ſmæle · ᵹeðo þonne ön þæþ
ſeleſtan pineſ .IIII. bollan ſulle · hæte þonne oþ þ hit
ſie ſpa hat ſpa þïn ſinᵹeþ ſoþbeþan mæᵹe ſele þonne
ðþincan · ðo ſpa þþiy ðaᵹaſ. Þiþ toþþoeenum Inno-
ðum · eellenðþeſ ſæð þel ᵹeᵹniðen ⁊ lytel ſealteſ ᵹeðo
on ſeeaþþ ſïn · ᵹeðo on ⁊ ᵹeþyþine mið hate ᵹloþenðe
iþene ſele ðþincan. Þiþ ſoþtoᵹeneþþe innän · heoþoteſ

---

[1] Read tinenum.

[2] Five lines found in Oribasius Synops, lib. ix., cap. xvi, in M.A.P.

and for tenderness of the naturalia of women. There
is a disorder of the wamb, *such* that a desire cometh
upon the sick man for discharging his bowels, and he
is not able, when he is shut into the outhouse. For
that, one must seethe in oil, or in butter, or in wine,
the slough of a snake in a tin vessel, and let him
smear the wamb with that. If the discharge be windy,
and watery, and bloody, let one foment the back gut
on the gang stool, with fenugreek and marsh mallow:
some smoke and foment with pitch: some work brewits
from rye meal, and cookings with salt: some chew
pennyroyal and lay it on the navel.

Book II.
Ch. xxxii.

This prescrip-
tion is found
in Marcellus,
376 a.

## xxxiii.

Of the dangerous disorder, in which a man, they
say, unnaturally speweth his fæces through the mouth.
He, they say, oft belcheth, and all the body stinketh
foully: let dill sodden in oil or in water be given him
to drink, and put a hot loaf of bread into the drink.
The blood of a reremouse *or bat* cut up, smudged on
the sick mans wamb, also withstandeth this disease.
For bowel wounds and sore of small guts; into good oil
sweetened, put the southern wormwood, that is, abrotanum, and other wormwood, and seethe it; let *the
man* take that as he most easily may. Again, for inwards wounds; melt harts marrow in hot water, give
it to be drunk. For broken and sore inwards; cleanse
part of wild mint well, as much as a man may take
up with three fingers, add a spoon measure of the
seed of fennel, and of marche, put all together, rub
small, then add four bowls full of the best wine, then
heat it so hot, as thy finger may bear, then give *it him*
to drink; do so for three days. For broken inwards;
put into sharp wine, seed of coriander well rubbed,
and a little salt; put *these* in, and warm with an iron
glowing hot, give *it the man* to drink. For inward

hopn ȝebɪepneð to ahſan ȝeȝnɪben ōn moʃteʃe · ꝺ
þonne aʃɪſt ꝺ mɪð hunɪȝe ȝepealcen to ſnæðum ʃele
neahtneʃtɪȝum to þɪcȝanne. Eſt nīm þa betan þe
ȝehʃæn peaxað ȝeʃeoð on pætʃeʃ ȝobum bæle · ʃele
þonne ðʃɪncan · .ɪɪ. ȝobe bollan ꝼulle ſcɪlbe hɪne pɪþ

cyle. he latʃe meltunȝe ɪnnan · nɪm ȝeaʃʃan ðʃɪnce
on ecebe þ̵ beah eac pɪð eallum blæðʃan aðlum. he
latʃe meltunȝe Innan þuban ʃæbeʃ .VIIII. cyʃnelu ȝe-
ȝnɪbene .ɪɪɪ. bollan ꝼulle ȝebo þa on ecebeſ ʃeʃteʃ
ꝼulne oʃeʃpylle ʃele þonne ðʃɪncan ōn ſume ʃaþe nɪȝon
baȝon. he latʃe meltunȝe nīm þæʃe ʃeaban netlan
ſpa mɪcel ſpa mɪð tʃam hanbum mæȝe beʃon · ſeoþe
ōn ʃeʃteʃ ꝼullūm pætʃeʃ ðʃɪnc neaht neʃtɪȝ. Ræð
bɪð ȝɪſ he nɪmð mealpan mɪð hɪʃe cɪþum ſeoþe on
pɪoteʃe ſele ðʃɪncan. þa þe þɪʃʃa læceboma ne ȝɪmað
on þɪʃʃe aðle þonne becymð līm ōn pæteʃ bolla · hʃeʃ
pæʃc ꝺ multeʃ ʃaʃ oþþe ȝeſpel mɪcȝean ꝼoʃhæʃðnɪʃ ·
paɪnbe ablapunȝ lenben pæʃc on þæʃe blæðʃan ſtanaʃ
peaxað ꝺ Sonb.

.XXXIIII.[1]

Be þæʃ monneʃ mɪhtum ʃceal mōn þa læcebomaʃ
ʃellan þe þonne ȝeʃoȝe ſynð heaʃbe ꝺ heoʃtan paɪnbe
ꝺ blæðʃan ꝺ hu ȝeaʃeʃ hɪt ſɪe · ſe þe ne beʃceaþað
þɪʃ ʃe hɪm ſceþeð ſpɪþoʃ þonne he hɪne bete. Se ʃceal
nyttɪan ȝeʃoʃobeʃ eleʃ ecebeſ ꝺ pɪneʃ ꝺ mɪntan leaſ
ȝeȝnɪben on hunɪȝ ꝺ þa unſmeþan tunȝan mɪð þy
ȝnɪban ꝺ ſɪʃɪþepan :·

Þɪþ latʃe meltunȝe. Olɪʃatʃɪum hatte pyʃt ſeo beah
to ðʃɪncanne. Eſt pyl on pætʃe lɪlɪan pyʃttʃuman
ʃele to ðʃɪncanne. ȝɪſ paɪnb ꝼoʃpeaxe on men · ꝼɪnol ·
coſt · elehtʃe · attoʃlaþe · ceʃlɪceʃ ʃæb · pyʃm melo

---

[1] In the margin are cyphers.

gripings ; harts horn burned to ashes, rubbed *small* in a mortar, and then sifted, and rolled up with honey into morsels, give *to the sick* after his nights fast to eat. Again, take the beet which groweth anywhere, seethe it in a good deal of water, then *give of this to the sick* two good bowls full to drink ; let him shield himself against cold. Of late digestion ; let a man drink in vinegar yarrow ; that medicine is also good for all diseases of the bladder. Of late digestion ; nine little grains of the seed of rue rubbed *small, with* three bowls full of *water* (?), add these to a cup full of vinegar, boil them, then administer to be drunk for nine days, in succession. Of late digestion ; take of the red nettle, so much as with two hands thou mayest grasp, seethe in a cup full of water, drink after a nights fasting. It is advisable if he taketh mallow with its sprouts ; let him seethe them in water, give this to be drunk. They who care not for these leechdoms in this disease, on them then cometh dropsy, liver pain, and sore or swelling of spleen, retention of urine, inflation of the wamb, loin pain, stones wax in the bladder, and sand.

### xxxiv.

According to the mans powers one shall administer the leechdoms which are suitable for the head and heart, for the wamb and bladder, and according to the time of the year; he who observeth not this, doth him more scathe than boot. He shall employ rose oil, vinegar, and wine, and mint leaves rubbed into honey, and with that shall rub and smear the unsmooth tongue.

For late digestion ; a wort hight olusatrum, which is good to drink. Again, boil in water roots of lilies, give *that* to be drunk. If the wamb wax too great on a man ; fennel, costmary, lupin, attorlothe, char-

ón calað ꞃele ðꞃincan. ᵹiꝼ món ꝼoꞃꞃunðoð ſie · ⁊ wið
bꞃeoſt þæꞃce · cuꞃmealle ⁊ ðile wyl on caloð. Eꝼt
ᵹꞃene þuðan lytlum oððe on huniᵹe þiᵹe. ᵹiꝼ mon
ſie ꝼoꞃblapen ꞃæ pinepinclan ¹ ᵹebæꞃnðe ⁊ ᵹeᵹniðene
ᵹemenᵹ wiþ æᵹeꞃ þ hꞃite ſmiꞃe mið. Þiþ þambe ᵹicþan · ðꞃeoꞃᵹe ðꞃoſtlan peoꞃp on peallenðe pæteꞃ læt
ꞃocian ón lanᵹe oþ þ mon mæᵹe ðꞃincan þ pæteꞃ.
Þiþ þambe pypꞃmum ·² nim þa miclan ſinꝼullan ꞃꞃinᵹ
þ ꞃeaꞃ óꝼ ꞃeoꞃeꞃ lytle bollan ꝼulle on pineꞃ anuni
bollan ꝼullum ſꞃa miclum ꞃele ðꞃincan þ ðeah wiþ
þambe pypꞃmum.²

### .XXXV.

Be cilða pambum ⁊ oꝼeꞃꝼylle ⁊ ᵹiꝼ him mete tela
ne mylte · ⁊ ᵹiꝼ him ſpat oꝼᵹa ⁊ ſtince ꝼule · þonne
mon þ onᵹite þonne ne ſceal him mon anne mete
ᵹebeoðan · ſie miꞃSenlice þ ꞃeo moꞃneꞃ þaꞃa metta
mæᵹe hím ᵹoðe beón · ᵹiꝼ hꞃa oꝼeꞃ ᵹemet þiᵹþ mete
þæꞃ món tilað þe eaðelicoꞃ þe mon ꞃaþoꞃ ᵹeðo þ he
ſꞃiꞃe · ⁊ ᵹelæꞃ ſie. ᵹiꝼ hiꞃ món ᵹetilað æt þæꞃe
yꝼelan þætan him becumað ón miꞃSenlica aðla · bꞃeoſt
þæꞃce · ſꞃeoꞃcoþu ſcalꝼ ³ aðl · heaꞃðeꞃ hꞃiꝼþo · healꝼᵹunð·
cyꞃnelu ſineaðlacnu ⁊ þam ᵹelic · ᵹiꝼ hi ꝼoꞃ þiſum ne
mæᵹen ſlaþan ðonne ꞃceal him mon ꞃellan hat pæteꞃ
ðꞃincan þonne ſtilð þ ᵹeꞃceoꞃ innan ⁊ clænꞃað ⁴ þa
pambe · Nyttiᵹen baþeꞃ meðmiclum · ⁊ mete þiᵹen ⁊
mið pætꞃe ᵹemenᵹeðne ðꞃincan þiᵹen.

---

¹ pinepinclan. Somner, Gl., p.
60 a, line 32, also prints pine; the
Junian transcript of the lost MS.
(Jun. 71, in the Bodleian) has pine.
The reprinter of the glossary [A.D.
1857] altered to pine, erroneously,
and silently. In the Colloquium
Monasticon, the MS. has pinepinclan, torniculi, where the printed
text [A.D. 1846, p. 24] gives pinepinclan, torniculos : the edition of
1857, pinepinclan, torniculi [p. 6].
Lye is quite correct. The present
MS. has always w.

² pypꞃnum in the contents.

³ Read ceaꞃl.

⁴ clæꞃnað, MS.

lock seed ; worm meal in ale ; give *him that* to drink.
If a man be badly wounded, and for pain in the breast;
boil in ale, churmel and dill, Again, take green rue, a
little at a time, or in honey. If a man be over much
blown out, mingle with the white of an egg sea
periwinkles, burnt and rubbed up, smear therewith.
For hicket or hiccup of the wamb : throw dwarf
dwostle into boiling water, let it soak therein long,
till a man may drink the water. For worms of the
wamb ; take the mickle sinful *or sedum,* wring out
the juice, four little bowls full, in one bowl full of
wine, as mickle *as the others ;* that is good for worms
of wamb.

## XXXV.

Of the wambs of children, and of overfilling, and if
their meat do not well digest, and if sweat come from
them, and stink foully. When a man understandeth
that, then shall not a single meat be offered them, but
various ones, that the newness *or novelty* of the meats
may be good for them. If one eateth meat over
measure, this *case* one tendeth the more easily, as one
the sooner bringeth about that he spew, and be empty;
if one tendeth him when troubled with the evil
humour *arising from overeating,* then come on him
various diseases, breast pain, neck disease, disease in
the jowl, scurf of the head, purulence in the neck,
churnels not easy to cure, and the like of those. If
for these they may not sleep, then shall one give them
hot water to drink, it will still the scour within, and
will cleanse the wamb. Let them employ the bath
moderately, and take meat and take drink mingled
with water.

## .XXXVI.[1]

Be milte pænce ꝼ ꝥ he bɪð ón þæꞃe pineſtꞃan
ſiðan ꝼ tacn þæꞃe aðle hu hiꝓleaſe hie beoð ꝼ ðolh
uncaðlácno · þa men beoð mæꝣꞃe ꝼ unꝓote · blace ón
onſyne þeah þe hie æꝓ ꝼꝛætte pæꞃon · ꝼ beoð hiðeꝓꞃ-
peaꞃðe · ꝼ pamb únꝣepealðen ꝼ unyþe micꝣe bɪþ hal ·
ac hio bɪþ ſpcaꞃtꞃe ꝼ ꝣꞃenꝓe · ꝼ blacꞃe þonne hiꞃe
ꝓiht ſie ꝼ ꝼnæꞃtiað ſpiþe beoþ ꝼoꞃtoꝣene · ꝣiꝼ 'ſio aðl
bɪþ to lanꝣSum · becymeþ þonne ón pꝛæteꝓ bollan ne
mæꝣ hine món þonne ꝣelacnian tunꝣe únꝣepealðen ꝼ
unſineþe ꝼ þa ðolh beoþ uneaðlácnu þa þe on lichoman
beoð ꝼ hie beoð on þa pinſtꞃan ſiðan mið ece ꝣeſpen-
ceðe ꝼ ón ðone hð þæꞃa eaxla betꝥeox ꝣeſculðꞃum bɪþ
micel ece ꝼ ón þám ꝣehꝓeoꝓꝼe þaꞃa bana ón þam
ſpeoꞃan habbað eac liꞃehte ꝼet cneop tꞃuciað · Ðu ꞃe
milte bɪð emlanꝣ ꝼ ꝣæðeꝓtenꝣe þæꞃe pambe hæꝼð
þyꞃne ꝼilmene ſio hæꝼð ꝼætte ꝼ þicce wðꞃa · ꝼ ꝼio
ꝼilmen bɪþ þeccenðe ꝼ pꞃeouðe þa pambe ꝼ þa inno-
ꝼaꞃan [2] ꝼ þa pyꞃmð · ꝼ iꝼ aþeneð on þoue pineſtꞃan
neꝓeſeoꞃan ꝼ iꝼ mið ſinehtum limum ꝣehæꝼð · ꝼ iꝼ ón
oðꞃe healꝼe bꞃað ꝣehꝓineð þæꞃe ſiðan · ón oðꞃe iꝼ
ðam innoðe ꝣetanꝣ · be hleahtꞃe þe óꝼ milte cymð
ſume ſecꝣaþ ꝥ ſe milte ðam ſinúm þeoꝓiꝣe ꝼ ꝥte ꞃe
milte ón ſumum ðæluin þain monnuin aðeaðiꝣe oþþe
óꝼ ſie · ꝼ ꝥ hi ꝼoꞃþon hlyhhan mæꝣen · Soþlice, on þa
ilcan piſan þe oþeꞃ limo þꞃoꝓiað untꞃumneꞃꞃa ꞃe milte
þꞃopað on þa ilcan piſan · Oꝼ cele [3] unꝣemetlicum oꝼ
hæto ꝼ óꝼ ðꞃiꝣneꞃſe oꝼ micelꞃe yꝼelꞃe pꝛætan ꝼoꞃþon
pixþ ꞃe milte oꝼeꝓ ꝣeſceap ꝼpouað ꝼ heaꞃðað ꝼ ſpiþoſt óꝼ
cele ꝼ oꝼ unꝣemetlicꝓe pꝛætan · þonne cumað þa óꝼtoſt

---

[1] This chapter, and many more that
follow, seem to be from Philagrios,
as preserved in Trallianus. But such
symptoms as "tongue uncontrolled,"
and "muscular feet," are not to
be found in the Greek, as printed.

[2] The letter or letters between
inn and ꞃaꞃan have been cut off
from the margin of the MS.

[3] The words of Philagrios, in
Alex. Trall., book viii., chap. x.

### xxxvi.

Of milt wark, *or acute pain in the spleen,* and that the milt is on the left side, and tokens of the disease, how colourless *the patients* are, and *there are* wounds not easy of cure. The men are meagre and uncomfortable, pale of aspect, though ere this they were fat, and still are *constitutionally disposed* that way; and the wamb is not under control, and scarcely *can it be that* the mic is healthy, but *rather* it will be swartish and greenish, and blacker than its right is to be, and the breathing is very hard drawn. If the disease is too longsome, then it turneth to dropsy, one may not then cure it; the tongue is uncontrolled and unsmooth, and the wounds which are upon the body are not easy of cure, and they are on the left side afflicted with ache, and in the joining of the shoulders, betwixt the shoulder blades, there is mickle ache, and in the turning about of the bones of the neck; they have also brawny feet, their knees fail *them.* *We tell* how the milt is alongside and adjacent to the wamb, it hath a thin film, which hath fat and thick veins, and the film covereth and embraceth the wamb and the inwards, and warmeth them; and it is extended on the left part of the lower abdomen, and it is held by sinewy attachments, and it is in the one quarter broad; it toucheth the side, on the other it is in contact with the viscera. Of the laughter which cometh from the spleen. Some say that the milt is the servant of the sinews, and that the milt in some parts is dead in men, or is wholly absent, and that for this reason they are able to laugh. In fact, in the same wise that other limbs suffer inconveniences, the milt in the same wise suffers. *We treat also* of immoderate cold, of heat, of dryness, of mickle evil wet, since the milt waxeth unnaturally, and diminishes, and hardeneth, and mostly of cold and immoderate wet; further,

óf mettum ꞃ óf cealdum ꝺꞃincan ſƿa ſƿa ꞃinꝺon cealꝺe
oſtꞃan ꞃ æpla ꞃ miꞃSenlice ƿyꞃta ſƿiþoſt on ſumeꞃa
þonne þa món þiꝫꝺ. bæþ him eꝫleꝺ ſƿiꝺoſt æfteꞃ
mete ꞃ hæmeꝺ þinꝫ on oꝼeꞃꝼyllo. Sió unꝫemetlice
hæto þæꞃ milteſ cymꝺ óf ꝼeꞃꝼaꝺlum ꞃ óf ꝼeꞃeꞃeſ[1]
ſƿolle ꞃ ón ylꝺo[1] ꝼoꞃ bloꝺe · biꝺ aþeneꝺ ꞃe milte ꞃ
aþunꝺen miꝺ ꝫeſƿelle ꞃ eac hat lyꝼt ꞃ ſƿolꝫa bꞃinꝫaꝺ
aꝺle ón ꝺam milte · þonne ꞃe mon ƿyꞃꝺ to ſƿiþe ꝼoꞃ-
hæt. Sƿa biꝺ eác ón ƿintꞃa ꝼoꞃ cyle ꞃ ꝼoꞃ þaꞃa
peꝺꞃa[2] miꞃſenlicneꞃꞃe ꝥ ſe milte ƿyꞃꝺ ꝫeleꝼeꝺ. ꝥ
maꝫon ƿiſe men ónꝫitan hꞃanan ꞃio aꝺl cume be miſ-
ꝫepiꝺeꞃum ꞃ óf metta ꞃ óf ꝺꞃincena þiꝫinꝫe ꞃ þuꞃh
þaꞃ þinꝫ þa yꝼelan ƿætan ꞃ ƿinꝺiꝫo þinꝫ beoþ acenneꝺ
on þam milte ꞃ aꝺla ƿeaxaþ :·

fol. 92 a.

.XXXVII.[3]

Đv món ꞃcyle þone monnan innan ꞃ utan lacnian
miꝺ hatum ꞃ cealꝺum innan miꝺ lactucan · ꞃ clatan ·
ꞃ cucuꞃbitan ꝺꞃince on ƿine · baþiꝫe hine on ſƿetum
ƿætꞃe. Utan he iſ to lacnianne miꝺ ꝫeꞃoſoꝺe ele ꞃ
to ſmiꞃꞃanne · ꞃ onleꝫena ꝫeꞃoꞃhte óf ƿine ꞃ ƿinꝺeꞃ-
ꝫum ꞃ óꝼt oꝼ butꞃan · ꞃ óf niꞃum ƿeaxe ꞃ óf yꞃopo ·
ꞃ óf ele onleꝫen ꝫeꞃoꞃht ; Œenꝫ ƿiþ ꝫoꞃe ſmeꞃu oꝺꝺe
ſƿineſ ꞃyꞃꞃle ꞃ ƿiꝺ ꞃecelſ · ꞃ mintan · ꞃ þonne[4] he hine
baþiꝫe ſmiꞃe miꝺ ele menꝫ ƿiꝺ cꞃoh. Œettaſ him beoꝺ
nytte þa þe ꝫoꝺ bloꝺ ƿyꞃceaꝺ ſƿa ſƿa ſint ꞃcilꝼixaꞃ
ꝼiꞃihte ꞃ ham[5] ƿilꝺa hænna ꞃ ealle þa ꝼuꝫelaſ þe on

---

[1] The Saxon has misread his text.
[2] ꝼeꝺnn., MS., with full stop.
[3] The words of Philagrios, as
before.

[4] þon, MS.
[5] Insert ꞃ.

these most often come of meats and of cold drinks,
such as are cold oysters, and apples, and various worts,
chiefly in summer, when one partaketh of such.   Bathing is harmful to them *who are splenitic*, chiefly after
meat, and copulation *following* on surfeit.   The unmeasured heat of the milt cometh from fevers and
from the swealing *or burning* of fever, and in old age
from *corruption of* the blood.   The milt is extended
and distended with swelling, and also hot air and hot
weather bring disease upon the milt; when the man
becometh too much heated.   So it is also in winter,
for the cold and for the variableness of the weather,
that the milt becometh corrupted.   *We next treat* that
wise men may understand whence the disease cometh
by bad weather, and from partaking of *unwholesome*
meats and drinks, and through these things the evil
humours and windy things are produced in the milt,
and diseases wax *therein*.


## xxxvii.

*We now explain* how one must apply leechdoms to
the man, within and without, with hot and cold *treat-
ments;* within, with lettuce, and clote, and gourd; let
him drink them in wine; let him *also* bathe himself
in sweet water.   Without, he is to be leeched and
smeared with oil of roses, and with onlayings *or
poultices made* of wine and grapes, and often must
an onlay be wrought of butter, and of new wax,
and of hyssop, and of oil; mingle with goose grease or
lard of swine, and with frankincense, and mint; and
when he bathes let him smear himself with oil; mingle
*it* with saffron.   Meats which work out good blood are
beneficial for him; such as are shell fishes,[1] and those
that have fins,[1] and domestic and wild hens,[2] and all

---

[1] Not in the Greek.       |       [2] Wild hens are pheasants.

ðunum libbað · ꞇ ƿipioneſ þ̷ beoð culꝼꞃena bꞃoððaſ ꞇ
healꝼealð ſpin · ꞇ ʒaꞇe ꝼlæꞃc ꞇ pyſena ꞃeap mið huniʒe·
hꝼæꞇ hꞃeʒa ʒepipeꞃoð · ꞇ eal ðaꞃ pæꞇan þinʒ bꞃeoſꞇum ꞇ innoþum ne ðuʒon ne þ̷ ƿin iſ ꞇo þicʒenne þ̷ꞇe
hæꞇeþ ꞇ pæꞇcþ þone Innoþ.

## .XXXVIII.[1]

Ðu mān ſceal þa pæꞇan ꞇ þa ponꞃceaꝼꞇan uꞇan lacnian mið aꝼꞃum ꞃealꝼum.  Pic ꞇ hluꞇoꞃ eccð ꞇ ʒepo-
ſoðne ele menʒ ꞇoſomne leʒe uꞇan ōn.  Þiþ þam pæꞇan
yꝼle þæꞃ milꞇeſ · nīm ꞃynðꞃiʒ ꞃealꞇ oððe pið peaxhlaꝼ
ſcalꝼe ʒemenʒ · ꞇ ʒepeꞃimeð ꞇ ōn blæðꞃan ʒeðon þ̷
lacnað þone milꞇe.  Eꝼꞇ nim ſ ꞃealꞇ ꞇ peax ꞇ eceð menʒ
ꞇoʒæðꞃe þ̷ ðeah · Nim eꝼꞇ ꝼiꞃleaꝼan[2] pypꞇꞇꞃuman · ꞇ
ðꞃiʒe peʒbꞃæðan ꞇ ʒebæꞃneð ſcalꞇ calꞃa emꝼela peſe
mið eceðe ꞇ ʒeſomna ðo ðꞃiʒe pic ꞇo · ꞇ peax · ꞇ ele
menʒ eal ꞇoʒæðeꞃe ðo ōn · Ne bið þ̷ an þ̷ þ̷ ðꞃiʒe þa
pæꞇan ac þa ahcaꞃðoðan ſpilaſ þa ðe cumað ōꝼ þiccum
pæꞇum ſlipeʒꞃum beꞇ ꞇ þꞃæn·ð.  Þiþ ſlipeʒꞃum pæꞇum
þæꞃ milꞇeſ ·  Nim acoꞃꞃencſ ꞃealꞇeſ[3] þ̷ pæꞇeꞃ þe þæꞃ
ōꝼ ʒæþ menʒ pið þa æꞃ ʒemenʒneðan[4] þinʒ.

## .XXXVIIII.[5]

Þiþ pinðiʒꞃe aꝼunðeneꞃꞃe þæꞃ milꞇeſ ꝼoꞃ æppla · ꞇ
hnuꞇa ꞇ pyſena æꞇe · ꞃoꞃ ꞇ ſmælþeaꞃme · pambe ꞇ
inneꞃoꞃan · ꞇ maʒan þa ʒeonð blapað.  Þiþ þon ðeah
pipoꞃ ꞇ cymen · ꞇ huniʒ · ꞇ ſealꞇ menʒe ꞇoʒæðeꞃe.

[1] Philagrios, as before.
[2] Abridged from Philagrios ap.
Alexandr. Trallian., p. 477, ed.
Basil.
[3] This is perhaps ἀλμή καὶ ἄφρος
ἁλός, as above.

[4] Read ʒenemneðan.
[5] An adaptation from Philagrios
in Trallianus, lib. viii., cap. 11, p.
479, ed. Basil.

the fowls which live on downs, and pigeons, that is, the young chicks of culvers, and half grown swine and goats flesh, and juice of peas with honey, somewhat peppered: and all moist things are not beneficial to the breast and the inwards, nor is such wine to be taken as heateth and moisteneth the inwards.

### xxxviii.

*Here we explain,* how one must treat the humours and the meagreness, on the outside, with sharp salves. Mingle together pitch, and clear vinegar, and oil of roses; lay on the outside. For the evil humours of the milt; take salt separately, or mingle it with a wax cake salve, *or cerote,* warmed and put upon *some* bladder; that healeth the milt. Again, take salt, and wax, and vinegar, mingle together, that is of benefit. Again, take a cinqfoil root, and dry waybroad, and burnt salt, of all equal quantities; soak them in vinegar, and collect them; add dry pitch, and wax, and oil; mingle all together *and* apply. Not merely doth that *remedy* dry the humours, but it bettereth and softeneth the hardened swellings,[1] which come of thick slimy wets *or crass viscid humours.* For viscid humours of the milt, take the water of carved salt, *or rock salt,* that namely which passeth from it, mingle with the things before named.

### xxxix.

For a windy distention of the milt from eating of apples, and of nuts, and of peas; they produce inflation through the long gut, and small guts, the wamb, and the inwards, and the maw; for that is useful pepper and cummin and salt, mingle them together.

---

[1] Scirrhous.

ƿiþ foᵹoþan ⁊ ꞃeadan[1] ⁊ ᵹeohſan þe oꝼ milte cymð. ᵹitte hatte ſuþeꞃne ƿyꞃt ſio iſ ᵹod on hlaꝼe to þic-ᵹenne ⁊ meꞃceꞃ ſæd ⁊ cellenðꞃan.[2] ⁊ peteꞃꞅilian on hlaꝼ becneden oþþe on pin ᵹeᵹniden. ⁊ eac ꝥ ðeah ƿiþ ablaƿunᵹe þæꞃ milteſ. ᵹiꝼ þonne ſio aþindunᵹ þæꞃ ƿindeſ femninᵹa cymð þonne ne maᵹon þaſ þinᵹ hel-pan. ꞃoꞃ þon ðe ꝥ ꞃile ƿendan on pæteꞃ bollan.[3] ᵹiꝼ mon to þam þa ƿyꞃmendan þinᵹ deþ þonne ycþ mon þa adle.[4] ƿiþ milte feocum men him mon ꞅceal ꞃellan eced on þam ſuþeꞃnan læcedome þe hatte oxumelle þe þe ꝑꞃiton ƿiþ þæꞃe healꝼdeadan adle ⁊ blædꞃan adle. Nim lauꞃeꞃ ꞃinde. ⁊ dꞃiᵹe mintan ⁊ ꞃiꞃoꞃ ⁊ ꞃudan ſæd.[5] coſt. ⁊ hunan. ⁊ centauꞃian. ꝥ iſ hyꞃdeƿyꞃt oðꞃe naman eoꞃþᵹealla ꞅꞃiþuſt þæꞃe ꞃeap. do þaꞃ ƿyꞃta on þone æꞃ neimdan læcedom ón ꝥ ꞃoꞃ þu meaht ᵹeſeon æt þam æꞃ ᵹenemdan adlum hu þu ðone oxumelle pyꞃcean ꞃcealt.[6] Aleꞃeꞃ[7] ꞃinde ſcoꝼ ón pæteꞃe oþ ꝥ þæꞃ pæteꞃeſ ſie þꞃiddan dæl unbeꞃelled. ⁊ ꞃele þonne þæꞃ ᵹodne ceac ꝼulne to dꞃincanne on þꞃy ſiþaſ læt ſimle dæᵹþeꞃne betꞃeonum. ƿiſ ilce deah lendenꞃeocum men. eꝼt þæſ blacan iꞃiᵹeſ[8] cꞃoꞃ-pan æꞃeſt. þꞃeo. eꝼt .V. þonne .VII. þonne niᵹon. þonne .XI. þonne .XIII. þonne .XV. þonne ſeoꞃantyne. þonne niᵹantyne. þonne .XXI. ſele ſpa ꞃeꞃteꞃ daᵹum dꞃincan ón pine. ᵹiꝼ ſe mán hæbbe eac ꞃeꞃeꞃ ꞃele þu þa cyꞃnlu þæꞃ eoꞃþiꝼiᵹeſ on hatum pæteꞃe dꞃincan. þiſ ilce deah ƿiþ lendenꞃeocum men. Eꝼt eoꞃðᵹeallan ón pine ᵹeſodenne ꞃele dꞃincan. Eꝼt betonican[9] ƿyl ón pine ꞃele dꞃincan. Sealꝼ ⁊ onleᵹen ƿið milte pæꞃce

---

[1] Κλύδωνας, *wavy movements*, much the same as βορβόρυγμα.

[2] ἄνισον, Al. Trall., p. 480.

[3] Ταδε γὰρ προσήκει, εἰ ὁ ὑδερὸς οὐκ αὐτίκα ἐνθίνδε τυγχανει εἰ δὲ ἐξαίφνης γεγένηται, τότε οὐδαμῶς ταὐτὰ συμφέρει.

[4] From Alex. Trall., viii. 11, p. 481.

[5] Many words are omitted, as

πευκέδανον: rue seed is πηγάνου ἀγρίου σπέρμα.

[6] So far from Alex. Trallianus or Philagrios.

[7] See Marcellus, col. 149 d.: *cyperus* for *alnus*.

[8] Marcellus, col. 349, A.

[9] Marcellus, col. 348, B.

For ill juices and wavy movements and yoxing, *or hic-keting*, which cometh from the spleen. A southern wort hight gith, which is good to eat on bread, and seed of marche and of coriander and of parsley kneaded up into bread or rubbed *fine* into wine : and also that is beneficial for inflation of the milt. If however the distention from the wind cometh suddenly, then these things cannot help, since that will turn into dropsy. If one applieth the warming *leechdoms* to that, then one eketh *or augmenteth* the disease. For a miltsick man, one must give him vinegar in the southern leech-dom which hight oxymel, which we wrote of[1] against the half dead disease and disease of the bladder. Take rind of laurel, and dry mint, and pepper, and seed of rue, costmary, and *hor*ehound, and centaury, that is herdwort, or by another name, earthgall, chiefly the juice of it, add these worts to the before named leech-dom into the ooze. Thou mayest see *where we have spoken* of the before named diseases, how thou shalt prepare the oxymel. Seethe in water rind of alder until there be of the water a third part unboiled away, and then give a good jug full of it to be drunk at three times ; leave always a days space between *the doses*. This same is beneficial for a loinsick man. Again, of the black ivy, first three berry bunches, next five, then seven, then nine, then eleven, then thirteen, then fif-teen, then seventeen, then nineteen, then twenty-one, give them so, according to the days, to be drunk in wine. If the man have fever also, give thou him the little grains of the ground ivy in hot water to drink. This same is good for a loinsick man. Again, give him to drink earthgall sodden in wine. Again, boil betony in wine, give *him that* to drink. A salve and a plaster for milt pain, work it up of honey and of

---

[1] As follows : II. lix.

ƿyrc of hunige ⁊ óf ecede dumelu[1] ⁊ linsæd to ⁊ beres grytta merces sæd lege ón ⁊ smire mid þys. do eác driges ƿermodes blostmān to.

.XL.[2]

Gif þonne se milte ablawen ƿyrð sona he ƿile aheardian ⁊ biþ þonne uneaþlæcne. þonne ꝥ blod aheardað on þam ædrūm þæs miltes. lacna hine þonne mid þām ær genemdan ƿyrtum. meng þa godan ƿyrta ƿið oxumelli þone suþernan eced drenc. ðe ƿe ær ƿriton þa lácniað þone milte ⁊ aweg adoð ꝥ þicce ⁊ lifrige blod. ⁊ þa yfelan ƿætan. næs þurh ða micgean ane ác eac þurh oþerne utgang. Hirdeƿyrt seo hnesse lege gebeatene utan. Nim eác clæfran ƿyrttruman do ón eced ⁊ gate tyrdlu[3] ƿyrc þonne to sealfe ⁊ beren melo do þærto. sele him þis eác on ƿine drincan.

fol. 94 a.

.XLI.[4]

Ƿiþ þære heardnesse ⁊ sare þæs miltes. sƿines blædran nim sƿa niƿe gefyl mid sceárpe ecede alege ofer ða heardnesse þæs miltes besƿeþe þonne ꝥ hio aweg ne glide. ác sy þreo niht þærón fæste gebunden. æfter þon onbind. þonne findest þu gif hit tela bið þa blædran gelære ⁊ ꝥ hearde tolnesced ⁊ ꝥ sar gestilled. Eft genim ifies leaf seoð ón ecede ⁊ oferƿylle on þam selfan ecede sifeþan. do þonne on blædran bind ón ꝥ sar. sele þonne æfter ƿyrtdrenc sona þus geƿorhtne; Ƿiþ heardnesse miltes. genim corðgeallan gebeat oþþe gegnid to duste sƿa sƿa þreo cucler mæl sien oððe ma. do safinan dustes to cúcler mæl þreo.

fol. 94 b.

---

[1] Read do melu.

[2] Alexander Trallianus, book viii., chap. xii., p. 481, ed. Basil.

[3] Alex. Trall., p. 500, line 8, ed. Basil; from Galenos.

[4] The next chapter of Alex. Tr. is on the same subject; but the receipts are not his.

vinegar, add meal and linseed, and barley groats, and seed of marche; lay on and smear with this. Add also blossoms of dry wormwood.

### xl.

Again, when the milt becometh upblown, soon it will harden, and then it is not easy to cure, when the blood hardeneth on the veins of the milt: then treat it with the before named worts, mingle the good worts with oxymel, the southern acid drink, which we before wrote of, they will cure the milt and will do away the thick and livery [1] blood, and the evil humours, not by the mie only, but also by the other *evacuation passage or* outgang. Lay on externally the lesser herdwort beaten up. Take also roots of clover, put them in vinegar, and goat treadles, then work them to a salve, and add thereto barley meal; give the man also this in wine to drink.

### xli.

For the hardness and sore of the milt; take a swines bladder so new, fill it with sharp vinegar, lay it over the hardness of the milt, then swathe up, that it may not glide away, but may be thereon, fast bounden, for three nights. After that unbind; then thou wilt find, if it be good, the bladder clear, and the hard *part* made nesh, and the soreness stilled. Again, take leaves of ivy, seethe them in vinegar, and boil in the same vinegar some bran, then put this into a bladder, *and* bind upon the sore; then soon after give a wort drink thus wrought: for hardness of the milt; take earthgalls, beat or rub them to dust, so that there may be three or more spoon measures, add three spoon measures of dust of savine thereto, and three

---

[1] Such as flows through the liver.

Ᵹ þeallenðeꞃ piceꞃ ðuſtꞃ þþeo cucleꞃ mæl · áꞃiꞅte eall
ꞃele þonne on pine neahtneꞃtiꞡum to ðꞃincanne cucleꞃ
ꝼulne · ꞡiꞃ he ſie eác on ꞃeꝼꞃe ꞃele him ón hatum
ꞃctꞃe ꞡeplecedum þa pyꞃta ðꞃincan þy læꞃ þ pic óꝼ-
ſtande mið þy oþꞃe ðuſte.  Eꝼt to milte ſeocum men
Ᵹ pið callum maðlum · cceð pið ꞡlæðenan ꞡemenꞡeð
pyꞃe þuꞃ ꞡlæðenán ꞃinde lytelpa ꞡeðo þꞃeo punð on
ꞡlæꞃ ꝼæt pel micel · ꞡeðo þonne þæꞃ ꞃccaꞃꞃeꞃtan pineꞃ
to .v. ꞃeꞃtꞃaꞃ áꞃete þonne on hate Sunnan on ſumeꞃa
Ionne þa hatoſtan peðeꞃ ſynð · Ᵹ þa ꞃciꞃan ðaꞡaꞃ
hpitan þe þe ꞡeꞃꞃitene habbað · þ hit ſipiꞡe Ᵹ ꞃociꞡe
.iiii. ðaꞡaꞃ oþþe ma · ꞃiþþan þæꞃ cceðeꞃ ꞃele þu milte
ſeocum inen cucleꞃ ꝼulne Ᵹ ſona ꞡiꞃ him ꞃeꝼtꞃ þám
ðꞃincan · ꝼoꞃ þon þe þ iꞃ ſpiþe ſtꞃanꞡ þam þe þ napa
æꞃ þꞡðe.  þonne ðeah þíꞃ pið hueniꞡe ꞡeycceð ꞡe pið
multe aðle · ꞡe pið maꞡan · ꞡe pið hꞃean ꞡe pið þon þe
món bloðe ſꞃiꞃe · ꞡe pið callum innan aðlum · eác þón[1]
ꞃueꝼþo Ᵹ ꞡicþa ſon apeꞡ ðeþ.  þeꞃ læceðóm ðeah ꞡe
pið hꞃieꝼðo Ᵹ ꞡicþan · pyꞃe óꝼ cceðe ꞃeaxꞃcalꝼc · ꞡením
þæꞃ cceðeꞃ .v. cucleꞃ mæl ðo ón niꞃne cꞃoccan ðo
cleꞃ bollan ꝼulne to ſeoð ætſomne ſceað niꞃeꞃ ſꞃeꞃꞃeꞃ
ꝼíꞃ cucleꞃ mæl · Ᵹ lytel peaxeꞃ oꝼeꞃ pylle eꝼt oþ þ
þæꞃ cceð ſie ꝼoꞃꞃeallen ·  ðo þonne óꝼ ꝼyꞃe Ᵹ hꞃeꞃe Ᵹ
ꞃiþþan ſnꞃe mið þy þa hꞃieꝼþo Ᵹ þone ꞡicðan.

### .XLII.

Ꞡíꞃ omihte bloð Ᵹ yꝼel ꝼæte on þam milte ſie þꞃ-
ðenðe þonne ꞃceal him mon bloð þuꞃ lætan.  Giꞃ þe
þince þ þu oþeꞃne maꞃan læceðom ðon ne ðuꞃꞃe · ꝼoꞃ

---

[1] Read þoū, that is, þonne.

spoon measures of the dust of "boiling pitch;"[1] sift all
this, then give a spoon full in wine to the man after his
nights fast to drink : if he be also in a fever, give
him the worts to drink in "hot" water made "lukewarm," lest the pitch form a concrete with the other
dust. Again, for a miltsick man, and for all inward
disorders ; vinegar mingled with gladden ; work it thus :
put three pound of little *bits of* rind of gladden in a
good sized glass vessel, then add thereto of the sharpest
wine, five sextarii, then set this in the hot sun, in summer, when the hottest seasons are, and the clear white
days of which we have written, that it may macerate
and soak for four days and more ; afterwards give thou
to the sick man of the vinegar a spoon full, and after
the dose soon, give him *something* to drink, since that
is very strong for him who never before tasted it. Further, this eked out with honey is of benefit, either for
milt disease, or for maw *disease*, or for rawness,[2] or in
case a man spew blood, or for all inward diseases : it also
further soon doth away roughness *of skin*, and itch.
This leechdom is good either for roughness or itch :
work of vinegar a wax salve, *or cerote*; take five spoon
measures of the vinegar, put *it* into a new crock, add
a bowl full of oil, seethe together, shed *therein* five
spoon measures of new brimstone, and a little wax,
boil it strongly "again," till the vinegar is boiled
off, then remove from the fire, and shake, and afterwards smear therewith the roughness and the itch.


## xlii.

If inflamed blood and evil humour be in the milt,
distending it, then shall *the sick* be thus let blood.
If it seem to thee, that thou dare not to do another

---

[1] Our Saxon has made some mistake : the receipt is similar to one
given by Marcellus, col. 348, B.,

where we read " ex picato mero vel
" nigro tepefacto."

[2] Probably *cruditas, indigestion.*

unmihte þær mannes oððe for unmeltunȝe oþþe for
ylbe · oþþe for ȝioȝoðe · oþþe for unȝeriðerum · oþþe
for útȝrihtan · ȝebið þonne oþ ꝥ þu mæȝe · oððe[1]
ðyrre · ȝif hæto oþþe meht ne pyrne læt him blod
ón þam pineſtran earme oſ þære uferran æðre · ȝif
þu þa findan ne mæȝe læt óf þære miðinertan roðre ·
ȝif þu þa findan ne mæȝe læt oſ þære heafod æðre.
Þonne ȝif mon þa findan ne mæȝe læt oſ þære pineſtran handa neah þam lytlan finȝre óf æðre · ȝif hit
ſprðe read ſie oþþe pon þonne bið hit þy þe ſpriþor to
lætanne · ȝif hit clæne oþþe hluttor ſie læt þy þe
lærre. Iſ hraþere ſpa to lætanne ſpa ꝥ liflice mæȝen
ne aſprinȝe.

.XLIII.

Þurſ[2] him món ſceal þurſ mettaſ ſellan ón þære
aðle ȝeſeape pyſan Ᵹ hlaf ón hatum pætere Ᵹ oxumelle þe pe ƿriton ær beforan piþ blæðran aðle ſu-
þeþne eceð ðrenc · merce on pætere ȝeſoden Ᵹ ſpilca
pyrta Ᵹ miȝole ðrincan Ᵹ þynne pín him iſ to ſellanne pel ſcir ꝥ bet ꝥ mæȝen þeſ milteſ Ᵹ ſcellihte
fiſcaſ him ſint to þicȝenne · Ᵹ fuȝlaſ þa þe on fen-
num ne ſien. þiſ him iſ to forȝanne · ne þicȝen hie
fen fixaſ · ne ſæ fixaſ þa þe habbað heard flæſc · Ᵹ
þicȝen hie þa for ȝenemðan mettaſ · oſtran · Ᵹ pinepinclan ·[3] ne þa mettaſ þa þe ablapan monnan mæȝen.
ne hriþeſleſ flæſc · ne ſpineſ ne ſceapeſ ne · þicȝean
hie · ne ȝate · ne ticceneſ · ne ðrince[4] þicce pín · ne
mete ne to ſprðe hatne · ne eſc to cealðne.  Erſt[5]

fol. 95 b.

fol. 96 a.

---

[1] oðð, MS.

[2] Þiſ, MS. With the text compare,
Ἐκώλυσα δὲ πάντα τὰ γλισχροὺς καὶ
παχεῖς χυμοὺς γεννῶντα, ὡσαύτως [δὲ]
καὶ τὰ κρέα [τὰ] βόεια, χοίρεια, προ-
βάτεια, αἴγεια καὶ ἐρίφεια, καὶ τῶν
ὀρνίθων τὰ ἐν λιμνώδεσιν ὕδασι διαιτώ-
μενα, καὶ τῶν ἰχθύων πάντας ἐλεώδεις
καὶ πελαγίους, ἄλλως τε [καὶ] τοὺς

σκληρὰς καὶ παχεῖς.  Opp. Alex.
Tralliani, p. 496, ed. Basil.

[3] p not þ ; see note, p. 240.

[4] ðrincan would be better.

[5] Καὶ αὐτίκα κατ' ἀρχὴν τοῦ ἦρος
αἷμα πολὺ ἐκ τοῦ ἀριστεροῦ ἀγκῶνος
ἀφῆρουν.  Opp. Alex. Tralliani,
p. 427, ed. Basil.

greater leechdom, for the want of might in the man,
or for want of digestion, or for old age, or for youth,
or for bad weather, or for diarrhœa, then wait till that
thou may so do· or dare. If heat, or *his* capacity to
bear it, forbid it not, let him blood from the left arm
from the upper vein ; if thou canst not find that, let
*him blood* from the midmost vein ; if thou canst not
find that, let *him blood* from the head vein. Further,
if that cannot be found, let *him blood* from the left
hand, near the little finger, from a vein. If *the blood*
be very red or livid, then must it be let flow more
plentifully ; if it be clean or clear, let it *flow* so much
the less. *Blood* however is so to be taken *from the
man* as that his vital power may not be unsettled.

xliii.

Thus shall the sick mens diet be administered in
that disease; juicy peas, and bread in hot water, and
oxymel, of which we wrote before, *when speaking* of
bladder disease, *the* southern acid drink; marche *also*
sodden in water, and such worts and diuretic drinks,
and thin wine must be given them, and sheer *or clear;*
that will better the power of the milt ; and shell
fishes are to be taken, and fowls, those, *namely,* which
are not *dwellers* in fens. This *that followeth* is to
be foregone; let them not partake of fen fishes, nor
sea fishes which have hard flesh, and let them take
the before named meats, oysters and periwinkles, not
the meats which puff up a mans strength, nor let
them take flesh of bullock, nor of swine, nor of
sheep, nor of goat, nor of kid, nor let them
drink thick wine, nor food either too extremely hot

bloð bið ᵹoð to lætanne ón ꝼoꞃan lenctene oꝼ þam
ꝑinſtꞃan eaꞃme.

## .XLIIII.

Eꝼt læcedom ꞃe þ yꝼel ut tıhð oꝼ þam milte ᴉ ꞃe
ðeah to maneᵹum oþꞃum aðlum · ᵹenīm ᵹꞃene ꞃuðan
ane ðꞃᴂᵹe ᴂꝑ ᵹeꞃomna ᴉ meðmicel ꝑıꝑoꝑeꞃ · oþeꞃ ſꝑıc
cymeneꞃ oððe ma · ðo þ cymen ane ðꞃᴂᵹe ᴂꝑ oððe
tꝛam oþþe þꞃım ón eceð aðꝑıᵹe ᴉ aᵹnıð to ðuſte calle
þaꞃ ꝑyꞃta · menᵹe pıð hunıᵹ aꞃꝑen · ᵹeðo þonne ón
ᵹlᴂꞃene ampullan ᴉ ꞃele þonne cucleꝑ ꝼulne þeꞃ ðeah
pıþ maᵹan aðlapunᵹe ᴉ ınnoþa · hneꞃceþ þa ꝑamðe ·
þynnað þa omán bıtꞃe hꞃᴂcetunᵹe aꝑeᵹ ðeþ ᴉ ðꞃeoſt
coþe · ᴉ ꞃıð pꞃꝛce · ᴉ lıꝼeꞃ aðle · ᴉ lenðen pꞃꝛce · ᴉ
milte pꞃꝛce eal þ lıht.

## .XLV.

Læcedomaꞃ ᴉ ſpıð ðꞃenc pıþ aſpollenum milte · accele
ðu ꝑealhat ıꞃen þonne hīt ꝼuꞃþum ſıe óꝼ ꝼyꝛe atoᵹen ·
ón pıne oþþe ón eceðe ꞃele þ ðꞃıncan þ þu mealht eꝛe
ꞃellan þam þe habbaþ heaꞃðne lıchoman · ne ꞃeeal
món hꞃᴂþeꞃe ꝼıꞃne ðꞃıncan ꞃellan ón ꝼoꞃeꞃeaꞃðne
þone ece ᴉ þa aðle áe ymb ꝼela nıhta.

## .XLVI.[2]

Her ſınðon læcedomaꞃ pıþ ᴂᵹhꝛᴂþeꞃꞃe ſıðan ꞃaꞃe ᴉ
taen hu ſıo aðl topeaꞃð ſıe · ᴉ hu þ mon ónᵹıtan
mᴂᵹe · ᴉ hu hıoꞃa[3] mon tıhan ꞃcyle · þaꞃ læcedomaſ
ꞃeeal món ðon pıþ ſıðan ꞃaꞃe · ᴉ þıꞃ ſınðon þᴂꝑe aðle

fol. 96 b.

---

[1] Καὶ μὴν καὶ στομώματος λεπὶς,
ἢν ἐκεῖνο ἐν χαλκείοις πυρούμενόν τε
καὶ σφύρᾳ κοπτόμενον ἀποβάλλει, σὺν
ὕδατι ἀναμεμιγμένη ἐν ποτῷ συμφέρει.
Opp. Alex. Trall., lib. viii., 13,
p. 506, ed. Basil.

[2] Alexandros of Tralles, lib. vi.
chap. 1, treats of the diagnosis between pleurisy and disease of the
liver.

[3] This plural may refer to the tacn
or the sidan.

or too cold.   Again, it is good to let blood in early
lent *or spring* from the left arm.

## xliv.

Again, a leechdom which draweth out the evil from
the milt, and which is efficacious for many other disorders.   Take green rue one day before *it is used*,
collect it and a moderate quantity of pepper, so much
also of cummin, or more, put the cummin one day
beforehand, or two or three, into vinegar, dry it and
rub to dust all the worts, mingle *this* with honey
strained, then put them into a glass pitcher, and so
give *the man* a spoon full.   This is good against upblowing of the maw and of the inwards; it maketh
nesh the wamb; it thinneth the corrupt gastric juices,
it doth away breakings, and breast disease, and side
pain, and liver disorder, and loin pain, and milt pain :
all that it lighteneth.

## xlv.

Leechdoms and strong drink for a swollen milt; cool
thou a fiercely hot iron, when it is just withdrawn from
the fire, in wine or in vinegar, give *the man* that to
drink.   Thou mayest also give that to them who have
a hard body : notwithstanding, this drink shall not
be given in the early stage of the ache and the disease,
but after many days.

## xlvi.

Here are leechdoms for sore of either side, and tokens
how the disease approaches, and how a man may understand that, and how a man shall treat it.   These leechdoms shall be done for sore of side, and these are the

tacn[1] ᵹelic lunᵹen able tacnum ⁊ hƿeㄖ ㄖæþceㄖ tacnum. þa men beoþ mið hㄖuþinᵹum ſㄖㄖþe ſtㄖanᵹum
pæcebe · ⁊ micel ſaㄖ on bam ſiðūm. Dㄖilun cnyㄖㄖeþ
ꝥ ㄖaㄖ on þa þið · hㄖilūm oㄖeㄖ ealle ſiðan biþ ꝥ ㄖaㄖ ·
hㄖilūm becyinð on þa peoþoban ⁊ eㄖt ymb lytel ᵹe
þa ᵹeſculðㄖu ᵹe eſt þone nepeſeoþan ꝥ ㄖaㄖ ᵹㄖㄖct · ⁊
hㄖoㄖað[2] ᵹelome · hㄖilum bloðe hㄖæcaþ · ㄖinᵹale þæc-
cean þㄖoㄖað · tunᵹe bið ðㄖㄖᵹe · ne maᵹou ᵹelicᵹean
ōn þㄖeㄖe þmeſtㄖan ſiðan · ᵹㄖꝼ ōn þㄖeㄖe ſㄖiðㄖan ꝥ ㄖaㄖ
bið · ne maᵹon eāc eㄖt ōn þa ſㄖiðㄖan · ᵹㄖꝼ on þa þin-
ſtㄖan ꝥ ㄖaㄖ biþ · ᵹeㄖclað ꝥ þa innoþaㄖ hㄖ penðaþ mið
hㄖoㄖa heㄖᵹneㄖㄖc ⁊ on þa ㄖiðan ꝼeallað þe he on lic-
ᵹeað · ㄖeþ þㄖeㄖe able þaㄖ tacn beoþ · biþ eāc ᵹeond
ㄖㄖㄖᵹㄖㄖㄖ[3] cele ⁊ cneoþa unmehꞇ eaᵹan ㄖeaðㄖað ㄖeoð[4] ⁊
beoþ heoþ ⁊ ㄖamㄖᵹ uꞇᵹanᵹ micᵹe aᵹeolþod ⁊ lytel biþ
þㄖeㄖ innoþeㄖ melꞇunᵹ ⁊[5] ㄖðㄖㄖa chæppeꞇunᵹ · eþunᵹ bið
ㄖaㄖhㄖc ᵹehnycneð neb ⁊ þaㄖa bㄖeoſta biþ ðcaㄖㄖᵹ þㄖeꞇunᵹ
ſþa ſþa ſie ᵹeſþaꞇ · moðeㄖ elhyᵹð ceolan hㄖㄖſꞇunᵹ ⁊
hㄖeounᵹ · hㄖybenðe ſþㄖㄖuſꞇ mnan þㄖſꞇlað oㄖ þam ðㄖele
þe ꝥ ㄖaㄖ bið hㄖmunᵹe ⁊ hㄖㄖᵹㄖㄖnᵹe þㄖð þㄖþeㄖㄖㄖㄖ · ᵹㄖꝼ
þㄖㄖ tacn lanᵹe þㄖnㄖað · þonne biþ ſeo aðl to ㄖㄖeccen-
lㄖco ⁊ ne mæᵹ him mōn ᵹeꞇㄖlㄖan · ahㄖa hㄖㄖþþㄖㄖ þone
mㄖㄖnan þe þㄖㄖ þㄖoㄖað hㄖㄖþㄖㄖ he ㄖㄖþㄖe þㄖeㄖe ㄖleᵹen
on þa ㄖiðan oðð ᵹeſꞇunᵹen oþþe hㄖㄖþㄖㄖ he lenᵹe ㄖeþ
aㄖeolle oðð ᵹebㄖoceu þㄖㄖðe · ᵹㄖꝼ hㄖꞇ ꝥ þㄖㄖne þonne
bㄖð he þy eaðㄖㄖㄖna ·[6] ᵹㄖꝼ hㄖꞇ biþ oㄖ cyle cumen oþþe oㄖ
yㄖelㄖe mㄖㄖtan hㄖꞇ bið þe uneaþㄖㄖㄖㄖa.[7] ᵹㄖꝼ he þonne
biþ ㄖeþ on þㄖㄖe hㄖㄖㄖe oþþe on þām lunᵹenum ᵹeſaㄖㄖᵹoð

---

[1] These symptoms are fully stated
in nearly the same words by Aretæos, Acut. I. x. Possibly the
diagnosis and the symptoms were
stated, as they are in the text, by
Philagrios. The Saxon author
mentions mechanical causes for the
sore of the side, as well as nosolo-
gical ; he does not therefore confine
himself to pleurisy.

[2] Read hㄖoㄖtað.

[3] Aretæos accompanies us no far-
ther.

[4] Read ⁊ biþ heoþ ㄖeoð ?

[5] Deaþð or some word to express
Σκληρός is wanting.

[6] Read eaðㄖeacnㄖa.

[7] For uneaðㄖeacnㄖa.

tokens of the disease, like unto the tokens of lung disease, and the tokens of liver pain. The men are afflicted with very strong fevers, and mickle sore on both sides. At whiles the sore striketh[1] upon the ribs, at whiles the sore is over all the side; at whiles it cometh up on the collar bones, and again, after a little, the sore greeteth either the shoulders or the lower belly, and they cough frequently, at whiles they break up blood, they suffer a constant wakefulness, the tongue is dry, they cannot lie on the left side if the sore is on the right side, nor again can they lie on the right, if the sore is in the left; they feel that their viscera by their weight shift place, and fall upon the side on which they lie. These tokens are before the disease. There is also cold all through their fingers, and powerlessness of their knees, their eyes are red, and red is their hue, and their discharge[2] is foamy, their mic is turned yellow,[3] and the digestion of the inwards is little, and *hard* the pulsation of the veins, the breathing is sorelike, the face twitched, and there is a dewy wetting of the breast, as if it sweated, a delirium of the mind; a spasmodic action, and roughness of the throat, sounding chiefly from within, whistleth from the part on which the sore is; the disease is unfavourable to a leaning posture and to laughing. If these tokens continue long, then is the disease too dangerous, and one can do nothing for the man: notwithstanding, ask the man, who endureth this, whether he ever were stricken or stabbed in the side, or whether he long before had a fall, or got a breakage; if it were that, then will he be easier to cure. If it is come of cold or of inward evil humour, it is so much the harder to cure. If further the man have been before troubled with soreness in the liver, or in the lungs, and the

---

[1] Νύσσει, doubtless.          [3] Thus the Saxon.
[2] Expectoration ?

Ᵹ þanan cymeð fio[1] ꞃiðꞃæpc þonne biþ ꝥ ſpiðe ꝼꞃecne.
Ᵹiꝼ hit on þam milte biþ æp þonne biþ hit þy eaþ-
lacꞃe · ᵹiꝼ he þonne biþ æp on þæꞃe lunᵹene ᵹepundoð
Ᵹ þanan cymð ſe ꞃiðꞃæpc þonne biþ ꝥ ſpiðe ꝼꞃecne ·
ᵹiꝼ hit on þam milte bið æp · þonne cymð ꝥ ꞃap on
þa pinſtꞃan ſidan · ᵹe þa habbað[2] heꞃiᵹe ꝼꞃecenneꞃꞃe ·
ahſa hine h�whþeꞃ him ſe milte ꞃap ſie oððe h�wæþeꞃ
him ſpeoꞃcoþu ſie · ſpa þu meaht onᵹitan ꝥ þæꞃ ſidan
ꞃap cymð oꝼ yꝼelꞃe pætan Ᵹ biþ ſpiðe ꝼꞃecne. Ᵹiꝼ him
ſe utᵹanᵹ ꞃoꞃſeten ſie oððe ᵹemiᵹan ne mæᵹe mid
ſineþꞃe ᵹnðounᵹe pyꞃtðꞃenceꞃ þuꞃh hoꞃn oððe piꞃan
ſio ꞃanib biþ to clænſianne · ꝼꞃecne bið eac þonne
þæꞃ ꞃeocan manneſ hꞃaca bið mamᵹeꞃ hiꞃeꞃ Ᵹ bleo ꞉[3]


Be þiꞃum tacnum þu meaht h�w}p ſe man to lac-
manne ſie onᵹitan h�wæp ne ſie · h�wæꞃ mōn unſoꝼte
ᵹetilað ōn ꝼoꞃeꞃeaꞃðe þa aðle þonne ꝥ ſap æꞃeſt
ᵹeſtihð on þa ſculdꞃu Ᵹ on þa bꞃeoſt. Sona ꞃceal
mōn blod oꝼ æðꞃe lætan. Ᵹiꝼ ꝥ ꞃap ᵹepuniᵹe ōn þam
bꞃeoſtum anum oþþe on þam uꝼeꞃan hꞃiꝼe oþþe on
þam miðljnꝼe · þonne ꞃceal him mōn pyꞃtðꞃenc ꞃellan
Ᵹ nimān ſpete pæteꞃ mid ele ᵹeðon ōn ſpineſ blæðꞃan
Ᵹ beþꞃan ꝥ ſaꞃ mið.


### . XLVII.

Læcedomaſ þa þe þynnunᵹe mæᵹen hæbben Ᵹ ſmal-
unᵹe · þam lichoman þa ða hæto meðmicle oþþe ſtꞃanᵹe
þꞃoꞃian Ᵹ hu him mōn ſcyle ſpineſ blæðꞃan ōnðon.
Ᵹenim hunan Ᵹ peax Ᵹ ele ᵹemenᵹe oþþe ᵹeᵹnið to-
ᵹæðꞃe cælꞃa emꝼela ꝥ hit an ſie ſmiꞃe mið Ᵹ ðo on
clæþ leᵹe ōn. Þiþ ſaꞃe ſiðan eꝼt ᵹenīm ꞃuðan leaꝼ Ᵹ

---

[1] Read ſe.
[2] hab, MS., at the end of a line, the writer forgetting to complete the word.
[3] In I. xlv. 5, the genitive was bleor. Bleo, by a zeugma, may be genitive plural.

side pain cometh thence, then is that very dangerous ; if it has been ere that on the milt, then it is the easier to cure. Further, if *the man* have been before wounded in the lung, and thence cometh the side pain, then is that very dangerous. If it have been formerly in the spleen, then the sore cometh on the left side, yea, those *tokens* have heavy mischief; ask him whether the milt be sore, or whether he hath neck disease. So thou mayest understand that sore of the side cometh from evil humour and is very mischievous. If his anal discharge be stopped, or if he may not mie, the wamb must be cleansed by an always easy application of a wort drink, *in this case a clyster*, through a horn or pipe. There is danger also when the sick mans *expectoration or* hreak is of many a hue and complexion.[1]

2. By these tokens thou mayest understand in what case the man is curable, in what case he is not. In case one treateth *a man* unsoftly in the early stage of the disease, then the sore first mounteth into the shoulders and into the breast. Soon must one let blood from a vein, if the sore continue on the breast alone, or in the upper belly, or in the midriff; then must one give *the man* a wort drink, and take sweet water with oil put into a swines bladder, and warm the sore therewith.

## xlvii.

Leechdoms which have the power of thinning and of making small, for the bodies which suffer the heat, *either* moderate or strong, and how one must apply a swines bladder to them. Take *hore*hound, and wax, and oil, mingle or rub together equal quantities of all, that it, *the mixture*, may be one ; smear therewith, and put *also* on a cloth *and* apply. For sore of side, again :

[1] Πάντα ὀναπτύεται κεχρωσμένα.   Alex. Trall.

lauþer cþoppan ʒebeat ſmæle ⁊ ſeoð on huniʒe leʒe
on clað oþþe ōn ſel þ hıt ealle þa ſıðan ⁊ þ ſaſ oſeſ-
lıcʒe leʒe ōn ⁊ beþe mıð þy ⁊ beleʒe æſteſ þæſe
beþınʒe mıð hatte pulle · ⁊ bınd peaxhlaſ ōn · ʒıſ þ
ſaſ þonne ne ſıe þe læſſe teolı þonne mıð ʒkeſe ōn
þa ſculðſu · ⁊ ſceaſſa þæſ hıt ſaſ ſıe ſpıþuſt · ⁊ ſeſeſ
þ blob oſ ſpıðe · ⁊ ʒıſ hıt þonne ʒıt ſpıþoſ ſaſ ſie ·
ne ðo þu þonne mıð ſealte þa blæðſan ōn · ſıc on ſoſe-
peaſðe þa aðle þenðen þ ſaſ læſt ſie. Ruðan ʒeſeoð
on ele oððe on pıne · ⁊ ðıle ſmıſſe þa ſıðan mıð þy
neoðlıce · ⁊ beþe mıð hneſcſe pulle ⁊ mıð þy ele ⁊
ðo þonne þa blæðſan ōn · ðo peaſm ſealt to ðo eſc
ſeoſoþa ōn ſealt ſſæteſ ðo on þa blæðſan aleʒe on þ
ſaſ ðo þıſ þſeo nıht.

## .XLVIII.

Ʒıſ þaſ ſultumaſ ne ſyn helþe · læt[1] bloð þonne
ōn æðſe ōſ earme næſ on þa healſe þe þ ſaſ bıþ · ⁊
þa pambe mān ſceal clænſıan[2] mıð ſmeþe pyſtðſence.
Eſt eoſoſſpıneſ[3] cpeað þ mōn ſınt ōn puða ʒemylte
ōn ſæteſe aſeoh ðo on hıſ ðſıncan · oþþe ðſıʒe ʒemenʒ
⁊ ʒeʒnıð on hıſ ðſıncan þ hælþ þæſe ſıðan ſaſ. Eſt
celenðſeſ[4] ſæð ʒeʒnıð ⁊ ſeoþ on hunıʒe oþ þ hıt ðıcce
ſie · ʒenīm þæſ þonne ōn moſʒenne ⁊ ōn æſenne þſeo
cucleſ mæl ſele to þıcʒenne.

## .XLVIIII.

Læcedomaſ ⁊ peaxſealſa ⁊ ſſeaſſunʒa pıþ ſıðan ſaſe ·
⁊ hſæt hım ſıe to þıcʒenne. Eſc þu ſcealt þonne þu
on þam ſculðſum tylıſt bloð teon ſpıðe ōn þæſe ſıðan

---

[1] Trallianus, p 85, ed. Lutet, recommends φλεβοτομία and the κά-
θαρσιν τῆς κοιλίας, after Hippokrates.

[2] clærnian, MS.
[3] Marcellus, col. 351, n.
[4] Marcellus, col. 351, c.

take leaves of rue and bunches of laurel heads, beat them small and seethe them in honey, lay on a cloth or on a skin so that it may overlie all the side and the sore; lay on and foment with that *mixture*, and cover after the fomenting with hot wool, and bind on a cake of wax. Then if the sore be not the less, then draw with a *cupping* glass on the shoulders, and scarify where the sore is most, and scrape the blood off thoroughly; and if it then be still more sore, do not thou then apply the bladder with salt, but *do this* in the early period of the disease, while the sore is least. Seethe rue in oil or in wine, and dill; anoint the sore with that, of necessity, and foment with nesh wool and with oil, and then apply the bladder: add warm salt, put bran also into salt water; put it on the bladder: lay it on the sore, do this for three nights.

### xlviii.

If these remedies are no help, then let blood on a vein from the arm, *but* not on the side on which the sore is, and the wamb shall be cleansed with a smooth wort drink. Again, melt in water the dropping of a boar swine, which one findeth in a wood, strain it, put it into his drink: or dry it, mingle and rub it into his drink, that will heal the sore of the side. Again, rub *small* some seed of coriander, and seethe it in honey, till it be thick, then take of that, at morning and at even, three spoon measures; give *the man* this to swallow.

### xlix.

Leechdoms and wax salves and scarifyings for sore of side, and what *the sick* are to take for diet. Also thou shalt when thou drawest blood on the shoulders, draw it strongly on the side, and for about three days

⁊ ymb .iii. niht fceappian ⁊ peax rcalfe ⁊ ele on lec-
ȝean ⁊ rellan ðpencaɲ þa þu ƿite þ̵ ƿið rið pæɲce

fcylen · ȝif þe pyɲt ðpenc ne limpe rele ftɲanȝne ·
leohte mettaf þieȝe ⁊ ȝeɲeap bɲoþu [1] ⁊ ȝeɲeape pyɲan
⁊ ȝeɲleȝen æȝɲu ⁊ bɲead ȝebɲocen on hāt ƿæteɲ [2]
pɲeƿmelan [3] aðon of rcellum mið pyɲūm.

### .L.

Eft ƿiþ rıðan rape betonican leaf ȝeɲeoð ōn ele ⁊
ȝebɲyte aleȝe ōn þa rıðan.

### .LI.

Þeɲ æfteɲ fint lunȝen aðla laðlicu tacn ⁊ hɲaɲan
fio cume ⁊ hu mōn læcedomaf ƿiþ þon [4] pyɲcean rcyle ·
bɲeoft aðlaƿen ⁊ rap þeoh ⁊ lıpa · ⁊ hīm fe maȝa
micla þinðeþ ⁊ ban ⁊ bæt rela fpellenðe yfcle fpılaf
unfelenðe ⁊ hine ðpeceþ þyɲpe hɲoftan ⁊ hīm ōn þam
hɲoftan hɲılum loɲað fio ftemn.    Smıɲe þone mannan
mıð ele · ⁊ eac mıð nıppe pulle beþe þa rıðan ⁊ jub ·
⁊ betɲeox fculðɲum hɲene æp æȝenne · læt þonne on
pefan · æfteɲ þōn læt him bloð of þam halan haþolıp-
þan In opne þæɲ him ne eȝle fyɲ · ȝif þu him to rela
lætft ne bıþ him þonne feopeɲ pen.    Þyɲe hīm bɲıf
ōf rcalpyɲte moɲan · ⁊ of fleaþan pyɲte · ⁊ hunan

⁊ ðıle raeð reoþ þaɲ on butɲan rele etan colne on
moɲȝen ⁊ on niht bɲıf hif mete ƿiþ ele ⁊ eal hıf
ðɲınca fıe cealð.    Ɵaneȝum men lunȝen ɲotað on
ðɲınce · [5] he fpıɲleɲ ðpenceef ⁊ rela henne æȝɲu ȝeɲlea
on an fæt fpa hɲıeap · ȝeþþeɲe þonne ⁊ þieȝe ⁊ ȝemenȝe æp ƿiþ fletan ⁊ nan opep molcen þieȝe.    Leoht
ðpene · ȝenīm ȝaȝellan fyl ōn pyɲte læt þonne hɲon

---

[1] Πτισσάνη, Alex. Tr.

[2] ψίχες, crumbs, Alex. Trall., p. 87,
line 15, ed. Lutet.

[3] Marcellus, col. 351, B.

[4] þon, we expected a feminine.

[5] The stop is misplaced thus in
MS.

scarify and lay on cerote and oil, and give such drinks as thou knowest are suitable for side pain. If a *mild* wort drink do not suffice, give a strong one. Let *the man* take light meats and juicy broths, and juicy peas, and beaten eggs, and bread broken in hot water, *and* periwinkles removed from the shells, with peas.

## l.

Again, for sore of side, seethe in oil leaves of betony, and bruise them, lay them on the side.

## li.

1. Hereinafter are *set forth* the loathly tokens of lung disease, and whence it cometh, and how one must work leechdoms against it. The breast is upblown, and the thigh and muscle is sore, and *the mans* maw distendeth much, and his legs and his feet swell much with evil unfeeling swellings, and a drier cough vexes him, and in the cough at whiles his voice is gone. Smear the man with oil, and also warm the sides and the ribs with new wool, and between the shoulders, a little before evening, then let *the oil* remain on him; and after that let him blood from the sound elbow " in an oven, where the fire cannot harm him;" if thou lettest him too much blood, there will be no hope of his life. Work him a brewit from roots of wall wort, and from fleath wort, and *hore*hound, and dill seed; seethe these in butter; give him *this brewit* to eat cold in a morning; and at night dress his meat with oil, and let all his drink be cold. In many a man the lung decayeth. Let him drink some emetic drink, and beat up many hens eggs into a vessel, all raw, then let him curdle it and eat it, and previously mingle with curds, and let him take no other milk diet. A light drink; take gagel, *or sweet gale*, boil it in wort *of beer*, then let it stand a little, remove the

ȝeſtandan do oꝼ þa ȝaȝellan do þonne nıpne ȝılt ōn
bepꝛeoh þonne þ hıt alıebbe ꝼell · do þonne eolenan ·
ꝉ ꝛeꝛmod · ꝉ betonıcan · ꝉ meꝛce · ꝉ antꝛan to ꝛele
dꝛıncan.

ȝepẏꝛc beopyꝛt ƿıþ lunȝen ꝛunde · ꝉ banꝛyꝛt ſeo
þe hæbbe cꝛoppan ȝecnua þa ꝛyꝛta tꝛa ꝼyl on butꝛan. dꝛenc ƿıð lunȝen adle ȝenı̄m hındheoloþan leaꝼ ·
ꝉ hınd beꝛȝean · ꝉ ȝaꝛclıꝼan heoꝛbꝛemleſ¹ leaꝼ ꝼyl
on ꝛyꝛte læt dꝛıncan.

Ƿıþ lunȝen adle · hınd beꝛȝean leaꝼ ꝉ hꝛeodeſ ſpıꝛ
ꝛeade hōꝼan · bīꝛceoꝛꝛyꝛt dolhꝛunan · neꝼtan on cle-
num pætꝛe ealle þaꝛ ꝛyꝛta ꝛylle ꝉ dꝛınce. Ƿıþ lunȝen
adle ꝛyꝛc ꝛealꝼe on buteꝛan ꝉ þıȝe ōn meolcum · nım
bꝛune ꝛyꝛt meodoꝛyꝛt · beꝛc ꝛaȝo · neꝼte · ȝaꝛclıꝼe.

fol. 100 a, Ƿıþ lunȝen adle bꝛune ꝛyꝛt eneoþholen · betonıca ·
ꝛudu meꝛce ſuꝛe · eoꝛoꝛ ꝼeaꝛn · acumba · ȝaꝛclıꝼe ·
tꝛeȝen bꝛemlaꝛ · uouelle · ƿad · ꝛyꝛc to dꝛence ꝉ to
ꝛealꝼe. ȝenım eoꝼoꝛꝼeaꝛn ȝecnuꝛa ꝉ aꝛylle on butꝛan
do þa ꝛealꝼe ōn aꝛyllede ȝate meolūc ꝉ þıȝe on nealıt
neꝛtıȝ · ꝉ on uꝼan mete. Dꝛenc ƿıþ dꝛuȝꝛe lunȝenne · holen ꝛınde · ꝉ .v. leaꝼan · dıle · ꝉ ꝛedıc ȝeenua to duſte · ꝉ ōꝼ ȝeōt mıd ealoð ꝛele dꝛıncan
ȝelome. Eꝼt dꝛenc · maꝛubıan · ꝉ betonıcan · meꝛce
ꝛude · ſuꝛaꝛuldꝛe ꝛınde · ꝛlah þoꝛn ꝛınde dꝛınce ōn
ealað. bꝛıꝛ ƿıþ lunȝen adle · ōntꝛan · eolonan · maꝛubıan · penꝛyꝛt · þa elıꝼıhtan · ꝛude · meꝛce · pıꝛoᵹ ·
hunıȝ. Ƿıþ dꝛuȝꝛe lunȝenne · ōꝼ ꝛealꝛyꝛte moꝛan · ꝉ
ōꝼ ꝼleoþan ꝛyꝛte · hunan · dıleꝛ ꝛæd · ſeoþ on butꝛan
ꝛele etan colne on moꝛȝenne · ꝉ on nıht · ꝉ bꝛıꝛ hıꝛ
mete ƿıþ ele. Eꝼt nı̄m alꝛeꝛ ꝛınde ſeoþ on pætꝛe oþ
þ þæꝛ pæteꝛeſ ꝛıe þꝛıddan dæl onbeꝛylleð ꝛele þonne

---

¹ heoꝛbꝛem bꝛemleꝛ, MS.

gagel, then add new yeast, then wrap it up that it
may rise well, then add helenium, and wormwood, and
betony, and marche, and ontre; give *the man this* to
drink.

2. Work together beewort, for a lung wound, and that
bonewort which hath bunches of flowers; pound the
two worts, boil in butter. A drink for lung disease;
take leaves of hindheal, and hind berries, *or raspberries*,
and garclife, *or agrimony*, and leaves of the hip
bramble, *or dogrose;* boil them in wort *of beer;* make
*the man* drink.

3. For lung disease; leaves of hind berries, *or raspberries*, a spike of a reed, red hove, bishopwort, dol-
hrune, nepeta; let *the man* boil all these worts in clean
water, and drink. For lung disease, work a salve in
butter, and take *the same* in milk; take brownwort,
meadwort, birch lichen, nepeta, garclife, *or agrimony*.
For lung disease; brown wort, knee holly, betony, wild
marche, sorrel, everfern, oakum (ashes), garclife, the
two brambles, *the dogrose and blackberry*, wowelle,
woad; work *these* into a drink and into a salve. Take
everfern, pound it, boil it in butter, put "the salve"
into boiled goats milk, and let *the man* take it at
night fasting, and on the top of that *his* meat. A
drink for a dry lung; pound to dust rind of holly and
cinqfoil, dill and radish, and pour them all over with
ale; give *the man that* to drink frequently. Again,
a drink; let him drink in ale, marrubium and betony,
marche, rue, rind of crab apple tree, sloe thorn rind.
A brewit for lung disease; ontre, helenium, marrubium,
wenwort, that *namely* which is bulbed, rue, marche,
pepper, honey. For a dry lung; some root of wallwort,
and of fleath wort, *horehound*, seed of dill; seethe these
in butter, give *the brewit to the man* to eat cold, in
the morning and at night, and dress his meat with
oil. Again, take rind of alder, seethe in water till a
third part of the water be boiled away, then give *the*

cælic fulne to ðpinceanne on þpiy piþaf · læt finle dægþepine betpeonum. Piþ lunzen punde · þæp blacan ipizep cjoppena ꝼ copna æpeſt þpieo on dæz .v. on mopzene ſcoꝼan þy þpiddan dæze þonne nizon · þonne .xi. þonne þpeottyne · þonne ꝼiꝼtyne · þonne ſcoꝼontyne · þonne nizantyne · þonne .xxi. pele ſpa æꝼtep dazum dpincan on pine. Eꝼt piþ lunzen punde betomican pyl on pine pele dpincan. Piþ þon ilcan zenim muzepypt iþepeapde · ꝼ bpunepypt pyl on butepan. Piþ lunzen adle zenim cpican · ꝼ ac pinde · ꝼ zapiclpan zeenupa tozædepe · bepylle þonne [1] þpiddan dæl on hpætene pynte ſupe æꝼtep amylte butepan.

Eꝼt zenim bpiune pypt · ꝼ bipccop pypt · puðu mepce · puðu cepꝼillan · coꝼop ꝼeapin · hind hioloþe · acumba · attoplaþe · peaðe hoꝼe · ꝼ mædepe. Piþ lunzen adle · dolhpune · ꝼ æꝼeiþe moþopeapð · ꝼ bpiune pypt · ꝼ peaðe hoꝼe · ꝼ peaðe netlan apylle on hunize ꝼ on cubutepan ſup on meolcum. Eꝼt zeniphim pædicep .iii. ſnæda · ꝼ bpaðe leacep zelice ꝼ ſpicep .iii. do þ .iii. dazaſ oþþe nizon.

### .LII.

To ſpip dpince .vi. copn alpan .xxx. lybcopna ꝼ þa zpeatan pypt moþopeapðe · hpepꝼe hatte dpize þa on ſunnan ꝼ ellen pinde iþepeapðe dpize eac · ꝼ zetpiꝼula ſpiþe ſmæle · do healpne bollan caloð to · ꝼ ſpete mið hunize · do hpon butepan · ꝼ pipopep hpon · ꝼ zehæte þ calu ꝼ do hpon pealtep to. Eꝼt piepimoð ꝼ coloman keppe kæt ſtandan tpa niht on caloþ dpince þonne. Eꝼt zlædene · hoꝼe ꝼleotpypt cnupa on calaþ ꝼ zeſpet dpince þonne. Zip mon hine bpiece oꝼep zemet to ſpipanne ſiþþan him ſpip dpienc oꝼ ſie · zeniphim ꝼættep ꝼkepcep pele tpa ſnæda. Pece dpience · clene þone læp-

---

*man* a chalice full to drink at three times ; leave
always a days space between. For lung wound ; of
the berry bunches of the black ivy and of its grains,
at first three a day, five on the morrow, seven the
third day, then nine, then eleven, then thirteen, then
fifteen, then seventeen, then nineteen, then twenty-one ;
give them so, according to the days, to be drunk in
wine. Again, for lung wound, boil betony in wine,
give it to be drunk. For the same ; take the netherward part of mugwort and brownwort, boil in butter.
For lung disease ; take quitch, and oak rind, and agrimony ; pound them together, then boil to the third part
in wheaten wort *of beer* ; sip afterwards some melted
butter.

4. Again, take brownwort, and bishopwort, wild
marche, wood chervil, everfern, hindheal, oakum (ashes),
attorlothe, red hove, and madder. For lung disease ;
dollrune, and the netherward part of æferth, and brownwort, and red hove, and red nettle ; boil them in honey
and in cows butter ; sip this in milk. Again, take
three slices of radish, and the like of broad leek, and
of bacon three : do that for three days or nine.


lii.

1. For an emetic ; six grains of aloes, thirty of libcorns, and the netherward part of great wort, wherve
it hight, dry it in the sun, and elder rind, the netherward part, dry it also, and triturate it very small, add
half a bowl of ale, and sweeten with honey, add a
little butter, and a little pepper, and heat the ale, and
add a little salt. Again, wormwood, and helenium, but
less of it ; let them stand for two nights in ale, then
let *the man* drink. Again, gladden, hove, float wort,
pound these in ale, and sweeten it, then let *the man*
drink. If a man strain himself overmuch to spew, after
a spew drink is *past* off from him, take some fat flesh,
give him two slices. A weak emetic drink ; helenium,

ꞇan ꝺæl þunȝeſ · cūmmōc ƿyl þ on ealaƿ ꞃele þ lytlum ſuþan þonne hiꞇ col ſie oþ þ he ſƿiꝼe. þ iſ hoꝼe
niþeꝛeaꞃꝺ beſcꝛeꝛen ꞇ ȝecnuaꝺ · ꞇ ellen ƿyꝛꞇꞇꝛuman
ꝛinꝺe aꝛæꞃc þa clæne ꞇ beſcꝛeꝛene · aꝛenꝺ þonne oꝼ

5 þam ƿyꝛꞇꞇꝛuman · ꞇ ȝecnua ȝoꞇꝛoþan · ꞇ ƿenƿyꝛꞇ ſio
ƿeaxeþ ōn ealꝺum lanꝺe · ȝeoꞇ þonne hluꞇꞇoꞃ eala ꞇo ·

ƿylle ſƿa ſƿiþꝛe meꝺo ȝiꝼ hebbe heꝛꝛeo ꞇ læꞇ ſꞇanꝺan nihꞇeꝛne aꞃeoh bollan ꝼulne ȝeſƿeꞇe þonne miꝺ
huniȝe aꞃeoh þonne eꝼꞇ · bebinꝺe þonne ȝenoh ƿeaꝛꝛne ·

10 læꞇe þonne ſꞇanꝺan neahꞇeꝛne. Ꝺꝛince þonne on
moꝛȝen ꞇ hine Ꝓꞃēo ƿeaꝛme ꞇ him ꝛlæꝒ beoꝛȝe ſƿiꝼe
ȝeoꝛne · lanȝe he mæȝ on þam ƿyꝛꞇum ſꞇanꝺan ꞇ
þonne hine mōn ꝺꝛincan ƿille ōnhꝛꝛeꝛe eꝼꞇ. Ƿyꝛce
þonne in þæꝛ bollan ꝼulne ſꝒa he æꝛ Ꝓoꝛhꞇe · ȝiꝼ he

15 ſie ꞇo unſꝒiꝺ ȝeȝꝛnꝺe he ꝼiꝼꞇiȝ lyb coꝛna ȝeſƿeꞇe
þonne. Ƿyꝛce ſꝒiꝺꝛan ȝiꝼ he Ꝓille · aꝺelꝼe þa ȝꝛeaꞇan
ƿyꝛꞇ aſcꝛeꝒ þa ȝꝛeaꞇan ꝛinꝺe ōꝼ ȝecnuꝛa þonne ſmæle
ȝeōꞇ þonne hluꞇꞇoꝛ eala ōn. Ꞇe ꝺꝛenc biþ ſꝒa ꝛelꝛa
ſꝒa þ ealu ꝛelꝛe biþ. ꞆꝒiꝼe ꝺꝛenc · ȝenim ellenꝛinꝺe

20 niþeꝛeaꝛꝺe · ꞇ hāmƿyꝛꞇe ꞇ hunꝺꞇeonꞇiȝ lybcoꝛna ȝecnua ſꝒiþe ƿel ealle þa ƿyꝛꞇa ꝺo on ealo menȝe þonne ·
ȝenim þonne Ꝓah mela hæꝛleſ oþþe alꝒeꞃ aꝛiꝼꞇ þonne
ꝼul clæne ꞇela micle hanꝺ ꝼulle ꝺo on ȝemanȝ læꞇ

neahꞇeꝛne ſꞇanꝺan ahlyꞇꞇꝛa ſꝒiþe ƿel · ȝeſƿeꞇ miꝺ
huniȝe ȝeꝺꝛinc ſcenc ꝼulne ꞇela micelne. ȝiꝼ ꞃe ꝺꝛenc
nelle ōꝼ ȝeꝒīn ōnꝛeꝺ ꞃelle ōn ealaꝺ ꝺꝛincan ſcenc ꝼulne
ƿeaꝛꝛeſ ꞃona biþ ꝛel. Ƿyꝛc ſꝒiꝛꝺꝛenc. ȝenim lybcoꝛn
ꞇ ꝒiꝒoꝛ coꝛn ꞇ hꝛiꞇ cꝛuꝺa ꞇ alꝒan ȝꝛinꝺ ꞇo ꝺuſꞇe
þa ƿyꝛꞇa ſꝒiꝼe · ꝺo on beoꝛ ſꝒa on Ꝓīn ſꝒa on þeoꝛꝼe

the least bit of thung *or aconite,* cammock *or peuce-danum;* boil that in ale; when it is cool, give *the man* that to sip little by little, till he spew. . . . that is, hove, the nether part of it scraped and pounded, and the rind of elder roots; wash them clean, and *have them* scraped, then rend *the rind* away from the roots, and pound goutweed, and wenwort, that *namely* which waxeth in old land, then pour thereon clear ale, boil *it,* or strongish mead if thou have it, wrap it up and let it stand or the space of a night, strain out a bowl full, then sweeten with honey, then strain again, then bind it up warm enough, then let it stand for a nights space; then let him drink it the morning, and let him wrap himself up warm, and let him very earnestly beware of sleep. Long may *the drink* stand upon the worts, and when a man hath a mind to drink it, let him shake it up again: then let him work thereinto a bowl full, as he before wrought it; if it be too weak let him rub small fifty libcorns,[1] *and* then sweeten it. Let him work it stronger if he will; delve up the great wort, scrape away the great rind, then pound it small; then pour clear ale upon it: the drink is the better according as the ale is better. An emetic; take the netherward part of the rind of elder, and home-wort, and a hundred libcorns, pound them very well, put all the worts into ale, then mix; then take fine meal of the hazel or alder, then sift it full clean, put in a good large handful amidst *the rest,* let it stand for a nights space, clear it very thoroughly, sweeten with honey, drink a good mickle cup full. If the drink will not *be thrown* off, take onred, give in ale a cup full of it warm *to the man* to drink; soon he will be well. Work a spew drink *thus;* take libcorns, and pepper-corns, and mastich, and aloes, grind the worts to dust thoroughly, put into beer, or into wine, or into skim

---

[1] Seeds of *Momordica elaterium.*

meoluc ꝟ þu þaꞃa oꝼeꞃꞃa naꝼꝥeꞃ næbbe · ꝟ þu on
ꝥine ꝛyꞃce oþþe ón meolce ꝛeꞃꝥeꞇ mꞇꝺ hunꝛe ꝺꞃꞇnce
ꞇela mꞇcelne ꞃcene ꝼulne.

Spꞇꝥe ꝺꞃꞇenc ꝥyꞃe óꝼ beoꞃe ꝺo coꞃꞇ ꞇo ⁊ alꝥan ⁊
lybcoꞃꞇna ꝼꞇꝼꞇyne þaꞃa oꝥeꞃꞇa ꝛelꞇce.

Spꞇꝥe ꝺꞃꞇenc hamꝥyꞃꞇe .III. ꞃnæꝺa · ⁊ ellen ꞃꞇnꝺe be-
ꞃenꝺe ꝛelꞇce mꞇcel .XXV. lybcoꞃꞇna[1] ꝛeꝛmꞇꝺ ꝺo hunꝛeꞃ
ꞃꝥꞇce an ꞃnæꝺ ꞃꞇe on eꞇe þonne mꞇꝺ cucleꞃe ón ꞃuꝥ
haꞇeꞃ ꝥæꞇeꞃeꞃ oꝸꝺe cealꝺeꞃ. Ꝥꞇꝼ ꝺꞃꞇenc óꝼ men nelle ·
ꝛenꞇm meꞃce · ⁊ ceꝥꝼꞇllan ꞃeoþ ꞃꝥꞇþe ón ꝥæꞇꝥe ꝺo ꞃealꞇ
ꞇo ꝺꞃꞇnce þonne. Ꝥꞇꝼ hꞇne mnan ꝥæꞃce · ꝛenꞇm nꞇꝛeꞃ
calaꝸ amꝥeꞃ ꝼulne ꝺo hanꝺ ꝼulle hamꝥyꞃꞇe ón · læꞇ
on hebban ꝺꞃꞇnce oþ þ þu ꞃꝥꞇꝥe · ꞃꞇꞇꝛ þonne ꝼeþꝥe
ón muꝸ ꞇeoh þa ꝛelleꞃꞇꝥan ꞇꞇꞇ ꝺꞃꞇne eꝼꞇ Sona :.

fol. 102 b.

Nꞇm ꞃcamonꞇam þ þenꞇꝛ ꝛeꝥeꝛe ⁊ ꝛeꝛmꞇꝺ ꞃꞇnæle ⁊
hꞃeꞃ henne æꝛ ꞃꝥꞇꝸe ꞃealꞇ ꝺo þa ꝥyꞃꞇ ón ne læꞇ ꝛeyꞃ-
nan þ æꝛ ac ꞃꞇuꝥ. Ꝥyꞃꞇꝺꞃꞇenc · ꞃcamonꞇam ꝛeceoꞃ þuꞃ
þꞃec on ꞇu ꝺo hꞃoꞃ ón þꞇne ꞇunꝛan ꝛꞇꝼ hꞇo hꞃꞇꞇe oꝼeꞃ-
þꞃeꝛꝺeþ ꞃꝥa meluc þonne hꞇo bꞇþ ꝛoꝸ · ꝛeꝛmꞇꝺ þonne
on ꞇꞃeoꝥenum ꝼæꞇe næꞃ on nanum oþꞃum mꞇꝺ ꞃꞇꞇccan
oþþe mꞇꝺ hæꝼꞇe ꝺo óꝼ þ mꝺn ꝛeꝛmꞇꝺan ne maꝛe þ
bꞇþ ꝛeuꞃꞇnen · ꝺo caulꞇceꞃ ón .II. ꝺꞃoꝥan oꝸꝺe þþy ·
oþþe eleleaꝼeꞃ ꞃꞇelan ꝛeꞃyl ꞇoꞃꝺmne · ꝛꞇꝼ hꞇo bꞇþ ꝛoꝸ ·
ꝺꞃꞇenc bꞇꝸ ón penꞇnꝛe · ꝛꞇꝼ mæꞇꞃa bꞇꝸ on oꝸꞃum heal-
ꞃum oꝸꝺe ón ꞇꞃam auuꞇꝼeþꞃꞇmænemæ.[2] Spꞇꝥe ꝺꞃꞇenc ·
hoꞃan ⁊ onꞃeꝸ · ⁊ ellen ꞃꞇnꝺe ꝛeenua ꞇo Somne ellen
læꞃꞇ · ꝺo þonne ꞇo .XXX. ꝥꞇꞃoꞃ coꞃꞃna ꝛeꞃꝥeꞇ mꞇꝺ hunꝛe
ꞃele ꝺꞃꞇncan.

---

[1] cybcoꞃꞇna, MS.
[2] Read auꝸ ꝛꞇꝼ ꞇꞃel þꞃꞇm ac ne
ma ? Yet the letters of the text
are quite legible and clear.

milk, if thou have neither of the others; if thou work it in wine or in milk, sweeten it with honey; let *the man* drink a good mickle cup full.

2. Work a spew drink of beer, add costmary, and aloes, and fifteen libcorns, of the others similarly.

3. An emetic; of homewort three pieces, and rend up elder rind, the same quantity, twenty-five libcorns, rub *them to dust*, and of honey as much as would be one piece *or proportion*, then eat thereof with a spoon, sip some water hot or cold. If *such* a draught will not *pass* from a man, take marche and chervil, seethe them thoroughly in water, add salt, then let *the man drink*. If there is inward pain, take a jug full of new ale, add a hand full of homewort, have *the jug* held up and drink till thou spew; then poke a feather into thy mouth; draw the bad matter out, drink again soon. Take scammony, so much as may weigh a penny, and rub it small, and half cook a hens egg, salt it thoroughly, put the wort into it, let not the egg congulate, but sip it. A wort drink; choose scammony thus, break it in two, put a bit on thy tongue, if it bursteth out white as milk, then it is good; rub it then in a treen vessel, not in any other, with a spoon or with a handle, remove what cannot be rubbed down, that *part* is congulated, add two or three drops of κωλικόν,[1] or boil together *with it* a stalk of olive leaf: if it be good the dose will be one pennyweight; if moderately good, one and a half or two pennyweights; if bad, three; no more than that. A spew drink; hove, and onred, and elder rind; pound these together, *put* least *of* elder, then add thirty peppercorns, sweeten with honey, give *the man* to drink.

---

[1] " Est etiam medicamentum . . . " quod κωλικὸν nominatur... magis " prodest potui datum." Celsus, IV.

xiv. See the mention of θηριακὴν. Book II. lvi. 4.

.LIII.

To leohtum ꝺꞃence ælꝼþonan ȝyþꞃiꝼan · betonican
þa cluꝼyhtan penꝼyꞃt · coꞃoþꝺꞃotan · heah hꞃoloþan ·
ealehtꞃan · eolonan ꞇꞃa ꞅnæꝺa · claꞇan · peȝbꞃæꝺan ·
ónꞇꞃe · cꞃopleác to pæꞇan healꝼ haliȝ pæꞇeꞃ · healꝼ
ꞃꞮe hluꞇꞇoꞃ eala. To leohꞇum ꝺꞃence · biꞅceop pyꞃꞇ
elehꞇꞃe · peꞃꞮmoꝺ · pulꝼeꞃ camb pyl ón meolcum ꞅꞃꞮþe
aꝼꞃꞮnȝ þonne þuꞃꞮh claꝺ ꝺꞃyp ealo ón oꝺꝺe ꝼín ꞃele
ꞅuꝼan. Leohꞇ ꝺꞃenc biꞅceop pyꞃꞇ onꞇꞃe eolone ·
maꞃubꞮe · ꝺꞃeoꞃꞷe ꝺꞃoꞅꞇle · meꞃꞮce · æꞃꞅꞃꞃoꞇꞮ · betonica ·
heah hꞃoloꝺe · hꞮnꝺ hꞃoloþe · ȝaȝꞮlle · mínꞇe · ꝺꞮle · ꝼꞮnul ·
ceꞃꝼꞮlle · ꝺꞃꞮnce on ealuꝺ ȝeꞃoꞃꞮhꞇe. UnꞅꞃꞮꞃol ꝺꞃenc
biꞅceop pyꞃꞇ · peꞃꞮmoꝺ · aꞇꞇoꞃlaꝺe · ꞅꞃꞃꞮnȝ pyꞃꞇ ȝyꝺ-
ꞃꞮꝼe · ꝺꞃeoꞃꞷe ꝺꞃoꞅꞇle · ꝼꞮnul · ȝebeaꞇen pꞮpoꞃ · ȝeꝺo þa
pyꞃꞇa ealle on an ꝼæꞇ ȝeꝺo þonne ealꝺ ꝼín hluꞇꞇoꞃ
on ꝺone ꝺꞃenc oꝺꝺe ꞅꞃꞮꝺe ȝoꝺ meꝺo ꝺꞃꞮnce þonne þone
ꝺꞃenc neahꞇneꞃꞇꞮȝ · ꝫ ꞅpa beꞇeꞃe hꞮm íꞅ ꞅpa he óꝼꞇoꞃ
ꝺꞃꞮnce ꝫ eꞇe þone bꞃꞮp þe heꞃ áꞃꞃꞮꞇen Ɪꞅ · byꞃꞮȝ eolonan ómꝼꞃan · onꞇꞃe · ȝoꞇꞃoꝼe hꞃꞮomȝeallan · ȝeꞅcaꝺ-
pyꞃꞇ moþoꞃeaꞃꝺe · ȝecnua þa pyꞃꞇa ꝺo ꞅealꞇ ón pyl on
buꞇꞃan. Eꝼꞇ unꞅꞃꞮꞃol ꝺꞃenc · biꞅceoppyꞃꞇ · ȝyþꞃꞮꝼe ·
ꞅꞃꞃꞮnȝ pyꞃꞇ .v. ꝺaȝaꞅ ꝺꞃꞮnce æꞇꞅomne ꞅꞮmle on moꞃȝne
ꞃoꞃꞃlæꞇe oꞃꞃe ꝼꞮꝼe .v. ꝺꞃꞮnce. Leohꞇ ꝺꞃenc ȝením
peꞃꞮmoꝺ · ꝫ betonican · ꝫ hꞃoloþan¹ læꞅꞇ ꝫ hꞮnꝺ hꞃoloþan
ꝺo on eala. SꞇꞮlle ꝺꞃenc · betonican · eolone · peꞃꞮmoꝺ ·
onꞇꞃe · hune · elehꞇꞃe · penꝼyꞃꞇ · ȝeaꞃꞃe · ꝺꞃeoꞃꞷe
ꝺꞃoꞅꞇle · aꞇꞇoꞃlaꝺe ꞃelꝺmoꞃꞮu.

.LIIII.

ÞꞮþ ꞮnꞅꞇꞮce · ȝením aꞃꞃoꞇanan · ꝫ aꞇꞇoꞃlaꝺan · biꞅceop
pyꞃꞇ þa ꞅuþeꞃꞮnan · ȝehæꞇe on beoꞃe ꝫ ꞅuꞃe. Ȝiꝼ ꞅꞇꞮce

_____

¹ Read ch hꞃoloþan.

### liii.

For a light drink, *use* elfthon, githrife, betony, the
cloved wenwort, everthroat, horse heal, lupins, two proportions of helenium, clote, waybroad, ontre, cropleek,
for liquid let half be holy water, half clear ale.  For
a light drink; bishopwort, lupin, wormwood, wolfscomb, boil thoroughly in milk, then wring through a
cloth, drop ale or wine upon it, give it *the man* to
sip.  A light drink; bishopwort, ontre, helenium, marrubium, dwarf dwostle, marche, ashthroat, betony, horse
heal, hind heal, gagel *or sweet gale*, mint, dill, fennel,
chervil, let *the man* drink *them* wrought up in ale.   A
not emetic drink; bishopwort, wormwood, attorlothe,
springwort, githrife, pennyroyal, fennel, beaten pepper,
put all the worts into one vessel, then put clear old
wine into the drink or very good mead, then let the
man drink the draught after his nights fast, and it is
the better for him according as he oftener drinketh, and
let him eat the brewit which is here written; borough-
helenium, ompre *or sorrel*, ontre, goutweed, raingall,
the nether part of oxeye, pound the worts, add salt,
boil in butter.  Again, a not emetic drink; bishopwort,
githrife, springwort; let *the man* drink for five days
together, always in the morning, let him leave it alone
for other five, and drink for five *more*.  A light drink;
take wormwood, and betony, and horse heal, the least
*of this*, and hind heal, put them into ale.  A quieting
drink; betony, helenium, wormwood, ontre, *horehound*,
lupin, wenwort, yarrow, dwarf dowstle, attorlothe, fieldmore *or carrot*.

### liv.

For an inward stitch; take abrotanon and attorlothe,
the southern bishopwort, *that is, ammi*, let *the man*
heat them in beer and sip.  If there be a stitch, but

butan inноðe ſie · ᵹenim þonne þa ꞃeaðan netlan ꞇ
ealðe ꞃapan ᵹebeat toſomne ꞇ ſmiꞃe mið ꞇ beþe mið
to ꝼyꞃe.

. LV.

Dꞃenc ᵹiꝼ món innan ꝼoꞃhæꝼð ſie · ᵹecnua eolonan
ꝥyl ón ealoð ꞇ betonican · peꞃmoð ꞇ þa cluꝼihtan [1]
ꝥenꝥyꞃt ꞃele ðꞃincan.   Ꝥiþ Incoþe coſteꞃ ᵹoðne ðæl ·
ꞇ ꝼinoleꞃ ꞃæðeꞃ oþeꞃ ſpile ᵹebeat ſmæle ꞇ ᵹeᵹnið to
ðuſte.   Ᵹenim þær cucleꞃ ꝼulne · ᵹeðo ón ealð ꝥín oþþe
caꞃꝥen ðꞃince þonne neahtneꞃtiᵹ þꞃy ðaᵹaꞃ.

Ꝥiþ ꞃæꝥcoþe biꞃceoꝥꝥyꞃt · peꞃmoð · betonica · þeðíc ·
meꞃce · coſt · ꞃuðan ꞃæð ꝥyꞃc to ðꞃence.

. LVI.

Ᵹiꝼ món ne mæᵹe ūtᵹeᵹan · ᵹením uman · ꞇ eac
ᵹeꞃꝥte hanð ꝼulle · ꞇ meðmicelne bollan ꝼulne ealað ·
beꝥyl þꞃimme ꝥ ealo on þæꞃe ꝥyꞃte ðꞃince þonne
neahtneꞃtiᵹ.   Eꝼt ᵹiꝼ món ſyþ ᵹaꝼleāc on henne
bꞃoþe ꞇ ꞃelð ðꞃincan þonne to læꞇ hio ꝥ ꞃaꞃ.   Eꝼt
ᵹate meoluc ꞇ eceð ſeoþ æꞇᵹæðeꞃe ꞃele ðꞃincan.   Eꝼt
ᵹate meoluc ꞇ huniᵹ ꞇ ꞃealt ꞃele ðꞃincan.   Eꝼt ꝥylle
ᵹeaꞃꞃan on huniᵹe ꞇ ón butꞃan ete þa ꝥyꞃt mið.

Ꝥiþ ūtꞃæꞃce eꝼt eꝼelaꞃtan uꝼeꞃcaꞃðe · ꞃeᵹbꞃæðan
ellenꞃinðe ꞃealt ón ealo ᵹeᵹniðen.
Tácū [2] be utꞃihtan ᵹe on þam uꝼeꞃꞃan hꞃiꝼe ᵹe ón
þam niþeꞃꞃan.   þa aðle món mæᵹ onᵹitan be þam
utᵹanᵹe hꞃiꞃe ꞃe ón ónſyne ſie.   Sum biþ þynne ſum
mið þiccum ꞃætum ᵹeonð ᵹoten.   Sum mið þæꞃ in-
noþeꞃ · ꞇ mið þaꞃa ſmæl þeaꞃma ᵹebꞃocum [3] ᵹemenᵹeð ·

---

[1] The MS. has a stop after cluꞃ-
ihtan.

[2] Nearly as Trallianus, book x.,

cap. i. p. 167, line 27, ed. Lutet.;
book viii., p. 455, ed. Basil.

[3] ξύσματα, Trall.

not in the inwards, then take the red nettle and old
soap, beat them together and smear therewith, and
foment therewith at the fire.


### lv.

1. A drink, if a man be costive within; pound helenium, boil in ale it and betony, *and* the cloved wenwort; give *the man* to drink. For inward disease; a
good deal of costmary, and as much more of seed of
fennel, beat small and rub to dust; take a spoon full
of this, put it into old wine, or wine boiled down one
third, let *the man* drink this after his nights fast for
three days.

2. For sudden sickness; bishopwort, wormwood,
betony, radish, marche, costmary, seed of rue; work
*these* into a drink.


### lvi.

1. If a man may not discharge his bowels; take
" uman," and also a contracted hand full *of it*, and a
moderately mickle bowl full of ale; boil strongly the
ale on the wort, then let *the man* drink it after his
nights fast. Again, if one seetheth garlic on chicken
broth, and giveth it *the man* as a drink, then it removes
the sore. Again, seethe together and give *him* to drink
goats milk, and honey, and salt. Again, let him boil
yarrow in honey and in butter, let him eat the wort
with *those.*

2. For painful evacuation; the upper part of everlasting, waybroad, elder rind, salt, rubbed up into ale.

3. Tokens of dysentery either in the upper part of
the belly or in the nether. One may understand the
disease by the faecal discharged, *observing* what like
it is in appearance: some is thin; some is suffused
with thick humours; some is mingled with fragments of
the inwards, and of the small guts; some is much

rum ſpiðe ȝeꝼylleð mið þoꞃmſe. Sum ſpiðe blodiȝ.
Sum cymð oꝼ þam uꝼeꞃꞃan hꝛiꝼe. Sum oꝼ þam
niþeꞃꞃan · þam þe oꝼ þam uꝼeꞃꞃan hꝛiꝼe cymð ꞃe
utꞃæꝼe þiſ tacn bið · þ̅ ꞃe man ꞃaꝛ ȝeꝼelð æt hiſ
naꝛolan Ᵹ on hiꞃ ſculdꞃum heꝼiȝ ꞃaꞃ · Ᵹ þuꞃſt Ᵹ
unluſt Ᵹ þuꞃh biec þeaꞃꞃin lytel blod dꞃoꝛað;

fol. 104 b.

Sio utꞃiht adl cymð maneȝum æꞃeſt oꝼ to miclum
utȝanȝe · Ᵹ þonne lanȝe hꝛile ne ȝymð mon þæſ oþ þ̅
ꞃe innoþ ꝛyꞃð ȝe onbuꞃꞃen ȝe þuꞃh þ̅ ȝeꞃunbod ·
hꝛilum onȝinneð oꝼ þam midhꝛiꝼe ꞃe iſ betꞃeox þæꞃe
ꞃambe Ᵹ þæꞃe liꝼꞃe · Ᵹ þa ꞃeaꞃ þa ðe beoð ȝemenȝedu
oꝼ mettum ꝛiþ blod Ᵹ ꝛiþ oman ȝeondȝeotaþ þone
Innoþ ꞃyꞃceað yꝼelic utȝanȝ Ᵹ ꝼoꞃ þæꞃe ȝꝛimneꞃꞃe
þaꞃa omena ne mæȝ beon ȝehæꝼð þy ſe mete ac beoþ
ꞃomod þa innoþaſ bedꞃiꝼen þonne ꝛyꞃð þ̅ to utꞃæꞃce.
Du mon þa utꞃꞃꞃenban men ꞃcyle lacnian þam mon
ſceal ꞃellan þa mettaꞃ þa ðe ꞃambe ncaꞃꞃan Ᵹ þam
maȝan ne ſceþþan · cauleꞃ ſeaꝛ · hꝛilum ꝛyſena bꞃoþ
Ᵹ eceð · Ᵹ ꝛoꞃ mid ꝛeȝbꞃædan ȝeſoden Ᵹ ealdne cyſe
ȝeſodenne on ȝate meolce mid þy ſmeꞃꞃe ȝate · hꝛilum
bꞃæde þone cyſe Ᵹ dꞃiȝne hlaꝼ Ᵹ pæteꞃ þ̅ ꞃe ꞃoſe on
ȝeſoden hꝛilum ꞃceaꞃꞃ ꝛin dꞃince. Pync him onleȝena
to clame ȝepoꝛht · beꞃen melo oþþe hꝛæten mid huniȝe
ȝeſoden · mid medmicle   *   *   *   *   *

*   *   *   *   *   *   *   *   *

*Here many folios have been taken from the MS. In the margin "hic lacuna eſt," now erased, may be read.*

filled with ratten; some is very bloody; some cometh
from the upper belly,[1] some from the lower: of that
in which the discharge cometh from the upper belly, this
is a token, that the man feeleth sore at his navel, and
heavy sore on his shoulders, and thirst, and loss of
appetite, and a little blood droppeth through the back
gut *or rectum.*

4. The disease dysenteria cometh to many first from
too mickle fæcal discharge, and then a man for a long
while attendeth not to this, till the inwards become
either inflamed, or through that neglect wounded.
At whiles it beginneth from the midriff, which is
betwixt the wamb and the liver, and the juices from
meats which are mingled with blood and with bad humours, pour themselves through the inwards and cause
an evil fæcal discharge, and for the grimness of the
inflammatous matters the food cannot be contained,
but the inwards,[2] along with it, are driven down,
then that turneth to dysentery. *We say now,* how
one must cure the man thus afflicted; to him one must
give the meats which restrain the wamb and do not
scathe the maw, juice of colewort, at whiles peas broth,
and vinegar, and porrum *or leek* sodden with waybroad,
and old cheese sodden in goats milk, along with the
grease of goat. At whiles roast the cheese and dry
bread, and let him drink water which has been sodden
upon roses, at whiles sharp wine. Work him poultices
wrought to a clammy mass, barley or wheaten meal
sodden with honey, with a moderately mickle        *

\*    \*    \*    \*    \*    \*    \*    \*    \*    \*

---

[1] 'Εξ ὑψηλῶν ἐντέρων, *bowels* correctly.

[2] That is ξύσματα, *abraded por-*

*tions* of the intestines, and τῶν
ἐντέρων ἡ φυσικὴ πιμελή, *the fat
naturally* adhering to them.

* ※ ✳ ⁂ ✲

## .LIX.

### MS. Harl. 55., fol. 1 a.

Πάρεσις or
Παράλυσις.

Ƿið þære healf deadan adle ⁊ hƿanon seo cume · seo adl cymð on þa sƿiðran healfe þæs lichoman · oððe on þa ƿynstran · þær þa sina toslupað ⁊ beoð mið sƿiȝre ⁊ þiccere færtan yfelre ⁊ yfelre þiccere ⁊ myccelre.¹

Þa sƿetan man sceal mið blodlæsum ⁊ drencum ⁊ læcedomum on feȝ adon · þonne seo adl cume æþest on ðone mannan þonne ontyne þu his muð sceapa his tunȝan þonne bið heo on þa healfe hƿittre þe seo adl on beon ƿile · lacna hine þonne þus · Gefeþe þæne mannan on sƿiðe færstne cleofan ⁊ ƿearmne ȝefeste him sƿiðe ƿel hleope þær ⁊ ƿearmne ȝleda beþe man ȝelome ínn.

Onþƿeoh hine þonne ⁊ sceapa his handa ȝeopne · ⁊ sƿa hræþere sƿa ðu cealde finde læt him sona blod on þære cealdan æðre · æfter þære blodlæse · huhƿeȝa ymb .III. niht sele him þýrst drenc útýpnende ðú ȝiðcopna sƿa feala sƿa hecas piton þ to þýrtðþence seulon ⁊ sƿa ȝeƿaðe þýrta.

Ðrilum alpan æfter hire juhte · him mon sceal sellan hƿilum sceamoniam · hƿilum eft æfter þýrtðþencum · þonne he ȝepiest sý · læt eft blod on æðre sƿa þu on frunnan dýðest · hƿilum þu teoh mið ȝlæye oððe mið hoppne blod of þam sapan stopum abeaðodum.

fol. 1 b.

Ƿiþ þære healfdeadan adle · beþe hƿilum þa sapan stope æt heopðe oððe be ȝledum · ⁊ smere mið ele · ⁊ mið halpendum sealfum · ⁊ ȝmð sƿyðe þ þa sealfa

---

¹ The MS. thus.

\* \* \* \* \* \* \* \* \* \*

## lix.

*The MS. seems to have been written about A.D.* 1040.

1. For the half dead disease and whence it cometh. Hemiplegia. The disease cometh on the right side of the body, or on the left, where the sinews are powerless, and are *afflicted* with a slippery and thick humour, evil, thick, and mickle.

2. The humour must be removed with bloodlettings, and draughts, and leechdoms. When first the disease cometh on the man, then open his mouth, look at his tongue, then is it whiter on that side on which the disease is about to be; then tend him thus: carry the man to a very close and warm chamber, rest him very well there in shelter, and let warm gledes be often carried in.

3. Then unwrap him and view his hands carefully, and whichsoever thou find cold, on that cold vein let him blood. After the bloodletting, somewhere about three nights, give him a purging wort drink, put in as many githcorns[1] as leeches know must be put into a wort drink, and suitable worts.

4. At whiles must be given him aloes after their proper method, at whiles scammony; at whiles again after wort drinks, when he is in repose, let blood again on a vein as thou didst at first; at whiles draw blood with a *cupping* glass or a horn from the sore deadened places.

5. For the half dead disease. Warm at whiles the sore place at the hearth or by gledes, and smear with oil, and with healing salves, and rub smartly so

---

[1] Berries of the *Dafne laureola.*

ın beꞃincen. Þẏꞃe ꞇo ꞃealᵹe ealᵭne mẏꞃſle ꞃealꞇne heoꝑ-
ꞇeꞃ meaꞃh · ᵹoꞃe ꝑẏꞃſle · oᵭᵭe hænna · ꞇ ᵭo ᵹoᵭe ꞃẏꞃꞇa
ꞇo beᵭe þa ſaꝛaꝛ ſꞇoꝛe æꞇ ᵹẏꝛe.

Ƿilum onleᵹe ꞇ oubınᵭ ꝑıc · ꞇ ꝑeax · ꝛıꝑoꝛ · ꞇ
ſıneꝛu · ꞇ ele · ꞇoᵹæᵭeꝛe ᵹemılꞇeᵭ. Ƿilum on þa
ꝛaꝛan ſınua ꞇ aꝛꝑollenan leᵹe on ꞇ bınᵭ on ᵹaꞇe
ꞇẏꝛᵭelu ᵹemenᵹeᵭ ꝑıᵭ hunıᵹ · oᵭᵭe on eceᵭe ᵹeꝛoᵭen ·
þonne þꝛınaᵭ þa aſlaꝛenan ꞇ þa aꝛꝑollena¹ ſına.

Þẏꞃe hım ꝑẏꝛꞇ ᵭꝛenc þe ne bıᵭ uꞇẏꝛꝛenᵭe · ne
ſꝛıꝑol ac ꞇoᵭꝛıſᵭ ꞇ lẏꞇlaᵭ þa ẏſelan pæꞇaꝛ · on þam
ꝛeocum men þe bıþ ſꝛa ſꝛa hoꝛh oᵭᵭe ꝛıꝛoᵭa oᵭᵭe
ᵹıllıꝛꞇꝛe.

Genım hunıᵹeſ þıſ¹ lẏꞇle punᵭ ᵭo þonne ꞇo þan ᵹe-
beaꞇen ꞇ aſıſꞇ ꝛıꝑoꝛ · ſẏle þonne ꞇo þıᵹᵹanne þam
unꞇꝛuma¹ men. Eſꞇ ẏmbe þꝛeo mıhꞇ ſẏle hım on
þam ılcan ᵹemeꞇe oᵭᵭe maꝛe · ꞇ ſꝛa ẏmb ſeoꝛeꝛ
mıhꞇ.

Ƿıᵭ þæꝛe healſ ᵭeaᵭaꝛ aᵭle · ᵭo þu hꝛılum ſealꞇeſ
cucleꝛ mæl ꞇo menᵹe ꝑıᵭ hunıᵹ ꞇ eſꞇ ꝛıꝑoꝛ · cunna
ſꝛa æᵹþeꝛ ᵹe on þıſum læceᵭome ᵹe on oᵭꝛum þæm
þe ıc eac ꝑꝛıꞇe hu hıꞇ on nıman ꝑolᵭe · ᵹıſ þ̷ he
heaꝛᵭ ſı uꞇan leᵹe on þane læceᵭom þe þ̷ heaꝛᵭ ſoꝛᵭı
hꝛelıᵹe ꞇ þæꞇ ẏſel uꞇ ꞇeo. ꞇeoh hım bloᵭ oſ ᵹıſ þæꞇ
neb oᵭᵭe þ̷ heaꝛoᵭ ſaꝛ ſı on þam hneꝛcan · ꞇ nıꞇꞇa²
þaꝛa læceᵭoma þe þanc hoꝛh oſ þam heaꝛᵭe ꞇeo · ¹ oþþe
þuꝛh muᵭ · oᵭᵭe þuꝛh noꝛu · ꞇ þonne he þa mıhꞇ
hæbbe ᵹeᵭo þ̷ he ᵹelome ᵹeſꝛeſe · ſẏle hım þa meꞇꞇaſ
þe ſẏn eaᵭmẏlꞇe · ꞇ ᵹoᵭ ſeaꝛ hæbben ꞇ he ſꝛam þam
meꞇꞇım mæᵹe ſınalıᵹan · þæꞇ ſẏn ᵹeꝛoᵭene ꝑẏꝛꞇa.
ꝑẏll · ᵹeoꞇe man þ̷ æꝛeſꞇe ꝑoſ ꞇ þ̷ aſꞇeꝛe onꝑeᵹ · ᵭo

fol. 2 a.

---

¹ MS. thus.     |     ² Corrected to nȳtta, MS.

that the salves may sink in. Work into a salve some old salt grease, some horse marrow, some goose fat or hens, and add good worts, and warm the sore places at the fire.

6. At whiles lay on and bind on pitch, and wax, and pepper, and grease, and oil melted together. At whiles lay on and bind on the sore swollen sinews goats treadles, mingled with honey, or sodden in vinegar; then the paralyzed and swollen sinews dwindle *to their proper size.*

7. Work him a wort drink, which is not purging nor yet emetic, but which driveth off and diminishes the evil humour in the sick man, which is, as it were, foulness, or rheum, or mucus.

8. Take of honey this small pound,[1] then add to it beaten and sifted pepper; then give it to the infirm man to eat. Again, about three nights *after*, give it him in the same quantity, or more; and so about four nights *after that.*

9. For the half dead disease; at whiles, apply a spoon measure of salt; mingle with honey and pepper besides. Try both in this leechdom and in others, which I also write, how it will hold; if the body be hard on the outside, lay on the leechdom that the hard part by it may turn to ratten, and may draw out the mischief. Draw blood from him, if the face or the head be sore, in the tender place; and make use of the leechdoms, which may draw the foul matter from the head, either through the mouth or through the nose; and when he hath the power, cause him to sneeze often; give him the meats which are easy of digestion, and have a good succulence, and *that* he by means of the meats may grow slender; that is to say, *give him* sodden worts; boil them; let the first and the second

---

[1] That is, a pound by weight, not a pint by measure: see Leechbook, II. lxvii.

þonne ȝod foſ tō · ⁊ ſýle to þýȝanne do lytel ſealt ·
⁊ ele · ⁊ mепce tō ⁊ pōſſſ · ⁊ þæm ȝeliee. healð þonne
ȝeoпne þ ſe mete ſ̄ ȝemýlt ſ̄eſ̄ he him eſt ȝýſe ·
foſðan þe ſe unȝemýlta mete him pýſið mýcel ýſel ·
ſeſ̄eſ piпeſ dſunce ſot hſæȝa ȝiſ he mā пille · dſunce
hāt pæteп. healðe hine ȝeoпne pið bæþ · ⁊ hſ̄lum
þonne he hit ȝeþſoſian mæȝe kete him blod on iпnan
eaпne ⁊ ſeeappiȝe þa ſeanean · ſeſ̄ele læeebom · ⁊ hu
ſeo healſ deade aðl · ſeſ̄ſ ſeopeſtiȝum oðde ſiſtiȝum
piпtſa naſſпe on men ne beeume.

Sume bēe kæpað pið þæſe healſdeadan aðle þ man
piпtſeoſ bæſпe to ȝlebum ⁊ þonne þa ȝleda ſette
toſoſan þam ſeoeum men ⁊ þ he þonne outýпduм
eaȝum ⁊ opene muſe þane ſēe ſpelȝe þa þſaȝe þe he
mæȝe · ⁊ þonne he mā ne mæȝe onſende hiſ neb
apēȝ lýthpon ⁊ eſt pende tō ⁊ onſō ðam ſteme ⁊ ſpa
ðō ælee dæȝe oð þ ſe bæl þæſ liehoman þe þæп aðea-
ðoð ſæ⁊ ⁊ ȝeleped to þæſe æппan hælo beeume.

fol. 2 b.

Soðliee ſeo aðl cýmð on monnan æſteп ſeopeſtiȝuм
oðde ſiſtiȝum piпtſa ȝiſ he bið cealdſe ȝeeýnðo þonne
cýmð æſteп ſeopeſtiȝum eleoп cýmð æſteп ſiſtiȝum
piпtſa hiſ ȝæſȝetaleſ · ȝiſ hit ȝinȝſan men ȝeliпpe
þonne bið þ eaðlæeneſe · ⁊ ne bið ſeo ýlee aðl
þeah þe unȝleape læcaſ peпan þ þ ſeo ýlee healſ-
deaðe aðl ſ̄. hu ȝehe aðl on man beeume on ȝeo-
ȝoðe on ſumum hine ſpa ſpa ſeo healſdeade aðl on
ýlðo beð. пe bið hit ſeo healſ deade aðl ae hpile
æthpeȝa ýſel pæte bið ȝeȝoten on þ lim þe hit on
ȝeſit · ae bið eaðlæeneпe · ſe ſeo ſoðe healſdeade aðl
cýmð æſteп ſiſtiȝum piпtſa.

Giſ mon ſ̄ þæſe healſdſeðan aðle ſeoe · oððe bſæe
ſeoe · pýſe him oxumelli ſuðeſпe eeeð dſиене eeeðeſ ·
⁊ humiȝeſ · ⁊ pæteſeſ ȝemanȝ.

infusion of them be poured away; then add some good
decoction, and give it him to partake of; add a little
salt, and oil, and marche, and leek, and such as those.
Observe then carefully that the meat be digested, ere
one give him *any* again; since the undigested meat
worketh him much evil: let him drink some sheer wine;
if he want more, let him drink hot water. Let him
hold back carefully from the bath, and at whiles, when
he may endure it, let him blood on the inner part of
the arm, and scarify his shanks.   A noble leechdom!
And *now*, how the half dead disease never cometh on
a man before forty or fifty years of age.

10. Some books teach for the half dead disease, that
one should burn a pinetree to gledes, and then set the
gledes before the sick man, and that he then, with
eyes disclosed and open mouth, should swallow the
reek, for what time he may; and when he is no longer
able, he should turn his face away a little, and again
turn it to the *hot embers*, and accept the glow; and
so do every day, till the part of the body which was
deadened and injured come again to its former health.

11. Well, the disease cometh on a man after forty
or fifty winters; if he be of a cold nature, then it
cometh after forty; otherwise, it cometh after fifty
winters of his tale of years; if it happen to a younger
man, then it is easier to cure, and it is not the same
disease, though unclever leeches ween that it is the
same half dead disease.  How can a like disease come
on a man in youth in one limb, as the half dead
disease doth in old age?  It is not the half dead
disease, but some mischievous humour is effused on the
limb, on which the harm settles; but it is easier of
cure; and the true half dead disease cometh after
fifty years.

12. If a man be sick of the half dead disease, or
epileptic, work him ὀξύμελι, a southern acid drink, a
mixture of vinegar, and honey, and water.

Nim eceþer anne dæl · hunizer tpezen dælar ƿel
zeclæꝑnoder · pæteꝑer ꝼeoꝑðan · ꝑeoð þonne oð ꝥ
þꝑiddan dæl þæꝑe pætan · oððe ꝼeoꝑðan · ⁊ ꝼleot
ꝥ ꝼam ⁊ ꝥ ꝑot ꝼýmle[1] oꝼ oðþæt hit zeꝑoden ꝑi ·
ziꝼ þu pille þone dꝑenc ꝑtꝑenzꝑan pýꝑcan · þonne
dō þu ꝑpa mýcel þæꝑ eceþer ꝑpa þæꝑ hunizer ⁊ nýtta
þæꝑ læcebomaꝑ ze pið þiꝑꝑe adle ze pið ælceꝑe ꝼul
neah. Nim ꝑimble þæꝑ eceðꝑenceꝑ ꝼpa zepoꝑhteꝑ
ꝑpa mýcel ꝑpa þe þince · ðō pið þiꝑꝑum adlum ꝑædic

fol. 3 a.

on ꝥ ꝑeap þæꝑ dꝑinceꝑ læt beo nihteꝑne ōn · sýle
þonne on moꝑzenne þam ꝑeocum men · neahtneſti-
zum þanc ꝑædic ꝼpā zeſcaꝑne to þicᵹanne ꝼpa he
ꝼpýðuſt mæze · ⁊ ꝥ þu þanne læꝑe þæꝑ seapeꝑ
ꝑýððan ꝑe ꝑædic oꝼc[2] ꝑý · zeot hat pæteꝑ on sýle
dꝑincan þam seocum men to ꝼýlle. And þonne ýmbe
aneꝑ dæzeꝑ hpile ſtinze him mon ꝼeþeꝑe on muð
oððe ꝼinzeꝑ nebe hine to ꝼpipanne. Nim eꝼt eleꝑ
anne dæl · peaꝑmeꝑ pæteꝑeꝑ tpezan · ꝑealteꝑ tpezan
cucceleꝑ[3] ꝼulle menz tozædeꝑe ꝑýle to dꝑincanne ceac
ꝼulne ⁊ þanne ſtinze ꝼinzeꝑ on muð bꝛæde to ꝼpipanne · læt þanne ꝼpipan on þane ýlcan ceac þe he
æꝑ oꝼ dꝑanc zeſceapa þonne hpꝛeðeꝑ þe[4] ꝼpiða ꝑý
ꝑpa micel ꝑpa he æꝑ zeðꝛanc · ziꝼ he maꝑa ꝑý týla
hiꝑ ꝑpa · ziꝼ he emmicel ꝑi þane[5] þe he æꝑ zeðꝛanc
ꝑýle eꝼt on ða ilcan piꝑan oðþæt he ma ꝼpipe þanne
he zeðꝛince æꝑ · þis ꝑecal ꝼpiþuſt pið blædꝑan adle
⁊ þæm ſtanum þe on blædðꝑan ꝑýn.


Þꝛð þꝑne healꝼðeadan [adle]. Nim ꝥ pæteꝑ þe
pýoꝑan jueꝑan on zeꝑodene oꝼeꝑ pilleda ꝑýle dꝛincan
ꝼpiðe þonne peeð[6] ꝥ þone innoð ⁊ clænꝑað. Eꝼt ꝑýn-

---

[1] ſinýle, MS.

[2] Read oꝑ, for oꝑc.

[3] Read cuclepaꝑ.

[4] On this form, see St. Marharete, p. 84.

[5] Read þam.

[6] Perhaps peꝑcð, *washeth*.

13. Take of vinegar, one part; of honey, well cleansed, two parts; of water, the fourth *part;* then seethe down to the third or fourth part of the liquid, and skim the foam and the refuse off continually, till the *mixture* be *fully* sodden. If thou wish to work the drink stronger, then put as much of the vinegar as of the honey, and use the leechdom either for this disorder, or for full nigh any one. Take always of the acid drink, so wrought, as much as may seem good to thee. For these disorders put a radish into the liquor of the drink; let it be in it for the space of a night; then give in the morning to the sick man, after his nights fast, the radish so liquored to eat, as he best may; and then, when the radish is gone, pour thou hot water on the remains of the liquor; give it to the sick man to drink to the full. And then, after about a days space, let some one poke a feather into his mouth, or a finger; let him compel him to spew. Again, take of oil, one part; of warm water, two; of salt, two spoons full; mingle them together; give to drink a jug full, and then poke a finger into his mouth; bid him spew; let him spew into the same jug from which he before drank; then examine whether the vomit be as much as he ere drank. If it be more, tend him then; if it be just as much as he before drank, give him again in the same wise, till he spew more than he drank before. This must be applied chiefly for disease of bladder, and for the stones which are in the bladder.

14. For the half dead [disease]. Take the water on which peas were sodden, *and* overboiled; give it *the man* to drink. That strongly waketh up and cleanseth

fullan leaf on ƿín gegníden ꝥ clænsað þane innað. Ƿið þan ilcan eft· ellenes blostman genim ⁊ gegnid ⁊ gemenge ƿið hunig ⁊ gedó on box· ⁊ þonne þearf si genim bollan fulne hluttres gesƿettes ƿínes gemenge ƿið ꝥ ⁊ aseohhe sýle drincan. Ƿið þan ilcan betan mid hire ƿýrtruman seoð on ƿætere butan sealte· sýle þonne þæs ƿæteres bollan fulne to gedrinceanne.

* * * * * * * * *

.LXIV.

* * * * * * * * *

fol. 105 a. Ƿte oferne healfne pening geƿege gegnid sƿiþe smale do þonne on hluttor æg ⁊ sele þam men to supanne· hió is sƿiþe god eác on þas ƿisan ƿið hƿostan ⁊ ƿiþ springe do þas ƿyrte on he biþ sona hal. Þis is balzaman smyring ƿiþ eallum untrumnessum þe on mannes lichoman biþ· ƿiþ fefre· ⁊ ƿiþ scinlace ⁊ ƿið eallum gedƿolþinge. Eal sƿa sume se petra oleum he is god ⁊feald to drinceanne ƿið innan tiedernesse ⁊ utan to smerƿanne on ƿintres dæge for þon þe he hæfð sƿiðe micle hæte for ðy hine mon sceal drincan on ƿintra· ⁊ he is god gif hƿam seó spræc oðfylð nime þonne ⁊ ƿyrce cristes mæl under his tungan ⁊ his an lytel sƿelge· gif món eác of his geƿitte ƿeorðe þonne nime he his dæl ⁊ ƿyrce cristes mæl on ælcre[a] lime butan eine on þam heafde foran se sceal on balzame beon ⁊ ofer on þam heafde ufan. Tyriaca ís god drenc ƿiþ eallum innoð tydernessum· ⁊ se man se þe hine sƿa begæþ sƿa hit her on segð þonne mæg he him miclum gehelpan. To þam dæge þe he

fol. 105 b. ƿille hine drincan he sceal fæstan oþ midne dæg ⁊ ne læte hine ƿind beblaƿan þy dæge· ga him þonne ūn

[a] ælcum ?

the inwards. Again, leaves of houseleek bruised in wine; that cleanseth the inwards. For the same again; take blossoms of elder, and rub them, and mix them with honey, and put them in a box, and when need be, take a bowl full of clear sweetened wine, mingle with that and strain: administer. For the same; seethe beet with its roots in water without salt; then administer a bowl full of the water to drink.

\*   \*   \*   \*   \*   \*   \*   \*   \*

## lxiv.

\*   \*   \*   \*   \*   \*   \*   \*   \*

so much as may weigh a penny and a half, rub very small, then add the white of an egg, and give it to the man to sip. It (*balsam*) is also very good in this wise for cough and for carbuncle, apply this wort, soon shall the man be hole. This is smearing with balsam for all infirmities which are on a mans body, against fever, and against apparitions, and against all delusions. Similarly also petroleum is good to drink simple for inward tenderness, and to smear on outwardly on a winters day, since it hath very much heat; hence one shall drink it in winter: and it is good if for anyone his speech faileth, then let him take it, and make the mark of Christ under his tongue, and swallow a little of it. Also if a man become out of his wits, then let him take part of it, and make Christs mark on every limb, except the cross upon the forehead, that shall be of balsam, and the other *also* on the top of his head. Triacle (θηριακόν) is a good drink for all inward tendernesses, and the man, who so behaveth himself as is here said, he may much help himself. On the day on which he will drink *triacle*, he shall fast until midday, and not let wind blow on him that day : then let him go to the bath, let him sit there

bæþ sitte þær on oð ꝥ he swæte · nime þonne ane cuppan do an lytel wearmes wæteres on innan nime þonne ane lytle snæd þæs tyrnacan ⁊ gemenge[1] wiþ ꝥ wæter ⁊ seoh þurh þynne hrægl drince þonne · ⁊ ga him þonne to his reste ⁊ beþreo hine wearme · ⁊ licge swa oþ he wel swæte · arise þonne ⁊ sitte him úp ⁊ scrype hine ⁊ þicge siþþan his mete to nones ⁊ beorge him geornne wiþ þone wind þæs dæges · þonne gelyfe ic to gode ꝥ hit þam men miclum gehelpe. Se hwita stan mæg wiþ stice ⁊ wiþ fleogendum attre · ⁊ wiþ eallum uncuþum brocum · þu scealt hine scafan on wæter ⁊ drincan tela micel ⁊ þære readan eorþan dæl scafe þær to ⁊ þa stanas sint ealle swiðe gode óf to drincanne wiþ eallum uncuþlicu þing ·[2] þonne ꝥ fyr óf þam stane aslegen hít is god wið ligetta · ⁊ wið þunorrada ⁊ wið ælces cynnes gedwol þing · ⁊ gif mon on his wege biþ gedwolod slea him ænne spearcan beforan biþ he sona on rihtan. Þis eal het þus fol. 106 a. secgean ælfrede cyninge domne helias patriarcha ón gerusalem.

. LXV.

Gif hors ofscoten sie · Nim þonne ꝥ seax þe þæt hæfte sie fealo hryþeres horn ⁊ sien .III. ærene næglas ón · Writ þonne þam horse on þam heafde foran cristes mæl ⁊ on leoþa gehwilcum þe þu ætfeolan mæge · Nim þonne ꝥ winestre eare þurh sting swigende · þis þu scealt don · genim ane girde sleah on ꝥ bæc þonne biþ ꝥ hors hal · ⁊ awrit on þæs seaxes horne þas word · Benedicite omnia opera domini dominum. Sy ꝥ ylfa þe him sie þis him mæg to bote. Wiþ utwærce bremel þe sien begen endas

[1] After gemenge, MS. has þe wiþ. | [2] Read ealle.

till he sweat; then let him take a cup, and put a little warm water in it, then let him take a little bit of the triacle, and mingle with the water, and drain through some thin raiment, then drink it, and let him then go to his bed and wrap himself up warm, and so lie till he sweat well; then let him arise and sit up and clothe himself, and then take his meat at noon, *three hours past midday*, and protect himself earnestly against the wind that day: then, I believe to God, that it may help the man much. The white stone is powerful against stitch, and against flying venom, and against all strange calamities: thou shalt shave it into water and drink a good mickle, and shave thereto a portion of the red earth, and the stones are all very good to drink of, against all strange uncouth things. When the fire is struck out of the stone, it is good against lightenings and against thunders, and against delusion of every kind: and if a man in his way is gone astray, let him strike himself a spark before him, he will soon be in the right way. All this Dominus Helias, patriarch at Jerusalem, ordered *one* to say to king Alfred.

## lxv.

If a horse is elf shot,[1] then take the knife of which the haft is horn of a fallow ox, and on which are three brass nails, then write upon the horses forehead Christs mark, and on each of the limbs which thou may feel at: then take the left ear, prick a hole in it in silence; this thou shalt do; then take a yerd, strike *the horse* on the back, then will it be hole. And write upon the horn of the knife these words, "Benedicite omnia opera domini, dominum." Be the elf[2] what it may, this is mighty for him to amends. Against dysentery, a

---

[1] Elf shot in the Scottish phrase.
[2] The construction as in Ic hit eom, *I am he*; combined with the partitive, as Hpile hæleða, *what hero.*

on eoþþan · ȝenim þone neoþþan pyptþuman delf up
þpit niȝon fþonaf on þa pinftþan hanð ꝛ ꞃinȝ þꞃipa
miSeþeþe mei deuꞃ · ꝛ niȝon fiþum þaceꞃ nofceꞃ ·
ȝenim þonne mucȝpypt · ꝛ eꝺelaftan · þyl þaꞃ þꞃeo[1] on
meolcum oþ þ hy ꞃeaðian fuþe þonne on nealic neꞃciȝ
ȝoðe bleðe fulle hpile æꞃ he oþeꞃne mece þicȝe · þefce
hine ꞃofce · ꝛ þꞃeo hine þeaꞃme · ȝif ma þeaꞃf fie ðo
eꝼc fpa · ȝif þu þonne ȝic þuꞃfe ðo þꞃiððan ꞃiþe ne
þeaꞃfc þu ofceꞃ. Ȝif ucȝanȝ foꞃfecen fie ȝenim ȝið-
coꞃneꞃ leaꝼa ȝoðe hanð fulle ꝛ þa ꞃuꞃan peȝbꞃæðan
moþoþeaꞃðe · ꝛ ðoccan þa þe fꞃimman pille · þyl þaꞃ
þꞃeo on ealðum ealað fꞃiþe ꝛ ðo ꞃealce buceꞃan on
þylle þicce læc ðꞃincan ȝoðe bleðe fulle hpile æꞃ oðꞃum
mece ꝛ þꞃeoh hine þeaꞃme · ꝛ þefce fcille ðo þuꞃ þꞃiþa
ne þeaꞃf ofceꞃ.

Piþ lunȝen aðle læceðom ðun cæhce · ꞃaluic · þuðe he
healꝼan þꞃeþe ꞃaluian · ꝼeꝼeꞃ ꝼuȝian emmicel þaþa cꞃeȝea
pyꞃca þꞃeþe ꞃaluian þꞃeo fpelc ðꞃeoꞃȝe ðꞃofclan hieꞃe þe
nu[2] calꞃa pyꞃca ꝼyꞃmeꞃc on þa ꞃealꝼe þe hum þyꞃef
læceðomeꞃ þeaꞃf fie healðe hine ȝeoꞃne piþ ȝefpec eala
ðꞃince hluccoꞃ eala ꝛ on þꞃer hluccꞃan ealað pyꞃce
þylle ȝeonȝe ãcꞃinðe ꝛ ðꞃince. Piþ ûcꞃæꞃce ȝenim
unfmeþiȝne healꝼne cyfe ðo enȝlyꞃeꞃ huniȝeꞃ .III.
fnæða to · þylle on þannan oþ þ bîc bꞃuniȝe · ȝenim
þonne ȝeonȝꞃe acꞃinðe hanð fulle ꝛ fpa fpiȝenðe æc
ham ȝeðꞃinȝ ꝛ næꞃꞃe in on þone môn ꞃceaꝼe þ ȝꞃene
on ucan þylle þa fæþ fþone on cu meolce ȝefpece mið
þum fnæðum huniȝef þone ðꞃenc þicȝe þonne mið ðy
cyꞃe æꝼceꞃ ðꞃence .VII. niht eala foꞃȝa ꝛ meoloc
þicȝe unfuꞃe. Piþ unlybbum fuþe cu buceꞃan .VIIII.

fol. 106 b.

fol. 107 a.

---

[1] Two herbs are named : the chips
are third.

[2] These words are scarcely without error.

bramble of which both ends are in the earth;[1] take
the newer root, delve it up, cut up nine chips into the
left hand, and sing three times the Miserere mei, deus,
and nine times the pater noster; then take mugwort
and everlasting, boil these three, *the worts and the
chips*, in milk till they get red, then let *the man* sip
at night fasting a good dish full, some while before he
taketh other meat; let him rest himself soft, and wrap
himself up warm; if more need be, let him do so
again: if thou still need, do it a third time, thou wilt
not need oftener. If the fæcal discharge be lodged,
take of the leaves of githcorn a good hand full, and
the nether part of the rough waybroad, and the dock
which will swim; boil these three in old ale thoroughly
and add salt butter, boil it thick, let *the man* drink
a good dish full a while before other meat, and let
him wrap himself up warm, and let him rest quiet;
do this thrice, no need *to do it* oftener.

2. For lung disease, a leechdom; Dun taught it;
sage, rue, half as much as of the sage; feverfue as
much as of the two worts; of pennyroyal three
times as much as of the sage; take thee of it of
all worts foremost *to put* into the salve. Let *the
man*, who hath need of this leechdom, withhold himself earnestly from sweetened ale, let him drink
clear ale, and in the wort of the clear ale let him
boil young oak rind, and drink. For dysentery, take
an ungreasy half cheese, and four parts of English
honey, boil in a pan until it browneth, then take a
hand full of young oak rind, and so in silence bring
it home, and never *bring* it in to the mans presence,
shave off the green outside *the house*, boil the sappy
chips in cows milk, sweeten it with three parts of
honey, let *the man* take the drink with the cheese,
afterwards let him drink: for seven days let him forego ale and take milk 'not *turned* sour. For poisons;
let him sip cows butter for nine mornings, for three,

---

[1] Frequently seen: spontaneous propagation

morgnas .III. sopan .VIII. morgnas cerfillan gemetlice on wine þridda dæl wæteres nime þonne hwerhwettan nioþoweardne gnid on wylisc[1] ealo swete mid hunige drince þære teoþan niht · to mete þone drenc on þreo þicge æt þam þrim honeredum.

Wiþ þære geolwan adle · genim nioþoweardne eolenan gedo ꝥ þu hæbbe on þam forman dæge þonne þu hire ǽrest brucce on morgen nim þreo snæda ⁊ þreo on niht ⁊ hire sculon beon on hunig gesnæd · ⁊ þy æfteran mergen .IIII. snæda ⁊ IIII. on niht · ⁊ þriddan mergen .V. snæda ⁊ . V. on niht · ⁊ þy feorþan mergen. .VI. ⁊ VI. on niht. Þes drenc sceal wiþ þon ilcan. genim alexandrian ⁊ grundeswelgean cnua smale ⁊ do to drence on hluttrum ealað. Gif men sie færlice yfele wyrce .III. cristes mæl an on þære tungan oþer on þam heafde · þridde on þam breostum sona bið sel. To gehealdanne lichoman hælo mid drihtnes gebede · þis is æþele læcedom · genim myrran ⁊ gegnid on win swilce sie tela micel steap ful ⁊ þicge on niht nestig · ⁊ eft þonne restan wille ꝥ gehealdeþ wundorlice líchoman hælo ⁊ hít eac deah wiþ feondes costungúm yflum.

fol. 107. b.

Þonne is eft se æþelesta læcedom to þon ilcan · genim myrran ⁊ hwit recels ⁊ safinan · ⁊ saluian · ⁊ rudan ⁊ þæs recelses ⁊ myrran sy mæst · ⁊ þa oþre syn ũwegene þara sien emfela · ⁊ ætsomne on mortere gegnide to duste wette under weofod þonne cristes tid sie ⁊ gesinge mōn .III. mæssan ofer þa .III. dagas on midne winter ⁊ æt stefanes tide ⁊ Sēe Iohannes euangelista ⁊ þa þry dagas þicge on wine on neaht nestig ⁊ ꝥ þær to lafe sie þæs dustes hafa ⁊ geheald; hit

[1] wylisc, MS.

soap, for eight mornings of chervil, a moderate quantity, in wine, a third part *also* of water; then let him take the netherward part of cucumber, rub it up into foreign ale, sweeten with honey, let *the man* drink *that* the tenth night, for meat let him take the drink at three *times* at the three cock crowings.

3. For the yellow disease; take the netherward part of helenium, contrive that thou mayest have it on the previous day; when first thou usest it, take three pieces in the morning and three at night, and they shall be *bits* of it sliced into honey; and the second morning four pieces, and four at night; and the third morning five pieces, and five at night; and the fourth morning six, and six at night. The following drink shall avail for the same; take alexanders and groundsel, pound them small, and form them into a potion in clear ale. If a man have sudden ailments, make three marks of Christ, one on the tongue, the second on the head, the third upon the breast, soon he will be well. To keep the body in health with prayer to the Lord: this is a noble leechdom: take myrrh and rub it into wine, so much as may be a good stoup full, and let *the man* take it at night fasting, and again when he will rest; that wonderfully upholdeth the health of the body, and it also is efficacious against the evil temptings of the fiend.

4. This is the noblest leechdom for the same; take myrrh and white frankincense, and savine and sage, and dyeweed, and of the frankincense and of the myrrh let there be most, and let the others be weighed, of them let there be equal quantities; and have them rubbed to dust together in a mortar, have them set under the altar, when it is Christmas tide, and let one sing three masses over them, for three days in midwinter, and at St. Stephens tide, and St. John the evangelists *day*, and for those three days let *the man* take the *leechdom* in wine at night fasting, and what there is left of the dust hold and keep; it is power-

mæȝ þiþ eallum fæþ[1] untꝑymneꝑꝑum · ȝe þiþ ꝼeꝑꝑie ȝe þiþ leucten aðle ȝe þiþ atꝑe · ȝe þiþ yꝼelꝑe lyꝼte. Ȝeꝑꝑiꞇu eác ꝑecȝeaþ ꝑe þe þone læcebom beȝa þ he hine mæȝe ȝehealban . XII. monaþ þiþ ealꝑa untꝑymneꝑꝑa ꝼꝑeceneꝑꝑe.

Þonne eꝼꞇ pið ȝicþan þ eal ꝑe lichoma ꝑy claneꝑ hiþeꝑ ꝭ ȝlaðeꝑ ꝭ beoþhꞇeꝑ· ȝenim ele ꝭ caldeꝑ þineꝑ ðꝑæꝑꞇan emꝼela ðo on moꝑꞇeꝑe ȝemenȝ ꝑel ꞇo ꝼomne ꝭ ꝼmiꝑe mið þy þone lichoman on ꝼunnan. Pið ꞇelꝼe ꝭ þiþ uncuþum ꝼiðꝑan[2] ȝmið myꝑꝑian on þꝼn ꝭ hꝑiꞇeꝑ ꝑecelꝑeꝑ em micel · ꝭ ꝑeeaꝼ ȝaȝaꞇeꝑ ðæl þæꝑ ꝼꞇaneꝑ on þ þꝼn ðꝑunce . III. moꝑȝenaꝑ neahꞇ neꝑꞇiȝ oþþe . VIIII. oþþe . XII. Þiþ lonð aðle þyl ꝑeꝑmoð ꝼpa ðꝑiȝne ꝼpa ȝꝑenne ꝼpa þeꝑ he hæbbe on oleð [inꝼiꝑmoꝑum][3] oþ þ þæꝑ eleꝑ ꝼie þꝑuððan ðæl beþylleð ꝭ ꝼmiꝑe mið þone lichoman ealne æꞇ ꝼyꝑe · ꝭ mæꝑꝑe þꝑeoꝼꞇ ꝑeeal ðon þone læcebom ȝiꝼ man hæꝑþ. Þiþ ȝonȝel pæꝑꝑan biꞇe ꝼmiꞇ on ꝑen ꝼpaꞇ. Þiþ uꞇꝑihꞇe meꝑ ȝeallan · blæe ꝼneȝl þyl on meolcum ꝑꝰp on æꝼenne ꝭ on moꝑȝenne. Ðeaꝼoð ꝑealꝼ muꝑꝑie ꝭ alꝑe libania ealꝑa ȝehee ꝼela menȝ þiþ eeeð ꝼmiꝑe mið þ heaꝼoð. Þiþ þon ilean ꝼpeꝑl ꝭ ꝼpeȝleꝑ æꝑꝑel muꝑꝑie · ꝭ æȝhꝑilceꝑ eynneꝑ ꝑecelꝼ niȝon þyꝑꞇa enȝliꝼœ · polleie · bꝑembel · æꝑꝑel · elehꞇꝑe · biꝑeeoþ þyꝑꞇ · ꝼinul · ꝑuꝑe ꝑeȝbꝑæðe · haꝑan ꝼꝑꝑeeel · ꝼio haꝑe þyꝑꞇ · liþ þyꝑꞇ · ealꝑa þiꝑꝑa emꝼela · oleum [inꝼiꝑmoꝑum] ·[3] haliȝ pæꞇeꝑ · haliȝ ꝑealꞇ · oþeꝑ ele · ꝼmiꝑe þe mið þyꝑ uꝼan þonne þu hi ȝniðe.

### . LXVI.

Cf. Marbodæus. Be þam ꝼꞇane þe ȝaȝaꞇeꝑ haꞇꞇe iꝑ ꝑæð þ he . VIII. mæȝen hæbbe. An iꝑ þonne þunoꝑꝑað biþ ne ꝑeeþeð

---

[1] Read ꝑæþhenn.
[2] Perhaps miswritten.

[3] The letters have been paled away purposely.

ful against all dangerous infirmities, either against fever, or against typhus, or against poison, or against evil air. Writings also say, that he who employs the leechdom is able to preserve himself for twelve months against peril of all infirmities.

5. Then again, against itch, and that all the body may be of a clean, and glad, and bright hue : take oil and dregs of old wine, equally much, put them into a mortar, mingle well together, and smear the body with this in the sun. Against an elf and against a strange visitor,[1] rub myrrh in wine and as mickle of white frankincense, and shave off a part of the stone *called* agate into the wine, let him drink *this* for three mornings after his nights fast, or for nine, or for twelve. For land disease *or nostalgia*, boil wormwood so dry (*or*) so green, as he hath there, in oleum infirmorum, *the oil of extreme unction*, till a third part of the oil is boiled away, and smear all the body at the fire with it, and a mass priest shall perform the leechdom, if a man hath means to get one. For a bite of gangweaving spider, smudge hydromel[2] on iron. For diarrhœa, boil in milk horse gall and black snail, sip in the morning and evening. A head salve ; myrrh and aloes, and libanum *or frankincense*, of all a like quantity, mingle with vinegar, smear the head therewith. For the same ; sulfur and swails apple, myrrh and frankincense of every sort ; nine English worts, pulegium, bramble, apple, lupin, bishopwort, fennel, rough waybroad, vipers bugloss, the hoar wort, lithewort, of all these equal quantities ; oil of unction, holy water, holy salt,[3] common oil, smear thyself with this upwards *on the head*, when thou hast rubbed *them*.

### lxvi.

Of the stone which hight agate. It is said that it hath eight virtues. One is when there is thunder, it

---

[1] Interpreted by Herbarium cxi. 3.
[2] Perhaps *Sweat*.

[3] Salt which has had the formula of benediction pronounced over it.

þam men þe þone ſtan mið him hæfð. Oþer mæʒen
iſ on ſpa hpilcum huſe ſpa he biþ ne mæʒ þæþ inne
ꝼeonð peſan. þriððe mæʒen iſ þ nan attoþ þam men

fol. 108 b.

ne mæʒ ſceþþan þe þone ſtan mið him haꝼaþ. Feoþþe
mæʒen iſ þ ſe man ſe þe þone laþan ꝼeonð on him
deaʒollice hæfþ ʒiſ he þær ſtaneſ ʒeſceaꝼeneſ hpilcne
dæl on prætan onꝼehð þonne biþ ſona ſpeotol æteopoð
on him þ æþ deaʒol mað. Fiſte mæʒen iſ ſe þe
roniʒne able ʒeðꝛeht biþ ʒiſ he þone ſtan on prætan
þiʒeþ him biþ ſona ſel. Syxte mæʒen iſ þ dꝛycꞃæſt
þam men ne deꞃeþ ſe þe hine mið him hæfð. Seoꝼoþe
mæʒen iſ þ ſe þe þone ſtan on dꝛince onꝼehð he hæꝼþ
þe ſineþþan hehoman. Ealtoþe iſ þæſ ſtaneſ mæʒen
þ nan næðꝛan cynneſ bite þam ſceþþan ne mæʒ þe
þone ſtan on prætan byꞃiʒþ.

## LXVII.

ðimitte.

Punð eleſ ʒepihð . XII. peneʒum læꞃꞃe þonne punð
prætneſ · ꝺ punð caloð ʒepihð . VI. peneʒum maꞃe þonne
punð prætneſ · ꝺ . I. punð pineſ ʒepihð . XV. peneʒum
maꞃe þonne . I. punð prætneſ · ꝺ punð huniʒeſ ʒepihð
. XXXIIII. peneʒum maꞃe þonne punð prætꞃeſ · ꝺ . I.
punð buteꞃan ʒepihð · lxxx. peneʒum læꞃꞃe þonne punð
prætꞃeſ · ꝺ punð beoꝛeſ ʒepihð . XXII. peneʒum læꞃꞃe
þonne punð prætꞃeſ · ꝺ I. punð meloꝛeſ ʒepihð . cxv.
peneʒum læꞃꞃe þonne punð prætꞃeſ · ꝺ I. punð beana
ʒepihð . lv. peneʒum læꞃꞃe þonne punð prætneſ · ꝺ XV.

fol. 109 a.

punð [1] prætneſ ʒaþ to ſeſtꞃe :·

balð habet hunc[2] libꝛum cilð quem conſcꞃibeꝛe iuſſit;
Ðic pꝛecoꝛ aꞃꞃiðue cunctiſ in nomine cꞃiſti ·
Quo[3] nulluſ tollat hūnc libꝛum peꞃꝛiðuſ a me ·
Nēc ui nec ꝼuꞃto nēc quoðam ꝼamine ꝼalſo ·
Cuꞃ quia[4] nulla mihi tam caꞃa eSt ꝺptima ʒaza ·
Quam caꞃi libꝛi quoſ cꞃiſti ʒꞃatia comit.

---

¹ An error, read yntꝛan, *ounces*.    ³ Read Quod.
² huuð, MS.    ⁴ Read as Cur? Quia.

doth not scathe the man who hath this stone with him. Another virtue is, on whatsoever house it is, therein a fiend *perhaps enemy* may not be. The third virtue is, that no venom may scathe the man who hath the stone with him. The fourth virtue is, that the man, who hath on him secretly the loathly fiend, if he taketh in liquid any portion of the shavings of this stone, then soon is exhibited manifestly in him, that which before secretly lay hid. The fifth virtue is, he who is afflicted with any disease, if he taketh the stone in liquid, it is soon well with him. The sixth virtue is, that sorcery hurteth not the man, who has *the stone* with him. The seventh virtue is, that he who taketh the stone in drink, will have so much the smoother body. The eighth virtue of the stone is, that no bite of any kind of snake may scathe him who tasteth the stone in liquid.

### lxvii.

A pint of oil weigheth twelve pennies [1] less than a pint of water; and a pint of ale weigheth six pennies more than a pint of water; and a pint of wine weigheth fifteen pennies more than a pint of water; and a pint of honey weigheth thirty-four pennies more than a pint of water; and a pint of butter weigheth eighty pennies less than a pint of water; and a pint of beer weigheth twenty-two pennies less than a pint of water; and a pint of meal weigheth 115 pennies less than a pint of water; and a pint of beans weigheth fifty-five pennies less than a pint of water; and fifteen ounces of water go to the sextarius.[2]

---

[1] This is the Saxon silver penny of twenty-four grains, our pennyweight.

[2] "Sextarius medicinalis habet "uncias decem." Plin. Valer. Pref.

[*Book III.*]

Ƿiþ heafod ece · ⁊ ƿiþ ealdum heafod ece · ⁊ ƿiþ
healfes heafdes ece. II. Ƿiþ aspollenum eaȝum ⁊ ȝod
eah sealf · ⁊ ƿið miste on eaȝan ⁊ ƿið flie · ⁊ ƿið pyp-
num on eaȝum ⁊ ƿiþ þæm ȝif flæsc on eaȝum peaxe ·
⁊ ȝif on eaȝum peaxan neade sponȝe · ⁊ ȝif eaȝan
typen ⁊ sceaðe sealf to eaȝum · ⁊ smeþe eah
sealf.

.III. Ƿiþ earpæree ⁊ ƿiþ þæm ȝif pyrmas syn on
earan ⁊ ȝod eap sealf. IIII. Ƿiþ toþ ece ⁊ ȝif teþ syn
hole.

.V. Ƿiþ innan tobpocenum muðe .VI. Ƿiþ ceoc adle
⁊ ƿiþ ceol pærce. VII. Ƿiþ healf pærce. VIII. Ƿiþ
lite. VIIII. Ƿiþ hpostan. X. Ƿiþ þam þe mon blode
hpæce. XI. Ƿiþ seondum ȝeallan. XII. Ƿiþ þære
ȝeolpan adle. XIII. Ƿiþ bpeost pærce. XIIII. Ƿiþ
hpostan ⁊ ƿiþ lunȝen adle. XV. Ƿiþ maȝan pærce ⁊
ƿiþ aþundeneÿre. XVI. Ƿið milt pærce.

fol. 109 b.

.XVII. Ƿiþ linden pærce. XVIII. Ƿiþ pambe pærce
⁊ nyrel pærce. XVIIII. Ƿiþ blæddeþ pærce.

.XX. Ƿiþ þam ȝif man ne mæȝe ȝemiȝan ⁊ þam
men þe stanas peaxan on þære blædpan. XXI. Ƿiþ
þam ȝif men sie se utȝanȝ forseten. XXII. Ƿiþ utsiht
adle dpenc ⁊ bpip. XXIII. Ƿiþ þam pyrmum þe beoþ
on mannes innoþe. XXIIII. Ƿiþ hð pærce. XXV. Ƿiþ
peaptum. XXVI. Ƿið þam miclan hce smipinȝ ⁊ bæþ
⁊ dpenc ⁊ bpip. XXVII. Ƿiþ sinȝalum þupste un-
tpumpa manna. XXVIII. Ƿiþ innan foptoȝe ⁊ smæl
þeapma ece. XXVIIII. Ƿiþ þam þe man sie mid fype
anum forbæpned ⁊ ƿiþ þam þe man sie mid pætan
forȝbæpned · ⁊ ƿiþ sunbpyne. XXX. Ƿiþ þeore dpenc

ᵃ Read þeoþe.

⁊ eft ƿiþ þæpeᵃ ⁊ sceotendum penne ⁊ eft bepinȝ ƿiþ
þam ȝif þeop ȝepunȝe on anpe stope. XXXI. Ƿiþ
penne sealf. XXXII. Ƿiþ dolȝe sealf. XXXIII. Ƿiþ þam

## Book III.

1. For head ache, and for old head ache, and for ache of half the head, *commonly called megrim.* 2. For swollen eyes, and a good eye salve, and for mist in the eyes, and against white speck, and against worms in the eyes, and in case flesh wax upon the eyes, and if red sponges wax on the eyes, and if the eyes are bleared, and a salve for obscure vision of the eyes, and a smooth eye salve. 3. For pain of ear, and in case worms are in the ears, and a good ear salve. 4. For tooth ache, and if the teeth are hollow. 5. For a mouth broken out within. 6. For cheek *or jaw* disease, and for pain in the jowl. 7. Against neck pain. 8. Against cancer. 9. For cough. 10. In case a man break up blood. 11. For flowing gall. 12. For the yellow disease *or jaundice.* 13. For breast pain. 14. For cough and for lung disease. 15. For pain in the maw *or stomach,* and distention. 16. For pain of spleen. 17. For loin pain. 18. For wamb *or belly* pain, and for pain in the fat about the belly, *where the kidneys are lodged.* 19. For bladder pain. 20. In case a man may not mie, and for the man in whose bladder stones wax. 21. For the case where a mans fæcal discharge is obstructed. 22. For diarrhœa, a drink and a brewit. 23. For the worms which be in a mans inwards. 24. For joint pain. 25. For warts. 26. For leprosy or elephantiasis, a smearing, and a bath and a drink, and a brewit. 27. For the constant thirst of men out of health. 28. For gripe and ache of small guts. 29. In case a man be burnt with fire only, and in case a man is burnt with liquid, and for sun burning. 30. A drink against the "dry" disease, and again for that, and for a shooting wen, *with shooting pains,* and again a fomentation for it, if the "dry" disease remain in one place. 31. A salve for a wen. 32. A salve for a wen. 33. In case a man be wounded in

ȝiꝼ man ſie uꝼan on heaꝼod ƿund ꝺ ſie ban ȝebꞃocen ꝺ ƿiþ þam ȝiꝼ ſio eaxl upſtiȝe . ꝺ ȝod dollh ꝺꞃenc ꝺ ȝiꝼ ȝebꞃocen ban ſie on heaꝼde ꝺ oꝼ nelle. XXXIIII. Ƿiþ hundeſ ſlite ꝺ ƿiþ þon ȝiꝼ ſmþe ꝼoꞃcoꝼꝼene ꝺ ƿiþ þam ȝiꝼ ſinþe ſien ȝeſeꝼuncene. XXXV. Ƿiþ ȝonȝe-piꝼꝼan bite. XXXVI. Ƿiþ cancꞃe. XXXVII. Ƿiþ þam þe ſiꝼ ne mæȝe beaꞃn acennan ꝺ ȝiꝼ oꝼ ƿiꝼe nelle ȝan æꝼteꞃ þam beoꞃþꞃe þ̷ ȝecyndelic ſie . ꝺ ȝiꝼ oꝼ[1] ƿiꝼe ſie dead beaꞃn . ꝺ ƿiþ þam ȝiꝼ ƿiꝼ blede to ſƿiþe æꝼteꞃ þam beoꞃþꞃe. XXXVIII. Ƿiþ þam þe piꝼum ſie ꝼoꞃſtan-den luꞃa monað ȝecynd ꝺ ƿiþ þam ȝiꝼ ƿiꝼe to ſƿiþe oꝼꝼloꞃe ſio monoþ ȝecynd. XXXVIIII. Ƿiþ ſmeaȝea ƿyꞃme ſmiꞃinȝ ꝺ anleȝen . ꝺ beþinȝ ꝺ ſealꝼ. XL. Ƿiþ þam þe man ſie monaþ feoc. [XLI.][2] Ƿiþ ealle ꝼeondeſ coſtunȝa ꝺꞃenc ꝺ ſealꝼ. Ƿiþ þon ilcan ꝺ hu man ꞃcyle ȝepiꞇſeocne man lacniau . ꝺ hu mon ꞃcyle pyꞃcean ſꞃiꝺꞃenc uꞇyꞃꞃnendum. XLII. Ƿiþ þam ȝiꝼ ſꞃiꝺꝺꞃenc on men ȝeſiꞇꞇan[3] ꝺ he nelle uꞇȝan. XLIII. Ƿiþ aꞇꞇꞃeſ ꝺꞃence. [XLIIII.][4] Ƿiþ luꝼum. XLV. Ƿiþ þam ȝiꝼ þoꞃn ſꞇinȝe mon on ꝼoꞇ oððe hꞃeod ꝺ þonne nelle oꝼȝan. XLVI. Ƿiþ æꞃmælum ꝺ ƿiþ eallum eaȝna pꞃeꞃce. XLVII. Ƿiþ lyꝼꞇ adle ȝiꝼ ſe muþ ſie ꞃoh oþþe ƿon læcedom ꝺ beþinȝ ꝺ bæþ ſealꝼ ꝺ leah ꝺ blodeſ læꞇ. XLVIII. Ƿiþ ſie adle ꝺꞃenc ꝺ beþinȝ. XLVIIII. Ƿiþ ſculboꞃ pæꞃce ꝺ eaꞃna. L. Ƿiþ eneoƿa ꞃaþe. LI. Ƿiþ ꝼota ꞃaþe. LII. Ƿiþ þam ȝiꝼ þu ne mæȝe blod dolȝ ꝼoꞃþꞃiþan. LIII. Ƿiþ þam ȝiꝼ meoloc ſie ȝeꞃeꞃd. LIIII. Ƿiþ niht ȝenȝean ſealꝼ. LV. Ƿiþ þam ȝiꝼ men beo ſio heaꝼod panne ȝehleneed. LVI. Ƿið þam ȝiꝼ men nelle meltan hiꞃ meꞇe. LVII. Ƿiþ ƿiꝼ ȝemæblan. LVIII. Ƿiþ ꝼeondeſ coſtunȝa. LVIIII. Ƿiþ þeoꞃ penne ȝiꝼ he ſie men on cneoƿe oþþe on oþꞃum lime. LX. be þam hu mon ꞃcyle eaꞃ ꞃealꝼe pyꞃcean.

. LXI. Ƿiþ ælꝼ cynne ſealꝼ ꝺ ƿiþ niht ȝenȝan . ꝺ

---

[1] Read on.
[2] XLI. is omitted in MS.
[3] Read ȝeſiꞇꞇe.
[4] XLIIII. is omitted in MS.

the head and bone be broken, and in case the shoulder rise *by dislocation*, and a good wound drink, and if a broken bone be in the head and will not come away. 34. For tear by a hound, and if sinews be cut through, and in case sinews be shrunken. 35. For the bite of the gangwayweaving spider. 36. For cancer. 37. In case a woman may not kindle a child, and if, after the birth, that which is natural will not come away from a woman; and in case there be a dead bairn in a woman, and in case a woman bleed too much after the birth. 38. In case womens natural catamenia be stopped, and in case the natural catamenia flow too freely. 39. A smearing, and an onlaying, and a fomentation, and a salve against a boring worm. 40. In case a man be a lunatic. 41. A drink and a salve for all temptations of the fiend. For the same, and how one must treat a deranged man; and how a man shall work a spew drink for those that have diarrhœa. 42. In case a strong dose lodge in a man and will not come away. 43. Against a drink of poison. 44. Against lice. 45. In case a thorn, or a reed, prick a man in the foot, and will not be got rid of. 46. Against imminutions and all pain of eyes. 47. Against palsy, if the mouth be awry or livid, a leechdom and a fomentation, and a bath salve, and ley and bloodletting. 48. Drink and fomentation for "fig" diccase. 49. For pain of shoulder blade and arms. 50. For sore of knees. 51. For sore of feet. 52. In case thou be not able to bind up a bloodletting incision. 53. In case milk is turned sour. 54. A salve against night comers, *incubi, etc.* 55. In case a mans skull is "linked," *or seems to feel bound round.* 56. In case a mans meat will not digest. 57. Against womens prating. 58. Against temptations of the fiend. 59. Against a "dry" wen, if a man hath it on his knee or on another limb. 60. Of this; how a man must work an earsalve. 61. A salve against the elfin race and night goblins, and for the *women,*

þam monnum þe deoƀol mid hæmð. LXII. Ƿiþ ælƀ
able læcedom ⁊ eƀt hu món ſceal on þa ƿyrte ſingan
æ̃ɼ hi món nime ⁊ eƀt hu mon ſceal þa ƿyrta don
under peoƀod ⁊ oƀeɼ ſinȝan · ⁊ eƀt tacnu be þam
hƿæþeɼ hit ſie ælƀ ſoȝoþa ⁊ tacn hu þu onȝitan
meaht hƿæþeɼ hine món mæȝ ȝelacnian ⁊ drencaſ ⁊
ȝebedu ƿiþ ælcɼe ƀeondeɼ coſtunȝe. LXIII. Tacnu hu
þu meaht onȝitan hƿæþeɼ món ſie on ƿæteɼ ælƀ able ·
⁊ læcedom ƿiþ þam ⁊ ȝealdoɼ on to ſinȝanne ⁊ þ ilce
món mæȝ ſinȝan on þunda. LXIIII. Ƿið deoƀle liþe
drenc · ⁊ unȝemynde · ⁊ ƿiþ deoƀleſ coſtunȝa. LXV.
Ƿiþ þon ȝiƀ mon ſie ȝeȝymed ⁊ tacnu hƿæþeɼ he
libban mæȝe. LXVI. drenc ƿiþ þam ȝiƀ þeoɼ ſie on
men. LXVII. Ƿiþ deoƀle ſeoce ⁊ ƿiþ deoƀle. LXVIII.
Ƿiþ ƿeden heoɼte leoht drenc. LVIIII. Ƿiþ þam¹ ȝiƀ
men ſie maȝa aſuɼod ⁊ ƀoɼþunden · ⁊ ƿiþ maȝan
ƿæɼce · ⁊ ȝiƀ man biþ aþunden. LXX. Ƿiþ þambe
ƿæɼce · ⁊ ƿiþ maȝan ƿæɼce · ⁊ ƿiþ þambe heaɼdneɼɼe.
LXXI. Ƿið ſpɼinȝe ſmiɼinȝ ⁊ ſealƀ. LXXII. Ƿiþ atteɼe
drenc ⁊ ſmiɼinȝ. LXXIII. Ƿiþ þeɼe ȝeolpan able.
LXXIIII. Ƿiþ þam ȝiƀ innelƀe ſi ute. LXXV. Ƿiþ
ælcɼe innan untɼymneɼɼe ⁊ ƿiþ heƀiȝneɼɼe ⁊ ƿiþ
hleoɼblæce. LXXVI. be þam hu mán ſcyle haliȝe
ſealƀe ƿyɼcean.

. I.

Ƿiþ þon þe món on heaƀod ace · ȝenim moɼo-
ɼenɼde ƿɼætte do on ɼeadne ƿɼæd binde þ heaƀod mid.
Ƿiþ þon ilcan · nim ſeneɼeɼ ɼæd ⁊ ɼudun ȝeȝnid on ele
do on hat ƿæteɼ þƿeah ȝelome þ heaƀod on þam ƿætɼe
he biþ hal. Ƿiþ caldum heaƀod ece ȝenim dɼeoɼiȝe

---

¹ Ƿiþa, MS.

with whom the devil hath commerce. 62. Against elf
disease, a leechdom; and again, how one must sing
upon the worts, ere one take them; and again, how
one must put the worts under the altar, and sing over
them; and again tokens of this, whether it be elf
hicket, and tokens how thou mayst understand, whether
one may cure the man; and drinks and prayers against
every temptation of the fiend. 63. Tokens how thou
mayst understand whether a man be in the water elf
disease, and a leechdom for that, and a charm to be
sung upon it, and that ilk may be sung over wounds.
64. A lithe *or soft* drink against the devil, and want
of memory, and against temptations of the devil. 65.
In case a man be overlooked, and tokens whether he
may live. 66. A drink in case the "dry" disease be
on a man. 67. For the devil sick *or demoniac*, and
against the devil. 68. A light drink against the wild
heart. 69. In case a mans maw be soured and distended; and against pain of the maw, and if a man
be inflated. 70. For pain of the wamb, and for pain
of the maw, and for hardness of the wamb. 71. Against
carbuncle; an ointment and a salve. 72. A drink and
smearing against venom. 73. For the yellow disease,
*jaundice.* 74. In case the bowels be out. 75. For
every inward infirmity, and for heaviness, and for cheek
blotch. 76. Of this, how a man must make a holy
salve.

## i.

In case a man ache in the head; take the netherward part of crosswort,[1] put it on a red fillet, let him
bind the head therewith. For that ilk, take seed of
mustard and rue, rub into oil, put into hot water, wash
the head often in the water, *the man* will be hale.
For an old head ache, take pennyroyal, boil in oil, or

---

[1] *Galium cruciatum.*

ðpoſtlan pyl on ele oððe on butꞃan ſmiꞃe mið[1] þa
þunꞃonꞡan ꞇ buꞃan þam eaꞡum on uꞃan þ heaꞃoð
þeah him ſie ꞡemynð oncypped he biþ hal.    Þiþ ſpiþe

fol. 111 b.

caldum heaꞃoð ece nim ꞃealt ꞇ ꞃuðan ꞇ iꞃiꞡ eꞃoꞃ cnua
ealle to ꞃomne[2] ðo on hunꞡ ꞇ ſmiꞃe mið þa þunꞃan-
ꞡan · ꞇ þone hniꞇel ꞇ uꞃan þ heaꞃoð.    To þon ilcan
ꞃec lytle ſtanaſ on ſpealpan bꞃiðða maꞡan ꞇ heald þ
lne ne hꞃinan eoꞃꞃan ne pætꞃe · ne oþꞃum ſtanum
beꞃcoꞃa hꞃa . III. on þon þe þu ꞃille ðo on þone mon
þe him þeaꞃꞃ ſie him biþ ꞃona ꞃel · hi beoþ ꞡoðe þiþ
heaꞃoð ece ꞇ þiþ eaꞡꞃæꞃee ꞇ þiþ ꞃeonðeꞃ coſtunꞡa ꞇ
nihtꞡenꞡan · ꞇ lencten aðle ꞇ maꞃan ꞇ pyꞃtꞃoꞃþoꞃe ·
ꞇ malſcꞃa · ꞇ yꞃlum ꞡealðoꞃ cꞃæꞃtum · hit ſculon beon
micle bꞃiððaꞃ þe þu hie ꞃcealt on ꞃinðan · ꞡiꞃ mon on
healꞃ heaꞃoð ace ꞡecnua ꞃinðan ſpiþe ðo on ſtꞃanꞡ eceð
ꞇ ſmiꞃe mið þ heaꞃoð uꞃan ꞃihte.    Þiþ þon ilcan aðelꞃ
peꞡbꞃæðan butan iſene æꞃ ſunnan upꞡanꞡe binð þa
moꞃan ymb þ heaꞃoð mið pꞃæte ꞃeaðe pꞃæðe ꞃona
him bið ꞃel.

.II.

Þiþ aſpollenum eaꞡum eaꞡum ꞡenim cucune hꞃeꞃn[3] aðo
þa eaꞡan oꞃ ꞇ eꞃt cucune ꞡebꞃinꞡ on pætꞃe ꞇ ðo þa
eaꞡan þam men on ſpeoꞃan þe him þeaꞃꞃ ꞃie he biþ
ꞃona hal.    Þyꞃe ꞡoðe eaꞡꞃealꞃe xim celeþonian ꞇ
biꞃceop pyꞃt · peꞃmoð · puðu meꞃice · puðu binðeꞃ
leaꞃ · ðo ealꞃa emꞃcla enuꞃa ꞃel ðo on hunꞡ · ꞇ on
þiñ · ꞇ on æꞃen ꞃæt oððe on cypeꞃen ðo tꞃæðe þæꞃ
fol. 112 a.    ꞃineꞃ · ꞇ þꞃiððan ðæl þæꞃ hunꞡeꞃ ðo þ ꞃe pæta mæꞡe
ꞃiꞃþum oꞃeꞃ yꞃinan þa pyꞃta læt ſtanðan .VII. niht
ꞇ ꞃꞃeoh mið bꞃeðe aſeoh þuꞃh clænne claþ ðone ðꞃenc
ðo eꞃt on þ ilce ꞃæt nytta ſpa þe þeaꞃꞃ ꞃie.    Se mon

[1] The MS. has a stop after mið.
[2] ꞃōme, MS.
[3] Nearly as Marcellus, col. 269 f.

in butter, smear therewith the temples, and over the
eyes, and on the top of the head; though his intellect
be deranged, he will be hale. For a very old head
ache; take salt and rue, and a bunch of ivy berries,
pound all at once, add honey, and therewith smear the
temples, and the forehead, and the top of the head.
For that ilk; seek in the maw of young swallows for
some little stones, and mind that they touch neither
earth, nor water, nor other stones; look out three of
them; put them on the man, on whom thou wilt, him
who hath the need, he will soon be well. They are
good for head ache, and for eye wark, and for the fiends
temptations, and for night *goblin* visitors, and for
typhus, and for the *night* mare, and for knot, and for
fascination, and for evil enchantments by song. It must
be big nestlings on which thou shalt find them. If a
man ache in half his head, pound rue thoroughly, put
it into strong vinegar, and smear therewith the head,
right on the top. For that ilk; delve up waybroad
without iron, ere the rising of the sun, bind the roots
about the head, with crosswort, by a red fillet, soon
he will be well.

## ii.

For swollen eyes, take a live crab, put his eyes out,
and put him alive again into water, and put the eyes
upon the neck of the man, who hath need; he will soon
be well. Work a good eye salve *thus;* take celandine
and bishop wort, wormwood, wood marche, leaves of
woodbind; put equal quantities of all, pound them well,
put them into honey, and into wine, and into a brazen
vessel, or a copper one; put in of the wine two parts
in three, and a third part of the honey, order it so
that the liquor may just overrun the worts; let it
stand for seven nights, and wrap it up with a piece
of stuff; strain the drink through a clean cloth, put it
again into that ilk vessel, use as occasion may be.

ɾe him ȝeðeþ ymb .xxx. mihta ɟoxeɾ ȝelynðeɾ ðæl
on þa eaȝan he biþ ece hal ;

ȝiɟ miſt ɾie ɟoɾe eaȝum nim cilðeɾ hlonð ꝸ huniȝeſ
teaɾ menȝ toſomne beȝea emɟela ſmiɾe mið þa eaȝan
Innan ;

Eɟt hɾeɟneſ ȝeallan ꝸ leaxeſ ꝸ eleſ ꝸ ɟelð beon
huniȝ menȝ to ſomne ſmiɾe mið þæɾe ɾealɟe innan þa
eaȝan ;

Þiþ ɟlie ȝebɾeɟneð ɾealt ꝸ ſpeȝleſ æppel ꝸ attɾum
calɾa emɟela ȝnið to ðuſte ꝸ ðo on þa eaȝan þɾeah
leohtlice mið ƿylle ƿætɾe ꝸ ſmiɾe æɟteɾ mið ƿiɟeſ
meolce ;

ȝiɟ ƿyɾmaſ ſien on eaȝum ɾeeaɾɾa þa hɾæɾaſ innan
ðo on þa ɾeeaɾɾan celeþonian ɾeaɾ · þa ƿyɾmaſ bioþ
ðeaðe ꝸ þa eaȝan hale. ȝiɟ ɟlæɾe on eaȝum ƿeaxe
ɾɾinȝ ƿyɾm ƿyɾte on þa eaȝan oþ ꝥ him ɾel ɾie.

ȝiɟ on eaȝan ƿeaxen ɾeaðe ſponȝe ðɾype on hat
eulɾɾan bloð oþɟe ſɾealɾan oððe ƿiɟeſ meoluc oþ ꝥ þa
ſponȝe apeȝ ɾynð. ȝiɟ eaȝan tyɾen nim ðɾiȝe ɾuðan
ꝸ huniȝeſ teaɾ menȝ toſomne læt ſtanðan .iii. niht
aɾɾinȝ þuɾh ɾiene cla∂ hnenne ꝸ ðo on þa eaȝan
ɾiþþan. Þyɾc ȝoðe ðɾiȝe ſeaðe ſealɟe nim ſpeȝleſ
æɾɾel ꝸ ȝebɾeɟneð ɾealt ꝸ ɾiɾoɾ ꝸ attɾūm ꝸ hɾit
cɾuðu ȝeȝnid to ðuſte aɾiɟt þuɾh cla∂ ðo lytlum on.
Eɟt hɾit cɾuðu ꝸ ȝebɾæɟneð oɟteɾ ɾcyl ȝnid to ðuſte
ꝸ nytta ſɾa ɟe þeaɾɟ ſie æȝþeɾ mæȝ aðon ɟlie uɟ
eaȝan. Þyɾc ſmeþe eaȝɾealɟe nim buteɾan ƿyl on
ɾannan aɟleot ꝥ ɟam uɟ ꝸ ahlyttɾe þa buteɾan on
bleðe ðo eɟt ꝥ hluttɾe on ɾannan ȝeenua celeþonian

fol. 112 b.

The man who putteth upon his eyes for about thirty nights, part of the suet of a fox, he will be for ever healthy.

2. If there be a mist before the eyes, take a childs urine and virgin honey, mingle together of both equal quantities, smear the eyes therewith on the inside.

3. Again, mingle together a crabs gall,[1] and a salmons, and an eels, and field bees honey, smear the eyes inwardly with the salve.

4. Against a white spot in the eye; rub to dust burnt salt, and swails apple, and olusatrum, of all equal quantities, rub to dust, and put on the eyes, wash lightly with spring water, smear afterwards with womans milk.

5. If there are worms in the eyes, scarify the lids within, apply to the scarifications the juice of celandine; the worms will be dead and the eyes healthy. If flesh wax on eyes, wring wormwort into the eyes, till they are well.

6. If red sponges wax on the eyes, drop on them hot culvers blood, or swallows, or womans milk, till the sponges be got rid of. If eyes are bleared, take dry rue and virgin honey, mingle together, let it stand for three nights, wring through a thick linen cloth, and afterwards apply to the eyes. Work a good dry salve for dim vision thus: take swails apple, and burnt salt, and pepper, and olusatrum, and mastich; rub to dust, sift through a cloth, apply by little and little. Again, reduce to dust mastich, and burnt oyster shell, and use as need be; either hath power to remove white spot from the eyes. Work a smooth eyesalve *thus;* take butter, boil in a pan, skim the foam off, and purify the butter in a dish; put the clear part again into a pan; pound celandine

---

[1] " Corvi marini fel." Marcellus, col. 277. F. If that passage were in view, this fish would be the mullet, *Mugil cefalus:* but I follow the passage in Wanley, p. 168 a. Hæpepu is another spelling.

⁊ bɩſceop ƿyɼc · ꝥuðu meɼce · ƿyl ſƿɩþe aɼeoh þuɼh
claꝺ ɳyꞇꞇa ſƿa þe þeaɼꝼ ſie ;

<h2 style="text-align:center">.III.</h2>

Þɩþ eaɼ pæɼ̣ce ȝenɩm henne ȝelynꝺo ⁊ oſꞇeɼ ɼcylle
ɼeꞇe on ȝleꝺa ȝepyɼm hɼon ⁊ ꝺɼyp on þa eaɼan ꞇona
beoꝺ hale ; Eꝼꞇ celenꝺɼan¹ ɼeap ⁊ pɩꝼeɼ meoluc ȝepyɼm
on ɼcylle ⁊ ꝺɼyp on þa eaɼan · ȝɩꝼ pyɼmaſ ɼɩen on
eaɼan ꝺo belenan ɼeap peaɼɩn on þa pyɼmaſ hɩe beoþ
ꝺeaꝺe ⁊ ꝼeallaꝺ óꝼ ⁊ þa eaɼan hale.

Eꝼꞇ ɼɩɩɩȝ cuɼmeallan ɼeap on oþþe maɼubɩan oꝺꝺe
ɼeɼɩɩɩoꝺ peaɼɩɩnɩɩe Sona hɩ́ɩɩ bɩꝺ ɼel. Þyɼe ȝoꝺe eaɼ
ɼcalꝼe · ȝeɩɩɩ baɼeɼ ȝeallan · ⁊ ꝼeaɼɼeſ · ⁊ ele calɼa
eɩɩꝼcla læꞇ ꝺɼyɼan peaɼɩɩ on ꝥ eaɼe.

<h2 style="text-align:center">.IIII.</h2>

fol. 113 a.

Þɩþ ꞇoþ ece ceop pɩɼoɼ ȝelome ɩɩɩꝺ þaɩɩ ꞇoɼɩɩɩ
lɩɩɩ bɩþ ɼona ɼel. Eꝼꞇ ɼcoꝺ beolcnan ɩɩɩoɼan on
ꝼꞇɼaɳȝuɩɩ ececꝺe oþþe on pɩnc ɼeꞇe on þoɳe ɼaɼan ꞇoþ
⁊ hɼɩluɩɩ ceoɼe ɩɩɩꝺ þy ɼaɼan ꞇoþe he bɩꝺ hal. ȝɩꝼ þa
ꞇeþ ſyɳꝺ hole ceop boþeneɼ² ɩɩɩoɼan ɩɩɩꝺ ececꝺe on þa
hcalꝼe.

<h2 style="text-align:center">.V.</h2>

Þɩþ ɩɩɩnan ꞇobɼocenum muꝺc nɩɩɩ plúɩɩ ꞇɼeopeɼ leaſ
pyl on pɩnc ⁊ ſpɩlc ɩɩɩꝺ þone ɩɩuþ :·

<h2 style="text-align:center">.VI.</h2>

Vɩꝺ ccoc aꝺle nɩɩɩ þone hɼeoɼꝼan þe ꝼɩꝼ ɩɩɩꝺ
ſpɩɩɩɳaꝺ bɩɩꝺ on hɩꝼ ſpeoɼaɩɩ ɩɩɩꝺ pyllenan þɼæꝺe ⁊

<hr />

¹ Read celeþenian.
² boȝeneɼ, with ȝe dotted, and þe written above, MS.

and bishopwort, wood marche, boil thoroughly, strain through a cloth; use as need may be.

### iii.

1. Against earwark; take a hens fat and oyster shells, set them on gledes, warm a little, and drip into the ears, soon they will be hale. Again, warm juice of coriander (*celandine rather?*) and womans milk in a shell, and drop *them* into the ears. If worms be in the ears; apply juice of henbane warm, to the worms, they will be dead and fall off, and the ears will be well.

2. Again, wring juice of centaury upon them, or marrubium, or wormwood warm; soon they will be well. Work a good earsalve *thus:* take a boars and a bulls gall, and oil, of all equal quantities, have *this* dropped warm into the ear.

### iv.

For tooth ache; chew pepper frequently with the teeth, it will soon be well with them. Again, seethe henbane roots in strong vinegar or in wine, set this into the sore tooth, and at whiles chew with the sore tooth; it will be well. If the teeth are hollow, chew rosemary roots with vinegar on that part.

### v.

For a mouth troubled with eruption within; take leaves of plum tree, boil in wine, and swill the mouth therewith.

### vi.

For cheek disease, take the whorl, with which a woman spinneth, bind on *the mans* neck with a woollen thread, and swill him on the inside with hot

ſpile man mið hate ȝate meolce him biþ ꝼel. Þið
ceol ꝼæꝛ̈ce adelf æꝛ ſunnan ūꝛȝanȝe peȝbꝛædan bind
on hiſ ſpeoꝛan. Eꝼt bæꝛn ſpealꝛan to duſte · ⁊ menȝ
piþ ꝼeldbeon humȝ ſele him etan ȝelome.

### .VII.

Þiþ healſ ꝼæꝛce pyl neoþeꝛeaꝛde netelan on oxan
ſmeꝛpe ⁊ on buteꝛan þonne ¹ þone heallſpæꝛc ſmiꝛe ða
þeoh · ȝiſ ſa þeoh ꝼæꝛce ſmiꝛe þone healſ mið þæꝛe
ſealꝼe. Eꝼt pyl uꝺþeꝛeaꝛde netelan on ecede ꝺo oxan
ȝeallan on þ eced ⁊ þa pyꝛte oꝼ ſmiꝛe mið þone
healſ.

### .VIII.

Þiþ bite pyꝛe ſealꝼe · nim ſaꝛ pyꝛte ꝛaꝼenan ⁊
meꝛſe mealpan ⁊ attoꝛlaþan ⁊ peoþobend ⁊ hꝛeꝛhꝛet-
tan ⁊ cluꝼþyꝛt ⁊ ſiȝel hꝛeoꝛꝼan · lund heoloþan ·
mucȝpyꝛt · puꝺu ꝼillan · ȝaꝛchꝛan · ꝛꝛactte · luꝼeſtice ·
maȝeþan · ȝiþcoꝛn · ꝛað · ꝼinul · þeꝛan þoꝛn · ꝛelꝼacte ·
coꝛoꝛþꝛote · ciccna mete · dulhꝛune · pylſe moꝛu ·
hnut beanicꝛ leaꝼ · næꝛ · ȝeaꝛꝛe · hoꝼe · hōc leaꝼ ·
alexandꝛe · ꝛiea peꝛꝛica ·² ſe ꝼula peꝛmoð · ſio ȝꝛeate
banpyꝛt · acleaꝼ · peȝbꝛæðe · ȝiunde ſpelȝe · ꝛcad
claꝼꝛe · leahtꝛic · þuꝼe þiſtel · taꝛu · heȝe clꝛꝼe · cluꝼ
þunȝ · enȝhꝛe moꝛu · ꝺyniȝe.

### .VIIII.

Þiþ hꝛoſtan pyl maꝛubian on pætꝛe ȝoðne ꝺæl ȝe-
ſꝛet hꝛon ſele ꝺꝛincan ꝛeene ꝼul.³ Eꝼt maꝛubian ſꝛiðe
pyl on hunȝe do hꝛon buteꝛan on ſele .III. ſnæda
oþþe .IIII. etan on neaht neꝛtiȝ beꝛup ſcene ꝼulne mið
ꝛeaꝛmeꝛ þæꝛ æꝛꝛan ꝺꝛenceꝛ.

---

¹ Read þonne ꝛið þone.
² A stop after ꝛiea in MS.

³ ꝛeene is masc. Read ꝛulne.

goats milk; it will be well with him. For jowl pain; delve up waybroad before the rising of the sun, bind upon *the mans* neck. Again, burn a swallow to dust, and mingle *him* with field bees honey; give the man ᴀpis silvarum. that to eat frequently.

### vii.

For neck pain; boil the netherward part of nettle in fat of ox and in butter, then for the hals wark, smear the thighs; if the thighs be in pain, smear the neck with the salve. Again, boil the netherward part of nettle in vinegar, add ox gall to the vinegar and remove the wort; smear the neck therewith.

### viii.

For cancer, work a salve; take these worts, savine, and marsh mallow, and attorlothe, and withywind, and cucumber, and clovewort, *or ranunculus*, and turnsol, hindheal, mugwort, wild chervil, agrimony, crosswort, lovage, maythe, githcorn, woad, fennel, tufty thorn, wildoat, everthroat, chickenmeat, pellitory, carot, leaves of the nut tree, nepeta *cattaria*, yarrow, hove, hollyhock, alexanders, vinca pervinca, *or periwinkle*, the foul wormwood, the great bonewort, oak leaves, waybroad, groundsel, red clover, lettuce, tufty thistle, tar, hedge clivers, cloffing, wild parsnip, * * * *

### ix.

For host *or cough*; boil marrubium in water, a good deal *of it*, sweeten a little, give *the man* to drink a cup full. Again, boil marrubium strongly in honey, add a little butter, give three or four bits for *the man* to eat; at night fasting let him sup up a cup full of the former drink warm therewith.

.X.

Viþ þon þe mon blode hræce ȝ spiwe · ȝenim ȝod
beþen mela · ȝ hƿit sealt do on þeam oþþe ȝode flete
hƿer on blede oþ þ hit sie þicce sƿa þynne lþƿþ sele
etan .VIIII. smeda .VIIII. morȝenas on[1] neaht nestiȝ ·
do þær meluƿes træde ȝ þæs sealtes þriddan dæl ƿyne
ælce dæȝe niþne.

.XI.

Þiþ feondum ȝeallan ete þædie ȝ piþoȝ on neaht
nestiȝ · ȝ apylleð liþræð on meolce suþe miþ[2] do þus
ȝelome him biþ sona sel.

.XII.

Við þæpe ȝeolpan adle sio cymð of feondum ȝeallan
ȝenim þæs sceappan þistles moran ȝ betonican · ȝ æt-
toplaþan hand fulle · ȝ ȝyþþiþan hand fulle ȝ .VIIII.
smeda moþorcaþe scpeþpotan of ȝeot miþ stpanȝan
beope · oþþe miþ stpanȝum calað ȝ drince ȝelome sele
him etan ȝepyptodne henfuȝel ȝ ȝesodenne capel on
ȝodum bpoðe do þus ȝelome him biþ sona sel.

Þyne ȝodne dust drenc piþ þæpe ȝeolpan adle · nim
meþceþ ræd · ȝ finoleþ ræd · dile ræd · eoxopþpotan
sæd · feldmoþan sæd · sæþeþian ræd · petoþþilian ræd ·
alexandþian sæd lufesticeþ ræd · betonican sæd · cauleþ
ræd · costeþ ræd · cymeneþ ræd · ȝ pipoþeþ mæpt
þaþa oðeppa emfela ȝeȝnid ealle pel to dufte nim þæs
dufteþ ȝodne euclen fulne do on stpanȝ hluttoþ eala
drince scene fulne on neaht nestiȝ · he iſ ȝod piþ
ælcþe liman untpumneſſe ȝ piþ heafod ece ȝ piþ un-

___

[1] Unless morȝenas, morrows, can be taken in the sense of successive
days, on must be omitted. Observe, a new page begins.
[2] In margin heþto.

fol. 114 a.

fol. 114 b.

### X.

In case a man hreak up and spew blood; take good barley meal, and white salt, put it into cream or good skimmings, agitate in a dish, till it be as thick as thin brewit, give *the man* to eat, nine doses for nine mornings after his nights fast : apply of the meal two parts in three, and of the salt a third part; prepare it every day new.

### xi.

For bile straining out; let the patient eat radish and pepper at night fasting, and let him sup besides linseed boiled in milk ; do this frequently ; it will soon be well with him.

### xii.

1. For the yellow disease, *jaundice*, which cometh of effusion of bile; take roots of the sharp thistle, and betony, and a handful of attorlothe, and a handful of githrife, and nine bits of the netherward part of ash-throat, pour them over with strong beer, or with strong ale, and let him drink *this* frequently : give him to eat a pullet dressed with herbs, and colewort sodden in good broth ; do this frequently, soon it will be well with him.

2. Work *thus* a good dust drink for the yellow disease. Take seed of marche, and seed of fennel, seed of dill, seed of everthroat, seed of fieldmore, seed of satureia, *savory*, seed of parsley, seed of alexanders, seed of lovage, seed of betony, seed of colewort, seed of costmary, seed of cummin, and of pepper most, of the others equal quantities ; rub all well to dust, take a good spoon full of the dust, put it into strong clear ale, let *the man* drink a cup full at night fasting. This *drink* is also good for every ailment of limb, and for head ache, and for want of memory, and for eye

ᵹemynde ⁊ ƿiþ eaᵹꝼæꞃꝼce ⁊ ƿiþ unᵹehyꞃnꞅꞅe ⁊ bꞃeoꞅt
ꞃæꞃce ⁊ lunᵹen adle ⁊ lenden ꝼæꞃce · ⁊ ƿiþ ælcꞃe
ꝼeondeꞅ coꞅtunᵹa ᵹeꝼyꞃe þe duꞅt ᵹenoh on hæꞃꝼeꞅte
þonne þu þa ƿyꞃta hæbbe nytta þonne þe þeaꞃꝼ ꞅie.

### .XIII.

Þiꞅ bꞃeoꞅtꞃæꞃce maꞃubie · neꞅꞇe · onꞇꞃe biꞅꞅcop
ƿyꞃꞇ · ꝼenꝼyꞃꞇ · ꝼyl on huniᵹe ⁊ buꞇeꞃan do þæꞃ
huniᵹeꞅ ꞇꞃæde · ⁊ þæꞃe buꞇeꞃan þꞃiddan dæl nytta
ꞅꞃa þe þeaꞃꝼ ꞅie.

### .XIIII.

Ƿiþ hꞃoꞅꞇan ⁊ lunᵹen adle · ᵹenim ꞅpeᵹleꞅ æppel ⁊
ꞅpeꝼl ⁊ ꝼeceꝼl ealꞃa emꝼela menᵹ ƿiþ ƿeaxe leᵹe on
haꞇne ꞅꞇan dꞃiᵹne þuꞃh hoꞃn þone ꞃec ⁊ eꞇe æꝼꞇeꞃ
ealdeꞃ ꞅpiceꞅ .III. ꞅꞃæda oððe buꞇeꞃan ⁊ ꞅuꞃe mid
ꝼleꞇum; Ƿiþ lunᵹen adle · ᵹenim beꞇonican · ⁊ maꞃubian · aᵹꞃimonian · ꞃeꞃmod · ꝼel ꞇeꞃꞃe · ꞃude · aᵹꞃind·
ᵹaᵹollan · ꝼyl on ꝼæꞇꞃe · bepyl þæꞃ ꝼæꞇeꞃeꞅ þꞃiddan
dæl · do oꝼ þa ƿyꞃꞇe dꞃince on moꞃᵹenne ꝼeaꞃuneꞅ
ꞅcene ꝼulne eꞇe .III. ꞅꞃæda mid þæꞃ bꞃꝼeꞅ þe heꞃ
æꝼꞇeꞃ ꞅeᵹþ :·

fol. 115 a.

Ƿyꞃꞇ bꞃꝼ ƿiþ lunᵹen adle nim beꞇonican · ⁊ maꞃubian · ꞃeꞃmod · hindheoloþan · ꝼenꝼyꞃꞇ moþoꞃeaꞃd ·
elehꞇꞃe · elene · ꞃædic · coꝼoꞃþꞃoꞇe · ꝼeldmoꞃe · ᵹecnua
ealle ꞅꞃiþe ƿel ⁊ ƿyl on buꞇeꞃan ⁊ apꞃinᵹ þuꞃh claþ
ꞃcead on þ̅ ꝼoꞃ beꞃen mela hꞃeꞃ on blede buꞇan ꝼyꞃe
oþ þ̅ hiꞇ ꞅie ꞅꞃa þicce ꞅꞃa bꞃꝼ eꞇe .III. ꞅꞃæda · mid
þy dꞃence ꝼeaꞃuneꞅ.

Eꝼꞇ ꝼyl on huniᵹe anum maꞃubian do hꞃon beꞃen
mela ꞇo eꞇe on neahꞇ neꞅꞇiᵹ ⁊ þonne þu him ꞃelle

wark, and for dull hearing, and for breast wark, and
lung disease, loin wark, and for every temptation of
the fiend. Work thyself dust enough in harvest, when
thou hast the worts, use it when thou hast need.

### xiii.

For pain of breast; marrubium, nepeta, ontre, bishopwort, wenwort, boil in honey and butter; put two
parts in three of the honey, and of the butter a third
part; use as need may be.

### xiv.

For host, or *cough*, and lung disease; take swails
apple, and brimstone, and frankincense, of all equally
much, mingle with wax, lay on a hot stone, let *the
man* swallow the reek through a horn, and afterwards
eat three pieces of old lard or of butter, and sip *this*
with cream. For lung disease; take betony, and marrubium, agrimony, wormwood, fel terræ *or centaury*,
rue, oak rind, sweet gale; boil them in water, boil off
a third part of the water, remove the worts; let *the
man* drink in the morning of *this* warm a cup full,
let him eat therewith three pieces of the brewit that
is here afterwards mentioned.

2. Work *thus* a brewit for lung disease; take betony,
and marrubium, wormwood, hind heal,[1] the lower part
of wen wort, lupin, helenium, radish, everthroat, fieldmore; pound all thoroughly well, and boil in butter,
and wring through a cloth; shed on the decoction barley
meal, shake it in a dish without fire till it be as thick
as brewit; let him eat three pieces, with the drink
of the warm *liquor*.

3. Again, boil in honey alone, marrubium, add a little
barley meal, let *the man* eat at night fasting; and when

---

[1] *Eupatorium cannabinum.*

 speno oððe bytp sele him hatne ⁊ læt ᵹenestan þone
man æstep tide[1] dæᵹes on þa spiðran siðan ⁊ hasa þone
eatm aþeneð.

. XV.

Þiþ maᵹan wærce wyl pīc on cu meolce abo þ̵ pic
ós supe hpon peatm sona biþ sel. Þiþ aþundenesse ⁊
[ᵹis][2] men nelle myltan his mete wyl on wætepe
polleian ⁊ leac cepsan sele dpincan him biþ sona
sel ;

. XVI.

Viþ milte wærce cnua ᵹpene sealhpinde seoð on
huniᵹe anum sele him etan . III. snæda on neaht
nestiᵹ.

. XVII.

Þiþ lenden wærce manubie . neste . boᵹen em sela
ealpa ðo on ᵹoð ealu pype to dpence spet hpōn sele
dpincan heᵹe uppeapð æstep þon ᵹoðe hpile.

. XVIII.

fol. 115 b.

Þiþ pambe wærce ⁊ nysel wærce þæp þu ᵹeseo topð
pisel on copþan sip peoppan ymbso lune mid tpam
handum mid his ᵹepeoppe pasa mid þinum handum
spiþe ⁊ cpeð þnipa ∙ Remedium facio ad uentpis dolopem.
Peopp þonne ofep bæc þone pisel on seᵹebehealð þ̵
þu ne lociᵹe æstep ∙ þonne monnes pambe wærce oððe
nysle ymbsoh mid þinūm handum þa pambe him biþ

thou givest him drink or brewit, give it him hot; and
make the man rest after an hour, by day, on the right
side, and have the arm extended.

### xv.

For pain in the maw; boil pitch in cow milk, remove the pitch, let him sip a little warm, soon *the
man* will be well. For distention, and if a mans
meat will not digest; boil in water pulegium and leek
cress,[1] give *this* to the man to drink, soon it will be
well with him.

### xvi.

For milt pain; pound green sallow rind, seethe in
honey alone, give *the man* to eat three pieces at night
fasting.

### xvii.

For loin wark; marrubium, nepeta, thyme, of all
equal quantities, put into good ale; work to a drink,
sweeten a little, give *to the man* to drink; let him
lie with face up afterwards for a good while.

### xviii.

For wamb wark and pain in the fatty part of the
belly; when thou seest a dung beetle[2] in the earth
throwing up *mould*, catch him with thy two hands
along with his casting up, wave him strongly with
thy hands, and say thrice, " Remedium facio ad ventris
" dolorem;" then throw the beetle over thy back away;
take care thou look not after it. When a mans wamb
or belly fat is in pain, grasp the wamb with thine

---

[1] *Erysimum alliaria.*
[2] Our Saxon must have had Tal-
pam, or ʼΑσπάλακα before him in
this sentence; but he names the
*Scarabæus stercorarius.*

ƿona ƿel · XII. monaþ þu meaht ſƿa ðon æꝼꞇeꞃ þam
ꝼꝛꝼele

### XVIIII.

Ƿiþ blæðꝺeꞃ ƿærce. Ƿudu meꞃce · ⁊ leacceꞃſe ƿyl
ſꝛꝛe on ealað ſele ꝺꞃincan ⁊ eꞇan ȝebꞃæꝺne ſꞇæꝼ.

### .XX.

Ȝiꝼ man ne mæȝe ȝemiȝan ⁊ him ꝛeaxan ſꞇanaꞃ on
þæꞃe blæðꞃan ƿyl ꝼunꝺcoꝛꝛ on ealað ⁊ peꞇeꞃſilian ſele
him ꝺꞃincan.

### .XXI.

Ȝiꝼ men ſie ſe uꞇȝanȝ ꝼoꞃꝼeꞇen ƿyl ꝛeꞃmoð on
ꞃuꞃum ealaþ ⁊ ðo buꞇeꞃan þæꞃ to him biþ ſona ſel
ȝiꝼ he hiꞇ ꝺꞃincþ.

### .XXII.

Ƿiþ ſꞇꝛꝛiht aðle · v. leaꝼan · hleomoce · cuꞃmealle ·
elehꞇꞃe. Ȝeonna þa ƿyꞃꞇa · ⁊ ƿyl on meolce ſele him

fol. 116 a.

ꝺꞃincan ꝛeaꞃin on moꞃȝenne ⁊ on æꝼen ; Ƿꝛꝛe bꝛꝛiꝛ
ꞇo þon ilean ƿuꝺu cunellan · hleomoðe · beꝛyl þaꞃa
meolce þꝛiꝺꝺan ꝺæl þæꞃe ƿyꞃꞇe oꝛ þam meolcum[1]
ſeeað hꞃæꞇen mela þæꞃ on ⁊ eꞇe þone bꝛꝛiꝛ cealꝺne ·
⁊ ꞃuꞃe þa meolúc him bið ſona ſel ȝiꝼ ſe bꝛꝛiꝛ ⁊ ſe
ꝺꞃene iune ȝeꞃuniað þu meaht þone man ȝelácnian
ȝiꝼ him ðꝼꝼleoȝeð him bið ꞃelꝼe þ þu hine na ne
ȝꝛeꞇe him biþ hiꞃ ꝼeoꝛh aðl ȝeꞇenȝe.

### . XXIII.

Ȝiꝼ ƿyꞃmaꞃ beoþ on manneſ innoðe ƿyl on buꞇeꞃan
ȝꞃene ꝛuꝺan ꝺꞃine[2] on neahꞇ neꝛꞇiȝ ſeene ꞃulne hi

---

[1] Read as before beꝛyl on meolce oþ þꝛiꝺꝺan ꝺæl · ðo þa ƿyꞃꞇa oꝛ
þam meolcum.

[2] Vowel dropped.

hands, it will soon be well with *the man;* for twelve months after the beetle thou shalt have power so to do.

### xix.

For bladder pain; wood marche and sauce alone; boil *them* strongly in ale; administer to drink, and to eat a roasted starling.

### xx.

If a man cannot mie, and stones wax in the bladder; boil sundcorns[1] in ale, and parsley; give *him* this to drink.

### xxi.

If a mans excrement be lodged; boil wormwood in sour ale, and add butter thereto; it will soon be well with him, if he drinketh it.

### xxii.

For diarrhœa; cinqfoil, brooklime, churmel, lupin; pound the worts, and boil them in milk; give *this* to the man to drink warm in the morning and in the evening. Work *thus* a brewit for the same: wild cunila, brooklime; boil in milk to a third part, remove the worts from the milk, shed wheaten meal thereon, and let him eat the brewit cold, and let him sip the milk, it will soon be well with him. If the brewit and the drink remain within him, thou mayst cure the man; if they flow away, it will be better for him, that thou should not meddle with him, his death sickness is upon him.

### xxiii.

1. If worms be in a mans inwards; boil green rue in butter, let the man drink at night fasting a cup

---

[1] *Saxifragia granulata.* Prescribed because saxa frangit.

geƿitað ealle aƿeg mid þy utgange ⁊ he bið sona hal;

To þon ilcan genim cymenes dust meng to gate geallan ⁊ fearres gnid þone nafolan mid ealle hi geƿitaþ niþer; ōf þæm men.

.XXIIII.

Ƿiþ lið ƿærce sing .VIIII. siþum þis gealdor þær on. ⁊ þin spatl spiƿ on. Malignus obligauit. angelus curauit. dominus Saluauit. him biþ sona sel.

To þon ilcan genim culfran tord. ⁊ gate tord drige sƿiðe ⁊ gnid to duste meng ƿiþ hunig ⁊ ƿiþ butran smire mid þa leoþu.

.XXV.

Ƿiþ ƿeartum genim hundes micgean ⁊ muse blod meng to somne smire mid þa ƿeartan hi geƿitaþ sona aƿeg :·

fol. 116 b. .XXVI.

Ƿiþ miclan lice genim moþoƿearde elenan ⁊ þung. ⁊ ōmpran þa þe sƿimman ƿile ealra emfela. ⁊ gecnua ƿel. ⁊ ƿyl on buteran do ƿel sealtes on ⁊ smire mid. Ƿyrc bið[1] ƿiþ þam miclan lice. elene. ælfþone. marubie. curmealle. ellen tanas. ⁊ ac tanas ƿyl sƿiðe on ƿætre ⁊ beþe on sƿiðe hatum þ lic. Ƿyrc drenc ƿið þam miclan lice hindhioloþan. curmeallan. bogen. nefte. agrimonia. betonica. finul. dile. do on god ealo sele drincan on dæge .III. scencas fulle. Ƿyrc driƿ ƿiþ þon ilcan. genim moþoƿearde elenan. ⁊ eofor þrotan. ƿedic. ⁊ þa readan netlan moþoƿearde scearfa smæle ⁊ gecnua ƿel. ƿyl siþþan on buteran do clæne ifig taran þær on gif þu hæbbe. ⁊ hƿon berenes melƿes do on blede mid þam ƿyrtum ⁊ hrer mid sticcan oþ

[1] That is, bæð.

full; they will all depart away with the evacuation, and he will soon be well.

2. For that ilk. Take dust of cummin, mingle it with goats and bulls gall, rub the navel with them all, the *worms* will all disappear from the man downwards.

### xxiv.

1. For joint pain; sing nine times this incantation thereon, and spit thy spittle on *the joint:* "Malignus " obligavit; angelus curavit; dominus salvavit." It will soon be well with him.

2. For that ilk. Take doves dung and a goats tord, dry them thoroughly and rub to dust, mingle with honey and with butter, smear the joints therewith.

### xxv.

For warts; take hounds mie, and a mouses blood, mingle together, smear the warts therewith, they will soon depart away.

### xxvi.

For elephantiasis, take the netherward part of helenium and aconite, and dock, that *namely* which will swim, of all equal quantities, and pound well and boil in butter, add a good spice of salt, and smear therewith. Work *thus* a bath against the mickle body *brought on by leprosy*, helenium, enchanters nightshade, marrubium, churmel, elder twigs, and oak twigs; boil strongly in water, and bathe the body in it very hot. Work *thus* a drink against the mickle body; put hindheal, churmel, thyme, nepeta, agrimony, betony, fennel, dill, into good ale; administer to be drunk in a day three cups full. Work a brewit for that ilk; take the netherward part of helenium and everthroat, radish, and the netherward part of the red nettle, scrape them small, and pound them well. Afterwards boil them in butter; add ivy tar besides if thou have it, and a little barley meal; put this on a dish with the

ꝥ hit col sie ꝼele etan on neaht neꝼtiʒ . III. snæða
ꝼele þone bꞃiꝧ ꝺ þone dꞃenc æꝛ þam bæþe þy læꝛ hit
mꞃlca æꝼteꞃ þam baþe.

### . XXVII.

Ƿiþ ꞃinʒalum þuꞃꝼte [1] untꞃumꞃa manna · Nim peꞃmoð ꝺ hind hꞃoloþan ꝺ ʒyþꞃꝺꝼan ꝼylle ōn ealaꝧ ʒeꝼꝛete
liꝺon ꝼele him dꞃincan hit hælꝧ þone þuꞃꝼt [2] pun-
ðoꞃlice.

fol. 117 a.

### . XXVIII.

Ƿiþ innan ꝼoꞃtoʒe [3] smæl þeaꞃma ece · ʒenim betonican · ꝺ peꞃmoð · meꞃce · ꞃæðic · ꝼinul · ʒecnua ealle ·
ꝺ ðo on eala sete þonne ꝺ beꞃꝛeoh dꞃinc on neaht
neꝼtiʒ ꝛcene ꝼulne.

### . XXVIIII.

Ƿiþ bꞃyne ʒiꝼ mōn sie mid ꝼyꞃe ane ꝼoꞃbæꞃned
nim puðuꞃoꝼan · ꝺ hlian · ꝺ hleomoc ꝼyl on butꞃꞃan
ꝺ smiꞃe mid. ʒiꝼ mon sie mid ꝛætan ꝼoꞃbæꞃned nime
elm ꞃinde · ꝺ hlian moꞃan ꝼyl on meolcum smiꞃe mid
þꞃiꞃa on dæʒ. Ƿiþ sunbꞃyne · meꞃꞃe iꝼiʒ tꞃiʒu ꝼyl
on butꞃꞃan smiꞃe mid.

### . XXX.

Ƿyꞃc ʒoðne ðꞃoꞃ dꞃenc · peꞃmoð · boʒen · ʒaꞃclꞃan ·
polleian · penpyꞃt · þa smalan ꝼel teꞃꞃe · eaʒwyꞃt ·
þeoꞃwyꞃt · ceasteꞃ æꞃcef . II. snæða · elenan . III. com-
mucef ⁵ III. puðu peax ān ʒoðne ðæl · cuꞃmeallan ·
ʒeꞃceaꞃꝼa þaꝼ pyꞃta on ʒoð hluttoꞃ eala oꝧþe pylisc
ealu læt standan . III. niht beꞃꞃiʒen ꝼele dꞃincan
ꝛcene ꝼulne tiðe æꞃ oꝛꞃum mete. Ƿiþ þeoꞃe ꝺ piꞃ
ꝛeotenðum penne · nim boʒen · ꝺ ʒeaꞃꞃan ꝺ puðu peax

fol. 117 b.

---

[1] ðuꝛ, MS.
[2] þꞃꝼt, MS.

[4] Read ꝼoꞃtoʒennerꞃe ꝺ.

worts, and stir it about with a spoon till it be cool; give *the man* to eat at night fasting three bits of it; give the brewit and the drink before the bath; let it strike inwards after the bath.

### xxvii.

For the constant thirst of ailing men; take wormwood, and hind heal, and githrife, boil in ale, sweeten a little, give to the man to drink, it healeth the thirst wonderfully.

### xxviii.

For inward griping and small guts ache; take betony, and wormwood, marche, radish, fennel; pound all and put into ale, then set it down and wrap it up; drink at night fasting a cup full.

### xxix.

For a burn; if a man be burnt with fire only, take woodruff, and lily, and brookline; boil in butter, and smear therewith. If a man be burnt with a liquid, let him take elm rind and roots of lily; boil them in milk, smear therewith thrice a day. For sunburn; boil in butter tender ivy twigs; smear therewith.

### xxx.

Work a good "dry" drink *for the "dry" disease;* wormwood, thyme, agrimony, pennyroyal, wenwort, the small centaury, eyewort, inula conyza, two proportions of black hellebore, three of helenium, eight of cammock, wood wax, a good deal of it, churmel; scrape these worts into good clear ale, or foreign ale, let it stand wrapt up for three nights, give *the man* a cup full to drink an hour before other meat. Against the "dry disease" and against a shooting wen; take bothen, and yarrow, and wood wax, and ravens foot, put into

ꝺ hneꝼneꞅ ꝼoꞇ ꝺo on ȝoꝺ ealu ꞅele ꝺnincan on bæȝe
. ııı. ꞅcencaꞅ ꝼulle.　ȝıꝼ þeoꞁ ȝepunıȝe on anꞁc ꞅꞇope
pync beþınȝe nım þ ıꝼıȝ þe on ꞅꞇane peaxe · ꝺ ȝeanpan ·
ꝺ puꝺu bınꝺeꞁ leaꝼ ꝺ cuꞅlyppan ȝecnua ealle pel leȝe
on haꞇne ꞅꞇan on ꞇꞁoȝe ȝcoꞇ hꝛon pæꞇeꞁeꞅ on læꞇ
ꞁeocan on þ lıc þꞁeꞁ þꞁꞁ hım þeanꝼ ꞅıe þonne ꞅe col
ꞅıe ꝺo oþeꞁıne haꞇne on beþe ꞅpa ȝelome hım bıþ
ꞅona ꞅel.

### . XXXI.

Þynꞇ ȝoꝺe penꞅealꝼe nım puꝺu meꞁce · ꝺ hneꝼneꞅ
ꝼoꞇ · ꝺ peꞁınoꝺ nıoþopeaꞁꝺne · cu ꞅlyppan · ꞁuꝺan ·
puꝺu bınꝺeꞁ leaꝼ · ıꝼıȝ leaꝼ þe on eonþan pıxþ · þa cluꞅ-
ꞅıhꞇan · penpynꞇ · ȝecnua ealle · pyl on ꞁammeꞅ ꞅmeꞁꞁe
oþþe on buccan ꝺo þꞁıꝺꝺan bæl buꞇeꞁan apꞁınȝ þuꞁh
claþ ꝺo þonne ȝoꝺne ꞅcıp ꞇaꞁan ꞇo ꝺ hꞁeꞁ oþ þ lıꞇ
col ꞅıe.

### . XXXII.

Vynꞇ ȝoꝺe ꝺollı ꞅealꝼe nım ȝeaꞁpan · ꝺ puꝺu ꞁoꞅan
nıoþopeaꞁꝺe · ꝼelꝺ moꞁan · ꝺ nıoþopeaꞁꝺne ꞅıȝel hpeoꞁ-
ꝼan pyl on ȝoꝺꞁe buꞇeꞁan apꞁınȝ þuꞁh claꝺ ꝺ læꞇ ȝe-
ꞅꞇanꝺan pel ælc ꝺollı þu meahꞇ lacnıan mıꝺ.

### . XXXIII.

fol. 118 a.
Ȝıꝼ mon ꞅıe uꞁan on heaꝼoꝺ punꝺ ꝺ ꞅıe ban ȝe-
bꞁocen nım ꞅıȝel hꞁeoꞁꝼan · ꝺ hpıꞇe clæꝼꞁan pıꞅan ·
ꝺ puꝺuꞁoꞁan ꝺo on ȝoꝺe buꞇꞁan aꞅeolı puꞁh claꝺ ꝺ
lacna ꞅıþþan.　　　　　　　　　　　　　：·

Ȝıꝼ ꞅıo eaxl uꝼꞅꞇıȝe nım [1]　þa ꞅealꝼe ꝺo hꝛon peaꞁme
mıꝺ ꝼeþenc hım bıꝺ ꞅona ꞅel.　Þynꞇ ȝoꝺne ꝺollı ꝺꞁenc
nım aȝꞁımonıan ꝺ puꝺu ꞁoꞁan ꝺo on ȝoꝺ ealo ꞅele
ꝺꞁıncan ȝoꝺne ꞅcenc ꝼulne on neahꞇ neꞅꞇıȝ.　ȝıꝼ ȝe-

---

good ale, give *the man* to drink three cups full a day : if the "dry disease" remain in one place, work a fomentation *thus ;* take the ivy, which groweth on stone, and yarrow, and leaves of woodbind and cowslip ; pound all *these* well, lay *them* on a hot stone in a trough, pour a little water upon *them,* let it reek upon the body, where need may be ; when *the stone* is cool, put another hot one in, foment *the man* so frequently. It will soon be well with him.

## xxxi.

Work a good won salve *thus ;* take wood marche, and ravens foot, and the netherward part of wormwood, cowslip, rue, leaves of woodbind, ivy leaves, that ivy which groweth on the earth, the cloved wenwort ; pound *them* all, boil in rams grease, or in bucks grease, put a third part of butter, wring through a cloth, then add good ship tar, and shake till it be cool.

## xxxii.

Work a good wound salve *thus ;* take yarrow, and the nether part of woodruff, fieldmore, and the nether part of solwherf ; boil in good butter, wring through a cloth, and let it stand. Pretty well every wound thou mayst cure therewith.

## xxxiii.

1. If a man be wounded in his upper quarter, in his head, and *some* bone be broken ; take solwherf, and white clover plants, and woodruff ; put into good butter, strain through a cloth, and so treat *the patient.*

2. If the shoulder get up out of place, take the salve, apply a little warm with a feather : it will soon be well with the man. Work a good wound drink *thus ;* take agrimony, and woodruff, put *them* into good ale, give *the man* to drink a good cup full, at

bpocen ban fie on heaꝑde ꝫ óꝼ nelle cnua ȝꝑene betonican ꝫ leȝe on ꝥ dolh ȝelome oꝥ ꝥ þa ban oꝼ fyn ꝫ
ꝥ dolh ȝebatod.

### .XXXIIII.

Þiþ hundeꝼ ꝛlƚe cnupa ꝛibban leȝe on ꝥ dolh ꝫ
ꝛudan ꝑyl on butꝛan lǽcna mid ꝥ dolh. ȝiꝼ finpe fyn
ꝼopcopꝼene nim ꝛenꝑyꝛmaꝛ ȝecnupa ꝑel leȝe on oꝥ ꝥ hi
hale fynd. Ȝiꝼ ꝛinpe ꝛen ȝeꝛcꝛunccne nime ꞑemeꞇꞇan
mid hiopa bedȝeꝛide ꝑyl on ꝑæꞇꝛe ꝫ beþe mid ꝫ ꝛece
þa ꝛinpe ȝeopnlice.

### .XXXV.

Viþ ȝonȝeꝛꝼꝛan biꞇe nim henne ǽȝ ȝmid on ealu
hꝛeaꝛ ꝫ ꝛceaꝛeꝛ topd nipe fpa he nyꞇe ꝛele him dꝛincan
ȝodne fcenc ꝼulne.

### .XXXVI.

Þiþ cancꝛe nim ȝaꞇe ȝeallan ꝫ huniȝ menȝ ꞇo
fomne · beȝea emꝼela do on ꝥ dolh. To þon ilean nipe
hundeꝼ heaꝼod bæꝛn ꞇo ahꝛan do on dolh · ȝiꝼ hiꞇ
nelle ꝥ nim monnef dꝛoȝan dꝛiȝ fpiðe ȝmid ꞇo duſte
do on ȝiꝼ þu mid þyꝛ ne meahꞇ ȝelacnian ne meahꞇ
þu him ꞇꝛꝛꝛe nahꞇe.

### .XXXVII.

Þiþ þon þe ꝛíꝼ ne mǽȝe beaꝛn acennan · nim ꝼeld
moꝛan mioþoꝛeaꝛde ꝑyl on meolcum ꝫ on ꝑæꞇꝛe do
beȝea emꝼela ꝛele eꞇan þa moꝛan ꝫ ꝥ ꝑoꝛ fuꝛan. To
þon ilean bind on ꝥ ꝑinſꞇꝛe þeoh up ꝛið ꝥ cennende
lím mioþoꝛeaꝛde beolonan oþþe .XII. coꝛn cellendꝛan
ꝛǽdeꝛ ꝫ ꝥ ꝛeal don cnihꞇ oððe mǽden · fpa ꝥ beaꝛn
ꝛe acenned do þa ꝑyꝛꞇa aꝛeȝ þy keꝛ ꝥ innelꝼe uꞇꝛiȝe.

night fasting.  If there be a broken bone in the head,
and it will not come away, pound green betony and
lay it on the wound frequently, till the bones come
away and the wound is mended.

### xxxiv.

For rending of hound ; pound ribwort, lay it on the
wound, and boil rue in butter, tend the wound therewith.  If sinews are cut through ; take worms, pound
them well, lay on till *the sinews* be restored.  If sinews
be shrunken ; take emmets with their nest, boil them
in water, and beathe therewith, and earnestly reek the
sinews *with the vapour*.

### xxxv.

Against bite of gangwayweaving spider ; take a
hens egg, rub it up raw into ale, and a sheeps tord
new, so that *the patient* wit it not, give him a good
cup full to drink.

### xxxvi.

Against cancer ; take goats gall and honey, mingle
together of both equal quantities, apply to the wound.
For that ilk ; burn a fresh hounds head to ashes,
apply to the wound.  If *the wound* will not *give way
to* that, take a mans dung, dry it thoroughly, rub to
dust, apply it.  If with this thou art not able to cure
him, thou mayst never do it by any means.

### xxxvii.

In case that a woman may not kindle a bairn ;
take of fieldmore the nether part, boil it, in milk and
in water, apply of both equal quantities, give the roots
*to her* to eat and the wash to sip.  For that ilk.
Bind on her left thigh, up against the kindling limb,
the netherward part of henbane, or twelve grains of
coriander seed, and that shall give a boy a or maiden :
when the bairn is kindled, remove the worts away, lest

ȝif óf piƿe nelle ȝan æftep þam beopþpe þ ȝecyndelic
fie · feoþe eald fpic on pætpe beþe mid þone cpiþ oððe
hleomóc oþþe hoccef leaf pyl on ealoþ fele dpincan
hit hat. ȝif on piƿe fie dead beapn pyl on meolce ꝥ
on pætpe hleomóc ꝥ pollerán fele dpincan ón dæȝ tupa.
ȝeopine if to pyppanne beapneacnum piƿe þ hio aht
fealtef ete oððe fpetef oþþe beop dpince · ne fpinef flæfc
ete ne naht fætef · ne dpuncen ȝedpincc ne on peȝ ne
fepe · ne on hopfe to fpiðe pide þy læf þ beapn óf
hipe fie æp pliht tide. ȝif hió [1] blede to fpiþe æftep
þam beopþpe moþopcapde clatan pyl on meolce fele
etan ꝥ fupan þ pof.

## . XXXVIII.

Ƿiþ þon þe piƿum fie fopftanden hipa monaþ ȝecynd
pyl on ealað hleomóc ꝥ tpa cupmeallan fele dpincan
ꝥ beþe ꝥ fíf on hatum baþe ꝥ dpince þone dpenc on
þam baþe hafa þe æp ȝepopht clam óf beop dpæptan
ꝥ óf ȝpenpe mucȝpypte ꝥ mepce · ꝥ óf bepene melpe
menȝ ealle tofómne ȝehpep on pannan clæm on þ
ȝecynde lím ꝥ on þone cprð moþopcapdne þonne hio
óf þam baðe ȝæþ ꝥ dpince fcenc fulne þæf ilcan
dpencef [2] peapmef ꝥ beppeoh þ fíf pel ꝥ læt beon fpa
beclæmed lanȝe tide þæf dæȝef do fpa tupa fpa þpipa
fpaþep þu fcyle · þu fcealt fimle þam piƿe bæþ pyp-
cean ꝥ dpenc fellan on þa ilcan tíb · þe hipe fio ȝecynd
æt þæpe ahpa þæf æt þam piƿe.

ȝif piƿe to fpiþe ófflope fio monað ȝecynd · ȝenim
nipe hoppef topd leȝe on hate ȝleda læt peocan fpiþe

---

the matrix prolapse. If what is natural will not come away from a woman after the birth, seethe old lard in water, bathe the vulva therewith; or boil in ale brooklime or hollyhock, administer it to drink hot. If there be a dead bairn in a woman, boil in milk and in water brooklime and pulegium, give it *her* to drink twice a day. Earnestly must a pregnant woman be cautioned, that she eat naught salt or sweet, nor drink beer, nor eat swines flesh, nor aught fat, nor drink to drunkenness, nor fare by the way, nor ride too much on horse, lest the bairn come from her before the right time. If she bleed too much after the birth, boil in milk the netherward part of clote, give *it her* to eat, and the ooze to sip.

### xxxviii.

1. In case mulieribus menstrua suppressa sunt; boil in ale brooklime, and the two centauries, give "*her*"[1] *this* to drink, and beathe "the woman" in a hot bath, and let her drink the draught in the bath; have ready prepared a poultice of beer dregs, and of green mugwort, and marche, and of barley meal; mix them all together; shake them up in a pan, apply to the natura, and to the netherward part of the vulva, when she goeth off the bath, and let her drink a cup full of the same drink warm, and wrap up the woman well, and leave her so poulticed for a long time of the day,[2] do so twice or thrice, whichever thou must. Thou shalt always prepare a bath and give the potion to the woman at that ilk tide, at which the catamenia were upon her; inquire of the woman about that.

2. Si muliebria nimis fluunt; take a fresh horses tord, lay it on hot gledes, make it reek strongly

---

[1] The Saxon text varies the numbers, plural and singular.
[2] By a transposition in the text, we should get "twice or thrice a "day."

betꞃeoh þa þeoh ūp undeꞃ þæt liꞃæʒl þ ꞃe mōn
fpꞁꞻce fpꞁþe.

## . XXXVIIII .

fol. 119 b.

Vꞁð fmeaꞃynme fmꞁꞃinʒ · nim fpꞁneꞃ ʒeallan ꞇ
fiꞃceꞃ ʒeallan · ꞇ hꞃefneꞃ ʒeallan · ꞇ haꞃan ʒeallan
menʒ ꞇo ꞃomne fmꞁꞃe þa ðolh miꞁ blaꞁ miꞁ hꞃeoꝺe on [1]
þ ꞃeaꞁ on þ ꝺolh cnua þonne heoꞃoꞇ bꞃembel leaꝼ leʒe
on þa ꝺolh. Þyꞃc beþinʒe ꞇo þon ilcan nim æꞁꞃ ꞃinꝺe ·
ꞇ ꞃiꞃ ꞃinꝺe · cꞃic ꞃinꝺe · ꞃlah þoꞃn ꞃinꝺe · pꞁꞃꞃinꝺe · [2]
beꞃc ꞃinꝺe · cnua ealle [3] þa ꞃinꝺa pyl on cyꞃe hꞃæʒe
þꞃeah miꞁ ꞇ beþe þ lꞇm þe ꞃe pyꞃm on fie · ꞇ æꞃꞇeꞃ
þæꞃe beþinʒe aꝺꞃiʒ ꞇ fmiꞃe miꞁ þæꞃe ꞃealꝼe · ꞇ blaꞁ
þa ꞃealꝼe on þa ꝺolh ꞇ leʒe ða bꞃembel leaꞃ ōn ꝺo fpa
on ꝺꞃæʒe ꝺꞃꞁꞃa on fumeꞃa ꞇ on pinꞇꞃa ꞇꞃiꞃa.

Þyꞃc þa blacan ꞃealꝼe ʒiꞃ þe þeaꞃꞃ fie · ʒeꞃimna
þe ꞇu ambꞃu hꞃyꞃꞃa micʒean · ꞇ ambeꞃ ꝼulne holen
ꞃinꝺa · ꞇ æꞃcꞃinꝺa · ꞇ þunʒeꞃ · pylle ꝼonne on ceꞇele
oþ þ ꞃe pæꞇa fie ꞇꞃæꝺe on beꞃylleꝺ aꝺo ōꝼ þa ꞃyꞃꞇa
ꞇ þa ꞃinꝺa · pyl eꝼꞇ oþ þ lꞁꞇ ꞃie fpa þicce fpa molcen
ꞇ fpa fpeaꞃꞇ fpa col fmiꞃe miꞁ ꞃiþþan þ ꝺolh ꞇ haꝼa
clꞚm ʒeꞃoꞃhꞇ ōꝼ mealꞇeꞃ fmeꝺmꞚn ꞇ oꝼ hꞃiꞇinʒ melꞃe ·
ꞇ elehꞇꞃan cluꝼa cnua ꞇ ʒniꝺ ꞇoꞃomne pyꞃc ꞇo clame

fol. 120 a.

ʒiꞃ he fie ꞇo ꝺꞃꞁʒe ꝺo on bꞃeoꞃenꝺe pyꞃc lꞃon clæni
on þa ꝺolh ꞇ uꞇan ymb · ꞃiþþan hie ʒefinyꞃeꝺ fynꝺ
feo ꞃealꝼ pile æꞃeꞃꞇ þa ꝺolh ꞃyman ꞇ þ ꝺeaꝺe ꝼlæꞃc
ōꝼeꞇan ꞇ þone fpile aꞃꞃænan ꞇ þone pyꞃm þæꞃ on
ꝺeaꝺne ʒeꝺeþ oþþe cꞃicne oꝼꝺꞃiꝼð ꞇ þa ꝺolh ʒelꞚcnaꝺ. :.

---

[1] ō þ ꞃeaꞁ, MS.                    [3] elle, MS.
[2] pꞁꞃꞃinꝺe is thus repeated in MS.

between the thighs, up under the raiment, that the woman may sweat much.

## xxxix.

1. A smearing for a penetrating worm; take swines gall, and fishes gall, and crabs gall, and hares gall; mingle them together, smear the wounds therewith; blow with a reed the liquid into the wound; then pound hart bramble[1] leaves, lay them on the wounds. Work up a fomentation for that ilk; take aspen rind, and myrtle rind, quickbeam rind, sloethorn rind, birch rind; pound all the rinds together, boil them in cheese whey, wash therewith and foment the limb on which the wound is, and after the beathing dry and smear with the salve, and blow the salve into the wounds, and lay on the bramble leaves; do so thrice a day in summer, and in winter twice.

2. Work up the black salve, if need be, *thus;* collect two buckets of bullocks mie, and a bucket full of holly rinds, and of ash rind, and of aconite; then boil in a kettle till the liquor be boiled to two thirds, remove the "worts" and the rinds; boil again till it be as thick as milk porridge and as swart as a coal; afterwards smear the wound therewith, and have a plaster *ready* wrought of fine smede of malt, and of whiting meal, and lupins; cleave, pound, and rub *them* together, work them into a paste; if it be too dry, add brewing wort, a trifle *of it;* dab it on the wounds and round about them. After they are smeared, the salve will first enlarge the wounds, and eat off the dead flesh, and soften the swelling, and it will do to death the worm therein, or drive him away alive, and will heal the wounds.

---

[1] *Rhamnus.*

.XL.

Ƿiþ þon þe mon fie monaþ feoc nim meþe fpinef fel
pyþc to fpipan fpinȝ miö þone man fona biö fel·
amen.[1]

.XLI.

Vyþc[2] ȝoöne öþenc piþ eallum feonöef coftunȝum·
Nim beconican· bifceop pyþc· elehcpan· ȝyþþifan·
accoþlaþan· pulfef camb· ȝeaþþan· leȝe unöeþ peoþoö
ȝefinȝe .VIIII. mæffan ofeþ ȝefceaþfa þa pyþca on
huliȝ pæceþ felc öþincan on neahc neþciȝ fcenc fulne·
ꝛ öo þ haliȝ pæceþ on ealne þone mece þe fe man
þicȝe. Ƿyþc ȝoöe fealfe piþ feonöef coftunȝa· bifceop
pyþc· elehcþe· haþan[3] fpþecel· ftþeaþbeþian piþe· fio
clufihce penpyþc eoþöþima· bþembel æppel· polleþan·
peþmoö· ȝecnua þa pyþca ealle apylle on ȝoöþe
buceþan pþinȝ þuþh claö fece unöeþ peoþoö fþinȝe
.VIIII. mæffan ofeþ· fmiþe þone man miö on þa þun-
ponȝe· ꝛ bufan þam eaȝum ꝛ ufan þ heafoö· ꝛ þa
bþeoft ꝛ unöeþ þam eaþmum þa fiöan. þeoþ fealf
if ȝoö piþ ælcþe feonöef coftunȝa ꝛ ælffiöenne ꝛ
lencten aöle. ȝif þu pilt lacnian ȝepifceocne man
ȝeöo bydene fulle cealbef pæcþef öþyp þþipa on þæþ
öþencef· beþe þone man on þam pæcþe ꝛ cce fe man
ȝehalȝoöne hlaf· ꝛ cyfe· ꝛ ȝaþleac· ꝛ cþopleác ꝛ
öþince þæf öþencef fcenc fulne ꝛ þonne he fie
bebaþoö fmiþe miö þæþe fealfe fpiþe· ꝛ fiþþan him
fel fie pyþc him þonne fpiöne öþenc ücyþnenöum.[4]
Ƿyþc þuf þone öþenc nim lybcoþnef leaf· ꝛ celeþonian moþan· ꝛ ȝlæöcnan moþan· ꝛ hoccef moþan·
ꝛ ellenef pyþccþuman þinöe pyl on ealaö læc ftanöan
neahceþne ahlyccþe þonne ꝛ ȝepyþm öo buceþan co ꝛ

fol. 120 b.

---

1 amen is in a different hand.           3 haþa, MS.
2 Vþc, MS.                                4 Read ucyþnenöe, for -önc.

xl.

In case a man be lunatic; take skin of a mereswine
or *porpoise,* work it into a whip, swinge the man
therewith, soon he will be well. Amen.

xli.

Work *thus* a good drink against all temptations of the
devil. Take betony, bishopwort, lupins, githrife, attorlothe, wolfscomb, yarrow; lay them under the altar,
sing nine masses over them, scrape the worts into holy
water, give *the man* to drink at night fasting a cup
full, and put the holy water into all the meat which
the man taketh. Work *thus* a good salve against
temptations of the fiend. Bishopwort, lupin, vipers
bugloss, strawberry plant, the cloved wenwort, earth
rine, blackberry, pennyroyal, wormwood; pound all the
worts, boil them in good butter, wring through a cloth,
set them under the altar, sing nine masses over them;
smear the man therewith on the temples, and above
the eyes, and above the head, and the breast, and the
sides under the arms. This salve is good for every
temptation of the fiend, and for a man full of elfin
tricks, and for typhus fever. If thou wilt cure a wit
sick man, put a pail full of cold water, drop thrice into it
some of the drink; bathe the man in the water, and let
the man eat hallowed bread, and cheese, and garlic, and
cropleek, and drink a cup full of the drink; and when
he hath been bathed, smear with the salve thoroughly;
and when it is better with him, then work him a
strong purgative drink. Work the drink thus; take
leaves of libcorn, and roots of celandine, and roots of
gladden, and root of hollyhock, and rind of root of
elder; boil in ale, let it stand for the space of a night,
then clarify, and warm *it,* add butter and salt, ad-

ɼealt ɼelé ðɼincan.  Þyɲc ſpɪpe ðɲenc ũⱬyɲneðne nɪm
ɼeopeɲⱬɪᵹ lybcoɲna beɲenð ɼel ⁊ ᵹeᵹnɪð on nɪoþoɲeaɲðe
celeþonɪan ⁊ hõcceɼ moɲan ⁊ ⱬɼa cluɼe þæɲe cluɼehⱬan
penɼyɲⱬe ⁊ hɼeɲhɼeⱬⱬe nɪþeɼeaɲðe an lyⱬel · ⁊ ham-
ɼyɲⱬe moɲan meðmɪcel · ᵹeðo calle þa ɼyɲⱬa ſpɪþe ɼel
clæne ⁊ ᵹecnua ðo on eala beþɲeoh læⱬ ſⱬanðan neah-
ⱬeɲne ɼele ðɼɪncan ɼcenc ɼulne.

fol. 121 a.

.XLII.

Ᵹɪɼ ſpɪððɲenc on man ᵹeɼɪⱬⱬe ⁊ he nelle õɼᵹan
nɪm nɪþeɼeaɲðe celeþonɪan · ⁊ lybcoɲneɼ leaɼ oþþe
aɲoð ɼyl on ealað ðo buⱬeɲan ⁊ ɼealⱬ ⱬo ɼele ðɼɪncan
ɼeaɲɪneɼ ɼcenc ɼulne.

.XLIII.

Þɪþ aⱬⱬɼeɼ ðɼɪnce ſeoþ henne ⁊ hõcceɼ leaɼ on
ɼæⱬɲe aðo þone ɼuᵹel õɼ ⁊ þa ɼyɲⱬa ɼele ſuɲan þ̄
bɼɪoð ɼel ᵹebuⱬeɲoð ſpa he haⱬoſⱬ mæᵹe · ᵹɪɼ he æɲ
hæɼþ aⱬⱬoɲ ᵹeðɼuncen ne bɪþ hɪm ahⱬe þe ɼyɲɼ ᵹɪɼ
he þ̄ bɼɪoð þonne æɲ ſyɲð ne meahⱬ þu hɪm þy ðæᵹe
aⱬⱬoⱬ ᵹeɼellan ;

.XLIIII.

Vɪþ luɼum ɼele hɪm eⱬan ᵹeſoðenne capel on neahⱬ
neɼⱬɪᵹ ᵹelonie he bɪþ luɼũm beþeɲeð.

.XLV.

Ᵹɪɼ þoɲn ſⱬɪnᵹe man on ɼõⱬ oþþe hɲeoð ⁊ nelle
õɼᵹan nɪme nɪɲe ᵹoɲe ⱬoɲð · ⁊ ᵹɲene ᵹeaɲɲan cnuɪᵹe
ſpɪþe ⱬoɲonne clæm on þ̄ ðolh ſona bɪþ ɼel ;

minister to drink. Work *thus* a purgative spew drink; take forty libcorns, rend them well, and rub them *small* upon the netherward part of celandine and mallow roots, and two cloves of the cloved wenwort, and a little of the netherward part of cucumber, and a moderate quantity of the root of homewort; make all the worts thoroughly well clean, and pound *them;* put them into ale, wrap up, let it stand for a nights space, give *the man* a cup full to drink.

## xlii.

If a strong potion lodge in a man, and will not come away, take the netherward part of celandine, and leaves of libcorn or arod,[1] boil in ale, add butter and salt, give to drink a cup full of it warm.

## xliii.

For drink of poison; seethe a hen and leaves of mallow in water, remove the fowl and the worts, give *the man* the broth to sip, well buttered, as hot as he can *take it.* If he hath drunken poison before, it will be none the worse with him. If he suppeth the broth beforehand thou mayst not that day give him poison (effectually).

## xliv.

Against lice; give *the man* to eat sodden colewort at night fasting, frequently: he will be guarded against lice.

## xlv.

If a thorn or a reed prick a man in the foot, and will not be gone; let him take a fresh goose tord and green yarrow, let him pound them thoroughly together, paste them on the wound, soon it will be well.

---

[1] Aron ?

.XLVI.

Þiþ ꞃymmælum · ⁊ þiþ eallum eaᵹna ꞅaꞃ·ce · ceoꞃ
þulꝼeꞃ comb ꞃꞃinᵹ þonne þuꞃh hæþenne claꝺ ꝼyllenne
on þa eaᵹan þ ꞃeaꝛ on niht þonne he ꞃeꞅꞇan þille ⁊
on moꞃᵹen ꝺo ꞅeᵹeꞅ þ hꝛiꞇe þæꞃ on.

.XLVII.

Viþ lyꝼꞇ aꝺle ᵹiꝼ ꞅe muꝺ ꞅie poh oþþe ꞃon · nim
cellenꝺꞃan ᵹniꝺ on piꞃeꞅ meolce ꝺo on þ hale eaꞃe him
biþ ꞃona ꞅel. Eꝼꞇ nim cellenꝺꞃan aꝺꞃinᵹ ᵹeꞃyꞃc ꞇo
ꝺuꞅꞇe ᵹemenᵹ þ ꝺuꞅꞇ þiþ piꞃeꞅ meolꞅc þe ꝛæꝛneꝺ ꝛebe
aꝛꞃinᵹ þuꞃh hæþenne claꝺ ⁊ ꝛmiꞃe þ hale ꞃonᵹe miꝺ
⁊ ꝺꞃyꝛe on þ eaꞃe þæꞃlice. Þyꞃc þonne beþinᵹe ·
ᵹenim bꞃembel ꞃinꝺe ⁊ elm ꞃinꝺe · æꞃc ꞃinꝺe · ꞅlah-
þoꞃn ꞃinꝺe apulꝺoꞃ ꞃinꝺe · iꝛiᵹ ꞃinꝺe · ealle þaꞅ
moꞃoꞃeaꞃꝺe ⁊ hꞃeꞃhpeꞇꞇan · ꝛmeꞃu ꝛyꞃc · eoꞃoꞃ ꝛeaꞃꞃ ·
elene · ꞅelꝼþone · beꞇonice · maꞃubie · ꞃeꝺic · aᵹꞃi-
monia ᵹeꞅceaꞃꝛa þa ꝛyꞃꞇa on ceꞇel ⁊ ꝛyl ꝛꝛiꝺe · þonne
hiꞇ ꞅie ꝛꞃiþe ᵹeꝛylleꝺ ꝺo oꝛ þam ꝛyꞃe ⁊ ꞃeꞇe ⁊ ᵹeꝛyꞃc
þam men ꞅeꞇl oꝛeꞃ þam ciꞇele ⁊ beꝛꞃeoꞃ ꝺone man
miꝺ þ ꞅe æþm ne mæᵹe ꝛiꞇ nahꝛꞃꞃ buꞇan he mæᵹe
ᵹeeþiaꞃ · beþe hine miꝺ þyꞃꞃe beþinᵹe þa hꝛile þa he
mæᵹe aꞃꞃæꝛnan. Daꝛa him þonne oþeꞃ bæþ ᵹeaꞃꞃa ·
ᵹenim æmeꞇ beꝺ miꝺ ealle · þaꞃa þe hꝛilum ꝛleoᵹaꝺ
beoþ ꞃeaꝺe · ꝛyl on ꝛꞃꞇꞃe beþe hine miꝺ · onᵹemeꞇ·
haꞇum. Þyꞃc him þonne ꞃealꝛe nim ꞅelceꞅ þaꞃa
cynneꞅ ꝛyꞃꞇa ꝛyl on buꞇeꞃan ꝛmiꞃe miꝺ þa ꞃaꞃan
hꞃꞃu hiꞃ cꞃiꞅiaþ ꞃona. Þyꞃc him leaᵹe oꝛ ellen ahꞃꞃan
ꞃꞃeah hiꞃ heaꞃoꝺ miꝺ colꞃe him biþ ꞃona beꞇ · ⁊ ꞅe
man læꞇe him bloꝺ ꞅelce monþe on ·v· nihꞇa ealꝺne
monan ⁊ on ꝛiꝛꞇyne ⁊ on ·xx·

### xlvi.

For imminutions,[1] and for all pain of the eyes; chew wolfscomb, then wring the ooze through a purple cloth upon the eyes, at night, when *the man* has a mind to rest, and in the morning apply the white of an egg.

### xlvii.

For palsy, if the mouth be awry or livid, rub coriander in womans milk, put it into the sound ear, it will soon be well with *the man*. Again, take coriander, dry it, work it to dust, mingle the dust with milk of a woman, who brought forth a male, wring through a purple cloth, and smear the sound cheek therewith, and drip it on the ear warily. Then work a fomentation; take bramble rind, and elm rind, ash rind, sloethorn rind, appletree rind, ivy rind, all these from the nether part of the trees, and cucumber, smearwort, everfern, helenium, enchanters nightshade, betony, marrubium, radish, agrimony; scrape the worts into a kettle, and boil strongly. When it hath been strongly boiled, remove it off the fire and set *it down*, and get the man a seat over the kettle, and wrap the man up, that the vapour may get out nowhere, except only so that the man may breathe; beathe him with this fomentation as long as he can bear it. Then have another bath ready for him, take an emmet bed, all at once, *a bed* of those *male emmets* which at whiles fly, they are red ones, boil them in water, beathe him with it immoderately hot. Then make him a salve; take worts of each kind of those *above mentioned*, boil them in butter, smear the sore limbs therewith, they will soon quicken. Make him a ley of elder ashes, wash his head with this cold; it will soon be well with him: and let the man get bled every month, when the moon is five, and fifteen, and twenty nights old.

---

[1] Contraction of the pupil.

.XLVIII.

D�enc ƿiþ fic adle nim bulut · ⁊ eoforþrotan
nioþoƿearde · ⁊ ƿudu fillan · ⁊ ȝeacer ꞅuran · ⁊
æfexiþan ȝeꞅceaꝛꝼa þaꞅ ƿyꝛto toSomne do on ȝellet
mnan læt ꞅtandan neahteꝛne æꝛ þu hine dꞅince.
Þyꝛe beþinȝe nim þ neade ꝛyden do on tꝛiȝ hat
þonne ꞅtanaꞅ ꞅƿiþe hate leȝe on þ tꝛiȝ mnan ⁊ he
ꞅitte on ꞅtole oꝼeꝛ þæꝛe beþinȝe þ hio hine mæȝe
tela ȝeꝛeocan þonne ꝼeallað þa fic ƿyꝛmaꞅ on þa
beþinȝe him biþ ꞅona ꝛel · dꞅince þone dꞅenc æꝛ
þæꝛe beþinȝe · ȝiꝼ he þonne þa beþinȝe þuꝛhteon ne
mæȝe dꞅince þone dꞅenc ælce dæȝe oþ þ him ꝛel ꞅie.

.XLVIIII.

Ƿiþ ꞅculdoꝛ ƿæꝛce ⁊ eaꝛma · ƿyl betonican ón ealoð
ꞅele dꞅincan ȝelome ⁊ ꞅnnle ꞅmiꝛe hine æt ꝼyꝛe mið
ꝛenƿyꝛte.

.L.

Ȝiꝼ cneoƿ ꞅaꝛ ꞅie cnua beolenan ⁊ hemlic beþe mið
⁊ leȝe on.

.LI.

Giꝼ ꞅe ꝼot ꞅaꝛ ꞅie ellen leaꝼ · ⁊ ƿeȝbꝛædan ⁊
muȝƿyꝛt ȝecnua ⁊ leȝe on ⁊ ȝebind hat þæꝛ on. ⁘

.LII.

Ȝiꝼ þu ne mæȝe blod ðolh ꝼoꝛþꝛiþan nim niꝛe
hoꝛꞅeꞅ toꝛð adꞅiȝ on ꞅunnan ȝeȝꞅnd tu duꞅte ꞅƿiþe
ƿel leȝe þ duꞅt ꞅƿiþe þicce on linenne claþ ƿꝛiþ mið
þy þ ðolh.

.LIII.

Ȝiꝼ meoluc ꞅie apyꝛð bind toSomne ƿeȝbꝛædan · ⁊
ȝiþꝛiꝼan · ⁊ ceꝛꞅan leȝe on þone ꝼildcumb ⁊ ne ꞅete þ
þæt niꝛeꝛ on eoꝛþan feoꝛon nihtum.

### xlviii.

A drink for the "fig" disease; take bulot, and the netherward part of everthroat, and wild chervil, and cuckoosour, and æferth; scrape these worts together, put them into a basin, let it stand for the space of a night, ere thou drink it. Work a fomentation *thus;* take the red ryden, put it in a trough, then heat stones very hot, lay them within the trough, and let *the man* sit on a stool over the fomentation, that it may reek him well, then the "fig" worms will fall on the beathing, and it will soon be well with him. Let him drink the drink before the beathing; if then he cannot pull through the beathing, let him drink the drink every day till it be all right with him.

### xlix.

Against pain of shoulders and arms; boil betony in ale, give *it the man* to drink frequently, and always smear him at the fire with wenwort.

### l.

If a knee be sore, pound henbane and hemlock, foment therewith and lay on.

### li.

If the foot be sore, pound and lay on elder leaves, and waybroad, and mugwort; and bind hot upon *the foot.*

### lii.

If thou be not able to stanch a bloodletting incision, take a new horses tord, dry it in the sun, rub it to dust thoroughly well, lay the dust very thick on a linen cloth; wrap up the wound with that.

### liii.

If milk be spoilt; bind together waybroad, and githrife, and cress, lay them on the milk pail, and set not the vessel down on the earth for seven nights.

### . LIIII.

Þýpc ſealſe pið nihtᵹenᵹan · ſyl on butepan
elehtpan · heᵹepiſan · bifceop pypt · peaðe maᵹþan ·
cpopleác · ſealt ſmipe mið him bið ſona ſel.

### . LV.

Ᵹiſ men ſio heaſod panne beó ᵹehlenceð aleᵹe þone
man ſippeapð ðpiſ . II. ſtacan æt þam eaxlum leᵹe
þonne bpeð þpeopeſ oſep þa ſet ſleah þonne þpipa on
mið ſleᵹe bytle hio ᵹæþ on piht Sona.

### . LVI.

Ᵹiſ men nelle myltan hiſ mete nipepeapð clate ⁊
mepce ⁊ ſundcopneſ leáſ pyl on ealaþ ſele ðpincan.

### . LVII.

Viþ ſíſ ᵹemæðlan ᵹebepᵹe on neaht neptiᵹ pædiceſ
mopan þy dæᵹe ne mæᵹ þe ſe ᵹemædla ſceþþan.

### . LVIII.

Þiþ ſeondeſ coſtunᵹe pnð molm[1] hatte pypt peaxeþ
be ypnendum pætpe · ᵹiſ þu þa on þe haſaſt ⁊ undep
þinum heaſod bolſtpe · ⁊ oſep þineſ huſeſ dupum · ne
mæᵹ þe deoſol ſceþþan Inne ne ute.

fel. 123 a.

### . LVII[II].

Þiþ þeop penne ᵹiſ he ſie men on cneope oþþe on
oppum lime pypc clam óſ ſuppe piᵹeppe ᵹput oððe
daᵹe ᵹedo æᵹeſ hpit to ⁊ bpoc cepſan leᵹe on þ̵ þu
oþ þ̵ ſe clam hatiᵹe do oſ þone leᵹe oþepne þæp on.

---

[1] Read molm.

### liv.

Work a salve against nocturnal *goblin* visitors; boil in butter lupins, hedgerife, bishopwort, red maythe, cropleek, salt; smear *the man* therewith, it will soon be well with him.

### lv.

If a mans head-pan, or skull, be *seemingly* iron-bound lay the man with face upward, drive two stakes into *the ground* at the armpits, then lay a plank across over his feet, then strike on it thrice with a sledge beetle, *the skull* will come right soon.

### lvi.

If a mans meat will not digest, boil in ale the netherward part of clote, and marche, and leaves of saxifrage, give *him that* to drink.

### lvii.

Against a womans chatter; taste at night fasting a root of radish, that day the chatter cannot harm thee.

### lviii.

Against temptation of the fiend, a wort hight red niolin, *red stalk*, it waxeth by running water : if thou hast it on thee, and under thy head bolster, and over thy house doors, the devil may not scathe thee, within nor without.

### lix.

For a "dry" wen; if it be on a man's knee, or on another limb, work a paste of sour rye groats or dough, add the white of an egg and brook cresses, lay on the limb till the paste gets hot, remove it then and lay another on.

## .LX.

Wyrc ȝode eaȝrsealfe hunder tunȝe uiþeweard ⁊ finȝrene ⁊ finȝulle · tunhofe moþorcarð · celeþonian leaf · ȝarlece · cropleac do on win oððe on eceð þþinȝ þurh hærenne clað on þ eaȝe læt standan .iii. niht ær þu hine on do. Eft nim cropleac ⁊ finȝullan ȝecnua¹ hron piner to ⁊ prinȝ on þ eaȝe him biþ rona sel

## .LXI.

Þyrre realfe wiþ ælfcynne ⁊ nihtȝenȝan ⁊ þam mannum þe deoful mid hæmð · ȝenim eorohumelan · peþmed biscoppyrt · elehtre · ațeþþote · beolone · hare wyrt · haran spriecel · hæþ benȝean piran · crop-leac · ȝarlece · heȝerisan corn · ȝyþþrice · finul. do þar wyrta on an fæt fete under weofod rinȝ ofer .viiii. mæssan apyl on butepan ⁊ on recaþer smeriþe do halȝes realtes fela on arcoh þurh clað · peorþ þa wyrta on ymende þætep. ȝif men hpile yfel cortunȝ peorþe oþþe ælf oþþe niht ȝenȝan · smire his ȝlitan mid þyrre realfe ⁊ on hir eaȝan do ⁊ þær him re lichoma rar rie · ⁊ recelfa hine ⁊ sena ȝelome hir þinȝ biþ rona relpe.

## .LXII.

Wið ælfadle nim biscop pyrt · finul · elehtre · ælfþonan uiþoþcaride · ⁊ ȝehalȝodes crirter mæles paȝu · ⁊ ftop do ælepe hand fulle · bebind calle þa wyrta on claþe bedyp on font pætere ȝehalȝodum

---

¹ to is to be added.

### lx.

Work a good ear salve *thus* ; the netherward part
of hounds tongue, and singreen, and sedum, the netherward part of garden hove, leaves of celandine, garlic,
cropleek ; put *them* into wine or vinegar, wring them
through a coloured cloth into the ear ; let *the liquor*
stand for three nights before thou apply it.   Again,
take cropleek and sedum, pound them, add a little
wine, and wring into the ear, it will soon be well
with it.

### lxi.

Work thus a salve against the elfin race and nocturnal *goblin* visitors, and for the women with whom the
devil hath carnal commerce ; take the ewe hop plant,
*probably the female hop plant*, wormwood, bishopwort,
lupin, ashthroat, henbane, harewort, vipers bugloss,
heathberry plants, cropleek, garlic, grains of hedgerife,
githrife, fennel ; put these worts into a vessel, set
*them* under the altar, sing over them nine masses,
boil *them* in butter and sheeps grease, add much holy
salt, strain through a cloth, throw the worts into running water.   If any ill tempting occur to a man, or
an elf or *goblin* night visitors *come*, smear his forehead
with this salve, and put it on his eyes, and where his
body is sore, and cense him with incense, and sign
him frequently with the sign of the cross ; his condition will soon be better.

### lxii.

Against elf disease ; take bishopwort, fennel, lupin,
the lower part of enchanters nightshade, and moss or
lichen from the hallowed sign of Christ, and incense,
of each a hand full ; bind all the worts in a cloth, dip
it thrice in hallowed font water, have sung over

þþiþa · læt finȝan ofeþ .III. mæffan · ane omnibus
Scīf · oþþe contþa tþibulatjonem · þriddan þþo in-
piþimiS · do þonne ȝleða an ȝleðfæt ⁊ leȝe þa pyþta
on · ȝeþee þone man mið þam pyþtun æþ undeþn ⁊
on niht ⁊ finȝ letania ⁊ cþeðan ⁊ þateþ noþteþ ⁊
pþit hun cþifteþ mæl on ælcum lime ⁊ nim lytle hanð
fulle þæf ilcan cynneþ pyþta ȝelice ȝehalȝoðe ⁊ pyl on
meolce ðþyþ þþiþa ȝehalȝoðeþ pætþeþ on ⁊ fuþe æþ
luf mete hun biþ fona fel. Þiþ þon ilean · ȝanȝ on
þunþeþ æþen þonne funne on fetle fie þæþ þu piþe
clenan ftanðan finȝ þonne beneðicite · ⁊ pateþ noþteþ ·
⁊ letanian · ⁊ ftinȝ þin feax on þa pyþte læt ftician
þæþ on ȝanȝ þe apeȝ ȝanȝ eft to þonne ðæȝ ⁊ niht fuþ-
þum feaðe on þam ilcan uhte ȝanȝ æþeft to cþicean
⁊ þe ȝeþena ⁊ ȝoðe þe bebeoð ȝanȝ þonne fþiȝenðe
⁊ þeah þe hþæt hþeȝa eȝeflicef onȝean cume oþþe man
ne cþeþ þu hun æniȝ poþð to æþ þu cume to þæþe
pyþte þe þu on æþen æþ ȝemeaþcoðeft finȝ þonne
beneðicite · ⁊ pateþ noþteþ · ⁊ letania aðelþ þa pyþt
læt ftician þ feax þæþ on · ȝanȝ eft fpa þu þaþoft
mæȝe to cþicean ⁊ leȝe undeþ peoþoð mið þám feaxe
læt licȝean oþ þ funne uppe fie · apæþe fiþþan ðo to
ðþence · ⁊ biþceoþ pyþt ⁊ cþifteþ mælef þaȝu apyl
þþiþa on meolcum ȝeot þþiþa haliȝ pæteþ on finȝ on
pateþ noþteþ · ⁊ cþeðan · ⁊ ȝloþia in excelþiþ ðeo · ⁊
finȝ on hine letania · ⁊ hine eac ymb þþit mið fþeoþiðe
on .IIII. healfa on cþuce · ⁊ ðþince þone ðþenc fiþþan
hun biþ fona fel. Eft þiþ þon leȝe undeþ peoþoð þaþ
pyþte læt ȝefinȝan ofeþ .VIIII. mæffan · þeeelþ ·
haliȝ fealt .III. heafoð cþoþleaceþ ælfþonan moþe-

fol. 124 a.

it three masses, one "Omnibus sanctis," [1] another "Contra tribulationem," [2] a third "Pro infirmis." [1] Then put gledes in a glede pan, and lay the worts on: reek the man with the worts before nine in the morning, and at night, and sing a litany, and the credo, and the Pater noster, and write Christs mark on each of his limbs, and take a little hand full of worts of the same kind similarly hallowed, and boil in milk, drop thrice some hallowed water into it, and let him sip of it before his meat; it will soon be well with him. For that ilk. Go on Thursday evening, when the sun is set, where thou knowest that helenium stands, then sing the "Benedicite," and "Pater noster," and a litany, and stick thy knife into the wort, make it stick fast, and go away: go again, when day and night just divide;[3] at the same period go first to church and cross thyself, and commend thyself to God; then go in silence, and though anything soever of an awful sort or man a meet thee, say not thou to him any word, ere thou come to the wort, which on the evening before thou markedst; then sing the Benedicite, and the Pater noster, and a litany, delve up the wort, let the knife stick in it; go again as quick as thou art able to church, and lay it under the altar with the knife; let it lie till the sun be up, wash it afterwards, and make into a drink, and bishopwort, and lichen off a crucifix; boil in milk thrice, thrice pour holy water upon it, and sing over it the Paternoster, the Credo, and the Gloria in excelsis deo;[4] and sing upon it a litany, and score with a sword round about it on three sides a cross, and then after that let *the man* drink the wort; soon will it be well with him. Again for that; lay these worts under the altar, have nine masses sung over them, incense, holy salt, three heads of cropleek, the netherward part of enchanters nightshade,

---

[1] In the missal.

[2] The same as "Pro quacunque necessitate"?

[3] In early morning.

[4] Luke ii. 14.

ƿearde · elenan · nim on morgen scenc fulne meoluce drync þriƿa haliges ƿæteres on swa he hatost mæge · ete mid .III. snæda ælfþonan ⁊ þonne he ƿestan ƿille hæbbe gleda þær inne lege stor ⁊ ælfþonan
fol. 124 b. on þa gleda · ⁊ rec hine mid ꝥ he sƿæte · ⁊ ꝥ hūs geond rēc ⁊ georne þone man gesena · ⁊ þonne he on reste gange ete .III. snæda eolenan · ⁊ .III. cropleaces · ⁊ .III. sealtes · ⁊ hæbbe him scenc fulne ealað ⁊ drype þriƿa halig ƿæter on · besupe ælce snæd · gereste hine siþþan · do þis .VIIII. morgenas · ⁊ .VIIII. niht him biþ sona sel. Gif him biþ ælfsogoþa him beoþ þa eagan geolƿe þær hi reade beōn sceoldon. Gif þu þone mōn lacnian ƿille þæne his gebæra ⁊ ƿite hƿilces hades he sie · gif hit biþ ƿæpned man ⁊ locað ūp þonne þu hine ærest sceaƿast ⁊ se ƿlita biþ geolƿe blac · þone mōn þu meaht gelacnian æltæƿlice gif he ne biþ þær on to lange · gif hit biþ ƿīf ⁊ locað niþer þonne þu hit ærest sceaƿast · ⁊ hire ƿlita biþ reade ƿan ꝥ þu miht eāc gelācnian · gif hit bið dægƿerne leng on þonne .XII. monaþ ⁊ sio onsyn biþ þyslicu þonne meaht þu hine betan to hƿile · ⁊ ne meaht hƿæþere æltæƿlice gelācnian. Ƿrit þis geƿrit · Scriptum est rex regum et dominus dominantium · byrnice · beronice · lurlure · iehe · aius · aius · aius · Ses · Sēs · Ses · dominus deus Sabaoth · amen · alleluiah. Sing þis ofer þam drence ⁊ þam geƿrite · Deus om-
fol. 125 a. nipotens pater domini nostri iesu cristi · per Inpositionem huius scripture expelle a famulo tuo N ·[1] Omnem Impetum[2] castalidum ·[3] de capite · de capillis · de

[1] nomen.
[2] impetū, MS.
[3] Castalides, dun elfen, Gl. Somn. p. 79 b. *Elves of the downs.*

helenium; take in the morning a cup full of milk,
drop thrice some holy water into it, let *the man* sup
it up as hot as he can : let him eat therewith three
bits of enchanters nightshade, and when he hath a
mind to rest, let him have in his chamber gledes, let
him lay on the gledes στύραξ and elfthone, and reek
him therewith till he sweat, and reek the house all
through ; earnestly also sign the man with the sign of
the cross, and when he is going to bed, let him eat
three bits of helenium, and three of cropleek, and three
of salt, and let him have a cup full of ale, and thrice
drop holy water into it; let him sup up each bit, *and*
afterwards rest himself.  Let him do this for nine
mornings and nine nights, it will soon be well with
him.  If *a man* hath elf hicket, his eyes are yellow,
where they should be red.  If thou have a will to
cure the man, observe his gestures, and consider of what
sex he be ; if it be a man and looketh up, when thou
first seest him, and the countenance be yellowish black,
thou mayst cure the man thoroughly if he is not too
long in the disease ; if it is a woman and looketh
down, when thou first seest her, and her countenance
is livid red, thou mayst also cure that ; if it has been
upon *the man* longer than a twelvemonth and a day,
and the aspect be such as this, then mayst thou amend
it for a while, and notwithstanding mayst not entirely
cure it.  Write this writing, "Scriptum est, rex regum
" et dominus dominantium Veronica,[1] Veronica, . . . IAO,[2]
" ἅγιος, ἅγιος, ἅγιος, sanctus, sanctus, sanctus, domi-
" nus, deus sabaoth, amen, alleluiah."  Sing this over
the drink and the writing, "Deus omnipotens, pater
" domini nostri Iesu Christi, per impositionem huius
" scripturae expelle a famulo tuo, *here insert the name*,
" omnem impetum castalidum de capite, de capillis, de

---

[1] The miraculous portrait on the
kerchief of St. Veronica.

[2] יהוה

cepebjio · be ꝼꞃonte · be lingua · be ꞃublingua · be ʒuttone ·
be ꝼaucibuſ · be bentibuſ · be oculiſ · be naꝛibus · be
auꝛibus · be manibus · be collo · be bꞃachuſ · be coꞃbe ·
be anima · be ʒenibus · be coxiſ · be pebibus · be com-
paʒinibus · omnium membꞃoꞃum intuſ et ꝼoꝛiſ · amen.
Ƿyꝛe þonne bꞃenc ꝼont pæteꝛ · ꞃuban · Saluian · caſꞃuc ·
bꞃaconʒan · þa ſmeþan peʒbꞃæban niþepeaꞃbe ꝼeꞃeꝛ
ꝼuʒian · bileſ cꞃop · ʒaꝛleaceſ · III. clufe · ꝼinul · peꝛmob ·
luꝼeſtice · elehtꞃe · calꝛa emꝼela · pꞃit · III. cꞃucem mib
oleum inꝼiꞃmoꞃum ꝰ cꝛeð · pax tibi · ꜱim þonne þ
ʒepꝛit pꞃit cꞃucem mib oꝼeꝛ þam bꞃince ꝰ ſinʒ þiſ þæꝛ
oꝼeꝛ.    beuſ omnipotenſ pateꝛ bomini · noꝛtꞃi · iesu
cꞃiſti þeꝛ Inpoſitꞃonem huiuſ ſcꞃiptuꞃæ[1] et þeꝛ ʒuſtum
huiuS expelle biabolum a ꝼamulo tuo · ꜱ · [2] ꝰ cꞃebo ·
ꝰ pateꝛ · noꞃteꝛ · þæt þ ʒepꞃit on þam bꞃence ꝰ pꞃit
cꞃucem mib him on ælcum lime ꝰ cꝛeð ſiʒnum cꞃuciS
xꝓ conꞃeꝛuate In uitam eteꞃnam · amen.    ʒiꝼ þe ne
lyſte hæt hine ꞃelꝛne oþþe ſpa ʒeꞃubne ſpa he ʒeſibboſt
hæbbe ꝰ ſeniʒe ſpa he ꞃeloſt cunne · þeſ cꞃæꝼt mæʒ
ꝛiþ ælcꝛe ꝼeonbeſ coſtunʒe.


.LXIII.

Ʒiꝼ mon biþ on pꞃæteꝛ ælꝼable þonne beoþ him þa
hanb næʒlaſ ꞃonne ꝰ þa eaʒan teaꝛiʒe ꝰ ꝛile locian
uꝛeꝛ · bo him þiſ to læcebome · eoꞃoꝛþꞃote · caꝛſuc ·
ꝼone moꞃoꞃeaꝛb · eoꝛbeꝛʒe · elehtꞃe · eolone · meꝛſc-
mealpan cꞃop · ꝼen minte · bile · lilie · attoꝛlaþe ·
polleie · maꝛubie · bocce · ellen · ꝼel teꝛꝛe · peꝛmob ·
ſtꞃeaꝛbeꝛʒean leaꝼ · conꝛolbe · ɖꝼʒeot mib ealaþ · bo
haliʒ pꞃæteꝛ to ſinʒ þiſ ʒealboꝛ oꝼeꝛ þꞃiꝛa · Ic binne
aꝛꝛat[3] beꞃeſt beabo pꞃæba ſpa benne ne buꝛꞃon ne

¹ –ꝛa, MS.
nomen.

³ From þꞃiðau rather than þꞃitan.

" cerebro, defronte, de lingua, de sublingua, de gutture, de
" faucibus, de dentibus, de oculis, de naribus, de auribus,
" de manibus, de collo, de brachiis, de corde, de anima,
de genibus, de coxis, de pedibus, de compaginibus
" omnium membrorum intus et foris. Amen." Then
work up a drink thus ; font water, rue, sage, cassuck,
dragons, the netherward part of the smooth waybroad,
feverfue, a head of dill, three cloves of garlic, fennel,
wormwood, lovage, lupin, of all equal quantities ; write
a cross three times with the oil of unction, and say,
"Pax tibi." Then take the writing, describe a cross
with it over the drink, and sing this over it, " Dominus
" omnipotens, pater domini nostri Iesu Christi, per im-
" positionem huius scripturæ et per gustum huius expelle
" diabolum a famulo tuo;" *here insert the name*, and the
Credo, and Paternoster. Wet the writing in the drink,
and write a cross with it on every limb, and say,
" Signum crucis Christi conservet te in vitam æter-
" nam. Amen." If it listeth thee not *to take this
trouble*, bid *the man* himself, or whomsoever he may
have nearest sib to him, *to do it*, and let him cross
him as well as he can. This craft is powerful against
every temptation of the fiend.

lxiii.

If a man is in the water elf disease, then are
the nails of his hand livid, and the eyes tearful, and
he will look downwards. Give him this for a leechdom ; everthroat, cassuck, the netherward part of fane,
a yew berry, lupin, helenium, a head of marsh mallow,
fen mint, dill, lily, attorlothe, pulegium, marrubium,
dock, elder, fel terræ, *or lesser centaury*, wormwood,
strawberry leaves, consolida ; pour them over with ale,
add holy water, sing this charm over them thrice :—

> I have wreathed round the wounds
> the best of healing wreaths,

burston ne fundian ne feologan · ne hoppetan ne ƿund ƿaco sian · ne dolh diopian · ac him self healde hale ƿæge · ne ace þe þon ma þe eorþan on eare ace · Sing þis manegum siþum · eorþe þe on bere eallum hire mihtum ⁊ mægenum · þas galdor mōn mæg singan ōn ƿunde.

.LXIIII.

Ƿiþ deofle liþe drenc ⁊ ungemynde do on ealu cassūc · elehtran moran · finul ontre · betonice · hind heoloþe · merice rude · ƿermod · nefte · elene · ælfþone · ƿulfes comb · gesing .XII. mæssan ofer þam drence ⁊ drince him biþ sona sel. Drenc ƿiþ deofles costunga · þefan þorn cropleac · eleþre · ontre · biscop ƿyrt · finul · cassuc · betonice · gehalga þas ƿyrta do on ealu
fol. 126 a. halig ƿæter · ⁊ sie se drenc þær inne þær se seoca man inne sie · ⁊ simle ær þon þe he drince sing þriƿa ofer þam drence · deus In nomine tuo saluum me fūc.

.LXV.

Gif man sie gegymed ⁊ þu hine gelacnian scyle · geseoh ꝥ he sie toƿeard þonne þu ingange þonne mæg he libban · gif he þe sie framƿeard ne gret þu hine ahte · gif he libban mæge ƿyl on buteran betonican ·

that the baneful sores may
neither burn nor burst,
nor find their way further,
nor turn foul and fallow,
nor thump and throb on,
nor be wicked wounds,
nor dig deeply down;
but he himself may hold
in a way to health.
Let it ache thee no more,
than ear in earth[1] acheth.

Sing *also* this many times, [2] " May earth bear on
" thee with all her might and main." These charms
a man may sing over a wound.

### lxiv.

A lithe drink against a devil and dementedness.
Put into ale cassuck, roots of lupin, fennel, ontre,
betony, hindheal, marche, rue, wormwood, nepeta, helenium, elfthone, wolfs comb; sing twelve masses over
the drink, and let *the man* drink, it will soon be well
with him. A drink against temptations of the devil;
tuftythorn, cropleek, lupin, ontre, bishopwort, fennel,
cassuck, betony; hallow these worts,[3] put into some ale
some holy water, and let the drink be in the same
chamber as the sick man, and constantly before he
drinketh sing thrice over the drink, " Deus! In
" nomine tuo salvum me fac."

### lxv.

If a man be overlooked, and thou must cure him,
see that his face be turned to thee when thou goest
in, then he may live; if his face be turned from thee,
have thou nothing to do with him. If he may live,

---

[1] In the grave.
[2] This seems intended to quell the
elf.

[3] By a formula of benediction.

ᵹyþþıꝼan · ᵹeaꝛꝛan · polleıan · ðolhꝛunan · apꝛınᵹ þuꝛh
claþ læt ꞅtanðan · ᵹehæꞇ ꞅcenc ꝼulne cu ꝛeaꝛmꝛe meolce
ðo þꝛꝛe ꝛealꝼe .v. ꞅnæða þæꝛ on ꞅuꝛe on neahꞇ neꝛꞇıᵹ
⁊ eꞇe ꝼeꝛꞅc ꝼlæꝛc þæꝛ þæꝛ hıꞇ ꝼæꞇoꞅꞇ ꞅıe · ⁊ þıcᵹe on
nıhꞇ þa ꝛealꝼe ⁊ ꝥ ðolh ꝛeꞇ mıð ealðan ꞅpıce oþþe mıð
ꝼeꝛꞅcꝛe buꞇeꝛan þonne hıꞇ ꞅıe clæne ⁊ ꝛel ꝛeað · lacna
mıð þa ılcan ꝛealꝼa · ⁊ ne læꞇ ꞇoᛋomne ᵹıꝼ hıo ꞅıe
clæne · læt ꝛıþþan ꞇoᛋomne. ᵹıꝼ hıꞇ nelle ꝼoꝛ þıꞅū
læceðome baꞇıan · ꝛyl on meolcum þa ꝛeaðan ᵹeaꝛꝛan
⁊ ꝼınul · hınꝛyꝛꞇ · ealꝛa ᵹehce læꞇ aꝛeallan .v. ꝛıꝛum
apꝛınᵹ þuꝛh clað ᵹebꝛꝛıꝛ ꝛel ꞅꝛıꝛne bꝛıꝛ þæꝛ on mıð
hꝛæꞇe melꝛe ⁊ ᵹeꝛceaꝼ ᵹoðeꝛ ꝛeaꝛeꞅ ane ꞅnæðe þæꝛ
on ⁊ hꝛeꝛ ꞇoꞅomne læꞇ ᵹecolıan · ᵹenım haꝛan ꝛulle
lyꞇle ꞅnæðe .iii. beꝛınð mıð þy bꝛıꝛe uꞇan ꝥ he mæᵹe
fol. 126 b. ꝼoꝛꞅꝛelᵹan ⁊ beꞅuꝛe mıð cu ꝛeaꝛmum.[1]

### . LXVI.

Dꝛenc ᵹıꝼ þeoꝛ ꝛıe on men nım þaꝛ ꝛyꝛꞇe nıoþe-
ꝛeaꝛðe · ꝼınol bıꞅceop ꝛyꝛꞇ æꝛcꝛꝛoꞇan ealꝛa emꝛela
þıꝛꝛa ꞇꝛeᵹa mæꝛꞇ · uꝼeꝛeaꝛðe ꝛuðan · ⁊ beꞇonıcan ðꝼ-
ᵹeoꞇ mıð hıluꞇꞇꝛum ealaþ ⁊ ᵹeꞅınᵹe .iii. mæꝛꝛan oꝼeꝛ
⁊ ðꝛınce ymb .ii. nıhꞇ þæꝛ þe he oꝼᵹoꞇen ꞅıe æꝛ
hıꞅ meꞇe ⁊ æꝼꞇeꝛ.

### . LXVII.

Vıþ ðeoꝼol ꞅeoce ðo on halıᵹ ꝛæꞇeꝛ ⁊ on eala bıꞅceop
ꝛyꝛꞇe hınðhıoloþan · aᵹꝛımonıan · alexanðꝛıan · ᵹyþ-
ꝛıꝼan ꝛele hın ðꝛıncan. Eꝼꞇ caꝛꝛuc · þeꝼan þoꝛn · ꞅꞇan
cꝛoꝛ · clehꞇꝛe · ꝼınul · coꝼoꝛþꝛoꞇe cꝛoꝛleꝼc oꝛᵹeoꞇ
ᵹehce. Eꝼꞇ ꞅꝛıꝛe ðꝛınc ꝛıð ðeoꝼle · nım mıcle hanð

---

boil in butter betony, githrife, yarrow, pulegium, pellitory; wring through a cloth, let it stand, heat a cup full in milk warm from the cow, put five pieces of the salve into it; let *the* man sup up that at night fasting, and let him eat fresh flesh in the part where it is fattest: and at night take the salve and comfort the wound with old lard or with fresh butter; when it is clean, and a good red, leech with the same salve, and let it not unite, if it be clean; make it unite afterwards. If it will not for this leechdom get better, boil in milk the red yarrow, and fennel, and flaxwort, of all equal quantities, let them boil five times, wring through a cloth. Brew up a pretty strong brewit upon this, with wheat meal, shave a piece of good wax into it, and shake up together; let it cool, take three little bits of hares wool, wind them on the outside about with the brewit, that he may swallow them, and let him sup it up with milk warm from the cow.

### lxvi.

A drink, if the "dry" disease be on a man; take the netherward part of these worts, fennel, bishopwort, ashthroat, of all equal quantities; of these two *following* more than of the others, the upward part of rue, and betony; pour them over with clear ale, and sing three masses over them, and let *the man* drink about two days from the time when it was poured over, before his meat and after.

### lxvii.

For one devil sick; put into holy water and into ale, bishopwort, hind heal, agrimony, alexanders, githrife; give *to the man* to drink. Again, cassuck, tufty thorn, stonecrop, lupin, fennel, everthroat, cropleek; pour over them similarly. Again, a spew drink against the devil; take a mickle hand full of sedge, and gladden,

z 2

fulle secges · ⁊ glædenan do on pannan · geot micelne bollan fulne ealaþ on beƿyl healf gegnid. xx. lybcorna do on þ þis is god drenc ƿiþ deofle.

[LXVIII.]

Leoht drenc ƿiþ ƿeden heorte elehtre · biscop ƿyrt ælfþone · elene · cropleac · hind hioloþe · ontre · clate · nim þas ƿyrta þonne dæg ⁊ niht scade · sing ærest on circean letania · ⁊ credan · ⁊ pater noster · gang mid þy sange to þam ƿyrtum ymbga hie þriƿa ær þu hie nime · ⁊ ga eft to circean gesing . XII. mæssan ofer þam ƿyrtum þonne þu hie ofgoten hæbbe.

. LXVIIII.

Gif men sie maga asurod ⁊ forþunden · genim holen leafa micle tƿa hand fulla gesceafena sniþe smale ƿyl on meolcum oþ þ hie syn ƿel mearuƿe ƿyrla snæd mælum ete þonne .VI. snæda · on morgen . III. ⁊ on æfen .III. ⁊ æfter his mete · do þus .VIIII. niht leng gif him þearf sie. :·

Gif mon biþ aþunden ete rudan ⁊ drince he biþ hal. :·

Wiþ magan ƿærce rudan sæd ⁊ cƿic seolfor ⁊ eced bergen on neaht nestig. Eft gnid on eced ⁊ on ƿæter polleian ƿele drincan sona þ ƿær toglit.

. LXX.

Wiþ ƿambe ƿærce ofgeot polleian ⁊ drince ⁊ rume binde to þam nafolan · ⁊ ƿite georne þ hio ƿyrt aƿeg ne aglide sona biþ ƿel.

put them into a pan, pour a mickle bowl full of ale upon them; boil half, rub *fine* twenty libcorns, put them into it; this is a good drink against the devil.

### lxviii.

A light drink for the wood heart; lupin, bishopwort, enchanters nightshade, helenium, cropleek, hindheal, ontre, clote. Take these worts when day and night divide; sing first in church a litany, and a Credo, and a Pater noster, with the song go to the worts, go thrice around them, before thou touch them; and go again to church, sing twelve masses over the worts when thou hast poured —[1] over them.

### lxix.

1. If a mans stomach be soured and swollen; take holly leaves, two mickle hands full, scrape them very small, boil them in milk till they be pretty tender, pick them out by a bit at a time; then let the man eat six bits, in a morning three, and in evening three, and after his meat. Thus do for nine days, longer if need be.

2. If a man be swollen, let him eat rue and drink it; he will be well.

3. For pain of maw; let the man taste at night fasting, seed of rue, and quicksilver, and vinegar. Again, rub pulegium into vinegar and into water, give *the man* to drink, soon the soreness glideth away.

### lxx.

1. For wamb wark; drench in ——[2] pulegium, and let him drink it and bind some to his navel, and let him earnestly beware that the wort do not glide away. Soon he will be well.

---

[1] Not mentioned; to be supplied from above.

[2] The liquid is not mentioned.

Þiþ maȝan ƿæɲce puðu þiſtleſ þone ȝɲenan[1] meaɲh
þe biþ on þam heaɲðe ſele him etan mið hatan ele.

Uiþ ƿambe heaɲðneɲſe ȝeclænſa ȝiþcoɲn ȝnið on
cealð ƿæteɲ ſele him ðɲincan.

Þiþ ſþɲinȝe ȝnið ſaluian þiþ huniȝ ſmiɲe mið Sona
biþ ſel. Eſt ƿyɲc ſealſe nim hanð ſulle ſþɲinȝ
ƿyɲte · ⁊ hanð ſulle peȝbɲæðan · ⁊ hanð ſulle maȝþan ·
⁊ hanð ſulle niðepeaɲðe ðoccan þɲepe þe ſmnuian
ƿille on butɲan ahlyttɲe þ ſealt óſ ⁊ þ ſam ðo hɲon
humȝeſ to enȝliſceſ · ðo oſeɲ ſyþ apyl · þonne hit
ƿealle· ſinȝ .III. ſæteɲ noɲteɲ oſeɲ ðo eſt oſ ſinȝ
þonne .VIIII. ſiþum ſæteɲ noɲteɲ ón ⁊ þɲiɲa apyl ⁊
ſpa ȝeloine óſ aðo ⁊ lacna mið ɲiþþan.

Viþ þɲope ȝeolþan aðle óſȝeot þaſ ƿyɲte mið ſþiþe
beoɲe · ɲibban hanð ſulle · cþic ɲinða hanð ſulle .VIIII.
ſnæða niþeþeaɲðɲe æɲcþɲotan · ⁊ .VIIII. niþeþeaɲðɲe
colenan.

Eſt ðile · celenðɲe · Salmian mæſt ƿyl ón ſþiþum
beoɲe þ hit ſie þɲicce · ⁊ ȝɲene · nim niþeþeaɲðe colenan
ȝeſiuþ on huniȝ ete ſpa maniȝe ſnæða ſpa he mæȝe
ȝeðɲince þæſ ðɲenceſ ſcenc ſulne æſteɲ ⁊ eal þ ſæc
ete ſceaþen ſlæɲc ⁊ nan oþeɲ.

Ȝiſ men ſie mnelſe ute ȝecnua ȝallúc aþþiȝ þuɲh
clað on cu peaɲme meolce · ƿæt þine hanða þæɲ ón ⁊
ȝeðo þ mnelſe on þone man ȝeſeoɲe mið ſeolce ƿyl him
þonne ȝallúc .VIIII. moɲȝnaſ butan him lenȝ þeaɲſ
ſie ſeð hine mið ſeɲſce hænne ſlæɲc     *     *     *

*     *     *     *

---

[1] The MS. has a stop after ȝɲenan.

2. For maw pain; give *the man* to eat the green marrow which is in the head of a wood thistle, with hot oil.

3. For hardness of wamb; cleanse githcorns, rub them *fine* into cold water, give *to the man* to drink.

### lxxi.

Against carbuncle; rub sage with honey, smear therewith, soon he will be well. Again, work a salve, take a hand full of spring wort, and a hand full of way broad and a hand full of maythe, and a hand full of the netherward part of dock, that *namely* which will swim; boil in butter, clear off the salt and the foam, add a little English honey, put over a fire, boil *it;* when it boileth sing three Pater nosters over *it,* remove it again, then sing nine Pater nosters, and boil it thrice, and so frequently; remove it, and after that cure *with it.*

### lxxii.

1. For the yellow disease; souse these worts in strong beer, of ribwort a hand full, of quickbeam rind a hand full, nine bits of the netherward part of ashthroat, and nine of the lower part of helenium.

2. Again, boil dill, coriander, most of sage, in strong beer, that it may be thick and green; take the netherward part of helenium, cut it up into honey, let the patient eat as many bits as he can; let him drink after it a cup full of the drink, *as above;* and all the time let him eat sheep flesh and none other.

### lxxiii.

If a mans bowel be out, pound galluc, wring through a cloth into milk warm from the cow, wet thy hands therein, and put *back* the bowel into the man, sew up with silk, then boil him for nine mornings galluc, *that is,* *comfrey,* except need be for a longer time, feed him with fresh hens flesh.

*Perhaps one folio is missing.*

There is some writing along the margin of the last page, the few readable syllables of which are unintelligible.

ᵹıla ᵹpa bınᵭ þ . . . . . . poᵭ þı . . . . . . . . Λ Býp m ıp bpen.

# GLOSSARY.

# GLOSSARY.

THE following glossary relies almost entirely upon original authorities; upon a collation of the manuscript ancient extant glossaries with their printed editions, which have been falsified by ignorant conjectures; and upon a careful examination of many Saxon volumes never yet published. No reliance has been placed on modern productions, in the way of dictionaries; they will be found full of errors.[1] Every article either supplies a deficiency or corrects an error; but our limits will not admit of the insertion of every correction prepared for the press. Corrections were, of course, to be accompanied by their proofs, and this adds to the length of the various articles. Some refer to genders or declensions or terminations, for an exact knowledge of our Oldest English is impossible, as long as students are deceived on these elementary points. The most important printed texts of Saxon works have been collated from beginning to end, letter by letter, with the original manuscripts. The modern editions in particular are, sometimes, very faulty.

In the names of plants the reader will observe that a name, however wrong, is within its own bounds, still

---

[1] See SHRINE (Williams and Norgate).

a name. Mistakes often thrive, and even overpower a true old tradition. Many decided spirits would have all error thrown over, but to do so, would render our collection less complete.

The order of the letters is so arranged that K goes with C, Y with I, and þorn is last of all.

---

# TABLE OF CONTRACTIONS.

## PRINTED BOOKS.

---

° Æ.G. Ælfrics Grammar, ed. Somner, quoted by pages and lines.

A.R. Adrian and Ritheus, ed. Kemble, by pages.

A.W. Ælfreds Will, reprint 1828, by pages.

° Bw. Beowulf, ed. Gruudtvig, collated with MS., by lines.

* Crd. Cædmon, if Cædmon, by the pages and lines of the original MS.

C.D. Codex Diplomaticus, by numbers.

° C.E. Codex Exoniensis, by pages, ed. Thorpe.

° Ch. Charms, Leechdoms, Vol. I.

° DD. (Dooms) Laws and Institutes, ed. 1840, by pages.

Dief. Glossarium Diefenbachii.

D.R. Durham Ritual, by pages.

° F.F. Fight at Finnesburg, ed. Thorpe.

G. Goodwins Andrew and Veronix.

° Gð. Goodwins Guðlac.

° Hb. Herbarium, Leechdoms, Vol. I., by articles.

Hom. Ælfrics Homilies, ed. Thorpe.

° Lb. Leechbook, Leechdoms, Vol. II., by chapters.

M. Mones Glossaries in Quellen und Forschungen, von F. J. Mone, 1830.

M.Sp. Mannings Supplement to Lye, paged for the purpose, from Testamentum Elfhelmi, page 1.

N. Narratiunculæ, 1861. (Russell Smith.)

° O.cl. O clerice, in preface to Leechdoms, Vol. I. p. lviii.

° O.T. Orosius, ed. Thorpe, by pages and lines.

° Quad. Medicina de Quadrupedibus, Leechdoms, Vol. I.

* Rnnl. The Runlioð, or Runelay. quoted by articles.

SH. Shrine, where some Saxon pieces are printed.

S.S. Solomon and Saturn, ed. Kemble.

SSpp. Spoon and Sparrow, for etymology.

## IN MANUSCRIPT.

*Generally cited by folios.*

xii.Ab. De xii. Abusivis. MS. C.C.C.

BL. Blooms, or Flores Soliloquiorum.

D.G. Dialogues of Gregorius, MS. C.C.C.

° Διδαξ. The treatise περὶ διδάξεων, in Leechdoms, Vol. III.

F.D. De Falsis Dis. MS. C.C.C.

° F.L. Fourth Leechdoms, for publication in Leechdoms, Vol. III.

G.D. Dialogues of Gregorius, MS. Cotton.

IIID. Liber de Hida.

° Lacn. Lacnunga, in Vol. III. of Leechdoms, by articles.

M.II. Minster Homilies of Ælfric, except Sigewulfi responsiones, de xii. Abusivis, and de Falsis Dis.

P.A. The Liber Pastoralis of King Ælfred, MS. Hatt.

R.M. Rule of Mynchens.

Sc. Liber Scintillarum.

SMD. Somniorum Diversitas.

## GLOSSARIES.

Gl. Brux. A Brussels Glossary, printed by Mone, p. 314, by Thorpe, unpublished, p. 36, by Wright, p. 62.

Gl. C. An early Glossary in MS.

Gl. Dun. An old Glossary in the library of the cathedral at Durham. The compiler had used the Saxon Herbarium, as in Lactuca leporina.

Gl. E. Glossaries printed by Eckhart, in Commentarii de rebus Franciæ Orientalis, Wirceburgi, fol., 1729, 2 vols.

Gl. Hoffm. Althochdeutsche Glossen, von A. H. Hoffmann, 1826.

Gl. M. A manuscript on vellum, the property of Rev. W. D. Macray.

Gl. M.M. Glossary of Moyen Moutier, printed, but unpublished.

Mone. Glossaries printed by Mone, in Quellen und Forschungen, Aachen und Leipsig, 8vo., 1830. The herb glossary fetches from. IIb. Used MS. B.

N. Bakers Northamptonshire Gl.

Gl. Prud. Glossary on Prudentius, printed but unpublished.

Gl. R. Junius transcript of the Rubens MS. Glossary, MS.

Gl. Somn. The Glossaries printed by Somner, in Dictionarium Saxonico-Latino-Anglicum. Oxonii, fol., 1659, printed with errors from Gl. R.

Other manuscript Glossaries numbering about fifteen.

# GLOSSARY.

## A.

A, as prefix, is a shorter form of—1. And, as in abidan, for andbidan.

2. On, as in among, for onmang, and aweg, for onweg, both of which are occasionally parallel MS. readings. *See* MII. 115 a, with var. lect.

3. Un, as in atynan, *open*, for untynan.

4. Of, as in acalan for ofcalan. Hom. II. 248.

5. Embe, as in ymbutan, abutan, and by apokope buton.

6. Ge, as in alefed, for gelefed.

Acumba, -an, masc.? *oakum, stupa.* Cf. " Coarse fibres among wool are kemps," Gl. N. Putamina, acuman, æcumba, Gl. Mone, p. 398 a, p. 407 a, as consisting of coarse fibres. Νάφθα is an approximation only, explained in SII. p. 10. Similarly "Napta, genus fomenti, *i.e.* " tyndir," Gl. M.M. p. 159 b. Acumba in ashes seems administered as a substitute for Σπόδιον. Lib. I. i. 15 ; xxxiii. 1 ; xlvii. 3.

Æ, as a prefix, is commonly a shorter form of Æf, which answers to the Latin Ob, in the sense of annoyance, as in Officere and the like. Thus Æbylgan, Æcyrf. Bed. 552, l. 13 ; Æmod.

Æc, Ac, gen. -e, fem., *oak, quercus robur.* Sume ac astah, Hom. II. 150, *got up into an oak.* Of ðære éc, C.D. 570, p. 78. þeoɼ ac, Æ.G. 7, 48. Gen. Acc,

Æc—*cont.*
Lib. I. xxxviii. 11. Vowels dropped. C.D. 588, 624, etc. Gen. pl. Acana, C.D. 126.

2. As a letter of the alphabet the same word is masc., gen. -es. Acaɼ ʈɼeʒen hæʒelaɼ ɼpa ɼome, C.E. 429, *two As and two Hs along with them.*

Æcelma, gen. an, masc.? *a chilblain, mula.* Gl. Mone, p. 359 b. " Mula est quædam " infirmitas in homine quæ vocatur " gybehos," Gl. Harl. 3388, that is, *kibe of heel.* In Italian, " mule, kibes, chil- " blanes " (Florio). In French, "mule, " a kibe " (Cotgrave). Palagra, æcilma, Gl. Cleop., where understand podagra and *footsore.* The word is compounded of Æ for Æɼ, signifying annoyance, cel, *chill,* and the participial man. SSpp., art. 943.

Ædre, vein, *vena*, gen. both -e, and -an, fem., Lb. I. i. 13 ; II. xviii.; II. xxxii., etc. IIb. iv. 4. On oþrum monþe þa ædron beoð geworden, N. p. 49, *in the second month the veins are formed.* S.S. 148, 192.

2. pl. *kidneys, rencs.* R.M. 69, a. IIb. lxxxvi. 3; cxix. 3. Paris Ps. cxxxviii. 11.

3. In the sense of water spring found neut. þæt wæteræddre, perhaps by attraction. Hom. II. 144. Ealle corðan æddre onsprungon ongean þam heofonlican flode. MS. C.C.C. 419, p. 42.

Æferðe, gen. -an, fem.? *an herb unknown.* Lb. I. xxxiii. 2, etc.

Ægwyrt, gen. -e, fem., *eggwort, dande-*
*lion, leontodon taraxacum* ; like Germ.
Eyerblume, from the round form of the
pappus. Lacn. 40.

Ælfsibenne, from ælf, *elf*, and sido, masc.
*manners*, as Boet. p. 45, l. 21, p. 131, l. 10,
often taken in a good sense as *morals*.
Lb. I. lxiv. The termination -en, like
-*ivos*, -inus, does not always relate to
metals and materials, but as in fyrlen,
*distant*, myrten, *mortuary*, is more general.
We may therefore take this word as the
accusative of an adjective. It is, however, possible that it may be a substantive. Lacn. 11.

Ælfsogoða. *See* Sogoða. Lb. III. lxii.

Ælfðone, gen. -an ; fem. ? probably *cir-*
*cœa lutetiana, enchanters nightshade,*
which in old Dutch is Alfrancke. Lb.
I. xxxii. 4; II. liii.

Æpening, masc., gen. -ey, *a medlar*, fruit of
*mespilus germanica.* Lb. II. ii. 2. See
the passage and the glossarial openæpy,
*mespilum.*

Æppel, gen. -ples, masc. in sing. pl. -pla,
*apple, malum.* Numb. xi. 5. P.A. 19 b.
*Also a soft fruit,* as *fruit of the bramble.*
Lb. I. lxiv.; III. xli. Fingeræpla, *dates,*
M.H. 131 b. A translation of Δακτυλοι.
Copðæppel, Numb. xi. 3, *a cucumber.*
Fic æppel, *a fig* (Lye), pl. ꞃicæppla,
Matth. vii. 16 ; Luke vi. 44. Palmæpla,
Gl. Cleop. fol. 66 d. Gl. Mone, p. 409 b.
Lb. II. i. ; II. xxxvi. SSpp. 543.

2. *A dumpling.* IIb. cxxxiv. 2.

3. *The ball of the eye,* with pl. masc.
On ðæʒ ꞃipenlʒean eaʒum beoð ða
æpplaꞃ hale. Ac ða bꞃæꞃaꞃ ꞅpeaꞇꞁʒeað,
P.A. 15, a. *In the eyes of the bleareyed*
*the balls are healthy, but the lids swollen.*
Se oðeꞃ æppel ꞃæꞃ ʒeemꞇꞁʒoð, M.H.
98 b, *the ball of one eye was emptied*
of its crystalline, aqueous, and vitreous
humours. Applied less exactly as a
translation of *pupilla*, Boet. p. 132, l. 25.

Æpse, gen. -an, fem. ? *the aspen, populus*
*tremula.* Lb. I. xxxvi. SH. 25. The
last syllable in the modern name represents the case endings. Æps. occurs in

Æpse—*cont.*
the glossaries, and Lb. III. xxxix; it is
regarded by Ælfric in Gr. as Abies.

Æsc, gen. -es, masc. C.D. 461, *the ash,*
*fraxinus excelsior.* Se ꞃophꞇa æsc. C.E.
429.

Ceaster æsc, *helleborus niger, black*
*hellebore,* which has leaves like those of
the ash. " Eliforus (*read* Helleborus),
" pebe bepʒe (*mad berry*) vel ceaꞅꞇep
" æꞃc," Gl. Cleop. fol. 36 b. Lacn. 39.

Æscee, gen. -an, fem., *ash, cinis.* Lb. I.
xxxviii. 4. Quad. iii. 4. Axe þu eapꞇ
꞊ on axan leoꞃa. Cinis es et in cinere
uiue. Sc. 11, a. Æ.G. 11, 47. C.E. 213,
line 27. Cf. Aska, fem., old Dansk.

Æscþꞃoꞇu, gen. -an, fem. 1. *Verbena*
*officinalis.* IIb. iv., with the drawing.
Verbenaca, in MS. Bodley 130, is drawn
and glossed Verbena, vervain. Also
Veruyn in MS. T. Verbenaca in
Dodoens is Vervain. " Verveyne,
" Veruena vocatur grece ierobotanum
" vel peristerion et dicitur verbena
" quia virtutibus plena," MS. Douce,
290. MS. G. has a gl. " Taubencropf,"
which, as I learn from Adelung, is
Verbena. " Hiera quam Latini Ber-
" benam uocant ideo a grecis hoc
" nomen accepit qued sacerdotes eam
" purificationibus adhibere consueve-
" runt." MS. Harl. 5264, fol. 56, b.
" Verbena, æscwert," Gl. Mone, p. 442 a.
" Berbenaces, eascvyrt," Gl. Dun. Lb.
III. 72.

2. Annuosa, which is found in a few
glossaries, is a mere blunder for anchusa,
translated in IIb. ci. 3, by ashthroat.

3. *Goutweed, œgopodium podagraria.*
Ashweed is this in Mylnes Indigenous
Botany. This plant I take to be meant
by the Ferula of Gl. M.M., Gl. Dun.,
Somner Lex., Gl. Brux. The Ferula
communis, or fennel giant, is not a
native of England, and under all cir-
cumstances, would either not have an
English name or one extended to plants
of a similar aspect, even if smaller.
This ægopodium is often called Angelica.

Æseþþoru —*cont.*

even down to Ray, and the angelicas are also large and hollow. Throat seems to imply hollowness, and Ash either size or similar leaves.

The fennel giant is, however, mentioned in the life of St. Godric as affording walking staves for pilgrims, (A.D. 1159), p. 163.

Æsmælum, dat. pl., a disease of the eye, *contraction of the pupil, oculorum imminutio.* "Evenit etiam ut oculi, vel ambo " vel singuli, minores fiant quam esse " naturaliter debeant." Celsus, VI. vi. 14. "Pupillæ malum est, quum an- " gustior ac obscurior rugosiorque effi- " citur." Actuarius, 184, c. Lb. I. 2, and contents. A comp. of Æ, for Æf, implying mischief, and Smæl.

Æþelreþðincgþ̄ypt, fem., gen. -e, *stichwort, stellaria holostea,* with *s. graminea.* Æþelreþðincþ̄ypt in IIb. lxiii. 7, translates "agrimoniam," and lxxviii. 1, " argemonitis." *See* Plinius, xxvi. 59. " Agrimonia alpha, cathelferthing vyrt " vel glofvyrt," Gl. Dun. " Alfa, æðel- " reþðincgþ̄ypt," Gl. Somn., p. 64 b, 7. Some supposed agrimonia to be stichwort, though as the translator of the Herbarium had called it ȝaþclȳfe, a very appropriate name, we should not have expected this uncertainty from him. " Agrimonia, ȝ̄teþ̄ýpt," Gl. Somn. p. 64 a, 65. In Lacn. 29, æþelreþðincg- þ̄ypt is glossed "auis lingua." " Lingua " avis. i. pigle, stichwort," Gl. M. " Lin- " gua auis . i . pigle," Gl. Rawl. C. 607. " Lingua auis, stichewort," Gl. Sloane, 5. The name describes the leaves.

Afreoðan, *to froth.* Lb. I. xlvii. 2.

Ahwænan, præt. ede, p.p. ed, *to trouble, contristare.* IIb. xx. 7, where Lat. contristatus. "Herof þe lauedies to me meneþ, An wel sore me ahweneþ, Wel nch min heorte wule tochine, Hwon ich beholde hire pine. Owl and Nightingale, 1562. *Of this the ladies to me moan, and pretty sorely distress me; well nigh my*

Ahwænan—*cont.*

*heart will break* (tocinan), *when I behold their pain.* Vtan þþeþ̄þian aliþænebe ⁊ hyptan oþmobe, MS. C.C.C. 419, p. 246. *Let us comfort the distressed and encourage the despairing.* Cf. DD. 139, xlvii.

Aleþþan, *to lather.* Lb. I. liv. *See* Leaðor. It is for Geleþþan.

Alor, Alr, gen. -es, masc., *the alder, alnus glutinosa.* Lb. I. ii. 14 ; alres, Lb. II. li. 3 ; masc. C.D. 376.

Ananbeam, gen. -es, masc., *the spindle tree, euonymus Europæus.* Lb. I. xxxii. 4. Germ. anisbaum. " Ƿanabeam, fusa- " num, *spindle tree, pricktimber.*" Somner Lex. " Fusarius, uuananbeam," Gl. M.M.

Anapym, Ons *worm,* masc. Lb I. xlvi. 1. In the Ynglinga Saga, Anasott is said to have taken its name from On, a king of Sweden, who prolonged his own life by sacrificing from time to time one of his sons to Woden. Siðan andæðist On konúngr, ok er hann heygðr at Uppselum. Þat er siðan kallut Anasott er maðr deyr verklaus af elli. Heimskringla, Ynglinga S. xxix. *Then expired king On, and was buried at Upsal. It was afterwards called On-sickness, when a man dies from old age, without agony.* That the former element in Anapym, Anasott, is the same cannot be doubtful.

Anpilbe, *unique (unicus, singularis).* Lb. I. ii. 9. Cf. Zwispild, geminus, biformis. (Graff.)

Antre. *See* Ontre. Lb. II. li.

Arendan. Lb. II. lii.

Argesweorf, gen. -es, *brass filings.* Lb. I. xxxiv. 1. *See* Gesweorf.

Arod, an herb, probably *arum,* Ἄρον. Lb. III. xlii. Lacn. 2. Thus Cyned for Cynen.

Aþ óm, *copperas.* The reading of the MS. in Lb. II. xv. is saþ óm, translating μετὰ χαλκάνθου λείου (καὶ μέλιτι ὀλίγῳ ἀναλαβών). Χάλκανθος is *green vitriol.* But it is also *brass rust, ærugo,* and the

Aр óm—*cont.*

true reading may be aр óm. The word copperas is commonly used for either the green rust of copper, or the green vitriol with which the kitchenmaid cleans brass pans ; from its ambiguity it was convenient. Λϵίου points to the levigated rust.

Asaru, *asarabacca, asarum Europœum.* Lb. II. xiv. Foles foot is Tussilago farfara.

Asiftan, *to sift.* Lb. I. ii. 20.

Aslawen, *struck, stricken,* from aрlean, for † aрlaᵹan, a collateral form. Contents, Lb. I. lvi. =aрlaᵹen in text. So cnucan becomes cnupan, cnuan.

Asprindlad, *ripped up and spanned open with tenter hooks.* Lb. II. xxiv. From sprindel, *tenticum,* Gl. C., *a tenter hook.* Cf. Spreisseln, Schmeller, Bayerisches Wörterbuch, IV. p. 593.

Aрpum, a Latin word, *Smyrnium olusatrum.* Lb. I. ii. 20, etc.

Aррoplaþe, gen. -an ; "venom-loather," *panicum crus galli.* In IIb. xlv. aррoplaþe is galli crus, and were there doubt, it seems removed by MSS. G. T. A., which draw the *p. sanguinale, Linn.,* now called *digitaria sanguinalis.* These two grasses are included together in the "cocksleg," hahnenbein of the Germans. The corresponding article in MS. Bodley, 130, gives the name sanguinaria, and the old gloss is Blobwrt, with a later of the 14th century, "Blodwerte." Sanguinaria is often glossed as shepherds purse, thlaspi or capsella bursa pastoris, or as tormentilla, these being esteemed stanchers of blood, or as polygonum ; but in this instance it must be as above, *d. -sanguinalis.* With these testimonies it is vain to consider how such virtue was attributed to a grass. Did they confuse panicum with panacea ? The glossaries give no real help. "Atrilla, "attorlathe," Gl. Dun., where atrilla seems to be aррoplaþe with a Latin termination. "Astrilla," Gl. Sloane, 146.

Aррoplaþe—*cont.*

"Cyclaminos, attorlathe," id., but cyclamen is in Herbarium "slite." "Galli "crus, attorlathe," id., a quotation from our book. "Fenifuga, attorlathe," id., understand venenifuga, a translation of the Saxon word. "Venenifuga, aррeplaþe," Gl. Somner, p. 66 [63] b. 27. "Morella, "atterloþe," Gl. Harl. 978, but morella is atropa belladonna, and poisonous itself. Aрeplaᵭe, betonica, Lyc, from a Gl. ; but betony and attorlothe are separately named in Lb. I. i. 15. The claims of asclepias vincetoxicum are set aside by its being a foreign plant. The heal all of the old Dansk, Laukr, has no support from our authorities. Lyc prints, by some error, sattorlaþe also. The small attorlothe occurs in Lb. I. xlv. 6.

Auruᵹo is interpreted by Du Cange *la jaunisse, the jaundice.* This rendering is supported by the etymon aurum, *gold,* and by authority ; aurugo, *color in auro, sicut in pedibus accipitris,* i . gelesouch, Gl. E. vol. ii. p. 992 a, *the colour one sees in gold, as in a hawks feet, the yellow sickness.* Gelisuhtiger, *ictericus, auruginosus,* Graff. vol. vi. col. 142. Our text, however, interprets aurugo, as *a tugging or drawing of the sinews,* IIb. Perhaps this may be explained by observing that auriginosus is glossed arcuatus, Du Cange ; auruginosus, arcuatus, Gl. Isid. Not very differently from our text ; "Artuatus, рƀmyole "aᵭl," Gl. R. p. 11, ult., read arcuatus and it may be, ᵹeole, or muscle ; whence it might well be supposed that ὀπισθότονος was meant, a term applied to bows, bent back the opposite way to their natural curvature, especially true of horn bows, Gortynia cornua, and to persons suffering under that extreme form of tetanus, in which the feet and head are drawn back till they touch. Aurigo is also, in Apul. lxxxvii., *morbus regius,* which was another mediæval name for the jaundice ; Graff. vol. vi.,

Aurugo—*cont.*

141. Graff's mark of interrogation at the word Gelbsucht, would be removed by the publication of our texts.

Aþrepan, † -þreap, -þupen, *turn, coagulate.* See Þrepan. Lb. I. xlv. 5.

Aþyn, *press.* Lb. I. viii. 2. His eyes ꞃæp ꞃæꞃon uꞇaꝺyꝺe oꝼ þam eahhꞃingum, MH. 98 b, *were before thrust out of their sockets.* See Þyn.

## B.

Ban—1. *A bone.*

2. *A leg,* neut., pl. ban. Lb. I. i. 15; I. xxvi.; II. li., where it is *leg,* so Cædm.? Daniel, MS. p. 195, 5. Pseudo Cædm. II.II. MS. p. 223, 20, *their legs failed them.* "Tibialis, banꞃyꞇ," Gl. M.M.

Banꞃyꞇ, fem., gen. in -e. 1. *bonewort, viola,* not blue voilet, but *viola lactea, white violet,* and *v. lutea, Heartsease.* In IIb. clii. 1, bonewort is in the Latin version of Dioskorides, (not existing in the Hellenic) "viola alba:" in IIb. clxv. it is also distinguished from viola purpurea in art. clxvi. Lb. I. i. 15.

2. *Bellis perennis, daisy,* ꝺæꝣeꞃ eaꝣe; but at a period later than our text; and perhaps by error. "Consolida minor, "daysey, venwort, idem bonewort," Gl. Harl. 3388. "Consolida minor . i. bon-"wort," Gl. M. "Consolida minor, days-"y꞉e," Gl. Bodley, 178. "Consolida "minor. Daysei is an herbe þat sum "men callet hembrisworte oþer bone-"wort," Gl. Douce, 290. "Consolida "minor . i . petit comferi . anglice dayis-"hege . habet florem album," Gl. Rawlinson, c. 607. Benwort, daisy, (Dickinsons Cumberland Gl. in add.)

3. *Erythræa centaureum,* if we trust "centaurea minor, banꞃyꞇ," Gl. Somn., p. 64 b, 18. The wort is said to have eꞃoppan, *bunches,* either racemes or

Banꞃyꞇ—*cont.*

umbels or cimes, which applies better to this lesser centaury than to heartsease or to daisy. Lb. II. li. 2.

4. "Filia aurea, banꞃyꞇ." Gl. Cleop. *Fila aurea, Solidago virgaurea, Bot.,* sometimes called consolida Saracenica.

Baꝺian, *to bathe,* is to be distinguished from Beꝺian, *to beathe* or *warm.* In the Lb. MS. fol. 92 a, the penman first had written e, but this he erased to put a. But as the old idea of a bath did not include cold water, the words are nearly allied.

Belene, beolene, gen. -an, fem. ? *henbane, hyoscyamus niger.* IIb. v. Lb. I. ii. 22; I. iii. 3. Another name is henne belle, from its bell shaped capsules, which are drawn in MS. V., and from them the name belene, seems derived; belle, *a bell;* bellen, *furnished with bells;* and the final e is the usual final distinctive form of names of worts. The modern name henbane is independent, and derived from its poisonous qualities; another is henne-pol, with the same sense.

Beope, *bark, latratus.* IIb. lxvii. 2. Gebeope, Sc. 55 b. Æ.G. 2, 44.

Beorꝺor, byrꝺor, gen. -res. 1. *the embryo, fœtus.* Quad. iv. 4; Bed. 493, 40. "Fœtu, ꞇuꝺpe vel mꝺ beopþpe," Gl. Cleop. 40 b. N. 50.

2. *Childbirth, partus,* Quad. iv. 6. Beopꝺoꞃeꝑelnaꞃ, *abortivi,* Lyc. Lb. III. xxxvii. Cf. Mone, p. 411 a.

Beopꞃyꞇ, fem., beewort, sweet flag, *acorus calamus.* IIb. vii. "Marubium, hunc "vel beopꞃyꞇ." Gl. Cleop. fol. 61 a, wrong. In IIb. vii. a synonym in the Latin is Veneria, and the mediæval marginal annotations on Dioskorides give on Ἄκορον (not Acorus), οἱ δὲ, χόρος, Ἀφροδισίας, Ῥωμαῖοι βενέρεα, οἱ δὲ, ναυτικὰ ῥᾶδιξ, Γάλλοι πεπερακιουμ; that is, Acorum is called in Latin Veneria, and by the Gauls peper apium (for apum), *bees pepper:* (for the Celtic use of kappa instead of pi, see SSpp. art. 20). What our text says about bees, is to be under-

Beopýpꞇ—*cont.*

stood, as that the wort will induce an
unsettled swarm of bees to reconcile
themselves to an offered hive ; hence it
was reasonably called beewort : and so
Dioskorides, of Acorum says, that the
roots are not in smell unpleasant ; τῇ
ὀσμῇ οὐκ ἀηδεῖς. In MS. V. the root
chiefly is drawn, and the figure corresponds minutely with the description in
Dioskorides, that they, for he uses a plural,
are not straight grown, but oblique and
superficial, divided by knots ; οὐκ εἰς εὐθὺ
πεφυκυίας ἀλλὰ πλαγίας καὶ ἐξ ἐπιπολῆς,
γόνασι διειλημμένας. That he adds
ὑπολεύκους, whitish, while the English
drawing has a strong red, may be set
down to the artistic tastes of the painter.
The drawing in MS. A. is very similar.
Somners Gl. p. 63 a, line 59, translates
apiago by beowyrt. In MS. Bodley,
130, veneria is drawn as acorum, with a
large creeping root, and glossed "lemre"
for the English name. Dorsten calls the
roots of acorus "rubicundas," as coloured in MS. V., and on this ground
several glossaries make acorus = madder.
The χόρος of the margin of Dioskorides
is another form of acoros, and Ἀφροδισίας
has the same sense as veneria. MS. G.
figures a crow foot, with gl. "honefus."

2. *Acanthe.* Hb. cliv. figured as *stellaria holostea.*

Besengian, *to singe.* Lb. I. li. *See* Sengian.

Besoreadan, *to empurple.* Lb. I. xlvii. 1;
from baso, *purple,* and read, *red.*

Byden, gen. -e, fem., *a bucket:* used in
Lb. I. xxxii. 2, with a perforated stool,
and thus evidently the modern bidet.

Binꞃꝛyꞃꞇ, fem., gen. in -e, *a rush,* a *iuncus*
or *carex* or *butomus umbellatus,* as in
German.

Byꞃꝼꝺbeꝛꝺe, fem., gen. -an, -can, *a mulberry.* Lb. II. xxx. 2. Moros, *mulberry
trees,* Ps. lxxvii. 52, is translated by
byꝛꝼꝺ and by maꝛbeamaꝛ. Spelm.
Beꝛꝼꝺbꝛene, diamoron, Gl. in Lye, a
drink made from mulberries with honey.

Bypla, masc., gen. -an, *the barrel,* in the
horse keepers sense ; Lb. I. lxxxviii. 3,
from the context and the modern word.
As, however, there is but this known
example, it may be *perineum,* like *bære,*
in Molbech. Cf. "Burlings, the tails
"and other parts, which are taken from
"lambs when sheared. Burl, to take such
"wool from lambs as is dirtied, or liable
"to additional deterioration from their
"laxity of body." Salopia antiqua Gl.

Biꝛceoppyꞃꞇ, fem. gen. in -e, *bishopswort,
ammi maius.* (Skinner, Nemnich, Florio,
Cotgrave, Lovell, Culpeper.) This is
medicinal, but foreign, and must be
taken as cultivated by our "herborists,"
as Lyte says of it. Bishops weed = ammi.
Skinner. So we read "the southern"
bishopwort, Lb. II. liv.

2. *Verbena officinalis?* if we trust Gl.
Somn. p. 64 a, 1, with p. 66 [63] b, 32.

3. "Hibiscus?" *tree mallow.* Gl. Cleop.
Gl. M.M. *Vitex* "*Agnus castus,*" Gl.
Arund. 42, fol. 92. "Puleium mon-
"tanum," Gl. Arund. 42.

Biꝛceoppyꞃꞇ ꝛeo læꝛꝛe, *the lesser
bishopswort, betonica officinalis.* "Beto-
"nica," Gl. Somn. p. 64 a, 49 ; Gl. Arund.
42; Gl. Dun. ; Gl. Mone, p. 320 b ; Gl.
Faust; IIb. i. ; but Skinner says "be-
"tonica aquatica," which is *scrophularia
aquatica, Bot.* ; and Culpeper says,
"water betony, in Yorkshire bishops
"leaves."

Biꞇe, gen. -eꞃ, masc. 1. *a bite.* 2. *a
cancer.* 1. pl. biꞇaꝛ, Quadr. xiii. 7; Isl.
bit, *a bite,* is neuter (B.H.). Biz, ohg.,
biss in Germ., are masc. The word is
followed by heo, Quadr. xi. 7, but that
will be an error. Sliꞇe also and others
have final e. Lb. I. xliv. 1.

Blæc, gen. -eꞃ? *a blotch.* Lb. Contents,
I. xxxii., with article þam. "Vitiligo,
"blec," Gl. M.M. p. 154 b, 39, where
is added þꝛuꝛꝼel, *leprosy,* the same as
Goth. þrutsfill, λέπρα. Similarly id. p.
164 b, 3, but bleceb.

2. *Ink, encaustum,* DD. 395.

Blopan, præt. † bleop, pp. blopen, *to blow,* *bloom, blossom, florere.* Tpeopa he ðeþ ꞃæþlice blopau, M.Sp. p. 16, Trees he shall *cause suddenly to bloom.* Mid blowendum wyrtum, Hom. II. 352, *with blooming worts.* Oð þ hi becomon ꞇo ꞃunum ꞃemenðum ꞃelba ꞃægꞃe Ɡeblopen, M.II. 99 b, *Till they came to a shining plain, fair and blooming* ("fairly blown"). C.E. 199, 200, etc.

BoꞬen. *See* Boðen, convertible, Lb. p. 310, note. Lb. III. iv. xxvi. xxx. lxii. 1.

Box, neut. ? Lb. II. lix. 14. ꞇobꞃocenum ꞃealꞃboxe, Mark xiv. 3. Buxus, box ꞇꞃeop. Buxum, ꞃopcaꞃuen box, ÆG. 5, ult. It is therefore direct from the late Latin, and seems to follow its gender.

Boðen, gen. -eꞃ; probably *wild thyme, thymus serpyllum.* Boþeneꞃ, Lb. III. iv. In IIb. lxxxi. boðen is rosemary, which is a native of the south of Europe. In IIb. cxlix. it is employed to translate *thyme,* and this is native to England. "Lolium, boþen," Gl. Somn., p. 77 a, but darnel is not to the unskilled eye at all like thyme and rosemary; it seems however to be considered only as a mean herb by the glossator. The drawing in MS. V., fol. 39 d, has not simple leaves as for either rosemary or thyme it should have (II.), but it may be the artists view of either. "Rosmarinus, sundeav vel bothen vel "feld medere," Gl. Dun. "Rosmarinus, "sundeaw," Gl. Mone, p. 322 b.; this is a failure to translate ros marinus as sea dew; our sundew or *droscra* is wholly different. In MS. Bodley, 130, there is no drawing of rosmarinus, but a hand of the 14th century has glossed the article "feld modere;" this seems to come of very careless observation. "Rosmari- "num, feld mædere," Gl. Mone, p. 322 a. White bothen is great daisie, says Gerarde.

Bꞃeað, *brittle.* IIb. cxl. 1. εὔθραυστος.

Bꞃecan, verb reflexive, bꞃecan hine, *make an effort to spew.* Lb. II. lii. 1.

Bꞃecan—*cont.* "Brakyn or castyn or spewe, *vomo* "*evomo,*" Prompt. Parv. "Brakynge or "parbrakynge, *vomitus, evomitus,*" id.

Bꞃeðe? *a particoloured cloth;* mid bꞃeðe. Lb. III. ii. 1. Cf. Bꞃædelꞃ, *stragulum,* Gl. in Lye. Cf. BꞃꝼꞬð, C.E. 218, line 9. BꞃeꞬðen, C.E. 219, line 13.

BꞃeꞬðan, præt. bꞃæð, p. part. bꞃoꞬðen, *to do anything with a sudden jerk or start.* Lb. II. li. 3. etc.

Bꞃyꞃepyꞃꞇ, fem., gen. -e, *pimpernel, anagallis.* "Anagallis, brisewort," Gl. Rawlinson, c. 506. Gl. Harl. 3388. Leechdoms, vol. I. p. 374.

2. *Bellis perennis,* MS. Laud. 553, fol. 9. Plainly for Hembriswyrt. *See* Banꞃyꞃꞇ, 2.

Bꞃipan, *to brew,* præt. bꞃeop, p. part. bꞃopen. Lb. I. xlvii. 3, *make a brewit, a lomentum, dress.* Lb. I. xxxvi. Bꞃip his meꞇe ꞃiþ ele. Lb. II. li. 1, 3. O.T. 254, 9. Hom. I. 352.

Bꞃyþen, neut., *what has been brewed.* Lb. I. lxvii. 2. C.E. p. 161, 4 = MS. fol. 47 a, 8, where the use of barm is mentioned. He Ɡeann . . . an bꞃyþen mealꞇes; *one brewing of malt;* malt for one brewing, Wulfgeats Will, unpublished.

Bꞃocmuꞇe, -an, fem., *mentha hirsuta, Bot.* IIb. cvi. "Sisymbrium, an herbe, "wherof bee two kyndes, the one is "called Sisymbrium alone, whiche is also "called Thymbrea, in englishe water "mynte." Elyots Dict. by T. Cooper. See the synonyms from mediæval sources in the Flora Britannica, with the words " In aquosis vulgaris."

Bꞃom, gen. -eꞃ, masc.? *broom, cytisus scoparius,* (Hooker). Lb. I. ii. 14.

Bꞃoþepꞃyꞃꞇ, fem., gen. -e, *penny royal, mentha pulegium,* Gl. Brux.

Bꞃuneþan, a dative: Lb. I. iv. 6, a disease, *brunella;* as I conclude from the following; "oris vitium cum linguæ "tumore, exasperatione, siccitate et "nigredine; unde et nomen teutonice "habet, vulgo brunella." Kilian in

Bpunꝑan—*cont.*

bruyne. Album Græcum, prescribed in
Lb. for this disease, is said by Salmon
(Engl. Phys. p. 753) to cure "Diseases
" of the Throat and Quinsies : for a sore
" throat called *Pruna*, you may use it."

Bpunpypꝥ, fem., gen. in -e, *brown wort,
scrofularia aquatica, water betony.*
(Skinner, Lyte, Nemnich, Culpeper.) So
braunwurtz in Dodoens. I suppose " the
" broad leaved brownwort which waxeth
" in woods," Lb. I. xxxviii. 4, to be
*scrofularia nodosa.*

2. IIb. art. lvii. makes bpunpypꝥ the
fern called splenium or asplenium, and
Gl. Dun. copies that. *Ceterach officina-
rum* is meant. It has a brown under
surface, but the drawing in MS. V. is
not a fern at all. Spimon vel reverion,
Gl. Brux., where spimon is a misreading
of splenion.

3. Also the vaccinium or bilberry
shrub, Gl. Somn. p. 66 [63] b, 12, where
bpunpypꝥ is printed. Gl. Dun.

4. *Prunella vulgaris,* where prun is
*brown.* So the Mæstricht Gl. in Mone,
p. 285 a. Nemnich. *See also* Bruyne
in Kilian.

Bulenꝝe, a wort. Lb. I. xlvii. 2. There
must have been more than one of the
name, as the passage mentions the small
sort.

Buloꝥ, Lb. I. lviii. 2 ; Bulur, Lb. III.
xlviii. ; *the root of lychnis flos cuculi?
See* Plinius xxi. 97 = 26. *Ballota,* Βαλ-
λέτη, *nigra?* Boletus?

# C.

Cæpen, neut. ? a Latin word, *carenum,
wine boiled down one third and sweetened.*
" Cypen, i.e. apuleð pin . dulcisapa," Gl.
in Lye. Mið þam cepenum þæꝑe goð-
ꝛpelliean ꝛpeꞇnyꝛꝛe, St.Guðlac, cap. xvii.
= p. 72, l. 7. Gen. -eꝝ. Lb. I. i. 17.

Cæpꝛe, gen. -an, fem. ? *cress, water cress,
nasturtium officinale.* The drawings in
V. A. have opposite leaves and a stout
tripartite terminal fruit or inflorescence,
so that they are " most like caper spurge,
" euphorbia lathyris," (II.) But the opposite leaves with a racemose arrange-
ment of the flowers, which latter may be
seen in MS. T., is sufficient for us, with
the synonym in Hb. xxi. " Nasturtium."
In MS. G. is a gloss, " Cart chresse,"
where the former word may stand for
κάρδαμον, cress. The drawing in MS. G.
is a good deal like the herb, and that in
MS. T. is meant for it. " Cardamon,
" cearse," Gl. Dun. Tun cæpꝛe, *garden
cress, lepidium sativum;* Dutch, Tuinkers.

Camecon, *cammock?* which see. Lb. I.
xlvii. 3. Cf. Illeomoc, Illeomocan.

Cammoc, Commuc, gen. -eꝝ. 1. *Sulfur
wort, harestrang, peucedanum officinale,*
IIb. art. xcvi., and so drawn MS. V. fol.
45 a. Peucedanum, gl. dogge fenell,
MS. Bodley, 130, adding " or balde-
" monie," which is gentian. "Peuce-
" danum, cammok," Gl. M. ; Gl. Dun.,
dog fenell (Grete Herbal). The fine
linear leaves are meant in a bad drawing
in MS. Harl. 5294, where is gl. hand
fenell. Peucedanum is harstrang in
Hollands Plinius (index, vol. ii.), and
in Dutch and German, and in Cotgrave.
Harestrong is *peucedanum officinale* in
Mylnes Indigenous Botany, 1793. Peu-
kedanum was also rightly read as *hogs
fennel,* in a Welsh Gl. of the 13th century (Meddygon Myddfai, p. 291). The
name fennel is derived from its linear
leaves. The genitive. Lb. III. xxx.

2. *Anonis, rest harrow,* Gl. Harl. 3388.
Gl. Arundel, 42. Gerarde. Gl. Sloane,
405. Gl. Dorsetshire, Culpeper. *See*
Cammoc whin, which is the correct word.

3. *Hypericum,* also *pulicaria dysenterica,*
also *senecio Iacobæa;* Gl. New Forest.

Cammoc whin, *rest harrow, anonis,* MS.
Laud. 553, fol. 18. The leaves are ternate like those of the true cammock.

Caꞃꞃuc, gen. in -eꞃ, masc., *hassock, aira*
*cæspitosa.* Lb. III. lxii., lxiii., lxiv.
Hassuc, masc., C.D. 655. Cf. Nemnich.
A confirmation in Laen. 79.

Cauhc, gen. -eꞃ, a medicine of which two
or three drops are prescribed, Lb. II.
lii. 3, perhaps κωλικόν, κολικόν.

Capel, masc., *colewort, brassica oleracea,*
Lb. III. xii., xliv.

Ceac, gen. -cs, masc., *a jug, urna:* pl. cea-
caꞃ. Bed. p. 520, l. 6, with Smiths note,
p. 97. Lb. I. ii. 11. Hom. I. 428.
2. *Laver* of the temple of Solomon ;
luter, λουτήρ. P.Λ. 21 b.

Cealpe, ceolpe, ceolöpe, acc. -e, nom. pl.
-as, masc., *pressed curds, curds crumbled
and pressed into a cake.* " Calmaria,
" cealpe ; Caluiale, cealepbpiꞃ," Gl.
Cleop. "Mulnetra, ceolöpe," Gl. C. The
dat. occurs, Lb. I. xxxix., acc. I. xliv. 1.
Laen. 57, pl. Διδαξ. 51. Compare Germ.
Gallerte, fem., *jelly.*

Ceaꞃꞇeꞃ æꞃc. *See* Æꞃc.

Ceaꞃꞇeꞃ ꞃypꞇ, fem., gen. -e, *black hellebore, helleborus niger.* Lb. I. xxxix. 2.

Cebelc, *Mercurialis perennis.* IIb. lxxxiv.
from the text and drawings. " Mercuri-
" alis, cedele vel merce," Gl. Dun., where
the insertion of marche or celery arose
from its similarity to the first syllable
in mercurialis. "Mercurialis, cebele.
" cyphe," Gl. Mone, p. 320 b ; but the
tradition of our people forbids us to believe that mercury is charlock.

Celenöpe, fem., gen. -an, *coriander, corian-
drum sativum.* Lb. I. iii. 9. Also celen-
öeꞃ, Lb. I. iv. 2, probably after the Latin
and neuter ; dat. -öpe, Lb. I. xxxv.

Celeꞃenie, celeꞃonie, cyleꞃenie, fem., gen.
-an, *celandine, chelidonium maius,* by
English tradition. But Glaucium luteum
is the χελιδόνιον μέγα of Dioskorides,
according to Sprengel. The drawing
in MS. V. fol. 38 a, is meant perhaps for
*chelidonium maius* (II.) IIb. lxxv. Lb.
I. ii. 2, and often.

Ceꞃꞃꞃꞁle, cyꞃꞃꞃꞁle, fem., gen. -an ; *garden
chervil, anthriscus cerefolium, Bot.*

Ceꞃꞃꞁle—*cont.*

Ɣubuceꞃꞃꞁle, *wild chervil, anthriscus
silvestris,* Lb. II. li. 4. Laen. 62.
See peaöe puön ꞃꞁle, Laen. 68. Ɣubu
ceꞃꞃꞁle, IIb. lxxxvi., is in both places
*sparagia agrestis, wild asparagus,* or as-
*paragus acutifolius, Linn. Asparagus
agrestis,* becomes coꞃönaꞃola, IIb. cxxvi.
2, by neglecting *agrestis.* Sparagia gres-
tis, rude cearfille. Sparago, nefle, Gl.
Dun.

Cicel, masc., *a cake.* Germ. Kuchen, masc.,
*a cake.* Quadr. ix. 17. Lb. I. xlvi. 2.
" Buccella," Gl. in Lye ; masc. Laen.
44. Διδαξ. 63, 21. A word still in use ;
Moores Suffolk words, Bakers Northants
Gl. Kersey. "*A flat triangular cake.*"
Moore.

Cicena mete, masc., gen. -eꞃ, *chickenmeat,
chickweed, stellaria media,* formerly called
alsine media, Linn. Hippia minor, etc.
" Ispia minor, [*read Hippia*], chyken-
" mete," Gl. Rawl. c. 607. " Ipia minor,
" chykynmete album florem [habet]."
Gl. Harl. 3388. Similarly, Gl. M., Gl.
Sl., 1571. "Modera," Gl. Dun. Muronis,
Gl. Brux.

Cymeb for Cymen ? N and D being kindred
dentals. Lb. I. xxxix. 2. Lye conjectured for chamædrys, *germander.*

Cymen, neut. (as Lb. II. xliv.), *cummin,*
κύμινον, *cuminum cyminum,* a foreign
plant.

Kincean, Lb. I. xvi. 1. I find " Kinnock,
" the artichoke, cynara scolymos,"
(Nemnich). " Cariscus, kinhbeam," Gl.
Sloane, 146. "Cariscus, cꞃebeam," Gl.
Somner, p. 64 b, 54, all agree that the
quickbeam is the (sorbus or) *pirus aucuparia.* The reader will suspect I
should have read kuihbeam, but the MS.
marks the i. " Virecta, cincae," Gl.
M.M. In these times virecta are green
shoots, as in Vita Godrici, p. 43, line 1,
applying well to the parts of the artichoke that are eaten. Kinphen, grem-
sich, Gl. Mone, p. 289 a, and Grensing,

Kincean—*cont.*

*nymphæa*, Graff. Gl. Mone, p. 290 b, 6, corrected.

The spelling qince in Lacn. 4, makes us suspect *quince*.

Cypnel, masc., gen. -er, *kernel* of a nut. " Nucli, cypnlar," Gl. Cleop. fol. 66 a, read *nuclei*.

Cypnel, neut., pl. cypnelu, *kernel*, *hard glandular swelling*, *churnel*, *grumus*. IIb. iv. 2, 3 ; xiv. 2 ; lxxv. 5.

Cyrlybb, neuter ? *rennet*, Quad. iv. 14. *See* Lib. Rennet is the substance which turns milk to curd, for which purpose is often used a calfs stomach ; hapan cyrlyb implies that the stomach of a hare or leveret would have the same effect. Otherwise cyrgepunn, Colloquium, p. 28 ; not *caseus*, nor yet *a cheese*, but *rennet*. Unlibban is otherwise declined, Hom. II. 504 ; lyb is in Gl. C.C.C. Cf. Lacn. 18.

Clæppe, gen. -an, fem. ? *clover, trifolium pratense*, Lb. I. xxi. Amid a wilderness of confusion, the ternate leaves of the figure in MS. Bodley, 130, at IIb. lxx. ; the close relationship between hares foot and clover in the old herbals, as Lytes, the similarity of the drawings in MS. V. at art. lxx. and art. lxii. ; a comparison of the drawings of clover, art. lxx., and hart clover, art. xxv., have convinced me that I have rightly determined the worts meant by hapan hige and Clæppe. Κίρσιον to which clæppe is equivalent, IIb. lxx., was in Dioskorides a pappose plant, *carduus parviflorus* (Sprengel). Lindley makes cirsium a cynaraceous genus. The *trifolium pratense* or purple clover is in German Kleber, Klever, Kleve, and -klee, Rothe-, Gemeiner- and Brauner-Wiesen-klee ; in Dutch Roode klaver, etc. ; in Dansk Röd-klever, etc. ; in Swedish Klöfver, etc. The drawing in MS. V. IIb. lxx. by itself " won't do for " Trifolium ; corresponds as far as it " goes with Thymus serpyllum," (H.) J. Grimm makes clæppe *clover*.

Clare, fem., gen. -an ; 1. The greater, *the burdock, arctium lappa*. " Blitum vel " lappa, clare," Gl. Somn. p. 66 [63] b, 30. " Bardane la grande, the burrdock, " slote [*read* clote] burr, great burr," Cotgrave. " Bardona.i.clotes.vel burres " secundum aliquos," Gl. Rawl. c. 607. " Elixis.i.lappa bardana.i.clote," Gl. Harl. 3388. " Lappa maior.i.bardana, clote," Gl. Harl. 3388.

2. The lesser ; *clivers, goosegrass, catchweed, little bur, galium aparine*. "Amorfolia, clare," Gl. Somn. p. 66 [63] b, 44, that is, *love leaves*, from cleaving to passengers ; so Gl. Dun. IIb. clxxiv. MS. O. The drawing, MS. V. fol. 64, is " a very neat representation of aspe-" rula odorata," (H.), but the asperula is not a burr plant, and the nearly akin G. Aparine must have been in the draughtsmans intention. It is called φιλάνθρωπος, as sticking to men and women. " Philantropium, lappa, clare," Gl. R. 41.

Lappa, *the catcher*, from λαβέσθαι, *lay hold of*, is applied like clote to both these herbs, in other particulars unlike. Clote itself must have the same sense, and with exceptional vocalisation is a derivative of cleopan, and for † cleopre, as slire for † rhhre, is from slean, † rlegan.

Clire, fem., gen. -an ; *clivers*. The greater is *burdock, arctium lappa*. The lesser is *galium aparine*, Lb. I. l. 2. The same as clirpypr. " Apparine, cliue." Gl. Dun.

Clirpypr, fem., gen. in -e, *burdock, arctium lappa*. Assuming the syllable clir to signify *cleaving*, the Xanthium strumarium and the Asperugo procumbens are too rare ; the Galiums or the Arctium lappa are common ; the equivalent roxer clire (Lacn. 112), seems to suit better the burdock, which will grow in the wet shore of a river, and so be eapypr. " Blitum vel lappa, clare vel clirpypr," Gl. Somn. p. 66 [63] b, 30. Lb. I. xv. 3.

2. *Galium aparine*, written clrðpypr, Lacn. 69, where occurs a gloss, Rubea minor.

Cluꝼe ? fem., pl. in -e, *a clove*, the bulb or tuber of a plant. Lb. III. xli., etc.

Cluꝼiht, cluꝼeht, *cloved, having a clove, bulbed, tuberous.* Lb. III. xli., etc.

Cluꝼþunᵹ, cluꝼþunᵹe, fem., gen. in -e, also -an, *cloffing, ranunculus sceleratus*, IIb. ix. In MS. G. the true herb is drawn ; in MS. A. the flowers are at least yellow, with five petals ; but in MS. V. fol. 21 a, all likeness is lost. Þunᵹ is *poison*, cluꝼ- is *clove*, the tuberous root ; as of some of this tribe. Cluꝼ-þunᵹan, IIb. ex. 3, where the Latin again makes the wort a ranunculus. " Mortali veneno, mid œttrigere cluf- " þunᵹe," Gl. Mone, p. 349 b, an erroneous version ; but an example of the feminine. " Scelerata herba vel apium " risus, anglice cloftong," Gl. Sloane, 405. " Scelerata, gl. cloftunge," MS. Bodley, 130. " As yellow as a claut," that is, marsh ranunculus (Wilts.). " Batra- " chium," Gl. Brux.

" Cicuta, cloftunke," Gl. Harl. 3388, an error, cicuta is hemlock ; the poisonous quality misled the writer. " Cloffing, the plant hellebore." Halliwell and the English Macer, MS. in Prompt. Parv., vol. i. p. 198 ; a similar error occurs, Lb. I. i. 7.

Cluꝼꝼyꝼt, *clovewort*, fem., gen. -e, *ranunculus acris*. In MS. G. the figure is that of ranunculus as in " scelerata," but here the root is tuberous, so MS. T., but less well ; MS. A. preserves a resemblance, which is almost lost in MS. V. IIb. x. " Batrocum," Gl. Dun., that is βατράχιον.

Cneopholen, masc., *knee holly, knee holm, -holn, -hulver, butchers broom, Ruscus aculeatus*, IIb. lix. The gender is determined by C.E. p. 437, 19, where the translation " alder," is an unfortunate blot. Two kinds are mentioned, Lb. I. xlvii., but one only is native to England. The second may be presumed to be R. Alexandrina of the middle ages, which included *R. hypoglossum, R. hypofyllum, R. racemosus*, of the Bot.

Corꞇ, gen. -es, *costmary, alecost, tanacetum balsamita*. Lb. II. lv. 1, etc.

Crawleac. *See* Leac.

Cꝛimman, præt. cꝛam, p. part. cꝛumen, *to reduce to crumbs, to crumble*. Cꝛim. Lb. I. lxi. 1.

Cropleac. *See* Leac.

Cꝛuc, masc., *a cross*. Lb. II. lvi. 4.

Cu, gen. cue, fem., *cow, vacca*. The declension is often contracted ; gen. Lb. I. xxxviii. 11, by contr. cu ; Sæꞇ an ꝺeoꝼol on þæꝑe cu hꝛycᵹe, M.H. 194 a, *There sat a devil on the cows back*. Dat. cý. Feꝺe oꝼ ꝺæꝑe cý, ibid., *the devil went off from the cow* ; gen. pl. cuna ; ꝛeoꝑeꝑiᵹ cuna, Gen. xxxii. 15 ; dat. pl. cum ; unꝺeꝑ ꝛolcum, Par. Ps. lxvii. 27, for ꝛolc cum, as Grein suggests ; acc. pl. cy ; ic hæbbe . . . ᵹecelꝼe cy, Gen. xxxiii. 13, where ᵹe is con ; SSpp. 261, *cows with their calves*.

Culmillan, for cupmellan ? Lb. I. xvi. 1.

Cumb, masc., gen. -eꝛ, *a vessel, " dolium,"* MS. St. Joh. Oxon. 154 ; SSpp. art. 1026. Lacn. 37. Cf. ꝼlꝺcumb. Lb. III. liii.

Cumulu, pl., *glandular swellings*, translates σκιῤῥώματα. IIb. clvii.

Cunelle, fem., gen. -an, a Latin word, cunila, a thymiaceous plant, say *Thymus vulgaris*, a garden herb, but it is not rue, as the glossator of the Lindisfarne Gospels, Luke xi. 42, says, nor chervil, as another Gl. says.

Ꝥuꝺu cunelle, *thymus serpyllum, wild thyme*. Lb. III. xxii.

Cupmelle ꝛeo maꝑe, *Chlora perfoliata*, Bot. ; Cupmelle ꝛeo lœꝑꝛe, *Erythræa centaureum*, Bot. IIb. xxxv. xxxvi. All the MSS., V., A., G., T. figure in both these articles, the same wort, and in all they are the *Erythræa centaureum*. The mediæval glossaries make no difficulty of the lesser, but they had lost the clue to the greater. The tradition is from Plinius, xxv. 30, 31. Though some of the continental botanists make no hesitation in identifying the greater centaurion of Plinius, with centaurea, yet his

Cuþmelle—*cont.*

expression, "caules geniculati," seems irreconcileable with the genus. The interpreter of our MS., however, and the draughtsman did not know what plant to name for the greater, nor did Fuchsius, the botanic reformer. Of the less, Plinius says, "Hoc (*minus*) centaurion nostri " fel terræ vocant propter amaritudinem " summam." " The whole plant is ex- " tremely bitter, and when dried is used " in country places as a substitute for " gentian root," (Lindley). Lyte (p. 375) describes Eryth. c., and mentions (p. 436) its bitterness, calling it "the small cen- " torie." " Centaurea minor, horse galle," Gl. Sloane, 5, where " horse " means *wild.* " C. maior, cristes ladder," Gl. Sloane, 5, but minor, Gl. Sloane, 135; Christs ladder cannot be polemonium cœruleum, which is nowise to the pur- pose. " C. þe more is not well knowen," Gl. Sloane, 5, fol. 18 b. " Centaurea " maior, anglice more centori or yrthe " galle, it hathe leuys like lasse centori " whytt, with on [*one*] stalk and yolow " flowrys and he flowryth nott in þe " topp," Gl. Sloane, 135; and so Harl. 3840, this is *chlora perfoliata.* Centaurea maior coniungit folia iuxta stipitem, florem habet croceum, MS. T., fol. 63 a. " Centaurea minor, anglice lasse centori, " with lasse leuys and grener þen þe more " centori, and hath mony branches com- " yng out of on, with flowre some dele " redde," Gl. Sloane, 135, plainly *eryth- ræa c.* The [H]ortus Sanitatis figures for centaurea, the *erythræum c.* Sibthorp iu the Flora Græca sustains the assertion. Centaurea, erthegalle, is drawn in Grete Herbal as *C. cyanus.* Dorsten says the greater centaury is unknown, yet draws it as C. cyanus.

Cuþlyppan, obl. case, *cowslip, primula veris;* fem. ? is a compound of cu, perhaps in the genitive, and slyppan. *See* Oxanþlyp- pan, Lb. III. xxx. Slyppan is probably the sloppy dropping of a cow.

Cþæð, neut., *dung.* Lb. I. l. 2 ; II. xlviii. Þynne is also neuter.

Cþelðeht, *full of evil matter, of pestilence.* Lb. I. liv. The termination as in cœp- riht, *cressy* ; cluþiht, *cloved;* cneoeht, *kneed;* bœþiht, *hairy* ; hœþiht, *heathy* ; hreodiht, *reedy* ; helmiht, *leafy* ; stæn- iht, *stony* ; þoþniht, *thorny.* For cþylð, see Lye.

Cwicbeam, gen. -es, masc. 1. By tradition the *rowan tree, Pirus aucuparia.*

2. *Iuniperus communis,* many glos- saries.

3. *Furze,* or *gorse, Vlex Europæus,* Lb. I. xxxi. 3. Prompt. Parvul. *See* IIb. cxlii.

4. The aspen, *Populus tremula,* Pref. vol. I. p. lxxxvi.

Cþrð, gen. in -eþ, masc., *the matrix, uterus, vulva.* Lb. III. xxxvii. xxxviii.

Cþrð, Lb. I. xlvii. 3, *Matricaria* ? Read cþice ?

# D.

Dæl, gen. -es, neut. *a dale, vallis, "barath- "rum."* C.E. p. 93, l. 26, p. 94, l. 18. Cœdm. if Cœdm., p. 16, line 11, p. 22, l. 10.

Dæl, gen. -es, mostly masc., sometimes neut., like Germ. Theil, *part, pars.* The masc. occ. everywhere. Exx. of neut. Διδαξ. 52, unless nominatival apposition is there used ; as is perhaps the case in Lb. II. xxx. Heo nænig dæl leohter reiman geþeon mihte, Bed. 578, 20. Sum dæl oðþer reoþcef to þyþcanne, D.G. 23 b.

Deaþe, gen. -e, fem. ? *deafness, surditas,* Lb. I. iii. 2, 5. Cf. Isl. Deyfa, fem. id. (B.H.)

Dile, gen. -es, masc., *dill, anethum graveo- lens.* Lib. I. i. 8 ; II. xxxiii. Leechd. vol. I. p. 374, where hæpene is for hæpenne by suppression of consonant; Pref. vol. I. p. c. ci.

Dile—*cont.*

Hæpen dile ; perhaps *Achillea tomentosa* ; for Cotgrave explains Anet as secondly, " little or yellow harrow," for which I read yarrow, the finely divided leaves of which might obtain it this name.

Dylsꞇa ? *mucus* ; pl. dylsꞇan. Lb. I. xxxi. 5. Cf. II. xxix.

Dylsꞇihꞇ, *mucous, slimy.* Lb. I. xxix. 1.

Dyniᵹe, it seems, an herb. Lb. III. viii. Read pyniᵹe ?

Dyþhomaꝑ, *papyrus.* Gl. Somn. p. 64 a, 39. Lb. I. xli.

Docce, gen. -an, fem., *dock, rumex ;* commonly *R. obtusifolius,* but often in medicine for Supdocce. Lb. I. xxxviii. 9, probably also *R. pulcer,* which is drawn in MS. T. ; fem. in Gl. Cleop. fol. 71 c.

Fallow dock. Lb. I. xlix. ; perhaps *R. maritimus,* and *R. palustris.*

Red dock. Lb. I. xlix. *R. sanguineus,* and perhaps for Supdocce.

The dock that will swim frequently occurs. Lb. II. lxv. 1 ; I. xxxvi ; also the Ompre that will swim, which is the same plant. Lb. III. xxvi. Gerarde calls " swimming herbe," duckes meat = *Duckweed = Lemna,* which is doubtful.

Supdocce, *sorrel, Rumex Acetosa* is the gl. in MS. T. Hb. art. xxxiv., and a bad sorrel is drawn.

The Saxons did not botanize on modern principles, and it easily follows that their genus Dock is not of the same reach as the modern Rumex. Thus Crousope, which is Saponaria officinalis, is glossed fomedok, Gl. Harl. 3388. The word " foam " shows that the writer knew his plant, which he calls a dock. As in this instance, and in Cammock whin, and many others, similarity of leaves seems to have been the chief guide to Saxon nomenclature. I cannot therefore believe that Cabocce (spelt docca) is Nymphæa, Gl. Somn. p. 64 a, 61. The word Nymphæa, like many others, must have been misunderstood ; I therefore believe that,

Docce—*cont.*

Cabocce is the great *water dock, rumex aquaticus* of Smith, and *R. hydrolapathum* of Hudson.

Dockenkraut in German is *Arctium lappa,* and dockcresses are *Lapsana communis.*

Dolh, gen. -es, mostly neuter, rarely masc., *wound, scar, vulnus, cicatrix.* Hb. x. 3. Lb. I. xxxi. 7, xxxviii. 9, 10 ; III. xxxiii. xxxiv. C.E. p. 68, 24, p. 89, 10. Syꝺꝺan re dolh ꝑær ᵹeopenod. M.II. 93 b.

Dolhꝑune, gen. -an, fem.? *pellitory, parietaria officinalis.* Hb. lxxxiii., as perdicalis, which is the same herb ; Lb. often.

Dora, masc., gen. -an, *the humble bee, bumble bee, dumble dore,* bombus generically. The mediæval glosses Burdo, Fucus, Attacus, mean this insect or some nearly allied. The commonest is *Bombus terrestris,* which stores honey. "Bourdon, " a drone or dorr bee," Cotgrave. Lb. often.

Dꝛacenꞇꝛe, gen. -an, fem.? Dragons, *arum dracunculus,* Hb. xv. Dragons was a name applied by English herbalists, 1. to *Polygonum bistorta,* which is, I think, the herb figured in the Latin Apuleius, MS. Bodley, 130, as dracontea ; 2. to *ofioglossum vulgatum,* Hb. art. vi. ; and 3. to *arum maculatum.* All these three have a resemblance to a snakes erected head and neck. The figure in MS. V., art. xv. is intended for *arum dracunculus,* and, this being so, it is impossible not to concede the name. That plant is not of English birth, but neither is the name.

Dꝛaconꞇjan, *gum dragon ;* Lb. II. lxiv. contents.

Dꝛiᵹe, ꝺꝛyᵹe, *dry, siccus, aridus,* Bed. 478, 14. Andreas, 1581. Lb. II. xlvi. (In C.E. 426, 22, ꝛoꞇum ꝺꝛiᵹe is ꝛ. ꝺꝛiᵹum).

Dꝛince, gen. -an, fem., *a drink, potus.* Lb. I. li. 1. ; I. xli. Hom. II. 180.

Dꝛopa, -an, masc., *palsy of a limb.* Lacn. 9. The Saxon interpreter was wide of his original in Hb. lix. 1, where "Ad " hæmata intercidenda," in cxxiv. " tussi

Dɲopa—*cont.*

"medendo" (so). Drop, droppe, *paralysis* (Kilian); Troppf, *gout* (Wachter). The original sense remains in the "drop- "ped hands," "wrist drop" of painters, paralysis of the extensor muscles of the wrist. Root Drapan, *to strike*, p. part. Dropen, Bw. 5955, MS.

2, *A drop, gutta.* Lb. I. ii. 21. Hence "colera" meaning lymph, in Sc. 30 b.

Duɼꞇ, neut., *dust, pulvis, powder.* Neuter everywhere ; Mark vi. 11, Luke x. 11, Psalm i. 5, Matth. x. 14.

Dɲeoꞽ̇ɠe ꝺpoɼꞇle, ꝺꞃeoꞽ̇ꝺ̇ge ꝺpoɼle, *penny royal, mentha pulegium.* Hb. xciv. clvi. 2, as pulegium. So Gl. Dun. So Διδαξ. 30, 51. " Pulegium regule, puliole " reale," Gl. Harl. 3388. " Pulegio, " peniroyall," Florio ; so Cotgrave. " The smallest of its genus," Sir J. E. Smith, and therefore well called "dwarf." " Much used in medicine," (All). Penny royal is only puliole royale. Flea bane is not this plant, nor is the reading ꝺꞃeoꞽꝺ̇ɠeꞃ.

*Mentha pulegium* is called, Hb. xciv. a male and female plant, but this has no reference to the sexual system of Linné, which make it didynamous not diœcous. Some notion of strength influenced Theofrastos and Dioskorides in giving these names. The drawing in MS. V. is like the herb intended. The flowers are sometimes white.

Dɲoɼle seems in the German glossaries to be Origanum.

# E.

Caꝫꝛyꝓꞇ, fem., gen. -e, *eyebright, eufrasia officinalis.* Lb. III. xxx. Germ., augentrost ; Dutch, oogentrost ; Dansk, "oientrost;" Swed., "ogontröst."

Calaꝺ, caloꝺ, calo, ealu, eala, neut. undeclined in sing., *ale, cerevisia;* gen. ealaꝺ,

Cala̓ꝺ—*cont.*

DD. 63; O.T. 256, 5; Lb. I. xiv. and often ; dat. ealaꝺ, DD). 357 d; Lb. often; gen. pl. caleꝺa, DD. 487, where it is used of *fermented liquor* generally. Gen. Alꝺes, D.R. 116, but the forms of D.R. are abnormal, or late.

Some interesting information on ale and beer is collected by that learned and accurate antiquary, Mr. Albert Way, in the Prompt. Parv. p. 245. The frequent mention of Wort (as I. xxxvi), that is, the warm malt infusion in the mash tub, prepared for fermentation, shows plainly enough that the Saxons brewed for themselves. The Alevat (I. lxvii.) is the vessel in which the ale was left to ferment. Double brewed ale (I. xlvii. 3.) was brewed on ale, instead of on water, and gave them then a very Strong ale (III. xii. p. 314, twice). Even without hops such ale would keep till it became Old ale (II. lxv. 1, p. 292, line 12). Keeping and careful treatment would secure its being Clear (I. lxiii.; II. lxv. 2, etc.). Sweet ale is opposed to the clear (II. lxv. 2), and so was thick. Ɏilɼe calu, foreign ale, is often mentioned (I. lxx., etc.). Ale is much more frequently named than beer ; strong beer is opposed to strong ale (III. xii.). Hopping drinks is mentioned, Hb. lxviii. ; further, *see* Þymele.

Cahɼeꝓ, *cileber, alliaria, sauce alone* (Gerarde). *Erysimum alliaria.* Lb. II. xxiv., etc. But Callitrichum, Gl. Dun.

Calla, *gall, fel.* Cf. Gealla. So Euang. Nicod., xxvi.

Caꝓban, pl. *tares, ervum* and *orobus.* Well made out by Somner. " Rolon," in Gl. Mone, is doubtless a corruption of orobus, ὄροβος, which, though divided by Bot., is every way the same as ervum. Lb. I. xxvi.

Caꝓꝓeꝫa, -an, masc., *earwig, forficula auricularis.* Lb. I. iii. ꝥ, followed by he.

Cɏelaɼꞇe, fem., gen. in -an, *Gnaphalium.* Somner found some authority for " Mer-

Crelayre—*cont.*

"curialis, the herb mercury, D.," and so Gl. Harl. 978, yet all the gnaphaliums have very lasting blooms, retaining their colour when dry ; the G. margaritaceum is specially our modern Everlasting, and found "near Bocking, on the banks of "the Rhymney, in Wire forest, and near "Lichfield." Skinner also, Gnaphalium Americanum, which is a misnomer by Ray. The genus is in Dansk, Evigheds-blomster.

Croppeapn, neut., gen. -er, polypody, *poly-podium vulgare.* IIb. lxxxvi., where it = Radiolus ; "Alii filicinam dicunt, "similis est filici, quæ fere in lapidetis "nascitur vel in parietinis, habens in "foliis singulis binos ordines puncto-"rum aureorum," Lat. In MS. Bodley, 130, a fern, as polypodium is drawn and a Gloss. in a hand of the 12th century gives "wilde brake." "Felix (read "Filix) quercina pollipodium . i. ewer-"wan," Gl. M. "þe iii.d is ouerfern, "and þat groys on walles," MS. Bodley, 536. "Polypodyn . i. ouerferne 't it "grewiþ on okys þis is lest," id. "Poly-"podium murale, euerfern," MS. Raw-linson, c. 506. To the entry, "Polypo-"dium arborale, pollipodie ; Pollipodium "murale, euerferne," MS. Harl. 3388, has been added a cross, so as to invert the in-terpretations. "Polypodium rubeas ma-"culas habet et uocatur filix quercina . "i. euerferne," id. "ffilex quercina pol-"lopodium, euerferne idem (sunt)," id. "Filix a[r]boratica, eyoppeapn," Gl. Somn. p. 64 a, 14. Culpeper, under polypody of the oak, describes at length and cleverly, pol. vulg. (II.), and his mention is one link in a long medicinal tradition. "And why, I pray, must "polypodium of the oak only be used, "gentle college of physicians ? Can "you give me but a glimpse of reason "for it ? It is only because it is "dearest." Culpeper. Polypodium vul-gare is "very frequent on the tops of

Croppeapn—*cont.*

"walls, old thatched roofs, shady banks "and the mossy trunks of rotten trees." (Sir J. E. Smith.) Its fructification forms a double row of golden spots on each frondlet. See also his allusion to tradition in English Botany, 1149. The older names were, "polypodium quer-"cinum ; filix arborum ; filicula ; herba "radioli." (Nemnich.) Italian, felce-quercina. The figure in MS. V. "would "do very well for plantago lanceolata, "(II.), it is not a fern at all." The gender neuter, Boet. p. 48, l. 31 ; Lb. I. lvi.

Crheoloþe, heahheoloþe, gen. -an, fem. ? *elecampane, inula helenium;* from eh, *horse, equus,* = heah, *horse,* ἵππος. "Ele-"campana ys an erbe þat som men "calleþ horshele, he beryth grene levis "and longe stalkys and berith yelowe "floures." Gl. Sloane, 5, fol. 22 c ; so Gl. Bodley, 178. Lb. I. xxxii. 2 ; I. i. 5, etc.

Clepa, *latter,* comp. adj. Lb. II. i. 1, re-lated to Clean, *be late* ; Cleung, *late-ness* ; Cleop, *later,* adverb.

Clehrpe, gen. -an, *lupin,* the cultivated sort of course, *lupinus albus;* so trans-lated, IIb. cii. 3. Given for diarrhœa, Lb. III. xxii. "Electrum multos habet "stipites folia virid[i]a et flores cro-"ceos," Gl. Harl. 3388. "Syluestres "lupini candida habent folia. Sativi "foliis non adeo albicant," Dorsten. "Lypinus . i. lyponys, þis erbe has "leuys lyke to þe v. levyd grass, bote "þe erbe fore the more party has v. "leues and a whyt floure, etc.," MS. Bodley, 536. "Clehrpe, moura," MS. in Somner. "Walupia, electre," Gl Dun.

Clhyzþ, *strange thought, distraction.* Lb. II. xlvi. Dyzþ is found fem. neut.

Clm, masc., gen -er, *elm, ulmus campestris;* perhaps also u. *sativa.* Gen. elmer, Lb. I. vi. 8, therefore like old Dansk, Almr, *elm,* masc.

Coɲopþþoꞇu, also -e, fem., gen. in -an; *carlina acaulis*, Eberwurtz, *carlina acaulis* (Adelung). "The Carline thistle, "formerly used in medicine, is not this "(carlina vulgaris), but *carlina acaulis* "of Linnæus. It was reported to have "been pointed out by an angel to Charle- "magne, to cure his army of the plague. "Ilis name is the origin of the generic "one." (Sir J. E. Smith, English Botany, plate 1144). Everwortel, chamæleon, Kilian; that is χαμαιλέων (λευκός), which was identified, rightly or not, by Spren- gel, as *carlina acaulis*. " Eberwurz, "cardo [*read carduus*] rotunda. Ener- "wurz, cardo pana, al. chamæleon," Gl. Hoffm. " Scissa," a gl. in Lye, perhaps a genuine name. " Scasa, ebopþþoræ," Gl. M.M. p. 162 b. " Colucus," Gl. Brux. "Coliens," Gl. Cleop. " Colitus vel Colo- "ens," Gl. Dun.; which I take to be mis- readings of Cō, for Cardo, and that for Carduus, λευκός. "Scasa vel scafa vel "siscu," further, Gl. Dun.; these are attempts to read a crabbed MS. Also "Anta," also "Borotium," Gl. Dun., the last being the English word eoɲoþ, boar, with a Latin termination. Lb. I. i. 6; xxxviii. 10.

The χαμαιλέων, which, by its name must have hugged the ground, is wrongly interpreted in IIb. xxvi., cliii., as a teazle, which has a strong long stem.

Colone, Clene, gen. -an; fem., *elecampane*, *inula helenium*. Lb. I. xxxiv. 2, and everywhere.

Colone læɲɲe, *flea bane, pulicaria dysen- terica*, doubtless. Lb. II. lii. 1.

Coꞁnlice, *earnestly*, "diligenter." IIb. lxxxvii. 2.

Coɲðꞅealla, masc., gen. -an, *Erythræa centaureum*, *Bot.* This is made the same as Centaurea maior, IIb. xxxv., and the drawings in MSS. V. G. T. A. represent *Erythræa centaureum*, which is "intensely bitter." It is, however, C. minor, not maior. In the pictorial Apuleius, MS. Bodley, 130, Se maꞃe

Coɲðꞅealla—*cont.*

curmelle, is intended for feverfue, *Pyrethrum Parthenium*, which is "herba "amara, aromatica," Flor. Brit. "Cen- "taurya maior. i . þe more centore or "erthe galle, his flowrs ben ꞅolow in þe "tope, etc." MS. Bodley, 536. Dorsten agrees with us. He figures Eryth. cent., and says the greater centaury has leaves like the walnut, green as the cabbage, and serrated. "Fel terræ. centaurea. "idem. muliebria educit..habet in sum- "mitate plures flores rubros," MS. Rawlinson, c. 607, which describes Erythræa. "Centauria, copð ꞅealle [a], Gl. Somn. p. 64 a, 5. Lb. II. viii., etc.

Coɲðnaꞃola, masc., gen. -an, *earth navel, asparagus officinalis*. IIb. xcvii. 1, "asparagi." So cxxvi. 2, masc. Oros. iv. 1 = p. 380, 30.

Coɲðꞁꞃma, gen. -an ? masc. Lb. III. xli. conjecturally *potentilla reptans*, since ꞁꞃma stands for ꞁeoma masc., as in roðꞁꞃma, gl. for roðꞁeoma, cf. Germ. Riem, masc., *a thong, a strap*. The signification is therefore " *Earth cord;* " this is not ap- plicable to the dodder, which does not touch the earth, and has its own Saxon name ꝺoꝺꝺeꞃ, Mone, 287 a ; the straw- berry, which is almost a potentilla, has also its old English name ; the com- mon *potentilla reptans* is therefore most likely.

Coɲð yꞁꞃ, neut., gen. -eꞃ, *ground ivy, glecho- ma hederacea*, the equivalent is Hedera nigra, IIb. c., according to our botanists, our common climbing ivy is Hedera helix, which name, however, in Plinius, lib. xvi. 62, is given to a sort which has no berries, "fructum non gignit." The plant eoꞁð yꞁꞃ would not be ground ivy, for its eꞁoppaꞃ or corymbi are mentioned, IIb. c. 3, but there is no getting over the common voice of England, which calls by the name ground ivy, what is not ivy at all. Hedera is of constant occurrence as ꞁꞃꞃ, and to be correct, the interpreter should

Cορᵬ yɲʓ—*cont.*

have added nothing. Glechoma is German Erd epheu ; French, le lierre terrestre ; Italian, ellera terrestre ; Spanish, hiedra terrestre ; Portuguese, hera terrestre. The errors lie perhaps in our misunderstanding of the words κισσός, Hedera, when used for that which is not ivy.

Coρ, Iρ, masc., gen. -eρ, *the yew, taxus baccata.* Masc., C.E. p. 437, line 18. "Ornus eop," Gl. Somner, p. 65 a, 40, only proves that the glossator did not understand the word ornus as we do ; whether current notions are correct appears questionable ; but at any rate the old folk of England know the yew out of which they made their victory giving bows. Cf. ohg. Iwa ; mod. g. Eibe, fem., *the yew* ; Fr. If, masc. ; Iρ is masc., C.D. 652.

Coρ beρɢe, *yew berry.* Lb. III. lxiii.

Coρobumele. Lb. III. lx., *the female hop plant. See* Þymele.

# F.

Fæρ, Feρ, gen. -es, masc., *fever, febris,* Lb. I. contents, lxii., a contraction of ɟeρoρ.

Fæτelρian, -oᵬe, -oᵬ, *put into a vessel, bottle off.* Quad. i. 3.

Feaρn, neut., *fern,* Boet. p. 48, line 31.

Þæx micle ɟeaρn, *the mickle fern, bracken, aspidium filix.* Lb. I. lvi.

Feaρ, Lb. I. xxxv., as opposed to micel, is *paucus, pauculus, paullus, little,* like Goth. Faws, 1 Timoth. iv. 8. Hence, perhaps, its construction with a genitive, Feaρa ɲxa, Matth. xv. 34, a few of fishes, like a Few of us.

Feban, Lb. I. lxiii., see Pref. vol. I. p. xl. Matter for conjecture. Se ᵬeopa ρeaᵬ ᵬpeoρɢe ρebeᵬ, C.E. 94, 25, *the deep pit feedeth* or keepeth *them dreary.*

Feρeρɟuɢe, gen. -can ; fem. ? *erythræa centaureum.* IIb. xxxvi. Gl. Harl. 585. Any wholesome bitter might be called feverfue, serving the purpose now served by quinine.

Felᵬmoρu, "fieldmore," *carrot or parsnep, daucus cariota,* or *pastinaca sativa.* Though pastinaca, IIb. lxxxii., is now decided to be a parsnep, yet the weight of nearly cotemporary authority stands for carot. In MS. Bodley, 130, the glosses are "a carott," "ffeldmore." "Daucus, wildmoren," Hortus Sanitatis, and figures a carot. The Gl. Somn. p. 64 a, 32, distinguishes "pastinaca, "ρelᵬmopa," (read -ρu, as Gl. Dun.), "Daucus, pealmopa [-ρu] cariota ρalᵬ-"mopa ;" but the distinction between a field root and a weald root is over fine. "Pastinaca, mallumopae," Gl. M.M. The words should include both. "Pastinaca domestica . i . parsnep." Gl. Bodl. 536. The p. silvatica has been improved by cultivation into *p. sativa.*

Felᵬρyρτ, gen. -e, fem., *gentian, gentiana,* IIb. xvii., where the marginal note, erythræa pulcella, describes the drawing in MS. V. The reading ρelρyρτ of Skinner and others, from Fel, gall, gives us a hibrid word. Probably, as in Esthonian, the earliest name was ρelᵬ-hymele, *field hop,* the plant being employed as a substitute for hops in embittering ale. Then as the appearance and leaves negatived this name, it was exchanged for ρelᵬρyρτ.

Fellepæρe, ρyllepæρe, masc., *epileptic convulsions.* Lb. II. i. 1. The word must be interpreted in harmony with ρylleseoc, ρylleseocnyρ. I had written so much before I detected the equivalent ἀρχομένας ἐπιληψίας in Alex. Trallianus.

Felτρyρτ, fem., gen. in -e, feltwort, *verbascum thapsus.* IIb. lxxiii. The reading ρelᵬρyρτ is a mistake, the felty leaves give it the name, whence it is also called in German Wollkraut ; mullein also is supposed to be woollen. Felτ

Feltρyρꞃ—*cont.*

was Latinised (Gl. Somn. p. 59 a, 58)
as feltrum, filtrum (John de Garlond,
p. 124); Dansk, filt, *felt*; Swedish, filt,
masc. *felt*; Germ., filz, masc. felt. The
drawing in MS. V. fol. 37 d, represents
the plant. "Filtrum terre, anglice felt-
"wort vel molayn idem." Gl. Rawl.
c. 607. "Thapsus barbastus [*read bar-*
"*batus*], G. moleyn, A. felwort." Gl.
Sloane, 5; so Gl. Sloane, 405. In Gl.
Somn. 63 b, 38, read Anadonia, ꝼelt-
ρyρꞃ. Feltwort vel hegetaper, Gl.
Arund. 42.

Feρðꞃyρꞃ, fem., gen. in –e. Lb. I.
lxxxvii.

Feρþe, masc., *sound part?* Lb. I. i. 15.
"Probus ferth," Gl. M.M. p. 160 b, 20.
Leasꞃeρðnes, *false probity*, P.A. 59 b.
*See* ꞃeρe, Chron. 1016, and Layamon,
1052, 1075, 1055. But there is also a
syllable ꞃeρð in "ꞃeoluꞃeρð, *torax.*" Gl.
C., that is, θώραξ, from perhaps Lorica,
p. lxxii. Cf. Gl. Cleop. fol. 85 b, and
ꞃeluꞃeρð, *centumpellio*, Gl. Cleop. fol.
26 b, which appears to be an altered
form of centipedem. In these two words
it is possible that ꞃeρðe may signify
*ring*, which would suit Lb. well. So,
Fleoꞇenðpa ꞃeρð, C.E. 289, line 26, *a
ring of floating ones.* ? = ferd-fird, y ... 4 y

Fic, Geꞃꞁ, masc., a disease known as ficus,
Συκῆ, Σῦκον, Σύκωμα, Σύκωσις. In the
Lb. I. ii. 22, the disease "fig" is said to
be χύμωσις, *a moisture in the skin en-
closing the eyes* (Florio), but without
exactly negativing that statement we
must bend to an overwhelming weight
of testimony, and accept it as *an excre-
scence like a fig with an ulcer*, so called
from a fig bursting with fatness, "ficus
"hians præ pinguedine." It affects all
parts of the body which have hair, especially the eyebrows, beard, head, and
anus; and it was sometimes called
marisca. Dioskor. i. 100; Pollux from
Apsyrtus, iv. 203; Celsus, vi. 3; Paulus
Ægineta, iii. 3; Psellus in Ideleri Phys.,

Fic—*cont.*

vol. i. p. 223, 704; Pollux, iv. 200;
Aetius; Martialis; Hippokrates, p. 1085
II.; Oribasius ap. Phot., p. 176, 3;
Schol. Aristoph. Ran., 1247. These
references I have taken from the Paris
ed. of Etienne. The name was in constant technical use among mediæval
medical writers. "Contra ficum arden-
"tem," "Contra ficum sanguinolen-
"tum," "Contra ficum corrodentem."
"Contra ficum nomere facientem." MS.
Sloane, 146, fol. 28. Hæmorrhoids are
ficblattern in the [H]ortus Sanitatis. In
Florios time (1611) fico in Italian had
been reduced to "a disease in a horses
"foot." Cotgrave (1673) has "fic, a
"certain scab, or hard, round, and red
"sore, in the fundament." "Fijck,
"tuberculum acutum cum dolore et
"inflammatione," (Kilian). It was a
running sore, Lb. I. xxxix.; it was
equivalent to þeoρaðl, Lb. I. ii. 22.
Written Uic, and masc., Lacn. 6; 44,
following the Latin usage.

　"Dicemus ficus quas scimus in arbore
　　"nasci,
　"Dicemus ficos, Cæciliane, tuos."
　　　　　　　　　　　Martialis, I. 66.

Hic fygus, *the fyge.* Wrights Gl. p. 224.

Filb, Lb. I. lxvii., with Filbcumb, Lb. III.
liii., may be taken to mean *the milk
drawn at one milking from how many cows
soever;* commonly called *the mornings
milk, the evenings milk.* In a dairy every
several milking is kept separate.

Fille, an apocopate form of ceρꝥille, *chervil,
anthriscus cerefolium,* as clearly appears
from a comparison of the poetical names,
Lacn. 46, with the same in prose. "Cer-
"folium . i . cerfoil . i . villen," Gl. Harl.
978 (A.D. 1240).

Fleaþe, ꝼleoþe, fem., gen. -an, *water lily,
Nymphæa alba, N. lutea.* Lb. II. li. i. 3.
"Nimfea, i . ꝼleaρeꞃꞇ," MS. Ashmole,
1431, fol. 19. "Nympha, ꝼleathorvyrt,"
Gl. Dun. But "flatter dock, pondweed,
"potamogeiton," Gl. Chesh.

Fleoȝan, *flow*, not "fly." Lh. III. xxii.

Fleoꞇpypꞇ, fem., gen. -e, "floatwort," Lb.
II. lii. 1. " Algea, flotvyrt," Gl. Dun.
" Alga," Gl. M. I fear the description
is too vague, *Potamogeiton fluitans?*
*Sparganium natans? Lemna?*

Fleꞇan, ꝥhecan. 1. Found only in pl., *fleetings, hasty curds*, skimmed, but yet not
cream, Lb. III. x. ; I. ii. 23. " After the
" curd for making new milk cheese is
" separated from the whey, it is set over
" the fire, and when it almost boils, a
" quantity of sour butter milk is poured
" into the pan, and the mixture is gently
" stirred. In a few minutes the curd
" rises to the surface, and is carefully
" skimmed off with a fleeting dish into
" a seive, to drain." (Carrs Craven Gl.)
" Sarrasson, fleetings or hasty curds,
" scumd from the whey of a new milk
" cheese." (Cotgrave.) Cf. Wilbraham
and Mr. Ways Promptorium.

2. In singular, *cream*, as Lye ; used
in this sense, Lb. I. xliv. 2. The common notion of these two senses, is
*skimmings.*

Fnæꝥꞇıaꝺ, Lib. II. xxxvi. If the passage
be without error, which is hardly to be
supposed, ꝼnæꝥꞇıaꝺ must be a plural.
Fnæsꞇ is masc., and makes acc. ꝥone
ꝼnæsꞇ, Δıδaξ. 28, 51 ; therefore we should
perhaps read ꝼnæsꞇas.

Foꝥbepan, præt. bæꝥ, p. part. boꝥen, *restrain, cohibere, continere.* Ilb. iv. 9.
Lib. I. xlv. 6, in a special sense, *continere, render continent, tie with a knot of
poison.* See preface, on knots. To this
binding down the instincts by herbs,
allude the glosses, " obligamentum, lyb-
" lyꝝefn ;" " Obligamentum, lyb," Gl.
Cleop. fol. 69 a, fol. 71 b ; Gl. M.M.
p. 160 a, 22, where lib is φάρμακον and
liꝝesn, φυλακτήριον, *an amulet ;* ȝaldoꝥ
oꝺꝺe liꝝeꝼne, Beda, p. 604, 9. In the
Njal saga, Una, virgin wife of Hrut,
thus tells her tale, attributing the mis-
fortune to something that had poisoned
him :

Foꝥbepan—*cont.*

Vist hefir hringa hristir
Hrutr likama ꝥrutinn
eitrs ꝥa en linbeꝺs leitar
lundygr munuꝺ dryia.

Known has Hrut,
the ring bestower,
his body bloat
with venom vile,
when he would, with all goodwill,
in linen white,
in bleached bed,
the bliss enjoy
of loves delights
with me the lass
he wooed and wed.

Cf. ꝥyꝥꞇyoꝥboꝥe. Lb. III. i. Foꝥbepan
is *restrain*, Bw. 3748.

Foꝥcuuolꝼꞇan, *to swallow.* Lb. I. iv. 6.
Cf. Qvolk, *gullet, throat* (Molbech).

Foꝥneꞇeꝝ ꝥolm, " Fornjots palm," some
herb ; Lb. I. lxx. lxxi. Gl. Cleop. fol.
65 b, which gl. only translates ꝥolm,
*manus.* Cf. Gorꝼꞇers nægler, Ꝥıhrmæꝥeꝝ
ꝥyꝥꞇ, Sigmærts cruyt=Sigmunds kraut.

Foꝥꝥeaxen ; that this word has been
rightly read *overgrown*, appears by Ilb.
ii. 4, and by ꝺy læꝝ hie ꞇo ꝺæm ꝝoꝥ-
peoxen ꝺæꞇ hie ꝝoꝥꝝeaꝥoꝺen ꝺy
unꝥæꝝꝺmbæꝥꝥan ꝥæꝥen, P.A. 54 b,
*Lest they overgrew to that degree that
they withered and were thus less fertile.*

Foꝥꝥylmian. See Ꝥelma.

Foꞇ, masc., *foot*, pl. ꝼeꞇ, as Mark ix. 45 ;
but ꝼoꞇas, Gꝺ. 114. Lb.

Foxeꝝ claꞇe, fem., gen. -an, " fox clote,"
*Arctium lappa.* Lb. I. lxix. See Claꞇe.

Foxeꝝ ꝝoꞇ, *bur reed, Sparganium simplex.*
In Ilb. xlvii. is ξίφıον. By the drawing
in MS. G. this seems to have been
understood as the German Schwertel-
ried = *Sparganium simplex*, the burs on
which may account for the name foxes
foot. Hares foot is a name similarly
given. The drawing in MS. V. is much
eaten out. " Xifion, foxes fot," Gl. Dun.,
copied from Ilb. So Gl. Land. 567.

Foþoþn, masc., gen. -eᵹ, *tenaculum*, in a surgeons case of instruments. Lb. I. vi. 7. Taken as a compound of ᵹon, *to catch*, and þoþn.

Fᵹampeaþðeᵹ, *in a direction away from*, Lb. I. lxviii. 1.

Fulbeam, fulanbeam, masc., gen. -eᵹ, *the black alder, rhamnus frangula.* Lb. I. xxxii. 4.

## G.

Gaᵹel, Lb. I. xxxvi. ; Gaᵹelle, Gaᵹille, fem. ? gen. -an. Lb. II. li. 1 ; II. liii.; III. xiv., *sweet gale, Myrica Gale.* But ᵹaᵹeles, Laen. 4.

Galluc, masc., *comfrey, symphytum officinale.* "Simphitone, the hearbe Alo, " Confrey or wallwort of the rocke," (Florio). So Hb. lx., Gl. Dun. copying IIb. "Cumfiria," Gl. Harl. 978 (A.D. 1240). "Adriatica vel malum " terræ, ᵹalluc," Gl. Somn. p. 66 [63], l. 9. If this means that the earth apple, whether Cyclamen or Bunium, is galluc, the statements above must be preferred. Copied into Gl. Dun. Occ. Lb. 1. xxvii. 1, masc.

Gaþcliᵹe, *agrimony, agrimonia eupatoria.* IIb. xxxii. Gaþcliᵹe is also the gloss of Agrimonia in Gl. Dun. and Lb. II. viii. Gl. Sloane, 146. MS. G. draws a rude likeness of agrimony, and MS. T. attempts ἀργεμώνη, *papaver argemone.* The word Agrimonia is said to be a corruption of Argemone, Plinius, xxvi. 59, but those who choose to enter into the subject of the Latin names had better compare Dioskor. ii. 108, who speaks of a poppy. Gaþ, *a spear*, is evidently the first element in the name of the plant, the spike of which rises like a narrow dagger above the grass: cliᵹe is, perhaps, connected with our Cliff, and with Illyrian, *to tower.*

Gaᵹetþeoþ, neut., gen. -eᵹ, *the nettle tree, the tree lotus, celtis australis.* Lb. I. xxxvi. Somners conjecture is wholly an error, his tree is the Gattridge tree. " Geizpoum, lothon ; [λωτός, genus " arboris, latine mella]," Gl. Hoffm.

Geaceᵹ ᵹuþe, gen. -an, *cuckoo sorrel, wood sorrel, oxalis Acetosella.* Proofs abound. Lb. I. ii. 13, 22.; III. xlviii.

Geaᵹl, neut. and masc, gen. -eᵹ, *the jowl, the fleshy parts attached below the lower jaw.* Lb. I. i. 16, 17.; iv. 3.

Gealla, masc., gen. -an. 1. *Gall, bile.* 2. *A gall, a fretted place on the skin, intertrigo.* Lb. I. lxxxviii.

Geaþuᵹe, ᵹæþuþe, ᵹaþþe, fem., gen. -an, *yarrow, Achillea millefolium.* Seo þeaðe ᵹaþþe, *red yarrow, Achillea tomentosa.* Lb. III. lxv.

Gebþæceo, *cough, tussis*, IIb. cxxiv., cxxvi. Gl. in MS. 11. Hoſc, *cough*, SII. p. 26.

Gebþocum, *with fragments*, Lb. II. lvi. 3. Cf. Scipgebþoc, Lye.

Gecyþnað, *granulated*, Lb. I. lxxv. Cf. ohg. Kirnjan, *nucleare ;* Isl. at Kyrna, *to granulate.*

Geceþyþan, præt. -þte, p.p. -þt, *contract* = Old Dansk Kreppa, *contrahere.* Lb. II. lvi. Hence Cripple.

Geᵹoᵹ, Geᵹeh, neut. 1. *a joining, a joint, commissura, compago.* (Lye, etc., ÆG. often.)

2. *glue.* Lb. I. ii. 2. Cf. Umbifangida, *glutinum*, in Graff., and Kauahsa (= gefahsa), *purgamenta*, the parings of hides and hoofs from which glue is made, id. III. 421. Cf. also many entries in 422.

Geþþþeð, *dense with boughs*, from ᵹþþ, *forest, opacus*, Hb. i. 1, where the Saxon made no error. Þa þæᵹ an þinᵹþeoþ þð þ þempl ᵹeᵹþþðeð, M.II. 183 b. *There was then a pine tree opposite the temple thick with foliage.*

Geᵹyman, præt. -eðe, p. part. -eð. *to overlook*, Lb. III. lxv. A man is overlooked when one having the power of witch-

Geᵹyman—*cont.*

craft has set designs against him. An approach to this sense of the Saxon word is found in Ꝺe eoꝺe on ꞃumeꞃ Faꞁꝼꞃea ealꝺꝑeꞃ huꞁ on ꝥærꞇeꝺæᵹe ꝥ he hlaꞁ æꞇe . ⁊ hiᵹ beᵹymbon hýne. Luke xiv. 1. Warlock hatred has a blasting effect. This faith is strong in Devonshire ; they say that the witch has no power over the firstborn.

Geheꝑan, *to extol, laudibus ampliare.* IIb. lvii. 2. Simple vb. in dictt.

Gehlenceꝺ, *linked,* Lb. III. lv. *See* the passage. Ꝺlencan, *links,* found as yet in pl. only; Elene, 47, Cædm. ? MS., p. 154, line 9, but probably masc., as old Dansk, Illekkr, *a chain,* masc.; Dansk, Lænke, not neuter ; Swed., Lænk, masc. Translate in Cædm.? *have their linked mail coats.*

Gehnæcan, præt. -ꞇe, p. part. -ᵹꝺ, *to twitch.* IIb. cxlviii. 1., clxiii. 6. Paris Ps. ci. 8, *allidere.* Cf. Hnykkja in Egilsson, prose sense, *vellere.*

Gehꝑeoꝑᵹ, gen. -es, *a turning,* also *a vertebra.* Lb. II. xxxvi., so Laws of Æꝥelstan, 10, var. lect. Cf. Ꞁꞃioꝑꞃban, *Lorica,* lxxi.

Geleꞃeꝺ, *corrupted.* Lb. II. xxxvi. p. 244. Root Leꞃ, *mischief.*

Gehehc, *proper, consentaneus.* Lb. II. xvi. 1.

Geloꝺꝑꞏꞇ, fem., gen. -e, *silverweed, potentilla anserina.* Its leaves resemble the human spine, ᵹeloꝺꝑe, with the ribs. "Heptaphyllon," Gl. in Lyc. Gl. Dun. Lb I. xxxii. 3 ; xxxviii. 11.

Gemæꝺla, masc., gen. -an, *talk.* Lb. III. lvii., from mæꝺlan, *to talk,* C.E. 82, 14, MS. reading.

Genæꝺa, pl. *ephippia, a packsaddle.* O clerice, p. lx. Visibly related to ohg. Ginait, *consutus.* That Ge signifies and is identical with Con, *together, see* SSpp. art. 261, a large induction. The German Nähen, *to sew,* exhibits the remainder of the root. But, as Wachter truly says, it is sufficiently manifest, that the word

Genæꝺa—*cont.*

has suffered sincopation, and that in its original form it had a D or T, as Neten, or Neden. So that it is related to Næꝺel, *needle.* "Ouh sih tharzua ni nahit | "uuiht thes ist ginait." *Et se ad hoc non approximat quicquam eius, quod est netum.* Otfrid Euangel. IV. xxix. 17, ed. Schilter ; "ioh' unginaten redinon ; *et inconsutili arte.* Ibid. 64.

Geoꝑman leaꞃ, all the gll. interpret *mallow,* but gl. C. writes ᵹeaꝑꝑan leaꞃ, *yarrow-leaf,* or *leaves ;* explaining the word ᵹeoꝑman, but rendering the tradition doubtful, for no mallow has leaves like yarrow. Ld. vol. I. p. 380. Lb. I. xxvii. I. ; xxxiii. 1., etc.

Geꞃeaꝺꝑyꝑꞇ, fem., gen. -e, an herb uncertain. "Berbescum [*read Verbascum*], "gescadvyrt," Gl. Dun., Gl. Sloane, 146. " Herbescum," id. "Talumbus, ᵹeꞃealꝺ-"ꝑýꝑꞇ," Gl. Cleop. ; ᵹeꞃeaꝺꝑýꝑꞇ, Gl. M.M., p. 164 a, 4., read βούφθαλμον, ᵹeꞃeaꝺꝑꞃꝑꞇ, that is to say, Oxeye, whether *Anthemis tinctoria,* as in IIb. clxi., or *Chrysanthemum leucanthemum,* not distinguished from the other by our folk. Lb. II. liii.

Geꞃceoꝑꞃ, neut., *abrasion,* Lb. II. i. xxxv.

Geꞃeaꝑ, *juicy,* Lb. II. xliii., as ᵹeꝺeaꝑ, *dewy.*

Gesꝑæꞇ, *see* Sꝑær, Lb. I. i. 15.

Gesꝑaꞇ, *sweaty,* Lb. I. xxvi. Cf. Geꞃeaꝑ.

Geꞃꝑeoꝑꞃ, geꞃꝑyꝑꞃ, gen. -eꞃ, *filings, limatura,* IIb. ci. 3. *See* Sꝑyꝑꞃan, *also* Aꝑ-.

Geꞃꝑoꝑunᵹ, fem., gen. -e, *swooning,* Lb. II. i. 1, in Trallianus συγκοπή, the syncope of modern medical phraseology, Lb. II. xvi. 1. Geswogen betwux ꝺam of-slegenum, Hom. II. 356, *in a swoon among the slain.* From this form comes SWOON.

Geꞇaꝑa, pl. only (as yet), *tools, instruments,* DD. p. 470, 2. Lb. I. xxix., where it is *instrumenta virilia.*

Geꞇeaꝺ, *prepared, paratus.* Lb. II. xxix. *See* Teaᵹan.

Gecenʒe, *incident*, CONTINGENT, which is
of the same component parts ; so also
Τυγχάνειν, where the NG sound is radical.

Getpipulan, *to rub down*, *triturare*, Lb. I.
i. 9, etc. Cf. Τρίβειν.

Gepealð, neut., *the natura*, *inguen*, IIb. civ.
2, pl., IIb. v. 5 ; Gl. Prud. p. 140 b.
The devil got a horn of an ox, ⁊ mið
þam hopne hine þýðe on þ gepealð fþýðe,
MII. 190 a, *and with it struck* a monk of
St. Martins *in the private part severely.*

Gepune, as a pl. adj., *customary*. IIb. lxviii.

Gebþepan, præt. ʒebþeop, p. part. ʒebþopen,
ʒebþupen, *to turn*, as cream to butter, milk
to curd, *to alter*, *convertere*, Lb. I. xliv. 2.
Bucepʒebþeop translates " butyrum " in
the Colloquium M., p. 28, but not quite
correctly. Hamepe ʒebþupen, Beowulf,
2504, poetically *consolidated by the hammer.* C.E. 497, 16.

Giceþa, masc. ? *hicket*, *hiccup*, Lb. contents,
I. xviii., answering to ʒeoesa, ʒeohsa, in
the text ; ʒoxing for hicketing is frequent in English, in a later stage. Hick,
hickse, *singultus*, *convulsio ventriculi*
(Kilian).

2. Masc., *itch*, *prurigo*, Lb. II. xli. ult. ;
II. lxv. 5 ; Hom. I. 86, where the true
translation is ascertainable from the
original passage of Josephus, κνησμός.
Translates *prurigo*. P.A. 15 b.

Gilhþcep, ʒeolbþcop, neut., *ratten*, *pus*,
*matter*, *sanies*, Lb. I. i. 17 ; Beda, p. 589,
line 3, var. lect. Virus, ʒeolcep (*so*), Gl.
Mone, p. 430 a. Dansk, Qualster, *thick
moist slime.* þa ʒilscpe. Laen. 1.

Gilhþepe, fem., gen. -an, *ratten*, etc. Lb. I.
i. 3. Virus, ʒeolþepe, Gl. Mone, p. 432 b.
" Pituita," Gl. M.M.

Gipc, masc., *yeast*, *fermentum* ex cerevisia.
Lb. II. li. 1. IIb. xxi. 6.

Gicpipe, ʒyðbþoþe, fem., gen. -an, *cockle*,
*Agrostemma githago*. The syllable pipe,
as in Hedgeriffe, refers to the roughness
of the plant. " The whole is rough,
" with hoary upright bristles," (Sir
J. E. Smith). " Gith, cokkell," Gl.

Gicpipe, ʒyðbþoþe—*cont.*
Harl. 3388. But in Gl. Cleop. Lassar
vel æsdre ; where Laser is *Ferula assa-
fœtida*. Lb. I. i. 5 ; xxxviii. 4, 5, etc.

Gicce, an herb, probably Gið. Lb. II.
xxxix.

Giðcopn, the seeds of *daphne laureola, the
spurge laurel.* IIb. cxiii. ; Plinius, xiii.
35. They are taken medicinally, and are
like poppy seeds (Theofrastos, ix. 24).
They are so hot they were wrapped in
fat or crumb, Ibid. More exactly the
seeds of *D. Gnidium ;* see the Latin of
Apuleius ; but that is not English, and
I have not supposed it imported. The
name κόκκοι Κνίδιοι refers to their employment as purgatives by the early
Knidian school of medicine.

2. *Agrostemma githago*, drawn to IIb.
cxiii. in MS. V. fol. 49 a, and in MS.
A. A plant is mentioned, Lb. II. lxv.,
not a grain. MS. Bodley, 130, glosses
" Lathyris, febecorn," *sieve corn.*

Glædene, gen. -an, *gladden, Iris pseuda-
corus.* As a Latinism I would have
passed by this word ; but Sir J. E.
Smith in Flora Britannica has made
" Gladwyn " *Iris fœtidissima :* hence
I quote. " Gladiolus . i . . . . habet cro-
" ceum florem . yris . purpureum florem
" gerit . alia alba. Gladiolus croceum
" sed spatula frætida nullum," MS. Rawlinson, c. 607. " Gladiolus florem habet
" croceum spatula fœtida nullum," MS.
Harl. 3388. " Gladiolus Acorus . gla-
" dene," id. I observe, however, that
if we take Sir J. E. Smiths words,
" stinking iris or gladwyn," as the same
words were understood in the old herbals, they mean *stinking iris* or *stinking
gladden.*

Glappan, perhaps from ʒlappe, as herbs
commonly are feminine in the an declension : perhaps *buckbean, menyanthes trifoliata*, Germ. Klappen, vol. I., p. 399,
where the construction may be plural.
Cf. ʒlæppan, C.D. 657. Thorpe compared
Lappa, but that is clarc, everywhere.

Gloɲpypτ, fem., gen., -e ; 1. *convallaria
maialis, lily of the valley :* drawn, but
without the blooms, at IIb. art. xxiii., in
MSS. A., G., T. glossed "clofwort" in
a hand of the 14th century, MS. Harl.
1585, a copy of Apuleius. The blooms
are drawn MS. Bodley, 130, and glossed
" foxes glove," but it is *convallaria,* not
digitalis, that is drawn. " Apollinaris,
" goldwort," Gl. Rawl. c. 506. " Apol-
" linaris, golewort," Gl. Harl. 3388.
" Apollinaris, glofwert," Gl. M.

2. *Buglossa,* IIb. xlii. 1, the same as
" houndstongue," *cynoglossum officinale,*
or perhaps *lycopsis arvensis.*

Goman, pl. 1. *the fauces, the back of the
mouth :* it translates φάρυγγα, IIb. clxxxi.
2. Paris Ps. lxviii. 3, cxviii. 103. C.E. p.
363, 31 ; p. 364, 26. Luporum faucibus,
ɲulɲa ᵹonium, Reg. Concord. Fauces,
ᵹoman, Gl. Cleop.

2. *the gums ;* see Lye. The gums are
mostly toðpeoman, *tooth straps.*

Gonᵹepæɲɲe, gen. -an, *a gangway weaver,
a spider, aranea viatica.* Lb. III. xxxv.

Gɲeacepypτ, fem., gen. -e, *meadow saffron,
colchicum autumnale.* In IIb. xxii. Hieribulbus, which according to Zedler is
colchicum ; and this plant is drawn in
MS. G. ; with broader leaves in MSS.
V. T. : the artist in MS. A. has taken
the liberty of turning the bulb into a
costly flower pot. " Hieribulbum, greate
" vyrt. Hierebulbum, cusloppe," that is,
*cowslip!* Gl. Dun. " Hierobulbus, col-
" chicum," Humelberg, an editor of Apuleius. If the Saxon translator put the
name on the sight of the drawing only,
he may have meant by greatwort, man-
gold würzel. Some make Hieribulbus,
*allium Ascalonicum,* eschallot, but that
will not pass for greatwort. *See also*
Hɲeɲɲe.

In Lb. II. lii. 1, greatwort has a rind
to be scraped off: it is to be dug up too.

Gɲunðeɲpylᵹe, fem., gen. -an, *groundsel,
senecio vulgaris,* Lb. I. ii. 13 ; I. xxii.
IIb. lxxvii. etc.

Gɲuτ, fem. neut., Boeth., p. 94, 3, indecl.,
*grout, the wet residuary materials of malt
liquor, condimentum cerevisiæ.* Dutch,
grauwt (Kilian). Lb. III. lix. The term
is now applied also to the settlings in a
tea or coffee cup. " Wort of the last
" running," Carr.

Guuð, masc., *rotten, virus, virulent matter.*
Lb. I. iv. 2, 3.

## H.

Hæɲepn, Hæbepn, masc., gen. -ey, *a crab
(cancer),* masc. Lb. I. iv. 2.

Hæɲτe, neut., *a haft, manubrium,* Lb. II.
lxv. Somner cited it right.

Hæɲɲocapð, neut., *hairlip.* Lb. I. xiii.

Hæsel, gen. -es, -les, masc., *the hazle,
corylus,* C.D. 624. Lb. I. xxxviii. 8 ;
II. lii. = p. 270.

Hæslen, *of hazle, colurnus ;* Lb. I. xxxix. 3.

Hæɲen hyðele ; Hb. xxx. The various
reading is instructive ; Hnyðele, which
is close akin, apparently, to Neτele, and
Κάνναβις : and the Brittanica of the
Vienna drawings (See pref. Vol. I., p.
lxxxi.) is so much like *Lamium purpureum, the red dead nettle,* that there arises
a fair presumption this is the true identi-
fication. Laen. 2. The gll. support
*Cochlearia Anglica.* (Lyte, index)
Flora Britannica, by Sir J. E. Smith.
Florio. Fig. in MS. V. There were
other Brittanicas. Sprengel holds that
the Βρετοννική of Dioskorides is *Rumex
aquaticus.*

Hæþbepᵹean pipe, gen. -an, fem., *heath
berry plant, bilberry plant, vaccinium.*
Lb. III. lxi.

Haɲocɲypτ, fem., gen. -e ; perhaps *hawk-
weed, Hieracium.* Lb. I. xiv. In all
Teutonic languages.

Halan, "secundæ," secundinæ, the after-
birth. Quad. vi. 25. The analogies
require Hamlan. " Inluvies secundarum,
" hama," Gl. C. " Hamme, secundæ,"
(Kilian). " Heam, secundinæ," Nemnich.
Germ. Hamen : etc., etc.

Ðalɲypt must have been *Campanula trachelium*, which in Dansk is Halsurt; in German, Halswurz, Halskraut ; in Dutch, Halskruid. It is said to have obtained these names from being used for inflammations in the throat. In English it is Throatwort.

2. *Buplcurum tenuissimum*, Haresear, " auris leporis, halɲypt," Gl. Somn. p. 63 b, line 48. " Auricula leporina, " halswort," Gl. Harl. 3388. " Auri-" cula leporina, halswort," MS. M. So Gl. Dun.

3. *Scilla autumnalis*, MS. G. figure, fol. 18 b. = Narcissus, Herb. lvi. = Bulbus, text of IIb. cix. Narcissus, Gl. Dun., probably from IIb.

4. Symphytum album, IIb. cxxviii., seems unsupported. Epicosium, Gl. Dun.

The figure in MS. V. lvi. to my sense is C. Trachelium, with the bell flowers spoiled ; to Dr. II. " a boraginaceous " plant."

Ðamoɲɲypt, fem., gen. -e, *parietaria officinalis?* as appears by a gl. in MS. II. on Herb. art lxxxiii. So Gl. Brux., and Gerarde. Grimm Mythol. speculates (126), thinking that perhaps Thors hammer is alluded to in the name. Lb. I. xxxi. 9. Since hamoɲɲypt and ðolᴈpune are mentioned together in Lb. I. xxv. 1, there is much doubt in the interpretation. Leechdoms, Vol. I. p. 374. Laen. 1, 2, 6.

Is not hamoɲɲypt the same as Hembriswort, *bellis perennis*, and derived from Hamop, a bird, such as the Yellow-hammer, Emberiza? *See* Secᴈ.

Ðanðpypm, masc., gen. -er, *an insect supposed to produce disease in the hand ;* [*cirio*], *curio, cirus*. Wrights vocab. p. 177, p. 190., from χείρ. " Surio vel brien-" sis vel sirineus, hanðpypm," Gl. Somn. p. 60 a, 25, which is to read by the preceding, the hissing sound being given to the letter C. So Gl. Harl. 1002. Prompt. Parv., vol. I. p. 225.

Ðapan hyᴈe, " *haresfoot*" (trefoil), *Trifolium arvense*. In IIb. lxii., Leporis pes, haresfoot ; the connexion of hyᴈe with the verb " to hie " is plain. Gl. Dun. copies. The artist in V. has omitted, as was the manner, the third leaflet of the trefoil, and the heads are eaten up. MS. A. has clover heads. MS. G. draws *Geum urbanum*, another harefoot, and glosses it, " Hasin unobh " " Benedicta," *herb bennet.* The later hand in B. also glosses Avens. But Fuchsius, the link between us and the middle ages, is clear as to the trefoil both by name and figure.

Ðapanɲpecel, -ɲpecel, *vipers bugloss, Echium vulgare.* Speckle in our usage, the verb frequentative, in this case the frequentative adjective of speck, ɲpecca, masc. (as MS.) is very applicable to this herb : hare only means that where hares live, it lives. Lb. I. xxxii. 2, 4 ; lxxxvii. Spreckle is now a Scotch and Suffolk form for Speckle. " Eicios, haran-" speccel," Gl. Mone, p. 321 a. " Echius, " Echium," Gl. in Lye. " Ecios, haran-" sveccel," Gl. Dun. Eicios, hapan ɲpeccel, Gl. Brux.

Ðapanpypt, Ðapepypt, fem., gen. -e. The little harewort oftenest groweth in gardens, and hath a white flower. Lb. I. lxi. 1 ; I. lxxxviii. ; III. lx. ; II. lxv. 5.

Ðapðbeam, masc., gen. -er, *sycomore, acer pseudoplatanus.* The translation of sycomore in the Lindisfarne Gospels, Luke xix. 4. The true sycomore is not English. Vol. I., p. 398, where the separation of the elements makes no difference.

Hares lettuce, *Prenanthes muralis.* IIb. cxiv. Lactuca or Lactuca siluatica, MS. T. The prenanthes m. is drawn in MS. T., and it is equivalent in German to Hasenlattich, in Dansk to Vild latuk. It is also drawn in MS. Bodley, 130, and glossed " slepwert." " Lactuca leporina " i . wyld letys, and he has leues like

Hares lettuce—*cont.*

" sow thestyll," MS. Bodley, 536. The figures in MSS. V., G., A. are of no account.

Hazian, translates *gravari*, Lb. II. xxv.

Ꝼaþolþe ? fem. ? declined in -an; probably *elbow joint.* The word is compounded of the syllable haþ, which is found in Ꝼeaðeꝼian, *cohibere* (Boet. xxxix. 5 ; Beda, iv. 27 ; C.E. p. 401, 17, where the fac simile of the MS. reads mee not me, p. 482, 5, and in Umbehaþhlichiu, *nexilis*, in Graff. iv. 805,) and of Lıþ, *a joint*; it signifies, therefore, the *nexile joint*, or *the fast tied joint*. The patient was to be bled on it. The fastest tied joint on which a patient can well be bled is the elbow. Somner conjectured, probably from knowledge of the Latin, *vena axillaris*; that is the same vein, τὴν ἐν ἀγκῶνι, τὴν ὑπὸ μασχάλην, says Trallianus (p. 127, ed. 1548).

Ꝼeahhealeþe, Ꝼeahhıoloþe, *inula helenium*; *See* Ch. Lb. I. xxxix. 2, etc. " Hinnula " campana, hoꝛfellen," Gl. Laud, 567, *i.e.*, Horse Helenium.

Ꝼealeƀe, *belly bursted, herniosus*, Gl. Somn. p. 71 b, 60. IIb. lxxviii. 2, where *ad ramicem pueri*, Lat. ; " Ponderosus," in Lye, which means not " weighty," but *bursted*; " Ponderosus, hernia laborans " (verba improbata in Bailey) ; Haull, masc., *hernia* (Islandic) ; þ cılƀ brð hoꝛoꝼoƀe ꝛ healeƀe (MS. Cott. Tiber. A. iii. fol. 41), *the child shall be humpbacked and bursted.* SII. 23.

Ꝼealꝼ, neut., *the half, dimidium, pars dimidia*, Lb. II. ii. 2. Ꝼealꝼ, *side, quarter* is fem.

Healꝼ heaꝛoƀ, *half head;* Æ.G. 14, line 24, distinctly defines as the *sinciput, the forward half*; (hoc sinciput), healꝼ heaꝛoƀ ; hoc occiput, ꝛe æꝛ̌tꝛa ꝺæl þæꝛ heaꝛƀeꝛ.

Ꝼealꝼ þuƀu, masc., gen. -ƀeꝛ, *field balm, calamintha nepeta*, Lb. I. xlvii. 2.

" Ƿdebalme . i . halue pude," Gl. Harl. 978. This plant was placed by Linnæus as Melissa ; it is perennial.

Ꝼealm, neut., *halm, calamus.* Gaðꝼıon hımꝛ̌ylꝛe þ healm. Exod. v. 7. Lb. I. lxxii.

Heaꝼ, Lb. l. ii. 21, *austere.* Cf. Heoꝼo, *sword*, C.E. 346, and its senses as a prefix.

Heƀelað, *a coarse upper garment*, Quad. iv. 17. " Heƀen, casla," gl. C., that is, *a chasuble.* " Heƀen gunna," gl. C. *gunny cloth.* Ne hæbbe he on heƀen ne cæppan, DD. 348, ix. *Let him have on neither chasuble nor cope;* the English rite. Cf. Heðinn, *a kirtle or cape of skin*, in Islandic. (Jonsson.)

Ꝼeꝣeelꝛe, fem., gen. -an, *hedge clivers, cleavers, clivers, Galium aparine*, Lb. I. ix.

Ꝼeꝣeꝵꝛe, gen. -an, fem. ? " hedgeruff," " hayreve," *Galium aparine.* " Rubia " minor, Hayreff oþer aron [*read* Hay- " renn ?] is like to wodruff, and þe sed " tuehid will honge in oncis cloþis," MS. Sloane, 5, fol. 29 a. " Rubia minor " cleuer heyreue," Gl. Harl. 3388. Lb. I. xxxii. 4; I. lxiv.

Ꝼelƀe, *tansy, tanacetum vulgare*, " Tana- " ceta," Gl. Somn. p. 66 [63] b, 22. So Gl. Jul., Gl. Dun., Gl. Harl. 978 (A.D. 1240); Tenedisse, Gl. Brux., also " Arti- " mesia hilde," Gl. Dun., but the tansy is generically akin to the mugwort. Lb. I. xxvi. Διδαξ. 58.

Ꝼemlıc, gen. -e, also -an ; *hemlock, conium maculatum.* Other plants may be sometimes called hemlock, for the umbellate herbs require educated eyes, but this is the starting point for English notions. *Cicuta virosa* is water hemlock (Sir J. E. Smith); " Cicuta," Gl. Somn. p. 64 a, 47, classically right, though botanically wrong ; for it follows from Plinius, xxv. 95, that Κώνειον =cicuta. Acc. Hymlican. Lb. I. i. 6. Has a masc. adj. Laen. 71; dat. hymlıce. Lb. I. lviii. 1.

Ꝼeoꝼoꝵþꝵembel, masc., gen. -eꝛ, *the buckthorn, rhamnus.* " Ranno, Christs thorne, " Harts thorne, Way thorne, Bucke " thorne, or Rainberry thorne," Florio

Deorɴbɲembel—*cont.*

Lb. III. xxix. 1. The berries are exceedingly loved by stags, Cotgrave, *v.* Bourdaine. Gerarde.

Deopoɲ eɴop, Lb. I. vi. 3, probably a bunch of the flowers of hart wort, or seseli. (Nemnich, Cotgrave.)

Deopɲ clæɲɲe, *hart clover or melie, medicago maculata.* In IIb. xxv. Hart clover is made germander, *teucrium chamædrys,* and there is no doubt about the identity of germander with the chamædrys of the Latin ; the name germander is a gradual alteration from the Hellenic word, and in MS. G. the plant is drawn. In MSS. V. and A. we see something more like anagallis arvensis, but we must make concessions to these old artists. There is, however, no doubt but that clæɲɲe is *clover,* " trifillon [*trefoil*], clæ-" ɲɲe," Gl. Somn. p. 64 a, 3. " Trifo-" lium rubrum, reade cleanre," Gl. Dun. " Calesta vel calcesta, hvit cleaure," Gl. Dun. That we find " trifolium, ɢeace-" ɲuɲe," Gl. Somn. p. 66 [63] b, line 11, may be satisfactorily explained by looking at the *Oxalis Acetosella,* which is a trefoil sorrel, abounding in groves and thickets in the spring. The same wort is meant by " Calcitulium, geaces " swre," Gl. Dun. ; for calta is *clover* with the Saxons ; " Calta siluatica, vnde " cleaure," Gl. Dun. ; " wood sorrel " is a frequent name of it at this day ; it was panis cuculi, Fr. pain de cocu (Lyte). The tradition of the word " hart " is sufficient for us ; probably, however, *m. falcata* and *m. sativa* were embraced under the name. These were once known as " horned clauer," or clover (Lyte); and since the melilot *m. officinalis,* was called hart clauer in Yorkshire (Gerarde), that also may have been set down for a variety. Culpeper calls melilot, kings clauer. " Cenocephalcon [*read* Cyno-], " heort cleaure," Gl. Dun., may be a misreading of a drawing, since toadflax and melilot hang their heads in the same

Deopɲ clæɲɲe—*cont.*

manner. " Camedus," Gl. Brux., that is, chamædrys, germander.

Dyɢ ? gen. -e, fem., *hive.* IIb. vii. 2. Lyc. Lecehd. Vol. I. p. 397.

Dillpyɲɲ, fem., gen. in -e, " hillwort, *calamintha nepeta.* Hillwort is pulegium montanum in the glossaries, to be distinguished by name and habitat from pulegium regale or penny royal. Now the Bergpoly of the Germans, Teucrium polium, is not a native of England, we must then select, as above, a plant which grows on " dry banks and way " sides on a chalky soil," with " odour " strong resembling mentha pulegium," (Hooker). But if the words be of the savour of a version from the Latin, then hillwort will be *teucrium polium. See* IIb. lviii. ; Promp. Parv. p. 399.

Dymele, gen. -an, *the hop plant, humulus lupulus* = humle (Dansk) = humall, masc. (Islandic). IIb. lxviii. The female plant is evidently meant by the ewehymele, copohumelan, Lb. III. lx.

The statement that men mix hymele with their ordinary drinks, shows what plant the writer of Hb. had in his mind. That he identifies it with bryony is an error in his Greek. Lovells Herball (1659) thus, " Hops, *lupulus.* In fat " and fruitfull ground, the wild among " thornes. The flowers are gathered in " August and September. Βρύον καὶ " βρυωνία, lupus salictarius et reptitius." Most of the early glossaries translate however, bryonia by Wilde nep, and Dioskorides (iv. 184, 185) describes what is certainly not the hop plant. Columella is charged with having confused the bryony with the hop, Lib. x. p. 350.

" Quæque tuas audax imitatur Nysie
" nites,
" Nec metuit sentes, nam nepribus
" improba surgens
" Achradas indomitasque Bryonias
" alligat alnos."

The lines hardly support the charge.

Dymele—*cont.*

According to the present usage of those who speak rural English, the hop is the fructification of the female plant, and the plant itself has no name but hop plant. It is quite incorrect according to the country folk to speak of the plant as the hop. No such name as Humble seems to be known.

The contrasted Degehymele, hedge-humble, affords presumption that there was a cultivated kind, and other proofs exist that the Saxons grew this plant.

Dymele, *hop trefoil, trifolium procumbens.* In IIb. lii. we had a problem to solve; polytrichum was hair moss, and hymele was hop, and yet the two plants must be the same. The trefoil leaves of polytrichum in MS. G. suggested a solution; it is hoped the right one. The text in IIb. lii. speaks plainly of hair moss; but the drawing in the MS. has nothing of the sort; in this difficulty the interpreter solved not the Hellenic word, but the drawing, and named it hymele; as it has no resemblance to the hop, nor to geum rivale. Jordhumle in Swedish is trifolium agrarium (Nemnich). The name Humble was not confined to the hop, *see* yeldpypt; and in Islandic Valhumall is achillea millefolium. (Olaf Olafsens Urtagards Bok, p. 88.)

Dindhælepe,-heolope, -an, *water agrimony, liverwort, Eupatorium cannabinum.* "Ambrosia." IIb. lxiii. 7; so Laen. 69. Gl. Sloane, 146. Our gll. make this ambrosia maior to be widely distinguished from chenopodium botrys, which is also ambrosia, but not an English plant. Hindheal is Hirschwundkraut in Germ. "stag-wound-wort." "Eupatorium lilifagus [*understand* "ἐλελίσφακος], ambrosia maior, wylde "sauge, hyndhale," Gl. Harl. 3388. "Ambrosia, hindhelethe," Gl. Dun. "Ambrose . salgia agrestis [*read salvia*], "lilifagus . eupatorium . idem," Gl. Rawl. c. 607. So Gl. M. "Hintloipha,

Dindhælepe—*cont.*
"ambrosia," Gl. Hoff. "Euperatorium, "ambrose, is an erbe that som men "calhp wilde sauge oper wode merche "oper hyndale," Gl. Sloane, 5, fol. 15 a. Similarly Gl. M.

2. *Sanicle, Sanicula Europæa,* as above; the plants have very similar foliation.

Dyphepypt, fem., gen. -e, *herd-* (shepherd) *wort, Erythræa centaureum,* Lb. II. viii., etc.

Hip, gen. -es, neut., *hue, complexion, color.* IIb. cxli. 2. Hom. II. 390. Hpy íp ðip gold abeopeað . Ᵹ ðæt æðelefte hiep hpy peapð hit onhpoppen, P.A. 26 a, *Why is this gold darkened, and why is its noble colour changed?* Lamentations iv. 1. *See* N. p. 71. Διδαξ. 58.

Dleomoce, Dleomoc, fem. gen., -an; *brooklime* (where lime is the Saxon name in decay), *Veronica beccabunga,* with *V. anagallis.* Lb. I. ii. 22. "It waxeth in "brooks," Lb. I. xxxviii. 4. Both sorts Lemmike, Dansk. They were the greater and the less "brokelemke," Gl. Bodley, 536. "Fabaria domestica . i . lemeke. "Fabaria agrestis similis est nasturtio "aquatico et habet florem indum [*blue*] . "i . faucrole et crescit iuxta aquas," Gl. Rawl. c. 607. In those words the *v. anagallis* is described. The following agree more or less, Gl. in Lye; Gl. Dun.; Gl. Cleop.; Gl. Harl. 978; Gl. Harl. 3388; Gl. Mone, p. 288 a, 27: *read lemicke;* Islandic, Lemiki.

Dlyt, masc., gen. -ep, *hearing;* masc. DD. 41, xlvi. Lb. I. iii. 7; Hom. II. 374; also fem., gen. -e, Lb. I. iii., contents; and in old Dansk.

Dluttop ðpene, masc., gen. -es, "clear "drink," *claret, made of wine, honey, aromatic herbs, and spices.* "Accipe "ergo hirtzunge [*hartstongue*] et eam "in vino fortiter coque, et tunc purum "mel adde, et ita iterum; tunc fac semel "fervere, deinde longum piper et bis "tantum cynamomi pulverisa, et ita

Ðluttoþ þpene—*cont.*

" cum prædicto vino fac iterum semel
" fervere, et per pannum cola et sic fac
" LUTER DRANCK." St. Hildegard. Phys.
xxx., and similarly ciii.

Ðniȝel, masc., *forehead,* Lb. III. i.

Hoc, gen. hocces, *one of the mallows, malva.*
Lb. III. xxxvii., xli. Many gll.

Ðoȝe, gen. -an, fem., *alehoof, hove, ground
ivy, glechoma hederacea.* Lb. I. ii. 19.
Seo peaðe hoȝe, the same.
2. Meþþe hoȝe, *stachys palustris?*
Lb. I. xxxviii. 5.

Hoþþec, hoþþæc, neut., *hoof nick, hoof track.*
Vol. I. p. 392. A parallel charm has
ȝorspoþ.

Ðoleæþþe, fem., gen. -an, *field gentian,
gentiana campestris.* Lb. I. ii. 17. The
same as the Holgræss of Œder, Icones
Plantarum, vol. 3, where he gives the
local Norwegian names.

Ðomoþþecȝ, masc. Lb. I. lxxvi. 2. *See*
Secȝ.

Ðoþh, Ðoþ, gen. -eȝ, also Ðoþeþes, masc.;
*foulness, filth, foul humour, flegma, pituita,*
is masc., Lb. II. xvi. 2 ; xxviii. and in
hoþaȝ, *pituita,* Gl. in Lye. Gl. Somn.
p. 72 a, 55. Written Oþaȝ, Quadr. viii.
6. *See* corrections, Vol. I. Neuter, Lb.
II. xvi. 1.
Flegmata, hoþh, Gl. M.M., p. 156 b,
5. Gl. Cleop. fol. 39 d. Horewes, Gl.
Mone, p. 404 b.

Hoþȝȝ, *mucous, purulent.* Gl. Prud. p.
146 b.

Ðoþn aðl, *a disease of foul humours in the
stomach.* Lb. II. xxvii. From hoþh,
*filth.*

Hþacu, gen. -an, fem., *throat, guttur.* Þæþ
ȝýnuðe on Ðaþe hþacan ȝȝýlce þæþ
hþýlc ȝeað þæþe. G.D. 226 b. *There
yawned in the throat as if there had been
a sort of pit.* Lb. I. i. 17. K. prints a
masc. SS. p. 148, line 32.

Hþæȝean, acc., *breaking, exscreatio,* Lb. I.
i. 16.

Ðþæctunȝe, *the uvula,* Lorica, lxx. Lb.
I. . 4. Hþacan, *fauces,* Gl. in Lye.

Ðþæctunȝe—*cont.*

+ tunȝe, tongue. Hþæcetunȝ is different,
Lb. II. viii. Hþæcan, *to clear the throat,
screare,* + ec frequentative, + unȝ, participial termination.

Ðþæȝneȝ ȝoc, masc., "ravens foot," *pilewort,
ranunculus ficaria, Bot.* In Hb. xxviii.
made Chamædafne, which, literally
translated, is "ground laurel or bay,"
and determined by Sprengel to be *ruscus racemosus.*" That it is indeed a
ruscus is quite evident by the words of
Dioskorides ; καρπὸν δὲ περιφερῆ ἐρυθρόν,
τοῖς φύλλοις ἐπιπεφυκότα, nor can we doubt
from the rest of the description but that
the species is correctly determined.
Plinius, however, having more knowledge of words than things, while citing
the description ; " semen rubens an-
" nexum foliis" (xxiv. 81), which makes
the chamædafne a ruscus, yet has misled
many of the later inquirers by declaring
it to be periwinkle ; " vinca pervinca
" sive chamædafne," (xxi. 99.) In this
error he is followed by many, as a Welsh
gl. of plants in Meddygon Myddfai,
(p. 283 a.), and Coopers Thesaurus.
The Latin Apuleius, MS. G. draws, I
think, a periwinkle. The species R.
racemosus, is a native not of England,
but of the Archipelago. Our concern,
however, being with Ravens foot, it will
soon appear that it is neither Ruscus nor
Vinca. Ravens foot, like crowfoot, was
a name probably given from the shape of
the leaves ; whence it will follow at
once that ravens foot is neither chamædafne nor vinca maior. The old interpreter had before him a wholly different
drawing, having a resemblance in its
folded leaves to Alchemilla vulgaris.
The unfolded leaves are deeply cut, and
so " Pentaphilon, refnes fot," Gl. Dun.
Quinquefila. Gl. Brux. So Gl. M.M.
p. 161 b, 34, showing that the leaves were
like those of cinqfoil. MS. T. has a gl.
" Rauen fote, crowfote," to the same effect,
with a drawing which I take to intend

Hræfnes fot—*cont.*
periwinkle, "quinquefolium, hraefnaes "foot," Gl. Moyen Moutier, p. 164 b; so p. 161 b. "Pes corui apium moroi-"darum, ravenys feete," MS. Bodley, 178. "Apium emoroidarum vel pes "corui idem ravnys fete," MS. Harl, 3388. "Apium emoroidarum, pes corui "idem," MS. Rawlinson, c. 607. The tubers at the root of this plant were compared to piles, hæmorrhoids, fici, whence the names Pilewort, Apium hæmorrhoidarum, Ficaria. "Pes pulli, "Gallice pepol, Anglice remnies fote," Gl. Sloane, 146. "Pied poul, the "round rooted or onion rooted crow-"foot." Cotgrave. Similarly Gl. Harl. 3388. Thus authority and early tradition run strongly for ranunculus ficaria; at the same time we cannot but feel a difficulty in observing that the leaves of this species are not crowfoot in shape, and the plant is so unlike most of the crowfoots, that on ancient principles it should hardly be called by a similar name.

Hrean, acc., Lb. II. xli., I suppose to be = Isl. Hrai, masc., *cruditas*, as perhaps not *rawness*, but *indigestion*. Somner, however, may have had authority for *φθίσις*.

Hreofol, fem., gen. -le, *roughness of the body, leprosy.* Lb. I. lxxxviii.

Hriesca, gen. pl., Lb. I. xxxi. 5, from some nom. s. signifying it seems *a crick*, which is a small *wrench*, a *twist*, accompanied usually with a small sound; a little crack, a crick, produced by the overstraining of some articulation. *See* Lye in Hriscian.

Hrif, neut., *the abdomen.* Lb. II. xxviii.; II. xxxii.

Hrifing, fem., gen. -e, *scab, crust of a healing wound.* Lb. I. xxxv. at end, the context requires this sense. Cf. Hriefþo, *scabies.*

Hristung, fem., gen. -e, *spasmodic action.* Isl. at Hrista *quatere*, in the reflexive, *contremiscere.* Lb. II. xlvi.

Hryt, *febricitat.* Lb. II. xxv.

Hryðeren, *bovinus.* Lb. II. viii.

Hrot, neut., *moisture, mucus, thick fluid.* Lb. II. xxviii.; ohg. Roz, *mucus, inrheuma.*

Hruð. Lb. II. xxiv.

Hundes heafod, "hounds head," *snapdragon, antirrhinum orontium, Bot.* In Hb. lxxxviii., Canis caput. The German Hundskopf is *A. orontium*, and according to Kilian in kalfs-snuyte, canis caput is antirrhinum. The drawings in MSS. V. and T. represent, I hold, this plant. "Cynocephaleon, heorotclæfre," Gl. Somn. p. 63 b, 56, *hart clover*, melilot, which might be made in a drawing to cluster its flowers as snapdragon.

Hundes tunge, fem., gen. -an, *houndstongue, cynoglossum officinale.* In Hb. xlii. this is made = bugloss; in MS. V., allowing for conventional and incorrect drawing, the figure (fol. 30 c.) seems intended for *lycopsis arvensis, Bot.*, or small bugloss; similarly MS. A., fol. 24 b. MS. G. draws *echium vulgare*, or vipers bugloss. MS. T. has given us, instead of bugloss, a picture of houseleek. The houndstongue family of plants is akin to the bugloss race, and our Saxon interpreter was, perhaps, unable to discriminate. "Buglossan, glosvyrt "vel hundes tunga. Canis lingua, hun-"des tunga," Gl. Dun. "Lingua bobule "(*bubula*) oxan tunge," id., "buglossa "hertestunge, ossentunge," Gl. in Mone, p. 283 a. "Bugilla, hundestunge," id. p. 285 b. (*bugle, ainga reptans, Bot.*), "lingua cervina, huntzunge," id. p. 289, (a mistake, read *hertszunge*). "Buglosse, "foxes glofa," id. p. 320 a; "canis "lingua, hundestunge," id. ibid. That *cynoglossum officinale* is houndstongue in German, Dutch, Dansk, Swedish, may have arisen from translation and instruction; but why not so also with the Saxons? The drawing in V. is more like borage (H., from a pen and ink sketch), but the blooms have no blue colour.

Þune, gen. -an, *horehound, marrubium vulgare*. Lb. I. iii. 11., etc.

Þunigteap, gen. -es, masc., *destillation from the comb*, without squeezing, *virgin honey*, mel purissimum, e favo sponte quod effluxit. "Mell stillativum," Lb. I. ii. 1. "Nectareum, hunigteapenne," Gl. Prud. p. 140 b. "Nectaris, hunigteaper," Gl. Mone, p. 384 b, 4. "Favum nectaris. "hunig camb teaper," Regularis Concordia.

Þpeopya, masc., *a whorl, verticillus*. Lb. III. vi.

Þpeppe, fem.? gen. -an? Lb. lii. 1, is a "great wort;" the radical syllable implies roundness, as in Þpep, *a kettle*, Þpepperte (*a gourd, a calabash*, and then) *a cucumber*. See Hb. xxii. Is it then the bulb, *colchicum autumnale?*

Þpopyban, neut., *knee cap, patella*. In the Lorica, Vol. I. lxxi., the gloss of poples, which is an error. See þeoh hpeopya.

Þpiteoðu, -ceoðu, gen. hpiter cpiðuer, *mastich*, the gum of the *pistacia lentiscus*. So the Gll. Lb. II. iii., Gl. Dun., etc.

Þpiting, *whiting, chalk and size*. Lb. III. xxxix.

## I.

Iþig, neut., gen. -er, *ivy; hedera helix* is the only species native to England; neut., Lb. III. xxx. Graff also marks the ohg. Ebah, *ivy*, neuter. Iþer, gen. Lb. I. ii. 10 ; I. iii. 7, etc.

Iþigtapo, masc., gen. -an, *ivy tar*. Lb. III. xxvi. ; masc., Cf. Lb. III. xxxi. "It is "produced from the Body of the larger "Ivy, being cut or wounded, and some-"times dropping forth of it self." Salmons English Physician, 1693, p. 991. "Oleum cyfinum (*read* κίσσινον) idem "de bagis (*read* baccis) hederæ confi-"citur sic. Sumis in ianuario mense "cum ceperunt hederæ grana crescere, "etc." MS. Harl. 4896, fol. 70 a.

Innoþapan, pl. *viscera*. Lb. II. xxxvi.

Inþipan, pl., *flavouring, condimentum*, Lb. II. vi., from þipan, *herbs*.

## L.

Læcepypt, 1. generally *a herb of healing, herba medicinalis*, M. II. 137 a.

2. *Campions*, or *ragged robin*, or one of that kindred, IIb. cxxxiii. ; but, I fear, only from the syllables Læc- and Lych-.

3. *Plantago lanceolata*, "læcepypt, "quinquenervia," Gl. Cleop. fol. 83 a. Gl. M.M. Läkeblad, *plantago maior*, in West Gothland (Nemnich). The plaintain was famed for healing power. Lb. I. xxxii. 3.

Læs, *a letting, missio*, Lb. III. cont. xlvii. fem. ? Cf. þa bloblæse, Lb. II. xxiii. ; blobblæspu, Beda, 616, 12, on ðæpe bloblæspe, 616, 5.

Lamber cœppe, gen. -an, is said, Lb. I. i. 17. to be the same as Cress.

Lapep, labep, *laver*, IIb. cxxxvi., is called Sium by Lyte also ; the botanists now call sium water parsnep, and the eaten laver, porphyra laciniata. Laver is a Latin word.

Leac, gen. -es, neut. 1. Originally *a wort, herba, olus*, whence are derived leacceppe, leactun, "hortus olitorius," leacpeoð, *a gardener*. Houseleek and holleac are not alliaceous. Aarons leek is arum maculatum, Gl. Sloane, 5.

2. *A leek, allium porrum*, Lb. II. xxxii. vol. I. p. 376, where I cannot now find a verification for the masculine gender, unless by resorting to the old Dansk, Laukr, masc. Þep, in Æ.G. is a misprint.

Bpaðeleac, probably *leek, Allium porrum*, from the breadth of its leaves. Lb. II. li. 4. Laen. 12.

Leac—*cont.*

Cpapleac, *crow garlic, allium ursinum,*
or *vineale,* vol. I. p. 376. " Centum ca-
" pita, asfodillus, ramese, crowe garlek,"
Gl. Rawl. c. 506.

Cpopleac, *allium sativum.* A gl. gives
" serpyllum," but that is an inadmis-
sible talc, for cpop means *bunch,* as of
berries, and leac means *leck ;* we must
therefore make our choice among asfodelaceous plants ; and as those which
answer the description best are open to
objection, for allium ampeloprasum is
by far too rare, and allium vineale is
crowleek, we fix on a common foreign
but cultivated species. Lb. I. ii. 13, 15;
I. iii. 11; I. xxxix. 2; III. lxviii. The
German Knoblauch has the same sense,
and is this plant.

Gapleac, *allium oleraceum?* See Lb. I.
ii. 16 ; III. lx. lxi.

Holleac, " hollow wort," *fumaria bul-
bosa,* the " radix cava " of the herborists;
Runde Hohlwurzel, Germ.; Huulroed,
Dansk ; Holwortel (Kilian) ; Hällrot.
Swed. Laen. 23, 61. Lb. ——. It
is not corydalis, the root of which is not
hollow. See English Botany, 1471.

Seegleac, Lb. I. lviii. 1, Laen. 37, is
of course *chive garlic, allium schœnoprasum,* the English and Hellenic names
having the same sense.

Leac cepse, fem., gen. -an. Lb. III. xv.
*Erysimum alliaria* is both leek and cress.

Leah, gen. leage, fem., *ley, lixivium.* Quad.
ix. 14. Leechd. vol. I. p. 378. Lb. III.
xlvii. Læg, Gl. C.

Leapop, neut.? *lather, spuma saponacea ;*
see Lybpan, not fem. Laen. 1. Islandic
Löðr, neut. *lather.* Cf. Lybpan, Alyb-
pan. St. Marharete.

Leapoppypc, fem., gen. -e, *lather wort, soap-
wort, saponaria officinalis.* " Borith
" herba fullonum, leaðoppypc," Gl.
Cleop. The plant yields lather freely.
Lb. I. iii. 11.

Leonpoc, masc., gen. -ep, *lion foot, alchemilla vulgaris,* IIb. viii. This name is

Leonpoc—*cont.*

foreign, and a translation of λεοντοπόδιον
in Dioskorides. Leontopodion is *alchemilla vulgaris* in Dorsten, in Lyte, in
Dansk; " Alchemilla vulgo appellatur et
" pes leonis," Cæsalpinus xiv. 249. Sibthorp says, alchemilla alpina is to this
day called Λεοντοπόδιον. Sprengel says,
that the Leontopodium of Dioscorides
is " Gnafalium leontopodium," and the
figures in V. G. T. Bodley, 130 (lxii.)
agree.

Lib, lyb, neut.? *something medicinal and
potent, a harmful or powerful drug,*
φάρμακον. Cf. lib-lac, *sorcery;* oxna-
lib, " *medicine of oxen,*" *black hellebore ;*
libcopn, *cathartic grains.* " Luppi, neut.
" *venenum,* succus lethiferus, etc.," Graff.
Ouglуppi, *eye lib,* collyrium, *eye salve,* id.
Goluppeten pfil, *venenata sagitta,* Gl.
Schilter. " Coagulum, lap," a gl. in
Mone, p. 287 a. Coagula, cýrlibbu, Gl.
Prud. 141 a, as if τυροφάρμακον ; it is the
runnet to turn milk to curd.

Libcopn, neut., gen. -er, *a grain of
purgative effect, especially* the seeds of
various *euforbias,* probably also the seeds
of some of the gourds, as *momordica elaterium, cucumis colocynthis.* Lb. I. ii. 22;
II. lii. 1, 2, 3.

Carthamo, also citocasia, also lacte-
rida, also catharticum, Gl. Dun. ; lacy-
ride, Gl. Brux. ; these are the milky
spurges.

Lim, mostly neut., but also fem., *a limb,
artus ;* fem., Lb. II. lxiv. p. 288 ; fem.
also in Islandic. Cf. Lb. I. xxv. 2, xxvii.
1, xxxi. 7, lxxiii.; III. xxxvii.

Limung, fem., gen. -e, *an attachment, car-
tilago.* Lb. II. xxxvi.

Lið, neuter and masc., *joint, articulus.* Lb.
I. lxi. 1 ; II. xxxvi. In old Dansk.
Liðr, masc.

Lið, *drink,* gen. -es, neut. Lb. I. xix.
Boet. 110, 33. Cýc ða him ðæc lið
geferped pæp, P.A. 55 a, *when the drink
was gone from him.*

Lıð ᵹyᵽꞇ, fem., gen. -e, lithewort, *dwarf elder, sambucus ebulus.* IIb. xxix. This is made Ostriago. *See* Pref. vol. I. p. lxxxv. : from the drawings, nothing can be learnt. " Ostriago, lith výrt. " Chamedafne, leoth výrt," Gl. Dun., read χαιμαιδκτη, that is, *ground elder.* " Ebulus, wall wort," in later hand " lyᵽe " wort," MS. Harl. 3388. In IIb. cxxvii. lıᵽᵽyᵽꞇ is erifia, which is unknown, and from the drawing probably nothing but dwarf elder was understood. Viburnum lantana was never known by this name.

Lyᵽꞃan ? *to lather, spumam e sapone conficere, aut ex quovis eiusmodi.* Lyᵽᵽe, imperat., Lb. I. 1. 2. Alyᵽᵽe, Lb. I. xxii. 2. Aleᵽᵽe, Lb. I. liv.

Lıᵽule, Lb , I. lxi. 2. Somner said *fistula,* which is a disease ; Lyc, *fistula, enema;* it has been translated in connexion with the foregoing leechdoms, as if lıð-ele, *joint oil, synovia.*

Lonð aðl, fem., gen. -e, *nostalgia,* Lb. II. lxv. 5.

Lunᵹenᵽyᵽꞇ, fem., gen. -e, *lungwort, pulmonaria officinalis.* Germ., Lungenwurz; Dansk, Lungurt; Swed. Lungört. 2. A sort mentioned, Lb. I. xxxviii. 4, " yellow upwards," *hieracium murorum* and *pulmonarium, golden lung wort.*

Luscmoce, fem., gen. -an, not in the gll., possibly by corruption of syllables, *Ladys smock, cardamine pratensis,* Lb. I. xxxviii. 3. 10. A kind with a cropp or bunchy head, Lb. I. xxxix. 2 ; I. xxxviii. 3.

# M.

Mæl, gen. -es, neut., *measure.* Orientis Mir. ix. Chron. p. 354, line 31, anno 1085. Lb. I. ii. 1 ; II. vii. " Circinum, " mælꞇanᵹe," Gl. Somn. p. 65 b, 4, *a pair of compasses, measure tongs.* Where hæᵹmælaꞃ is printed, the MS. has dæᵹmæl uꞃ.

Maᵹeᵽe, Maᵹoᵽe, fem., gen. -an, *maythe, Anthemis nobilis.* 2. ᵽılðe maᵹeᵽe, *maythe, Matricaria chamomilla.* 3. *maythe, maythen, Anthemis cotula.*

1. Chamæmelon is translated maᵹeᵽe, IIb. xxiv. " Camemelon, magethe," Gl. Dun. " Beneolentem," Gl. Brux. p. 41 a, the distinctive mark of true chamomille. " Chomomilla, megede " blomen," a Gl. in Mone, 286 b.

2. ᵽılðe maᵹᵽe, Lb. II. xxii., *wild maythe,* must be wild chamomille, for I do not find that No. 3 was ever supposed to possess medicinal properties; it is therefore *matricaria chamomilla.*

3. The *anthemis cotula* is now called maythen, the final being, to speak after our grammars, derived from the termination of the oblique cases ; country folk say it may be always distinguished from the true camomille by its bad smell. The glossaries agree, " Camomilla " i . camamille similis est amarusce [*read* " -æ] sed camomilla herba breuis est et " redolens et amarusca i. maythe fetit " [fœtet], MS. Rawlinson, c. 707. " Herba " putida, mæᵹðn," Gl. Somn. p. 64 a, line 11. " Mathers, May weed, Dogs " cammomill, Stinking cammomill, and " Dog fenel." Lyte (A.D. 1595).

Perhaps the Saxons included *pyrethrum parthenium.* These plants are so much alike that it requires much technicality to distinguish them ; the artist in MS. V. took the liberty of making the flowers blue. Calmia, mayᵽe, MS. Sloane, 146, with i marked. " Culmia, " magethe," Gl. Dun., whence correct Somner. Gl. p. 66 [63] b, line 6. Calmia is calamine, ore of zinc, and these glosses are blunders.

Reaðe maᵹeᵽe, *anthemis tinctoria.* Lb. I. lxiv.

White maythe, *pyrethrum inodorum.* " Buestalmum [*read* βούφθαλμον], hvit " megethe," Gl. Dun.; printed buestalinum, Gl. Brux. p. 41 a.

Ƿape, Lb. I. xxxi. 7, perhaps *potentilla* as Mara, in Iceland now (Olaf Olafsens Urtagards Bok) ; the cottony potentilla will be *silverweed, p. anserina*, with *argentea.*

Ƿarepypt, max-, fem., *mashwort, the wort in the mash tub*, Laen. 111. Lb. II. xxiv. On the malt boiling water is poured, and allowed to stand three quarters of an hour ; the liquid is wort, or mashwort. Braxivium atque bulita cum braseo nondum cerevisia, *vert ;* a Belgic Gl. in Mone, p. 304 a.

Ƿeaph, meapȝ, masc. and neut., *marrow ;* masc., old Dansk Margr, Lb. III. lxx. ; neut., Germ. Mark, Lb. I. ii. 22.

Ƿeapre meap ȝealla, masc., gen. -an, belongs, from its bitterness implied in " gall," to gentianaceous plants, and from its habitat in marshes may be, *gentiana pneumonanthe.* Lb. I. xxxix. 2; I. l. 2.

Ƿeðo, gen. meðeper, neut., *mead.* Lb. II. lii. 1 ; II. liii. In old German, Mete, and in old Danish, Miöðr, are masc. Gen. Gl. Mone, p. 395 b.

Ƿeðopypt, fem., gen. -e ; 1. *Meadow sweet, spiræa ulmaria.* " Regina prati, Germ. " Wiesenkönigin; Dansk, Miödurt " (Nemnich). " Melissa, medwort, regina " prati." Gl. Harl. 3388. So Gl. Bodley, 178. " Melletina," Gl. Somn. 63 b, 53. " Regina medpurt," Gl. Harl. 978 (A.D. 1240). " Mellanna," Gl. Dun. Lb. I. xxxviii. 10.

2. *Melissa officinalis, balm.* " Nas- " turtium [h]ortolan[um] medwort," Gl. Harl. 3388.

Ƿen, masc. ? *a part, a proportional part =* Swedish, Mån, masc. *a part.* Lb. I. l. 2. The construction with a numeral admits either a plural or a singular.

Meox, Meohs, neuter, *muck, dung, fimus, stercus.* Ðæt meox ıs þær ȝemynð hıs ȝulan ðæða, Hom. II. 408, *The dung* of the parable *is the memory of his foul deeds.*

Ƿepee, gen. -er, masc., *marche, apium.* IIb. xcvii., cxx. ; Gl. Somn. p. 64 a, 11 ; IIb. cxxix.

Scan mepee, *parsley,* Apium petroselinum. Gl. Brux.

Ƿuðu mepee, *wood marche, sanicle,* Sanicula Europæa, a gloss in Laen. 4. also Gl. Laud. 553, fol. 18. Gl. Harl. 978, which was overlooked, so that note 9, p. 35, requires correction. It is a suitable name. Lb. I. i. 15 ; I. xxxix. 2 ; I. lxi. 2 ; III. ii. 6.

Ƿer ? = mıpt, *a mess, dung.* Lb. I. xxxviii. 11. Mes, *stercus, fimus* (Kilian).

Micel lic, *elephantiasis.* Sona puþðon ðuphrleȝene mıð þape able þær myclan licep, G.D. 210 a, *Soon were smitten with " elephantinus morbus."*

Mylse ? or Mylsce ? *mild, mitis.* Lb. I. xlii. ; II. xvi., p. 194. Gemılseeð, Lb. II. xix. xx.

Ƿılte, masc., gen. -er, also -an, *the milt, the spleen.* Lb. II. xxxvi. with gen.-er ; but gen. -an, Laen. 110 ; Quad. ii. 8 ; IIb. xxxii. 6 ; and fem., IIb. xxxii. 6 ; lvii. 1.

Mynet, neut., *money, moneta.* Bed. 532, 1. Lb. II. xv.

Ƿınte, fem., gen. -an, *mint, mentha.*

Fenmınte, *mentha silvestris.* Lb. I. iii. 2.

Sænmınte. Lb. I. xv. 4.

Tunmınte, *mentha sativa.* Lb. I. ii. 23.

Ƿıptel, masc. ? *basil.* 1. *Clinopodium vulgare.* In IIb. cxix., cxxxvii. equivalent to ὤκιμον, *basil.* " Ocimum, mistel," Gl. Mone, p. 321 b, is a repetition not a support. " Ocimus, mistel," Gl. Dun., another echo. " Mistil, basilice," MS. Bodley, 130, on Ocimum : an independent statement. Ƿıptel is a derivative of Ƿıpt, *muck*, and the *clinop. vulg.* is called in German, Kleiner dost, from Doste; old high g. Dosto, *marjoram,* and that may be compared with Dost *cænum, dirt.* Copð mıptel, Lb. xxxvi., seems to distinguish this from the mistletoe ; a few lines lower is Acmıptel.

Ꝣyꞃꜩel—*cont.*

2. *Misteltoe, viscum album.* Germ. Swed. Mistel, masc ; Dansk, Mistel (en ). "Viscarugo, mɪꞃꜩɪlꞇan," Gl. Somner, p. 64 a, line 56. "Mɪꞃꜩelꜩa, chamœleon, " viscus, Cot. 175, 210." Lye. Chameleon is þɪꞃꜩel, not mɪꞃꜩel. " Mistil, " viscus," Graff. ohg. Lb. I. xxxvi.

The mistle or mistletoe is propagated by being carried in the dung of birds.

Ꝣyxenplanꜩe, fem. ? gen. -an ? Lb. I. lviii. 4. " Morella," Gl. Sloane, 146 ; so MS. T., fol. 62 b, that is, *atropa belladonna.*

Ꝣoꞃoꝺ, Ꝣoꞃaꝺ, *a decoction,* the ζέμα of the medical writers ; glossed *carenum,* Gl. Somn. p. 62 a, 11, which is *must boiled down to one third part of its bulk and sweetened.* But this gloss is not quite appropriate in the first example in Lb. I. xxxv., which requires τὰ ἐκ ζέματος, like ἰχθῖς ἀπὸ ζέματος in Trallianus. Occ. Lb. I. xlviii. 2. Moraz in the Nibelunge Not., 1750, is interpreted by the Germans *mulberry wine,* Do schaucte man den gesten . . . . mete môraz unte win ; *then was poured out for the guests mead, moraz and wine.*

Ꝣoꞃu, fem., gen. -an ; 1, *a root.* 2, the root, the edible root, namely, *carrot,* δαῦκον. Lb. I. xviii. ; I. li. 23. Cf. Felꝺmoꞃu, Germ. Möhre, fem. " þis erbe " [squill] haþ a rounde more lyk to an " onyon." MS. Bodley, 536.

" Ne beoþ heo nowt alle forlore, " That stumpeþ at þe flesches more." Owl and Nightingale, 1389.

Ꝣaghꞃe moꞃu, *parsnep, pastinaca sativa,* Lb. I. ii. 23 ; III. viii.

Ᵹylhꞃe moꞃu, pealmoꞃu, *carrot, daucus cariota,* Lb. III. viii. Gl. Somn. p. 64 a, 33.

Ꝣoꞃꞃypꜩ, fem., gen. -e, " moor wort ;" the small moor wort occurs Lb. I. lviii. 1. Somner says, Moor grasse is ros solis, that is, sundew, drosera, which grows on moist heaths. " Silver weed,

Ꝣoꞃꞃypꜩ—*cont.*

" or cotton grass " (Nemnich), that is, potentilla anserina or crioforum.

The German interpreters of St. Hildegard make it the *Parnassia palustris.*

Mucgꞃypꜩ, IIb. art. xiii., *artemisia Pontica.* See Anzeiger für Kunde tentscher Vorzeit, 1835.

Ꝣuꞃꞃa, fem., gen. -an ? *cicely, myrrhis odorata.* Lb. I. i. Μυῤῥίς, οἱ δὲ μύῤῥαν καλοῦσιν, Dioskor. lib. iv. c. 116, which is " scandix odorata " (Sprengel), now named as above.

# N.

Næꝺꞃe ꞃypꜩ, fem., gen. in -e, *adderwort, polygonum bistorta.* In IIb. vi. næꝺꞃeꞃypꜩ = viperina. Our adderworts are those plants which resemble an irritated snake raising its head, the * oficglossum vulgatum,* the *arum maculatum,* the *polygonum bistorta.* In MS. G., the German gloss is " Naterwure," and the German Natterwurz may be *polygonum bistorta,* or provincially *sedum,* or again provincially *echium vulgare.* (Adelung). We are therefore to conclude that the two glossators, agreeing, made the herb *p. bistorta.* The figures in MSS. V., A., G., T. have much the appearance of alisma plantago. In MS. Bodley, 130, the figure and gloss are " Sowethistell." From MS. G. fol. 8 a, the Germans called the Satirion orchis " Natarwure," which must be applied to enlarge Adelung.

Næꞃe, *a fawn skin ; a piece of fawn skin,* Lb. I. ii. 20 ; I. xxxix. 3. " Nebris," Gl. Cleop., that is, νεβρίς, and support is had from Gl. Somn., p. 61 a, line 27. So Gl. Jul. If we take nebris for a piece of soft leather, as a " tripskin," a " rybskin," it comes to the same at last. Næꞃe in the Lib. Med. corresponds to " Phœnicium " in Marcellus.

Naꝩa, *never*, Lb. II. xli. Ne, *not* + Aꝩa, *ever*.

Neahꞇ neꞃꞇiᵹ, *fasting for a night, with fast unbroken; see* Lb. II. lxv. 5, and II. vii. at beginning.

Neꞇle, fem., gen. -an, *nettle, urtica.* ꝼo miele poppiᵹ neꞇle, *u. dioica.* Lb. I. xlvii.

Neupuꞃne, acc., a disease. Lb. I. lix. and contents.

Neꝺeꞃeoþa, Nu-, masc., gen. -an, *that part of the belly which lies between the navel and the share* or pubes, *the pit of the belly.* Lb. II. xxxvi., xxxi., xvii. and contents, xlvi. " Ilium," Gl. M.M., p. 137 b, 15.

## O.

Oꝼeꞃᵹyllo, neut., *overflow, overfilling, spuma vas coronans.* Lb. I. li.

Oꝼeꞃꞅæpiꞃc, *from over sea, transmarinus.* Lb. I. vi. 6. M.II. 100 a. The reading Oꝼeꞃꞅæpiꞃc is not in the MS. nor agreeable to analogy.

Oꝼneꞇ, (gen. prob. -eꞃ), *a close vessel.* In Lb. I. ii. 11, oꝼneꞇe translates " vas- " culo clauso vel operto." The word may be connected with oꝼen, *oven*; the κλίβανος was a close vessel covered up in the hot embers, and an oven at the same time.

Oꝼꞃcoꞇen, properly *badly wounded by a shot*, but specially used, Lb. I. lxxxviii. 2., II. lxv. i., for *elf shot*, the Scottish term, that is, *dangerously distended by greedy devouring of green food.* It is spoken of cattle; sheep are very subject to it, if they get into a clover field at full freedom. " The disease consists in " an overdistension of the first stomach, " from the swelling up of clover and " grass, when eaten with the morning " dew on it."

Oꝼꞃcoꞇen—*cont.*

  Next you'll a warlock turn, in air
    you'll ride,
  Upon a broom, and travel on the tide ;
  Or on a black cat mid the tempests
    prance
  In stormy nights beyond the sea to
    France ;
  Drive down the barns and byars,
    prevent our sleep,
  Elfshoot our ky, and smoor mang drift
    our sheep. Falls of Clyde, p. 120.

" The approved cure is to chafe the parts " affected with a blue bonnet. The bas- " ting is performed for an hour without " intermission, by means of blue bonnets. " The herds of Clydesdale, I am assured, " would not trust to any other instru- " ment in chafing the animal." Jamie- son in Elfshot, and Suppl. " When " cattle are swollen they are said to be " degbowed. I have frequently known " a farmer strike a sharp knife through " the skin, between the ribs and the " hips, when the cow felt immediate " relief from the escape of air through " the orifice, so that the distended car- " case instantly collapsed, and the ex- " crements blown with great violence " to the roof of the cow house." Carrs Craven Gl. " Deggbound, mightily " swelled in the belly." Yorkshire dialogue, Gl. 1697, A.D.

Ome ? -an ; fem. ? *corrupt humour*, es- pecially *gastric*, the *pituita* of the medical and classical authors ; also *Erysipelas*, the external symptom of such a humour. Lb. I. xxxv. Dat. pl. Omum; gen. pl. Omena. The analogy of the Islandic suggests a feminine form.

Omppe, fem., gen. -an, *dock, rumex*; the German Ampfer, masc., *dock, rumex*. " Rodinaps, ompre, docce," Gl. Mone, p. 322 a. " Cocilus,' Gl. Cleop. If καυκαλίς, not likely. Of the Omppe, that will swim, *see* Docce. Lb. I. viii. 2 ; III. xxvi. Laen. 23.

Onᵹealle, *fellow*. Lb. I. xxxix., xli., obl. cas., from the contents.

Onꝥeð, gen. -es, some wort ; herba quædam. Lb. I. xl. i.; II. lii. 1.

Onꞃꝑꞃenᵹan, *to administer a clyster*. Lb. I. iv. 6. From Sꝑꞃinᵹ, *a gush of water*, hence, *a lavement, a sousing, a washing*, a κλυσμός.

Onꞃæꝑi ? *unripe*. Lb. I. ii. 14.

Oꝑaꞃ, Quad. viii. 6, plural of Hoꝑh.

Oxanꝛlyppe ? fem. ? gen. -an, *oxlip, primula elatior*. Lb. I. ii. 15.

Oxnaliɓ, neut. ? *oxheal, Helleborus fœtidus* and *H. viridis* (Cotgrave in Ellebore). Oleotropius, Gl. Dun. Lb. I. xxxii. 2. ; I. x.

# P.

Pic, gen. -es, neut., *pitch, pix*. Lb. I. xxxviii. 9 ; II. xli. ; III. xv.

Piꝑoꝑ, gen. -es, masc., *pepper, piper;* Lb. II. vii.

Poc, gen. pocces, masc., *a pock, pustula* ut in variola. Lb. I. xl.

Punð, gen. -es, neut.; 1. *a pound*, as Lexx. 2. *a pint*. Lb. II. lxvii. So " Norma, " pæteꝑ punð," Gl. Somn. p. 68 b, 11., that is, a pound of water is a pint of water, and a pint of water is a pint for all liquids.

Puꝛlian, *to pick out the best bits, optima quæque legere*. Lb. III. lxix. " Peuse-" len, (among kindred senses) *summis " digitis varia cibaria carpere*," (Kilian).

# R.

Ræᵹeꝑeoſe, fem., Lb. II. xxxi. ; also Ræᵹeꝑeosa, masc., Lb. I. lxxi.; pl. -an ; *the two ridges of muscles on either side of the spine up and down the back*. " Pissli,

Ræᵹeꝑeoſen—*cont.*

" reosan," Gl. Mone, p. 321 b, ult. Pissli is a contraction of Paxilli ; similarly " Peysel, *pieu, échalas*," Roquefort. But, as we know from Cicero, Paxillus was also contracted into Palus, and these muscles were called Palæ, like Pala, *stipes, palus*, in Du Cange. " Rugge—bratun, *palæ*, sunt dorsi dex-" tra lævaque eminentia membra," Gl. Hoffmann. " Palæ Ugutioni 'Dorsi " ' dextra lævaque eminentia membra, " ' dicta sic, quia in luctando eas pre-" ' nimus, quia luctari vel luctam " ' Græci dicunt l'alim.' 'Palæ sunt " ' dorsi dextra lævaque eminentia " ' membra ; dicta quod in luctando " ' eas preminus, quod Græci παλαίειν " ' dicunt.' Isidorus," and so on (Du Cange). The sense suits the passages where ꞃæᵹeꝑeoꞃan occurs, Lb. I. lxxi., lxxxi. ; II. xxxi. " Palæ, ᵹeꞃenlðꝑe," Gl. Somn. p. 71 a, 44, *the shoulder blades*, and in this sense the dictionary to Cælius Aurelianus, who often uses the word, understands it. " Palæ, riegrible," Gl. Mone, p. 317 b.

Ræꝑ ? *row, ordo, series:* dat. ꝛæꝑe, C.D. vol. iii. p. xxv. ; acc. ꝛæꝑe. Lb. II. xxxiii ; also Gl. in Lye.

Raᵹu, Raᵹe, *lichen*, λειχήν. Lb. I. xxxviii. 8 ; I. lxviii.

Raᵹu ꞇ meoꞃ, Deuteron. xxviii. 42, neither word is used there with precision. The Gl. give Massiclum, Mossidum, which are formatives of our Moss, lichen being considered a sort of moss.

Ramᵹealla, masc., gen. -an, " *ramgall*." From the name gall, no doubt a gentianaceous plant ; said Lb. I. li. to be particoloured. This description answers to *Menyanthes trifoliata*, which is very bitter and much administered by herb doctors. (Sir J. E. Smith.)

Renðꝑian, I presume to be the still current Render, applied to suet. Suet is full of films, thin membranes, with some other

Renðpian—*cont.*
not fatty substances ; to render it, is to
make it homogeneous by melting. The
word may be a derivative of Hrein,
*clean.* Gepenðpian is applied to elm-
rind, Lb. I. xxv. 2. ; to the black alder,
I. xv. 4.

RenƷpypin, Ren-p., RænƷ-p. *See* Fypin.

Rib, neut., *a rib.* Lb. II. xlvi. S.S.
p. 198, 11.

Ribbe, gen. -an, fem.? *ribwort, plantago
lanceolata.* IIb. xxviii. Lb. I. ii. 22.

Ryðen ; þ peaðe pyðen. Lb. III. xlviii.

Rinð, gen. -e, fem. ; *rind, cortex.* Lb. I.
xxxviii. 5, 6.; II. lxv. 2, and often.
Hom. II. 8 and 114. Lyes quotation
was false, Lb. I. xlv. 5, and the more
recent deduction from him.

Ripoða, *rheum,* ρευματισμός, *a flowing.*
Lb. lix. 7. *See* Brem. Worth. p. 502. 4.

Rop, masc., gen. poppes, *the colon, wide
intestine.* Lb. II. xxxi. often.

Ror, neut., *scum, spuma, reiectamentum.*
Lb. II. xx. as Hpor.

Ruðe, fem., gen. -an, *rue, Ruta graveolens.* Foreign, but adopted. Filðe
puðe, Lb. I. ii. 1, is foreign, but a
garden herb, *Peganum harmala.*

Ruðmolin, read Ruðurolin, Lb. III. lviii.,
a Norse word signifying *Red stalked,*
from poð, *red,* nioli *stalk.* It is said, to
grow by running water ; and it is *Polygonum hydropiper,* called Redshanks or
Water pepper in Bailey's dictionary.

Run, gen. -e, *secret, heathen mystery,
arcanum quid,* Bw. 363.
Leoð pune, gen. -an, fem., *the same,
idem.* Lb. I. lxiv.

## S.

Sæþepie, Suðepiʒe, fem., gen. -an, *savory,
satureia hortensis.* The interpretation,
" Satirion," Gl. Somn., p. 64 b, 16, is
an evident error. Savory is in England
a garden plant, and retains its foreign

Sæþepie—*cont.*
name. All the orchis tribe are "bal-
" loc " worts. Lb. III. xii. 2.

Sap, gen. -es, neut. everywhere : *See* acc.
Sapan, Lb. II. xxviii. It is also, as
Sio sap, sometimes put for Sio soph ;
Bw. 49, 29. So G.D. 201 b. C.E. 134,
line 23.

Sapepen, *disposed to soreness.* Lb. II. i. 1.
There is no corresponding word in
the Hellenic text ; this is epexegetical,
and must be interpreted accordingly.

Scapu, fem., gen. -e, *the share,* that is,
*the pubes.* Lb. II. xxxi, xxxii. It is a
word well known to those who have
heard pure English spoken, and is neither
" Ilium " nor " Penis " nor " Alvus,"
but something near each of those. The
books generally make a confusion, but
Sharebone is always, I think, Os pubis.
See a quotation in Halliwell, but strike
out " of a man." Compare also Penil,
pubes, with Penul, a schare, in Garlande
and Biblesworth, p. 121, p. 148.

Sceaðan, præt. Sceað, p. part. Sceaðen, *to
shed, let fall* ; also intransitively *fall ;
infundere, inspergere.* Lb. I. ii. 23.;
I. lxi. 2.; II. iii. IIb. ii. 6. Cf. Lyc,
Sceðan. Æpceða, *migma,* Gl. in Lye,
which is doubtless to be understood
as the substantive of 'Απομύττεσθας,
Emungi.

Sceapen, adj., *of sheep, ovinus.* Lb. I. lviii.

Sceappian, *to scrape, radere.* IIb. lxxxi.
5. The L is frequentative.

† Sceappan, præt. † Sceapp, *scrape,* es-
pecially scrape herbs fine. Gepceapp,
IIb. lvii. 1. The same in substance as
Sceapian, IIb. i. 2.

Sceappe, fem., gen. -an, *a scarification,
incisura in cute.* Lb. I. lvi.; I. xxxv.

Sceappian, *to scarify, in superficie cædere.*
Lb. I. xxxii. 2.

Sceopran, *to scarify, rodere, mordere.*
Scyprð, Scyppenðum, Lb. I. xviii. Þa
ʒæpircrðar ʒ þa pýpicpuman receoppenðe
pæpon, O.T. 270, line 32, *began gnawing
the grass sprouts and the roots.*

c c 2

Scinlac, gen. -es, neut., *an apparition, visum*; gen. Gl. Mone, p. 402 b. ; peaflaces, Matth. xxiii. 25. Boet. p. 55, 7 ; accus. ænig reinlac, Quad. x. 1 ; plur. -laen, SMD. 27 b ; constr. neuter, DD. 437 foot, M.Sp. 8, plur. Scinlac, Quad. ix. 1. But *see* lyblacas, DD. 344.

Scytel, *dung*, from Sciran. Quadr. iii. 14, xi. 13. *See* the passages, where Somners notion of testiculus would require some drying process not mentioned.

Scpimman, *to shrink*, a synonym of Scpincan. Lb. I. xxvi., contents. " Skrim-" pen, adj. som vrider eller undslaaer " sig for Arbeide, som er meget kiælen " eller emtualig," Molbech, *one who flinches from work*, etc. Cf. Shrammed, *chilled* (pinched with cold, O.C.) Wilts. Scrimd ; Devon, (heard by myself).

Scpur, Gerceopr, neut., *scurf*. Lb. II. xxxv. IIb. clxxxi. 3.

Seaðan, Seaðan, *a feeling as if the cavity of the body were full of water swaying about*, κλύδωνes, *undulationes*, Lb. I. xiv.

Sealh, Scalh, masc., gen. -er, *the sallow, salic-em, salix*, of which seventy English sorts are reckoned. The termination of the gen. shows the word is not fem., and few names of trees are neuter.

Red Sallow, Laen. 89, *Salix rubra. See* also *S. repens*, of Smith.

Seap, neut., gen. -er, *juice*. IIb. v. 2. Lb. I. ii. 14, and frequently.

Secg, masc., gen. -er, *sedge*; " carex, " gladiolus," Gl. in Lyc ; masc., Lb. I. xxiii. ; gen. I. xxxix.

Bomoprecg, " hammer sedge." Lb. I. lvi. 2. Homop is probably a bird, as in yellow hammer. " Scorellus, omep," Gl. C. Emberiza. Cf. clobhamep, Gl. Mone, 315 a ; also Gl. Dief.

Read secg, " red sedge," Lb. I. xxxix.

Selpæce, gen. -an, *avena fatua? wild oat?* Lb. I. xxxiii. 2 ; III. viii., and perhaps by emendation for realr ræran, Lb. I. xlvii. 2.

† Sengian, *singe ; see* Berengian ; ohg. Sengjan, Bisengjan, and Bireng is what grammarians would have end in a vowel.

Sybe, masc., *decoction*, ἀφέψημα, IIb. cliii. 4, from Seoðan.

Sibsam, Lb. II. lxv. 5.

Sire, *sieve*, constr. as neut. Lb. I. xxxviii. 5, as Germ. Sieb, neut. Yet Dutch Zeef is fem.

Syreðan, Syreðan, Sioreðan, pl. *bran, furfures*. Boet. p. 91, line 23. Gl. Cleop. In IIb. clv. 1, it translates ὠμὴ λύσις, which is said to be flour ; but here is a tradition that it is *bran*.

Sigelhpeopra, gen. -an, masc. 1. *Yellow milfoil, Achillea tomentosa*, masc., as Lb. III. xxxii. In IIb. I. = Heliotropion. All plants turn to the sun, which of them is meant ? In MS. V. " Achillea ser-" rata " (II.) seems to be drawn ; the other drawings do not at all resemble this. " Eliotropia, sigelhverpha. Elio-" trophus, sigel hveorfa. Nimphea, collon " croh vel sigelhveorna. Solsequia, si-" gel hveorna. Achillea, collon croch," Gl. Dun. Most of these are translations, and so equivalents : nymphea is the yellow water lily, and croh is crocus, yellow also. The testimony of the drawing falls in so well with that of the old glossary, that we must accept Achillea ; and as we must also attend to the hints for yellowness, it must be *A. tomentosa*.

2. *Scorpiurus heliotropion*, for IIb. cxxxvii. is founded on Dioskorides, ἡλιοτρόπιον τὸ μέγα, ὃ ἔνιοι ἐκάλεσαν σκορπίουρον. The figure in MS. T. for art. 1. agrees. The drawing in MS. V. art. cxxxvii. is nearly destroyed, what remains looks like " Polygonum couvol-" vulus." (II.) The " round" seed " forbids us to think of sunflower, Helianthus, which is also Mexican.

3. *Cichorium intybus?* Often Turnsol and Heliotrope in glossaries. So Germ. Sonnen wendel (Adelung).

4. *Euphorbia helioscopia*.

A small Sigelhpeopre, Lb. I. xliv. 2.

Sıȝronȝe, a wort, herba quædam ignota. Lb. I. xxxi. 7.

Sineþe, _ever easy_; ɼın-eþþe, Lb. II. xlvi.

Sınɼulle, gen. -an, _houseleek, Sempervivum tectorum._ The syllable sın like sem in Semper, means _always_; as also in Sınȝȝene. Sınɼulle is Sempervivum, Hb. cxxv. That herb is drawn in MS. V., explained, as the green pigment has left only the external cast in the vellum, by MS. A., and in MS. G., where it is glossed " hufwure," that is, Hauswurz, and in MS. T. These all point the same way. Singreen seems only a more generic term, in later times, but " The mickle " sinfulle," Lb. II. xxxiv., shows that this term also in early times would include Sedums, as _S. Telephium,_ Lb. I. iii. 11.

Sınȝpene, fem., gen. -an, _singreen,_ any sort of Sedum, with _sempervivum tectorum,_ literally _always green._ Hb. lxxxvi. " Sedo magno, Houseleeke or Sen- " greene," Florio. " Joubarbe, House- " leek, Sengreen, Aygreen, etc." Cot- grave. In Hb. xlix. = Temolus, that is, Moly, the Homeric μῶλυ, a garlic, _Allium moly._ In Dansk. the evergreen periwinkle, _Vinca._ Þa ɼmalan ɼınȝɻenan, Lb. I. viii. 2, shows that Singreen was a gene- ric name. " Colatidis," also " Temolus " vel titemallos," Gl. Dun. " Temolus," Hb. xlix., saying the root is bulbous, drawing it large, and with leaves and stem in MS. V., like Pinguicula vulgaris (II.), with no resemblance to Vinca.

Sınɼpænbel, masc. ? _a bolus,_ " _turundula,_" Lat. Hb. xiv. 2. Sın, as in Sınepealȝ, _round;_ Tɼenbel has a masc. termina- tion.

Slaɼne ? gen. -an, _Salvia sclarea,_ Lb. I. xv. 5.

Sleeȝeȝan, _palpitate with strong beats,_ Lb. II. xxvii ; from Sleeȝe, a _sledge_ hammer, and the frequentative termination -eȝan, -eȝȝan.

Slýpe ? gen. -an, _a viscid or sloppy sub- stance._ Masc. Lb. I. i. 6. Fem. Laen.

Slýpe—_cont._
46. Cf. Slıpıȝ. Cf. Cu slyppan, Oxan slýppan.

Smeȝaɼyȝın, Smoeȝa -, Smea-, masc., gen -eɼ, Lb. I. liii. ; III. xxxix., _a worm or insect that penetrates, that eats its way, a burrowing insect;_ cf. Norse, Smjúga, 1. _irrepere,_ 2. _penetrare,_ E. Smuȝan, _to creep,_ Smyȝelaɼ, _cuniculi, conies or their burrows._ Somn. Gl. M.M.

Smeɯopýɼȝ, 1. _Aristolochia rotunda,_ for- eign, and _A. clematitis,_English. Hb. xx., Lb. III. xlvii., with several glossaries and MSS., Gl. Dun., Gl. Harl. 3388, Gl. Sloane, 5. _A. longa,_ Gl. Sloane, 405.

2. _Mercurialis,_ Gl. Rawl. C. 607. Gl. Harl. 3388 in margin. G. de Bibles- worth, p. 162. Gl. Sloane, 5, fol. 34. Gl. Sloane, 135.

3. From the qualities, _Pinguicula, butterwort._

Smıȝȝan, _to smudge, illinere,_ Lb. I. xxxi. 3 ; related to modern Smut ; in Lye Smıȝȝa.

Snæb, fem. gen. -e, _a bolus, a morsel,_ Laen. 81. Lb. I. xv. 6 ; I. lii. 3 ; II. lxiv. ; III. lxii. p. 348 ; III. lxv. Seo snæb, Hom. II. 272. S.S. p. 169, line 809. But ða snæbas, C.D. 207.

Soȝoða, gen. -an, _corrupt humour, pituita_ with _hiccup, hicket, sobbing,_ λυγμός, _sin- gultus,_ Hb. xc. 11 ; Lb. I. ii. 1 ; II. xxxix., where the original is μετὰ δὲ ταῦτα λύζουσι, Alex. Trall. p. 480, ed. Basil. From Suȝan.

Ælɼȝoȝoða, _elvish hiccup,_ the same thing gone to a frightful extreme. Thus πάντα γὰρ ἐποίησα ταῦτα καὶ ἐπὶ μεγάλου λυγμοῦ τοσοῦτον, ὡς ὑπονοεῖν ἐκτὸς κλίνης ἐξάλλεσθαι τὸν κάμνοντα. Alex. Trall. p. 121, ed. Paris. = lib. vii. 15, _in an instance of so strong a hiccup that we supposed the patient was springing out of bed,_ Lb. III. lxii. p. 348.

Soloɼece, _Heliotropium Europæum._ Hb. lxxvi. Sprengel says that by Solse- quium, Charlemagne understood H.E. as above.

Soppiꝣan, *to sop, to dip in liquid.* Lb. II.
xxx. 1. Cf. Soppcuppe, fem., C.D. 593,
685, 721.

Spæran, *to syringe, spout, aquam proiicere;*
Lb. II. xxii. p. 208 ult., where the sense
hardly admits *spuere.* "Spoyte, sprützen,
" sprenken, so auch Süddän." Outzen.

Spepe pypꞇ, 1. *Ranunculus flammula.*
" Flamula . i. sper wortt or launsele, this
" erbe is schapyn as hit wer a sper all
" so . and in the crope of þe stalk
" commys aut mony smale branches ꞇ
" hit has a whyte floure, ꞇ hit groys in
" waters." MS. Bodl. 536. The flower
is yellow. " Flammula, anglice spere-
" wort," MS. Rawl. C. 607, similarly
C. 506, Harl. 3388, and again adding
" lanceola," id. " fflamula minor. Las
" sper wort hauith lewis shapid like a
" spere," Gl. Sloane, 5, fol. 32 c. Gl.
Sloane, 405.

2. *Inula Helenium,* IIb. xcvii. and
Gl. Harl. 978, make spearwort Inula
campana = *Inula Helenium, Bot.* Gl.
Dun. perhaps copies IIb. Gl. Brux.
agrees. MSS. V., G., A. draw spears
springing from a root.

In MS. Bodl. 130, is an explanation,
Centaurea, and a gloss in a hand of the
14th century, " Sperewert." The Centaurea Cyanus is so far like Inula II.,
that it may be mistaken in a drawing.
" Policaria minor," Gl. Harl. 3388.

3. *Carex acuta,* Germ. Spiessgras, is
probably meant in the following, " Fla-
" mula mynor . i. sperworte thys erbe
" has smale leuys lyke to grase, bot hit
" (*omit hit*) schape as hit were a speyr.
" and growes in feldys," MS. Bodl.
536.

4. † *Brassica rapa, turnep,* " Nap
" silvatica [*read* Napus silvaticus] ꝛpepe-
" pypꞇ," Gl. Somn. p. 64 a, 16. This
must be rejected.

Spicau, *spices,* Latinism? species. Lb. II.
lxiv., contents.

Sppacen, neut.? *berry bearing alder,
Rhamnus frangula.* Lb. I. xv. 4., xxiii.

Sppacen—*cont.*
Germ., Spreckenholz, Sporkenholz;
Dutch, Sporkenhout; Dansk., Spregner;
Swed. dial., Sprakved. " Apeletum,"
Gl. Cleop. for alnetum, misunderstood as
alnus nigra.

Sppung pypꞇ, fem., gen. in -e, "spring-
" wort," *Euphorbia lathyris.* "Sprincwrz,
" lacturidia. al. lactariola vel. citocasia,"
Gl. Hoffm. Graff. vol. i. col. 1051. "Cra-
" pucia [*read* cataputia] springwort,"
a Gl. in Mone, p. 287 a. Lb. I. xxxix.
2.

Stæþpypꞇ, fem. gen. -e, " staithwort;"
if we choose the commonest of the sea-
shore plants it will be *Statice,* compre-
hending *thrift* and *sea lavender.* Lb. I.
xxxii. 3. " Aster atticus," Somner, but
why?

Stanbæþ, neut., *a vapour bath,* contrived
by heating " stones " that would not fly,
and pouring on water. Lb. I. xli.

Stebe, masc., *strangury,* "stranguria," Lat.
of Quad. ii. 15., viii. 11. Radically; *the
being stationary, still standing;* as in
Sunnstebe, *solstice.* So Næpon þunc
heopða ꝛtebiꝣe, Gen. xxxi. 38., *thine
herds were not barren.*

Stemp, *stamp,* Leechd. vol. I. p. 378.

Stiece, neut., *sticky stuff, viscid fluid;* Lb.
I. xxxix. 2.

Stice, fem., gen. -e, *a pricking sensation, a
stitch, a stab;* Quad. xiii. 10. Instice,
Lb. II. liv. lxiv. contents. All cited
passages have this declension.

Scpælpypꞇ, fem., gen. -e, the commonest
*club moss, Lycopodium clavatum.* " Cal-
" litrichon," MS. ap. Somn., but in this
term were included the club mosses.
Scpæl as *arrow,* may have given name to
this moss, as the stems look like arrows
with the feathers up and the heads in
the ground. Were it not for this gl.
we might interpret *Galium verum,* from
Scpæl, *bed; our ladys bed straw.*

Scpeap, Scpeop, *straw,* neuter in Lh. I. iii.
12. Rushw. Matth. vii. 3. (streu), is
masc. Διδαξ. 46.

Sugan, *to moisten, macerare, madefacere,*
Syᵹð, IIb. xxxv. 3 ; p. part. Soᵹen, as
appears by Soᵹoða, Foᵹᵹoᵹen; cf. Socian
in Lexx.; also Isl. Söggr, *madidus,* Lb. II.
xv. Da ᵹoᵹᵹoᵹeðan þunðe ᵹuᵹe ꞇ clœn-
ᵹᵹe, P.A. 24 b. *Moisten and cleanse the
putrified wound.* Asoᵹen. C.E. 373. l. 19.
Sunðcoᵹn, gen. -eᵹ, neut., *Saxifraga granulata.* Sunðcoᵹn, IIb. xcix. is saxifraga,
and the statement is accompanied by a
remarkable drawing, represented in the
fac simile to Leechdoms, vol. I.; *see* pref.
lxxix. The word coᵹn itself, as signifying *grain,* assists our determination of the
herb. In the Latin Apuleius, MS. Bodley,
130, a gloss is " Sundcorn." MS. A. fol.
45 b, has also a portion of earths surface,
but figures the herb above ground, not
quite correctly. " Saxifrigia, suudcorn,"
Gl. Dun. The same gl. in the MS.
Lacn. 18, where fifteen grains are mentioned in the text. So Gl. Mone, p.
442 a.
2. Lithospermon officinale, IIb. clxxx.
It appears by a glossary in Anzeiger für
Kunde der teutscher Vorzeit. 1835, col.
247, that the false readings meant sunnan
coᵹn, Milium solis, which must be taken
as an emendation of the text.
Suᵹe, fem., gen. -an, *sorrel, Rumex Acetosa,* also *Oxalis.*
Geaceᵹ ᵹuᵹe, *cuckoos sorrel, Oxalis
Acetosella.*
Monneᵹ ᵹuᵹe, *Rumex Acetosa.* Lb.
I. li.
Suᵹmelᵹe, *sourish, sour sweet.* Lb. II. i.
" Malus matranus, ᵹuᵹmelᵹe apulðeᵹ,"
Gl. Somn., p. 64 b, 48 ; correct *Malus
matiana,* ᵹuᵹmelᵹe apulðᵹe ; *the crab
tree.* " Maciana . i. mala siluestria,"
Gl. Harl. 3388. " Mala maciana, po-
" mum siluestre, wode crabbis," id.
So Dorsten, Gl. Mone, p. 290 a. Melᵹe
is a separate word, " Melarium, milᵹe
" apulðᵹ." Gl. M.M. p. 159 a, 27, probably for mel-ᵹᵹe, formed on Mel, *honey,*
which therefore appears genuine English,
as in Melᵹeocel, Melðeaᵹ, St. Marh. Gl.,

Suᵹmelᵹe—*cont.*
not hibrid words ; related to Meðu, *mead,*
SSpp. art. 511.
Spane ᵹyᵹꞇ, fem., gen. -e. Lb. I. xxxi. 7.
Spaꞇ, gen. -es. 1. *sweat.* 2. *blood.* 3.
*hydromel.* IIb. 22 a. The gender has
been given only from other Teutonic
languages, as masc. ; but in Lacn. 111,
spa ða spaꞇ beoð miᵹᵹenheu, *as the
sweats are various,* the form makes it
neuter. Dutch Zweet, neut ; Isl. Sveiti ;
Germ. Schweiss ; Swedish Svett, masc.
Speᵹleᵹ æppel ; Lib. I. ii. 12, also 21 ; I.
xiv., I. xxiii. The receipt Lb. I. ii. 12,
pepper, salt, wine, and swails apple,
corresponds with the following words of
Alex. Trall., p. 48, line 4, ed. 1548.
Ἀλὸς ἀμμωνιακοῦ (our author often solves
his difficulties by omission) Γο ά, φύλλων
Γο γ΄, πεπέρεως Γο ϛ΄, ποιήσας ξηρίον
ὑπάλειφε καὶ ποιεῖ πρὸς ξηροφθαλμίας.
Φύλλα are the leaves of the malobathrum.
Plinius, xxiii. 43, also prescribes malobathrum for the eyes.
† Speðau, *to swathe,* not yet found, whence
Spaðil and Speðunᵹ, *a swathing,* Lb. I.
xxxi. 7, and Beᵹᵹeþan, id. I. i. 2 ; II.
xlii. C.E. p. 100, 19. Weak conjuga-
tion.
Spiᵹan, Speᵹan, præt. speoᵹ, spoᵹen, *to
invade, pervade, penetrate.* Read Spi-
ᵹende, Lb. II. xxiii. Secꞇe hine
ᵹylᵹne onᵹean þone (so) ᵹᵹeᵹenðan ᵹyᵹ,
M.II. 184 b. St. Martin *set himself in
opposition to the invading fire.* Ealle ða
ᵹullneᵹᵹa ðæᵹ ðᵹᵹeᵹan oᵹneᵹ ðe me æᵹ·
ðuᵹhᵹeoᵹh on ᵹeᵹ aᵹlymeðe, Beda,
629, 21. *Put to flight all the foulnesses
of the darksome furnace, which previously
had scorched me.* þ næᵹiᵹ biᵹceop oþeᵹ
buᵹceopᵹeᵹe onᵹᵹoᵹe, Beda, 575, 32,
*that no bishop invade another bishops
diocese.* Cf. Inᵹᵹoᵹenuyᵹ, *invasion,* Beda,
507.
Spyle, masc., gen. -eᵹ, *a swelling.* IIb. ix.
3. On mycelᵹe spyle, Bed. 616, 6, is
some error ; *see* 616, 38.

Sᵽýᵽꝛan, præt. Speoᵽꝛ, p. part. Sᵽoᵽꝛen, *to file, to grind away*, whether by a file or a grindstone; and so *to polish*. "Sᵽyᵽᵽþ *limat*," Gl. Prud., p. 144 b. " Aꝛᵽoᵽꝛen *expolitus*," *id*. p. 142 a. Sᵽoᵽꝛen C.E., p. 410, 24; p. 497, 18, also notes. Cf. Gothic Swairban; ohg. Swerban, Farswerban.

　Aꝛꝼeꝼꝛeoᵽꝛ, *brass filings*. Lb. I. xxxiv. 1.

　Geꝼꝛyᵽꝛ, gen. -eꝛ, *filings*. IIb. ci. 3.

Sᵽꞇᵽman, *swarm*, de apibus, *examen ex alveari educere*. Leechd. vol. I., p. 384. Cf. " Coaluissent, suoᵽnaðun." Gl. C. read suoᵽmaðun for sᵽeoᵽmaðon ?

Sᵽoᵽan, *to swoon*, see ꝼeꝼꝛoᵽunꝼ, swowe in Will. and Werwolf, p. 4.


# T.

-ꞇanꝼe, -ꞇenꝼe, -ꞇınꝼe, as a termination occurs in Geꞇenꝼe, *accidental to*, *quod accidit alicui*, in Inꞇınꝼa, *occasion*, in Geaðoꞇꞇenꝼe, *adjacent*, in Samꞇenꝼeꝛ, *continually*; the same syllable is seen in contingit, contigit, Τυγχάνειν, Τύχη, Tangere, Θιγεῖν, Touch.

Teaꝼan, *to prepare, parare*. þ lanð mıð ꞇo ꞇeaꝼenne :· Ða þ lanð ða ꝼeꞇeað ᵽæꝛ. Beða, 605, 33. Cuðbertht requested some husbandry tools wherewith *to till the land; so when the land was prepared*. præt. ꞇeoðe, CE. 335, 1. 16, 336, 1. 4.

Taᵽu, Teaᵽo, neut., gen. -oꝛ; *tar, gum, distillation from a tree; wax* in the ear; neut., Lb. I. xlv. 3, I. liv., I. lxi. 1, also makes ꞇaᵽan, masc., Lb. III. xxvi., xxxi. þone ꞇeaᵽ, Lacn. 3. Geclæm ealle þa seamas mid tyrwan, Hom. I. 20, *calk all the seams with tar*. So Gen. vi.14. Týᵽᵽan ꝛoᵽ ᵽeallum, Gen. xi. 3. Geᵽoᵽhꞇ oꝛ ꞇıꝼelan . ꝺ oꝛ coᵽðꞇyᵽeᵽan, OT. 304, 12, *wrought of tiles*, thin bricks, such as the Romans made, *and bitumen*.

Telꝼꝛa, masc., gen. -an, *branch, ramus*, Quad. i. 7. Sume þonne sneddun telgran of treowum, Matth. xxi. 8, Rushworth, ed K.

Teon, præt . ꞇeah, p.p. ꞇoꝼen, *draw, ducere*. The translation of ꝼeꞇoꝼen, Quad. vi. 11, as *tightened*, is justified by the context and by the following example. A monk calls on the devil to untie his sandals, and the devil does so : then the monk is frightened and backs out, but ða ꝼeᵽuncðon ða þꝛanꝼaꝛ on mıcelum ðæle onꞇoꝼene ꝺ onhꝛðoðe ; GD. 217 a., *the thongs remained in great part untightened and eased*.

Teꞇꝛa, Lb. II. xxx., appears to be an error for Teꞇeᵽ, masc., *tetter, impetigo*. Hæꝛð ꞇeꞇeᵽ on hıs hchoman, P.A. 15 b., *hath tetter on his body*. Se ꞇeꞇeᵽ buꞇan ꝛaᵽe he oꝛeᵽꝼæð ealne ðone hchoman, ibid., "Impetigo quippe sine dolore corpus " occupat." So Se. 46 a. The gll., Quad. ii. 10, IIb. xlvi. 6, cxxii.

Tıꝛe, fem ? *bitch*; Isl. Tik, *bitch*, fem. Dansk. Tæve, *bitch*. Lb. II. lx. contents.

Tyᵽðelu, Tyᵽðlu, pl., *little tords, treddles*; the droppings of sheep are called sheeps tredles in Somerset, trattles in Suffolk. *See* Moor Gl. ; further. Tridlins: Craven Gl. Lb. I. xxxi. 4, II. lix. 6, etc.

Toꝼeꞇꞇeð, *there are tuggings, spasms*. Lb. I. xxv.

Toᵽ beꝼeꞇe, *hard gotten*, Lb. I. xlv. 5. The expression goes to mark a Dansk admixture in the Lb. Cf. Torꝛenginn, *hard to get*, in the Laws of Magnus the law mender; Nú aꝛ því at viuno menn ero miök torfengnir í heraði, oc allir vilia nú i kaupferdir fara. Kaupa Bólkr.• 23, *Now since men for labour are very hard to get in the country, and all will now go a trading*. Tor, with o long, is frequent in later English, " It were tor for " to telle al here atyr riche," William and Werwolf, fol. 21 ; " It were toor for " to telle treuli al þe soþe," id. fol. 75, with the notes.

Toþþ, *a piece of dung, stercus conformatum*; neut., Lb. I. xlviii. 2 ; I. lxxii. ; III. xxxviii. Quad. vi. 14, 18, 19, 20, 21, 24, Laen.

Toþniӡe, *blear eyed*, with eyes inflamed and full of acrid tears. IIb. xvi. 3, " ad " lippitudinem oculorum," Lat. IIb. liv. 1, "ad epiphoras oculorum," Lat., that is, *excess of lacrymose humour.* A compound of τyþan, and eaӡe.

Toð, *tooth*, *dens*, makes dat. sing. τoþe, Lb. III. iv., but τeþ, Exod xxi. 24, and nom. pl. τeþ, Lb. III. iv., but τoþas, Gð. 34, SS. 141, acc. pl. τeð, Lb. I. vi. 5.

Toþӡaþ, *a tooth pick.* Lb. I. ii. 22. Gaþ is not a weapon originally, but αἰχμή, something at an acute angle, as in the Gore of a gown. *See* ӡaþa, Cod. Dipl. vol. iii.

Tþuӡ, neut., *a trough,* Lb. III. xlviii. þþuh, another form of the same word, is fem. in all the examples cited by Lye ; is neut. in C. D. 118, A.D. 770. Biððenðe aneþ lýτleþ τþoӡeþ, OT. 312, 32, *Begging for a little boat.*

Tulӡe, *root of tongue,* Lb. I. xlii., there is no notion of flesh, or muscle, or hypoglottis. It is Gothic, Tulgus, ἑδραῖος, στερεός. Gothic, Tulgiða, fem. ὀχύρωμα, ἀσφάλεια, ἑδραίωμα.

Tunӡilþinpyþτ,fem.,gen. -e, *white hellebore? Veratrum album,* for it seems probable enough, that Tunþuӡþyþτ, IIb. cxl. and Gl. Dun., is a contraction of this older form. Lb. I. xlvii. 3.

Tþæbe, *two parts in three;* Lb. III. ii. 1. ; III. x., xiii., xxxix.

Tþinihτ, *downy;* from Tþin *byssus,* Gl. Lb. I. xxxi. 7.

# þ.

þæþe, masc., gen. -eþ, *wark, pain.* Wark, in compounds at least, is in most of the modern gl. Dansk. Wærk, *pain.* Isl. Verkr., masc. Occurs masc. Lb. I. iv. 2 ; II. xlvi. 1. Also þeoþce, þeoþe, þþæc.

þæþe—*cont,*
See Pref. vol. I. p. xcvi. Not to be confounded with þeoþe, *work,* neuter. The feminine article in Lb. II. xlvi. 1, for *sidewark,* is an error, it is masc. in the next four lines ; such errors occurred by attraction, for þibe is feminine.

þæþcan, *be in pain.* Lb. III. xviii.

þæτeþholla, masc., gen. -an, *dropsy, dropsical humour,* ὕδρωψ ὕδερος, Lb. I. xxxix. ὑδερική παρέγχυσις, Lb. II. xxi., occ. I. xliii.

þæτeþþyþτ, fem., gen. in -e, *waterwort, Callitriche verna.* In IIb. xlviii. waterwort is made Callitriche, and we may perhaps trust our botanists in their own science for this herb. The figure in MS. V. is such that it resembles Raphanus raphanistrum stripped of leaves (II). " Waterwort Callitriche verna " (Nemnich). Sir W. Hooker says Water star wort.

þæτla, masc., gen. -an, *a cloth.* Lb. II. xxii.

þaþan, *ware, iactare.* Lb. III. xviii.

þah, in þahmela, Lb. II. lii. *finc,* ohg. Wahi, mhg, Waeke, *subtilis, expolitus, venustus,* künstlich, fem. schön.

þealþyþτ, fem., gen. -e, *wallwort, dwarf elder, Sambucus ebulus,* IIb. xciii. ; but *Intuba, endive, intubus,* Gl. Cleop. fol. 53 d.

þeaþ, masc., *bowl;* Lb. II. xxiv., the same as þþeþ = Norse Hverr, masc. It translates *uter,* a waterskin, Paris Psalter, Ps. cxviii. 83.

þeaþ, masc., pl. þeaþþas, *a hard pimple on the face; a hardened callosity;* varus. " Vari parvi ac duri sunt circa faciem " tumores." Paul. Ægin., col. 444 A. Lb. I. lxxiv.

þeaþӡ-, þeaþhbþæbe, gen. -au, fem ?, *a wide spread warty eruption,* IIb. ii. 18, " ulcus," Lat. xx. 8 ; " carcinoma," Lat. Lb. I. xxxiv.

þece, *weak, debilis,* Lb. II. lii. 1 ; þace, DD. p. 425 vi. Without the final vowel, Gl. R. 115 ; Sc. 10 b ; Boet. p. 176 a ; Cædm. (if Cædm.), 154, 20 MS.

Ƿebe, *mad, furious, phreniticus*, indeclinable in IIb. i. 25, in contents *see* var. lect. ii. 21, contents iv. 10, xxxvii. 5, etc. Lb. I. lxix.

Ƿeᵹbþæbe, fem., gen. -an, properly "way- "broad," but called *waybread;* 1. *Plan- tago maior;* 2. ƿeo pape peᵹbþæbe, *plantago media*, it it hoary, hirsute. IIb. ii., Lb. II. lxv., etc.

Ƿenᵹe, Ƿænᵹe, Ƿanᵹe, neut., gen. -an, *cheek, bucca;* Matth. v. 39 ; Luke v. 29 ; Lb. I. i. 8, 10 ; III. xlvii. ; Hom. II. 180. And hum ða ponᵹan bpiceð, S.S. 140.

Ƿenn, Ƿen, *a wen*, masc., pl. pennas. Lb. I. lviii, ; III. xxx. ; Laen. 12.

Ƿenpypt, fem., gen. -e ; " wenwort," is of sorts:—1. clupihᵹ, or cloved ; Lb. I. lviii., II. li. 3. 2. eneoehᵹe, kneed ; id. I. lxvi. Wenwort must be so called from curing wens ; for wens are good, says Salmon, " Alexander, Archangel, Asarabacca. " Celandine, Chickweed, Coriander, " Crow foot, Cresses, Darnel, Endive, " Figwort, Laser wort, Lentils, Melilot, " Purslane, Thorowwax, Turnsole, " Wound wort." Among these, for 1, *Ranunculus acris*, as crow foot, *Ranun- culus ficaria*, as the lesser celandine, and for 2, Darnel, *Lolium temulentum*, are the most likely.

Ƿepmoð, gen. -es, masc., *wormwood, Arte- misia absinthium.* Lb. II. xxii., lxv. 5 ; III. iii. 2, xxxi.
Se pula pepmoð, *Anthemis cotula ?* Lb. III. viii.

Ƿice, *wych elm, Ulmus montana*, occ. Lb. I. xxxvi. Declension and gender unas- certained.

Ƿifel, masc., *a beetle.* Lb. III. xviii.
Topðpifel, *Scarabaus stercorarius*, Linn. *Geotrupes*, others Lb. III. xviii. It feeds on and lays its eggs in dung.

Ƿilbe (with final vowel), *wild, silvestris.* Ƿilbe apra. Gl. R. 21. (Lye inexact). Ƿilbe bap. Gl. R. 20. (Lye inexact). Ƿilbe oxa. Gl. R. 19, which has also pilbe cynnep hopp, 20. Ƿilbe cÿpyet.

Ƿilbe—*cont.*
Gl. R. 39, but pilb, 44. Ƿilbe popiᵹ. Gl. R. 41. Hpit pilbe pinᵹeapð. Gl. R. 39. Ƿilbe laceuce. Gl. R. 44. (Lye inexact). Ƿilbe næp. Gl. R. 42 and 44. (Lye inexact). Ƿilbe pinᵹepð. Gl. R. 39. Ƿilbe pyp. Gl. R. 11. (Lye inexact). To some of Lyes quotations are attached no references. Ƿilbðeop is a compound, sometimes written pilbeop, and the geni- tive plural is pilbðeopa. The separate words are found Nan pilbe ðeop. Hom. I. 486. Ðapað pilbe moð. S.S. 168, line 755, where moð is neuter. Lib. I. xxxvii. 2. Probably more examples of e dropped, than as above, may appear.

Ƿilpen ? or -ne ? gen. -e, *a she wolf, lupa.* Quad. ix. 7. Germ. Wölfinn. Cf. Mynecenu.

Ƿyllecæpre, -cypre, fem., gen. -an, *fenu- greek, Trigonella fœnum græcum,* from Gl. Brux. Gl. Dun.

Ƿinbelᵹтpeap, neut., gen. -ep, *windle straw, cynosnrus cristatus.* Lb. I. iii. 12. Jamieson. Nemnich. The expression " two edged" belongs perhaps to the spike. But Mylne (Indigenous Botany) did, and the author of the name, Par- kinson, must have understood *Agrostis spica venti.*

Ƿypm, masc., gen. -ep, *any creeping thing, worm, snake, dragon, mite, insect, acarus, vermin.* Lat. Vermis and Vermiculus. So multipedæ are " many foot wormes," in Hollands Plinius. The numerous worms mentioned in the Saxon text are not all lumbrici.
Anapypm. *See* Ana.
Ðanðpypm, *hand worm*, perhaps trans- lating Κειριαι as if from Χειρ. Κειριαι occurs as *lumbrici lati* in Actios, 492 c Lb. I. l. " Teredo, urcius, surio, Gl. in Lyc. Surio, or Sirio, which is the name of the itch mite in many European lan- guages, seems to me to be only Cirio from χειρ ; but at the same time an error for Κειρία. The lumbricus latus is *Tænia solium* or *Bothriocefalos latus.*

Ƿyrm—*cont.*

In Cod. Exon. p. 427, 24, it is said to be
" delved," whence the translation " earth
" worm " seemed justified.

Smoeȝapyrm, *see* letter S.

Deaƿpyrm, *dew worm*, in Lb. I. l.,
infests the feet.

Renȝpyrm, Ren–, *ringed worm*, a kind
of *belly worm*. Alex. Trallianus divides
the worms which infest the human body
into three, of which this is one. Πρῶτον
τοίνυν ἡμᾶς εἰδέναι δεῖ, ὡς τριττόν εἰρήκα-
σιν οἱ παλαιοὶ τῶν ἑλμίνθων εἶδος, ἐν μὲν
τὸ μικρὸν πάνυ καὶ λεπτόν, ὃ καλεῖν
εἰώθασιν ἀσκάριδας, δεύτερον δὲ τούτων
στρόγγυλον, καὶ τρίτον ἄλλο τὸ τῶν
πλατειῶν. Ed. Ideler, p. 315. To the
same effect M. Psellus in the same
vol. p. 241. The moderns have more
sorts. IIb. lxv. *See* Lb. I. xlviii. xlix.
They seem to derive their name from
the rings of some of them. An earthworm is Aнȝelтɼꞩece.

Ƿyrmpyrt, *wormwort*, *Sedum album* or
*villosum*. *Wilde Prick madame*. (Lyte)
Lb. I. xxxix.; J. lvii.; III. ii. 6.
Chenopodium anthelminticum is American.

Ƿyrþ, gen. –e, fem., *recovery*, *valetudo in
melius conversa*. Lb. I. iv. 5. Nu ɪꞩ
ꝥær bæꞃm cymen aɼƿeneð ro ꝼyꝛꝥe
ꞃeoɼcum eꞃꞃea, C.E. 5, line 8, *now is
that bairn come, raised up for the recovery
of the Hebrews from their miseries.* The
passage is congratulatory. C.E. 336,
line 5.

Ƿyꞃꞇung, fem., gen. –e, *a preparation of
worts*. Quad. iv. 5.

Ƿꞃꞇmæɼeꞃ ꝼyꞃꞇ, ꝥɪhꞇmæɼeꞃ ꝼyꞃꞇ, " Wiht-
" mars wort." Lb. I, ii. 13. " Britta-
" nica Vihtmeres vyrt vel heaven hin-
" dele," Gl. Dun. It may therefore be
*spoonwort*, *scurvy grass*, *Cochlearia
Anglica*. *See* Dæɼen hyðele.

Ƿɪðe– Ƿɪðopɪnðe, gen. –an, fem. ?, *withywind*, *convolvulus*, both *Conv. sepium* and
*arvensis.* Lb. I. ii. 20; J. vi. 7; I. xlix.

Ƿɪðɪȝ, masc., gen. ꝼɪðɪeꞃ, *a withy, a willow,
salix.* Lb. I. lxxiv. ÆG. 13, line 54.

Ƿonɼceaɼꞇa and ꝥa ꝼonɼceaꞇan, J.b. II.
xxxviii. and contents, may be taken either
as *lividness* or *meagreness.* The passage
of Philagrios, does not exhibit the word.

Ƿꞃæꞇꞇe, gen. –eꞃ, *crosswort, galium cruciatum.* Lb. III. i., viii. Laen. 12, 29. Wa-
rantia ꝼꝛeꞇ, gl. Leechd. vol. I. p. 376.
" Vermiculum . i . parance . i . ɼrotte,"
Gl. Harl. 978, with " cruciata maior
" warence," Gl. M. The Galium tribe
were often called by names which mark
their relationship to the Madder, thus
Vermiculus, properly the cochineal insect
used to get a red dye, transfers its name
to Madder, Rubia tinctorum, and Madder gives its appellations to the Galiums
its relatives. " Cruciata maior . i .
" warence . anglice madir," Gl. Harl.
3388.

Ƿuðubenð, –binð, gen. –eꞃ, masc. ?, *woodbind.* IIb. clxxii.; Lb. I. ii. 21; III. ii. 1;
III. xxxi., *convolvulus*, from the leaves of
the drawing, the likeness to the caper
plant, and modern usage; which, besides
convolvulus, applies the name also to the
honeysuckle.

Ƿuðu cepulle, wood chervil, cow parsley,
*Anthriscus silvestris.* Cepulle being an
English adaptation of Cerefolium, Χαιρέ-
φυλλον (Columella), and ƿuðu being
taken in the sense of our wild, we as-
certain at once, that we have here the
Chærophyllum silvestre, which Koch
and Hooker now name *Anthriscus silv.*
Nemnich agrees, and Lytes description.
In IIb. lxxxvi. wood chervil is made to
be Asparagus agrestis, and the drawings
in MSS. V., T., A. have clearly the
characteristics of *Asparagus officinalis.*
If our Saxon interpreter held his opinion
with deliberation, he differs from the
rest of our English world. Asparagus
in MS. Bodl. 130, is drawn like the
mature plant.

Ƿuðu leeꞇꞇue, masc., wood lettuce, *wild
sleepwort*, *Lactuca scariola* is IIb. xxxi.

Ꝼuꝺu leeꝛpꞇe—*cont.*

Lactuca sylvatica. Masc. G.D. 11 a. The
gloss in II. Scariola must be accepted ;
Sir J. E. Smith turns it Prickly Lettuce;
Sir W. Hooker says it is found on waste
ground in Cambridgeshire, at Southend,
Essex, and formerly near Islington. He
adds that the garden lettuce, *L.* sativa, is
not a native of this country. " Lactuca,
" letuse, slepewort, idem ; domestica et
" campestris." Also " Lactuca agrestis,
" rostrum porcinum . mylk thistell." MS.
Harl. 3388. " Lactuca silvatica idem
" wild letys, þis erbe has lenys like to a
" thystell, and they ben scharpe 't ken 't
" hit has a floure of purpure colour, 't
" hit groys in feldes 't in whet," MS.
Bodl. 536, fol. 17. The word purpure
was in early times an exact repetition
of purpureus, which the Romans applied
to any bright colour. The flower of
Lactuca scariola is yellow. Lactuca silvatica has yellow rays in MS. Bodl. 130,
but the leaves are too like sword blades.
It is there glossed Suge þhiſtel, that is,
sow thistle. " Scarola . endiua . txᵉnna
(?) lactuca agrestis," Gl. M. The
drawing in MS. T is an exact representation of *L. scariola,* glossed Branca vrsina,
to which there is resemblance.

Ꝼuꝺu poꝛe, hpoꝛe, gen. -an: 1. *Asfodelus
ramosus.* In IIb. xxxiii., liii. Woodroffe
is astula regia, that is hastula regia, the
royal sceptre, and all accounts agree that
it is a kind of onion, an asfodelaceous
plant, with a vast number of bulbs,
" LXXX. simul acervatis sæpe bulbis,"
" Plinius, xxi. 68 ; and though it has
" transferred its name to the daffodil,
" yet not that plant, *Narcissus pseudo-
" narcissus,* is its equivalent. The As-
phodelus is figured in MS. V. fol. 28 a,
but the flower is gone ; the drawing, as
much as remains, matches that in Fuchsius, p. 121. " Asphodellus, wode hone"
(*so*), MS. Harl. 3388. " Astula regia . i.
" wode rove," MS. Rawl. C. 607. " Has-
" tyca regia . i . woderofe." MS. Bodl. 536.

Ꝼuꝺu poꝛe—*cont.*

" Affodillus vude hofe," (*so*), Gl. Dun.
So Gl. M. Fuchsius makes his goldwurz,
*asfodelus lutens,* Gl. R. 40. Laen. 69.

2. *Asperula odorata,* modern usage.
In MS. Bodl. 130 ; for hastula regia is
drawn a true *Asperula,* with gloss in
14th century hand " woodrofe." " Rubea
" minor woodroff," MS. Bodl. 178.

Ꝼuꝺupoꝛe, gen. -an, fem., *wild rose, dogrose, hedgerose, rosa canina.* Lb. I.
xxxvii. 1.

Ꝼuꝺu peaxe, gen. -an, fem ? *wood wax,
wood waxen, Genista tinctoria.* Lb. I.
xlvii. 2 ; III. xxx.

Ꝼulꝛes camb, masc., gen. -es, " wolfs-
" comb," *wild teazle, Dipsacus silvestris.*
In IIb. cliii. translates χαμαιλέων, which
in elvi. is turned by pulꝛeꞧ ꝛæꝛl ; as the
teazing wool is combing it, this has no
surprise. The figure in MS. V. art. xxvi.
is a teazle, so MS. T. The equivalent
χαμαιέλαια was misunderstood by our
interpreter. However χαμαιλέων is no
teazle at all, but a stemless thistle, the
Carlina acaulis, *see* eoꝛoþhꝛoꝛu, Masc.
Laen. 3.

Ꝼullhan, *wipe with wool, lana detergere,*
Quad. vii. 4.

Ꝼunꝺel ? *a wound,* pl. punꝺela, IIb. i. 11,
cont., iv. 10, ix. 2. Ꝼunꝺelan, DD. 417,
xxiii.

Ꝼupme?, fem. ?, gen. -an, *woad, Isatis
tinctoria.* Somn. in Lex. has a gloss,
" Lutum," which is *woad.* Lb. II. lxv. 4.
Ꝼupme being properly any thing having
the power of dying, not blue, but vermilion ; and representing the vermiculi
or cochineal insects.

# Þ.

Þeapꝛ, Þeopꝛ, *wanting in something,* ἐνδεής,
*cui quid opus est,* as they interpret the
Norse þarfi. Whence 1, *poor.* 2, *un-
leavened,* of bread. 3, *skimmed,* of milk.
Lb. II. lii. 1.

Feapm, *gut*, pl. -maɼ, *guts, intestina*. But
þ smælþeapme, I.b. II. xxxi. Da ðyððe
ꞃeꞃneþ hine unð hinðeꞃepðe ſceaꞃꞇe on
ðæꞇ fmælðeapme, P.A. 55. a, *Then
Abner stabbed him with the hinder end of
his spearshaft in the small gut*. Gl. R. has
both fmælþeaþmaɼ and smæle þeaþmaɼ,
74.

Feꞃeþoꞃn, þeꞃanþoꞃn, masc., gen. -eꞃ,
" tufty thorn," *buckthorn, Rhamnus ca-
tharticus* and *R. frangula*, Lb. I. lxiv.
"Ramni, i, þeꞃeþorn," Gl. Harl. 978,
So Gl. Arundel, 42, Gl. Dun., Gl. M. M.
p. 162 a, 24.

Feꞃꞁan for þꞁꞁan, *press, pierce*, by con-
traction þyn, which see. Lb. I. xvii. 1.
Fuþſꞇe ꞛeþeꞛeðe, C.E., p. 92. line 17.
Laen. 114.

Felma, masc., gen. by analogy in -an;
Lb. I. xxxv. Foþþylmau in the Lambeth Psalter is *obscurare*. Foþðou þe
þeoꞃꞇþu ne beoð ꞃoþþylmoðe *vel* ꞃoþ-
ꞃþoꞃeene ꞇo þe : ꞎ mihꞇ ꞃꞃa ꞃꞃa dæꞁ bið
onlihꞇeð. Quia tenebræ non obscura-
buntur a te, et nox sicut dies illumina-
bitur, Ps. cxxxviii. 11. Ne þeaþꞃ he
hoþian no · þyꞃꞇꞃum ꞃoþþylmeð · þ he
þonan moꞇe, Judith x. = p. 23, line 12,
Thwaites. Combined with burning brands
of fire in Cod. Exon. p. 217, line 23 =
MS. fol. 60 a, line 4. Compare Διὰ τὸ
ἐπιφέρειν τοὺς κατὰ πνιγμὸν κινδύνους καὶ
καίειν τὴν φάρυγγα, Dioskor. iv. 156, with
Ilb. clxxxi. 2, last words. Felma and heat
go together in the Lb. In Ilb, cxl. 1, I do
not find the words the Saxon had before
him, but translate as guided by clxxxi.

Feoh hꞃeoþꞃa, masc., *kneecap*, Lorica, Gl.
Harl., *genusculum*. So " Whirl booan,
the round bone of the knee, the patella,"
Gl. to Tim Bobbin. The bone has
some similarity to lumbar and caudal
vertebræ.

Feoþ, *the dry disease*, fem., gen. -e. *See*
þeoþabl. Fem. Lb. III. xxx., contents ;
if þæþe be correct.

Feoþabl, fem., *the dry disease* or *wasting
away*. Lb. II. lxiii. A different signifi-

Feoþabl—*cont.*

cation was assigned by Somner, whose
words are " Deoþ, Ꞛeoþe, morbus qui-
" dam, fortasse, inflammatio, phlegmone.
" an inflammation, a blistering heat of
" the blood or a swelling against nature
" being hot and red." Probably this
conjecture of Somners was founded
partly on the etymological considerations
which follow. Feoþ seems to have for
its kindred words þyþ *dry*, þyþꞃꞇ *thirst*,
that is, *dryness*, the German dorre, *dry*,
and a large number of other words, for
which *see* Spoon and Sparrow, arts 478,
592, etc. In the German Dürrsucht
(*dry sickness*) *atrophy, meagreness, consumption*, the withering effects of dryness have produced the expression. The
Latin equivalent for these ideas would
be Tabes, which is treated of by Celsus
(iii. 22) as having for its species ἀτροφία,
*atrophy*, καχεξία, *corrupt habit of body*,
and φθίσις, consumption. Feoþabl ap-
pearing in the feet, Lb. xlvii., is Tabes
in pedibus, such a wasting away of the
feet as arises from ulceration produced
by an over long journey on foot. That
the disease is spoken of as local sometimes follows from the teaching of
Celsus : " Huic (scil. cachexiæ) præter
" tabem, illud quoque nonnunquam ac-
" cidere solet, ut per assiduas pustulas
" aut ulcera, summa cutis exasperetur,
" vel aliquæ corporis partes intumes-
" cant." That worms belong to the
disease is paralleled in German, which
has its Dürremäden, worms which cause
a meagre habit and atrophy.

Feoþþyþꞇ, ðyoþþyþꞇ, fem., gen. -e, *plough-
man's spikenard, Inula conyza*, formerly
called C. squarrosa, Germ. Durrwurz,
Doorkrant ; which is as above. Lb. III.
xxx. Laen. 40.

Þymel, *a thumbstall*. Lb. I. lxxv. Thimble
is the same word, the material is not in
the syllables. Cf. Germ. Däumling, *a
thumbstall*; Dutch, Duymelinck, *teymen
sive munimen pollicis, theca pollicis*

Þymel—cont.

(Kilian). Þymel seems to have been originally an adjective, hence its use in Laws of Ine. xlix. Duymelinck in Kilian is also a wren, *a bird as big as ones thumb.*

Þýn, præt. þýðe, p. part. þýð; *squeeze, press, stab.* Lb. II. iii. v., Quadr. vi. 15. Norse at þjá. The infinitive þýðan of dictionaries has no existence. Geþýn, *squeeze,* Solom. and Sat. p. 150, line 34. Geþýð, id. p. 162, line 607. *See* Aþyn. It is a contraction of þigan. Beda, 611, 41. The present Ic þi, *fodio,* ÆG. 32, line 45.

Þinan, *grow moist;* the intransitive to þænan, *moisten,* as Lb. I. ii. 21.

Þure þistel, masc., gen. -les; "tufty thistle," *sow thistle, sonchus oleraceus, Bot.* Also þuþistel, Germ. Dudistel, Lb. III. viii.

Þunopclappe, fem., gen. -an; *bugle, aiuga reptans,* if we may rely on a gl. Leechdoms, vol. I. p. 374. "Consolida media, þundre clouere," Gl. Harl. 978. On consolida media, *see* Fuchsius, p. 386.

Þunorwyrt, fem., gen. -e, *houseleek, sempervivum tectorum,* so called from its averting thunderbolts; Grimm. Mythol. clxi.: an allusion to this is found in some copies of Dioskorides, iv. 189.

Þunwange, -wenge, gen. -an, neut. as wenge, *temple. timpus.* Lb. I. i. 8; III. 1.

Þunwange—cont.

Plural in -ge. Lb. III. xli. Gerloh þa mið annm byrle bugan hir þunwengan, Judges iv. 21, where, I presume, bugan is not for begen, but rather begeonð. ÆG. 12, line 16.

Þwænan, *make to dwindle, minuere,* it appears IIb. ii. 7, compared with Dwinan, IIb. ii. 4. So Lb. I. xxxi. 1. This signification now seems too conjectural.

2. *To soften, mollire.* Tiloðen hir læcar ꝺ ðone yrule mið yealrum ꝺ mið beþenum geþþænan þolðon, Bed., 611, 19, *Curabant medici hunc appositis pigmentorum fomentis emollire.* Ðone unʒeþþænan ryýle mið ðyʒðe ꝺ ðpende, ibid, line 40, *Tumorem illum infestum horum appositione comprimere ac mollire curabat.*

3. *Irrigate.* For þam ʒir þ þærery hi ne geþþænðe, ðonne ðruʒoðe hio, etc. Boet. p. 78, line 27. *If the water had not irrigated her,* the earth, *she would have got dry, etc.* Ða aðruʒoðan heortan ʒeðpænan mið ðæm rlorenðan yðon hir lape, P.A. 14 a, *Corda arentia doctrinæ fluentis irrigare.* Donne rio mildheortnes ðær lareorer geðpænð ꝺ ʒeleeð ða breost ðær ʒelnerenðer, P.A. 27 a, *Quando hoc in audientis pectore pietas prædicantis rigat.* Cf. þænan.

Þrepan, *turn.* See geþþepan.

# INDEX OF PROPER NAMES.

LONDON :
Printed by GEORGE E. EYRE and WILLIAM SPOTTISWOODE,
Printers to the Queen's most Excellent Majesty.

For Her Majesty's Stationery Office.

[2508.—1000.—1/65.]

# LIST OF WORKS

By the late Record and State Paper Commissioners,
or under the Direction of the Right Honourable
the Master of the Rolls, which may be pur-
chased of Messrs. Longman and Co., London;
Messrs. J. H. and J. Parker, Oxford and London; Messrs. Macmillan and Co., Cambridge and
London; Messrs. A. and C. Black, Edinburgh;
and Mr. A. Thom, Dublin.

---

## PUBLIC RECORDS AND STATE PAPERS.

---

ROTULORUM ORIGINALIUM IN CURIA SCACCARII ABBREVIATIO. Henry
III.—Edward III. *Edited by* HENRY PLAYFORD, Esq. 2 vols
folio (1805—1810). *Price* 25s. boards, or 12s. 6d. each.

CALENDARIUM INQUISITIONUM POST MORTEM SIVE ESCAETARUM.
Henry III.—Richard III. *Edited by* JOHN CALEY and JOHN
BAYLEY, Esqrs. Vols. 2, 3, and 4, folio (1806—1808; 1821—1828),
boards : vols. 2 and 3, *price* 21s. each; vol. 4, *price* 24s.

LIBRORUM MANUSCRIPTORUM BIBLIOTHECÆ HARLEIANÆ CATALOGUS.
Vol. 4. *Edited by* The Rev. T. HARTWELL HORNE. (1812), folio,
boards. *Price* 18s.

ABBREVIATIO PLACITORUM, Richard I.—Edward II. *Edited by* The
Right Hon. GEORGE ROSE and W. ILLINGWORTH, Esq. 1 vol.
folio (1811), boards. *Price* 18s.

LIBRI CENSUALIS vocati DOMESDAY-BOOK, INDICES. *Edited by* Sir
HENRY ELLIS. Folio (1816), boards (Domesday-Book, vol. 3).
*Price* 21s.

LIBRI CENSUALIS vocati DOMESDAY-BOOK, ADDITAMENTA EX CODIC.
ANTIQUISS. *Edited by* Sir HENRY ELLIS. Folio (1816), boards
(Domesday-Book, vol. 4). *Price* 21s.

[LEECH O. II.]                                      D D

STATUTES OF THE REALM, large folio. Vols. 4 (in 2 parts), 7, 8, 9, 10, and 11, including 2 vols. of Indices (1819—1828). *Edited by* Sir T. E. TOMLINS, JOHN RAITHBY, JOHN CALEY, and WM. ELLIOTT, Esqrs. *Price* 31s. 6d. each; except the Alphabetical and Chronological Indices, *price* 30s. each.

VALOR ECCLESIASTICUS, temp. Henry VIII., Auctoritate Regia institutus. *Edited by* JOHN CALEY, Esq., and the Rev. JOSEPH HUNTER. Vols. 3 to 6, folio (1810, &c.), boards. *Price* 25s. each.

\*\*\* The Introduction is also published in 8vo., cloth. *Price* 2s. 6d.

ROTULI SCOTIÆ IN TURRI LONDINENSI ET IN DOMO CAPITULARI WESTMONASTERIENSI ASSERVATI. 19 Edward I.—Henry VIII. *Edited by* DAVID MACPHERSON, JOHN CALEY, and W. ILLINGWORTH, Esqrs., and the Rev. T. HARTWELL HORNE. 2 vols. folio (1814 —1819), boards. *Price* 42s.

" FŒDERA, CONVENTIONES, LITTERÆ," &c. ; or, Rymer's Fœdera, New Edition. 1066—1377. Vol. 2, Part 2, and Vol. 3, Parts 1 and 2. folio (1821—1830). *Edited by* JOHN CALEY and FRED. HOLBROOKE, Esqrs. *Price* 21s. each Part.

DUCATUS LANCASTRIÆ CALENDARIUM INQUISITIONUM POST MORTEM, &c. Part 3, Calendar to the Pleadings. &c., Henry VII.—Ph. and Mary ; and Calendar to the Pleadings, 1—13 Elizabeth. Part 4, Calendar to the Pleadings to end of Elizabeth. (1827— 1834.) *Edited by* R. J. HARPER, JOHN CALEY, and WM. MINCHIN, Esqrs. Folio, boards, Part 3 (or Vol. 2), *price* 31s. 6d. ; and Part 4 (or Vol. 3), *price* 21s.

CALENDARS OF THE PROCEEDINGS IN CHANCERY, IN THE REIGN OF QUEEN ELIZABETH; to which are prefixed, Examples of earlier Proceedings in that Court from Richard II. to Elizabeth, from the Originals in the Tower. *Edited by* JOHN BAYLEY, Esq. Vols. 2 and 3 (1830—1832), folio, boards, *price* 21s. each.

PARLIAMENTARY WRITS AND WRITS OF MILITARY SUMMONS, together with the Records and Muniments relating to the Suit and Service due and performed to the King's High Court of Parliament and the Councils of the Realm. Edward I., II. *Edited by* Sir FRANCIS PALGRAVE. (1830—1834.) Folio, boards, Vol. 2, Division 1, Edward II., *price* 21s. ; Vol. 2, Division 2, *price* 21s.; Vol. 2, Division 3, *price* 42s.

ROTULI LITTERARUM CLAUSARUM IN TURRI LONDINENSI ASSERVATI. 2 vols. folio (1833—1844). The first volume, 1204—1224. The second volume, 1224—1227. *Edited by* THOMAS DUFFUS HARDY, Esq. *Price* 81s., cloth ; or separately, Vol. 1, *price* 63s.; Vol. 2, *price* 18s.

Proceedings and Ordinances of the Privy Council of England, 10 Richard II.—33 Henry VIII. *Edited by* Sir N. Harris Nicolas. 7 vols. royal 8vo. (1834—1837), cloth. *Price* 98*s.* ; or separately, 14*s.* each.

Rotuli Litterarum Patentium in Turri Londinensi asservati, 1201—1216. *Edited by* Thomas Duffus Hardy, Esq. 1 vol. folio (1835), cloth. *Price* 31*s.* 6*d.*
  \*\*\* The Introduction is also published in 8vo., cloth. *Price* 9*s.*

Rotuli Curiæ Regis. Rolls and Records of the Court held before the King's Justiciars or Justices. 6 Richard I.—1 John. *Edited by* Sir Francis Palgrave. 2 vols. royal 8vo. (1835), cloth. *Price* 28*s.*

Rotuli Normanniæ in Turri Londinensi asservati, 1200—1205 ; also, 1417 to 1418. *Edited by* Thomas Duffus Hardy, Esq. 1 vol. royal 8vo. (1835), cloth. *Price* 12*s.* 6*d.*

Rotuli de Oblatis et Finibus in Turri Londinensi asservati, tempore Regis Johannis. *Edited by* Thomas Duffus Hardy, Esq. 1 vol. royal 8vo. (1835), cloth. *Price* 18*s.*

Excerpta e Rotulis Finium in Turri Londinensi asservatis. Henry III., 1216—1272. *Edited by* Charles Roberts, Esq. 2 vols. royal 8vo. (1835, 1836), cloth, *price* 32*s.* ; or separately, Vol. 1, *price* 14*s.* ; Vol. 2, *price* 18*s.*

Fines, sive Pedes Finium ; sive Finales Concordiæ in Curiâ Domini Regis. 7 Richard I.—16 John (1195—1214). *Edited by* the Rev. Joseph Hunter. In Counties. 2 vols. royal 8vo. (1835—1844), cloth, *price* 11*s.*; or separately, Vol. 1, *price* 8*s.* 6*d.*; Vol. 2, *price* 2*s.* 6*d.*

Ancient Kalendars and Inventories of the Treasury of His Majesty's Exchequer ; together with Documents illustrating the History of that Repository. *Edited by* Sir Francis Palgrave. 3 vols. royal 8vo. (1836), cloth. *Price* 42*s.*

Documents and Records illustrating the History of Scotland. and the Transactions between the Crowns of Scotland and England ; preserved in the Treasury of Her Majesty's Exchequer. *Edited by* Sir Francis Palgrave. 1 vol. royal 8vo. (1837), cloth. *Price* 18*s.*

Rotuli Chartarum in Turri Londinensi asservati, 1199—1216. *Edited by* Thomas Duffus Hardy, Esq. 1 vol. folio (1837), cloth. *Price* 30*s.*

Report of the Proceedings of the Record Commissioners. 1831 to 1837. 1 vol. folio, boards. *Price* 8*s.*

REGISTRUM vulgariter nuncupatum "The Record of Caernarvon," e codice MS. Harleiano, 696, descriptum. *Edited by* Sir HENRY ELLIS. 1 vol. folio (1838), cloth. *Price* 31s. 6d.

ANCIENT LAWS AND INSTITUTES OF ENGLAND ; comprising Laws enacted under the Anglo-Saxon Kings, from Æthelbirht to Cnut, with an English Translation of the Saxon ; the Laws called Edward the Confessor's ; the Laws of William the Conqueror, and those ascribed to Henry the First ; also, Monumenta Ecclesiastica Anglicana, from the 7th to the 10th century ; and the Ancient Latin Version of the Anglo-Saxon Laws ; with a compendious Glossary, &c. *Edited by* BENJAMIN THORPE, Esq. 1 vol. folio (1840), cloth. *Price* 40s. Or, in 2 vols. royal 8vo. cloth. *Price* 30s.

ANCIENT LAWS AND INSTITUTES OF WALES; comprising Laws supposed to be enacted by Howel the Good ; modified by subsequent Regulations under the Native Princes, prior to the Conquest by Edward the First ; and anomalous Laws, consisting principally of Institutions which, by the Statute of Ruddlan, were admitted to continue in force. With an English Translation of the Welsh Text. To which are added, a few Latin Transcripts, containing Digests of the Welsh Laws, principally of the Dimetian Code. With Indices and Glossary. *Edited by* ANEURIN OWEN, Esq. 1 vol. folio (1841), cloth. *Price* 44s. Or, in 2 vols. royal 8vo. cloth. *Price* 36s.

ROTULI DE LIBERATE AC DE MISIS ET PRÆSTITIS, Regnante Johanne. *Edited by* THOMAS DUFFUS HARDY, Esq. 1 vol. royal 8vo. (1844), cloth. *Price* 6s.

THE GREAT ROLLS OF THE PIPE FOR THE SECOND, THIRD, AND FOURTH YEARS OF THE REIGN OF KING HENRY THE SECOND, 1155—1158. *Edited by* the Rev. JOSEPH HUNTER. 1 vol. royal 8vo. (1844), cloth. *Price* 4s. 6d.

THE GREAT ROLL OF THE PIPE FOR THE FIRST YEAR OF THE REIGN OF KING RICHARD THE FIRST, 1189—1190. *Edited by* the Rev. JOSEPH HUNTER. 1 vol. royal 8vo. (1844), cloth. *Price* 6s.

DOCUMENTS ILLUSTRATIVE OF ENGLISH HISTORY in the 13th and 14th centuries, selected from the Records in the Exchequer. *Edited by* HENRY COLE, Esq. 1 vol. fcp. folio (1844), cloth. *Price* 45s. 6d.

MODUS TENENDI PARLIAMENTUM. An Ancient Treatise on the Mode of holding the Parliament in England. *Edited by* THOMAS DUFFUS HARDY, Esq. 1 vol. 8vo. (1846), cloth. *Price* 2s. 6d.

MONUMENTA HISTORICA BRITANNICA, or, Materials for the History of Britain from the earliest period. Vol. 1, extending to the Norman Conquest. Prepared, and illustrated with Notes, by the late HENRY PETRIE, Esq., F.S.A., Keeper of the Records in the Tower of London, assisted by the Rev. JOHN SHARPE, Rector of Castle Eaton, Wilts. Finally completed for publication, and with an Introduction, by THOMAS DUFFUS HARDY, Esq., Assistant Keeper of Records. (Printed by command of Her Majesty.) Folio (1848). *Price* 42s.

REGISTRUM MAGNI SIGILLI REGUM SCOTORUM in Archivis Publicis asservatum. 1306—1424. *Edited by* THOMAS THOMSON, Esq. Folio (1814). *Price* 15s.

THE ACTS OF THE PARLIAMENTS OF SCOTLAND. 11 vols. folio (1814—1844). Vol. I. *Edited by* THOMAS THOMSON and COSMO INNES, Esqrs. *Price* 42s. Also, Vols. 4, 7, 8, 9, 10, 11 ; *price* 10s. 6d. each.

THE ACTS OF THE LORDS AUDITORS OF CAUSES AND COMPLAINTS. 1466—1494. *Edited by* THOMAS THOMSON, Esq. Folio (1839). *Price* 10s. 6d.

THE ACTS OF THE LORDS OF COUNCIL IN CIVIL CAUSES. 1478—1495. *Edited by* THOMAS THOMSON, Esq. Folio (1839). *Price* 10s. 6d.

ISSUE ROLL OF THOMAS DE BRANTINGHAM, Bishop of Exeter, Lord High Treasurer of England, containing Payments out of His Majesty's Revenue, 44 Edward III., 1370. *Edited by* FREDERICK DEVON, Esq. 1 vol. 4to. (1835), cloth. *Price* 35s. Or, in royal 8vo. cloth. *Price* 25s.

ISSUES OF THE EXCHEQUER, containing similar matter to the above; James I.; extracted from the Pell Records. *Edited by* FREDERICK DEVON, Esq. 1 vol. 4to. (1836), cloth. *Price* 30s. Or, in royal 8vo. cloth. *Price* 21s.

ISSUES OF THE EXCHEQUER, containing similar matter to the above ; Henry III.—Henry VI. ; extracted from the Pell Records. *Edited by* FREDERICK DEVON, Esq. 1 vol. 4to. (1837), cloth. *Price* 40s. Or, in royal 8vo. cloth. *Price* 30s.

NOTES OF MATERIALS FOR THE HISTORY OF PUBLIC DEPARTMENTS. *By* F. S. THOMAS, Esq., Secretary of the Public Record Office. Demy folio (1846), cloth. *Price* 10s.

HANDBOOK TO THE PUBLIC RECORDS. *By* F. S. THOMAS, Esq. Royal 8vo. (1853), cloth. *Price* 12s.

STATE PAPERS DURING THE REIGN OF HENRY THE EIGHTH. 11 vols. 4to., cloth, (1830—1852), with Indices of Persons and Places. *Price 5l. 15s. 6d.* ; or separately, *price 10s. 6d.* each.

> Vol. I.—Domestic Correspondence.
> Vols. II. & III.—Correspondence relating to Ireland.
> Vols. IV. & V.—Correspondence relating to Scotland.
> Vols. VI. to XI.—Correspondence between England and Foreign Courts.

HISTORICAL NOTES RELATIVE TO THE HISTORY OF ENGLAND; from the Accession of Henry VIII. to the Death of Queen Anne (1509 —1714). Designed as a Book of instant Reference for ascertaining the Dates of Events mentioned in History and Manuscripts. The Name of every Person and Event mentioned in History within the above period is placed in Alphabetical and Chronological Order, and the Authority whence taken is given in each case, whether from Printed History or from Manuscripts. *By* F. S. THOMAS, Esq. 3 vols. 8vo. (1856), cloth. *Price 40s.*

---

## *In the Press.*

CALENDARIUM GENEALOGICUM ; for the Reigns of Henry III. and Edward I. *Edited by* CHARLES ROBERTS, Esq.

---

# CALENDARS OF STATE PAPERS.

[IMPERIAL 8vo.  *Price* 15s. each Volume or Part.]

CALENDAR OF STATE PAPERS, DOMESTIC SERIES, OF THE REIGNS OF EDWARD VI., MARY, and ELIZABETH, preserved in Her Majesty's Public Record Office. *Edited by* ROBERT LEMON, Esq., F.S.A. 1856.
> Vol. I.—1547–1580.

CALENDAR OF STATE PAPERS, DOMESTIC SERIES, OF THE REIGN OF JAMES I., preserved in Her Majesty's Public Record Office. *Edited by* MARY ANNE EVERETT GREEN. 1857–1859.
> Vol. I.—1603–1610.
> Vol. II.—1611–1618.
> Vol. III.—1619–1623.
> Vol. IV.—1623–1625, with Addenda.

CALENDAR OF STATE PAPERS, DOMESTIC SERIES, OF THE REIGN OF CHARLES I., preserved in Her Majesty's Public Record Office. *Edited by* JOHN BRUCE, Esq., V.P.S.A. 1858–1864.
> Vol. I.—1625–1626.
> Vol. II.—1627–1628.
> Vol. III.—1628–1629.
> Vol. IV.—1629–1631.
> Vol. V.—1631–1633.
> Vol. VI.—1633–1634.
> Vol. VII.—1634–1635.

CALENDAR OF STATE PAPERS, DOMESTIC SERIES, OF THE REIGN OF CHARLES II., preserved in Her Majesty's Public Record Office. *Edited by* MARY ANNE EVERETT GREEN. 1860–1864.
> Vol. I.—1660–1661.
> Vol. II.—1661–1662.
> Vol. III.—1663–1664.
> Vol. IV.—1664–1665.
> Vol. V.—1665–1666.
> Vol. VI.—1666–1667.

CALENDAR OF STATE PAPERS relating to SCOTLAND, preserved in Her Majesty's Public Record Office. *Edited by* MARKHAM JOHN THORPE, Esq., of St. Edmund Hall, Oxford. 1858.
> Vol. I., the Scottish Series, of the Reigns of Henry VIII., Edward VI., Mary, and Elizabeth, 1509–1589.
> Vol. II., the Scottish Series, of the Reign of Elizabeth, 1589–1603 ; an Appendix to the Scottish Series, 1543–1592 ; and the State Papers relating to Mary Queen of Scots during her Detention in England, 1568–1587.

CALENDAR OF STATE PAPERS relating to IRELAND, preserved in Her Majesty's Public Record Office. *Edited by* HANS CLAUDE HAMILTON, Esq., F.S.A. 1860.

Vol. I.—1509–1573.

CALENDAR OF STATE PAPERS, COLONIAL SERIES, preserved in Her Majesty's Public Record Office, and elsewhere. *Edited by* W. NOEL SAINSBURY, Esq. 1860–1862.

Vol. I.—America and West Indies, 1574–1660.
Vol. II.—East Indies, China, and Japan, 1513–1616.

CALENDAR OF LETTERS AND PAPERS, FOREIGN AND DOMESTIC, OF THE REIGN OF HENRY VIII., preserved in the Public Record Office, the British Museum, &c. *Edited by* J. S. BREWER, M.A., Professor of English Literature, King's College, London. 1862–1864.

Vol. I.—1509–1514.
Vol. II. (in Two Parts),—1515–1518.

CALENDAR OF STATE PAPERS, FOREIGN SERIES, OF THE REIGN OF EDWARD VI. *Edited by* W. B. TURNBULL, Esq., of Lincoln's Inn, Barrister-at-Law, and Correspondant du Comité Impérial des Travaux Historiques et des Sociétés Savantes de France. 1861.

CALENDAR OF STATE PAPERS, FOREIGN SERIES, OF THE REIGN OF MARY. *Edited by* W. B. TURNBULL, Esq., of Lincoln's Inn, Barrister-at-Law, and Correspondant du Comité Impérial des Travaux Historiques et des Sociétés Savantes de France. 1861.

CALENDAR OF STATE PAPERS, FOREIGN SERIES, OF THE REIGN OF ELIZABETH. *Edited by* the Rev. JOSEPH STEVENSON, M.A., of University College, Durham. 1863.

Vol. I.—1558–1559.

CALENDAR OF LETTERS, DESPATCHES, AND STATE PAPERS relating to the Negotiations between England and Spain, preserved in the Archives at Simancas, and elsewhere. *Edited by* G. A. BERGENROTH. 1862.

Vol. I.—Hen. VII.—1485–1509.

CALENDAR OF STATE PAPERS AND MANUSCRIPTS, relating to ENGLISH AFFAIRS, preserved in the Archives of Venice, &c. *Edited by* RAWDON BROWN, Esq. 1864.

Vol. I.—1202–1509.

---

## In the Press.

CALENDAR OF STATE PAPERS relating to IRELAND, preserved in Her Majesty's Public Record Office. *Edited by* HANS CLAUDE HAMILTON, Esq., F.S.A. Vol. II.—1574–1585.

CALENDAR OF STATE PAPERS, DOMESTIC SERIES, OF THE REIGN OF ELIZABETH (continued), preserved in Her Majesty's Public Record Office. *Edited by* ROBERT LEMON, Esq., F.S.A. 1580–1590.

CALENDAR OF STATE PAPERS, FOREIGN SERIES, OF THE REIGN OF ELIZABETH. *Edited by* the Rev. JOSEPH STEVENSON, M.A., of University College, Durham. Vol. II.—1559–1560.

CALENDAR OF STATE PAPERS, DOMESTIC SERIES, OF THE REIGN OF CHARLES I., preserved in Her Majesty's Public Record Office. *Edited by* JOHN BRUCE, Esq., F.S.A. Vol. VIII.

CALENDAR OF LETTERS AND PAPERS, FOREIGN AND DOMESTIC, OF THE REIGN OF HENRY VIII., preserved in Her Majesty's Public Record Office, the British Museum, &c. *Edited by* J. S. BREWER, M.A., Professor of English Literature, King's College, London. Vol. III.—1519, &c.

CALENDAR OF STATE PAPERS, DOMESTIC SERIES, OF THE REIGN OF CHARLES II., preserved in Her Majesty's Public Record Office. *Edited by* MARY ANNE EVERETT GREEN. Vol. VII.—1667–1668.

CALENDAR OF STATE PAPERS AND MANUSCRIPTS, relating to ENGLISH AFFAIRS, preserved in the Archives of Venice, &c. *Edited by* RAWDON BROWN, Esq. Vol. II.

---

## *In Progress.*

CALENDAR OF LETTERS, DESPATCHES, AND STATE PAPERS relating to the Negotiations between England and Spain, preserved in the Archives at Simancas, and elsewhere. *Edited by* G. A. BERGENROTH. Vol. II.—Henry VIII.

CALENDAR OF STATE PAPERS, COLONIAL SERIES, preserved in Her Majesty's Public Record Office, and elsewhere. *Edited by* W. NOËL SAINSBURY, Esq. Vol. III.—East Indies, China, and Japan.

---

# THE CHRONICLES AND MEMORIALS OF GREAT BRITAIN AND IRELAND DURING THE MIDDLE AGES.

[ROYAL 8vo.   *Price* 10s. each Volume or Part.]

1. THE CHRONICLE OF ENGLAND, by JOHN CAPGRAVE. *Edited by* the Rev. F. C. HINGESTON, M.A., of Exeter College, Oxford. 1858.

2. CHRONICON MONASTERII DE ABINGDON. Vols. I. and II. *Edited by* the Rev. JOSEPH STEVENSON, M.A., of University College, Durham, and Vicar of Leighton Buzzard. 1858.

3. LIVES OF EDWARD THE CONFESSOR. I.—La Estoire de Seint Aedward le Rei. II.—Vita Beati Edvardi Regis et Confessoris. III.—Vita Æduuardi Regis qui apud Westmonasterium requiescit. *Edited by* HENRY RICHARDS LUARD, M.A., Fellow and Assistant Tutor of Trinity College, Cambridge. 1858.

4. MONUMENTA FRANCISCANA; scilicet, I.—Thomas de Eccleston de Adventu Fratrum Minorum in Angliam. II.—Adæ de Marisco Epistolæ. III.—Registrum Fratrum Minorum Londoniæ. *Edited by* J. S. BREWER, M.A., Professor of English Literature, King's College, London. 1858.

5. FASCICULI ZIZANIORUM MAGISTRI JOHANNIS WYCLIF CUM TRITICO. Ascribed to THOMAS NETTER, of WALDEN, Provincial of the Carmelite Order in England, and Confessor to King Henry the Fifth. *Edited by* the Rev. W. W. SHIRLEY, M.A., Tutor and late Fellow of Wadham College, Oxford. 1858.

6. THE BUIK OF THE CRONICLIS OF SCOTLAND; or, A Metrical Version of the History of Hector Boece; by WILLIAM STEWART. Vols. I., II., and III. *Edited by* W. B. TURNBULL, Esq., of Lincoln's Inn, Barrister-at-Law. 1858.

7. JOHANNIS CAPGRAVE LIBER DE ILLUSTRIBUS HENRICIS. *Edited by* the Rev. F. C. HINGESTON, M.A., of Exeter College, Oxford. 1858.

8. HISTORIA MONASTERII S. AUGUSTINI CANTUARIENSIS, by THOMAS OF ELMHAM, formerly Monk and Treasurer of that Foundation. *Edited by* CHARLES HARDWICK, M.A., Fellow of St. Catharine's Hall, and Christian Advocate in the University of Cambridge. 1858.

9. EULOGIUM (HISTORIARUM SIVE TEMPORIS): Chronicon ab Orbe condito usque ad Annum Domini 1366; a Monacho quodam Malmesbiriensi exaratum. Vols. I., II., and III. *Edited by* F. S. HAYDON, Esq., B.A. 1858–1863.

10. MEMORIALS OF HENRY THE SEVENTH: Bernardi Andreæ Tholosatis Vita Regis Henrici Septimi; necnon alia quædam ad eundem Regem spectantia. *Edited by* JAMES GAIRDNER, Esq. 1858.

11. MEMORIALS OF HENRY THE FIFTH. I.—Vita Henrici Quinti, Roberto Redmanno auctore. II.—Versus Rhythmici in laudem Regis Henrici Quinti. III.—Elmhami Liber Metricus de Henrico V. *Edited by* C. A. COLE, Esq. 1858.

12. MUNIMENTA GILDHALLÆ LONDONIENSIS; Liber Albus, Liber Custumarum, et Liber Horn, in archivis Gildhallæ asservati. Vol. I., Liber Albus. Vol. II. (in Two Parts), Liber Custumarum. Vol. III., Translation of the Anglo-Norman Passages in Liber Albus, Glossaries, Appendices, and Index. *Edited by* HENRY THOMAS RILEY, Esq., M.A., Barrister-at-Law. 1859–1860.

13. CHRONICA JOHANNIS DE OXENEDES. *Edited by* Sir HENRY ELLIS, K.H. 1859.

14. A COLLECTION OF POLITICAL POEMS AND SONGS RELATING TO ENGLISH HISTORY, FROM THE ACCESSION OF EDWARD III. TO THE REIGN OF HENRY VIII. Vols. I. and II. *Edited by* THOMAS WRIGHT, Esq., M.A. 1859–1861.

15. The "OPUS TERTIUM," "OPUS MINUS," &c., of ROGER BACON. *Edited by* J. S. BREWER, M.A., Professor of English Literature, King's College, London. 1859.

16. BARTHOLOMÆI DE COTTON, MONACHI NORWICENSIS, HISTORIA ANGLICANA (A.D. 449—1298). *Edited by* HENRY RICHARDS LUARD, M.A., Fellow and Assistant Tutor of Trinity College, Cambridge. 1859.

17. BRUT Y TYWYSOGION; or, The Chronicle of the Princes of Wales. *Edited by* the Rev. J. WILLIAMS AB ITHEL. 1860.

18. A COLLECTION OF ROYAL AND HISTORICAL LETTERS DURING THE REIGN OF HENRY IV. Vol. I. *Edited by* the Rev. F. C. HINGESTON, M.A., of Exeter College, Oxford. 1860.

19. THE REPRESSOR OF OVER MUCH BLAMING OF THE CLERGY. By REGINALD PECOCK, sometime Bishop of Chichester. Vols. I. and II. *Edited by* CHURCHILL BABINGTON, B.D., Fellow of St. John's College, Cambridge. 1860.

20. ANNALES CAMBRIÆ. *Edited by* the Rev. J. WILLIAMS AB ITHEL. 1860.

21. THE WORKS OF GIRALDUS CAMBRENSIS. Vols. I., II., and III. *Edited by* J. S. BREWER, M.A., Professor of English Literature, King's College, London. 1861–1863.

22. LETTERS AND PAPERS ILLUSTRATIVE OF THE WARS OF THE ENGLISH IN FRANCE DURING THE REIGN OF HENRY THE SIXTH, KING OF ENGLAND. Vol. I., and Vol. II. (in Two Parts). *Edited by* the Rev. JOSEPH STEVENSON, M.A., of University College, Durham, and Vicar of Leighton Buzzard. 1861–1864.

23. THE ANGLO-SAXON CHRONICLE, ACCORDING TO THE SEVERAL ORIGINAL AUTHORITIES. Vol. I., Original Texts. Vol. II., Translation. *Edited by* BENJAMIN THORPE, Esq., Member of the Royal Academy of Sciences at Munich, and of the Society of Netherlandish Literature at Leyden. 1861.

24. LETTERS AND PAPERS ILLUSTRATIVE OF THE REIGNS OF RICHARD III. AND HENRY VII. Vols. I. and II. *Edited by* JAMES GAIRDNER, Esq. 1861–1863.

25. LETTERS OF BISHOP GROSSETESTE, illustrative of the Social Condition of his Time. *Edited by* HENRY RICHARDS LUARD, M.A., Fellow and Assistant Tutor of Trinity College, Cambridge. 1861.

26. DESCRIPTIVE CATALOGUE OF MANUSCRIPTS RELATING TO THE HISTORY OF GREAT BRITAIN AND IRELAND. Vol. I. (in Two Parts) ; Anterior to the Norman Invasion. *By* THOMAS DUFFUS HARDY, Esq., Deputy Keeper of the Public Records. 1862.

27. ROYAL AND OTHER HISTORICAL LETTERS ILLUSTRATIVE OF THE REIGN OF HENRY III. From the Originals in the Public Record Office. Vol. I., 1216–1235. *Selected and edited by* the Rev. W. W. SHIRLEY, Tutor and late Fellow of Wadham College, Oxford. 1862.

28. THE SAINT ALBAN'S CHRONICLES :—THE ENGLISH HISTORY OF THOMAS WALSINGHAM, MONK OF SAINT ALBAN'S. Vol. I., 1272–1381. Vol. II., 1381–1422. *Edited by* HENRY THOMAS RILEY, Esq., M.A., Barrister-at-Law. 1863–1864.

29. CHRONICON ABBATIÆ EVESHAMENSIS, AUCTORIBUS DOMINICO PRIORE EVESHAMIÆ ET THOMA DE MARLEBERGE ABBATE, A FUNDATIONE AD ANNUM 1213, UNA CUM CONTINUATIONE AD ANNUM 1418. *Edited by* the Rev. W. D. MACRAY, M.A., Bodleian Library, Oxford. 1863.

30. RICARDI DE CIRENCESTRIA SPECULUM HISTORIALE DE GESTIS REGUM ANGLIÆ. Vol. I., 447–871. *Edited by* JOHN E. B. MAYOR, M.A., Fellow and Assistant Tutor of St. John's College, Cambridge. 1863.

31. YEAR BOOKS OF THE REIGN OF EDWARD THE FIRST. Years 30–31, and 32–33. *Edited and translated by* ALFRED JOHN HORWOOD, Esq., of the Middle Temple, Barrister-at-Law. 1863–1864.

32. NARRATIVES OF THE EXPULSION OF THE ENGLISH FROM NORMANDY, 1449-1450.—Robertus Blondelli de Reductione Normanniæ: Le Recouvrement de Normendie, par Berry, Herault du Roy: Conferences between the Ambassadors of France and England. *Edited, from MSS. in the Imperial Library at Paris, by* the Rev. JOSEPH STEVENSON, M.A., of University College, Durham. 1863.

33. HISTORIA ET CARTULARIUM MONASTERII S. PETRI GLOUCESTRIÆ. Vol. I. *Edited by* W. H. HART, Esq., F.S.A. ; Membre correspondant de la Société des Antiquaires de Normandie. 1863.

34. ALEXANDRI NECKAM DE NATURIS RERUM LIBRI DUO ; with NECKAM'S POEM, DE LAUDIBUS DIVINÆ SAPIENTIÆ. *Edited by* THOMAS WRIGHT, Esq., M.A. 1863.

35. LEECHDOMS, WORTCUNNING, AND STARCRAFT OF EARLY ENGLAND ; being a Collection of Documents illustrating the History of Science in this Country before the Norman Conquest. Vols. I. and II. *Collected and edited by* the Rev. T. OSWALD COCKAYNE, M.A., of St. John's College, Cambridge. 1864–1865.

36. ANNALES MONASTICI. Vol. I. :—Annales de Margan, 1066–1232 ; Annales de Theokesberia, 1066–1263 ; Annales de Burton, 1004–1263. *Edited by* HENRY RICHARDS LUARD, M.A., Fellow and Assistant Tutor of Trinity College, and Registrary of the University, Cambridge. 1864.

37. MAGNA VITA S. HUGONIS EPISCOPI LINCOLNIENSIS. From Manuscripts in the Bodleian Library, Oxford, and the Imperial Library, Paris. *Edited by* the Rev. JAMES F. DIMOCK, M.A., Rector of Barnburgh, Yorkshire. 1864.

38. CHRONICLES AND MEMORIALS OF THE REIGN OF RICHARD THE FIRST. Vol. I. ITINERARIUM PEREGRINORUM ET GESTA REGIS RICARDI. *Edited by* WILLIAM STUBBS, M.A., Vicar of Navestock, Essex, and Lambeth Librarian. 1864.

39. RECUEIL DES CRONIQUES ET ANCHIENNES ISTORIES DE LA GRANT BRETAIGNE A PRESENT NOMME ENGLETERRE, par JEHAN DE WAURIN. From Albina to 688. *Edited by* WILLIAM HARDY, Esq., F.S.A. 1864.

40. A COLLECTION OF THE CHRONICLES AND ANCIENT HISTORIES OF GREAT BRITAIN, NOW CALLED ENGLAND, BY JOHN DE WAVRIN. From Albina to 688. (Translation of the preceding.) *Edited and translated by* WILLIAM HARDY, Esq., F.S.A. 1864.

## *In the Press.*

LE LIVERE DE REIS DE BRITTANIE. *Edited by* J. GLOVER, M.A., Vicar of Brading, Isle of Wight.

THE WARS OF THE DANES IN IRELAND : written in the Irish language. *Edited by* the Rev. J. H. TODD, D.D., Librarian of the University of Dublin.

A COLLECTION OF SAGAS AND OTHER HISTORICAL DOCUMENTS relating to the Settlements and Descents of the Northmen on the British Isles. *Edited by* GEORGE W. DASENT, Esq., D.C.L. Oxon.

A COLLECTION OF ROYAL AND HISTORICAL LETTERS DURING THE REIGN OF HENRY IV. Vol. II. *Edited by* the Rev. F. C. HINGESTON, M.A., of Exeter College, Oxford.

POLYCHRONICON RANULPHI HIGDENI, with Trevisa's Translation. *Edited by* CHURCHILL BABINGTON, B.D., Fellow of St. John's College, Cambridge.

OFFICIAL CORRESPONDENCE OF THOMAS BEKYNTON, SECRETARY TO HENRY VI., with other LETTERS and DOCUMENTS. *Edited by* the Rev. GEORGE WILLIAMS, B.D., Senior Fellow of King's College, Cambridge.

ROYAL AND OTHER HISTORICAL LETTERS ILLUSTRATIVE OF THE REIGN OF HENRY III. From the Originals in the Public Record Office. Vol. II. *Selected and edited by* the Rev. W. W. SHIRLEY, D.D., Regius Professor in Ecclesiastical History, and Canon of Christ Church, Oxford.

ORIGINAL DOCUMENTS ILLUSTRATIVE OF ACADEMICAL AND CLERICAL LIFE AND STUDIES AT OXFORD BETWEEN THE REIGNS OF HENRY III. AND HENRY VII. *Edited by* the Rev. H. ANSTEY, M.A.

ROLL OF THE PRIVY COUNCIL OF IRELAND, 16 RICHARD II. *Edited by* the Rev. JAMES GRAVES, A.B., Treasurer of St. Canice, Ireland.

RICARDI DE CIRENCESTRIA SPECULUM HISTORIALE DE GESTIS REGUM ANGLIÆ. Vol. II., 872–1066. *Edited by* JOHN E. B. MAYOR, M.A., Fellow and Assistant Tutor of St. John's College, and Librarian of the University, Cambridge.

THE WORKS OF GIRALDUS CAMBRENSIS. Vol. IV. *Edited by* J. S. BREWER, M.A., Professor of English Literature, King's College, London.

HISTORIA ET CARTULARIUM MONASTERII S. PETRI GLOUCESTRIÆ. Vol. II. *Edited by* W. H. HART, Esq., F.S.A. ; Membre correspondant de la Société des Antiquaires de Normandie.

HISTORIA MINOR MATTHÆI PARIS. *Edited by* Sir FREDERICK MADDEN, K.H., Keeper of the Department of Manuscripts, British Museum.

ANNALES MONASTICI. Vol. II. *Edited by* HENRY RICHARDS LUARD, M.A., Fellow and Assistant Tutor of Trinity College, and Registrary of the University, Cambridge.

CHRONICON RADULPHI ABBATIS COGGESHALENSIS MAJUS; and, CHRONICON TERRÆ SANCTÆ ET DE CAPTIS A SALADINO HIEROSOLYMIS. *Edited by* the Rev. JOSEPH STEVENSON, M.A., of University College, Durham.

THE SAINT ALBAN'S CHRONICLES :—Vol. III., THE CHRONICLES OF RISHANGER, TROKELOWE, BLANEFORD, AND OTHERS. *Edited by* HENRY THOMAS RILEY, Esq., M.A., Barrister-at-Law.

CHRONICLES AND MEMORIALS OF THE REIGN OF RICHARD THE FIRST. Vol. II. *Edited by* WILLIAM STUBBS, M.A., Vicar of Navestock, Essex, and Lambeth Librarian.

YEAR BOOKS OF THE REIGN OF EDWARD THE FIRST. 20th, 21st, and 22nd Years. *Edited and translated by* ALFRED JOHN HORWOOD, Esq., of the Middle Temple, Barrister-at-Law.

RECUEIL DES CRONIQUES ET ANCHIENNES ISTORIES DE LA GRANT BRETAIGNE A PRESENT NOMME ENGLETERRE, par JEHAN DE WAURIN (continued). *Edited by* WILLIAM HARDY, Esq., F.S.A.

DESCRIPTIVE CATALOGUE OF MANUSCRIPTS RELATING TO THE HISTORY OF GREAT BRITAIN AND IRELAND. Vol. II. *By* THOMAS DUFFUS HARDY, Esq., Deputy Keeper of the Public Records.

## *In Progress.*

CHRONICA MONASTERII DE MELSA, AB ANNO 1150 USQUE AD ANNUM 1400. *Edited by* EDWARD AUGUSTUS BOND, Esq., Assistant Keeper of the Department of Manuscripts, and Egerton Librarian, British Museum.

DOCUMENTS RELATING TO ENGLAND AND SCOTLAND, FROM THE NORTHERN REGISTERS. *Edited by* the Rev. JAMES RAINE, M.A., of Durham University.

WILLIELMI MALMESBIRIENSIS DE GESTIS PONTIFICUM ANGLORUM, LIBRI V. *Edited by* N. E. S. A. HAMILTON, Esq., of the Department of Manuscripts, British Museum.

*January* 1865.

www.ingramcontent.com/pod-product-compliance
Lightning Source LLC
Chambersburg PA
CBHW030042130726
47901CB00005BA/1431